YOU CANNOT KILL A SWAN: THE LOVE STORY OF LYUBA AND IVAN

BY

URSULA HARTLEIN

This book is a work of historical fiction. Apart from the well-known actual people, locales, and events which feature in the narrative, all references to real people or real places are used fictitiously. All characters, events, incidents, and dialogues are products of the author's imagination. Any resemblance to actual events, locales, or persons, living or dead, is entirely coincidental.

Published by Purple Tarantula Press
ISBN 978-1-927967-30-0 (Kindle)
ISBN 978-1-927967-29-4 (Nook, Kobo, iBooks)
ISBN 978-1-927967-33-1 (paperback)
ISBN 978-1-927967-32-4 (hardcover)

10 9 8 7 6 5 4 3 2 1

Cover design by Ursula Hartlein

In memory of the real Mikhaila
and
In memory of my family's first computer, our 1984 128K Mac, on which I began this story so many years ago. A part of that dear machine, who was treated like a member of the family, will always live on in this book.

Finally, in loving memory of my favorite writer, Aleksandr Isayevich Solzhenitsyn (11 December 1918–3 August 2008). Had I not discovered his writing on 29 December 1995 and instantly taken him into my heart, soul, and mind as my favorite writer and one of my heroes, it's doubtful my Russophilia would've been reawakened so powerfully and thus inspired me to return to this juvenile story in September 1996, imbuing it with all the Russian culture and history which had previously been almost completely absent. May his beautiful memory be for an eternal blessing, and may his soul rest in peace.

A note on Russian pronunciation and names:

The transliteration style employed in this book is the modern, letter-for-letter style; e.g., Aleksandr instead of Alexander, Aleksey instead of Aleksei or Alexei, Katya instead of Katia, Anastasiya instead of Anastasia, Yuriy instead of Yury or Yuri. A and I are always long, and O is pronounced like a long A when unstressed; e.g., Ivan is Ee-VAHN and Boris is Bah-REECE. G is always hard; e.g., Georgiya is Gay-OHR-gee-yah. Kh is like the guttural Ch in loch or Chanukah. Accent marks were used as a pronunciation guide in the first two editions of this book, but they've been removed so as to avoid pedanticism and conform with all other mainstream transliterations.

Russians have an *otchestvo*, a patronymic, usually formed by adding one's father's name to -yevna or -ovna for a girl, -yevich or -ovich for a boy. Exceptions include Ilyinichna and Ilyich from Ilya; Yakovlevna and Yakovlevich from Yakov; Mikhaylovna and Mikhaylovich from Mikhail; Pavlovna and Pavlovich from Pavel; and Petrovna and Petrovich from Pyotr.

Though the titles Mr. and Mrs. are extremely unusual in Russian, those titles are used to distinguish the older characters from the younger characters in a way that's familiar to the non-Russian or non-Russophile reader.

The name of Ukraine's capital is rendered as Kiyev when referred to by a non-Ukrainian. However, out of respect for the Ukrainian people, the city's true name, Kyiv, is used in the narrative and when referred to by a Ukrainian or Ukrainophile. Likewise, Russia's capital and the scene of the majority of Part I is always referred to by its true name, Moskva, as is the city's historic fortress, the Kreml.

Though the overwhelming style in the English-speaking world is to "translate" the names of people in the Imperial Family, their Russian names are used throughout for the simple reason that it would be ridiculous for a Russian-speaker to use a foreign name like Nicholas, Catherine, Paul, or Peter.

Proper names of places, such as Patriarch's Pond, St. Basil's Cathedral, and the Tretyakov Gallery, are translated instead of rendered in Russian. Even my pretentiousness has limits. However, several churches in Tartu are referred to by their Estonian names, and translated in the Glossary.

Please refer to "The Story Behind the Story" in the back matter for details explaining the non-Russian names Kittey, Kat, Nikolas, and Ginny.

In the original edition of this book, the Tsar's son was referred to with the title of Tsarevich, though that title wasn't properly used to refer to a tsar's firstborn son and heir since 1721. It has now been changed to the correct Tsesarevich. Though the title Tsarevich is more familiar and widely-used in the English-speaking world, it wasn't the word actual Russians used to refer to their heir. Likewise, from 1721, the official titles for the Imperial couple were *Imperator* (Emperor) and *Imperatritsa* (Empress). Tsaritsa was never a legal title, but widely used informally and unofficially as a pet name for the Tsar's wife. The widely-used English word Tsarina isn't just legally incorrect, but doesn't exist in Russian.

Part I: Russia (3 April [16 April New Style] 1917–14 March 1921)

Part II: America (2 May 1921–14 March 1924)

Part One Characters

In order of appearance, all birthdates New Style:

Ivan Ivanovich Konev, the male protagonist, Lyuba's best friend and the love of her life, born July 5, 1898
Aleksey Vladimirovich Tvardovskiy, a friend of Lyuba's who becomes Eliisabet's husband and Ivan's best male friend, born November 17, 1899
Lyubov Leontiyevna Zhukova (Lyuba), the female protagonist, born December 11, 1899
Mikhail Grigoriy Mikhaylovich Kharzin (Ginny), Lyuba's badly-misbehaved younger cousin from East Prussia, born March 5, 1907
Pyotr Stepanovich Litvinov, their dear friend and one of Lyuba's admirers, who double-crosses his Bolshevik father and older brothers to help his White friends, born November 20, 1899
Basil Yakovlevich Beriya, an ethnic Georgian and Lyuba's most delusional admirer, born May 3, 1897
Eliisabet Martovna Kutuzova, a childhood friend of Katrin and Anastasiya who becomes Lyuba's best female friend, born November 14, 1899
Anastasiya Viktorovna Voroshilova, Katrin's brainless, self-centered best friend and Ivan's on-and-off pretend girlfriend, born May 15, 1899
Katariina Kaarelovna Nikonova (Katrin), a passionate Estonian nationalist and Socialist, born December 13, 1899
Viktoriya Kaarelovna Nikonova, Katrin's favorite sister, born April 23, 1907
Boris Aleksandrovich Malenkov, initially Lyuba and Ivan's best friend, later Ivan's bitter enemy, born March 1, 1900
Yekaterina Iosifovna Zhukova (Katya) (Mrs. Zhukova), Lyuba's mother, born February 3, 1882
Margarita Iosifovna Kharzina (Mrs. Kharzina), Ginny's mother, Lyuba's aunt, and Mrs. Zhukova's younger sister, born-March 1, 1883
Tram driver, principal of Aleksandrovskiy Gymnasium, various

teachers, and police

Aleksandr Sergeyevich Shepilov, initially Ginny's best friend but later his sworn enemy, born August 21, 1906

Georgiya Yuriyevna Savvina, Ginny's sweetheart and part of a well-known Bolshevik family, born February 2, 1907

Anna Afanasiyevna Koneva (Mrs. Koneva), Ivan's mother, born February 19, 1879

Katrin's parents and younger siblings

Katerina Aleksandrovna Godimova, a woman in the underground who assists Lyuba and her friends in hiding

Rudolf Godimov, her husband

Storekeeper of a boutique

Nikolay Alekseyevich Kutuzov-Tvardovskiy, the son of Aleksey and Eliisabet, born twelve weeks early on November 7, 1917

Nikolay Andreyevich Vishinskiy (Nikolas), a friend of Lyuba's who survives a labor camp, and Kat's fiancé, born November 3, 1899

Katerina Andreyevna Vishinskaya (Kittey), his younger sister, born September 10, 1906

Katriyana Dmitriyevna Vrangel (Kat), a friend of Lyuba's, born September 9, 1900

Aleksandra L'vovna Minina (Alya), a friend of Lyuba's, born October 7, 1899

Maksim Petrovich Gromyko, an insufferable young man who hopes to marry Alya, born November 8, 1899

Anna Pavlovna Furtseva (Anya), a friend of Lyuba's who survives a labor camp, born November 5, 1899

Leonid Yuriyevich Savvin, Georgiya's conceited much-older brother, born May 4, 1894

Yuriy Ignatiyevich Savvin (Mr. Savvin), their father, born 1874

Inna Stepanovna Savvina (Mrs. Savvina), their mother, born 1874

Priest who marries Eliisabet and Aleksey in a secret, illegal religious ceremony

Boris's friends he does shady odd jobs with

Tatyana Ivanovna Zhukova (later Koneva), the child of Lyuba and Boris, whom Ivan raises as his child from the beginning,

born January 23, 1919
Old woman at boardinghouse
Midwife
Katrin's maid
Doctor who treats Tatyana and Kittey after Ginny injures them
Ginny's babysitter
Bolsheviks in charge of a "baby prison"
Grigoriy Vasiliyevich Golitsyn (Mr. Golitsyn), manager of the third boardinghouse Lyuba and her friends stay at, and a deposed prince, born March 25, 1874
Branimir, Lyuba, Ivan, and Ginny's Kabardin horse, born 1916
Mikhail Yakovlevich Godunov (Misha), a sadistic scoundrel whom Lyuba and her friends knew at gymnasium, who runs an illegal brothel out of the house where he lives with his grandmother, born June 1, 1897
Konstantin Mstislavovich Godunov (Kostya), Misha's buffoonish younger cousin and lackey, born November 3, 1899
Pavel Lavrentiyevich Teglyov, their boarder who secretly despises them, born June 1, 1902
Nadezhda Osipovna Lebedeva, his girlfriend, the head prostitute, born May 3, 1902
Officer Bulyakov
Sofya Igorovna Godunova (Mrs. Godunova), Misha and Kostya's grandmother
Dr. Yavlinskiy
Mikhail Mikhaylovich Kharzin (Mr. Kharzin), Ginny's father and Lyuba's uncle, born January 25, 1883
Leontiy Leonidovich Zhukov (Mr. Zhukov), Lyuba's degenerate father, born January 3, 1879
Ivan Vasiliyevich Konev (Mr. Konev), Ivan's father, a former alcoholic, born February 8, 1879
Vasiliy L'vovich Fyodotov (Mr. Fyodotov), the manager of the hotel where Lyuba and Ivan stayed during the first week of their secret romance
Anton Alekseyevich Yatsenko, Lyuba and Ivan's neighbor at the hotel and the estranged, nonconsensual husband of Nadezhda's cousin Alla

Aleksandr Igorovich Maksimov, man in charge of recruiting office
Vladimir Maksimovich Gorshchenko, director of the Marx Center for the Crazies
Mariya Vladimirovna Gorshchenko (Miss Gorshchenko), his daughter and the co-director
Anna Rudolfovna Godimova (Anya), Katerina's daughter, born January 6, 1903
Vera Ilyinichna Lebedeva, Nadezhda's cousin, the eighth of ten sisters, born February 5, 1905
Natalya Ilyinichna Lebedeva, Nadezhda's cousin, the ninth of ten sisters, born February 11, 1909
Fyodora Ilyinichna Lebedeva, Nadezhda's cousin, the tenth of ten sisters, born February 1, 1914
Mrs. Darya Zyuganova, a sadistic orphanage warden in Minsk
Nina Ignatiyevna Medvedeva, an orphanage girl, born January 1909
Yelena Vasiliyevna Klykachëva, an orphanage girl, born 1911
Svetlana Yuriyevna Khrushchëva, an orphanage girl, born 1913
Valentina L'vovna Kuchma, a Ukrainian orphanage girl, born September 27, 1916
Inna Aleksandrovna Zhirinovskaya, an orphanage girl, born October 11, 1906
Inessa Andreyevna Zyuganova, a Belarusian orphanage girl and Mrs. Zyuganova's niece, born December 15, 1909
Olga Leonidovna Kerenskaya, an orphanage girl, born December 1910
Dinara Olegovna Nikolayeva, an orphanage girl, born 1909
Larisa Adolfovna Dietermann, an orphanage girl, born 1904
Klara Mikhaylovna Nadleshina, an orphanage girl, born 1909
Irina Samuelovna Brodskaya, an orphanage girl, born 1912
Lyudmila Dmitriyevna Zyuganova, Mrs. Zyuganova's oldest daughter, born 1892
Rufina, Ivana, and Kseniya (Ksyusha) Dmitriyevna Zyuganova, her next three daughters
Naina Antonovna Yezhova, an orphanage girl, born November 29, 1911

Yekaterina Karlovna Chernomyrdina (Katya), an orphanage girl and Naina's close friend, born October 27, 1907
Karla Maksimovna Gorbachëva, an orphanage girl and Naina's cousin, born October 9, 1917
Leontiy Rudolfovich Godimov, Anya's brother and Katerina's son, born August 3, 1911
Dmitriy L'vovich Zyuganov (*Dyadya* Dima), Mrs. Zyuganova's kind-hearted husband and Inessa's uncle, born April 18, 1870
Mrs. Brezhneva, a not entirely unsympathetic orphanage warden in Kyiv, born 1870
Andrey Vitaliyevich Andropov (Mr. Andropov), the manager of a boardinghouse
Yelena Vadimovna Yeltsina (Lena), a very young unwed mother whom Boris makes a sworn enemy of, born September 27, 1906
Yuriy Mikhaylovich Yeltsin, Lena and Misha's son, born February 18, 1919
Zinaida Vadimovna Yeltsina (Zina), one of Lena's older sisters, born August 15, 1889
Mrs. Voznesenskaya, a deranged, sadistic orphanage warden in Petrograd
Antonina Borisovna Petrova, who befriends Lena at the orphanage, born 1907
Klarisa Mstislavovna Baryshnikova, the deranged Mrs. Voznesenskaya's pet, who uses her privileged position to sneak many of the girls out of the country and to get nice things while they're there, born 1905
Priest in Lubyanka prison
Sergey Osipovich Gruzin, an interrogator and jailer at Lubyanka
Alla Ilyinichna Lebedeva, Nadezhda's cousin, the seventh of ten sisters, born September 16, 1900
Miss Goldmann, the Savvins' cook
Sofya Mitrofanovna Gorbachëva (Sonya), Karla's mother, later surrogate mother to Lena and Antonina, born May 9, 1890
Ilya Nikolayevich Lebedev (Mr. Lebedev), Nadezhda's paternal uncle, born February 18, 1872
Kroshka, Mr. Lebedev's little Pomeranian dog, who originally be-

longed to his daughter Svetlana, born 1908
Valeriya Afanasiyevna Koneva, Ivan's maternal aunt, who was also married to his father's brother, born May 7, 1877
Izabella Vartanovna Nahigian, an Armenian orphanage girl, born 1911
Maral Nahigian, Izabella's mother, who works in Mrs. Brezhneva's orphanage, born 1897
Sarah Mendelovna Katz, an orphanage girl
Ohanna Aramovna Zouranjian, an Armenian orphanage girl, born 1909
Alina Petropashvili, a Georgian orphanage girl, born May 1908
Zofia Kwaśniewska, a Polish orphanage girl, born 1908
Galina Ilyinichna Lebedeva (Galya), Nadezhda's cousin, the first of ten sisters, born May 22, 1890
Priest who hires and quickly fires Boris
Stepan Arkadiyevich Litvinov (Mr. Litvinov), Pyotr's father, born 1872
Leonida Stepanovna Litvinova, Pyotr's oldest sibling, born 1892
Kuzma Stepanovich Litvinov, Pyotr's oldest brother, born 1894
Venedikt Stepanovich Litvinov, the fourth-born sibling, born 1896
Viktor Stepanovich Litvinov, the fifth-born sibling, born 1897
Fredrikh Stepanovich Litvinov, the eighth-born sibling, born 1900
Rikhard Stepanovich Litvinov, the tenth-born sibling, born 1902
Dmitriy Stepanovich Litvinov (Mitya), Pyotr's baby brother and the penultimate sibling, born 1905
Manager of final Muscovite boardinghouse
Masha, Ida, and other prostitutes
Residents of the abandoned resort where Boris stays on his second illegal visit home
Yelena Ilyinichna Lebedeva (Lyolya), Nadezhda's cousin, the fifth of ten sisters, born December 29, 1898
Svetlana Ilyinichna Lebedeva, Nadezhda's cousin, the sixth of ten sisters, born October 13, 1899
Serafima Ilyinichna Lebedeva, Nadezhda's cousin, the fourth of ten sisters, born January 3, 1898
Dinara Ilyinichna Lebedeva, Nadezhda's cousin, the third of ten sisters, born February 1, 1897

Overlords of forced-labor mining camp and other *zeki*
Smirnov family, who takes Lyolya in after she's pushed off a bridge in Bulun
Director of the Manhattan orphanage Yuriy Yeltsin is at for a few months
Viktoriya L'vovna Yeltsina (Mrs. Yeltsina), Lena and Zina's mother, who runs a boardinghouse first in Moskva, then Tver, born May 3, 1866
Natalya Vadimovna Yeltsina, Lena's baby sister, born March 2, 1914
Father Spiridon Proshchenikov, priest who befriends Boris and hires him to teach religious school, born June 10, 1873
Aleksandr Timofeyevich Malenkov (Mr. Malenkov), Boris's father, born 1881
Aleksandriya Nikiforovna Malenkova (Mrs. Malenkova), Boris's mother, born 1881
Mazepa family
And assorted extras (Bolshevik marauders, police officers, Cheka men, Mr. Litvinov's henchmen, train conductors, Lubyanka jailers and prisoners, orphanage boys, merchants, etc.)

Part I: Russia
(April 1917–March 1921)

Chapter 1: Storm on the Horizon

Instead of walking to St. Basil's Cathedral to marry his dream girl, Ivan Ivanovich Konev is crying his eyes out in a broom closet.

His heartbeat quickens when he hears approaching footsteps and the door opening. *Perhaps my belovèd Lyuba already changed her mind*, he thinks as he turns around.

Instead his eyes fill with the sight of his good friend Aleksey Vladimirovich Tvardovskiy, one of the only people who knew about their clandestine romance.

"Lyuba jilted me when I asked her to marry me and go to America!"

"What? That doesn't make any sense! Why don't you dry your eyes. We can talk about this while we wait for the tram." Aleksey extends a handkerchief. "If only people really knew how overly sensitive you are."

"Not too long ago we skipped gymnasium and spent the day at Patriarch's Pond," Ivan says wistfully as he wipes his eyes and follows Aleksey outside. "We were watching the swans and talking about how they mate for life. When a swan finds its soulmate, the two swans swim together and their beaks form a heart shape. Well, you can't kill a swan's pair bond, and my beautiful swan will be back where she belongs no matter how long it takes."

"You'd have to be willfully blind to miss how she's always looked at you. I never bought her charade of preferring that short, chubby Malenkov. Anyone who knows what's what can see Lyuba only has romantic feelings for you."

"I suspect her mother got to her. She coerced my Lyuba into jilting me because I'm such a romantic dreamer and promise her so many idealistic things. I've never pretended all these things will come overnight, but at least we'd have love to get us through the tough times. And at least we'd be safe in America, however poor we might be at first. If she marries Boris, she won't have what really matters most. A girl doesn't jilt a guy out of the blue, for no good reason. Mark my word, Lyuba will be my wife no matter how long it takes before she gets tired of running away from what's in her heart."

Aleksey looks over at Lyuba standing with an azure-eyed, dark-haired little boy. "Since when does her cousin go to this school? I thought he lived on the other side of Moskva."

"Her *Tyotya* Margarita and that kid moved in with her and her mother yesterday, since her evil father is finally at the front. She didn't feel safe under the same roof as that degenerate. That aunt of hers is a very smart woman, though if she were really smart, she would've gone to America instead of home to Russia after the war broke out. She'd probably be safer in East Prussia than Russia now, the way things are going."

"I don't blame you for wanting to take Lyuba to America to escape this storm on the horizon. I've thought of going to America myself many times lately."

They stop talking as the tram comes up Arbat Street and pulls up to the curb. Aleksey's eyes light up when a girl with long brown hair and grey eyes smiles at him, and Ivan's insides twist with jealousy, remembering how Lyuba looked at him like that as recently as this afternoon. Aleksey smiles a lovestruck grin at her before she boards the tram, her long hazel skirt swishing around her ankles.

"She's one of those three new Estonian girls, and her name's Eliisabet. I can't believe an exotic foreign woman likes a plain Russian guy like me. Don't worry. With enough time, I'm sure Lyuba will look at you like that again."

Ivan has always sat beside Lyuba on the ride home, but now he doesn't have the heart for it. He finds a seat in back, as far away from Lyuba as possible. Eliisabet's friend Anastasiya, a delicate blonde who bit her nails all day, takes a seat next to him and smiles flirtatiously. He takes in this stranger, immediately sensing she's nothing like Lyuba. She looks like she stepped from the pages of a fashion magazine, with her painted face and nails, Jeanne Paquin gown, and tango shoes. She also has a very large sketchpad of dresses she spent the day drawing in lieu of classwork. Lyuba meanwhile has never painted her face or nails, wears comfortable over fashionable clothes, and enjoys reading newspapers and classic novels instead of keeping up with the latest fashions and the lives of the rich and famous.

Though Ivan has never dared tell her this, Lyuba has long reminded him of Theda Bara, both in appearance and personality, and that excites him deep down. He's more attracted by what the ruthless, man-eating, domineering, dark-haired, dark-eyed, voluptuous Vamp represents than what a sweet, innocent, virginal, blonde, blue-eyed ingénue like Mary Pickford represents. A so-called good girl might guarantee a safe, normal, predictable life, and an easily-attained happily ever after, but the so-called bad girl, the one with a haunted past and scars where no one can see them, represents a more interesting, complicated life, and the thrill of the chase. Just like Lyuba, Ivan too has scars where no one can see them, in addition to physical scars, which she's mercifully been spared. With their souls so thoroughly mottled with scars, it's obvious they belong together. So-called normal people would never understand them on such an intrinsic, deep, complete level.

Lyuba boards the tram near the end of the line, and loudly curses when she sees all the seats are taken. Having little choice, she grabs the rail and finds herself standing next to the third Estonian girl. The first thing she notices about the girl is her short blonde hair. Her short hairstyle isn't feminine like American dancer Irene Castle or French actress Polaire, but cropped as short as a man's, with nary a hair accessory like hair clips or a bandeau. It looks so modern next to Lyuba's mane of hair flowing past her knees.

"I'm Lyubov Leontiyevna Zhukova. What's your name?"

She looks up at Lyuba with piercing green eyes, and begins speaking with the most beautiful accent Lyuba has ever heard, a soft, singsongy lilt which blends sadness, poetry, and music. "Wow, you're tall. I never met such a tall girl before. My name is Katariina Kaarelovna Nikonova, though Yekaterina Karlovna is the name I'm forced to write on my schoolwork. *Pozhaluysta*, call me Katrin. I'm a big-time Estonian nationalist, and greatly looking forward to turning Russia upside-down! I miss Tartu, but I can't help admiring the perfect timing of my family's move to Russia. Was there ever a better time to live in Russia and change the future?" She indicates a younger girl in a nearby seat. "That's my little sister Viktoriya. She's nine. Vika and I are the only people in our family with any Estonian pride or modern values."

Lyuba takes this information in, nodding politely. "I'm a modern woman myself. After I graduate gymnasium next year, I want to go to university instead of getting married."

"You're our kind of woman," Viktoriya says. "May I ask how tall you are? I've never seen any girl who was nearly so tall."

"Five feet nine. I think my height helps in being taken more seriously instead of dismissed for my interest in modern ideas and masculine things."

"Only what's in your heart matters," Katrin says. "No matter what things might look like on the outside."

As the tram begins to move, Lyuba holds onto the rail and gazes back at Ivan, daydreaming about making love to him. She certainly had a week's worth of chances to do just that at the beginning of their secret romance, but she made him stop just as they were about to cross the point of no return because she's so terrified of pregnancy. Lyuba hopes she never has even one child. Still, her body shivers at the memory, his hands touching her so gently and lovingly, his soft, sweet, warm mouth on hers, cuddled up in one another's arms at that hotel every night during the first week of their romance…

But now isn't the time to dreamily think back to what a wonderful kisser he is, or how lovely it felt to be in his arms and be touched by him, Lyuba reminds herself. She hopes her jilted beau hasn't seen her longingly gazing at him just now.

As Lyuba goes over to an empty seat after the first stop, the tram makes a mad turn. The next thing she knows, she's sitting in her friend Pyotr's lap. She tries to get up, and lands on Boris's lap. Everyone is laughing.

Lyuba is so embarrassed, she rings the bell to let her off about ten blocks away from her house, while the tram is making its way through the beautiful Garden Ring. The sooner she gets off, the better. She storms ahead of her ten-year-old cousin Ginny Kharzin and her two best friends, livid at their continued laughter.

"You can all go to Hell if you can't shut up!"

"Even me?" Ivan asks, sounding wounded. "But I'm your best friend."

"If you were my best friend, you wouldn't take part in laughing at me when I was so humiliated in front of everyone!"

"Is there a public outhouse nearby?" Ginny asks. "I don't think I can hold it long enough to get home."

Boris rolls his eyes and drags him three blocks west. Lyuba and

Ivan stand waiting for them to get back.

"Maybe you're just having an overall bad day and that's why you rejected my proposal, *golubka*? Or is it because I didn't have an engagement ring, or you thought being proposed to on your way out of gymnasium wasn't romantic or special enough? If you want, I can take you someplace special and ask you all over again, and I'll buy you a nice ring. How about citrine, your birthstone? Or a dark-colored stone, like sapphire, emerald, or ruby? I know you like dark gemstones. I'll make it a white-gold band. Yellow gold doesn't look good on women with dark hair. It's better-suited to blondes. You don't really subscribe to that stupid superstition about Mondays being unlucky, do you? If you're that superstitious, I'll gladly ask again tomorrow."

"I told you to pretend this past month never happened, Vanya! Nothing you do or say will ever change my answer. My mother was right about you being a romantic dreamer with your head in the clouds. Why would I want to leave my comfortable life here and sail across the ocean, live in a cramped tenement in New York City, have nine children, and become a farm wife? You know I love you and wish we *could* be married, but there are too many things going against it. Even our astrological signs are ill-matched. You're Cancer, I'm Sagittarius. Water and fire are such diametrically opposed elements. We're best friends who happen to be of the opposite sex, and only Alyosha and Kolya knew about our clandestine romance. Now hush up. Borya and Ginny are coming back."

Ivan hates the idea of having to pretend the past month never happened, and how Lyuba has long pretended to all their friends she prefers Boris, but he's consoled by her assurance they're still best friends. Perhaps she'll change her mind over time, after he's demonstrated to her how he's the one who really loves her for all the right reasons. Still, it doesn't seem right to go to Lyuba's house after school as usual when he expected she'd say yes and they'd be on their way to St. Basil's to be married in the beautiful cathedral. Now he'll go to bed in his parents' house tonight, instead of enjoying his wedding night on board a ship taking them to America.

Maybe Lyuba gets her insistence on working instead of homemaking from her mother, he thinks as they enter the empty house, an imposing white and red stone building. Unlike his mother Anna, Lyuba's mother Katya has always been a working woman. She's worked at a cloth factory since the family relocated to Moskva nine years ago, and when she lived in the former St. Petersburg, she and her sister worked at a clothing store in the famous upscale department store The Passage. As much as Ivan hates Lyuba's mother, he suspects part of the reason she still works, even after years in upper-middle-class society, is the same reason Lyuba always brings him and Boris home with her after school. Both mother and daughter are scared to death Mr. Zhukov might be home early from work, though Mrs. Zhukova has much less to fear than Lyuba. She also has no other children to take care of, and while she has a few good friends among the Konevs' social circle, many people can't forget her origins as Katya Gammerova, a poor girl from the slums of St. Petersburg. Her repulsive husband doesn't help her reputation either.

Though Lyuba's father is now away at war, she hasn't stopped bringing Ivan and Boris home after school. They're best friends, not just male protection. Ivan in particular makes her feel safe, since he's over six feet tall and so strong he can bend a horseshoe with his bare hands. Lyuba has no doubt he could easily win a fight with anyone trying to harm her. Or even kill a man to defend her, she thinks, wishing he would've done just that when he found out what her father was all about when he was thirteen and Lyuba was eleven.

"I'd like a snack," Ginny says as Boris digs a large bowl of Olivier salad out of the icebox and puts a heaping serving on a plate.

Ginny's real name is Mikhail Grigoriy, but his mispronunciation of his baby nickname, Genie, stuck. His parents don't care that's a girl's name in the English-speaking world. To Lyuba, it's just her cousin's name, and a male name by virtue of belonging to him. It's about as normal as the fact that he has an actual middle name in addition to his patronymic.

Lyuba pulls a box out of the cupboard. "Why don't you take this coffeecake to your room? My mother just bought it at the bakery yesterday, and you'll be the first to eat it. It's made in the German style, so it'll remind you of home."

"I'm not stupid. You want me to leave because you want to talk about grownup things! Twenty rubles or I listen. And for ten kopeks I'll be nice to you."

"I'll pay him," Boris offers, throwing the money on the floor. Ginny picks it up and runs upstairs.

Lyuba takes a seat at the antique mahogany table and nervously looks at her two best friends. "I can't help thinking which of us will be next to disappear. God knows what happened to Anya and Kolya's families after that protest against our Tsar's abdication. It's not a crime to have different political opinions. I'd like to think they were abducted by people taking the law into their own hands, or arrested on trumped-up charges manufactured by people who never liked them. This can't be an official policy so soon after our Tsar gave up his Divine rights. Whyever it's happening, it's not good at all. It doesn't matter who these vigilantes are. I can't even celebrate the arrest of Vanya's father, as much of a scoundrel as he was. He probably could've continued his bootlegging without incident if the wrong people hadn't discovered his monarchist views. At least we're not in Petrograd. I wouldn't feel safe if I still lived in the capital."

"I've wanted to go to America for awhile," Ivan says. "This persecution and civil upheaval can only get worse, not better. This must be how our Jewish residents felt after all those *pogromy*. Now is the time to think about safety, not loyalty to the Motherland." He gives Lyuba a meaningful look. "For the first time in over three centuries, we're without a Tsar. I want to throw up when I think about how our Tsar gave up his throne without any fight, passively agreed to house arrest, and let radicals take over our government. I'm even more shocked his brother refused the throne in his place. I'd love to have a throne dumped in my lap. Anyone who's studied his Russian history knows how well it's turned out before when we've been without a Tsar."

Lyuba's eyes grow sad. "One of my happiest memories was hearing the cannon salute announcing the birth of our Tsesarevich. My mother, my aunt, and I all thought our dynasty was secure for another generation. Little did we know that long-awaited boy would be denied his rightful throne. It wouldn't have mattered if he'd been a fifth girl, since our dynasty was thrown in the trash heap. Even if our Tsesarevich had come to the throne with a Regency, the way it was supposed to happen, he's only twelve, and couldn't rule in his own right until his sixteenth birthday." She crosses herself. "I remember the entire empire praying for him when he was ill four and a half years ago, and how we rejoiced when he recovered. That was all for naught too. How could our Tsar not only give up his throne so passively, but deny his long-awaited only son his Divine birthright? God forgive me for speaking like this about our Tsar, but now I can almost understand why so many people hate him so much. Something horrible has been set in motion. I can just feel it."

"Could I have more Olivier salad?" Boris wipes his mouth across his sleeve.

"Big glutton, you ate it all! And you didn't leave any for us!" Lyuba is continually amazed at how quickly Boris's mind turns from serious subjects to his favorite subject, food.

"I couldn't help myself when it was so delicious!"

"Is that your excuse for why you're so chubby, you can never help yourself when there's food around?"

"I was born this size. I'm very familiar with the story about the rusty forceps the doctor used to pull my big head out. Hey, you have salad! Hand it over!"

As Mrs. Zhukova and Mrs. Kharzina enter the house, the bowl slips out of Boris's hands and breaks. Mrs. Zhukova runs into the kitchen, not bothering to take off her boots and black sable coat, and shakes her head at the sight of the shards of white and green glazed earthenware all over the dusky pink marble floor. At least the salad landed in one large, congealed chunk instead of being scattered all about too.

"Do you have the money to pay for a new bowl?" Mrs. Zhukova asks. "You're the clumsiest, most careless person I've ever met."

Boris pulls out another twenty rubles. "Unlike Konev, I have a ready supply of money."

"Yes, money is a very important asset in a husband." Mrs. Zhukova fixes Ivan with a meaningful look. "My daughter needs a husband who can provide for her and any future children, not someone full of idealistic, romantic promises about sailing to America, farms in the Midwest, and love being the only thing a couple needs to get through tough times."

Ivan stalks over to his house next door, cursing himself for being such a passive excuse of a man he just rolled over and took no for an answer when he put his heart on the line and proposed. Well, if Lyuba thinks he's going to give up on her this easily, she's got another think coming. He's the only left-handed student in the entire gymnasium because he always withstood the efforts of his teachers, since first grade, to try to make him write right-handed, even when they hit his hand with rulers and straps, thumped him on the head with heavy books, and threatened to beat him. He believes God made him left-handed for a reason, the same way he believes he and Lyuba were destined to be husband and wife. If he could stay true to his left-handedness under such intense attempts to switch him, he can be just as committed to staying the course until Lyuba gives in to her heart.

2

The next day after gymnasium, Lyuba and her friends find the tram driver leaning against the vehicle and smoking a cigarette. He scans the crowd as he blows smoke rings.

"I've decided I'm not going to let you patronize my vehicle anymore if you support that worthless Tsar. Don't think I don't know some of you are from reactionary families who want Russia to remain centuries behind the modern world. Your teachers are being very accommodating by letting you continue to attend their left-wing gymnasium in spite of your repulsive ideology. Understood? At least some of you are from modern families. Don't try to sneak on and think I won't know the difference. After enough years of ferrying most of you back and forth, I know these things."

"But some of us live past the Garden Ring, way up near the Moskva Zoo," Ivan protests. "You don't expect us to walk all the way home from Arbat Street."

"This isn't open for discussion. Now you know how the exploited proletariat has felt for centuries. It won't kill you to walk a few *vyorsty*."

Lyuba sighs and turns away, then stiffens when Boris puts his arm around her. She grins and bears it, remembering all her friends believe she prefers Boris to Ivan. And she can't very well complain or have any right to feel upset when she made the choice to jilt Ivan yesterday. Still, she doesn't look at him the entire way home. It galls her that he did that without asking if she'd mind.

Ivan asked her permission before he kissed her for the first time.

It's nearly 4:00 by the time they see the familiar sights of home. As soon as Lyuba opens the door, Boris goes right to the icebox, traipsing dirt all through the house. Lyuba slaps his hands.

"This may be the beginning of the end," she says. "What if we're expelled from gymnasium next?"

"We could always immigrate," Boris says. "I heard America's streets are lined with gold."

"You think America would give first priority to you?" Ivan asks. "They like tall, strong guys like me, not short, pudgy guys."

Ginny holds his hand out. "If you want me to go upstairs and leave you alone, you can give me the same price you did yesterday."

"Why not take money from your mother's room?" Boris suggests. "I have writing practice to do. My Russian teacher won't stop harping about how bad my penmanship is. Give me any word, and I'll show you how my writing is improving."

"Write *uvyortka*." Lyuba looks lovingly at Ivan starting his geology homework. She's never seen anyone else write left-handed. The only lefty in the entire school, Lyuba thinks with a touch of longing for this sweet boy with such a special characteristic. The way his hand glides over the page, creating that unique slant and smudge...

Ivan looks up at her, and Lyuba quickly looks away, trying not to make it look like she was just gazing at him with adoring eyes. Boris carefully writes увёртка on a piece of paper. Ivan has to smile over the fact that Lyuba asked Boris to write the word "ruse," and that Boris, in his usual thick-headed way, doesn't see the irony. If only Boris knew Lyuba's pretended preference for him is a ruse too, and that only yesterday, she and Ivan were holding and kissing one another.

Lyuba sneaks another look at Ivan writing. "Anyone want snacks?"

"I do," Boris says.

"Besides you. Vanya? Ginny?"

"Do I look fat to you?"

"Like the pigs we raised at the mission!" Ginny giggles.

The door opens, and the house fills with the sound of Mrs. Zhukova and Mrs. Kharzina chattering away about the latest political news. After they've taken off their boots and coats, they join the others in the kitchen.

"Today we were refused service on the tram," Ginny says. "Lyuba says soon we won't be able to go to school anymore. Is that true, *Matushka, Tyotya* Katya?"

Lyuba sends Ginny an icy-cold look.

"I said they could pay me to not listen, but no one gave me money."

"Mikhail Grigoriy Mikhaylovich Kharzin, you go upstairs right this minute!" Mrs. Kharzina yells. "How dare you try to extort money from your own cousin!"

Boris grabs his collar. "Better give me back my money too! That money I gave you yesterday didn't grow from a tree, and then I had to hand over more money to Mrs. Zhukova for breaking her damn bowl!"

Ginny pulls one kopek and three rubles out of his pocket.

"I gave you twenty rubles and ten kopeks!"

"I lost six rubles and nine kopeks to Aleksandr Sergeyevich Shepilov when we played poker."

"Well, now Aleksandr owes me! What about the other eleven rubles?"

"I used them to buy candy."

"Pay me all of it back by tomorrow, you little rat, or I'll give you the worst beating of your life!"

"Boris, I think that's enough!" Mrs. Kharzina says.

Lyuba stares at Boris as he pulls on his coat and leaves. The way he jumped on Ginny and screamed at him frightens her. This is the man she pretends she prefers over Ivan. But as her mother has long impressed on her, it's better to marry a man with solid goals and financial prospects, no matter his negative traits.

3

"My parents got taken away yesterday," Boris says the next day at lunch. "I came home and they were gone, the house a mess. My guess is all these neighborhood disappearances are the work of overzealous vigilantes. We all know there are plenty of radicals in our neighborhood, and plenty of radicals here at gymnasium. Those vigilantes can go to Hell. My parents have never been political, other than writing letters to several newspapers in support of the Tsar and against the government's takeover by radicals."

Lyuba crosses herself. "Why didn't you tell us immediately? Do you feel safe in the house without them, or would you like to move in with one of us?"

"I'm seventeen, old enough to get along on my own. I just hope I don't starve without my mother's cooking."

"Well, I'm sure you've got enough body fat to keep yourself warm for awhile," Ivan smirks. "And if you run out of food, you can always start feeding on yourself."

Lyuba smiles at her friend Pyotr Stepanovich Litvinov as he takes a seat next to her. Pyotr, a tall fellow with blonde hair and deep blue eyes, has long had a crush on Lyuba, but he's always put his friendship for her above any romantic feelings. The seventh-born of twelve children in a prominent Bolshevik family, he's somewhat of the black sheep of his family for how he maintains friendships with non-Bolsheviks and sometimes expresses rather unorthodox ideas in disagreement with the Party line.

"Petya, could you help me with trigonometry?" Lyuba asks. "My mathematics teacher will have my head on a platter if I don't have my homework done."

"Sure thing. You helped me with my English homework last week, and now it's my turn to help you."

"You're strange," Ginny says. "I never met any other girl who had so many male friends. Are you sure they're not secret beaux?"

"I get on better with guys than I do with the average girl. I have more in common with guys, since I was never a stereotypically feminine girl." Lyuba starts copying Pyotr's homework.

"Do you have to be so chummy with a Bolshevik?" Boris whines. "These people still aren't happy with that radical provisional government. They won't rest till they've taken over and turned Russia even more radical."

"Petya's nothing like his father and older brothers, in case you'd forgotten. He's one of the good guys. Petya wanted a constitutional monarchy, not an overthrow of the Tsar. He doesn't advocate violence or oppression against the other side. He's more of a Menshevik than a Bolshevik."

"You can count on me if things ever get really bad and you need someone from the other side to help you." Pyotr turns the page. "But right now, all we need to worry about is eating and finishing our trigonometry."

Eliisabet and Aleksey start making eyes at one another and holding hands. Ivan is insanely jealous, though Aleksey has long been one of his best friends besides Boris. He'd do almost anything to be holding hands and flirting with Lyuba right now, but instead he's forced to pretend the past month never existed and Lyuba is just a friend who happens to be a girl.

"Do you have a beau, Lyuba?" Katrin asks.

"She's got more than one," Ginny pipes up. "Boris and Ivan come over to her house every day, and that other day on the tram, you saw her sitting on Pyotr's lap, and Boris's. Yesterday Boris even had his arm around her while we walked home."

Ivan stares at her, unable to believe the girl who was his sweetheart just days ago is already letting another guy put his arm around her.

"Since your parents are missionaries, you ought to be quite familiar with the Biblical line 'Let he who is without sin cast the first stone,'" Lyuba says. "You've got Bolshevik friends too. You're staying upstairs this afternoon unless you want me to tell your mother about your Bolshevik associations. Is that understood?"

"Don't you think it'll come out eventually?" Ivan asks as he puts sugar in his tea. "Secrets do have a way of coming out, even if the people keeping the secrets don't want to confess. And it's unhealthy to keep some things secret."

"No, I'm very sure some things are better-off hidden and left in the past. Appearances and reputation matter more than honesty in certain cases."

***

That afternoon, when Lyuba sets out on the long walk home, Ginny runs away. They don't see him again until they're in front of Lyuba's house. Lyuba's jaw drops when she sees him getting out of a van, a bag of nougat candy in one hand and a bag of candied fruit slices in the other. She recognizes several of the children at the windows from radical neighborhood families, including Georgiya Yuriyevna Savvina, the top pupil in Ginny's class.

"You were in a car driven by *them*!" she admonishes him. "Where's your loyalty to your own family? We support the Tsar as

Christ on Earth while you cavort around with the people who coerced him into abdication! You can go in yourself. We won't hold the door for traitors."

"Was it true what Ginny said?" Ivan demands as they go inside. "That you let Boris put his arm around you yesterday?"

Lyuba steps into the living room with him and shuts the door while Boris is pulling out another bowl of Olivier salad and Ginny is helping himself to cookies. "How the hell many times do I have to tell you our relationship is over? We had a wonderful month together, but thank God my mother was able to get me to see sense before things went too far. Just because I still love and wish I could marry you doesn't mean it's what's best for me. I need a man like Boris, without lofty ambitions and silly romantic dreams about starting our own farm. Do you realize how poor we'd be if we left everything behind and started all over again in a foreign country? It might take ten or twenty years to save up enough money for that mythical farm you're always talking about! And having nine children on top of that? I wasn't made to be a wife and mother, and even if I did want that, you know full well what my degenerate father did to me. I love how you treated me so special, but I'm afraid I wouldn't know what to do if I had to stay forever with a man who treated me so wonderfully instead of abusing me. I'm too used to being hurt and abused by men. The sooner you get it through your head I'm no longer your girlfriend, the better."

"But I love you. You're the only girl I've ever kissed, held, caressed, been caressed by, seen naked, slept in the same bed as, or said '*Ya tyebya lyublyu*' to. Doesn't that mean anything to you?"

"This is the twentieth century, Ivan. A new world order is coming. Soon it'll be seen as laughably old-fashioned to expect to marry the first and only person you ever have feelings for or do those things with. We're still best friends, even if we're no longer a couple."

"I don't want to go back to being just friends. I want you to be my wife, the mother of my children, my lover, my partner in running a household, my Mrs. Koneva, the one I grow old with, the one I'll one day spend eternity next to six feet underground!"

"There you go again with your silly romantic speeches and attempts to guilt me into being with you! Now I'm going to go back into the kitchen to have something to eat. I think I just heard something break, which can only mean Boris owes my mother more money."

"Look." Ivan pulls a box out of his schoolbag. "I made you chocolates last night. My mother and I thought making chocolates would take our minds off my father's arrest. I thought you'd like it if I gave you some extras. Here, open your mouth. I'll feed a few to you."

"What am I, an invalid? And since when have I ever been the type to be won over by trinkets like flowers and chocolates?"

"You're just confused because of everything going on in the country, on top of everything you've been through at the hands of your father and the dastardly campaign your mother waged to coerce you into jilting me. But I know this isn't the real Lyuba talking. The real Lyuba still loves me."

"You know I do. You also know my reasons for why we can't be husband and wife. That astrology book was right when it said Cancer is the most sensitive sign, so easily-wounded, and like a leech on its love interest."

"Then why don't we sit on the davenport right now. Just let me kiss you once and see if you don't react to it."

Lyuba involuntarily smiles, then turns her head.

"You see? Even that suggestion made you happy and excited. I'm going to wait as long as I have to for you to sort things out in your head and come back to me. Why don't you come here and let me do it anyway. Maybe that'll make you change your mind and come back to me faster."

The door opens just as they've sat down and are leaning towards one another. Ivan jumps up when he sees Lyuba's mother and aunt, and Lyuba quickly gets up and goes into the kitchen, hoping they didn't see anything.

Her eyes fill with the sight of Boris scraping Olivier salad off the floor, broken glass everywhere. At least this means her mother will be distracted from what she might've seen when she came in.

"Boris Aleksandrovich Malenkov!" Mrs. Zhukova shouts. "Another broken bowl?"

"Ginny spilled his water, and I slipped on the puddle. I wasn't about to let good food go to waste, so I decided to eat it off the floor."

"If all you think about is food, you can no longer come to my house!" Lyuba says.

"Have some sympathy! My parents were gone when I came home yesterday."

"My father was arrested too, and do you see me acting like that?" Ivan asks.

"This bowl was more expensive than the last one," Mrs. Zhukova says. "I'd say it was at least a thousand rubles, since it was fancy glass. If your parents left enough money behind, you can use that to pay for it. You're lucky I'm not charging you four times extra in spite of this nauseating inflation."

"You're telling Boris to steal money from his imprisoned parents?" Mrs. Kharzina asks.

"Why not? They won't miss it, and if it bothers him so much, he can pay them back when they're together again." Mrs. Zhukova sees the box in Ivan's hand. "What's that, a present for Lyuba? You know I don't approve of you as a suitor for my daughter."

"Vanya and his mother made chocolates last night," Lyuba says. "He wanted to give me some extras."

Mrs. Zhukova sniffs. "That's another thing I don't like about you. My daughter needs a husband who engages in masculine pursuits only, like repairing machinery, fixing the house, hunting, and gambling. She doesn't need a pansy who likes cooking and baking."

"I like cooking. There's nothing wrong with a man who knows how to cook. A husband and wife are supposed to take care of each other; one spouse shouldn't be forced to only do certain things. That's not an equal relationship. Sure some things are women's domain, like childcare, but that doesn't mean I can't do some things traditionally associated only with women."

"Are you sure you weren't damaged by forceps or dropped when you were born? Or is this part of the sickness that caused your left-handedness?"

"Many famous artists, musicians, and writers were lefties. It's a special gift from God bestowed only on select few people." Lyuba takes Ivan's left hand and lovingly caresses it, remembering how the teachers used to leave marks and bruises on it because he refused to switch. "And God doesn't make mistakes."

"No, God never makes mistakes," Ivan says, gazing at Lyuba. "There's always a reason for everything, even hardships, even when mere mortals can't figure out why we can't get our happy ending handed to us right away. Maybe it'll make us appreciate our happy ending more, if we have to earn it."

4

The next day, Lyuba and her friends decide to have lunch off gymnasium grounds. Aleksey leads the way to a modest restaurant and goes inside to ask after a table. When he emerges, he informs them they'll have to eat outside, since the inside is full.

"I'm cold," Katrin says. "I reckon I'm the richest person here. Can't you go back inside and show them my money?"

"You're always talking about how much you love Socialism," Eliisabet taunts. "Here's a great opportunity to be one of the people and live your principles."

Boris plunks himself next to Katrin, takes his coat off, and puts it around her. "Did that warm you up?"

"Indeed. So much for that little boy's story that you're one of Lyuba's beaux. A fellow with a sweetheart would never do that for another girl."

"I'm cold too," Anastasiya says. "I should've worn my mink. Moskva in April is so much colder than Tartu."

Ivan takes his coat off and puts it around Anastasiya. Lyuba squirms in her seat, her heartrate quickening. Ivan is secretly pleased Lyuba is jealous.

"I'd think twice about getting too friendly with those fellows, ladies," Ginny says. "Though they're not Lyuba's beaux, Boris and Ivan like Lyuba. Her mother wants her to marry Boris, but the way she looks at Ivan makes me wonder which one she really prefers."

Anastasiya gasps, jumps off the bench, and throws Ivan's coat at him. "Using me to make another girl jealous, or just trying to have your hand in every pot? I'm a respectable girl, not someone content to be courted by a fellow who's already wooing someone else!"

Katrin jumps up also, throws Boris's coat at him, and follows Anastasiya up the street, though it's hard for them to run very fast in their tango shoes. Boris catches up to Katrin and grabs her arm.

Katrin whirls around, her dark green eyes flashing in anger.

"How dare you put advances on me when you're courting another woman! I'm a whole damn lot of things, but I'm not a *suka* who gets between two potential sweethearts!"

"Good riddance," Eliisabet says. "Nastya's a stuck-up little brat, and for all Katrin's talk about how she's one of the people and looking forward to turning Russia upside-down, she sure doesn't mind having a wealthy family and living a rich lifestyle!"

"I thought the three of you were best friends," Aleksey says.

"Oh, I can handle Katya in moderation, since she *is* very intelligent in spite of her naïve knee-jerk views and blatant hypocrisy, but Nastya is a spoilt fashion-plate. We grew up together, but that doesn't mean we're beholden to always being best friends. Regardless, I think I've found some better friends right here."

***

After lunch, Lyuba drops Ginny off at his class before going to her side of the building. Because of the kerfuffle, they were out longer than they were supposed to be, and now are twenty minutes late. Lyuba holds onto Ivan's arm, praying they're not going to be screamed at.

"You damn Tsarists are late." Mrs. Kosygina, the English teacher, folds her arms over her chest. "Is there a rational explanation for your tardiness without a note?"

"We're very sorry," Ivan says. "It'll never happen again. Next time we'll have lunch without certain people."

"You'd better not ever be late again. Now take your seats, you delusional Tsarists. If I had my way, you'd be sitting in a segregated area of my classroom."

"What gives you the right to talk like that about us?" Boris asks. "We're being good, patriotic Russians by standing by our Tsar right or wrong. Without him we're lost! Who in his right mind wants to be ruled by commoners? I sure don't!"

Mrs. Kosygina sharply breathes in. "I cannot believe such insubordination to your elders. Unlike you, I want Russia to move into the modern era, and we can't do that if we have a monarchy. I bet you were so late at lunch because you're so fat, and you were eating quadruple servings." She taps a random boy on the shoulder. "Would you mind fetching the principal? This gross behavior can't go unpunished."

He obediently gets up and returns with the principal. While he's saying something to Boris in a whisper, Anastasiya sticks her tongue out at Ivan.

"Anastasiya Viktorovna Voroshilova, one of the newest pupils at this gymnasium? You're already skating on thin ice with your archaic Tsarist views. I was just telling Malenkov he's got detention for the rest of the week. Now you do too. You're both damn lucky the very system you oppose, liberalism, is against corporal punishment in schools. If this gymnasium were run by one of your belovèd Tsarists, you'd probably be getting beaten right about now. Come to the office with me, both of you, and we'll discuss what detention entails."

Lyuba is secretly glad to see Anastasiya following Boris and the principal. The girl with sneaky designs on her belovèd is gone!

***

Ginny is surprised when Boris doesn't come out after school. Lyuba has her arm around Ivan's waist. *So much for her feelings for Boris!*, Ginny thinks.

"Where's Boris?"

"He sassed a teacher, so now he has detention for a week," Lyuba says. "Boy, I think I'm getting a headache."

"Why don't we go to the pharmacy?" Ivan asks. "It's closer than our houses, and I can buy you medicine there."

Lyuba nods, unable to believe the man she jilted days ago is still being so nice to her and carrying on as though they're still only best friends of the opposite sex instead of two people who were having a beautiful, sweet, tender relationship not too long ago. She wonders if his heart breaks every time he looks at her, the same way her heart often breaks when she looks at him.

As they're browsing the aisles of the pharmacy, they overhear two men in another aisle talking about people they arrested recently. Lyuba clings to Ivan's arm and desperately hopes these men won't discover there are three Tsarists in the aisle behind them.

"About two days ago, I arrested Aleksandr Timofeyevich Malenkov and Aleksandriya Nikiforovna Malenkova. Only the husband was supposed to be arrested, for his treasonous letters to newspapers in support of that damn Tsar, but the wife insisted on going with him. What a stupid woman. Just before I came here on my break, I told them if they were so in love they wanted to be together no matter what, they could enjoy the Solovetskiy Islands together in a labor camp."

Lyuba has always liked Boris's parents, and isn't surprised to hear Mrs. Malenkova insisted on being arrested with her husband. She can only hope, should such a situation arise, she too would have the courage to insist on going wherever Ivan goes so they'll never be separated.

"And then there was a bootlegger I hauled in, Ivan Vasiliyevich Konev. He was six feet seven inches tall, and made me feel like a dwarf. Well, his huge height doesn't count for anything now, since he's dead. He apparently has been in prison before, since he asked if he could be taken back to Lefortovo. I'm glad to know our jail made such a good impression on him he'd specifically ask for it the second time he got arrested."

"Did he kill himself? I've never heard of anyone dying so soon after getting to prison. Even if he started a hunger strike the moment he arrived, it takes a lot of time to die of starvation or thirst!"

"Who knows. This morning I found him dead on the floor of his cell. Perhaps he drank bad water, had food poisoning, or was ill. Since the only good Tsarist is a dead Tsarist, we're looking for his wife and son, Anna Afanasiyevna Koneva, birth name Akimova, and Ivan Ivanovich Konev. The son is eighteen and also over six feet tall, though not as massive as his father."

Lyuba grabs Ginny's arm and yanks him out of the store, forgetting all about her headache. Ivan has turned grey and holds onto Lyuba's other arm. He never had a great relationship with his father, due to Mr. Konev's raging alcoholism and how he used to abuse his only child horrifically for years. Ivan's animosity increased when he murdered his own brother, Ivan's *Dyadya* Igor, in a fit of drunken rage two and a half years ago. Still, no one expects to outlive his father, even if that father were a disgrace to fatherhood.

Mrs. Zhukova and Mrs. Kharzina are there when they get home. Lyuba sees letters on the table, in her father and uncle's handwriting. She's glad to know her *Dyadya* Mishenka is alive, but upset her father hasn't already been killed.

"Is Papa coming home soon?" Ginny asks. "It's not nice how

he left us to fight in a stupid war."

"He's serving our country," Mrs. Kharzina says. "East Prussia wasn't our real home. You should be very proud of him."

"At least he's still alive." Ginny smirks at Ivan.

"Oh, lucky you, to have a father who loves you," Ivan snaps. "Some of us aren't so lucky and have terrible fathers like mine and Lyuba's. Clearly you know nothing about how awful my father was if you thought you were pouring salt into supposed wounds with that little comment."

"Vanya's father just died in prison," Lyuba says. "Under any other circumstances, I'd be celebrating. Why did our enemies have to be the ones who killed him?"

"And now they're looking for me and my mother. I knew we should've gotten out of here. The longer we stay, the more dangerous it could get."

"Nonsense," Mrs. Zhukova scoffs. "Your father would've wanted you to stay and fight, not run away like a coward. This is why Lyuba needs a man like Boris. He might have uncouth manners and not be so handsome, but at least he's not a coward or defector."

5

The next day before school, Aleksandr Shepilov comes up to Ginny. "I can no longer be your friend, Tsarist rat!"

Ginny punches him. Aleksandr punches back, harder. As they're rolling around on the ground pulverizing one another, the principal comes by. Lyuba hangs her head as the principal drags them off to the office.

"Sasha was always a good boy. I saved him from a well when he was a little boy. What are his parents telling him to make him behave like that? If this continues much longer, it'll resemble the situation during the American Civil War, friends and neighbors turning on one another."

"If you'd said yes, we'd be sailing to America by now, free of all this," Ivan whispers.

"No one asked how my first day of detention went yet," Boris whines. "While I was getting a cramp in my hand from all the schoolwork I was forced to do, Anastasiya was fawning all over a bunch of pictures of American and French moviestars. Say, why don't you drive a car home today so you don't have to walk so far? I've got a buddy on Strastnaya Square who's let me borrow his car before. You'll know his house by the red roof."

***

That afternoon, they decide to have lunch in the courtyard to avoid any potential trouble in the cafeteria. Halfway through lunch, Boris gets up to smoke a cigarette. Ivan almost starts choking when he sees what his best friend is doing. Boris has never smoked in front of them before. He wonders where in the world Boris could've picked up such a bad habit.

"Lyuba, can I ask you a question?" Ginny asks.

"Sure." She sends a suggestive look to Ivan across the table and lets her leg touch his.

"Why does *Tyotya* Katya want you to marry Boris so much?"

"When you're older, you'll understand how sometimes we make choices based on security and appearances instead of being led by emotions. Some cultures still practice arranged marriages, where your spouse is chosen for deeper reasons than superficial attraction or heated love emotions. When your looks fall to pieces and you're no longer getting butterflies in your stomach after decades of marriage, that deeper connection is still there." She looks her belovèd right in the eyes as she says this. "And you can't support a family on just love."

Ginny senses movement and looks to his left. A man who's even shorter than Boris is lurking in the bushes and licking his lips, leering at Lyuba.

Lyuba shrieks and clutches Ivan's hands. "Why doesn't he leave me alone? His parents picked a wife for him two years ago!"

Aleksey's eyes narrow. "Is that creepy Basil Beriya hanging around again? He's not even a student here anymore!"

"Who is that?" Ginny asks.

"A delusional admirer named Basil Yakovlevich Beriya," Lyuba shudders. "He's convinced I'm in love with him and that we're going to get married. I don't think he'll understand I hate him. He frightens me so much. He's almost twenty and graduated gymnasium awhile ago, but he keeps hanging around to try to talk to me."

"And look how short he is for a man," Ivan scoffs. "Even Boris is two inches taller!"

"He's shorter than I am. No woman wants a fellow who's shorter than she is. Even if I weren't so tall for a woman, I'd still think he were too short for a real man."

"He's also a Bolshevik, and not a real Russian. Not a drop of Russian blood in his body. His parents couldn't even name him Vasiliy. They had to use a Georgian form of a proper Russian name."

"His family's been here for seven generations, but they've only married into other Georgian families. Even if I returned his disturbed affections, his parents would never approve of the match since I'm not Georgian."

"Oh, that's so creepy," Eliisabet says. "Sometimes unwanted suitors who don't get hints do really crazy, desperate things. I hope that never happens to you. I'd wondered why that guy was hanging around gymnasium grounds when he's not a student."

Ginny throws a rock in Basil's direction and laughs when Basil yelps and starts rubbing his head. Lyuba breathes a sigh of relief when Basil takes off without looking in her direction.

"You see, you can refuse a marriage prospect if you don't love the man," Ivan whispers. "I know you can come back to your senses and say yes to me. You know who the best man for you is, and it's not that uncouth glutton Malenkov or that deranged Beriya."

As she walks off to Strastnaya Square after school, she slips her hand into Ivan's, half-wishing she'd said yes to his recent marriage proposal. By now they could've been sailing across the ocean, married, on their way to America, and best of all making love every night in their cabin. She knows Ivan would take the appropriate measures to not get her pregnant, as he promised her, even though it'd mean denying himself full pleasure. Most men only care about their own selfish pleasure, instead of ensuring their lovers full pleasure by another avenue while cheating themselves. Instead she had to listen to her mother and stay here, where things are only getting worse.

Ivan stands back at the sight of Boris's friend. This man clearly isn't a gymnasium student, and he's smoking, something Ivan has always considered a repulsive habit. Ivan's eyes narrow when he sees the way this shady-looking fellow is looking at Lyuba. Before Ivan can ask how he and Boris know one another, the man throws him the keys and opens the garage door to reveal a beautiful sea-green Rochet-Schneider. Ivan's stomach is lurching as the man goes back inside. *People like that never come by beautiful French luxury cars by honest money*, he thinks as he starts cranking the car.

Lyuba gets into the backseat, while Ginny sits up front. Ivan looks back at her with a wounded look in his eyes before getting into the driver's seat. He's driven his father's Russo-Baltique many a time, and figures a Rochet-Schneider can't be much different.

Ivan brakes when he sees a police officer standing in front of the car and holding his hands out. His heart goes into his throat as he starts praying this isn't one of the people looking for him.

"What are you doing with such an expensive, foreign car?"

"Our tram driver won't let us ride anymore because we're Tsarists," Ginny says. "We wanted a car, since it's a long walk."

"I'm not surprised to learn you support that fool Tsar. How typically out of touch, to go around in a luxury automobile while the common man is starving. Get out now, and there won't be any trouble."

Ivan and Lyuba slide out and stand as far away from the officer as possible. Lyuba clutches Ivan's hand in a death grip.

"A man who lives in a red-roofed house on Strastnaya Square lent us this car. We were referred to him by Boris Aleksandrovich Malenkov, a student at Aleksandrovskiy Gymnasium," Ginny prattles.

The officer gets in the car and drives off.

"What is wrong with you?" Lyuba demands. "Do you just not know when to keep certain information private? This isn't how you were raised!"

Ivan grabs Ginny off his feet. "Understand you're never again going to do anything to threaten the safety of the woman I love, you little brat. Nor my safety, might I add. The authorities are looking for me and my mother, in case you'd forgotten. Now start walking, or I'll throttle you."

Ginny drags his feet all the way home, though in the midst of his sulking fit, he can't help but notice Ivan has his arm around Lyuba. Lyuba in turn has her arm around Ivan, and her hand is in his coat pocket. When they arrive home and Lyuba unlocks the door, she gazes up at Ivan like he's the only person in the world.

Ivan motions to the floor. "Sit, imbecile. I'm sure your mother will give you some sort of punishment when she gets home and finds out what you did."

"I'm not sitting on the floor."

"You are unless you want me to do you bodily harm. I learnt from the master how to do it."

Ginny sits on the floor sulking and reading the funny pages as Lyuba opens the assigned novel for her Russian class, *Smoke*, by Turgenev. Ivan rifles through the crate with phonographic cylinders and pulls out a few of his favorites. He grumbles as he turns the phonograph around so he can crank it without wrenching his arm.

"How come you're cranking it with that hand?" Ginny asks, looking up from the comics.

"Because God wanted to make me a *levsha*. We do exist, believe it or not. Not all of us give in to teachers trying to change us."

"You're strange. I had a few kids like that in my school back in East Prussia, and they all obeyed the teacher and learnt how to use their right hands."

"I'm not like those people who are so weak-willed they let other people shame and bully them out of this special gift from God. I've never been afraid to be different from the others. Now shut up unless we speak to you. I want to listen to music in peace."

Mrs. Zhukova and Mrs. Kharzina come home an hour later, as Beethoven wafts through the house. Ginny jumps up to greet them, then freezes in place when he sees the hard look Ivan and Lyuba are giving him.

"Guess what happened today," Ivan starts. "We were driving home in a car we borrowed from one of Boris's friends, and Ginny got us in trouble with a nearby police officer. He took our car, and we had to walk the rest of the way home. This little pipsqueak told him exactly where we got the car, and who pointed us towards the car in the first place. We're lucky we weren't arrested or followed."

"He was never this much of a handful when I visited you in East Prussia or Kuzminki," Lyuba says. "Is he acting up because he's upset over moving? If anything, he should've been more upset over moving from East Prussia, not moving to a different neighborhood within the same city."

"I think he misses his friends," Mrs. Kharzina says. "And it's never easy for a child to move to another country and have his father away at war. He got used to Kuzminki over the last two and a half years, and now he's been uprooted again. Maybe you can think of something to take his mind off all these heavy things."

"There's a gymnasium ball tonight. I guess he can tag along. This time it's Boris's turn to take me. I hope detention will bend for tonight."

"What is detention?" Mrs. Zhukova asks.

"It's a modern form of school punishment. Liberals don't like corporal punishment, so they punish students by keeping them after school."

"I don't think someone being punished will be allowed to go to a ball," Mrs. Kharzina says. "Besides, I happen to think Ivan is much more handsome than Boris. I can't tell you which one you should prefer, but if I were young and going to a gymnasium ball, I'd want to be seen on the arm of a tall, handsome man more than someone who's pudgy and short for a man. And isn't Ivan a little older than you? Boris is a few months your junior, and most girls your age prefer slightly older men."

"I guess this means I'm your escort for tonight." Ivan smiles at her, his whole face radiating love. "Lucky me, I get to take you to a ball twice in a row!"

"So you are," Lyuba says, looking at the floor. "So you are."

6

"Now remember, next time there's a ball, Boris has two turns to take me," Lyuba says as they arrive.

"When will we ever go to another ball?" Ivan asks. "The way things are going, we might not be at this school very much longer. I'm proud you're on my arm tonight. That chubby Malenkov doesn't deserve such a beautiful woman as his escort." His insides twist in jealously when he sees Aleksey with his arm around Eliisabet, who's wearing a long velvet dress matching her soft grey eyes.

Eliisabet smiles giddily. "I can't believe my luck, one of the new girls at school, and already the guy I like is taking me to a ball! We're going to get punch, but we'll be right back."

"Where's your friend Anastasiya?" Lyuba asks as she leans towards Ivan and lets him put his arm around her. "I see Katrin, but not Anastasiya. I'm surprised a fashion plate like that would miss a ball. Come to think of it, I didn't see her at school today either."

"I'll answer that," Katrin says as Eliisabet and Aleksey go towards the refreshments table. "Last night I was woken by horrific screams from next door. Vika and I ran to our window and lifted the curtain. Stasya's parents and older brother Gerasim were being murdered, and Stasya was screaming so loud you'd have thought she was being murdered too. They dragged her off with them. Hopefully they won't rape her. She might seem vain on the outside, but she's not as stupid as she appears. She could probably survive a labor camp. My guess is this happened because her fool father had to open his big mouth at work and denounce our wonderful new provisional government. Liza's father and my father have also expressed such views. They've only been at their new job for a matter of days, and are jeopardizing themselves in ways they can't imagine. Work isn't the place for political discourse."

Lyuba shudders and huddles closer to Ivan. "I hope they don't come for us next."

"Well, enough grim talk for tonight. Vika and I are going to discuss politics with your friend Pyotr. I've been to enough balls, it won't matter if I skip dancing one time out of a hundred." Katrin walks off with her wavy-haired little sister.

Eliisabet comes back looking very flustered. "You'll never believe what I saw Ginny doing. Making the *dulya* sign at that Shepilov boy and getting into his second fight of the day with him!"

"As long as he stays out of our way for the evening, there's no harm done," Aleksey says. "Why should we let a ten-year-old brat ruin our nice evening? This might be our last time we get to really enjoy ourselves for awhile, the way things have been going." He steps out onto the dance floor and beckons to Eliisabet, who smiles giddily at Lyuba before hastening to join her new beau in a dance.

"Would you care to dance too?" Ivan smiles. "Holy Mother of God, I can't wait to have you in my arms again, even if it's only for dancing."

"No, I'd rather prefer to just talk. I don't want irrational feelings to cloud my better judgment and influence me against what I know was the right decision. Only hedonists believe important decisions should be based on happy feelings and self-validation. The right decision isn't always the easiest one."

Lyuba stands all evening with her arm around Ivan, longing

for last week. He put his heart on the line and proposed. After a wonderful month, she rejected his love. She closes her eyes and remembers how sweet and gentle he was, and yet how passionate. If she'd just said the word, he would've let her take his virginity. If she'd said yes, by now they'd be sailing to America, husband and wife, and looking at the Moon and stars shining over the water on board the deck. Instead of dreaming about a rosy future in a world that welcomes her, she's now spending the night worrying about whether or not she has a future, the way things are going.

At the end of the evening, they go home in a carriage. Lyuba lets Ivan take her arm, and they stand outside the house.

"You know my offer will always be open," he whispers.

"I know, but marrying you isn't practical."

"How can it not be practical? We love each other, and I'll never throw you away after you've gotten older, or drink, or beat you!"

"Just remember I'll always love you and remember the past month fondly for the rest of my life."

"And *you* just remember I'm not going to rest easy until you're Mrs. Koneva! You can fight it all you want, but you know you're in love with me. I've caught you looking at me so many times since your rejection! The carriage isn't that far down the road. We can get back inside, and I'll pay the driver extra to take us to Petrograd, where we can take a ship to America!"

"That can never be possible."

"I want children. I want you to give me those children."

"My mother doesn't want you as a son-in-law, Vanyechka."

"Who cares what your mother thinks!"

"You're right," she whispers.

Mrs. Zhukova bangs on the window. "Lyuba, I told you your future is here in the Motherland, not running off to America with that pathetic dreamer! And I thought I'd made you understand he's too old for you at your age!"

"I hate you," Ivan snarls.

He goes next door to his house without getting to kiss Lyuba goodnight. Once home, he growls out the story to his mother.

"You're only a year and five months older than she is, Ivanok. I could understand her complaint if you were ten years older, but yours isn't a major age difference at all at your respective ages. She has to be using that as an excuse."

"Tell me another one!" He grabs a picture frame from a shelf and flings it to the floor.

"Calm down, Ivanok. You don't want to be a brute like your father."

"I love Lyuba more than anyone besides you, Mama, and Lyuba's mother says I'm too old for her and promise her too much! And that evil woman let Lyuba's father go on doing what he did to her for years and years! If I had a shotgun, I'd find Mr. Zhukov and blow his brains out, then do the same to his enabler, and take Lyuba, marry her, and go to America! Lyuba was traumatized so well by that *mudak* father of hers, she's scared of our love for each other! I hate that man more than I hated my father!" Ivan picks up a chair and throws it through the window. "The sight of Lyuba's mother repulses me, knowing she let her husband go on doing what he did all those many years! I hate both her parents!" He goes into the kitchen and grabs a knife. "I'm going to stab Mrs. Zhukova and rescue my love from the life of unhappiness, loneliness, and exploitation she's been trained to live by her *suka* of a mother!" He begins to toss various dishes and cups around the room.

"Stop that, Ivan, you're behaving like your namesake's grandson!"

"I have a right to rescue Lyuba from the degradation her father set her on the path to! It'll get harder and harder to win back her love as time goes on!"

"Quit it!" Mrs. Koneva grabs her son, who stands eight inches taller than she. "You'll regret doing any such things! Can't you be like your namesake, or at least his *prapradedushka*, Ivan the Meek?"

"Yes, Mama. I'll be your Ivan the Meek."

"It scared me when your father turned into Ivan Grozniy, and it scares me just as much to see you unleashing that *groznik* temper! Now you go to bed, and in the morning you'll feel different. If Lyuba truly is in love with you, she'll consent to be your wife sooner or later. She can't keep running away from what's in her heart."

Ivan kisses his mother and goes upstairs to bed, still shaking with rage.

7

Though there's normally never school on Saturday, one of the gymnasium administrators calls the next day and orders Lyuba and Ginny to report to school as soon as possible. Feeling there's little choice, she puts down her Turgenev novel and suits up for the long walk to Arbat Street. Aleksandrovskiy Gymnasium has been a hotbed of Bolshevism, Socialism, anarchism, liberalism, and radicalism in general since she started attending, and the tide doesn't seem likely to turn back anytime soon. Perhaps all these vigilantes arresting people in her neighborhood have been directed to old-guard Tsarist families by these radical students and teachers.

When Lyuba arrives at school, she only sees other students from Tsarist families. With the shambles the Russian Empire has fallen into during recent years, she and her friends constitute a distinct minority. Not counting those who've already been arrested and taken away for opposing the provisional government and protesting against the Tsar's abdication, there aren't even fifty students from Tsarist families left. She half-wonders if they're going to be arrested, and desperately wishes she could take Ivan's arm. But she mustn't betray her secret love for him in front of so many people, who've always believed she truly prefers Boris.

"We've decided to expel all the students from Tsarist families. I felt breaking the news in person was better than a crass letter of expulsion. This gymnasium prides itself on being modern, not reactionary and stuck centuries behind the modern world."

"Are you willing to make an exception?" Katrin asks. "I've been Communist since before I knew my feelings had a name. I promise I'm sincere in my intentions. Give me paperwork attesting to my support of the provisional government, and I'll sign it right now. I'll also happily join any applicable clubs and societies, at gymnasium, in Moskva, and in Russia."

The principal looks at her closely. "I don't recognize you. Are you a new student? That's definitely not a native Russian accent. It's too soft and singsongy."

"I just moved from Estonia. My name's Katariina Kaarelovna Nikonova. I no longer wish to go by the name on my official records, Yekaterina Karlovna. That's the equivalent of an American Negro's slave name." Katrin indicates four boys. "Those are my brothers. My favorite sister, nine-year-old Viktoriya, is home sick today. I think I can convince Vika to join me. She may be young, but she's got all the same viewpoints I do. Our parents are Karl Osipovich and Martina Leonidovna. You should easily find their address in my school records. They're serious Tsarists, and never listened when I tried to talk reason to them. They think this is still the Age of Kings, and are completely out of touch with modern reality."

The principal jots all this down and smiles. "My administrators will see to everything, and I'll contact the appropriate authorities. Would anyone else care to follow this principled, modern young woman's courageous example?"

"Unlike that traitor, I don't think any of us are going to up and spit on how we were raised, to view the Tsar as Christ on Earth!" Eliisabet shouts.

Katrin stifles a laugh. "I don't understand how any modern, thinking, rational person can still support the Tsar, or any monarch. He made a complete mess of the Russian Empire, and helped to keep it centuries behind the modern world. I can't understand the mental gymnastics which justify absolute monarchism while holding oneself as a modern, educated woman who supports progressive causes like women's suffrage and surname autonomy. Maybe you don't want to think about how contradictory your views are, since it would disrupt your safe, comfortable, established belief system too much. But good luck with your future endeavors."

Lyuba drags her feet as they walk out of the building and down the steps for the final time. Now there will be no final exams, no graduation ceremony for Ivan in June, no excited feeling of knowing she has only one year left of school. If she'd said yes to Ivan, they would've taken placement exams and finished school in an American high school, perhaps a night school. Now she's a seventeen-year-old with an incomplete scholastic record, barely better than a peasant who never went to gymnasium.

***

When they get home, Lyuba hears her mother and aunt's voices drifting from upstairs. It's not normal for them to be home on Saturday. She takes her coat and boots off and stumbles upstairs, where her eyes fill with the sight of suitcases and trunks all over the floor, and clothes, books, luxury items, and other things strewn all over the bed, the carpets, and the bureau.

"We were expelled from gymnasium," Lyuba mutters. "Would another gymnasium accept me so late in the year, and with only one year left?"

"You don't need to worry about that, since you're leaving the city," Mrs. Zhukova says. "Until this civil unrest dies down, you'll be safer outside Moskva. Your aunt and I are lucky enough to be going to America. While you were out, we went to the local White Star office and bought two ocean liner tickets."

"What?" Ivan demands. "Up until now, you kept insisting it was our duty to stay in the Motherland! And why can't you take Lyuba with you?"

"My husband and brother-in-law wrote us letters a few days ago, as you remember. They urged us to immigrate while there was still a chance. Lucky us, we got passage on a ship with only two more spots open. This won't be the first time only part of a family immigrates and has to wait awhile for the others to join them."

"But normally the younger people go first! A normal mother's instinct is to save her child, not herself!"

"She'll be safer here. This isn't open for discussion. Who stands a better chance of succeeding in America, a seventeen-year-old girl with an incomplete education and no job history, or a thirty-five-year-old woman who's been working for years and has plenty of money? Besides, I don't feel safe at work anymore. I'm the only person at that damned factory, either laborer or manager, who isn't a heartless radical. They all think I'm crazy and foolish for still supporting the Tsar in spite of being a factory worker. I'm the only one who never took part in any of those recent strikes, and they all think I'm a traitor."

"Can I go with them?" Boris asks. "My parents are gone."

"You can stay the night if you sleep downstairs. But understand I want no scandal with my only child while I'm out of the country and her father's at war. Lyuba will be going into hiding with Ginny and Ginny only. Don't think I don't know how both you and Ivan feel about her. With no adults to supervise, and you being the age you are, certain things often happen. Those certain things are more likely to happen if she lives with two unrelated men. Is all that clear, Mr. Malenkov? If you did give in to your natural urges regardless of where you lived, and the worst happened, you could emerge unscathed, but when an unmarried girl is caught having premarital relations, or God forbid gets pregnant out of wedlock, her reputation never recovers. Even if you do end up having contact with Lyuba, it is to be only chaste, proper contact. I'm trusting you to behave properly when you're on your own."

Boris rolls his eyes after she goes into another room. Lyuba is slightly alarmed he seems to think her mother's warning is a joke to be shrugged off. When she told Ivan to stop when they were about to go all the way, he respected her decision, and told her he'd do what he must to avoid getting her pregnant. Although right about now, she almost wishes she hadn't told him to stop, so she might be having his baby, a forever reminder of him, on the eve of having to go God knows where to wait out the unrest in Moskva. Like most guys, Ivan would prefer a boy first, especially since he's the last Konev. Lyuba falls asleep dreaming of a beautiful little boy with Ivan's deep brown hair and eyes, left-handed like his father, with the same gorgeous Slavic facial features, a miniature version of the man she loves to keep her company and remind her of the love they shared all too briefly.

8

Mrs. Zhukova gives Lyuba a map in the morning. "Put on as many layers of clothing as possible, and pack as much as you can. We don't want those godless radicals to ransack our house and steal any of our belongings. It may be a long journey, so arrive at the meeting-place as soon as possible. God will understand why you're not going to church today. Saving yourself is more important than hearing Divine Liturgy. Once you're in America, you'll be able to enjoy many more years of weekly churchgoing."

Mrs. Kharzina pulls Lyuba aside and whispers to her. "Remember what I said. Ivan is so much more handsome than Boris, and he's impressed me with his good manners and respectful treatment of you. He also has a very kind face, and I've seen the way you look at each other. If you're afraid of being with a nice boy because of what your degenerate father did to you, at some point you have to relax and trust Ivan's intentions. I don't get a very good feeling about Boris. I know he's your other best friend, and not outwardly mean or disrespectful, but I picked up on a lot of little things, like breaking the bowls, stuffing his face, losing his temper quickly, and rolling his eyes at your mother's lecture the other day. I advise you to choose very carefully when the day comes that your suitors inevitably force you to choose one of them. Sometimes what seems like a safe choice isn't always what's best for us or makes us happiest in the long run."

"Vanya knows what my father did to me. He used to watch from his window. Sometimes he'd walk across a rope between our windows and sit with me afterwards, holding me and comforting me. I would've pushed away any other boy touching me after something like that, but Vanyechka's special. He doesn't have a cruel bone in his body, and I knew from the first time I met him that he meant me no harm. I was really mean to him when I first met him, but I took back all my cruel words the moment I realized he's another wounded soul putting on a façade to the world. I don't trust any other man to touch me. He doesn't care I'm not a physical virgin or that I have that black mark in my past. Maybe it's because he was abused by his own father, in a different way, and wounded souls gravitate to each other through an unseen force overseen by God. Ivan is the only man I've ever loved, but I don't think I'd know what to do longterm with a man who treated me so special. I'm used to being abused, and scared of the thought of being in a relationship with a good man forever. That's another reason I've always surrounded myself by male friends. It was extra protection in case my father got any ideas when we weren't in private."

"You don't need extra protection from that degenerate brute anymore. I hope he's killed in battle. In the meantime, remember what I said. As scary as it might be given your history, the clear choice seems to be Ivan. When two people are meant to be together, God opens up a way for them to find their way home, no matter how long they're separated or how long it takes for them to realize they're meant to be. It's like the swan mating for life. If that's the true pair bond intended by God, you'll know it in your heart, and no one or nothing can tear it asunder."

"Come on, Rita, we're going to be late!"

Mrs. Kharzina gives Lyuba a meaningful look before she walks off to join her sister.

***

Lyuba and Ginny put on layer after layer of clothing and pack their entire lives into a limited amount of space. As she stuffs her jewelry box, medicine, and a hairbrush into a suitcase, Lyuba reflects upon how she could've been a Koneva, no longer carrying the same surname as her disgusting father, if she'd said yes to Ivan. She wonders if she'll ever see Ivan again, and if not, if she'll become a fallen woman and get old disgracefully, every day tortured by the memory of her belovèd Vanyushka, whose only offense ever was to fall in love with a girl who had so much psychological and emotional baggage at the tender age of seventeen that she had no choice but to reject his selfless love.

She looks at herself in one of the full-length mirrors and almost begins to cry upon realizing that by now she could've been pregnant with Ivan's baby. But there will be no wedding ring and no baby Konev or Koneva, because from now on she can have no more contact with Ivan, the only person who knows her deep secret and the only person who loves her.

After she's all packed, Lyuba opens the icebox and starts putting food into a large sack. Since it might take awhile to get to the safe place, she wants them to have enough to eat in the meantime. She tosses in hard-boiled eggs, smoked fish, cheese, ham, and apples. When she goes to the cupboard, she sees her mother and aunt already took everything. She wonders how long they were planning to go to America and leave her behind. Normally there's a lot more food stocked in their pantry, even with the ongoing food shortages.

Lyuba leads Ginny out of the house, fighting back tears as she struggles to hold onto her luggage. It's probably ridiculous to have packed so much, but if she can't have Ivan, at least she can have these reminders of her former life.

"Hey!" Boris calls. "Care to become a party of three?"

"Boris Aleksandrovich Malenkov, it would be improper to live together! Didn't you pay any attention to my mother's lecture?"

Across the street, a woman is yelling in a language that sounds vaguely like Finnish as she and her husband are herded into a van. Lyuba, Ginny, and Boris can clearly see what's going on inside the house because of the large, beautiful bay windows. Lyuba gasps when she recognizes Katrin's school-aged siblings, who are being shot one by one and crying hysterically. Katrin is standing against a wall, luggage at her feet, bearing what Lyuba hopes is the world's greatest poker face. It would be too abominable to imagine she truly feels no human emotion upon witnessing such a scene.

Lyuba swears she sees slight movement from Viktoriya after she slumps to the floor. She looks closer, and sees a bullet hole to Viktoriya's left on the wall behind her. Instantly she realizes Viktoriya's assassin misfired and Viktoriya instinctively knows to play dead till the villains are gone. But Katrin is too busy watching the vigilantes moving down the line to absorb this information. Lyuba sees Anastasiya's large sketchpad among Katrin's luggage and has hope that perhaps Katrin really isn't so cold and unfeeling after all. A fanatic would never have risked her hide to sneak over to the Voroshilov house to get Anastasiya's belongings. Lyuba imagines she's keeping them to give back to Anastasiya should she survive and come home, or as reminders of her best friend.

The three youngest, all girls, a three-year-old, a fifteen-month-old, and a three-month-old, are crying hardest of all. A vigilante breaks the neck of the three-year-old and throws her against the wall. Katrin continues to watch without a tear in her eye, not even upon hearing the three-year-old's bones breaking as the vigilante walks all over her limp body on the way to do the same thing to the other babies.

"My parents were always traitors, kowtowing to the Estonian rulers favored by the Tsar. I hope they finally see the light in prison. And as cold and heartless as this sounds, now there are nine less extra people taking up valuable land and breathing space." Katrin picks up her things and heads for the door as the vigilantes light torches and throw them into the corners of the living room. "My little sister Viktoriya was in sympathy with my views. I urged her to go with me last night, but she wasn't able to make up her mind in time. I'm sad about losing her, but not the others. There's no law that says you have to love your family."

"Boris, you can come with us, but only if you promise to behave!" Lyuba isn't too keen on the idea of living with him and having people assume scandalous things, but even if Boris isn't half as handsome or sweet as Ivan, after witnessing the carnage in Katrin's house, she isn't about to fling him to the wolves when she's in a very good position to provide sanctuary.

Aleksey runs out of a house in flames, carrying Eliisabet. Eliisabet is gagging on the smoke and tightly holding his neck, a terrified look on her face. A big, bulky, burlap parcel is strapped to his back, and he's holding a suitcase in one hand. Lyuba half begins to wonder if the Tsarist students were expelled to coincide with these vigilante attacks taking place in broad daylight. These villains knew they'd be at home around this time, and so feel emboldened to strike while more people are right where they want them. They must feel even more emboldened in their shameless vigilanteeism because their leader has just returned from exile, and is already advocating for the overthrow of the provisional government and the ascension of Bolshevik rule. There's no doubt left in Lyuba's mind just who these people are, at least this time. She can't see regular Socialists, Kadets, anarchists, or run-of-the-mill liberals as being so violent and taking the law into their own hands so brazenly.

"Look, that's Vanya's house! They're setting it on fire!" Lyuba's heart begins bleeding for her belovèd and his broken heart.

Lyuba's heart falls to her knees when she sees one of them getting into the Konevs' Russo-Baltique and driving it away. That car was where she and Ivan had their first kiss, she thinks with a gnawing sadness. Then three more Bolsheviks emerge from the house, dragging Mrs. Koneva. Lyuba knows full well Ivan loves his mother more than anyone except for her, and is baffled as to why he isn't trying to save her.

"*Blyakha-mukha*! Where is your son?" one of the butchers asks. "He ran away too fast for us to catch him!"

"God willing, he'll escape from you murderers. Even if I knew, I'd never give up my precious only child's whereabouts to the likes of you. God willing, my Vanyechka will live a long life, escape to safety in America, marry the woman he's loved since childhood, and have many beautiful children with her. Even if I'm not there to see it, I'll always watch over my beautiful boy. Go ahead and kill me in his place. My Vanyechka will only be nineteen this summer, but I'm already thirty-eight and have lived long enough."

"Fine, be stupid and sign your own death warrant. If your son gets out of that house alive, we'll find him at a later date and kill him too. Besides, we've heard your son's a *levsha*. He'll stick out in a crowd when people see him using the wrong hand. He's also over six feet tall, another reason for him to stick out. Believe us, your son is living on borrowed time."

One of the butchers hits her in the head with his rifle, hard enough to knock her unconscious to the ground. Laughing, the Bolsheviks drag her to a ditch filled with bodies, pour gasoline, and throw a match in. Suddenly Mrs. Koneva comes back to her senses and begins screaming, rolling around to try to put out the fire.

"May God watch over you, Vanya, and be with you every step of the way!"

Lyuba watches as the house is engulfed in flames, staring at it with sickened eyes. A maze of crazed thoughts are banging around inside Lyuba's brain like pinballs, all having to do with the fact that the man she loves was in that house that just went up in flames, and he could've been safe in her arms right now if only she'd said yes to his marriage proposal. She's absolutely sick to her stomach.

"Do you think Ivan's dead?" Ginny asks, his royal azure eyes sick with terror.

"His family said they'd hide in their sub-cellar if the Huns invaded," Boris says. He goes around to the back of the house, dodging errant flames, and opens a door in the ground.

Lyuba collapses onto the ground and grabs Boris by his boots. "Ivan is dead, Ivan is dead! Oh, Vanya! Vanya! Damned Bolsheviks! I hate them, I hate them, I hate them!"

In the midst of her hysterics, she notices Ginny descending into the Konev sub-cellar. Knowing her aunt will have her head on a platter if she loses her only child after only a few hours in her custody, she leaps up and chases after Ginny.

"Look at this strongbox with all the money in it!" he yells excitedly, tucking it under his arm.

"Boy, when I get done with you, you'll never disobey again—"

On the street above, Boris hears Lyuba screaming. Scared of the possibility of fire, but determined to investigate, he goes down.

"Watch where you're going!" Ginny cries as he bumps into portly Boris. "Maybe I'm a troublemaker, but I'm not stupid. I'm getting out of there before something bad happens. If Lyuba's smart, she'll come join us."

***

Lyuba is sitting on the cold stone floor, crying her eyes out. "I love you more than I love anyone, Vanya!" She hugs his knees and lays her head on his lap.

"Then prove it and marry me." He gets off the old Karelian birch chair and sits beside her. "I know I don't have much to offer you, but the only thing that matters is love. There's nothing of much worth in this valise I threw together, except maybe the two small paintings. Right now, the only thing of any worth I have to give you is my name. Wouldn't you be prouder to be the wife of a poor but honest man than the wife of an Esau? All the material riches in the world can't make up for poor social graces and a lack of love."

"I should've known you'd never die without making me your wife. My mother made arrangements for me and Ginny to go into hiding. *Pozhaluysta*, Vanya, love of my life, you have to go with us or you'll die!"

"Oh, great. Your mother. I bet she told them not to let you take this older man along!"

"You're only a year and a half older. She makes it seem like you're old enough to be my father!"

He wraps his arms around her. "I'll never let your father hurt you again. Once you're my wife, you're going to enjoy so much love and protection. Nothing can ever erase the pain and the memories of the past, but I'll try my best to spend the rest of my life making you feel like a Tsaritsa."

"If you don't come with us, I'll never be able to marry you!"

"Are you promising me you'll be my wife someday?"

"I like being an independent woman, and the thought of being with a good man forever terrifies me. I'm too used to being hurt and abused. But if I decide to get married, I'd never choose any other man but you."

"That's a challenge I'm willing to accept, no matter how long it takes."

"But, *pozhaluysta*, do keep your *groznik* temper under control. I don't want you to take out your easy rage on poor Boris. You really fluctuate between my Ivan the Meek and my Ivan Grozniy, but don't often act like my Ivan the Great." Lyuba stands up and gives him her arm. "Let me lead you out. I'll take your valise too."

As Lyuba emerges, Boris gets a wild look in his eyes and faints.

Ginny rushes over to him, yelling in a pipsqueaky voice, "Boris, are you alright?!"

"So I guess there will be four of us going into hiding," Ivan says. "Isn't Lyuba the best friend ever for risking her life to look for me before leaving? She'll do a great job as the woman of our house!"

"In the meantime, we have to get going," Lyuba reminds him.

There's no looking back as they start making their way towards the place on the map. Now they can only look ahead to their uncertain future, with the comforting knowledge they're in this uncertainty together.

****

Chapter 2: Hiding Out

A wagon comes over the horizon and halts in front of the weary foursome. In the bright sunlight, Lyuba sees Eliisabet and Aleksey in the wagon. Eliisabet is slumped against Aleksey, looking barely less terrified than when Lyuba last saw her earlier today.

"Are you Lyubov Leontiyevna Zhukova and Mikhail Mikhaylovich Kharzin?" the woman asks.

"Yes we are," Lyuba says.

"Then come on into the wagon. You're just the people we're looking for."

Boris glares at Ivan for helping Lyuba step into the wagon after tossing their luggage in. As soon as they're all aboard, the horses break into a canter.

"Thank God you're all still alive!" Aleksey says. "I didn't know if we'd ever see each other again."

"I'm Katerina Aleksandrovna Godimova, and that's my husband Rudolf. I take it you already know Aleksey and Yelizaveta. We're taking you to the outskirts of Ryazan. For the sake of safety, you won't all stay together. Two young men in the underground, Basil Yakovlevich Beriya and Pyotr Stepanovich Litvinov, will regularly come by with supplies and warn you of any potential danger." Katerina's voice trails off. "Who are these two men? Your mothers told me only you two would be going into hiding!"

"I'm Boris Aleksandrovich Malenkov, and that's my best friend Ivan. Lyuba saved us from being killed by the dirty Bolsheviks."

"A young woman alone with two unrelated men? I think I should arrange for you to stay someplace else. At least Aleksey and Yelizaveta are cousins."

Aleksey looks at his friends sheepishly. "God forgive me for lying, but I couldn't let my sweetheart stay somewhere alone, with no familiar faces," he whispers. "I wasn't about to have our courtship interrupted so soon when I like her so much."

"Let people talk," Ivan sneers. "It's their problem if they think there's something wrong with a woman living with two men!"

"I don't want to know what goes on with Mrs. Zhukova's daughter."

"Lyuba's a virgin," Boris says. "She'd never do anything so

scandalous as to have sexual relations outside wedlock! You can trust *us*."

Katerina sighs, feeling she has little choice but to accept the situation. These two young men need sanctuary, and it would be wrong to make them fend for themselves on the streets. "Your cover story is that you've just relocated from Tsaritsyn after your parents were killed. Lyubov, Mikhail, and Ivan are siblings, and Boris is her husband."

"Why do we need a cover story?" Ivan asks. "Won't that arouse suspicion if we tell locals a tall tale about how we came to be here?"

"You'll also need to think up false names. Maybe you can use Ukrainian or Belarusian names so people don't suspect you're ethnic Russians."

"Why can't we use our real names?" Boris asks. "No one will know us out here. I don't think we're important enough to be tracked."

"I'm already letting Miss Zhukova live with you and your friend. Don't push your luck, Mr. Malenkov."

Lyuba is uneasy at the prospect of being looked after by these people, but can't very well pick and choose when she's just gone from a comfortable upper-middle-class existence to the precarious situation of being hidden. She's also so grateful to have found her Vanya and be going into hiding with him, after spending a tense couple of hours believing she'd never see him again, she hardly cares about the details. Still, she wishes her mother and aunt had found someone who knows something about hiding people. This woman seems to know nothing about how to orchestrate an airtight ruse. Lyuba feels safer at the thought of Pyotr helping them. He's always been a good friend, and his friendship for her comes before his romantic feelings.

"So, Liza, how did you and Alyosha come to be here?" Lyuba asks. "That massacre along our street today was brutal. These neighborhood vigilantes are out of control."

Eliisabet crosses herself. "They set my house on fire while I was throwing some things into a suitcase, and my parents and older brother were trapped by the flames. I had just grabbed my rosebush when Alyoshka came by. He was taking a walk when he realized it was *my* house that was on fire." Eliisabet switches to French so Katerina and Rudolf won't find out the truth about her relationship to Aleksey. "I've got the best beau ever. I can't think of very many guys who'd risk their lives to run into a flaming house to save a girl they've only known for a week. I was having a hard time breathing, so he tied my rosebush to his back, picked up my suitcase, and carried me. By the time we got to his house, his parents were gone and the house had been looted. Alyoshka gathered up what he could find, put it in a suitcase, and we just started running until we came across Katerina."

"I wish I had a beau. I really, really like a certain man, but for reasons too complicated to explain, I don't know if I'll ever be able to become his wife."

"It's Ivan, isn't it? Alyoshka mentioned something about you and Ivan having a clandestine relationship recently. Maybe when we get to know each other better, you can tell me more about that and why you ended it. I knew Alyoshka and I were meant for each other when I looked into his eyes. I knew there was something special about him. I didn't need to make a list of all his positives and negatives or know him for years to decide this was the man God made just for me. Maybe it sounds flighty, but sometimes all it takes is a funny feeling one can't put into words."

"I have that feeling all the time with Vanya, but it's too late now to do anything about it. I jilted him when he proposed, and told him to pretend our secret romance never happened. I can't stop thinking about him, and I want to kiss and hold him so badly, it hurts me in my heart."

"It's never too late if that's the man you really love."

"What are you ladies whispering about?" Boris asks. "And why are you speaking French? What is this, the eighteenth century? Russians don't speak French anymore!"

"Sometimes women want to talk among themselves and not give away their personal secrets to men," Lyuba retorts.

Late at night, they arrive on the outskirts of Ryazan. Lyuba is amazed they've reached their destination so relatively quickly by horse-drawn wagon. The horses have been cantering and galloping for much of the journey, and several times Katerina has stopped with underground friends to change horses. This breakneck speed can only mean getting out of Moskva is a perceived matter of life and death, what with so many rail lines being out of service, or perhaps Mrs. Zhukova didn't have enough money to cover a journey of several days.

Aleksey and Eliisabet are dropped off at an old abandoned house first, and then Katerina returns to the wagon and Rudolf drives them a fair distance farther, until they reach an old dacha. Lyuba is rather impressed with how Katerina seems to be the one who wears the pants in her family, even if she's not so up to snuff on the finer details of hiding people.

When they get in, Katerina lights a lantern, shoves away a big four-poster bed, and points out a trap door. She then fixes Boris and Ivan with a very hard look and points out the room where they'll be sleeping, and the rooms for Lyuba and Ginny. Before leaving, Katerina points out onions and broth in a pot banking in ashes in the iron wood-burning stove. It's the poor person's version of French onion soup, without any cheese or croutons. Lyuba goes in search of tableware, and sets the table. She supplements the available food with the leftover food she brought from home, though onions in broth, smoked fish, and cheese aren't exactly the stuff of a filling, gourmet feast. Once the table is set, she lights all the candles she can find. Mercifully, several working kerosene lamps also present themselves.

As they take their seats at the table, Ginny screams when he sees the food. He wrinkles up his nose, pushes his chair back, pours his soup on the floor, and stamps on it, screaming, "*Govno*! Those *govnyuki* that made us this *govno* food! I will not eat any of it! Try to make me, why don't you, you *govnyuki*! All of you are *govnyuki*!" He throws himself on the floor and starts thrashing about like a wild animal, his face turning red as he gags and coughs. While this is happening, Boris goes to the stove for more food, as though nothing out of the ordinary is happening.

Ivan stands up. "Now that I'm the oldest one in our home, it's time to lay down some ground rules. You are to respect me at all times, and respect Lyuba as the woman of our home. When food is put on the table, you either eat it or starve. You're going to get a beating if you ever engage in such savage behavior again. Now sit down and eat, or go right to bed. I was always the best fighter on the schoolyard. Don't think I'm afraid to knock you around just because you're so much younger. Now apologize to your cousin and to me."

"Or what, you'll spank me?"

Boris drops his bowl on the floor. "What about respecting me?"

"You clumsy oaf, you broke another bowl!" Lyuba shouts. "You're a big glutton, and I bet you couldn't go a day without eating, could you, tubby?"

Boris scoops the onions into Ginny's bowl and sucks some of the broth off the floor. "After supper, maybe we can think up aliases. My mother's single name was Dobrolyubova. Perhaps we can use that as our assumed family name."

"Are you sure the doctor didn't squeeze your fat head with those rusty forceps and damage you as well as your mother? We're under no suspicion now, and only need to stay out of the way of soldiers and marauding Bolsheviks. It'll look *more* suspicious if we tell them an elaborate story about who we are and what we're doing in the area."

"You should listen to Lyuba," Ivan says. "She's very smart. But if we have to make up some kind of story to locals, I'd like to pretend to be her husband. They'd probably laugh at the idea of such a beautiful woman choosing a short, pudgy fellow as her husband."

"We're not making up any stories or names," Lyuba repeats firmly.

Ginny yawns. "Can I go to bed?"

"Sure, if you don't mind going to bed hungry. I'm too tired to go hunting for other food and turn it into an edible supper for a very spoilt boy. Or you can always eat the food that was so graciously provided for us."

Ginny starts screaming again, which results in Ivan promptly grabbing him and giving him a thrashing. Lyuba ignores them and goes to wash the road dust off. Once in her new room, she gratefully peels off all those layers of clothes and throws them on the floor, pulling on the purple cotton pajamas she wore during her week at the hotel with Ivan. To give her room a touch of home, she unpacks some of the drawings Ivan gave her when he still painted and drew. Before she has time to think about the potential to rekindle their relationship, she's fast asleep.

***

In the middle of the night, on her way to the indoor bathroom, Lyuba bumps into Ivan. He grabs her hands and looks into her eyes pleadingly.

"*Pozhaluysta*, Lyuba, I've lost my whole family. You're all I have left in this world. Why did you have to reject me last week?"

"Sometimes things don't work out the way we planned them. Go find a nice girl who can return your affections. I'll only bring you heartache because I'm so emotionally crippled from what my father did to me. I never wanted to be a wife and mother."

"You know you saved me because you love me."

"Vanya, we've discussed this! I'm not ready to be your wife, and probably never will be!"

He bursts into tears and grabs her. Lyuba hugs him back, wishing she never had to let go. After he finishes sobbing his broken heart onto her shoulder, he lets her go. Lyuba continues to the bathroom and curses when she sees the red stain on her pajama pants. She could've been pregnant with Ivan's baby by now instead of losing an unfertilized egg, she thinks in agony as she reaches into the bag with her cloth pads and menstrual belts.

2

The next morning, Pyotr and Basil drive up in a wagon full of canned goods and chicken meat. Ivan's skin crawls from the creepy way Basil is leering at Lyuba. Boris and Ginny notice a strange look in his hazel eyes too, and immediately wish only Pyotr were their helper. Although it would follow that Katerina wouldn't find anything off about Basil, given her brilliant idea to use fake names for no reason.

As soon as they're inside, Lyuba goes into the kitchen with Pyotr and closes the door. "What is that little man Beriya doing here? He's always looked at me like he's undressing me with his eyes. There's no doubt in my mind he only signed up to come around with supplies because the object of his weird obsession is here!"

"He was over to my house a few days ago when I was alone and talking on the phone to someone in the underground. He heard enough of the conversation to understand I was signing up to help Tsarists going into hiding, and of course, he knew you're a

Tsarist. He hates Tsarists otherwise, and threatened to turn me in to the authorities unless I let him come with me every time I go to help you out. That's the only reason he came along when we had our meeting with Katerina. I know it'll be tough to deal with, but think of it as the price to pay for keeping me out of jail so I can help you. I've always liked you, but I know you don't think of me that way, and I'm man enough to step back and just enjoy being friends with you. I'll try my best to never let Basil come here by himself. Besides, I think Konev would snap him in half if he ever did anything beyond those creepy looks."

Basil swings the kitchen door open and devours Lyuba with his eyes, running his hands through his reddish-brown hair and licking his lips.

"I don't like the way you're looking at my Lyuba," Ivan growls. "You're undressing her with your eyes. I know exactly what's on your mind and why you came here, and I am not going to sit back idly and let you leer at her. I don't want to know what you're imagining doing to her in your mind."

Pyotr keeps an eagle eye on Basil as he makes several trips back to the wagon to bring in the food, while Basil leans against a wall and continues leering at Lyuba.

"Did you have any useful reason for coming here, little man?" Ivan asks. "Boy, are you short. You're a foot shorter than I am. I don't even think you're physically strong despite your tiny height. If you don't put your eyes back in your head this instant, you're going to regret it."

"Do you think I wanted to waste the opportunity to gaze at my future wife? If she's this beautiful with her clothes on, imagine how much more gorgeous she must be without them."

"That's no way to talk to a lady, and she's going to be *my* wife, not yours! Lyuba, come over here and stand by me. I'll protect you from that deranged little man who only wishes a beautiful, perfect woman like you would even give him the time of day." He represses the urge to let Basil know he knows very well what Lyuba looks like naked and that she's just as gorgeous as Basil thinks.

"You see?" Lyuba scurries over to Ivan, slipping her hand into his and gazing up at him longingly. "When a decent, honorable man is interested in a woman, he talks to her in a respectful manner and treats her like a lady. He doesn't leer at her with a disturbing, scary, lecherous gaze."

"Can you kick him out of our house, Ivanych?" Ginny asks.

"Don't they teach you manners in East Prussia, you little *mudak*?" Ivan demands. "Don't you ever call me by the shortened form of my patronymic again, or I'll break your neck! Don't you know it takes decades of friendship to earn the right to call a man by his patronymic, let alone the familiar form? And you never address an elder that way!"

"Okay, Ivanych! I'll call you Ivanovich instead!"

Ivan is about to grab Ginny to give him another thrashing, then sees Basil is still leering at Lyuba and decides to focus on the more serious issue. "You know you wouldn't have come here if Lyuba weren't here. If I ever catch you near her, Basil Yakovlevich Beriya, you'll live to regret it."

Pyotr raps on the table to get attention. "I think Lyuba deserves a present to make up for leaving her comfortable life. Let's go into town and get her jewelry, perfume, that sort of thing."

"Can I buy toys?" Ginny asks. "I thought we'd be holed up like rats in a trap out here. I hope we get to go into town often."

"Mikhail Mikhaylovich Kharzin, you cannot go anywhere after last night," Lyuba says. "You deserve a punishment for all that cursing and those ridiculous temper tantrums."

"That little pipsqueak isn't going," Pyotr says. "You really deserve something nice, Lyuba. I know this wasn't how you pictured your life ending up. The least we could all do is buy you nice things to help take your mind off your situation."

Pyotr drives them to a fancy boutique with jewelry, paintings, vases, lamps, antique books, and globes in the display windows. While Pyotr browses perfume and Boris inspects necklaces, Basil leans over to look at a display case of china dolls and trips right into it. Ignoring the upturned case and the broken dolls littering the floor, Basil saunters up to Ivan and throws a punch. Ivan blocks it and punches him in the jaw. When Basil tries to throw another punch, Ivan pushes him, sending him knocking right into Boris, Pyotr, and another display case.

"This was just supposed to be a simple trip to a store to buy something nice for Lyuba, not yet another fight!" Pyotr shouts in frustration as Basil is ordered to pay for the broken merchandise.

Ivan looks despondently at the bracelet in his hand. "I wanted to buy her this citrine bracelet, since that's her birthstone, but I guess no amount of jewelry will turn her head after she jilted me and rejected my marriage proposal. My Lyuba only loves me as her best friend, not someone she wants to marry. Unlucky me."

"What month is citrine for?" the storekeeper asks. "We're finally converting to the Gregorian calendar, so our old Julian birthdays will have to be adjusted."

"Her birthday's November twenty-ninth. She was born in 1899. How many days are we behind the Gregorian calendar now, twelve?"

"Thirteen, though it was twelve in the last century. Your Lyuba has a December birthday now."

He rolls his eyes. "That means my own birthday changed its month. I was born June twenty-third of 1898, which must put my birthday into early July now. I liked having a June birthday. At least that doesn't change our astrological signs. I'm still Cancer and she's still Sagittarius."

"That's an awful match," the storekeeper says as he counts out the money Basil dug out of his pockets and wallet. "It's literally fire with water. We're not slaves to the stars, but that might be one of the contributing factors in why she jilted you. But it won't be over till a wedding band is slipped onto her finger. Some women have to be courted longer than others and asked more than once before they finally say yes. Here, take the bracelet half-off. You have a kind face, and you deserve something nice after that short little man started a fight with you for no reason. Perhaps in time the lady will return your affections. There's no shame in not marrying as soon as you're of age."

They return to the dacha an hour later. Pyotr hands Lyuba a bottle of perfume, and Boris hands her a necklace with a white china bauble. Ivan has decided to save the bracelet for a future date, maybe Lyuba's birthday or Christmas. He's too bashful to present it to her in front of everyone.

"Spasibo." Lyuba hopes Boris doesn't see her cringing. While she appreciates the perfume, she's not impressed with the necklace. Ivan always gives her birthday or Christmas jewelry with brightly-

colored stones. A plain gold chain with a white china bauble is so devoid of personality.

Basil enters in a huff. "I didn't have money to buy anything for you, and it's all his fault!" He points at Ivan. "Stupid *levsha*!"

"Don't you *dare* insult me because I'm a *levsha*, you arrogant right-handed *mudak*!"

"Basil had to pay for the damages he caused," Pyotr says. "Not to mention he started a fight."

"Beriya is so stupid," Boris says. "He forgot he was taking on a guy a foot taller than he is, and as strong as ten men. I've seen Konev bend a horseshoe with his bare hands, and Basil doesn't even know how to punch!"

"I thought he was trying to kill me," Ivan lies, hoping Lyuba's heart will flood with sympathy for him so she'll give him special treatment for the unexpected attack he was subject to.

"Liar," Basil says. "I started a fight, I *didn't* try to kill you!"

"The way Basil was swinging at him, you'd think he was spoiling for that fight for a long time," Pyotr says. "I think he's jealous of Konev because he was your neighbor for nine years, and is your best friend besides."

Lyuba shivers in horror when Basil saunters up to her and puts his arm around her. She wants desperately for Ivan to come to her rescue and snap Basil in half the way Pyotr suggested he probably could. In spite of her sincere belief that women can get along just fine without men and that the sexes are equal, deep down she can't help but like the idea of being protected and taken care of by the man she loves.

Ivan grabs Basil's collar and yanks him away from Lyuba. "I'll break your arm if you try that again. I'll kill you if you so much as lay a finger on her!"

"Get out of my house, *yebarishka*!" Lyuba shouts.

Ivan coughs in embarrassment at the mouth on his belovèd, though it's not a huge surprise from a woman so insistent on the equality of the sexes, who actively shuns most things traditionally associated with femininity. He's barking up the wrong tree if he wants a wife who's content to cook, clean, raise children, and go to society parties and teas in her spare time. Lyuba's been a tomboy since he's known her, always preferring male friends to female, unafraid to get dirty or use unladylike language, playing with model cars and planes instead of dolls or tea sets, and picking up worms and spiders to play with instead of running screaming at the sight. Not that he's one to talk, being rather atypical himself. He'd probably never hear the end of it if their friends found out how easily he cries, that he wanted to be an artist till his father beat it out of him, or how he's put up a façade so no one but Lyuba will ever find out he's a shy, sensitive boy deep down. After his father became an alcoholic and beat him within an inch of his life every day for years, his defense mechanism became having a volatile temper of his own and frequently fighting in the schoolyard.

"If we catch you around here again, you're going to be dead!" Ivan shouts as Basil stalks out. "Lyubonka, just scream for me if he hurts you, and I'll take care of the rest."

"I'm not taking any chances. If I had short hair, he might find me unattractive, and finally leave me alone. Who wants to cut my hair?"

"You can talk this out on your own," Pyotr says. "I should really be getting back home. I don't want my father to find out where I've really been and that I skipped gymnasium today. You're my friends, and I don't want you to get in trouble."

3

Basil returns while they're eating lunch the next day. Ignoring everyone's startled responses, he sets a large cookie jar on the kitchen table and pulls a wrapped parcel out of a knapsack.

"Mind if I join you? What delicious food did you make today? I love a woman who can cook!"

"I was the one who made lunch," Ivan volunteers, glaring at him. "Lyuba likes men who can cook. She wants a husband who's an equal partner in a marriage and running a household, not a lazy *svoloch* who sits around without lifting a finger while she breaks her back with chores."

Basil begins stroking her hair. "I can't wait for our wedding night, when I get to touch all of you."

Ivan stands up and storms towards Basil, hitting him with the back of his hand. "Didn't your parents ever teach you not to touch what's not yours? If you don't get the hell out of our house this instant, I'll break every bone in your little body, starting with the pinky finger on your writing hand. If you ever do anything beyond making inappropriate comments and touching my Lyuba, I'll break something else off your body. Understood?"

"Didn't your parents pick a wife for you when you were eighteen?" Lyuba asks. "Why don't you marry her and leave me alone?"

"He's leaving you alone right now." Ivan drags him to the door by his ear and shoves him out. "We'll lock all the doors and windows nice and tight, so that stalker can't get his hands on you. If he does break in, he'll have to get through me before he does anything to you." He looks derisively at Boris stuffing his pudgy face. "It won't take much to get through Malenkov, not that I mind being your only male protection. You poor thing, you're shaking. Here, you'll recover your nerves faster if you get something more to eat." He ladles more chicken soup into her bowl. "It's the recipe my mother taught me. It'll cure everything that ails you. For dessert, you can have an extra portion of the chocolate cake I made. It's a bad habit to eat sweets in the middle of the day, but you deserve chocolate after what just happened."

Lyuba tries to ignore the butterflies in her stomach as Ivan keeps looking at her and smiling during the rest of the meal. In spite of her pretended preference for Boris, he'd never be this protective and attentive. Ivan would take care of her if she got sick or became disabled, judging by how he just came to her rescue and is now making sure she eats her fill. A lot of men think a healthy appetite in a woman is a bad thing. To force herself to stop gazing at his beautiful deep brown eyes and sensuous mouth, she fetches scissors as soon as she's done eating.

"Vanka, *pozhaluysta*, cut my hair."

He takes the scissors and goes into his room, closes the door, and sinks down on the bed crying. Lyuba gives thanks Boris is still occupied with stuffing food down his gluttonous throat.

"Do you realize it's only been a week since you shattered my heart into a million pieces? How am I supposed to feel after waiting years to have my dream girl, only to be jilted after just one month? Do you know how special it is to me that you're the only girl I've ever loved? I even asked you for permission before I kissed you, unlike a lot of other guys! Why don't we go away in the night? You could be carrying our first child in no time at all!"

"You really don't understand the meaning of no, do you?"

"Have I ever done anything so awful to you I deserved to have my heart broken? All I ever did was love my Lyuba and want to take you to safety in America. I wanted to protect you from this national turmoil and to have a loving wife and darling baby to come home to every day. Is it that I'm not manly enough for you? I'm a lot more sensitive than normal men, but wouldn't you rather have a gentle husband than a brute who drinks and beats you and your children? The thought of spanking, switching, or whipping an innocent child makes me want to throw up. I'd treat you like a Tsaritsa and our kids like princes and princesses. There would be so much love in our house, even if we might not be wealthy."

"Love can never trump financial security. Now cut my hair and stop crying like a baby. I don't need a husband who cries at the drop of a hat. If only our friends knew how easily you cry and that you're so overly sensitive beneath your tough exterior. It hurts me too that we can't be together, but you don't catch me sobbing about it all the time and trying to fight against reality."

He takes the scissors and starts trying to cut it. "I can't do it." Ivan holds the scissors in both hands. "I'm no good with scissors. No one designs scissors for a *levsha*, I'm afraid."

"Cut my hair off! I don't want Basil to touch me again!"

"I'm here to defend your honor." Ivan tries to work the scissors again but fails. "This really is beautiful hair."

"Stop running your hands through my hair. You're making me think about our lovely month together."

"That's a good thing!"

"Do you want me to get Boris to cut it?"

Ivan crooks his left arm over and shifts to Lyuba's left so he can use his right arm to steady the direction of the scissors. Lyuba feels liberated to see the hair slowly falling onto the floor. Now she'll look like a modern woman, and people will take her seriously when she talks about how the sexes are equal and how she wants nothing to do with so-called traditional feminine things. Already she loves having short hair, and smiles as she thinks about how her mother can't do anything about it.

"It still flows a bit past my shoulders. Now I won't have to constantly push it out of my face. *Bolshoye spasibo*, Vanya."

"I've never seen you with such short hair before. You always had long locks, like a Tsaritsa, a goddess, or a fairy queen in a legend."

"So you don't like me anymore?" she teases.

"I'd love you even if you lost all your hair," he whispers in her ear. "I bet Boris can't say the same, *golubka*!"

4

Ivan has his birthday in July. His birthday has always fallen on the twenty-third of June, but now it falls on the fifth of July.

"I can't get used to that new calendar," he grumbles.

"How old are you?" Ginny asks.

"Nineteen."

"The way my aunt was talking to my mother, you're so much older than Lyuba! A year and a half isn't a big age difference at your age."

"Why the hell were your mothers talking about your age difference?" Boris asks. "How did *that* come up as conversation?"

"I always eavesdropped on them after I was supposed to be in bed. My aunt isn't one to talk about Ivan being too old for Lyuba at her age, since she's three years younger than *Dyadya* Leontiy and was married as soon as she was seventeen. But to answer your question, *Tyotya* Katya wants Lyuba to stay in Russia and marry someone like you, Malenkov. She said Lyuba can never marry Ivan."

"But Lyuba likes *me* better." A huge grin comes crawling over Boris's chubby face. "Didn't she *know* that?"

"Lyuba's mother can rot in Hell," Ivan says. "She hates me because she thinks I'm too old for Lyuba, too much of a dreamer, and not financially promising enough. Just because she married for money doesn't mean she has to force Lyuba to do the same."

"Don't be a sore loser, Konev. I stole Lyuba's heart. You never stood a chance against me!" Boris presents him with an apple.

"An apple? This is your birthday present?"

"Here's a little poem I made up," Ginny says, trying hard not to laugh.

Ivan turns white in rage when he reads it. "How dare you write this disgusting little verse and pass it off as poetry! Where did you learn such vulgar expressions, and how did you come up with rhymes for each and every one of these disgusting words?! And it's a poem about me, Boris, and Lyuba, don't try to deny it! Didn't you think I would guess who these three unnamed people are?!" He grabs Ginny and begins to punch him in the jaw.

"Look, Konev, he even added illustrations!" Boris laughs.

"Didn't your parents teach you to respect women? My mother would've washed my mouth out with soap had I used such expressions!" Ivan rips up the pornographic poem. "Your delicate eyes shouldn't see what he wrote!"

"I worked so hard on my poem!" Ginny starts crying.

"I made you *rassolnik* for your birthday," Lyuba says in a small voice. "I hope my cooking is as good as your mother's."

Ginny opens his mouth and begins to recite his poem. Ivan starts chasing him, and Ginny knocks into Lyuba carrying the pot of *rassolnik*. It spills all over the floor, and the pot breaks. Lyuba punches him in the face before stalking off to another room.

"See what you did to your cousin?" Ivan grabs Ginny by the ears and begins to slam him against the wall.

Lyuba comes back out after changing her dress. She immediately sets to work cleaning up the mess on the floor.

"Quit it, Konev! You really were named after the wrong Tsar! I'm telling my mother when I go to America that I was nearly killed by a spiteful man named for Ivan Grozniy!"

"You do and I'll stab you in the stomach and cook your innards for lunch, you horrible little urchin! Don't you respect your cousin? Don't you know I don't consider women mere objects of lust?!"

Ginny screams as Ivan starts battering him over the head with a horseshoe. Then they hear the singing of "The Internationale."

"Would anyone care to provide hospitality?" someone demands in a drunken voice. "We just deserted from the front, and are starving."

Ivan drops Ginny on the ground and stuffs a boot into his mouth to keep him quiet. He slings Ginny over his shoulder like a sack of potatoes and starts over to the four-poster bed, shutting the bedroom door just as the drunken deserters axe the front door open. Ivan slams Ginny on the floor, shoves aside the bed, opens the trap door, and throws Ginny down before jumping. Boris jumps down next. Lyuba is last.

Boris sends Ivan the evil eye as he catches Lyuba. "You've got designs on my woman, and I don't like it. Don't think I don't notice how much attention you've been paying her lately."

"*Your* woman?" Ivan laughs. "If you think she really likes *you* more, you're dangerously blind to the quite obvious!"

They stay there for endless moments listening to the deserters walking around upstairs. All the noise seems to be centered in the kitchen, where the intruders must be helping themselves to their food. Lyuba is shaking in terror by the time she finally hears them going away. While Boris has been keeping his hand tightly over Ginny's mouth to keep him quiet, Lyuba has been holding onto Ivan for dear life. Boris hasn't noticed this embrace is mutual. *He really* is *blind*, Ginny thinks in amazement.

5

The next time Basil and Pyotr come over, Basil stares at Lyuba. "What happened to your beautiful hair?"

"Vanya volunteered to cut it when I expressed interest in having a haircut. Modern women have short hair, and I'm a modern woman."

Basil stalks into the kitchen and smiles when he recognizes the tablecloth as Ivan's. He pulls a jackknife out of his pocket and starts cutting it.

Ivan clamps a hand on his shoulder. "Do you always cut up other people's heirlooms?" Before Basil has a chance to react, he throws a punch.

Pyotr leaves after putting canned goods on the shelves. He's confident leaving with Basil there since he's being pulverized by Ivan instead of standing around leering at Lyuba. Pyotr is almost as tall as Ivan, five feet eleven, and could probably win in a fight against Basil too, but he doesn't want to blow his cover. There's no telling if Basil would inform on him to his father or other authorities, and then three of Pyotr's friends, along with an innocent if very annoying little boy, would be thrown to the wolves.

Basil is black and blue by the time Ivan throws him out the door.

"Can you teach me how to fight good like that, Ivan?" Ginny

asks, gazing at him in admiration.

"Good fighters are born, not made. I've been tall and strong since I was a boy, and winning schoolyard fights always came naturally to me. Lyuba, aren't you proud such a brave, strong guy can easily win fights for your honor? You're pretty tall for a woman, but we all know men have more physical strength than women."

"And we all know I've never been the type of woman to feel incomplete or unwomanly without male attention. If I were to get married, I'd favor brains over brawn."

6

When Pyotr and Basil next come over several weeks later, Lyuba can immediately tell something's wrong, and when Pyotr starts speaking, her worst fears are confirmed.

"I came as soon as I could. I overheard my father, my brothers Kuzma and Venedikt, and a couple of my father's friends talking this morning. You'll have to join Eliisabet and Aleksey, because Katerina's family was arrested. I immediately recognized them from my father's descriptions. They were caught hiding peasants who took part in an uprising against their landowners. Now there's been yet another peasant uprising nearby, and the provisional government has sent out more of their forces to quash the rebellion. You'll be safest if you leave this area. There are no suspicions about Aleksey and Eliisabet's area, but if you're paid a housecall after you get there, don't make up any stupid stories or use fake names. Just act naturally and pretend you don't follow politics."

Lyuba starts trembling. Ivan wishes they weren't surrounded by so many other people, since otherwise he'd immediately rush to hold and comfort her, the way he used to when he walked across the rope between their bedroom windows after her degenerate father left for the night.

"Can I take Lyuba over?" Basil gives Lyuba his usual creepy leer.

"Not on your life, Basil Yakovlevich Beriya."

Pyotr glares at Basil. "You'd better start packing now." He hands Lyuba a map. "This is where we'll be waiting. Try not to be too long, since I can't lurk in this area indefinitely without my father finding out. I'd take you right from the house if I weren't so nervous about Bolshevik spies or Kerenskiy's thugs."

Ginny starts packing and pulling on layer after layer of clothing. As Lyuba packs her suitcases and pulls on as many clothes as can fit, she feels a bit guilty to have saved so many things from her former life. Boris only has one suitcase, mostly containing clothes, and Ivan also only has one valise, containing clothes, that tablecloth, a glass vase, coins, stamps, some poetry books, a few colored pencils, an ikon of St. Vladimir, and two small framed paintings, one of the Tsar and the other of Ivan's namesake. As she sees him depositing the colored pencils in their little box, Lyuba remembers how Ivan used to be an artist, often drawing pictures for her, and getting paint, charcoal, pastel, and colored pencil residue all over his left hand. A number of his drawings are in her own luggage. He told her some of the most famous lefties in history, the ones who weren't forced to switch, were artists, and that he'd like to be one too. But then his father beat it out of him, and now he hasn't picked up a paintbrush, charcoal pencil, or colored pencil in years. Perhaps these colored pencils remind him of happier days, when his heart was whole.

Just as they're about to leave, the air is punctuated with strange, loud, hostile voices, demanding all peasants and their sympathizers declare themselves. Lyuba tiptoes to the window and peers out to see where the enemy is so they'll know which door to leave by.

"You go on without me," Boris says. "I was so busy packing my belongings and the interesting stuff that came with the dacha, I forgot all about food and money."

"What if you're killed?" Ivan asks. "There'll be enough food at the new place, and we never spend money anyway."

"I'll be as fast as I can. Go on, I'll be right behind you."

As they start to walk away from the house in the dark, Lyuba is happy Boris isn't here. She almost hopes he's caught and killed, so she can be alone with Ivan. She feels strangely safe and protected walking by his side, for Ivan will meet Death before he'll let her be harmed. She cannot touch him because Ginny's there, but she sends him a longing look of love.

Pyotr and Basil are at the meeting-place, sitting in a haywagon. Ginny scrambles in and immediately falls asleep while Pyotr puts the luggage in.

"Won't you help me into the wagon, my Ivan the Great?" Lyuba asks.

He pulls her up. "There you go. Boris isn't half as strong as I am. He could never help you step into a wagon or carriage. Don't you want to have sons who are just as strong as I am?"

Lyuba sits in silence. Now is not the time to discuss such things.

"Where's Boris?" Pyotr asks.

"Getting money and food," Lyuba says. "Of all the times to think about insignificant things."

Boris comes panting over the horizon. "Sorry I'm late. I tried to get all the money, but I had to get out of the house because they set fire to it."

Pyotr shakes his head in disgust as Boris pulls his pudgy body into the wagon.

***

When they reach Eliisabet and Aleksey's house, Lyuba stares at Eliisabet's midsection. She definitely doesn't remember Eliisabet as overweight, and that concentration of weight in that place suggests only one thing.

Eliisabet smiles when she sees Lyuba staring at her. "I'm pregnant."

"You're only seventeen!" Lyuba says. "And not married!"

"I worry about my child sometimes, growing up in such a world we never knew. But Alyoshka's the most wonderful man I've ever met, so whatever happens in the world, my baby will have an incredible father." She goes over to Lyuba and whispers in her ear, "I hope you don't think I'm a whore because I slept with Alyoshka the first night we got here. He kissed me for the first time right after Katerina left, and one thing led to another. It hurt at first, but it got better over time."

"Of course I don't think you're a whore," Lyuba whispers back. "Christ said there's nothing higher than love, so how could love be a sin? You did what was natural."

"Wouldn't you love to be pregnant by me?" Basil asks.

"Never!" Lyuba slaps him.

"That's right, Basil," Ivan informs him. "She'll carry *my* children."

"I tell you, Lyuba, there's something missing in your life if you don't have someone to put his arms around you in the middle of the night," Eliisabet says.

Lyuba's mind drifts back to the week at the hotel, when she went to sleep every night in Ivan's arms. There's an aching twinge in her heart when she sees his beautiful deep brown eyes, his beautiful thick mop of dark brown hair, his beautiful face, his sensuous mouth...

"We'd better go," Pyotr says, dragging Basil out by his collar. "How many times do we have to tell you not to make unwanted advances on Lyuba?"

"We're women now, seventeen years old, not little girls anymore, and every woman deserves a good man who loves her, protects her, and makes her happy," Eliisabet continues. "I believe in women's suffrage and other progressive causes, just like you, but that doesn't negate my wanting more traditional things too."

"I'd feel too trapped and limited if I were nothing but a wife and mother. I don't want to die in childbirth or lose my mind after too many babies, or have nothing to fill my day with beyond cleaning, ironing, cooking, changing diapers, nursing babies, washing dishes, and being at a man's sexual beck and call. The only women who make history on their own merits are the ones who never married. I can only think of a few women who got famous in spite of having married, like Eleanor of Aquitaine or *Matushka* Mariya. Romantic attention makes me uncomfortable. I want to be seen as a friend, one of the boys, not a strange creature from another planet who only exists to be a future wife and mother. I was so uncomfortable at the first ball I went to with Vanya, when I was fourteen and he was sixteen. He kept saying things like, 'My arms were meant for holding you!'"

Lyuba sneaks a seductive look at him. She wishes he didn't have such beautiful deep brown eyes, since he always has such a wounded look in his eyes when he's sad. It's almost impossible not to feel sorry for him when he looks so forlorn.

"You're an oddity, but I still like you." Boris smiles. "I don't think I've ever known or read about any girl like you. All the other girls look forward to marriage as soon as possible instead of declaring they'll be better-off asexual."

"You read a book you weren't required to read?"

"I haven't much choice in how to amuse myself lately. There were a lot of good books back at the dacha."

"Well, *I* enjoyed reading long before you were forced to start reading for pleasure," Ivan says. "Lyuba also likes reading, and she likes men who like reading more than anti-intellectual boors who not too long ago spent more time stuffing their piggy faces than feeding their minds. I know her better than you ever will, and that must make you so jealous."

7

The next day, while Ivan and Eliisabet are preparing dinner, a knock sounds at the door. Everyone looks at one another, then around the house. There aren't any pictures of the Tsar or religious articles on display, so they're safe from both Bolsheviks and Kerenskiy's thugs. Finally, Aleksey goes to the window and peers out. Upon seeing a group of unarmed men wearing regular clothes, he breathes a sigh of relief.

"Just act naturally," he reiterates as he steps back. "For all we know, they're just regular travellers. They probably want lodgings for the night."

Boris gets the door. "Hello, good neighbors. I'm Andrey Vitaliyevich Gumilyov, and these are my wife Yuliya, her brothers Dmitriy and Maksim, and her cousins Mariya and Zakhar Rutskoy. We relocated from Tsaritsyn after our parents died. Our dinner is almost ready. Won't you come and sit down?"

"Of course. We just deserted, and hope to hide out in this area for awhile before travelling to Petrograd to meet up with our fellow Bolsheviks. That stupid provisional government can't be overturned soon enough."

Lyuba kicks Boris under the table after he plops into a chair. Pyotr specifically said not to make up a story or use fake names, yet Boris blazed ahead and did it anyway. At the rate he's going, he'll get them all in trouble.

"Why do you have a black eye?" one of the guests asks Boris.

"Oh, just a little horseplay between friends." Boris glares at Aleksey, who gave him a black eye and bloody nose last night. "Some men can't take a little joke and think they own their wives. God forbid another guy pay a little playful attention to his woman.

I've already got my own woman, *bolshoye spasibo*!"

Eliisabet brings out the food and forces smiles at the guests as Ivan sets the table. After everyone is seated, Ginny turns his nose up in disgust at the stuffed cabbage and onion soup.

"Do I have to eat this?"

"Of course, unless you want to be sent to bed without any food," Ivan says.

Ginny hurls himself from the chair and screams like a wild animal. "Make me!"

Ivan hauls him off to the closet, where they hear him whipping Ginny with his belt. He returns to the table dragging Ginny by his ear and pushes Ginny into his chair. After Ivan is seated, he brings a forkful of stuffed cabbage to his mouth, the guests staring. They record in their minds this left-handed rarity.

"Guess what," Boris says. "My wife is expecting and started having her pains just before you arrived. Isn't my wife amazing for how well she conceals her pregnant state? She's a bit early, but better a small baby than a big one."

Lyuba drops her fork, paralyzed by fear. Ivan sends Boris an icy-cold stare.

"Would you like us to fetch a doctor or midwife?" one of the guests asks.

"Thanks for the offer, but my wife doesn't need help doing what comes naturally to women. Our doctor trusts her to do it alone, so long as he monitors her progress beforehand." Boris kisses her on the cheek.

Lyuba shudders at his mouth on her face. If this is how repulsive a kiss on the cheek from him feels, she doesn't want to imagine how awful Boris would be if he ever kissed her on the mouth.

Boris abandons his food and pulls Lyuba up, Ivan trailing after them.

"Are you insane?" Ivan whispers once they're in Lyuba's room. "What will they say when there's no baby?! And saying she can do it without any help and that a doctor would agree to such an insane proposition? We're not in the jungles of the Pacific or the bushes of Sub-Saharan Africa!"

"We're supposed to be married, and this is excellent proof! Aren't you proud of me for thinking up such a clever story on the spur of the moment?"

"No, I'm more inclined to bash your head in for that stupid, stupid story! Can't you grasp the danger we're in?"

Full of terror, Lyuba begins screaming and moaning to go along with this ridiculous charade Boris roped them into. She's never witnessed a birth, but she knows enough to know women in labor usually make a lot of noise.

"My darling Yuliya had a stillbirth," Boris calls.

Ivan stares at him in cold horror. From what little he knows about birth, not even the fastest labor takes all of five minutes. There isn't even a body to show for this alleged stillbirth. If Boris got them all in trouble, he'll take Lyuba and run away with her as far as he can, not asking her permission. He'll drug her if he has to, just to make sure she'll be taken to safety. He's not about to stand idly by if the woman he loves is in danger because Boris can't keep his big mouth shut.

When Ivan returns to the table, the Bolsheviks announce their intentions to stay overnight. His heart is in his throat for the entire rest of supper and as the uninvited guests sit around talking with everyone until they retire to a spare bedroom. All night, he barely sleeps, constantly fearing they'll go into Lyuba's room and assault her, or find out they're upper-middle-class Muscovites who came here to escape the civil unrest and persecution of Tsarists. At least the Bolsheviks haven't wondered out loud why no doctor or midwife has come by to check on Lyuba after delivering alone.

At 5:00 the next afternoon, the guests leave after looking around in Lyuba's room. The room is very clean for supposedly having just been the site of a birth, but perhaps the birth fluids were already mopped up, the sheets thrown in the wash, and the placenta buried outside. There's some dried blood on the floor, but it's not very thick, and there isn't a lot of it. Nothing looks outwardly suspicious, but they can't shake the feeling these people have to be hiding something. They don't know what just yet, but they retain the mental note that Ivan has dark brown hair and eyes, is over six feet tall, and is left-handed, and the woman who supposedly had a stillborn is very tall for a woman, almost six feet tall herself, with raven hair and eyes.

Lyuba breathes a sigh of relief when they see the Bolsheviks' horses receding in the distance. "Everything we were told not to do to arouse suspicions, Boris did anyway. He'd better pray he didn't plant any doubts. I'd hate to have to go even farther away just to be safe." She pulls off the gloves she's been wearing all day. "We'll have to wash these to get the blood out. Borya cut our fingers to fake birthing fluids. He squeezed all the blood out on the floor."

"You did *what*?" Ivan takes Lyuba's hands and sees cuts on every single finger. "And you didn't cover them! I'll be right back with iodine and gauze. Malenkov, you're on your own if you want to cover your cuts."

"It's not a big deal," Boris says. "It's not like I amputated something."

"You're lucky you only did that instead of amputating anything, because otherwise I'd be very tempted to amputate something from your body. Now let me go to the medicine cabinet. I promised my Lyuba I'd get first aid."

8

Several days later, Pyotr and Basil return. Basil gives Lyuba his usual creepy leer, and Lyuba squirms under his gaze.

"Why again are you coming around with Petya? He's the only one doing the serious legwork in protecting us and giving us supplies. All you do when you come over is leer at me."

"I know it's annoying, but we have to put up with his unnecessary presence in exchange for my freedom." Pyotr drops a map on the table. "I overheard my father and some of his friends saying there are Bolsheviks moving through this area. There's no telling what'll happen, now that the Bolsheviks' Central Committee has voted to approve an armed uprising. The red dot shows where you're supposed to go, the town of Zaraysk. Boris and Aleksey should leave first, in case you're being watched."

"This is the third time we've been moved," Boris complains.

"Wouldn't you rather be moved a thousand times than be dead?"

"I think he just misses having a free range of cream puffs and other sweets," Ivan smirks. "Unlike some people, I appreciate how we're still together and alive."

***

Late at night, they hear loud, strange voices getting closer and closer. Ginny is indignant he's been woken up, and is screaming and jumping up and down.

"Liza, get up," Ivan says, gently shaking her awake.

"Where's Alyoshka?"

"He left with Boris and our luggage an hour ago," Lyuba says.

"I think I'm in labor. I know I'm early, but I think I'm feeling contractions."

"We have to get out of here. Even if you are in early labor, most women take a long time the first time, I've heard. We'll have plenty of time to find a doctor or midwife after we get to the new place."

"It hurts."

Nearby, screams fill the air and gunfire erupts.

"Ginny, go along without us," Lyuba orders.

Ginny starts running as fast as he can without looking back.

"Liza, get up."

She lifts her head up from the pillow. "I'm scared."

They hear the strangers shouting orders to burn the house down. It doesn't matter at this point if they're Bolsheviks or from the provisional government; all that matters is they're enemies.

"Liza, *pozhaluysta*!"

"I can't walk fast enough to escape them."

"Vanya, carry her."

Ivan lifts her and they leave by the back door just as the enemies torch the house. After what feels like an eternity, they finally find the others huddling around a campfire, wrapped in blankets and fur coats. Eliisabet is having her pains one minute apart by now, breathing fast. Her water has broken, and Ivan is having a hard time keeping a solid grip on her with the slippery amniotic fluids all over his hands and arms. She's so scared by the approaching forces, she's gone into precipitous labor at only twenty-eight weeks.

Ivan sets her on the ground after Lyuba unfurls an Arctic fox blanket from the wagon and everyone else clears away. To protect Eliisabet from the bitterly cold air, Lyuba drapes a polar bear fur coat over her, another warm, insulating treasure taken from the house they just left. Aleksey takes his place by the head of the makeshift birthing bed and holds Eliisabet's hands. Eliisabet doesn't want to be too loud, so she grits her teeth and squeezes Aleksey's hands so tightly he cries out in pain. Eliisabet's instincts are telling her to get on all fours to push and relieve some of the pain, but she doesn't want to lose the ability to look all around at a moment's notice. If her back is turned to the approaching Bolsheviks, she'll be the last to know.

"I have a strong maternal feeling it's a boy," she whispers as she pushes in a sitting position. "My little boy won't be taken from my arms because he was born out of wedlock! *Pozhaluysta*, Lyuba, don't let my baby die! I want you to be his godmother, and your husband can be his godfather! *Pozhaluysta*, don't let my baby die because he's so early!"

"Our Grand Duke Dmitriy Pavlovich was born at seven months too," Lyuba says, trying to be encouraging. "He's as healthy and handsome as can be, and safe in Persia."

"Liza, *ma armastan sind. Ya tyebya lyublyu*," Aleksey says. "Our son will know both of his cultures, Russian and Estonian. Since you're an advocate of women's rights, we'll give him both our surnames." He takes a ring out of his pocket. "I found this in the house. Turquoise isn't the most expensive stone, but the thought's still there. Will you, *pozhaluysta*, do me the honor of becoming my wife as soon as we find a priest?"

"Nothing would make me happier, my love."

She gives a cry of pain as the baby crowns. When Lyuba sees the head coming out, she quickly supports it with her hands and waits for Eliisabet to push the rest of the baby out, not wanting to take any chances with such a tiny baby by pulling on it to get it to come out faster.

"Well, you were right, Liza! It's a boy!" Lyuba wraps the tiny baby in a sable shawl and hands him tenderly to Eliisabet.

"Nikolay Alekseyevich Kutuzov-Tvardovskiy," she says, holding him next to her heart. "Your name will be Nikolay in honor of the Tsar!"

"Happy birthday, little fellow," Aleksey says. "You're a Scorpio just like me and your mother."

Eliisabet and Aleksey cry their eyes out as tiny Nikolay wraps his tiny little hands around their fingers. Lyuba looks proudly at her future godson, who doesn't appear as frighteningly underweight as she imagined.

"Why do I feel like I have to push again?" Eliisabet asks. "Am I having twins?"

"Gross!" Ginny shouts when he sees the placenta Eliisabet presently delivers.

"What do we do with *that*?" Aleksey asks, just as surprised as Ginny and Eliisabet to discover birth doesn't properly end with a baby. "Our enemies will know we were here if they find that."

"We'll carry it with us and cut it away later," Lyuba says. "He's early, so he probably needs extra time attached to it."

Aleksey takes him, supporting his little head, and leads Eliisabet over to the wagon. The others follow suit.

"Listen. My baby is crying very softly because he knows we'll be found out if he cries too loudly!" Eliisabet kisses him on his bald little head.

Boris takes the reins and drives to the place indicated on Pyotr's map. When they get there, Eliisabet collapses into the nearest bed, tears of joy in her eyes. Aleksey hands her Nikolay, and she nurses him. Lyuba makes the sign of the cross over her unofficial godson and whispers a prayer over him.

"He's so beautiful," Aleksey gushes. "It's hard to believe this happened so soon! We hadn't planned on this for twelve more weeks!"

"And he's named in honor of the Tsar," Lyuba adds. "What a beautiful turn of events these last few hours have been!"

"I don't like all this moving," Ginny whines. "There's nothing beautiful about being homeless and on the run from bad guys."

"We're alive and together, thanks to Petya. Didn't I tell you he was one of the good Bolsheviks? He's double-crossing his father and brothers every time he helps us. He's not getting any monetary reward for this. It's all about helping friends because he's such a good person. I wish Petya were our only helper, since we all know Basil only tags along because he's obsessed with me. The only thing stopping him from acting on his bizarre obsession, I'm sure, is that he knows he'll have to get through four of my male friends. The way he looks at me gives me a sick feeling in my stomach."

"You're safe with me, *golubka*," Ivan whispers. "Petya told me Basil's parents are sending him to school in Georgia, because they're tired of him not studying or working. Soon that creepy Beriya will just be a memory, and the only man who'll look at you will be me. I've never looked at you in a creepy or disturbing way."

"You look like you're in love every time you look at me. In another lifetime, I might be able to return the loving gaze."

"You'll be my wife in *this* lifetime if I have anything to say about it. God, if we weren't surrounded by all these other people, I'd take you to bed right now. I see the way you look at me when you think I'm not looking. When two people are meant to be together, even if they become separated, they always find their way back to each other no matter how long it takes. Remember that day we skipped gymnasium, before you jilted me, and we were watching the swans? The swan represents true, lifelong love, friendship, and loyalty, because it mates for life. You're my beautiful swan, my mate. Our pair bond may have been disrupted, but since we've already formed our bond, it's only a matter of time until it heals and you're back where you belong."

9

The next night, Pyotr and Basil come over with a huge haywagon. Pyotr's jaw drops when he sees the baby.

"What *happened*! She was only seven months along!"

"I got so scared, Petya, I went into labor early, and now here he is!"

"I proposed to Liza as she was bringing our baby into this world, and she said yes!" Aleksey adds.

"I named him after the Tsar. Isn't he the most beautiful baby anywhere?"

Pyotr gently rubs Nikolay's tiny arm. "Well, you three, get into the wagon. I'll arrange to have a doctor brought along to make sure nothing went wrong during the delivery. Little Kolya needs to be examined by a doctor also. At least he looks bigger than I'd expect a baby at that stage to be."

"Can you find a woman doctor?" Eliisabet pleads. "That's the next-best thing to a midwife."

"I sure can. I know someone who trained at St. Petersburg State Medical University, the women's medical school. She'll probably have progressive advice about how to keep a premature baby strong and healthy."

Aleksey, Eliisabet, and Nikolay get into the wagon and drive away with Pyotr and Basil. A few hours later, Pyotr returns to pick up the others. On the drive to Kolomna, he explains they're staying in different houses this time, hopefully only temporarily. He assures them he'll be on the lookout for a house in a relatively secure area, where they can resume normal life.

10

Lyuba serves cinnamon pancakes for breakfast, daydreaming about making and serving a hearty breakfast of strawberry, blueberry, or raspberry pancakes with thick maple syrup for Ivan and those mythical nine children of theirs in their farmhouse in the American Midwest. She's fantasizing about licking the excess maple syrup off his mouth when Pyotr comes through the door.

"Latest news out of Petrograd is that Kerenskiy was deposed. It looks like the Bolsheviks are going to take over power. The worst of the danger seems to be past, now that they've finally gotten what they wanted. So long as the transfer of power goes smoothly, I see no reason why you shouldn't go home. It's such a big city, no one will care about a few Tsarists in their midst. Just don't make waves and let on you want the Tsar returned to the throne."

"I want to see if it's true," Boris says after Pyotr leaves. "I'm going to find a paperboy."

"I hope it's not true," Lyuba says. "The best thing for Russia would be a return of our Tsar, but the next-best thing is Kerenskiy. At least he's not a raving Bolshevik."

"Well, someone has to check on the news, and I'm tired of relying on Litvinov to bring us all the news from the outside world. Don't worry, I'll be back soon. It's a good idea to talk to people on the street too, getting all the opinions instead of just the official one from the press."

They watch him leaving with mixed emotions, then decide to cut their potential losses and go back to breakfast before the food gets cold. It's unlike Boris to put current events before stuffing his face, but this means there'll be more food for them. They're not in the middle of a warzone, so it's probably relatively safe for him to walk around town. Like Pyotr said, the authorities and run of the mill Bolsheviks have greater priorities than tracking down expelled Tsarist gymnasium students.

Ginny finishes first and heads to his room to read the comic strips in the newspapers that were left lying around the house, not bothering to clear his dishes. Lyuba rolls her eyes and goes to clear his setting after she finishes eating. She jumps upon feeling Ivan pulling her around to face him.

"Don't you remember, during our beautiful month together, you finally gave in to your heart until your mother coerced you into jilting me? Let your heart do the talking again, and you'll see we belong together!"

"Let go of me, Vanya. That was months ago."

"Admit you love me! It's wrong to pretend we don't desire and adore each other!"

"It *is* wrong."

"How is it wrong for us to have a relationship if we really love each other? I know I'm a romantic dreamer with my head in the clouds and that I promise you a lot of things that probably won't happen overnight, but we'll have love in the meantime. I remember what you said to Ginny, how sometimes you're supposed to pick a husband who's socially safe even if he's not your first choice, and that you can't support your family and household on just love. But even if we are poor for a time, we'll have each other and our children to love. If you marry someone you don't love just for the sake of appearances and financial security, you won't have love to get you through the tough times. Are you a woman who knows what she wants, or a little girl who lets everyone else tell her who to love and what to do?"

Lyuba stares into Ivan's eyes with love. "You're right. I love none other than you. But it's not so simple, because something always gets in the way of our being together."

"It doesn't have to if you listen to your heart."

"Take me away from here. Be my lover. I would make love to none other than Ivan Ivanovich Konev."

Ivan slams the door in Ginny's face. Lyuba's soul cries from joy at finally getting to taste his soft, warm, sweet mouth again, and the maple syrup makes him taste even sweeter.

"I know just where to go. Alyoshenka and Liza can help us if we act immediately."

"Finish what you've started before we go!"

"I'd love to, but we need to leave before the will of God is ruined again by someone or something. Don't worry, we can get to work on trying for our first child tonight, so you don't have to wait too long. Holy Mother of God, I can't wait to become your lover."

Lyuba scampers off to her room to pack up her things and throws on her coat and boots. She's fantasizing about making love to Ivan as she rejoins him and slips her hand into his.

Basil comes in just as they're leaving through the back door. "That dunce Aleksandr Kerenskiy was deposed," he says. "Where are you going? Konev, what are you doing with her?"

"Do you always spring surprise visits on people?" Ivan asks.

Ivan holds Lyuba's hand more tightly and tries to leave by the window, but Basil notices that too. "Where are we going, Konev? Why are you taking Lyuba?"

"This isn't your house." Ivan tries to assert his authority over this trespasser. "We don't have to accept your unwanted company."

"I want to tell Ginny about Bolshevism." Basil flashes Lyuba one of his creepy grins, and her skin crawls. "I'm not going anywhere."

Feeling like the most incompetent, passive excuse of a man ever, Ivan takes a seat on the davenport with Lyuba, keeping a sharp eye on Basil across the room as he spews Bolshevik propaganda. Basil has the nerve to help himself to lunch, during which he talks with his mouth full and wipes his mouth across his sleeve. Even Boris doesn't talk with his mouth full.

Ivan is ready to burst into tears when Basil doesn't leave after lunch. He continues telling Bolshevik propaganda stories to Ginny, who listens with wide eyes. And of course, he just has to help himself to dinner as well, and then tell even more stories to Ginny till well into the night.

By the time Basil finally leaves, Lyuba has fallen asleep on the davenport. The only thing stopping Ivan from picking his sleeping love up and carrying her away is the uncertainty of travelling in the dark, not knowing if any roving Bolsheviks are lurking in the bushes. *At least she finally admitted she still loves me*, he thinks as he carries her to her bed and tucks her in.

11

Boris returns the next day, looking more chipper than the news would suggest. "It's true. The Bolsheviks chased Kerenskiy out, and there's going to be a victory ball organized by Katariina Nikonova. What a lucky guy I am, I get to take Lyuba this time!"

Ivan's heart stops beating for a moment. This could've been the perfect chance to sweep Lyuba off her feet and propose again, but because Boris had to open his big mouth in April, he got detention, and their usual order of taking Lyuba to balls was switched. He doesn't like the way Boris is looking at Lyuba, but he hopes Lyuba can stay true to her heart and resist any advances Boris might make on her.

****

Chapter 3: Trapped in Two Charades

In the afternoon, Pyotr arrives with a sleigh they'll take to the large social hall where the ball is to be held. Pyotr says it used to be the mansion of a Tsarist minister, but has been taken over by the opposition for social functions and Party meetings. Next door is a bombed-out hall where political meetings used to be held. Since Moskva is some distance from Kolomna, they'll take a steamboat along the Moskva River. Luckily, the river hasn't frozen over yet.

Lyuba hates the idea of having to be escorted by Boris, and how she let Boris have two turns in a row because their usual arrangement was thrown off in April. Not every man can be as handsome, tall, and strong as Ivan, but that doesn't mean she wants to be seen on the arm of someone who's short for a man, chubby, with large eyes, sickly-colored pasty skin, and terrible manners. To try to repulse Boris, she's worn an ordinary lilac wool dress instead of something fancy like her purple velvet ballgown.

"Do you have to be escorted by Boris?" Eliisabet whispers as the men climb into the sleigh. "I see how you look at Ivan when you think no one else is looking, and I know you had a clandestine romance in the spring."

"It's a long-standing arrangement we've had since gymnasium," Lyuba says in resignation. "They always took turns taking me, and since Boris had detention the last time, Ivan took over for him. If Boris hadn't had detention, Vanya would've taken me tonight."

"It's long past time you were honest with both of them. If you really prefer Ivan, it's dishonest to have them switch turns and pretend you only like both of them as friends. I can see it all over your face. That's the man you love. If you lead Malenkov on, things might get more complicated than you bargained for. It's easier to level with someone before things go too far than it is to jilt someone who thinks he's your beau."

"Just yesterday we were about to run away to get married and leave for America, but that creep Basil sprung a surprise visit on us and ruined everything. Vanya may have only ever kissed me, but he's as incredible as a man who's had a thousand prior girlfriends. I wish I were in his arms right now, doing all the things we used to do during our secret romance in the spring."

Eliisabet kisses two-and-a-half-pound Nikolay's head after he sneezes. "I can't go, because the doctor told me not to take out such a tiny premature baby, let alone in cold weather, but I want you to do the right thing and choose the man you love."

"Don't tell anyone. All my friends believe I've always preferred Boris. The only thing stopping me from being with Vanya is that I'm scared to death of being with a nice guy. You don't want to know why."

"Well, whatever your reason, I hope you're able to confide in me someday. I know we don't know each other very well yet, but I already consider you a good friend, and I'd never go around spreading my friends' personal business. You were my midwife, and yours were the first hands to ever touch my baby. We share a special bond after that. If it's because something awful was done to you to make you distrust nice guys' intentions, I'd never tell such a painful secret to anyone. And I would never judge or blame you if something horrible was done to you against your will. God knows there's a double standard. A man can have premarital relations with a hundred women and be lauded for it, while if a woman is caught just once having intimacy before marriage, people think she's a whore and fallen woman. Just remember what I told you, it's always better to choose the man you love, even if it hurts the feelings of your competing suitor."

Boris waddles into the house. "Aren't you coming, Lyuba? Liza's already got Alyosha staying behind to help her. Don't tell me you're trying to get out of being my date."

Lyuba sighs and follows him out to the sleigh. After she climbs in and Pyotr starts driving the horses, she sits in silence. The entire ride to Moskva, she looks longingly at Ivan. She's so absorbed in gazing at him, she doesn't realize the sleigh has stopped and they've arrived at the hall. Boris goes in first to help himself to *zakuski*, leaving Pyotr to help her out of the sleigh.

Ivan stops in his tracks as they enter. "Look who's here! Nikolas Vishinskiy and his little sister Kittey! I thought we'd never see them again!"

Nikolas, a longtime dear friend of Lyuba's, is a bookish intellectual, kind of scrawny in spite of his moderately tall height, and a lover, not a fighter. He's been going by the Greek form of his real name, Nikolay, since he fell in love with the ancient Greek philosophers at age twelve. It's a miracle the poor fellow wasn't eaten alive in Siberia. His gentle brown eyes are still warm and full of life, not empty and despondent.

Nikolas rushes up to them. "Long time, no see! Thank God Kittey and I are still alive. We were sent back home as part of a prisoner exchange, and Anya Furtseva was sent back with us."

Anna Pavlovna Furtseva, a rather strong-minded woman with strawberry-blonde hair, steps forward to hug Lyuba. "It's so good to be home, even if I'm alone in the world. At least I have friends to come home to. In the absence of blood relations, close friends take the place of family."

Lyuba surveys the crowd and sees a number of her other friends. She sighs when she sees Ginny scurrying off towards his old school friend Georgiya and a number of other children she recognizes as Bolsheviks.

"Is it okay if I steal your date for one dance, Malenkov?" Ivan smiles.

"What for? We always respected this agreement before and found other girls to dance with. What, are you scared Lyuba will fall for me so hard you'll never have a chance to escort her again?"

Lyuba grimaces when Boris puts his chubby arms around her. She sends a pleading look to Ivan, but he doesn't seem to notice as he walks off to talk with his friends. It's humiliating to dance with a man shorter than oneself, as opposed to Ivan, who stands now six inches taller than she is. Boris always wears inserts inside his thick-soled shoes to try to appear several inches taller, and he's never quite learnt how to balance on them while dancing. With any luck, this is the last time she'll ever have to dance with Boris, and by the end of the evening, she and Ivan will be on a train taking them to the coast and a boat to freedom.

***

"Hello, handsome. I see the woman you were interested in is on the arm of another man, so I have no more objections to you paying attention to me."

Ivan's eyes widen at the sight of Anastasiya Voroshilova, wearing an ordinary dress instead of the Jeanne Paquin gowns she wore in April. Perhaps Katrin was right, and she's not as stupid as she gives the impression of. If she survived a labor camp, she can't be completely harebrained.

"Don't say you can't remember me! Are you going to dance?"

Ivan begins to protest his heart belongs to Lyuba, then realizes he can use Anastasiya to make his belovèd turn green with jealousy. It won't be easy on him emotionally, but it's the perfect plot to win her back. There's no danger of developing feelings for Anastasiya, and it's not like he intends to get very physical with her. He and Lyuba held one another, kissed, touched, and slept in the same bed during that happy month in the spring, everything short of making love, but he's pretty sure Anastasiya's the type of girl who'd be offended by anything other than a chaste courtship. The main reason Lyuba didn't want to go all the way was because she was terrified of becoming pregnant, not because she wanted to wait for the wedding. Anastasiya would probably be scandalized at the thought of doing anything physical one moment before marriage.

Lyuba catches sight of her belovèd dancing with Anastasiya and feels a hatchet tearing into her heart. At the end of the evening, she intends to track down Ivan and let him know she accepts his offer of marriage and running away to America. If he's using that Voroshilova woman to make her jealous, he's doing a very fine job of it. Already Lyuba's heart is rending at the thought of anyone else being so close to the man she loves.

"I got you a present," Georgiya tells Ginny. "Your very own copy of *The Communist Manifesto*! If you have any questions, you can always come to my house. My *papashka*'s very important in the local Party, but he's so nice, he takes time out of his busy schedule to teach the next generation. It's too bad my annoying big brother Leonid can't be so generous with *his* time."

"Isn't this a grownups' book?"

"I didn't have much of a problem reading or understanding it, because it's so short and not full of boring statistics and lifeless examples like some of Marx's other books. And I just told you, my *papashka* explained the difficult parts. It's kind of funny Marx and Engels predicted the first Communist revolution would happen anywhere but here, because we were so backwards thanks to the Tsar."

"Stranger things have been known to happen, like Konev

dancing with that silly blonde Estonian girl."

"Girls like Anastasiya are a waste to any self-respecting Communist society. I'd be so humiliated if I'd been brought up to sit around primping myself, pining after handsome men, and doing nothing to contribute to society. She's the kind of girl who's washed-up by the time she's thirty, because she didn't do anything besides look beautiful and act helpless."

***

Lyuba can barely stand dancing with Boris, since he's not as good of a dancer as Ivan, and she hates how his pudgy arms feel around her, but this little charade won't last too long. Ivan will be jealous and come running to get her back, and forget he ever bothered with that Voroshilova woman. After what she feels has been a reasonable, respectable time, she excuses herself and goes to talk with Katriyana Dmitriyevna Vrangel and Aleksandra L'vovna Minina, having had enough of pretending to love dancing with Boris. Hopefully, her charade has already worked. She gave Boris amorous smiles every time Ivan looked in their direction and cuddled up nice and close to him while they were dancing. *Two can play at this game*, she thinks. *If Ivan wants to use Anastasiya to make me jealous, I can use Boris to make him jealous right back.*

"This sounds horrible, but I'm jealous of you for being on your own," Alya says. "Kat and I have both become betrothed against our will. At least you don't have parents around to arrange a marriage for you." She twists a strand of her bobbed red hair around her finger. "My parents took his side when he said he wanted me to grow my hair out after we're married. No way am I giving up the freedom of short hair. We've fought hard for the right to have shorter hair."

"Nikolas is my betrothed," Kat says. "All he does is read philosophy books. He's a nice guy, but being nice doesn't pay the bills. He wants to be a university professor or lawyer, and that won't exactly make us rich. And he goes by the Greek form of his name! Only nobles and royals go by non-Russian names! At least my excuse is that I didn't want to be just another Katya and needed some way to stand out from the crowd of fifteen sisters."

"My betrothed is Maksim Petrovich Gromyko. He cares more about books than people, and believes women are inferior to men.

Not that most men believe we're equals, but at least someone like Ivan or Nikolas is more benevolently old-fashioned instead of thinking we have no rights, intelligence, or feelings. We're supposed to get married in July. I wasn't made to be a wife and mother so young. Most of our mothers were married by our age, but it's a new generation. I want to work and go to university, not be chained to a man who thinks women are inferior."

"My life will be over once I start having kids. My poor mother has almost lost her mind on account of having fifteen kids. At least now there's a new drug that lets women go to sleep and wake up already having given birth. I hope that comes to Russia soon. I'd kill myself if I had to suffer through that many painful births."

"I don't want any kids," Lyuba says. "Not even one. My insides hurt just thinking about how your mother had fifteen pregnancies and deliveries. I hope Voroshilova's okay with Ivan's desire for nine."

"Nine children?" Alya asks. "That would be torture for me. I'd never get a moment's peace, and could never have a real job if I had to raise babies for thirty years."

"I'd go crazy at even five or six," Kat says. "And look how skinny I am. These hips weren't made for birthing babies. But you, Lyuba, you have a very womanly body. I think deep down you want that conventional life of marriage and motherhood, but you're too proud or modern to want to admit it. Out of all of us, I think you'd be most natural at it. And at least you can choose your husband, now that your parents are away."

"But make sure to choose the right one. You say you prefer Boris, but the way you and Ivan have always looked at each other tells another story. For the love of God, don't settle for Boris just because he promises more financially or has realistic ambitions. Love is the most important thing. I wish Kat and I had that option of marrying for love."

Lyuba grows cold with horror at the thought of being trapped in a charade with Boris. But the man she wants to marry, make love to, and grow old with is on the dance floor with her antithesis, and it doesn't seem like he wants to end his evening with Anastasiya anytime soon.

***

"I always wanted to marry a rich man or a royal," Anastasiya is gassing on, oblivious to the bored look on Ivan's face. "I used to dream about hosting teas and socials and mingling with the handsomest men at court. This ball is a dream come true after those seven months in Siberia. Hopefully I'll soon have beautiful clothes to wear again, and all the handsome men will cut in to dance with me. I'd love nothing more than to make the front pages of the society section, known as the wife of a rich man or prince."

"Is that all you think about, high society? There are far more important things going on in the world right now than worrying about marrying a prince or giving parties. I never liked women whose only interests lie in material things."

"But I'm not like that, Ivan! I'm not self-centered! I look beyond what's on the outside. Being in that labor camp made me a new person."

Ivan refuses to believe any of this spiel is remotely true, since leopards don't change their spots overnight. It's also ridiculous for Anastasiya to so clearly pretend to be someone she's not the moment she finds out her love interest's values are diametrically opposed to hers, and that she's far from the type of woman he's interested in courting. His one reassurance is that the woman he truly loves will come running back to him by the end of the evening, and he can soon forget he ever engaged in this charade to make Lyuba jealous.

***

Katrin is engaged in a shouting match with eleven-year-old Kittey Vishinskaya when Ivan and Anastasiya waltz past them later in the evening.

"You're out of touch with the modern Russia! The overthrow of your belovèd Tsar was a long time coming! The only people who liked him were upper-class people who never saw how the majority of real Russians lived, nor the people in the countries illegally occupied by the Tsar, like my own native Estonia!"

"Tell me how you sleep at night after you were responsible for the murders of your nine siblings and the arrest of your parents! You're living on blood money!"

Anastasiya wrinkles her nose. "That putrid traitor tried to hug me when she saw me earlier tonight. While I was imprisoned in the middle of nowhere, she was living like a princess in a damn mansion. The traitor gave me a bunch of my things and said she snuck over to my house after I was arrested. We're not best friends anymore. Though I'm not entirely sure she's a real Bolshevik."

"Are you sure about that? I seem to remember some very clear statements she made about hating the Tsar, being an Estonian nationalist, and resenting her parents for supporting the Tsar instead of agitating for an elected Estonian government."

"That's what she says, but I don't think she would've joined the Bolsheviks if she hadn't been forced into that corner at school. She's still living like a rich person! Bolsheviks hate the wealthy!"

Ivan looks up at the clock. "It's really late. I think I should go home." He cranes his neck to look for Lyuba.

"I should probably get home too. A lady never stays out past midnight, and the boardinghouse for single girls has a strict curfew. I only got to stay much later than the normal curfew when I presented proof I was going to a ball instead of compromising my reputation. Will you be my escort for the second ball tomorrow?"

"I hoped to escort another woman, but she's been having such a good time with her escort, she might come back with him. If you don't see me on another woman's arm, I'll be your escort."

Extremely hurt Lyuba hasn't approached him once during the evening, Ivan goes in search of Ginny. He stands back in the shadows when he sees Ginny talking to Georgiya, her twenty-three-year-old brother Leonid, and their parents by a carriage. As soon as they drive off, he taps Ginny on the shoulder.

"How does a warm train home sound? I have enough money for fare."

"Aren't we going to wait for Lyuba and Boris?"

Ivan looks back for a moment. "I'm sure they can find a carriage or steamboat heading our way. Besides, I think Lyuba's been having a good time with that chubby Malenkov. They might want to stay a bit longer. I was raised to be a gentleman, not a boor who horns in on another guy's date."

Ginny shrugs and follows Ivan.

Boris grabs Lyuba when he sees her starting towards the door. "Don't be in such a hurry to follow Konev. Wouldn't you rather ride home with me? Besides, here we have privacy."

Lyuba's heart starts racing. Perhaps this is what Eliisabet was trying to warn her about, leading on a guy she has no romantic interest in and then finding herself in too deep when the charade worked too well.

"I think I can still see Ivan. Vanya, wait up! I'll be right there!"

By the time she's out on the street, Ivan is gone. As the snow falls on her and she thinks of what a fine mess she's gotten herself into, Boris appears at her side. Her heart is in her throat as he pulls her back inside, dragging her into a corner. The nightmare reaches its peak when he lunges at her face and initiates a repulsive kiss. Lyuba recoils, but he pulls her back into his arms and holds her in an iron grip. Not only is she terrified of what Boris might do to her if she pulls loose, she's also nauseated at what an awful kisser he is. He's slobbering all over her and practically inhaling her mouth with a vacuum grip, no idea that real kissing is supposed to be a conversation. A first kiss isn't supposed to be like this. When Ivan first kissed her back in March, it was a soft, gentle, short kiss. Only after he knew she liked it and started getting the hang of how to do it did he go in for longer and deeper kisses. But now Lyuba fears she'll never enjoy another kiss with Ivan again, since Boris might spread around the story that she's a tramp and a tease if he finds out she's really in love with Ivan. She knows as well as anyone only disreputable girls let themselves be kissed by guys they don't have serious feelings for.

2

Ivan jumps out of bed and grabs a lantern when he hears the door creaking open and sees Lyuba and Boris come in.

"Praise Christ! I was so worried about my Lyubochka when you didn't come home. Are you okay, *golubka*? I hope you're not too mad at me for what you saw. I can explain what I was doing with Anastasiya. It's not at all what it might've looked like."

"I wanted to go with you and Ginny. Why couldn't you wait for me?"

"I'm so sorry we left without you. I had no idea you wanted to follow us. Now you must be even more upset at me."

Boris pushes Ivan away when he sees him moving to hug Lyuba. "*Pozhaluysta*, don't touch my woman. Lyuba's now my girlfriend, and you know how indecent it is to hug another man's woman. Tell me a decent, honorable girl like this would let a guy kiss her if she didn't really, really like him and want to be courted by him!" Boris lets out a very loud, obnoxious yawn. "I'm going to hit the hay. See you people tomorrow."

Ivan looks at Lyuba in shock, unable to believe just yesterday she admitted she still loves him, kissed and embraced him for the first time in seven months. The only thing stopping them from running away to elope and move to America was Basil's unwanted visit. She's just broken his heart in a million pieces yet again.

If only Boris hadn't had detention, it would've been my *turn to take her to the ball*, he thinks, feeling a sharp knife piercing through his already broken heart.

In her room, with the door closed, Lyuba cannot hear Ivan crying himself to sleep the same way she's doing. The man she loves just spent the entire evening dancing and talking with a woman with as much sense and intelligence as a pump handle, and now she feels she's lost him forever. Instead of being held and kissed by a handsome, sensitive man, she has little choice but to remain with a short, fat, less than handsome man with uncouth, impulsive manners. Ivan wouldn't have been able to take care of her financially as Boris could, and God knows her mother impressed on her over and over the need to marry a man with solid job prospects, unlofty ambitions, and money, but Ivan would've been a loving husband and father. Knowing this is all her fault for being so easily manipulated and afraid of being with a nice guy makes it even worse.

3

Lyuba can barely keep her breakfast down in the morning, and doesn't say a word while Ginny prattles about what he's read so far in *The Communist Manifesto* and Boris and Ivan ridicule him for switching teams just like that. She stays in her room the entire day, except for meals, and bursts into tears each time she thinks about that repulsive, forced kiss and the charade relationship she's been painted into. Even if it's what she always said she wanted, what her mother impressed on her she should want, it doesn't feel good to lose the man she really loves.

Pyotr once again brings them over to Eliisabet and Aleksey's house to visit before they leave for the second victory ball in the evening. As soon as they're done eating supper, making smalltalk, and fawning over tiny Nikolay, Lyuba rushes into a back room with Eliisabet and bursts into tears again.

"What happened, *golubka*? Why does that chubby man think you're his girlfriend just because he was your escort? Don't tell me you're still holding to that ridiculous agreement from your gymnasium days. If you really want Ivan to be your escort, you should say so, instead of saying Boris has to escort you twice in a row just because their usual order was thrown off in April."

"I feel like such a whore, Liza! Borya wouldn't let me leave with Vanya and Ginny, pulled me back inside, and forced this disgusting kiss on me! So now I have no choice but to be his sweetheart. Vanya spent the entire evening dancing with that lightheaded Voroshilova moron. He'll be her escort again tonight. I almost want to kill myself."

"What? A fellow kisses you, and you think that makes you beholden to him? Kissing is more personal than holding hands, but this is the twentieth century! What kind of people have you been associating with if you think you're only allowed to be kissed by a man you want to marry, or a serious beau? Not that I think you should go around kissing every man in the neighborhood, but it's not like you're a whore if you kiss a few guys you don't want to get serious with!"

"He'll tell people I'm a tramp and a tease. I brought it on myself by playing up the charade. All I wanted to do was make Vanya jealous and rue how he danced with Anastasiya. Now I'll look like a complete liar and whore if Boris finds out the truth. I was never a Lillian Gish or Mary Pickford type of girl, but I was never a Theda Bara or Valeska Suratt type either. I might be a modern woman who feels herself equal to men, but I have my limits. I don't want to be seen as a heartless, man-eating Vamp."

Eliisabet unbuttons her blouse and positions Nikolay at her breast. "Even a Lillian Gish type would be considered innocent if a man of ill repute forced a kiss on her. But you have to come clean as soon as possible."

Boris knocks on the door. "Aren't you coming, Lyubochka? I can't wait to spend all evening dancing with my new woman!"

Lyuba stands up and looks at Eliisabet in resignation. "This serves me right. I wouldn't have let any of this happen if I were serious about Ivan or as strong-minded as I claim to be. At least I'll have a good life financially, and in time I might grow to love him as I love Vanya."

Lyuba sits in silence as Pyotr drives the sleigh. She doesn't have the heart to fantasize about doing anything with Ivan. Though she was never very interested in balls and only attended them out of obligation and for the sake of appearances, it already seems as though the night will be endless.

Katrin greets them at the door. "How good to see you again. It is my fervent hope that after enough time of living under our glorious new régime, you'll come to your senses and embrace the new Russian order. You said you were a modern woman, Lyuba. No self-respecting modern woman would pick a reactionary monarchy over Socialism if she were fully educated on what Socialism has to offer the oppressed peoples of the world."

"Thanks to Socialism, I'm now oppressed myself," Lyuba mutters.

"You don't see anything ironic about suddenly being in the position the repressed masses were in for centuries? Now you know how they've always felt, and why they finally had the guts to throw off their chains. Anyway, I live in a requisitioned mansion on Povarskaya Street, near gymnasium. School administrators didn't feel comfortable letting a seventeen-year-old emancipated girl live alone, so I have a maid for the sake of appearances. You're all welcome to visit anytime you'd like, and we can discuss politics, news, philosophy, religion, literature, history, lots of enlightening subjects."

"We'll see about that." Lyuba walks away from Katrin as quickly as possible.

Ginny trips Aleksandr before going over to Georgiya. Lyuba gasps, but her attention turns when Anastasiya enters.

"That's Anastasiya Voroshilova," Lyuba tells Anya. "She's an Estonian who bites her nails and somehow survived a labor camp. I never saw the appeal of curly blonde hair and blue eyes. Dark hair and eyes have more personality. Holy Mother of God, if you even spend five minutes around this woman, you'll feel your intelligence shrinking. All she cares about are handsome moving picture actors, unmarried princes and grand dukes, fashion, and salacious news stories about the rich and famous."

"What's she doing with Ivan? I always thought he was in love with *you*!"

"All I know is I'm no longer the woman he loves."

Kat blanches. "Here comes Nikolas! I've been as rude to him as possible since our betrothal. I feel a little bad, since he lost his parents and must've gone through a really tough time in the labor camp, but he's not the man of my dreams. Someone like Leonid Yuriyevich Savvin is more my type. Even if he's a know-it-all and not very social, at least he has money and works a real job."

"But he's a Bolshevik!"

"I'm sure I could find that type of man among our people. And didn't you come here for the second night with a man you're not really in love with? We should each seek our own happiness and not feel compelled to stay with the first man who courts us."

"Kolya's a very nice guy, and it's only him and Kittey now. He's probably lonely and wants to start a family. Doesn't darling little Kittey deserve a big sister after losing her mother? Maybe you could grow to love him, like people did in the olden days. My mother always told me there's a lot more to marriage than lust or social outings."

"God knows he's not the type of guy most girls dream about, with all his philosophy books and intellectual debates," Anya says. "But at least he's not Maksim or Boris. A handsome prince won't warm your wool forever, but a man with a good heart will provide for you and love you no matter what."

"You know this is true. At least your betrothed is attractive, intelligent, and considerate." Lyuba fights away tears at the thought of being indefinitely stuck with Boris.

"I was often assigned to work duty with Nikolas at the labor camp, and he was always very protective. When we were being sent home, one of the guards loading us onto the boxcars tried to frisk me. Kolya told him in a low growl to lay the hell off me and Kittey. We boarded without molestation. I live with them in a squalid little hotel room, posing as his cousin, and he protects me and Kittey from unwanted male attention. He can act traditionally masculine when the need arises."

Kat considers the matter as Nikolas approaches them. She can't help noticing he's kind of cute, even if he's only moderately tall and isn't very muscular. She looks over at Lyuba and sees the pained expression on her face. In spite of Lyuba's longtime pretense of preferring Boris, Kat knows her real love is Ivan. She can't fathom why Lyuba would choose a man she doesn't seem genuinely happy with. At least her parents have matched her with someone she's always liked as a friend.

"Care to dance, or are you going to berate me again for not being as handsome as a moving picture actor and more interested in books than socials?"

"I'm sorry I've been rude to you, but I don't want to be forced to marry someone my parents picked. You're a really sweet guy, and maybe I was too harsh on you. Not everyone's meant to land a handsome prince, and as the last of fifteen daughters, I certainly can't have any delusions about my prospects. You're a nice guy, and the fact that you're an intellectual and an idealistic dreamer tells me you'll be nice and respectful, unlike a lot of other guys."

Nikolas's whole face transforms into a huge smile. "You're a nice girl, Kat. I'll do everything I can to prove I'm worth your time. What a lucky guy I am, to be matched with such a pretty girl who's willing to give me a second chance."

Lyuba feels almost crushed by the pain in her heart. If she had any sense, she would've leveled with Ivan the same way Kat just did with Nikolas. But instead she feels obligated to continue being courted by Boris, all because of that repulsive kiss and her terror of having her reputation ruined.

Alya comes in on Maksim's arm, looking very unhappy. As soon as he goes over to his friends, she rushes to Lyuba and Anya.

"I know I'm of marriageable age, but I wish I had a say in who my future husband is. I'm not against arranged marriage, but I want to at least like the potential husband instead of being told I have no choice and can't meet any other candidates."

"I'm going to America to join my mother and aunt as soon as possible," Lyuba says. "Maybe you could come with us so you can get out of this marriage. Ginny, Borya, and Vanya are coming too. I hope it's still possible to immigrate now that the Reds are taking over."

"What if Ivan decides to take Anastasiya?"

Lyuba looks over at Anastasiya and takes in her baby blue

eyes, painted face, and fluffy blonde curls. It's incomprehensible Ivan should've fallen for someone who looks like this, when he always used to tell her how much he loved her raven eyes and long sable hair, and how he was glad she doesn't paint her face like other modern women. He always told her how much he loved her natural beauty. And Anastasiya is about a foot shorter than Ivan, whereas Lyuba is almost six feet tall herself. Ivan has often told her he likes how she's tall for a woman and closer to his own above-average height.

Ginny suddenly appears at Lyuba's elbow. "Are you really interested in Malenkov romantically? I know you've said you like him more, but the way you look at Konev makes me think you really prefer him. What exactly happened last night?"

"Boris kissed me, and even you must be old enough to know only tramps do that with men they don't intend to be serious with. Now go away!" She feels weak in the knees remembering that delicious month in the spring, and the incident a few days ago, wondering if she'll ever be able to feel Ivan's arms around her and his soft mouth on hers again. She dares not confess to her friends and Ginny that Boris is actually the second, not the first, boy to have kissed her. She's afraid they'll think she's a whore, and she's worked so hard for so long on the façade that Boris is the one she likes most.

***

"Would you like to dance?" Boris asks Lyuba when he comes across her an hour later.

"Can't I take a little break? You know I never liked dancing that much. And I think Vanya might be upset, since tonight was supposed to be his turn." *And our rule is stupid*, she thinks. *Taking turns taking me to balls indeed. I wanted to be with Ivan. You, you tricked and trapped me!*

"He'll get over it. In the meantime, I have a dance card with your name on it."

Feeling more and more trapped by the moment, she lets him put his hands on her ribcage. She curses herself for not being strong enough to stay with the man she truly loves, her degenerate father for messing her up so badly for so many years, her mother for pressuring her into jilting Ivan, Anastasiya for ensnaring him,

Basil for springing that surprise visit on them when they'd been about to run away together, and most of all Boris for forcing that repulsive kiss on her last night. Now he believes they're a couple, and Lyuba can't very well come clean now without looking like a tramp, a tease, and most of all a liar.

Ginny and Georgiya are snooping around in the bombed-out hall next door, looking for any loot that might've been left behind or spared the raid, when they hear approaching footsteps. Upon recognizing Lyuba and Boris, Ginny runs outside to the veranda with Georgiya and crawls underneath. Their eyes widen at what happens next.

Boris starts kissing Lyuba's neck, unbuttons the first three buttons of her blouse, pulls her to the wall, and kisses her. Sick to her stomach, she tries to pretend he's Ivan. Ginny shrieks.

"Hey, get out of here!" Boris yells. "Can't a man have privacy to love his lady?"

"Privacy means in your own home," Georgiya says. "Or a respectable place like a hotel. I might be only in fifth grade, but I'm not stupid or naïve. Before I only thought you looked stupid. Now I know you're stupid and ill-mannered."

"You're just a child! What do you know about adult matters!"

"Trust me, I know plenty. I'm not a goody-goody who was shielded from reality, like you might've been at my age. Things like that are all going to come to an end soon. Bolshevism doesn't believe in raising children to be helpless, ignorant, and fearful of reality or adult life. My parents never had any part in this modern-day notion that children are delicate, fragile little glass things who need to be handled with kid gloves or they'll break. Only a few hundred years ago, people my age were routinely exposed to things that are now considered inappropriate for our ears and eyes." She turns and walks off with Ginny.

Boris looks at Lyuba.

"No thanks. I've lost the mood."

I never had the mood, she tells herself. *You're pathetic. Ivan's a lot better than you.* She remembers how they were that happy month in the spring. How sweetly and gently he would hold her close, yet how passionately he would kiss her, like a man who's been with dozens of women and has perfected his skills from so much experience. Yet

Ivan has never kissed any other woman. It's as though they were so wonderful together because they're soulmates.

Lyuba desperately looks over at Ivan dancing with Anastasiya and wants to fling herself into his arms, and she pictures them taking a cab and getting a room at an out of the way hotel, and then all night long they'll hold one another, tell one another secrets, and finally become lovers. With tears in her eyes, Lyuba imagines herself telling Ivan a few weeks later that she's pregnant. But she'll have no such thing happen. Ivan, unbeknownst to her, is only with Anastasiya to try to make her jealous, and Lyuba, unbeknownst to Ivan, is only with Boris because he trapped her into a relationship. *C'est la vie.*

***

Pyotr catches up to Lyuba at the end of the ball. "One of my underground friends alerted me to the existence of a big abandoned house in a valley, near the town of Mitino. You can move in tomorrow." He slips her six train tickets. "The best news is, as you might've heard, Basil is being forced to go to school in Tbilisi. His parents are sending him there in a few weeks so he can get moved into the dormitory before the winter semester starts. Hopefully he'll find a Georgian girl to obsess over and forget all about you."

Just like Vanya forgot all about me, she thinks despondently as she puts on her coat.

4

Lyuba is outraged to see Anastasiya is one of her housemates, but doesn't dare say anything for fear of upsetting Ivan. His charade also worked too well, and now Lyuba believes he's in love with Anastasiya. At least Anastasiya will be sleeping in her own room instead of cuddled up in his arms in Lyuba's place. She's much happier to see Alya is also one of her housemates. This can only mean she ran away from home to escape her arranged marriage.

"Since I'm the most beautiful woman here, I decided I'm going to be Snegurochka," Anastasiya announces. "I hope there are no objections. Because of the change in régime, I can't help Dyed Moroz hand out gifts, and last year's ban on Christmas trees is still in effect, but it'll be nice to have at least one tradition. Why don't we buy a sleigh and drive me around to sing at friendly houses?"

Ivan thinks Lyuba is the most beautiful woman there, but

dares not say anything in front of Anastasiya, who believes they're courting. For all he knows, Lyuba really did decide to take up with Boris for the reasons she laid out many a time—appearances, social advancement, better future financial outlook, and a basis of more than physical attraction or butterflies in the stomach. He thought he and Lyuba had a deeper connection because of their going on ten years of being best friends and their similar traumatic childhoods, the kind of connection that would indeed keep the home fires burning even at seventy or eighty. Whatever her reason, he's not going to stoop so low as to steal his best friend's girlfriend. If Lyuba truly loves him best, she'll come back to him eventually. His mother told him if you love someone, sometimes you have to let that person go, and if it's truly meant to be, that person will come back to you.

5

The next day when everyone sits down to breakfast, Ivan's seat remains empty. Aleksey goes upstairs to look for him, and finds him nowhere in the house, on the porch, or around the yard. Lyuba's stomach clenches at the thought of her belovèd going on a walk and being arrested by Bolsheviks. She can hardly stand the thought of her sweet, gentle Vanyushka being beaten, starved, and tortured in prison. Eliisabet rushes to the general store and places a frantic call to Pyotr, ordering him to look around the city for their missing friend. Lyuba's mind is going crazy with nightmare scenarios by the time Pyotr shows up with Ivan in tow very late in the evening.

"Our friend was at a jewelry store. I hope he hasn't caught something from being out in the cold so long."

"A jewelry store?" Lyuba demands. "You're already buying expensive jewelry for your brand-new girlfriend?"

"Yes, I do have that kind of effect on men." Anastasiya smiles.

Pyotr steps into the kitchen, motioning to Lyuba. In a whisper, he begins talking. "I have no idea what in the world happened, but I know it's not what either of you really wants. It's no secret I've always liked you, but I knew you really liked Konev best. Other people might've bought your act of liking Malenkov best, but I never did. If you're just using Malenkov to get back at him because he was sucked in by that Voroshilova woman, it's doing everyone a disservice. I've known women like Anastasiya. They delusionally think one conversation, one smile, one dance automatically equates a full-fledged relationship or being in love. They paste up pictures of film actors and unmarried princes on their bedroom walls and believe they might get lucky enough to marry one of those guys. I don't know why he feels obligated to fuel her fantasy, but it can only end badly the longer any of this continues. I'm still attracted to you, but I'm man enough to put my friendship for you above any romantic feelings. If Malenkov really likes you, he can do the same and let you go to the guy you really love. Just be careful, whatever happens. I like you too much to see you getting hurt by a relationship with the wrong guy or losing the guy you really love."

Lyuba steps back into the living room in time to see Anastasiya taking off Ivan's coat and giving him a heap of furry blankets. Aleksey throws more logs on the fire. Lyuba bristles to see another woman doing little things for her belovèd. If she had any sense, she would've accepted his marriage proposal in April or run away with him recently. Then *she'd* be the one fetching warm blankets for him, making him tea, bringing him hot chicken soup, taking his wet coat off for him, and sitting by him to keep him company. She wants to scream at how things are turning out between her and Ivan.

6

The next day, Kittey and Ivan stand on the veranda watching migrating birds, while the women sew and Ginny makes a voodoo doll of Aleksandr. The other men of the house read newspapers.

"You're not going to talk with your new girlfriend or hold her sewing supplies?" Kittey laughs. "I'm surprised she let you come out here to watch birds instead of being constantly by her side. Why are you with her? I may be only eleven, but I'm not stupid. You're with that silly Estonian woman to spite Lyuba for taking Boris as her beau. For all you know, maybe Lyuba's with Boris to try to spite *you* for courting Anastasiya. I really think you all got your signals crossed, and now feel obligated to continue these stupid charades. Don't look at me like that. I know you love Lyuba. God, the way you always looked at her was the look of a guy head over heels in love. It's how men in the moving pictures look at their sweethearts."

"Where did you get the idea I'm in love with Lyuba?"

Kittey rolls her eyes. "I think everyone knows it. You can pretend all you want with that empty-headed Voroshilova woman, and Lyuba can pretend with that short, fat Malenkov, but anyone with a set of eyes who's been around both of you long enough knows the truth. You're in love with each other, and have been for quite some time. My brother told me he and Alyosha caught you kissing and embracing a couple of times! I have no idea why neither of you has done anything about it, but the longer you put off getting back together, the harder it'll be. If you let these phony relationships with Voroshilova and Malenkov continue, it'll only get much more complicated to find your way back to each other."

Ivan crawls under the porch swing and pulls a blanket over himself when he sees someone approaching in the distance. Kittey hears his heart thumping out of his chest. She looks at the man curiously, wondering why he scared Ivan so much he felt the need to hide. Pyotr assured them this valley is a safe haven. Probably the man is just passing through and means them no harm. Certainly, no matter what his politics, he's either minding his own business or has much bigger fish to fry than tracking down run of the mill Tsarists.

"Excuse me, young lady, have you seen a tall young man with dark brown hair and eyes? I've been on the lookout for this man since he escaped from justice this April, and I'm very eager to close this case so my men and I can move on to bigger things."

"That could describe any number of men I've seen."

"Oh, you'd know this man right away if you saw him writing, eating, turning a key, you name it. He's a *levsha*. As if such a sickness weren't rare enough, this man is even rarer because he didn't have it successfully beaten out of him."

"Sorry, I don't think I know any *levshi*." Kittey hopes she has a very good poker face. "But I'm glad to be of service to you so you know where not to look."

He tips his hat and continues down the road.

Ivan is so shaken-up by the close call, he heads into the house as soon as Kittey whispers the all-clear. He flings himself down onto a davenport and lies there shaking.

"What happened?" Lyuba asks.

"Kittey just saved my life. One of the barbarians who killed my mother was just by, asking after a man of my description.

Thank God he didn't decide to enter the house or look around the veranda! And for the love of God, why do so many people think left-handedness is some kind of sickness? It's how God decided to make me and my late uncle, as well as many famous writers, artists, and musicians. It's not a mark of Satan; it's a special gift from God. I like being different."

Lyuba's eyes narrow when she sees something sparkling on Anastasiya's finger. "What's that? Is that what you bought her yesterday when you were out so late at the jewelry store?"

"It's an early Christmas present. Don't be jealous of her. Boris can easily buy you a nice piece of jewelry too. You don't even like diamonds. You always preferred dark-colored gemstones. I'm sure you'll get something equally nice for Christmas from your beau."

"We all decided we're not exchanging presents! We have no money to waste on things we don't need! How dare you waste good money on a foolish diamond ring for your new girlfriend! What makes her so special she deserves a Christmas present, and an expensive one at that, while everyone else does without?"

"I'm special." Anastasiya stands behind Ivan and rubs his shoulders. "You really lucked out. I got a tall, handsome beau with money to buy me nice things, while you got a short guy who's not that attractive and doesn't have any money to make up for his lack of good looks."

Lyuba's heart sinks. If she hadn't been tricked into a relationship with Boris, she and Ivan would've been engaged by now. But now he's giving that Voroshilova woman expensive Christmas presents in her place. Cold comfort is the knowledge that at least he isn't doing anything physical with that woman.

7

Any remaining hopes of Ivan and Anastasiya's relationship not being that serious are dashed when Lyuba walks past Anastasiya's room one afternoon and sees her modeling a floor-length white mink coat and matching hat with earflaps in front of the mirror. Even from a distance, Lyuba can see light reflecting off a diamond necklace nestled among the fur. Fuming, she throws on her shabby coat and boots and storms outside, where she knows Ivan is feeding the six horses Pyotr bought them.

"How much money did you spend on that *suka* this time?"

Lyuba demands. "I don't understand why you've become such a fool for that woman!"

"It's nice to buy things for a woman who actually welcomes my romantic attentions. Why should I be expected to live like a monk?"

"I never thought she was your type. Maybe I don't know you as well as I thought."

"And I never thought you liked Malenkov enough to choose him as your beau, so we're even." Ivan indicates the sleigh Pyotr gave them. "Would you care for a ride? Just because I'm courting someone else doesn't mean we're not best friends anymore."

"Don't insult me or try to cause a scandal. It would be unseemly for you to give another man's girlfriend a ride in a sleigh alone. I hope you have fun courting that empty-headed woman. At least Boris has made some new friends who've offered him work opportunities. My mother was right when she said I need to marry a man with money. Thank God I'm not the one being courted by someone without any money."

8

It's now 21 December, and Lyuba is still stewing at the memory of her eighteenth birthday ten days earlier, when Ivan only gave her a pair of mittens instead of his usual personal gifts like jewelry, silk scarves, or poetry. She'd like to throw those damned mittens in his face or beat him over the head with them instead of pulling them onto her hands as they get ready to go out. The Bolsheviks took over Moskva on 15 November, and fighting stretched on for two long weeks. Now that the city has turned Red, it's relatively safe to leave their small town near Mitino and go back into the big city. It won't be the Moskva she lovingly remembers, but at least she'll be able to walk there freely again.

As they walk around and make stops at a bakery, a dress goods shop, a boutique, a toy store, a bookstore, and a candle store, looking more than buying, Lyuba looks longingly at Ivan holding hands with Anastasiya. When they stop in front of a salon, the nightmare gets worse.

"You should wear a scarf in this sort of weather. Here, wear mine. Frostbite can kill you!" She fastens her scarf around his neck as Lyuba bristles at her belovèd being touched by another woman.

"I'm going in to buy some beauty products, and I'll probably be in there for awhile. Don't go anywhere, my handsome prince!"

Lyuba glares up at him when she sees him standing over her on the bench she's found behind the salon. "What do you want?"

"Can't I sit with my best friend while I wait for that empty-headed woman to come out?"

"If she's so empty-headed, why is she your girlfriend?"

"She was there and you weren't. I don't interfere in another man's relationship, even if I did once love his girlfriend. It's not right."

"Oh, so now you admit you don't love me anymore. I was wondering why you only got me a pair of mittens for my birthday and not something more personal. I'm glad to know you've completely forgotten how you were so crazy about me since you first saw me when you were nine years old."

"It's not like that. But if you didn't really care for Malenkov, you wouldn't be with him. If that's the man you really decided makes you happiest, I'm no one to argue with that. I'm man enough to let the woman I love go if I know she wouldn't be happy with me, even if you are with my old rival. Maybe in time I'll learn to love that vain blonde thing."

"I don't want to imagine you kissing and holding that moron. I'm jealous of her for getting a boyfriend who knows how to kiss. Boris is so awful, I can't even describe it."

"We have a very chaste courtship. I don't think she expects me to do anything to her until we're married."

Lyuba looks tearfully at Anastasiya's form behind one of the upper-level windows. "Just kill me now and get it over with. I can't live knowing another woman will be called Mrs. Koneva, making you meals, bearing you children, and making love to you in my place. I got what I deserved, hesitating so long on our relationship."

"Are you telling me you still have feelings for me?" he whispers. "Because if you are, I'll jilt that woman as soon as she comes out, and make you my wife before the year ends. I'll sell everything I own so we'll have enough money to go to America. Little Baby Konev might be growing inside you by next month at this time. I can't wait to be a husband and father. I promise I'll be the best father in the world. After how my father beat the hell out of me when he was drunk, every single day for years, I'll just about smother our kids with all the fatherly love I was cheated out of. I'd never even spank a child once if he misbehaved. The thought of hurting a child makes me want to throw up. Children deserve love and protection from their parents, not fists, kicks, belts, clubs, and switches." He struggles to compose himself upon remembering the brutal treatment he had to endure as a boy.

"It's too late now, Vanya. I'm not going to destroy my reputation by ending my relationship with Boris. No woman wants to be known as a tramp and a tease for getting involved with a guy she doesn't want to marry or have feelings for."

"I don't care what anyone says or thinks about you, *golubka.* Don't ever forget I'll be right here waiting for you to come back to me, no matter how long it takes you to decide you've had enough of Malenkov." He jumps to his feet as soon as he sees Anastasiya coming.

9

Anastasiya is up at five in the morning on Christmas. Lyuba wants to murder her when she loudly knocks on everyone's doors and screams at them to wake up. She would've thought Anastasiya would like to get as much beauty sleep as possible, eat a fancy breakfast Ivan doubtless made with expensive ingredients bought just for her, go back upstairs to take an hour-long bath, put on her outfit, and paint her face and nails. Lyuba rues the day she jilted Ivan. The thought of wearing any of the jewelry he bought her for past birthdays and Christmases makes her physically sick, knowing he's moved on to buying expensive diamonds for another woman.

"Did you forget I'm Snegurochka this year? Hurry up, or I'll drive the sleigh myself!"

All day they drive Anastasiya around to the houses they know to be anti-Bolshevik, and she sings Christmas carols at each stop. In return, she receives food, candy, and flowers, and many of the children ask Snegurochka where Dyed Moroz is and why she's not giving them any presents.

"I wish I could get flowers, sweets, and a hot meal just for a pretty face," Kat glowers. "I might have deep blue eyes like hers, but they're paired with hair the color of tar pits, not fluffy blonde curls."

"What are you talking about?" Nikolas asks. "You're far prettier than she is! The best part is, you don't need to paint your face and nails, style your hair, and don the latest fashions for your beauty to shine through."

"All you ladies are prettier than that vain blonde thing singing at the door," Aleksey says. "Even if she is physically attractive, she's got an awful personality. Her beauty only runs skin-deep, and she'll probably be washed-up in another ten years when her looks begin to fade."

"Why did Vanya have to choose *her*?" Lyuba whispers tearfully when Boris leaves to beg for food. "This is an awful Christmas, knowing the man I really love is courting another woman."

"This is what I warned you about," Eliisabet whispers. "For your own sanity, I urge you to jilt Boris sooner, not later. The longer these so-called relationships continue, the more scandalous it'll look to break things off, and the harder it'll be to break things off period, scandal or no scandal."

Some of the children run after the sleigh and throw flowers. Lyuba closes her eyes and imagines flowers being pelted at her and Ivan on their mythical wedding day, as they're led thrice around the Holy Table while the best man and maid of honor hold the crowns above their heads. But at the rate things are going now, she'll have no choice but to marry Boris, and Ivan will marry Anastasiya. The thought of never knowing what it feels like to make love to Ivan, and having to bear Boris's children, makes her want to scream in agony.

Ivan thinks guiltily that if Lyuba had accepted his proposal, they would've been in America by now and possibly have a little baby. Instead of spending Christmas as a married man with a darling little baby to love and spoil, safe in America, he's trapped here, stuck between Anastasiya and Lyuba, and with all these other people. He should've just drugged her, and by the time she came to herself, she would've been in the priest's office, and then he would've carried her onto the train and ship, and now they would've been husband and wife, poor but happy. Ivan curses himself for being more passive than even Nikolas. But he'll never give up on Lyuba, no matter how long it takes.

****

Chapter 4: Trapped in a Nightmare

3 April 1918 is Aleksey and Eliisabet's wedding day. Kat admires her new lapis lazuli engagement ring as she and the other women help Eliisabet get ready, while Lyuba burns with jealousy. She's sick to her stomach every time Boris kisses her. He hasn't gotten any better with time. It's still the same slobbery, nauseating, vacuum death grip style he's always used. When he touches her, it's not at all gentle and soft like Ivan's touch. Lyuba hopes she never has to find out how barbaric and nauseating Boris would be if they had intercourse. She'd never consider the act of sexual intimacy with him to be making love.

"I'm so glad you agreed to perform our marriage," Aleksey tells the priest. "It's nice to find a priest who's understanding about this sort of thing."

"You've committed no sin if you're marrying the woman you had your child with, the only woman you've ever known. The horse is already out of the barn, and the least I can do is make your relationship official and legitimize your child. Christ himself said nothing is higher than love, and your marriage is a celebration of that love."

"Will you get in trouble for performing a marriage during Great Lent without special permission? I was always a good Orthodox Christian, and would hate to think I'm causing a priest to sin."

"Performing a Sacrament is the most important thing in these uncertain times. God knows when you'll get another chance to do this, the way things are going now."

Aleksey smiles at Eliisabet as they take their places by the bank of the Moskva River. They lack rings, a wedding party, and a wedding gown, but it's a marriage. For fear of being spied on, there will be no Communion, no crossing themselves, no prayers, no crowns. The only religious aspect is the holding of candles. Ivan hands Aleksey his lit candle, and Lyuba hands Eliisabet hers.

Aleksey smiles at Eliisabet with his entire being before making his declaration of intent. "I, Aleksey Vladimirovich Tvardovskiy, have come of my own free will, with no prior commitments or constraints, to become the husband of Yelizaveta Martovna Kutuzova.

I knew she was the one for me the day I met her, and I'm so honored to have a child with her and become her husband. She's already my wife in my heart, but now she'll be my wife according to the laws of God and man as well. As long as God sees fit to bless us with life, I'll be the best husband I know how to be."

Eliisabet shyly smiles at him. "I, Yelizaveta Martovna Kutuzova, have come of my own free will, with no prior commitments or constraints, to become the wife of Aleksey Vladimirovich Tvardovskiy. I fell in love with him the moment I saw him, and I can't wait to become his wife! I'd want to marry him even if we didn't have a baby. Alyosha is the perfect soulmate God chose for me."

"Let's pretend there are actual rings and that I'm making the sign of the cross. Part of religion is imagination. After all, we cannot see God, yet there are many artistic representations of him!" The priest joins their right hands. "We'll have to forego reading the Epistle and the Gospel." He pours wine into a silver chalice.

Eliisabet and Aleksey drink from it, making eyes at one another over the chalice.

"We have no Holy Table with the Gospel and cross, so I'll ask you to pretend we have a Bible on that blanket. There's a very small medal depicting the Crucifixion on it."

Eliisabet and Aleksey walk around the blanket, gazing at one another and smiling.

"I hereby pronounce you man and wife. Be thou magnified, Aleksey, as Abram, and blessed as Isak, and increased as Yakov, walking in peace and working in righteousness the commandments of God. And thou, Yelizaveta, be thou magnified as Sara, and glad as Rebeka, and do thou increase like Rakhil, rejoicing in thine own husband, fulfilling the conditions of the law; for so it is well pleasing unto God."

Aleksey lifts the veil over Eliisabet's face, and they kiss, husband and wife a year to the day since they met. Now that the Gregorian calendar has been adopted, their true anniversary of meeting is 16 April, but 3 April is the date they're emotionally attached to. They're still not used to the calendar being thirteen days ahead.

The priest quickly puts away the few religious articles he snuck out, and then there's a modest reception with fish, sweet potato pudding, meat and potato salad, and mushrooms in cream. For drink, they have another bottle of wine provided by the priest. Under Orthodox rules, meat, wine, dairy, and oil are prohibited during Great Lent, but with the ongoing food shortages, they can't afford to be holy martyrs and starve.

Eliisabet snuggles up to her new husband. "I always looked forward to wearing a crown on my wedding day, displaying it at home, and at the end of my days being buried in it, but the most important thing is being your wife."

Ivan is jealous of the simple ceremony, since at least Eliisabet and Aleksey are married. If Lyuba had said yes to his proposal, they would've been celebrating their year-anniversary instead of involved with other people. He thinks heartbrokenly of the citrine bracelet, still sitting in the small box instead of on his belovèd's wrist. At this point, it would be inappropriate to give another man's girlfriend jewelry, and even if Boris were okay with it, Anastasiya would be quite displeased to see her alleged boyfriend giving jewelry to another woman. It'll have to continue languishing in the bottom of his valise, waiting for the day he and Lyuba are together again, however long that takes.

2

For a few weeks now, Ginny has noticed Lyuba and Boris have been avoiding one another a lot. He's also noticed Lyuba has been sleeping in, retiring early, complaining of headaches, and eating at odd hours. Ginny fears she's coming down with something more serious than just a cold, but she'll be mad at him for interfering in her affairs. He also doesn't have the greatest reputation with Lyuba's friends, so they might think he's making it up or exaggerating. But when she turns grey and starts retching over a bucket on a warm day in early June, he can't stay out of her business anymore.

"Are you going to throw up?"

"Did you just actually ask me that? Do you not know what an impolite question that is to ask a woman?"

"I know we haven't been the best of friends, but I'm worried about you. You've had all the normal diseases, right? Measles, mumps, whooping cough, chickenpox, rubella, scarlet fever, fifth disease, roseola, diphtheria?"

"How could I catch any disease in this isolated valley, even if I weren't already immune? If Borya finally got chickenpox, he couldn't give it to me or anyone else, since we recovered years ago." Lyuba starts throwing up into the bucket.

"Malenkov, Lyuba's sick!" Ginny shouts when Boris comes by, smoking a cigarette. "Why don't you stay home and take care of her?"

"That's not my concern. And I can't be late for work." Boris heads out the door.

Lyuba is mortified when Ivan and Anastasiya come in as she's vomiting profusely. She wishes she could crawl into a magical hatch leading to another world and never return. Forget Ginny's impolite initial question; actually vomiting in front of a man, to say nothing of the man she loves, is even more humiliating.

"Do you have food poisoning?" Ivan asks in concern. "Or maybe you were out in the sun too long?"

"She's been unwell for awhile," Ginny reports. "Always complaining of headaches, eating all the time, sleeping too much, and now vomiting! I think she's got a virus. At least that flu that's been going around America hasn't come overseas, so we know what's *not* wrong with her."

"Whatever you have, I hope I don't get it," Anastasiya says. "I'm never at my most beautiful when I'm sick."

Lyuba glares at her. "You won't come down with my symptoms unless you sleep with your boyfriend and don't take any precautions, because I'm going to have a baby."

Ivan's heart stops beating. This is just what he dreaded, and now his worst fear has come true. The woman he loves will be tied to another man forever, and not only that, he can't get the image of Lyuba and Boris in bed together out of his head. It's far too late for them to jilt their respective partners and reunite, since Lyuba having a baby by another man has changed their relationship dynamic. He'll look like a dog and homewrecker if he steals another's man's pregnant girlfriend, and Lyuba will look like a whore if she leaves the father of her baby-to-be for another man. Additionally, if they're ever able to get married, Lyuba will always be known as a woman who has children by two different fathers, and she'll have very unkind things said about her. Angrier in his own mind than he allows himself to let on, he asks Anastasiya and Ginny to go upstairs.

"Boris, right? Because if it's not Boris, I'll break every bone in the body of any excuse for a man who raped you."

"Who else? And don't you think I would've told you if I'd been raped?"

"I'll kill him. Did he rape you or get you drunk?" Though Lyuba's been with Boris for seven months now, and it looks on the surface like a contented relationship, Ivan refuses to believe for one moment that the woman he loves voluntarily went to bed with his best friend. Given the conversation they had while Anastasiya was in the salon, when Lyuba admitted she still loves him very much, it's impossible to believe she slept with Boris out of love or consent.

"That's frankly none of your business, Vanya!" Lyuba holds back tears at the memory of waking up next to Boris and realizing what was done to her the night before. Now not only does she feel like she's been unfaithful to her Vanya, she's having another man's baby. A baby who won't have his beautiful deep brown eyes and dark brown hair, who probably won't be a *levsha*.

He gets down on the floor beside her, puts his arms around her, pulls her close, and sobs into her hair. *If only I hadn't been ruined by my degenerate father*, she thinks. *Then I could've been safe in America, bearing the title Mrs. Koneva, carrying the child of the man I love, and assured of being treated like a special person instead of pushed aside after the newness of the relationship wears off.*

"I'm so sorry your first child had to be by that *mudak* Boris. Now he's *really* marked you as his own! There's no choice now but to marry him. I just lost you forever. I'll never know what it feels like to make love to you or what a child of ours would've looked like. Maybe in another lifetime we'll be more than friends."

"I'm sorry too. I wanted *you* to be the father of my children. *Pozhaluysta*, believe me, no matter what everything looks like, *you're* the man I love, my sweet, gentle Vanyechka. I dreamt about having a little boy with your dark brown hair and eyes, your beautiful face, left-handed like you."

"My Lyuba still loves me? The way a woman loves a man and not just as a best friend who happens to be a man? But then why get involved with another guy? I don't understand why you'd hurt me so much if you really love me in that way." Ivan rubs her back, tears flowing down his face, as she throws up. "You can tell me the truth, Lyuba. I know I'm a mouse and not a man. A real man wouldn't let anything stand in his way if he really wanted a woman. I should've kidnapped you so you would've had no choice but to go to America. We would've been married by now, living in a little apartment in New York, and saving up money for our farm in the Midwest. We probably would've had our own dear little baby by now too. Instead I was as passive and unmanly as always and let my best friend seduce you."

Lyuba starts sobbing even harder at the memory of seeing blood running down her legs when she woke up in the morning, with that terrific headache, in bed next to Boris, who looks even pudgier naked. Ivan would never have been so rough he drew blood. At least Ivan knows he wouldn't have been taking her physical virginity, which Boris no doubt believes he did, because of the blood. Boris has no idea what Mr. Zhukov was really all about, while Ivan wouldn't have cared he was getting "used merchandise," a woman without the factory seal. Making love to Ivan would've been Lyuba's first time as far as she's concerned, since there's no comparison between a loving, consensual act and having an act of sexual violence forced upon oneself.

He puts his arm around her back and walks her over to the davenport. "Don't you worry. He'll have to answer to all of us if he's not interested in doing the right thing."

The next day, Boris comes back, shifty-eyed and rather disinterested in Lyuba. Ivan is sick to his stomach to see how the woman he loves is being treated by her boyfriend after only seven months of courting. He can't imagine being away from Lyuba for a few days and not hugging and kissing her when he comes home.

"You'll never believe what Lyuba told us." Ivan's eyes are blazing.

"Totally dreadful news!" Anastasiya says. "Bad, bad news! So bad you'll never ever show your face in public again!"

"She told us she's carrying your child! Is that why you're avoiding her?"

"I'm sorry."

"Will you make me a respectable woman?" Lyuba asks.

"Sure. I don't think I'll marry you right away, but I'll do what I must."

Ivan can hardly believe Boris is so nonchalant about finding out he's going to be a father, and answering questions about his intentions to stick around as brusquely and matter-of-factly as though announcing the weather. If Lyuba told him she were expecting their child, Ivan would turn cartwheels in elation, hold her close, gaze at her adoringly, and spend money like a drunken sailor on baby toys, clothes, and supplies.

3

Ivan is forced to watch Lyuba carrying a child belonging to someone who doesn't care to be a father, but he's scared Lyuba and Boris will curse him out if he tries to interfere in their excuse of a relationship, and he has no idea how to get rid of Anastasiya. Boris cares less Lyuba is pregnant, and barely spends any time around the house. Ivan is a devout Russian Orthodox Christian, but he doesn't believe Lyuba's a sinner because she's pregnant out of wedlock. She didn't get pregnant by herself. Ivan suspects Lyuba isn't too happy about it either. For fear of alienating his belovèd, he doesn't say anything about how he thinks it may have been rape, but he has his suspicions, and can't wait to find backup for these feelings. He also sees Lyuba sitting alone crying more often as she begins to show a little bit, and lately she's been putting an awful lot of greasepaint on her face, as though trying to hide bruises. It makes him sick with heartache, but he can't do anything unless Lyuba comes to him and begs for help.

"We're going to the ballet today," Anastasiya says. "I've had enough of being cooped up in this stupid valley. It's high time we go out and do something normal people do. I miss going to ballets, moving pictures, operas, plays, and concerts."

"You spent money on ballet tickets instead of food?" Ivan asks. "With all this insane hyperinflation, we shouldn't spend our precious rubles on anything we don't absolutely need."

"Why not? When Pyotr came over last week with money for our groceries, I squirreled away enough to buy four tickets—for you, me, Lyuba, and Boris."

"Zhora and her family are going to the ballet today too," Ginny says. "Take me with you!"

"With what ticket?"

"I have my ways of getting money. I'll buy a child's ticket when we go in. I'm sure the show isn't totally sold out, and even if all the seats are full, I'll have a place with Zhora's family in their private balcony."

As they're getting into the sleigh to ride to the ballet, Ivan sees Lyuba trying to snuggle up against Boris, only to be pushed away. Boris was never this cold to Lyuba before. Ivan wonders if perhaps he was only interested in the chase, and has no idea what to do with Lyuba now that she's no longer just a best friend or brand-new girlfriend.

At the ballet, Georgiya flags down Ginny. "Would you like sit on my family's private balcony? We're with a friend of Lenin's who was a guest at our house." Georgiya looks scornfully at Boris. "Look at that body language. Your cousin's beau is a scoundrel. Even my stupid brother Leonid would immediately marry a girl if he got her in trouble, and he wouldn't treat her like a pariah. If that tall, handsome fellow got her in trouble, I guarantee *he* wouldn't treat her so coldly after the fact. Some men are dogs. It's too bad all your other friends have moved into their own houses, since there aren't as many pairs of eyes keeping watch on him."

***

After the ballet, Lyuba timidly comes up to Ivan when he's alone. She drops her voice to a whisper and looks around for Boris.

"Vanya, I'm scared for my life, and for my baby's life."

"It's Boris, isn't it? I'll kill him."

"Don't you do anything just yet. I'm just telling you right now, I'm scared. But don't you dare tell him I told you! I know how easily you get angry at people, my sweet *groznik*." Lyuba walks back off to join Boris.

As they climb back into the sleigh, Ginny smirks. "I'm going to meet a friend of Lenin's at Zhora's house."

"You should stay home and take care of Lyuba. I have to go out and meet my friends," Boris says.

"What is it with you and your new friends?" Anastasiya asks. "And how can an eleven-year-old be the man of the house?"

"I'm earning money to buy ship fare to America."

"What kind of job do you have?" Ginny asks.

"I do all sorts of things, like selling cigarettes and being a village guard."

Ivan strongly suspects Boris is involved in drug trafficking and other unscrupulous things, from his strange behavior and conversations he's overheard when Boris's friends have come by. He only hopes this has nothing to do with why Lyuba said she's scared for her life and her baby's life.

4

Lyuba is going out to get the newspaper on the morning of 22 July when she comes face-to-face with Basil. She wants to scream upon seeing her delusional, obsessed admirer standing there in the flesh. She thought he was just a bad memory since his parents shipped him off to school in Tbilisi, but his obsession runs deep enough to return to spring one of his trademark surprise visits on her.

"Good morning!" He grabs her hands and leers up at her, not embarrassed he's eight inches shorter than she is. "What a wonderful day. First I find out the most wonderful news ever, and then I get to see and touch my future wife!"

"What the hell are you doing here, Basil? I thought you were at college in Georgia. Let go of me, you creep."

"What, can't a man take a summer holiday to see the most beautiful woman in the world?"

"Do you realize how rude it is to spring a visit on someone? This isn't the first time you've come over by surprise."

"Have a look at your paper and read the good news. Would you like to go out to a dancehall to celebrate?"

Ivan storms downstairs. "I heard your voice upstairs, Beriya. Get the hell away from my Lyuba right this moment or I'll break every bone in your short little body." He gives Basil a push, sending him flat onto his back.

Lyuba picks up the paper and begins screaming uncontrollably when she sees the headline. She grows faint as she gasps for breath and plummets to the floor.

"What a typical out of touch reaction to the best news ever," Basil scoffs. "I couldn't stop singing when I heard about the triumphant Bolshevik victory."

Ivan rushes over to her. "Don't hyperventilate, Lyuba. It's not good for your condition. There's an innocent little baby depending on you to be calm and healthy." His eyes nearly fall out of his head when he picks the paper. "Regicide! I'll kill the murderers if I ever meet them! How dare they?!"

"What kind of animals are these?" Lyuba weeps. "Why couldn't they let him live out his days in peace? How could anyone have such little compassion for fellow human beings?"

"Why the hell are you still standing there, Beriya? Get the hell out of our house and leave us to mourn our Tsar in peace! Unlike you, *some* of us stood behind him right or wrong and would never dream of celebrating the barbaric murder of innocent children! Our Tsesarevich would've only been fourteen next month! How has a child that young done anything so awful he deserved to be brutally massacred! Get the hell out of our house before I brutally massacre *you*!"

"You haven't seen the last of me," he says as he walks back out.

"Does this mean we're going to lose the Civil War?" Lyuba asks. "We've lost our rallying-point. Things might start getting worse for us again."

"My offer to take you to America will always be open. Just say the word and I'll take you to safety. I could never live with myself if you fell victim to a barbaric killing squad like our Divinely-anointed."

5

At the beginning of August, Ivan gets his first conformation there's a lot more to Lyuba's relationship with Boris than meets the eye. When he comes home after leaving Anastasiya at the market, he hears loud shouts and screams upstairs.

"I told you, I don't want to take responsibility! How dare you get pregnant out of wedlock!"

"It wasn't my fault you wanted to go to that cabin, Boris!"

"You should've stopped me! Nice, respectable girls tell their boyfriends when to stop! You *wanted* me to continue! You *let* me!"

"Stop it! Don't you love our baby? You're going to kill her if you don't stop beating me every week!"

"I'm leaving. Maybe *this* will help you get rid of our problem."

Ivan watches in horror as Boris drags Lyuba to the top of the stairwell and pushes her down the stairs.

"I hope to God that mistake is dead by the time I get home!"

Boris shouts as he heads for the door.

Lyuba lies there, numb, listening for the car that comes by to pick up Boris for work. As soon as the car takes off, Ivan goes over to her and puts his hands over the bulge.

"Don't you get involved in the dispute Boris and I were having, Ivan! He'll kill you if you take me away from him!"

"Your baby is still moving. Praise God. I know that wasn't the first time Boris beat you up!"

"No, it wasn't. Is she really still moving?"

"I just felt the baby kicking. I'll protect you and your baby. If Boris tries to beat you again, I'll kill him."

"No, Vanya, I can't lose Boris's love!"

"He pushed you down a stairwell! You call that love!"

"He's been beating me so hard, it's like he wants me to lose our baby! And he puts bruises all over my face, beats me over the baby with a crowbar and bricks, and even sat on the baby once!"

"I'll tell Petya about this, and we can get away from here. The baby will be born in America, and I'll be its father."

"I pray it's a girl, so she won't be a bully like her father!"

Ivan helps Lyuba to the davenport and drapes a blanket over her. He insists she stay there and continue relaxing when the others sit down to supper, and brings her a tray of the supper he cooked. When Boris comes back at midnight, Ivan jumps on him, tackles him to the floor in the dark, and begins to whack him with a crowbar.

"We're best friends, Konev! Stop it!"

"You don't beat a pregnant woman, you *dryan*! That's your baby she's got inside her, and you could care less! She told me she's scared for their lives. Well, I will die before I let anyone hurt Lyuba or her baby, you *sukin syn*!"

"Stop it, Ivan, you're behaving like your namesake's grandson," Lyuba commands him from the davenport.

"That's right, Konev," Boris growls. "I can do what I want with Lyuba. It's none of your business what I do to her."

Ivan is forced to watch from the sidelines as Boris begins to beat Lyuba more and more over the next few weeks. The only times Boris is in the house are when he's coming to beat Lyuba, then quickly back off to work. Lyuba hides after Boris leaves, and

Ivan comes dutifully to her to make sure the baby is still moving. She begs him not to tell the others, and he washes the blood off her face and puts ointment and greasepaint over it. He curses himself for not taking matters into his own hands so many possible times in the past year.

6

In November, Georgiya comes for a visit and fixes Boris with a cold, hard stare when she takes off her influenza mask. He returns the hateful look.

"You're the one who got your girlfriend pregnant and plans to flee the country as soon as she has the kid? Grigoriy told me you started spending more time around the house last month, but that doesn't negate what a dog you were prior to that point. My papa says guys who get girls in trouble and don't do the decent thing almost never make a last-minute turnaround. We were just talking about this at supper the other night, and we all agreed you're probably going to take off for America on your own rather than stick around to be a man."

"Ginny, what have you been telling people about me?" Boris demands. "I thought we were buddies."

"Only the truth," Ginny says. "Anastasiya, can Zhora borrow some of your gossip and confession magazines?"

"Not unless you want me to do her bodily harm."

"Do you know you're in a White-controlled valley?" Boris asks. "None of us likes you, Georgiya. You're outnumbered here. One of my jobs is serving as a village tough, and I can easily call over a bunch of my work buddies to rough you up. Do you know we can have you put in an asylum?"

"An asylum is for nutcases," Georgiya scoffs. "I bet you're just jealous of me because I live in my own house, with my own family, a couple of servants, nice food, and nice clothes. You meanwhile are civilian refugees. The only reason you're relatively secure now is because the White Army has been winning recently. But make no mistake. My people will soon emerge victorious, and you'll rue the day you threw your hats in with out of touch autocrats. Although what am I talking about? You're not going to be here very much longer, so you probably don't care which side wins."

"We may be isolated in this valley and not living as comfortably as we did before the Revolution, but at least we're together with our friends, and we're better protected from that nasty influenza and typhus than we'd be in the big city. Aren't you scared to have to wear that mask every time you venture out?"

"My papa says we're descended from people who survived or avoided the Black Plague when it ravaged our country in the 1350s. I'm from hearty stock. I'm not afraid of a little Spanish flu."

Boris sees five of his friends walking by, swings the door open, and whistles loudly. The next thing Georgiya knows, these strangers are standing in the house and looking at her very menacingly.

"We're the leaders of this valley you're trespassing in," the toughest-looking one informs her. "Do you know Bolshevism is a worldview espoused by the mentally ill? You'll have to be cured of your insanity the hard way. Come with us, or there'll be trouble."

"You'd better listen to them," Boris says.

"My father is an important man—"

The ringleader grabs her and swings her over his shoulder like a sack of potatoes. Ginny stares in shock as she's toted away, screaming at the top of her lungs. Ivan is just as shocked to finally get an up-close and personal view of some of Boris's new friends. These definitely aren't characters he wants to bump into in the dark, even with his physical strength. They doubtless have knives and guns, and aren't just using their fists. But since Boris has been seeming to grow closer to Lyuba lately, he tries to push his fears out of his mind.

7

Boris stops growing closer to Lyuba at the beginning of December. He begins to beat her again. Lyuba fears for her life, and any future children.

"I'm telling you in strictest confidence, Vanyechka," she sobs after the latest beating. "I'm scared he's beaten me so much and so brutally he's ruined any chances I might've had to have another child!"

"I'll pack your things, and we'll leave tonight with your cousin," he whispers in her ear. "Flee the country, and I'll raise the baby as my own flesh and blood child! If that *mudak* Malenkov ruined your chances for having more children, we can always adopt. I wouldn't stop loving you more than I love anybody just because you might be unable to give me biological children!"

"He'll kill you, Vanya! I want to protect you from his mad rage!"

"I want to protect *you* from that very same rage! I'd rather him kill me than you!"

"I pray so much it's a girl. Will you pray with me?"

"I learnt a long time ago that praying for something that isn't happening is very futile. But remember, when you decide to break free from that scumbag Boris, I'll be here waiting to make you my wife and to treat you like a human being, not a punching bag!"

Boris still cares less she's carrying his child, even as she approaches the homestretch. He didn't get her anything for her nineteenth birthday on 11 December except a black eye and lash marks across her ribcage. Ivan meanwhile was too scared of his best friend's newly-revealed dark side to get Lyuba a birthday present, for fear Boris might've accused him of making advances on his woman. He had to make do with massaging her swollen ankles and aching back for the umpteenth time during the pregnancy, and Lyuba found it birthday present enough to savor the touch of his loving hands, however transitory it was before she fell back under the cruel hands of the other.

Lyuba has doubled over in pain several times and screamed in agony after he's left the house, and Ivan has ordered her each time to lie in bed until the pain goes away. On more than a few occasions, he's had to carry her upstairs to her bed because she's so scared she might put undue pressure on the baby by walking. Lyuba is frantic over what's happening to her. She fears her uterus is starting to rip from the rough handling it's received at the hands of Boris, and she's also begun to lose placental tissue. She stays in bed and cries all day, with her secret entrusted to only Ivan, who's helplessly watching Lyuba suffer at the hands of another abusive man, only this time Boris, not her father. He never once suspected Boris is so cruel.

"I have enough money for us to go to America," Boris says. "We'll see you other people when you scrape up enough money for ship fare."

"You want a woman about to have a child to go on a disease-ridden ship to another country at a minute's notice?" Anastasiya asks. "Aren't you scared of that flu that arrived here back in October? It's been killing so many people all over the world, and ships are notorious breeding grounds of disease. We're damn lucky we've managed to avoid it here in our secluded little valley, but you probably won't be so lucky if you expose yourself to the riffraff in the cities and on the ship. There's also a typhus epidemic."

"This isn't up for discussion. Besides, I'm eighteen and managed to elude chickenpox my whole life. I think I'll do fine avoiding another contagious virus. Lyuba's got a hearty constitution too."

"This isn't a normal disease! Most of the victims are healthy and young, not elderly, children, babies, or people with bad health!" Ivan shouts. "Haven't you seen the photos in the newspapers, of all those stacked-up bodies and coffins, and people wearing masks? A lot of the people getting it are dead within a day or two! And you dare to expose an innocent unborn baby and her innocent young mother to this pandemic by leaving our safe little spot in this valley! Lyuba's *dedushka* died of the last flu pandemic!"

"It's already decided. We're going to America, and no flu epidemic or threats from you can stop us."

Ivan grabs Boris by his throat. "Don't you dare take my Lyuba away from me. There's no way in Hell you're going to expose her to that scary epidemic that's been sweeping all around the world since the spring. You'd be killing both Lyuba and her innocent baby, though at this point I care less if you fall victim to it, so long as you don't infect them."

The thought of Lyuba being taken away from him and forced to go on a long transatlantic voyage with an abusive man while pregnant rends at his heart. There's no telling what might happen to her on that ship, either at the hands of Boris or any other unscrupulous men. Ivan has heard stories about many women getting assaulted on ships, particularly in third-class. If Lyuba were to give birth en route, there's no telling what might happen to the baby, either at the hands of Boris or because of the conditions on the ship. He wishes Lyuba would finally accept his offer to take her out of the country with Ginny, since so long as Lyuba became his wife while she were pregnant, the baby would be legally his child, no matter who the blood father is, and he could press charges against Boris if he showed up to try to hurt either Lyuba or the baby again. Never before did Ivan think there were a positive side to a woman being her husband's property.

8

It's now 23 January 1919, and Lyuba is in her ninth month. Ever since last night, she's felt intermittent contractions, but hasn't told a soul about it. Now, however, she's starting to feel very strong contractions coming much closer together, and forces herself to push through the pain without letting on. If Boris knew she were in active labor, there's no telling if he might snap again.

"Last night I decided it's stupid for me to take you on a ship when you're pregnant, so I think I should go alone and wait for you. Besides, I'm young. I don't want to be tied down by a baby or be forced into marriage."

Lyuba nods. There's obviously nothing she can do or say at this point to change his mind or make him stay, and secretly she's relieved he's going away. After a respectable period of time passes, perhaps she'll finally be able to reunite with Ivan.

"Goodbye." He kisses her and walks off the veranda.

As soon as he's left, her pains start increasing even more. She's no longer able to grin and bear it, and knows it's finally time to ask for help. Struggling to walk, she goes into the house and finds her cousin reading a children's Bolshevik propaganda story from Georgiya. "Ginny, go get Ivan and tell him to get a midwife. Make sure to ask for lots of chloroform!"

"Are you really in labor?"

"Yes! Do exactly as I tell you, or Vanya will rip you apart when he comes home and finds out you let me give birth unassisted!"

Ginny puts down his story, pulls on his coat, boots, and mittens, and heads out. He runs up the main thoroughfare until he sees Ivan and Anastasiya emerging from the only four-star restaurant in their valley. Anastasiya sighs when she sees Ginny approaching, and Ivan stiffens in fear, imagining Lyuba alone in the house with Boris when she's so close to her due date.

"Boris just left, and she's in labor! Get a midwife with chloroform!"

"Isn't there a hospital in this damned valley?" Anastasiya asks. "Don't tell me she intends to birth at home like a primitive woman. If I ever have a child, I'll insist on a modern, antiseptic hospital with a trained doctor and that twilight sleep drug."

"You're not the one in labor," Ivan snaps. "Lyuba is, and she wants a midwife to come to the house, the way women have done it for thousands of years. She might be a modern woman, but she's not so modern she's going to abandon all the tried and true old ways." He puts his hands on Ginny's shoulders. "Hurry back home and help Lyuba as much as possible. No woman deserves to be alone as she's birthing a baby, even if there's no birth attendant."

Ivan goes back into the restaurant to use their phone. He hopes Pyotr will get someone who won't make any moral judgments on an unwed mother. Ivan doesn't know much about birthing babies, but he does know most first-time mothers are supposed to take a long time and that it's unusual to go as fast as Eliisabet. He could coach Lyuba through her labor or catch the baby if he absolutely had to, but since he's not the father, it's best to let a professional handle it. If Anastasiya were there, she'd immediately pick up from his body language and speech that Lyuba is more than just a friend. Things might get ugly once she figures out he was using her to make Lyuba jealous.

Pyotr drives up twenty minutes later, and Ivan rushes out to the car. Anastasiya follows him but doesn't get in.

"I'm sorry, but I can't come. I get motion sickness very easily. You should've seen how much I vomited in that filthy cattlecar on the way to the Urals."

"Then wait here," Pyotr orders. "We'll be back very soon. I'd hope any decent midwife is willing to make an unexpected housecall at this hour, particularly since everyone knows babies come at all hours."

***

Too weak to waddle upstairs to her room, Lyuba is laboring in Anya and Alya's old room downstairs, located right off the front door. She lies down when she sees Ginny entering, and orders him to bathe her head with cold water. Ginny thinks the whole business of birthing babies is disgusting and scary, but obeys for fear of what she'll do to him, or what Ivan will do to him if he comes back and finds out he refused to help. For several hours, he bathes her head as she moans and rocks back and forth.

When Eliisabet gave birth, she barely made any noise, but now

Lyuba feels free to make all the noise she wants. Also unlike Eliisabet, she has absolutely no one to hold her hands. If only the baby belonged to Ivan, who'd be here holding her hands, she thinks in utter agony as she crouches on all fours and screams through the pain.

"Thank God, my baby came out alive!" Lyuba begins to cry. *"Bolshoye spasibo."* She crosses herself. "It's a girl!" She tenderly holds the tiny infant next to her heart. "You're so beautiful!" She begins counting her fingers and toes to make sure everything's where it should be.

"Are you going to push out that gross thing Eliisabet did? Because if you are, I don't want to look at it."

"It's a natural part of birth. It has to come out or I'll get an infection."

Ginny hides in another room when he sees Lyuba setting the baby down to start pushing out the placenta. Lyuba recoils in horror at the sight of it, partly because parts of it are missing. Boris beat her so badly, she lost placental tissue more than a few times, but at least she didn't lose the entire placenta and thus the baby along with it.

"Ginny, get scissors. Her cord has stopped pulsating. Now she's ready to breathe on her own."

***

Anastasiya is standing outside, wrapped in a shawl. Pyotr stops the car, unable to believe someone could be so stupid as to stand outside for that long in January. He assumed she'd head home and help Lyuba when he didn't come back in a reasonable time, but that assumed too much of this pathetic woman.

"Thank God, a proper doctor," Anastasiya says as she climbs in.

"He was all I could find at this hour," Pyotr says. "The woman doctor I found for Liza couldn't be reached, and I have no idea how to find a midwife, since I'm not a woman. He'll have to do for now."

"Good. Maybe this'll teach Lyuba a lesson about preferring outdated ways."

As they drive past the depot, Pyotr's eyes narrow. "I see Boris. What kind of degenerate leaves the mother of his child when she's in labor? Even if a guy's old-fashioned and doesn't want to watch, he can stay in another room!"

"I'm going to give him a piece of my mind," Ivan says.

"You don't have a mask to protect yourself from all the riffraff at that depot!" Anastasiya says.

Boris is carrying two suitcases and wearing an influenza mask as he approaches the train station. He stops in his tracks when he sees Ivan approaching, looking like a man possessed.

"Boris Aleksandrovich Malenkov, you are the world's biggest *govnyuk*! You impregnated an innocent woman, did God knows what with those shady new friends of yours, wanted her to go on a ship with you when the entire world is in the grip of an influenza pandemic, and now you've deserted a woman in labor! If both of them are dead, it'll be all your fault! Are you going to say anything besides an apology that should've been said months ago?"

Boris pulls the mask down. "I want you to take care of Lyuba and tell the child you're the father. *Do svidaniya*, Ivan."

By the time Ivan gets back to the car, the doctor has left. Ivan can just make out his form walking off in the distance. Part of him is secretly glad, since Lyuba would recoil at being seen or touched by a strange man, even a doctor, but he also worries Lyuba might need medical assistance. He starts imagining one horrific scenario after the other—a transverse breech, triplets, a cord wrapped three or four times around the neck, a baby born not breathing, a fifteen-pound baby.

"He left when he found out Lyuba's unmarried," Anastasiya says. "He asked why her husband was deserting her, and I said they were never married. What did you say to Boris?"

"Don't ask," Ivan mutters, too upset at Boris to redress Anastasiya for driving away the doctor. "He used to be a pretty decent fellow. I can only hope his guilty conscience will kill him where I failed to bodily kill him."

***

Ginny looks up when he sees the door opening. "Did you catch Boris?"

"He's gone," Anastasiya says. "I've read stories about what to do when this sort of thing happens in my gossip and confession magazines."

"While you were out, I packed for you. You'll find everything in this trunk. Don't forget your sketchpad or this influenza mask. It's high time you left. We all know you only moved in with us because of Konev."

"You heard my cousin," Lyuba says as forcefully as she can manage in her postpartum state. "Get out of my home. You never belonged here. Ginny is my cousin, all our neighbors have been my friends since I was a girl, and Liza is the mother of my unofficial godson. No one ever wanted you here. Now scram."

Anastasiya looks around in bewilderment, unable to believe the rug is being yanked from under her in the dead of winter and during a flu pandemic. She finds only the unfriendly faces of Lyuba and Ginny. Ivan is looking up at the ceiling, refusing to look at her. Feeling defeated, she clutches her oversized sketchpad and the trunk as she trudges through the snow.

Lyuba gazes down at her baby as she nurses. "That's right, sweetheart, drink as much milk as you want. You're safe now."

Ivan finally looks at the baby, and his heart melts. "What a beautiful new life. What is it?"

"A darling little girl. Thank God I got what I wanted. If it were your child, I'd have wanted it to be a boy, but since Boris is the father, I'm glad I got my girl. Malenkov doesn't deserve a child in his own image, and I wouldn't want to look at a boy and see that *mudak* every day."

"Thank God you're both alive! I had a horrible image of the woman I love and her innocent baby being dead when I came in! If I were a woman, I don't think I could be so brave as to have a baby all by myself with no doctor or midwife. I'm so proud of you for doing such a great job all by yourself, even if you were bringing Malenkov's child into the world and not mine."

"I'm surprised I was able to do it without any chloroform, ether, laughing gas, or whatever other drugs they use. Is Borya really gone?"

"He's waiting at the depot for a train. He might be on the train by now. Good riddance."

"Boris loved me in his own way. He just wasn't ready to have a child."

"Boris treated you like a dog! He never loved you!"

She clutches her daughter. Right after going through the intense experience of childbirth, her emotions are going crazy, and she isn't thinking of how much she loves Ivan. This baby is a physical reminder of the fact that she and Boris were together and had a physical union, even against her will.

"Ginny, get to bed," Ivan orders. "It's late, and your cousin and I need to have a talk in private."

Ginny obediently goes upstairs. After he's gone, Ivan looks longingly at Lyuba, asking the unspoken question with his deep brown eyes.

"I've just had a baby by another man. It's too late to marry anyone else."

"You can always come back to me. I'll wait forever. You're the only woman I'd marry. Anastasiya was just a distraction."

"But it'd be too scandalous. It doesn't matter if we love each other. Decent, respectable women have to marry the fathers of their illegitimate children."

"Are you already forgetting how Boris regularly beat you up? You came crying to me about it all the time! Before Boris ensnared you, my heart was only in a million pieces. Now it's in a trillion pieces. Isn't it obvious we're soulmates? We're two wounded souls who are scarred where no one can see it, and we understand what drives some of our seemingly confusing behavior. You're the only one who knows the real me, and I'm the only one who knows the real you. Holy Mother of God, I can't wait to become your lover."

"How many times do I have to tell you it's impossible for us to marry now? I'm already an unwed mother; I'm not about to increase the scandal and shame by marrying another man and denying my child legitimacy."

"I'll be twenty-one in July. Do you know how humiliating it feels to be my age and not know what it's like to make love to a woman? I'm cut off from the one defining experience that separates the adults from the kids, this secret world of knowledge I haven't been initiated into. You are too, since you've never known a consensual sexual union. Don't give me that look. I'd swear on my mother's unmarked grave Malenkov raped you, or coerced you into it by getting you drunk."

"That's none of your business." Lyuba starts up at a thud behind the house, followed by footsteps.

Ivan goes to the window and raises the curtain. In the dark, he sees Ginny running up the street. "I suppose he knows where he's going. We'll have peace and quiet if that little upstart is out. I assume he'll come back soon. I think we all know he's been stealing and begging since we've been in this valley."

"Thank God. He won't disturb me or my baby."

Ivan sits beside her, continuing where he left off. "My heart leapt out of my body the moment I first saw you when I was nine years old. It was my dream come true, that month we shared. You smashed my heart into a million pieces, but I knew deep down you still loved only me, and that you'd loved me since you met me too. *Pozhaluysta*, don't go back to being mean to me like you were the first month we knew each other."

"Why do you make me feel guilty about not loving you?"

"I'd never ignore you. You'd be up on a pedestal. If you give me your heart, I'd never betray you. *Pozhaluysta*, unbreak my heart and be my sweetheart again."

"It's indecent to speak like this to a woman who just had another man's baby. I don't want to see you again until you apologize for this inappropriate behavior."

Ivan wants her so badly it hurts him, even right after she's had another man's baby. He doesn't want her to see him cry, so he goes into another room, all the while keeping up hope she'll shed her iron walls and surrender her heart to him. As his mother said, if Lyuba truly loves him, she'll come back to him eventually. She can't keep running away from what's in her heart. After all, the swan mates for life, and they likened themselves to swans that afternoon they skipped gymnasium at Patriarch's Pond.

9

Katrin looks up in shock when she sees Anastasiya, an influenza mask over her face, dragging a trunk, her large sketchpad under her arm. "What in tarnation are you doing here, Nastya?"

"We're best friends, Katya! Ginny shoved me out right after Lyuba gave birth to her bastard, and this was the only place I knew I'd be welcomed."

"You really think we're still best friends, after the horrible reception I got when I last saw you? Do you know I risked my hide to sneak over to your house to gather up all your belongings so I could give them to you if you survived and came home? When I saw you at the first victory ball, I was trying to hug you and ask what happened to you, and you pushed me away and said you hated me. I guess you changed your mind about never wanting to associate with me ever again."

"How do you think I felt to hear the stories about you after I got home? I never dreamt my best friend since childhood was capable of watching her parents' arrest and her younger siblings' murders without a tear in her eye, nor that she was the one who turned in her family in the first place! Even your little protégée Viktoriya's life didn't count."

"I came to her the night before and asked her if she'd like to join me. I was on my way to try again in the morning when my new friends came in. Of course I miss *her*. Now as for you, I guess you can stay. I can't ignore seventeen years of being best friends, and it'd be pretty cold to make you stay on the streets in January. I'll ask the maid to make up a bed for you."

"I think Ivan was on the very verge of proposing. Why don't we take a train over tomorrow bright and early and try to rectify this misunderstanding?"

Katrin thinks she's as delusional as always, since any woman on the verge of being proposed to would've had her supposed boyfriend running after her and would never have let a child push her out of the house. She also isn't looking forward to going on a train and exposing herself to people who may have flu or typhus, but it won't be a very long ride, and she has a mask. In the meantime, she resigns herself to putting her old best friend up in her house for the night.

10

Ivan comes out from the other room, his whole face red and swollen. "Do you have a name for her yet?"

"Tatyana, after one of our murdered Grand Duchesses. Olga and Mariya are too common for my tastes, and of course I'd never call a child Anastasiya after knowing that vain blonde thing."

"Tatyana is a beautiful name."

Her heart softens, and she takes pity on him, remembering how he's the only man who's ever truly loved her, even when she's treated him like dirt and rebuffed his offers of marriage. "Poor

Ivanok."

He smiles, remembering his belovèd mother's pet name for him. "Can I hold the baby?"

"Of course." Lyuba gazes down at the baby at her breast. "If you don't like Tatyana, maybe I could call her Anna."

Ivan freezes. "After my mother."

"Would you prefer she be named for your mother? I know how much you adored her, and then she died so barbarically..."

"No, no, we're naming her Tatyana. It's already decided. It's a beautiful gesture, but nothing can ever replace my mother." He averts his eyes when Tatyana unlatches, though he's already seen Lyuba completely naked. "Is she Tatyana Borisovna Malenkova or Tatyana Borisovna Zhukova?"

"Neither. She'll get my surname, but her patronymic will be Ivanovna. That is, if you don't think it's inappropriate to give your name to a child who belongs to another man."

Ivan's entire face lights up. "Do I mind? Are you kidding me? Of course I'd love to give her my name! Hopefully one day you'll take my name too. Besides, love transcends biology."

"Here you go, my sweet *groznik*." Lyuba sits up slightly, pulls her blouse back over her breast, and hands him the tiny baby. "Sit next to me, so if you accidentally drop her, she'll only fall onto the bed and not the floor. Tanyechka, this is your *papashka* who loved you since before you were born."

He holds Tatyana Ivanovna Zhukova lovingly. When she stares right into his eyes, he breaks down crying. "Do you know how much I love you, Tanyechka? You're my beautiful firstborn child, and even more special than most firstborns because you're my daughter through love and not blood. Someday your mother and I will have blood children together, but you'll always be my firstborn. I'd die for both you and your mother. A very bad man was hurting you and your mother before you were born, but he's far away now, and he'll have to get through me before he ever hurts either of you again. Someday when we live in America, I'll buy you the most beautiful clothes, go on Easter egg hunts with you, decorate the Christmas tree with you, buy you the most beautiful dolls and toys, and help you with your schoolwork. When you're old enough for boys, I'll protect you from all the bad guys like your blood father, and only let nice, respectable boys court you. Maybe you'll grow up to marry your mother's godson Nikolay. He's only fourteen months older than you. But for now, all you need to worry about is being the most beautiful, special baby ever."

11

In the morning, Ivan comes downstairs to check on Lyuba and Tatyana, and smiles when he sees them both peacefully sleeping. Then he heads over to the laundry area to wash the bedsheets, which he threw into the largest wash tub to soak last night before Lyuba went to sleep. He wouldn't hear of her or Tatyana sleeping on sheets stained with blood and birthing fluids, and made Lyuba lie on the davenport while he stripped the bed and made it up with clean sheets, then found an old but thick blanket for her to lie on top of to catch any postpartum bleeding.

After putting the sheets through the wringer, he hangs them up on the indoor clothesline by the stove and heads outside with the basin containing the placenta and umbilical cord. Grabbing a shovel, he digs through the snow until he hits earth, and pushes as hard as he can to break ground. Once he's dug deep enough, he deposits the afterbirth in the ground and covers it back up. All that done, he heads back inside to start making breakfast for Lyuba. He savors the feeling of peace and quiet, only the two of them plus the baby in the house. It feels so right and natural, and he hopes they can stay this way forever.

The feeling of peace and quiet is soon broken by a very loud knock on the door, followed by the bell ringing several long times in a row. Tatyana begins crying loudly, which in turn wakes up Lyuba.

"What do we do if it's Boris?" Lyuba asks as she gives her breast to Tatyana.

"Don't you worry, he'll never hurt you again. He forfeited his right to both you and that precious newborn when he abandoned you last night." He peers through the peephole. "It's your cousin, Anastasiya, and that crazy Nikonova woman. I don't see the harm in letting them in. But first let me bring you your breakfast. I made you scrambled eggs, oatmeal, *syomga*, bread with strawberry jam, and soft goat cheese with herbs. You need to eat as hearty a breakfast as you can after that ordeal. It'll bring your strength back and give Tanyechka healthy milk. Tomorrow I'll make you blueberry pancakes."

Lyuba represses the urge to smile at him when he brings her breakfast on a tray. It would be unseemly to rush to reunite with him so soon after she's had his best friend's baby, and Anastasiya won't give up on him easily.

Anastasiya strides into the house and drapes her white mink coat over a chair. "I came back, because I know you were on the very verge of proposing—"

"What a delusional moron you are," Lyuba says. "I'm glad you're gone. I only put up with you because Vanya liked you, and if I said anything against you, I would've been out on the streets."

"Don't be silly." Ivan gently strokes the top of her head. "I'd never put my Lyuba out on the streets, particularly not during a pandemic."

Anastasiya holds out her hand. "Would anyone care to pay me back?"

"What for? No one told you to come back here. Lyuba and I are the master and mistress of this house now. You're dreaming if you think you're still welcome here after Lyuba had her baby."

"*Pozhaluysta*, let me finish eating in peace," Lyuba says. "I'm sure Katrin can give you return fare."

Anastasiya is indignant when Katrin opens her purse and pulls out some bills. Too shocked to start to formulate a plan for winning back the man who never really was hers, she takes the money and silently trudges back to the depot.

Ivan sits on the bed with Lyuba after she finishes breakfast and changes Tatyana's diaper, taking turns holding the baby he already loves like his own daughter. As Katrin educates Ginny on the finer points of recent political events, Lyuba nurses Tatyana. Ivan looks away in embarrassment and goes into the kitchen to make lunch.

"You can cook?" Katrin laughs.

"My mother taught me."

"I've heard about women like that. They're disappointed their only child is a boy, so they do all the girly things with them. Not that I have anything against men who do so-called traditional feminine things. I'd never marry a man who wants me barefoot and pregnant while he never lifts a finger to take care of the house or kids."

"You take that back right now. My mother, may she rest in peace, was a sweet, kind-hearted woman! She adored her only child and died in my place! I just so happen to like cooking. What's so wrong with a man with a sensitive side?"

Katrin ignores the question and goes back to telling Ginny all about Comrade Trotskiy's views on the Treaty of Brest-Litovsk. Ivan and Lyuba quickly shout her down for supporting it.

"That treaty was humiliating to our national pride," Ivan says. "Just wait till the people find out their new leaders are a bunch of barbarians. They'll be screaming for a return to monarchy."

"By the way, what did you call her?" Katrin changes the subject.

"Tatyana Ivanovna Zhukova," Lyuba says.

"A wise decision. That vile man doesn't deserve to have his name passed on. Not that I ever thought only men's names matter, but in a case like this, I'm even more opposed to automatically using a man's name instead of the mother's." She stands up and reaches for her coat. "Where are my manners? While I'm here, I ought to visit Liza and the others. I can't wait to see how big Liza's little miracle baby is now. I'm not too keen on the idea of God, but a higher force was at work when a baby born twelve weeks early survived infancy."

"I wouldn't visit anyone if I were you," Ivan says, dreaming of the day when Tatyana and Lyuba both change their name from Zhukova to Koneva. "Little Kittey Vishinskaya just caught polio. The doctor said she'll recover, but it'll take awhile, and she has to gradually relearn how to walk. In the meantime, we're quarantined. At least she caught a mild form of it instead of influenza or typhus."

Katrin grimaces. "I hope someday there are immunizations for scary diseases like that. It was no fun growing up the oldest of ten, all of us always having some disease we passed around—measles, mumps, diphtheria, scarlet fever. I should leave, since I don't want to take any risks being exposed to it. It's been lovely visiting, though."

After Katrin leaves, Ginny puts his coat and boots on. "I'm going out again. I need to use a phone."

"To call who?" Ivan asks. "Don't turn into a younger Boris.

The last thing we want or need is you hanging around shady characters and doing potentially illegal things."

"Take it easy. I'm only going to call Zhora at that asylum Malenkov's friends took her to."

Ginny trudges through the snow to the general store, the nearest public place with a phone. After giving the address to the operator, he waits a few minutes before he hears Georgiya's voice on the other end.

"Hello, Grigoriy. Today our brave Red Army men liberated us. The people responsible for our plight are going to pay. When the commander asked for names and addresses, I provided Malenkov's name and the general location of that valley. I advise you to get out of there and stay at my house. The soldiers will be after blood to revenge what was done to our people. If your cousin and her friends are smart, they'll get out of there too."

As soon as Ginny gets home, he relays the message to the others, ignoring their horrified expressions and complaints about how they have to flee with such little notice. This time they don't have Pyotr to take them to safety. Ivan in particular is furious at Georgiya for her role in this situation, since now there's an innocent newborn's life at stake, as well as a twelve-year-old girl recovering from polio. He spends the rest of the day packing his and Lyuba's things, and then goes to talk with the others to decide where they're going to go.

"Liza and Alyosha are going to a hotel on Tverskaya Street," he reports back to Lyuba. "They'll take the sleigh. We can't all leave at the same time, since our group is so large. We'll hide in different places, and God willing reunite when things settle down. Kat's group will go first, then Alya and Anya, then Alyosha's family, and finally us. We have to leave very early in the morning to get out of harm's way. I can't stand the thought of you being caught and raped by that marauding horde, or that innocent newborn being killed. In the meantime, I'll make you supper. Our final memories of this place should be as happy and normal as possible."

Lyuba falls into a deep, peaceful sleep after finishing the mushroom barley soup, rye bread with peach jam, stuffed tomatoes, broiled salmon, and apple tart. The next thing she's aware of, it's daylight and Ivan is sitting on the bed, shaking her awake, with the sound of shooting and screaming in the background.

"We both overslept. We have almost no time to get out of here. If I have to, I'll take a bullet to protect you and Tanyechka." He starts up at a loud knock on the door. "You have to throw your coat on and go. There's no time to get dressed."

Lyuba jumps out of bed and looks through the window. "Will wonders never cease. God sent us the most unlikely miracle-worker."

****

Chapter 5: On the Run

The Cheka are about to break the door down when they see Ginny running up with Georgiya.

"What can we do for you, Georgiya Yuriyevna?"

"My friend's cousin lives here. You're making a very big mistake! If you leave that house alone, I could arrange for you to meet a friend of Comrade Lenin's tonight. Are you that low you'll kill your fellow Russians over a misunderstanding? My parents are having a celebratory supper in honor of my homecoming, and several of Comrade Lenin's friends will be in attendance." Georgiya names each of these guests, along with brief summaries of who they are and what they've done. She speaks slowly, but not so slowly she risks being thought a moron or double-crossing authorities. "You and your men are welcome too."

"I'll be honored to dine with such distinguished guests, but these people need to open the door for me first."

In the time Georgiya has stalled the butchers outside, Lyuba has run upstairs and pulled on several layers of clothes. When she comes back downstairs, she sees her luggage waiting by the back door. She feels slightly guilty when she sees her suitcases, knowing Ivan only has one valise.

"Here. You take these two suitcases and I'll take the third. I don't want you to carry so much by yourself. I'll wrap Tanyechka up like an American Indian." He grabs a shawl and fastens it around the front of Lyuba's body as a baby-carrier, making sure Tatyana is snug. "Perfect. My mother said that's how everyone did it before prams were invented. I'm an old-fashioned guy, and if it worked for our ancestors, it's good enough for us, no matter how out of fashion it looks."

"Great. Another man is abandoning me, this time the one man I thought would never leave me."

Ivan takes her by the arm and marches her to the back of the house, opening the door to the freezing January weather. "I'm just taking an alternate route in case we're followed. They're more likely to go after a young guy like me than a woman alone with a baby. I'm the one who risks being thrown in prison or killed, not you."

"I'm too scared to go without you to protect me! I can hear

them inside the house now, in the rooms just off the front door!"

"You know how to get to Tverskaya Street from here. That's where Liza and Alyoshka went, to a twenty-five-story hotel. Now take this beautiful newborn and run. I'll join you as soon as I can, my love." He slips an influenza mask over her face, pushes her gently out the door, presses his ikon of St. Vladimir into her hand, and makes the sign of the cross over Tatyana.

Lyuba curses her bad luck as she runs away from the house, trying not to trip in the snow or drop her suitcases. She prays her barely-born child doesn't fall out or that the shawl doesn't come unfastened. If Ivan should die at the hands of the Bolsheviks, she'll lose the chance to someday marry and have children with a man she loves, and Ivan will go to his death never having had a blood child or knowing what it's like to make love with a woman.

Late at night she reaches the hotel and starts asking around, floor by floor, for Eliisabet and Aleksey. She finally finds them on the eighteenth floor. Lyuba drops her luggage from exhaustion once Aleksey leads her into their quarters. She takes Tatyana out of the shawl and begins nursing her, glad the newborn didn't succumb to frostbite, hypothermia, thirst, or hunger during the long flight. Aleksey leaves the room to give her privacy.

"Where are the others?" Eliisabet asks.

"Ginny went to Georgiya's house, and I don't know where Vanya is."

Nikolay is on a rug playing. He makes a gurgling sound. "Baby."

Eliisabet hands Nikolay a boy doll Alya made him for his first birthday. "You'll be amazed at how fast yours grows up too. It seems like only yesterday I was scared into premature, precipitous labor with him, and now he's fourteen months old, toddling, and saying a few words! Even if you adjust his age to account for his prematurity, he'd be eleven months old and doing those things anyway."

"Baby! Baby!" He turns bright red. "Baby! Baby!"

"He can hold her, I guess," Lyuba says. "Vanya was telling her she might grow up to marry your Kolya!"

Nikolay grins at the infant when Lyuba carefully places her in his arms. She and Eliisabet are supporting both babies when the floor caretaker calls into their quarters and says they've got a visitor.

"A very tall, handsome man with dark brown hair and beautiful brown eyes?" Lyuba asks.

"No, a rather short woman with curly blonde hair and blue eyes, and a young boy with black hair and azure eyes."

"You stay right here," Eliisabet says when she sees Lyuba starting up. "You're exhausted from your long, scary journey. I'll handle that *suka.*" She storms into the hallway.

"Hi! I heard you nearly got killed by the Bolsheviks! How'd you escape? Ivan just came over, and then Ginny showed up. I took the liberty of taking the brat here, since he wasn't moving on his own. Pity this isn't a modern hotel and doesn't have even one phone. I usually never spring visits on people unannounced. Katya knew where it was based on the description of a twenty-five-floor hotel on Tverskaya Street, so here I am."

"Oh, yes, I'm in such a fine mood to tell you the story of how we escaped with our lives from that marauding horde! What goes through that pea-sized brain of yours when you talk about matters of life and death in such a perky voice? Were you put on cocaine after you got out of the camp, and this is why you have such an unnaturally cheerful voice when talking about everything from celebrities to marauding Bolshevik hordes?"

"Excuse me, but my boyfriend—"

"You're only fooling yourself if you think Ivan loves you. At best, you were a distraction for him while the woman he truly loves was with another man. I have no idea why he came over there, but trust me, it's not about love."

"But we don't want Ginny. Can you *pozhaluysta*, *pozhaluysta* take him off our hands?"

Lyuba runs out. "What am I, an idiot? That child is the last thing I want or need after I just had a baby! My patience has been worn thin by him, and now it's your turn!" She points to the door.

"So I guess we know both of them are safe," Eliisabet says as Anastasiya trudges down the steps with Ginny.

"The Devil take Konev. I guess he did learn to love Voroshilova if he's living in her new house. He sure fooled me, the way he was taking care of me like I were his wife and Tatyana were his daughter the last few days. He's welcome to that *suka*, because I sure as hell won't waste my time daydreaming about getting back together with a man who emotionally cheats on me. I hope that blonde fool was worth it, because he's lost the best thing that ever happened to him. Vanya always dreamt of being a farmer in the American Midwest, with lots of kids. Voroshilova would probably think she'd lose her precious figure if she had more than a few kids, and would have a nervous breakdown at the thought of being a farm wife. If that man were in front of me now, I'd have some very choice expressions for him."

2

When Katrin opens the door the next day to get her mail, the newspaper, and the milk, she finds Ginny still there. He doesn't attempt to run away when he sees the anger in her green eyes, but just goes on chewing a loaf of bread.

"Maid, can you get the dogs to escort this child out?"

"The maid's busy with the new guests," Anastasiya says.

"What new guests?"

"The children who came in at midnight."

"What! I want those strangers out of my house! They might all have influenza or typhus!"

"Do you think Konev did it? He's a little too soft for his own good, though I have no idea how he could've left the house without our noticing and come back in just as stealthily." Anastasiya storms into his room. "Ivan Konev, how dare you invite in all these children!" she yells in his ear.

"What children?" Ivan has barely slept at all, so worried about Lyuba and Tatyana making it to safety without him to protect them. He's hardly thrilled to be so rudely awoken when he finally fell asleep for more than fifteen minutes.

Anastasiya's eyes narrow when she realizes the only other possible source of these strange guests. Storming outside, she grabs Ginny by his ear. "Start explaining right now! There are a bunch of strange children in our house, and you're the only person who could've done it!"

"I spent the night walking around the neighborhood, and they began to follow me because I had nice clothing. There they all were by the time I got back to the house!"

"This entire house could be infested with influenza and typhus from these strange children!" Katrin shrieks.

"Go away!" Anastasiya yells. "And get rid of these ragbag children while you're at it!"

Ivan is only too glad to get out of there. He's less than thrilled about getting such poor sleep, but now that he's up and it's morning, it's pointless to try to go back to sleep. He changes into day clothes, gathers his meager possessions into his tattered valise, pulls on his boots, scarf, hat, gloves, and coat, slips on a mask, and heads for the door, carrying his valise and Lyuba's other suitcase. Ginny likewise picks up his luggage and follows Ivan as he heads away from the mansion. The children trail after them.

3

Lyuba is sitting at the window with Eliisabet in the afternoon, both nursing their babies, when they see a large crowd approaching. At first they fear another horde of Bolsheviks, but quickly realize these are all children. Then Lyuba recognizes the familiar forms of her cousin and Ivan among them. Ivan has grown two inches since they left home and now measures six feet three, towering above everyone else in the crowd. He's also the only one wearing a mask. Lyuba prays these strange children don't decide to take up residence on the eighteenth floor, though she'll have to rub elbows with them when they go downstairs to take their meals in the big communal dining room.

"Where's Lyubov Leontiyevna Zhukova?" Ivan asks at the check-in desk in the lobby. "She's very tall for a woman, long sable hair and raven eyes, she came here with our newborn daughter within the last day."

"Up on the eighteenth floor. What kind of husband leaves his wife to flee to safety, and with a newborn no less?"

"I thought it'd be safest to go by different routes in case we were followed. I can't believe my poor Lyuba had to walk up eighteen flights of stairs with her luggage and a baby. I'm going to find her right now." He sets his valise on the desk and pulls out a ragdoll. "I bought this on my way over, my first present for my beautiful baby girl. I know newborns are too young for toys, but I couldn't wait to get my sweet baby a present. My father was a jerk who drank too much and beat me, so I'm going to go the other way in regards to my own children. I can't wait to start spoiling that darling baby."

Lyuba looks up when she sees her cousin and best friend coming in the door to their floor. She has no idea how they ended up together when Ivan told her he was taking a different route and Ginny announced his intentions to stay with Georgiya, but she already knows a certain vain blonde woman is involved.

"We came from Katrin's," Ginny says. "I stayed in the garage, and Konev slept in a guest bed. They tossed us out when I invited a bunch of stray kids. The kids followed us here." He looks around at his new surroundings. "Where are the others?"

"God knows if we'll see them again. In the meantime, there are still seven of us. Although right about now, I wish we had Kat and the Vishinskies in place of you and Konev. They never ran away all the time, fraternized with our enemies, or abandoned supposed best friends."

Lyuba is glaring at Ivan. As soon as they're alone in the room, she pounces on him with a tongue-lashing, never minding Tatyana begins screaming at the noise.

"You betrayed me. You didn't come here by a different route, you got hold of Ginny before he could defect to that girl's house, and the two of you went to Katrin's house!"

"I hate Anastasiya, and Katrin isn't much better! At least I can have an intelligent conversation or debate about politics, religion, or whatever with Katrin, but Anastasiya's only interests lie in clothing, cosmetics, and celebrities! I was only using her to make you jealous!"

"How convenient. I was only using Boris to make *you* jealous!"

"*Golubka*! I knew you didn't become his girlfriend because you loved him! We never knew we were using them to make each other jealous! I only stayed with Katrin to evade the Bolsheviks for a few days, until it was safe to come to you and the others!"

"It's far too late for apologies. We'll never stand a chance in Hell of being romantically involved again." Lyuba sets Tatyana on the mattress.

Ivan rushes up to her, taking her in his arms and kissing her. Though Lyuba doesn't reciprocate, he feels her quivering. This positive response emboldens him to become more dominating, taking what he wants instead of using a sweet, gentle technique. Lyuba pushes him away shortly after he forces his tongue into her mouth, a good five minutes after he started kissing her.

"Are you crazy! I've just had a baby by another man! You will not touch me, you will not do what you just did, you will not speak to me in romantic words, you will not do anything whatsoever to indicate you're still in love with me! I can't very well rush into your arms when just days ago I had a baby with another man!"

Ivan leaves the room feeling dejected, though comforted knowing Lyuba was only using Boris to make him jealous. Now probably isn't the time to present Tatyana with the doll he bought her, though he's a little cheered by how Lyuba let him kiss her for that long instead of immediately pushing him away. If she really didn't love him anymore, she wouldn't have let him continue or even start.

4

Several hours later, Ivan comes into Lyuba's room with an older woman. Lyuba is rocking Tatyana and telling her a Pushkin fable.

"Lyuba, my love, I'm very concerned about what happened to you during your pregnancy. You told me you were terrified you were beginning to miscarry several times. So I found a midwife to make sure nothing went wrong."

"I don't need any doctor, Vanya. She'll probably condemn me for having a child out of wedlock."

"She's an understanding woman. I told her about how Boris abandoned you, and she was in complete sympathy. Give her Tatyana."

Lyuba does so reluctantly. "I was so scared, you can't imagine."

Ivan fills the midwife in on all the details about how Boris abandoned Lyuba, neglecting to mention how he beat her up so many times. Now Lyuba is able to hold his hands as the midwife examines her. She's too terrified and traumatized by her recent ordeal to feel self-conscious or violated, though she closes her eyes and prays for this to be over soon.

Ivan curses himself for not going right back home as she was in labor. He would've coaxed her gently through the whole ordeal while waiting for Pyotr to come with a doctor. Lyuba looks even more exhausted than Eliisabet was. *Probably because of Boris*, he thinks in pain.

"Mother and daughter are doing just fine. Your Lyuba is lucky to have such a considerate friend. Poor girl, pregnant out of wedlock and abandoned by the father only days ago, the very night she gave birth!" The midwife drops to a whisper. "Ivan Ivanovich, I don't know if you should tell your friend this, so soon after the heartbreak she went through, but I noted serious cervical damage. If she has another pregnancy, much less carries it to term, it'll be a miracle!"

"Her boyfriend beat her during almost the entire pregnancy."

"That could explain it. I managed to guess you have feelings for her. Sometimes if a woman doesn't know about her problems, she isn't burdened by the sad knowledge. If you want her to give you at least one child of your own, perhaps you shouldn't tell her."

"I won't. If she gives me a healthy baby boy, I'll be very happy indeed."

"Such a pity, to lose the ability to have children all because of a hateful man, and at barely nineteen. I've seen women go insane because they're unable to have children, or more than one or two. Sometimes they spoil the only child rotten, and become insane with grief if they think something bad happened to that child."

"I'm an only child. My mother tried so hard to have another baby. I don't want Lyuba to find out just yet. This could kill her. I always wanted a big family, to make up for being an only child, but if she gives me at least one of my own, I'll be very happy. I just can't live if I never have at least one little child of my own. My family name will die with me, and she might ask for an annulment when we're married and no children are showing up. I can't live without Lyuba. I'll pray to God she gives me a son, and then we'll have a girl and a boy, even though they'll have different fathers."

"What are you whispering about?" Lyuba asks. "It's bad news, isn't it? I got so scared when I got those awful cramps, and I lost tissue, and sometimes Tatyana stopped moving!" She pulls Tatyana close to her body and kisses her on the head.

"Don't be fatalistic, my love. You'll have many more children. You remember I wanted nine. Well, we've got the first one, even though she isn't biologically mine, and there are eight more to go."

The midwife turns white. "Ivan Ivanovich, perhaps if she doesn't know, she might indeed be able to conceive and give birth to two or three if she's really lucky, but eight more?! I said you could deceive her for good intentions, not build up her hopes unrealistically!"

"We'll have a big family in America." Ivan ignores the midwife and goes back to Lyuba, kissing her on the eyelids. "If that lowlife Malenkov *did* ruin your chances to have more children, I'll kill him. Because I'll die of grief if I don't get my own children." He sends a warning glance to the midwife.

The midwife shuffles out of the room.

5

At supper later that day, Ginny sits far away from the others, slurps his beet and carrot stew loudly, and uses his filthy hands to wrest a hunk of sourdough bread from one of the large loaves. He eats as sloppily as possible, sloshing liquid all over the table and himself. When a piece of carrot or meat falls on the floor, he ducks underneath the table to retrieve it and cavalierly pops it into his mouth.

"Ginny, cut it out," Lyuba instructs.

He goes on making noises just to annoy her.

"Who is that boy's mother?" an old woman asks. "I advise her to whip him soundly when this meal is over!"

"Ginny, I said cut it out."

Ginny slurps his stew even louder and burps.

"Are these the table manners they taught you in the mission?"

Ginny stuffs too much food into his mouth and gags, spitting the excess back into the bowl. After he swallows that mouthful, he throws his spoon on the floor and begins eating with his hands, still making obnoxious noises. The only thing holding Ivan back from pummeling him is the fact that they're in front of so many other people.

"Mikhail Grigoriy Mikhaylovich Kharzin, cut those noises out right now or Ivan will whip you!"

Ginny hates being called Mikhail, so he shuts up, but a few minutes later he's back to his noise-making. Once he finishes his stew, he tilts the bowl into his mouth to drink the last few drops, then shoves his face into the bowl to lick up the last possible remaining liquid.

"Your son is the worst-behaved child I've ever met!"

"He's my cousin." Lyuba is horrified anyone would take her for someone old enough to have a child Ginny's age. She's been through hard times, but certainly not enough hard living to make her look *that* much older than nineteen!

"Where is his mother, or is she dead?"

"She and my mother went to America. Our fathers served in the war, but we haven't heard from them in a long time. If they're still alive and haven't immigrated, it's possible they joined the White Army."

"Has this child ever been whipped? A child this age who misbehaves like this clearly has never had a good spanking or whipping."

"That old *babushka* is so nosy," Eliisabet whispers.

Ginny wrests another hunk of bread from one of the communal loaves. "My parents never hit me, but that tall guy with the thick mop of brown hair has whipped and spanked me a few times. He's a damn hypocrite for doing that, since he's always going on about how horrible his father was to beat him as a boy."

"Your cousin's husband has sense. Maybe he'll finally beat some manners and respect into you one of these days, better late than never."

"That's not her husband. She's never been married."

"So then where did that baby come from? Is she living in sin with that man, or is that not her own child?"

"The baby's father abandoned her because she was having his child. He went to America. The tall guy is her best friend who lives with us."

"I have never in all my years heard of anything so scandalous! So you're a whore. A common piece of trash. No respectable man will marry you! Cheap slut!"

"Ginny!" Lyuba shouts. "I'm going to whip you myself, you *yebarishka*!"

The old woman gasps and crosses herself. "Have you always used such vulgar language, let alone in public and in the presence of your elders? Or did you start using obscenities after you began slutting it up outside of wedlock? Only whores think they deserve to keep their illegitimate brats. Decent fallen women always give the babies to orphanages. I wonder, are you already fornicating with this man and soon to produce another bastard?"

"Take your hate-filled diatribe back!" Ivan screams. "Apologize!"

"Oh, so finally you leap to my defense." Lyuba gives him a dirty look.

"Is this your new partner in sin?" She looks suspiciously at Ivan's utensils on the left side of his plate, but decides to pursue the so-called moral offense she uncovered first instead of adding a new one.

"No, he's my best friend, and my child carries his name as her patronymic." Given the hole Ginny dug for her, and the secretive nature of the relationship, Lyuba doesn't mention Ivan is her ex-boyfriend in addition to her best friend.

"Oh, great. More scandal!"

Ivan makes the *dulya* sign at her, shaking in rage. "Don't you know this beautiful woman was just days ago abandoned by the *mudak* who fathered her child? Don't you have any sympathy for her horrible ordeal? Like she got pregnant all by herself."

"Do you know who's the true father? If that baby has your name as her patronymic, who's to say if the missing partner in sin is really the father? If this slut were so sure that other man were the father, she would've given the baby his patronymic."

"We know it's Boris. I've never had relations with Lyuba. Why do so many people, women as well as men, believe if a woman has premarital relations with just one man, that automatically means she's slept with lots of others? It's not fair to punish a woman for that when men get away with it and are even cheered on."

"That woman is a common whore for having a child out of wedlock! If she were decent, the father would've married her! Seems to me he knew if she let him, she let others, and abandoned her to avoid having to marry a trollop and raise God knows which man's bastard."

"You apologize to her right now!" Ivan grabs her out of her seat and pins her against the wall. Lyuba is too shocked to chide him. "Are you calling the father a scandalous piece of trash too?! Can't you respect this woman?"

"She lost her respect when she procreated out of the bonds of wedlock."

"My best friend has had too much hard luck in her mere nineteen years! I'm the only person who's ever treated her with the respect she deserves! You're going to apologize to her right now!"

"I don't make apologies to sluts."

"If you weren't a woman, I would kill you." Ivan lets go of her and lets her walk away. "It must be nice to be completely perfect and never have lived in the real world, where bad things often happen to good people through no fault of their own."

"You assaulted an old woman to defend my honor." Lyuba begins to laugh. "There's a first for you!"

"I promise you." He stands behind her, drops to his knees, and puts his arms around her shoulders. "Whatever mud people wish to fling on you, they can fling on me too. Whatever horrors the Bolsheviks unleash, we'll experience together. I will never leave you!"

After dinner, they bump into the old woman again. She opens her mouth to say something, then sees Lyuba's menacing best friend with the *groznik* temper right at her side and thinks better of it. She doesn't even make a hex or cross herself.

"Mikhail Kharzin, I have never been so mad at anyone in my life!" Lyuba screams as soon as they get back to their room.

"I'm sorry," he says in a very insincere tone.

"I'm sure you'll find a band on the streets somewhere. Here. Take these coins, and I hope I never see you again!"

6

Katrin and Anastasiya are swooning over their pictures of their favorite American actor, Douglas Fairbanks, and their favorite royal, Grand Duke Dmitriy Pavlovich, when they're interrupted by loud, obnoxious knocking. Half-wondering if it might be her old maid, whom she fired for letting all those stray children in, Katrin abandons the pictures and goes to get the door, Anastasiya right behind her. Instead of the disgruntled former employee, they find Ginny.

"What do you want?" Anastasiya asks.

"Can I live here? My cousin kicked me out five weeks ago, and I had enough of roaming around on the streets. I want to live in a house again. Come on, I know you have lots of money and extra space."

"Forget it," Katrin says. "Stasya and I live here with our new maid and her husband. My home is not a hotel for wayfarers and *besprizorniki*."

"If I can't live with you in the house, I'll live on your property. I'll be in the garage if anyone wants me."

Ginny takes up residence in the garage, stealing food and eating grass buried under the snow. Katrin wants desperately to toss him out, but a tiny maternal part of her wonders how she'd feel if that were her favorite sister Viktoriya, who'd be Ginny's age now. Lyuba told her she swore she saw slight movement from nine-year-old Viktoriya after she fell to the floor when Katrin's siblings were being lined up and slaughtered. Lyuba also saw a bullet hole in the wall behind Viktoriya, which might suggest the assassin misfired and Viktoriya were playing dead till the coast was clear. If Viktoriya survived, escaped, and started a new life somewhere, Katrin would hate to learn she was evicted for the crime of trying to survive and getting on the nerves of her unwitting landlords just by existing.

7

Ivan is lying on a rug next to Tatyana after Lyuba has bathed and nursed her after supper. Every time she curls her fingers around his or gurgles, he smiles at her like she's the most special baby who ever lived.

"That's your ear," he smiles as she reaches up and explores her ear.

"Why don't you go back and be Ivan's girlfriend now that Malenkov's gone?" Eliisabet pesters. "He's such a natural with your baby, treating her like his own blood child, and I'd have to be blind to miss the way you look at each other. Not many men are willing to raise the baby of the woman they love when it was fathered by his best friend, or give the time of day to a woman who committed that ultimate betrayal. Your Vanya's a keeper, one in a billion among men. You'd be a fool to let such a diamond slip through your fingers."

"Of course I love him, Liza. But I have to adhere to society's rules. Everyone already thinks I'm a whore; why add fuel to the fire by getting involved with another man so soon after my illegitimate child's father left me? As if my other issues weren't bad enough."

"I hope we're close enough friends by now for you to tell me exactly what these issues are. I'd guess the reason you're so scared of being with a nice guy is because you were raped, and that made you distrust the intentions of every man ever since."

"You don't want to know. Trust me, it's too diabolical. But maybe someday I'll be able to get back together with the man I love. God must have some reason for keeping us alive and together this long, even if it isn't yet time for us to be together as husband and wife."

8

The next day, the hotelier and her staff are arrested by the Cheka. From the floors below, Lyuba and her friends hear shots and screams. A fire is set in the lobby before the butchers leave. Full of terror, Lyuba's party begins gathering their belongings together to get ready for escape. Aleksey goes first, carrying Nikolay down the fire escape.

"Lyuba, you and Tatyana go next," Eliisabet says. "I'll follow you."

"Vanya, can you wrap Tatyana up like an American Indian again?" Lyuba begs. "I can't carry my luggage and her at the same time."

"Anything for my Lyuba." He pulls a shawl out of one of Lyuba's suitcases and fashions it into a baby-carrier. "She'll be nice and snug. Prams are nice, but babies are happier and feel more secure and loved when they're carried the old-fashioned way. It lets the baby bond more closely to its mother instead of being kept at arm's length." He smiles at Lyuba. "You're the best mother in the world to Tanyechka. Say what you want about your feelings in girlhood, but from the moment our precious baby was born, you've adapted to motherhood like a fish to water. I bet you'll be a great wife too."

Eliisabet peers out the fire escape door and surveys what's going on below. "I know this sounds awful, but I have to ask Ivan to remain behind."

"What are you saying?" Lyuba screams, running back into the room. "Vanya promised me he'd never leave me! He's my best friend! And now you want me to leave him here to die!"

"I don't want all of us to go together, in case we're followed. Besides, Konev has the good sense to find another place to hide in the meantime instead of waiting around for the worst to happen."

"Go with the others," he begs her.

"*Ya tyebya lyublyu*," she whispers. "No matter what it looks like!"

***

There's an eerie stillness when they get back to the building three hours later. Lyuba is almost afraid to go back up, though the uppermost floors aren't blackened or gutted like most of the lower floors. The thought of finding her Vanya lying dead on the floor, either as a charred corpse or dead of smoke inhalation, tears at her soul and makes her curse herself for the umpteenth time in the last two years. If only she'd said yes to him, they would've been married, safe in America, and raising at least one child of their own. They could've easily had two children by now.

"Alyoshka, hold the kids," Eliisabet says.

They slowly ascend the fire escape to the eighteenth floor and push the door open. Lyuba hopes there aren't any Bolsheviks still lurking about as they tiptoe through the main hall and look into the rooms.

"In here. I read some of my poetry books while you were gone, Blok and Lermontov. Firemen came by soon after the murderers left, and they put out the fire so it wouldn't spread to the other buildings."

Lyuba's heart floods with joy at seeing Ivan alive. If she hadn't just had a baby by another man six and a half weeks ago, she'd be rushing into his arms right now. Her whole being tingles at the memory of finally being kissed by him again, and she wishes society didn't have so many stupid rules and that unbearable sexual double standard. Eliisabet knows full well Lyuba's heart burns for Ivan, and Lyuba and Aleksey have been friends since they were eight years old, but Lyuba still doesn't want to portray herself as a tramp. Tongues would wag if she started a relationship with another man so soon after having a baby and being abandoned.

"We found an old abandoned barn with a woodshed," Eliisabet says, smiling when she sees how Lyuba is gazing at Ivan. "It's close to Khimki Forest, in case we need to flee again. You know how crazy March weather can be, so it looks like we might be cuddled up like bugs in a rug tonight to keep warm."

"Show me the way!" Ivan smiles, taking Lyuba's hand.

***

Ginny, Katrin, and Anastasiya are standing there when Lyuba's party arrives. Lyuba wants to spit fire upon seeing Anastasiya, even knowing her belovèd was only using Anastasiya to make her jealous. At the rate she's going, she'll never be able to reunite with the man she loves.

"They evicted me because there were two Whites in the house," Katrin says. "They claimed I wasn't a true Bolshevik, but that's a damn dirty lie. I had Socialist leanings before I knew those feelings had a name." She goes into a corner and pulls a quilt over her head. "At least they let us take all our things before they evicted us. They took the maid's husband prisoner, but the maid came with us. She's over there on the wagon."

"Thank God I saved my cosmetics," Anastasiya says. "And all our pictures, so we can still swoon over Douglas and Dmitriy."

"When we came here earlier, you weren't here," Aleksey says. "I want you to get out and find somewhere else to stay. You expect us to believe this wild tale that a Bolshevik would get kicked out of her mansion?"

"They came to search all the houses, and they recognized Stasya from the labor camp," Katrin says. "Heads will roll when Comrade Lenin finds out about this appalling miscarriage of justice."

The others go into the barn, Lyuba dragging Ginny behind her. After they climb a ladder to the loft and deposit their luggage, Aleksey and Eliisabet claim some blankets and the mattress nearest the window. Lyuba sets Tatyana on the other mattress, not caring it has a hole or that it's right by the hay.

"Our barn on our farm in the American Midwest will be so much nicer," Ivan smiles. "Before you know it, we'll be safe in the land of the free, and as soon as we have enough money saved up, we can leave New York and move to a place that's not so crowded. Lots of our people move there after they leave the big city, so we won't feel lost in a sea of strangers."

"I suppose we're sleeping in our clothes?" Lyuba asks, ignoring his idealistic promises. "We don't have a curtain to put up for changing, and even if we did, there's no heat. We'd be too cold in just pajamas."

"We're all friends here, and our men are gentlemen," Eliisabet says. "If you want to put on pajamas, Alyoshka will look away, just like Ivan would look away if I were changing."

Tatyana and Nikolay start crying at a heavy, pounding sound. Aleksey creeps over to the window and peeks out. To his relief, it's only a heavy rainstorm, not another marauding horde of Bolsheviks.

"I suppose this settles the question about nightclothes. I don't think any of us are foolhardy enough to put on even wool pajamas during a rainstorm when we're in an unheated building."

Ivan lies on Lyuba's mattress and takes Tatyana's tiny hands in his. "That scary noise is only rain, *knyazhna*. You've got your *mamashka*, your *papashka*, your *Tyotya* Liza, and your *Dyadya* Alyoshka to protect you and your friend Kolya. As for that little delinquent, he's sleeping below us, so he won't bother us during the night." Ivan reaches into his valise. "Look, *knyazhna*, I got you a present. I bought this the day I arrived at the hotel, but I didn't know if it'd be appropriate to give it to you right then, after the less than amicable reception your mother gave me. I forgot about it over the next six weeks."

"You got my daughter a doll?" Lyuba asks. "That was really sweet of you. I like how she has dark hair. Too many dolls have blonde hair and blue eyes, as though that's the epitome of beauty."

"This is your first doll, my sweet Tanyechka. Now you'll have something to hold and cuddle at night when you're scared, and something to play with during the day. Someday, when we have our own little home, I'll be a guest at the tea parties you have with your doll, and all the other dolls and stuffed animals you'll have by then. Tonight will be your first night to sleep with your new friend, while your *papashka* and *mamashka* sleep on either side of you to protect you from all the bad guys."

"You're sleeping here?" Lyuba blushes as she maneuvers Tatyana under her blouse to nurse her.

"We're all friends here, remember?" Aleksey teases. "You know I was privy to your secret romance two years ago, and I knew you were in a hotel together the first week. Even if you didn't go all the way, you still slept in the same bed."

Lyuba turns even redder and doesn't say another word as she nurses or as she and Eliisabet change their babies' diapers, sticking the dirty ones out the window so the rain can clean them. She tries not to look at Ivan as she gets back on the mattress with Tatyana.

"Even if you get cold from all the rain, I'll keep you warm," he whispers.

"This is only temporary. As soon as we find more permanent lodgings, we'll go back to sleeping in different rooms instead of in such an inappropriate, scandalous fashion."

"Our romantic separation is only temporary too, Mrs. Koneva. Sooner than later, you'll come back right where you belong."

9

Lyuba wakes up in the morning to Ginny pacing about and devouring a hunk of bread. When the others wake up, he continues stuffing his face, not offering to share.

"Do you realize we haven't eaten since we left the hotel? Only the babies got to eat. I'm surprised you came up here to join us instead of running away to roam the streets again."

"Well, it was like this. I slept on a dirty pile of hay next to an old pipe. During the night, it made a noise, so I kicked it and it broke. The barn began to flood, and when I ran outside, it was still raining. Rather than take my chances outside, I came up here where it was safe and relatively warmer. Did you enjoy sleeping with your boyfriend?"

"You idiot! Are you sure you weren't dropped at birth or didn't have your head squeezed by forceps?"

"Where are the dimwits and their maid?" Eliisabet asks. "I love how Katrin is such a good Socialist, such a friend of the common people, that she relegated her servant to sleeping in the wagon while she and Nastya slept in the woodshed with their blankets and pillows."

"I think that's your answer," Aleksey says from the window.

The others go over to look and see the rain pounding down on a heavy wool blanket tied over the wagon as a tent. Even through the heavy rain, the closed window, and the distance from the wagon, they hear Katrin and Anastasiya screaming as the blanket collapses. When Katrin urges the horses on, the wagon goes right into a huge puddle, and the front wheels break off. Then the luggage falls out, the horses break free of their harnesses, and the maid tumbles into the puddle. The wagon begins moving backwards, in spite of the missing horses and front wheels. Lyuba and her friends, from the safety of the hayloft, feels as though they're watching a twisted Charlie Chaplin or Max Linder comedy short. Not having seen a moving picture in two years, watching their adversaries' unintentional dark comedy will have to suffice.

"Oh, finally Katrin shows she cares for the common people when she puts her mind to it," Eliisabet says as Katrin jumps off the runaway wagon to assist the unresponsive maid.

Anastasiya sloshes over to the barn, her long, heavy skirts impeding her movement more than usual due to being so waterlogged. She's also having difficulty walking with her tango shoes. The moment she opens the door, more water rushes out. Katrin, not wanting to wait around for the rain to get even worse, yanks Anastasiya off by the hand and rushes to gather up their suitcases.

"Oh, *no*," Ivan says. "Everyone be very quiet. There's a policeman coming."

The man sloshes through the water, fighting to control his umbrella, and makes a beeline for the barn. They hear him walking around while he waits for the rain to subside. After what feels like an eternity, the rain stops, and they hear his footsteps ascending each rung of the ladder, followed by his fumbling with the hatch.

Aleksey jumps out the window, and Eliisabet drops Nikolay into his arms. After sending down their two suitcases and her rosebush, she jumps with some discomfort. They start running softly to Khimki Forest after gathering up their belongings. Ginny jumps right into a pile of burrs and screams.

"Who's up there? Don't make me axe this hatch open!"

Ivan climbs down the wall after dropping the luggage out the window. Lyuba crosses herself, closes her eyes, and drops Tatyana into Ivan's waiting arms, then clings to the pane, too afraid to jump.

"Just jump!" Ginny yells. "He'll kill us if we don't scram!"

She lets herself drop to the ground, her fall somewhat broken by the water, and starts to gather up the luggage. Part of her wishes she only had one suitcase, like Eliisabet and Aleksey, and maybe one extra parcel, like Eliisabet's rosebush, but she's hung onto these reminders of her former life so long, and won't hear of discarding them.

"Oh, no, *golubka*, none of that. You're still too weak from your awful ordeal."

"How you can look at this shamed woman who has a child out of wedlock with another man and still love her escapes me."

"You carry Tanyechka, and I'll carry the luggage."

"Now you're behaving like your namesake." Lyuba smiles at him and takes Tatyana.

Shortly after they reach Khimki Forest, they hear the baying of a dog and many menacing footsteps rapidly approaching. Aleksey climbs up a huge tree with Nikolay clinging to him, Eliisabet after them. Ivan takes Lyuba by the arm and pulls her behind the tree. Ginny ascends the tree next, but in the dark, he cannot see he's reached the top, and falls out, landing with a sickening thud.

"Consider yourselves warned. If I catch you squatting in abandoned buildings again, you'll all be thrown in jail. I guess you're essentially harmless, even if you are squatters. Have fun sleeping outside tonight and finding food in the forest."

The officers turn and walk away, leaving Lyuba's party shaking in terror of the close call they just had.

"I think I broke a bone," Ginny moans. "I see bone poking out."

"Do you see a doctor nearby?" Lyuba snaps. "If Kat were with us, she could set your break. Her oldest brother-in-law's a doctor, and she knows some emergency medical techniques from watching him so often."

Aleksey climbs out of the tree and pulls a blanket out of one of Ginny's suitcases. He plasters mud over Ginny's left arm, then rips off a piece of the blanket.

"That was my blanket from East Prussia!"

"Look how worn it is. You know as well as anyone this is a rag. It's the best we can get for a cast at the moment." Aleksey wraps the rag around Ginny's injured arm. "Sweet dreams, delinquent."

"Doesn't anyone have any medicine?"

"All used up. We don't even have alcohol to numb the pain."

Lyuba sees a gleam in Ginny's eyes in the dark, but pushes it out of her head as she and her friends set up makeshift beds near the tree, using blankets and pillows as cushioning nests. Only the nearby presence of her belovèd takes away Lyuba's fear of being attacked during the night or ruining her back.

10

"Well, good morning!" Anastasiya says. She and Katrin are holding several baskets, Ginny thankfully nowhere in sight. "The maid died. Katya foraged for food, but I'm too good to eat bark, berries, leaves, and roots. At least she found some fruit and killed a few rabbits. Do you have anything for breakfast?"

"Only some apples, cheese, and eggs we took from the hotel," Eliisabet says.

"We can't subsist on that," Katrin says. "There's a market a short distance away. I've still got my money, even if I lost my house. I'll buy quality foods and ingredients, and we can all share them. Think of it as my treat. I got all my traitor parents' money after they were arrested, so I've got more than enough to cover expenses in spite of hyperinflation. In the meantime, you can eat the food I foraged. Rabbit's more filling than eggs, apples, and cheese."

Eliisabet looks at her in astonishment as she walks off. Pampered Princess Katrin really isn't so coddled and out of touch if she knows how to forage for food and doesn't consider eating bark, leaves, berries, and roots beneath her. As it now stands, Anastasiya is the most expendable member of their band, not Katrin.

Aleksey takes a knife out of his pocket and starts skinning the rabbits. "It's not as hearty as beef or lamb, but it's meat."

"Lyuba can have my portion," Ivan says. "I like rabbits. I always loved watching and talking to the bunnies who came to my backyard, and I always wanted to get my kids pet bunnies when we live on our farm in the American Midwest. I don't mind rabbit fur hats, but I can't eat them."

"My boyfriend and I have to catch up." Anastasiya saunters up to them and drags Ivan over to a tree. "We'll sit together and chat, since you won't be eating."

Lyuba fumes when she sees him obliging this empty-headed woman. The snatches of conversation she catches as everyone else enjoys roasted rabbit, fruit, and berries further confirm what a light-headed dunce Anastasiya is. Ivan has always appreciated and respected Lyuba's intelligence and smarts, and expects to have a wife who's an intellectual equal instead of someone who plays dumb and helpless to get a man. Like most men, he believes men and women have separate roles and that some things, like driving cars, are men's territory, while things like childcare are women's territory. But he doesn't think things like cooking, basic sewing, housework, and taking care of sick children are beneath him or a woman's domain only. He's about as enlightened a man as one can hope for without being an anti-establishment radical. Now that Anastasiya's back in the band, it looks like he's going to continue the charade of courting her, but at least now Lyuba knows it's just make-believe and that his heart truly belongs to her only.

"Ew." Anastasiya averts her eyes from Lyuba and Eliisabet nursing. "I thought all civilized, modern women used bottles. Most American and English women nowadays use bottles unless they're too poor."

"I don't like to look either, but it's how mammal mothers feed their babies. Why would you waste good money on something you can get for free?" Ivan imagines Lyuba nursing their future son, the little Baby Konev who'll carry on his family name, as she sits in a rocking chair in their farmhouse and waits for him to come in from a day in the fields. "I'm modern about some things, but I'm an old-fashioned guy at heart. The old ways of doing things worked just fine for hundreds or thousands of years, and it's silly to discard time-honored traditions just because a new fad comes along."

Several hours later, Katrin comes back with several baskets full of food. Lyuba still doesn't think of Katrin as one of her best friends, but she can't help but admire her little touches of generosity. After all, Katrin could've used her money and Bolshevik connections for selfish ends instead of helping people from the other side.

11

The next morning Ginny returns, a large sack on his back. "I have a ton of money, and it's all mine! Seven million rubles and five thousand kopeks! And a crate of jarred borshcht! Mine! I stole it, and I'll use it to make more money all for myself! You can't have any of it at all, but if you ask nicely, I might just—"

"Give us that money!" Lyuba yells. "We're all hungry and need things!"

"I just bought a lot of food," Katrin says. "Let the little urchin enjoy his stupid jarred borshcht. We're the ones who've got real food from the market, and we didn't steal our food."

Aleksey steps back from him. "Your breath smells funny. Have you been drinking?"

"What I did to get pain relief while I was gone is my business. Instead of hassling me about my private business, why don't you put yourself to good use by helping to pack up so we can get going?"

They walk many *vyorsty* that day. Anastasiya and Katrin get blisters all over and spend all day complaining about how they no longer have horses or a vehicle. Anastasiya in particular has difficulties keeping pace, since she's wearing her tango shoes as always. At least Katrin, for all her own complaining, is wearing sensible leather boots. Ivan is disgusted, unable to believe an alleged Socialist is demanding to be treated like a coddled princess or that someone who survived a brutal labor camp learnt nothing about toughness or self-sufficiency from her ordeal. If anyone deserves to complain, it should be Lyuba, after the difficult pregnancy she went through and still doesn't seem fully recovered from. He hopes they find a more permanent home soon, where she can finally relax and not have to worry about anything.

As the sun starts going down, Katrin and Anastasiya head for a big birch trunk lying on its side and set their luggage down. Typically, Anastasiya sits on the trunk while Katrin does the hard work of putting up a tent with blankets, ropes, and big, heavy branches. Aleksey and Ivan start a campfire and gather leaves for makeshift beds. Once the fire is crackling away, Ivan cooks some of Katrin's vegetables and cured meats. Lyuba puts Tatyana under a blanket with her doll, savoring the luxurious warmth from the fire and the delicious smells. The dinner they presently eat tastes almost as good as the gourmet food she enjoyed when she lived in St. Petersburg. Two years ago, she could never have imagined she'd one day soon find delight in such simple things.

"Would you like some of my leftover blankets for your own tent?" Katrin asks. "You shouldn't spend another night exposed to the elements, even if March isn't quite as unforgiving as December or January."

"We'll manage," Lyuba says in resignation. "But *bolshoye spasibo* for the offer. Maybe someday I'll be able to figure out how so many contradictions can reside in the same person. I wouldn't quite call you a Jekyll and Hyde, but you do seem to have quite a lot of different faces."

"Don't we all?" Katrin takes the last bite of her roasted potato. "I hope you sleep as well as you can, considering. If you change your mind, my tent is always open. Estonians are good at hospitality, even if our potential guests belong to the people who oppressed us for centuries." She stands up and heads off with Anastasiya.

"I'm taking up their offer," Ginny announces. "You people are insane to want to sleep without any kind of walls."

Katrin and Anastasiya are in the middle of changing into warm wool pajamas when Ginny bursts into their tent. Katrin is maneuvering around under her fur coat, and Anastasiya is changing under a blue silk blanket from Estonia.

"Sleep somewhere away from us." Katrin instinctively backs away from Ginny as though he has Bubonic Plague. "It's improper to sleep near unrelated males. My offer was for Lyuba, Liza, and their babies, not for you or the men."

Ivan and Aleksey lift the tent flaps.

"Ginny, it's high time we had a talk," Aleksey asks. "We want to know exactly where you've been and what you've been doing when you've been away from us. It's one thing to steal when you're homeless, but you've been sneaking away and stealing for a long time, even when we were being taken care of by Petya and didn't need to steal."

"It's none of your business what I do to get things."

"Lyuba asked us to talk to you about it. And why were you reading so much Bolshevik propaganda back at the house in the valley? Your friend Zhora was always a bright kid, intelligent and mature beyond her years, a bit like a younger Lyuba, but her family is Bolshevik! How could you go around with traitors to the Motherland when we're in this sorry state because of them!" Aleksey pulls a vodka bottle out of his coat pocket. "Maybe you can explain this too. Lyuba found this in that sack of money and food you refused to share with us. You had to get this from the black market, since only restaurants can sell hard liquor these days."

"That's for pain relief, since no one here loves me enough to take me to a doctor, and we're all out of medicine." Ginny stands up and tries to grab it. "It's not nice to snoop. That *govnyuk* will be sorry she did that."

"Mikhail Grigoriy Mikhaylovich Kharzin, you shouldn't use vulgar language to talk about a lady!" Ivan yells.

"I've heard you use that word yourself, and Lyuba herself curses! I want you both to go away, *pozhaluysta*!" He turns his head. "And don't you *dare* think I'm asking you this because I'm going to cry. Only tiny babies like Nikolay and Tatyana cry! Leave me alone! Go away, *pozhaluysta*! Get out of here now!" His face is red, his cheeks puffing out.

As they turn and leave, he runs after them with a devil expression on his face. He grabs a huge stick with his unbroken right arm and starts to raise it above them. Aleksey grabs him while Ivan grabs the stick and throws it away. Ginny tries to wiggle out of Aleksey's grasp.

"Let go of me now!"

"Why, so you can batter us?"

"I hate you!" He twists loose, runs to the encampment, and starts to kick the leaves off Eliisabet and Nikolay, red in the face.

"Stop that!" Lyuba grabs him. "I think it's time for him to go back to the streets, if this is the kind of evil person he's turned into."

"I'll steal a car in the morning and leave him somewhere far away from us." Ivan sends Ginny a look. "Lyuba, he called you a vulgar word and refused to apologize!"

"I'll go with you," Aleksey says.

True to their word, the next day Ivan and Aleksey leave early in the morning and return in a large car. Lyuba doesn't care her belovèd Vanya is a thief, since desperate times call for desperate measures. Ginny is ordered to collect his luggage and get into the backseat. He's pushed out, screaming, when they reach Sadovnicheskaya Street.

12

The next day, Lyuba wakes up to the sight of Kat and Nikolas walking through their encampment. Kittey is in a wheelchair. Lyuba quickly wakes the others, and they go around hugging their missing friends.

"We're heading to a boardinghouse near Sokolniki Park," Nikolas says. "We would've gone there already, but we wanted to scope out the area first, to make sure we weren't leaving any of our friends behind."

"We were at a White encampment the past six weeks," Kat says. "We knew you'd gone to that place on Tverskaya Street, but we thought it'd be safer in the meantime to stay in smaller groups, and influenza and typhus were still going around. Did you hear the sad news about Vera Kholodnaya dying of flu last month? She was always one of my favorite film actresses. When we heard your place was ransacked, we decided to look for you in the forest. That's a natural hiding place. God must want us to come back together if we found each other."

"Alya and Anya aren't following us," Kittey says. "We don't know where they went, but we can only hope it was another White stronghold, or that they haven't been captured, wherever they are."

"We lost our sleigh and the horses," Ivan says. "Alyosha found the stable empty. The Reds stole them, or another family took it when they fled. Luckily, we managed to steal a car yesterday."

"Do you think we'll all fit?" Eliisabet asks.

"We can try," Nikolas says.

Ivan gets into the driver's seat and beckons to Lyuba to sit next to him. Eliisabet climbs into the back with Nikolay, followed by Kat. Nikolas squeezes Kittey into a sitting position, then takes the final bit of space in the back. Aleksey ties Kittey's chair to the roof, passes their luggage into the backseat, and climbs into the rumble seat. Katrin squeezes in next to him, leaving Anastasiya to balance on their laps. During the five-hour ride, with many detours and side roads in case anyone's following them, Anastasiya gets carsick several times. They resign themselves to the reality of having to indefinitely live with her. Lyuba in particular hates the idea of living with her again, but it's not right to throw another human being out on the street and force her to fend for herself.

13

During the spring, they settle into life at the new place. Lyuba lovingly nurses Tatyana and rocks her to sleep, and by the beginning of May, she's well enough to start going out to Sokolniki Park with Tatyana in a pram, her doll tucked beside her. Ivan accompanies them, and his heart melts whenever he sees the baby.

"She has your eyes and hair, my love."

"What makes you so sure she takes after me and not her father? We've both got black hair and eyes."

"Give yourself more credit for making a beautiful baby. Boris only contributed his worthless seed, and you did all the rest of the work. Tanyechka's just as beautiful as you, and doesn't look anything like that ugly *morda* Malenkov."

They sit down on a bench. Ivan glares at the policemen leering at Lyuba.

"Don't turn back into Ivan Grozniy. I thought you were starting to act like your namesake, my Ivan the Great."

"Oh, you secretly like it when I get into fights. You're proud such a brave, strong guy loves you."

"Now you're deluding yourself!"

"Women without husbands or male relations are at greater risk of attack. Look at yourself. You're so beautiful."

"You know I can't give my heart away easily after what happened to me. I honestly don't think I'd know what to do with a nice guy for more than a short relationship. There's a reason you're my best friend, not my husband."

"Your father's going to Hell for what he did to you. Boris can go to Hell too for what he did to you, and I'm positive my father's already in Hell for what he did to both of us. I don't care how long it takes; you're going to call me your husband one day."

"It'd be nice to have a little boy in your image. Maybe someday I'll merit bearing you a son with your beautiful dark brown hair and eyes, your beautiful face, your thick mop of hair, a *levsha*."

"Ask and you shall receive." He squeezes her hand. "You're the only right-handed person I've ever known who *wants* a *levsha* for a child. Most of your kind think we're possessed of Satan, diseased, or deficient. Maybe you were a *levsha* in another lifetime."

She tenderly caresses his left hand. "My heart broke for you when the teachers hit your hand with straps and rulers, or thumped you on the head with heavy books. One *suka* substitute even tied your hand down with rope. My sweet Vanyechka didn't deserve to be abused for behaving the way God made you."

"The sooner you come back to me, the sooner we can be married, and the sooner we can have that little boy in my image. If I withstood years of mean teachers trying to change me, don't you think I have what it takes to wait as long as it takes for you to come back where you belong?"

Lyuba goes to sleep every night with Tatyana beside her, longing for Ivan to be there on her other side. But she's doing a very good job of putting up a charade for the other members of the band. The image of the wronged young woman who was left by her baby's father. No one except Ivan knows she almost miscarried at least five times, that Boris beat her during the entire pregnancy, or that she never loved Boris. Publicly she puts on the role of the scorned woman, then at night longs for Ivan. She'll let a few more months go by before rushing back into his arms. That way, it won't look rehearsed. Besides, she's still waiting for him to get rid of Anastasiya.

Ivan turns twenty-one on July fifth. Lyuba reflects on the fact that, in America, he'd be old enough to vote. In other words, a grown man. During his birthday dinner, Lyuba burns with lust for Ivan. She wishes she could give him herself as a birthday present. Yet she doesn't dream her wish will soon be helped along by the reappearance of one of her least-favorite people.

****

Chapter 6: Ginny's Reign of Terror

On a hot day in August, Lyuba and her friends are awoken by loud knocking on the door, followed by very obnoxious bell-ringing. While Katrin and Anastasiya moan about their beauty sleep being interrupted, Lyuba looks through the window and sees her cousin, his luggage in his hands. She's alarmed by the strange way he's holding himself, and wonders if the vodka she found in March was only the beginning of a downward spiral. After throwing on day clothes, she picks up Tatyana and knocks at Ivan's door.

"The young demon is back. I just saw him standing at the door. Will you help me get rid of him?"

"How did he find us?"

"I guess we're about to find out."

"Wait here while I change. I'll be right out to evict him."

Lyuba rolls her eyes as he shuts the door. It's not as though she's never seen him naked before. For someone who wants nine kids, he's awfully concerned with modesty.

"Okay, I'm ready. Let's go kick him out."

They walk downstairs, and both can instantly tell something's not right when Ivan opens the door. Ginny's pupils are very dilated, and his whole bearing looks very off. It's as though Ginny's body is here while his psyche is far away in a strange other zone.

"*Ukhodite*! No one here wants you." Ivan tries to shut the door, but Ginny sticks his foot inside, shoves past them, and runs upstairs.

By now the other members of the band have gotten up to see what the disturbance is. Ignoring everyone's gasps, curses, and shouts, Ginny grabs the handles of Kittey's wheelchair and pushes her downstairs.

"What the hell is wrong with you?" Kat screams, alarmed by his dilated eyes and the strange way he's holding himself. "That dear little girl will only be thirteen next month, and she's not fully recovered from polio!"

"*Blyakha-mukha*, there's nothing wrong with me!"

"And some people think *I'm* the one possessed by Satan for being left-handed?" Ivan asks as Nikolas runs down the stairs. "I think the real Satan-possessed person just walked in!"

"I want you to stop this right now!" Aleksey orders.

"Who are you to tell me what to do?" Ginny screams, grabbing Aleksey by his shirt.

"Get your hands off my husband this instant!" Eliisabet yells.

Nikolas tenderly lifts Kittey back into the wheelchair and pulls her backwards up the stairs. While everyone, even Katrin and Anastasiya, swarms around her offering sympathy, asking what hurts, and gently probing for possible broken bones, Ginny sees Tatyana on a blanket on the floor. Seizing the moment, he grabs her and starts running down the stairs. Ivan spies this out of the corner of his eye and runs after him. Ginny trips halfway down the stairs, and Tatyana slips out of his arms and lands on the floor. She begins to bawl very loudly.

"Oh my Lord, Mikhail Mikhaylovich Kharzin, what have you done to my baby?" Ivan puts Tatyana on his lap and rips off the bottom of one of his pant legs, wrapping it around her bleeding head. "Don't you worry, *knyazhna*, your *papashka* will take care of you, and you know you and your *mamashka* are the most important people in the world to me."

Lyuba storms downstairs, grabs Ginny, and shoves him against the wall. "What the hell did my baby ever do to you? And why are your eyes so huge? Are you drunk or using drugs?"

"He's damn lucky he's only twelve, since otherwise I'd contact the police right now to have him arrested for the attempted murder of a baby! Get the hell out of here now before I break all your limbs!" Ivan cradles Tatyana in his arms. "How dare that little upstart try to kill our baby! This child is as much mine as if I'd made her!"

***

That afternoon, Pyotr comes over with a doctor, who addresses Lyuba as Mrs. Koneva. She flashes Pyotr a smile of pure gratitude.

The doctor gently pulls away the makeshift bandage. "It's a good thing her father rescued her right away, or she might've bled to death. A lot of fathers aren't so attentive, and expect their children to be entirely cared for by their mothers. You're a very lucky woman to have such a wonderful husband, Mrs. Koneva."

"Yes, not a day goes by when I'm not thankful for my Vanya and how God decided to bless a nobody like me with an incredible man like that." Lyuba puts her arm around Ivan to play up the role of Mrs. Koneva. "Of all the men in the world, I'm so glad he was chosen to be mine. God made him special just for me, and made us a perfect match."

"She needs special care in a clinic. I'm one of the best doctors in Moskva, so don't worry she'll die while she's away."

"How about my little sister?" Nikolas asks. "She broke two bones in her right leg. My fiancée's oldest brother-in-law is a doctor, and she learnt from him how to set broken bones. But there's no substitute for a cast."

The doctor goes over to Kittey. "How old are you?"

"Nearly thirteen."

"And why are you in this wheelchair, because of that evil boy?"

"No, I had polio in January. I'm not paralyzed anymore, though. I can move my arms and legs, but I haven't practiced too much walking. My brother and his fiancée made me exercise my limbs and gave me hot wool compresses so my muscles wouldn't atrophy."

"Why don't you come with me and the baby, Katerina Andreyevna? You may be able to start using crutches and calipers."

Lyuba hugs and kisses Tatyana, then lets Ivan have a turn. She puts on a brave face as she sets Tatyana in Kittey's lap and watches them leaving with the doctor.

As soon as they're gone, Ginny goes over to Lyuba and says in a smug tone, "I hope that stupid baby dies!" He leaves the room, howling with laughter.

Ivan puts his arm around her when he sees her blinking away tears. Then he presses his luck and puts his other arm around her. Lyuba loves to be held by him, and pretends to be upset longer than she really is.

"I can tell you're pretending to cry," he whispers. "I think someone wishes we were more than friends again and that I could do a lot more than just hold you."

"Only in my dreams. You're with Anastasiya now, and I have a child with another man. Maybe in another lifetime we'll be married."

"You know my relationship with Voroshilova is just make-believe. As soon as you say the word, I'll be all yours again, and you can do whatever you want to me, if you know what I mean. I hope you let me do whatever I want to you too."

"Always the ones you least suspect." Lyuba blushes.

"Well, you know what they say about the quiet ones!" He abruptly releases her from his embrace. "That damned cousin of yours is still laughing that mad laugh. I'm going to try to talk with him, man to man, and I'll be right back to sit with you."

Ginny looks up when he sees Ivan entering the room he claimed. Ivan notices pills lying across the bed, which Ginny rushes to stuff into his pocket.

"What did Lyuba ever do to you to make you want to kill her darling little innocent baby?" Ivan notices Ginny's eyes are dilated again and that he's itching in spite of no visible rash. He doesn't want to know what in the world is behind this.

"I don't have to explain myself to anyone."

"Your behavior's at its all-time worst, and that's saying a lot. What are those pills I saw you trying to hide? Do they have anything to do with this violent behavior that's an all-time low even for you? You may have acted up before, but you never were so diabolical you tried to murder an innocent baby! We all know you were drinking vodka the last time you were with us. Have you moved on from drinking to addictive pills? What exactly happened to you those five weeks you roamed the streets before landing on Katrin's doorstep? And what happened to you the last five months?"

"That's none of your damn business! You have no right to lecture me about what I might do to make myself feel good when you're so moral it's sickening! You're twenty-one and have never smoked a cigarette, drank alcohol, used any kinds of drugs, or slept with a woman! Don't you dare live like a monk and get mad when I do things people in the real world do for fun!" Ginny starts itching even more furiously.

Ivan shakes his head in disgust and leaves the room.

"He's always back, no matter how hard we try to lose him!" Lyuba laments. "He might be family, but I've reached my limit with him! I can't deal with his degenerate, violent behavior!"

"I'll deal with him for you. Maybe I'm a big hypocrite for beating him up after my drunken father abused me so much, but there's no other way to try to drive sense or respect into that child. My father went after me completely unprovoked, and I'll never raise my hands against any child of ours. Dealing with your vile cousin is an entirely different story."

2

The next day, the doctor comes back with Tatyana, her head in a bandage. Lyuba rushes to take her baby, smothering her with kisses and cuddles, then very reluctantly hands her to Ivan so he can have a turn. It continually amazes her how good and natural he's been with Tatyana since she was born, even knowing he's always been sweeter, more sensitive, and more nurturing than most men. But then again, he's told her several times lefties are generally more sensitive people by nature, since they use the side of the brain associated with emotions. And Ivan's sign is Cancer, ruled by the Moon, the most sensitive sign in the Zodiac. Lyuba's a Sagittarius, which isn't a good match for Cancer. Regardless of what the stars say, she knows what her heart and soul say, that the man cuddling and crying over her baby is her soulmate.

Kittey slowly wheels her way into the room, her right leg in a cast, her left leg in a full-length caliper, a pair of crutches fastened to the back of the wheelchair. "The doctor told me I should practice with crutches for a few hours every day." She gives Ginny a very dirty look before going into her room.

Ginny ignores her and goes up to Lyuba. "I made you lunch. Trust me, it doesn't have poison in it."

"You did something nice for another person?" Ivan asks as he cuddles Tatyana. "If I find out you have a sinister ulterior motive for this, I'll wring your neck."

Ginny lights a candle, ladles borshcht into bowls, and pours drinks.

"I am so sick of borshcht," Lyuba sighs. "This is supposed to be a romantic candlelight meal?"

"Someday I'll take you to a grand restaurant in America," Ivan promises as he puts Tatyana in the highchair. "We'll have a romantic meal with candles, flowers, violins, and waterfalls. I'll let you order anything you want, even fancy, expensive food like lobster, caviar, chocolate mousse, and duck."

Lyuba makes a violent face as she drinks. "Vanya, does your water taste funny too?"

Ivan takes a sip and blanches too. "It does taste funny. Maybe the water supply is rank today."

"Well, I'm thirsty. We can't be too picky about where anything comes from these days, since we're lucky to be alive." Lyuba drinks her glass to the bottom and smiles an odd smile when she finishes. "Ginny, may I have more water?"

Ginny obediently ducks back into the room and refills her glass. "What's wrong, Konev, not thirsty?"

"No, the water tastes funny. I'm not as thirsty as Lyuba."

Lyuba starts drinking the second glass, and the room starts to spin. The glass slips out of her hand as her head crashes down onto the table. The contents of the glass spill all over. Ivan stares at her in horror as she slumps out of her chair. Lyuba tries to get up, but quickly topples over and starts giggling.

Ivan picks his glass up and takes another sip, physically recoiling. With a sick feeling in the pit of his stomach, he tries to help Lyuba up. He isn't prepared for her to began screaming hysterically and clawing at his face.

"Don't touch me! By God's cross, I'll never let you violate me again! Get your dirty hands off me, *Batya*!" She begins breathing in frantic, ragged gulps, blood rushing and pounding through her ears, as she continues flailing her limbs hysterically.

When Ivan gets a whiff of her breath, he immediately realizes Ginny poured vodka instead of water. Being a teetotaler, he didn't recognize the taste, but now he recognizes the smell as clear as day. Fighting back nightmarish images of his own father, he lies next to her and begins whispering in her ear, thankful everyone but Ginny and Kittey is out.

"Lyubashka, it's me, Vanya. Calm down. We're safe now. That *mudak* is gone, and my father is dead. They haven't touched you in over two years. I've been protecting you since we left home. Your evil cousin gave you vodka and tricked you into thinking it was water. He's damn lucky you didn't drink enough for alcohol poisoning. I'll stay with you till it gets out of your system, and take care of you while you're sick. You're just reliving bad memories in your head, but you've survived them. They're only memories."

Lyuba looks over at him through her fuzzy vision, still frantically gulping for breath. As his words start sinking in, she reaches out for him and gently strokes his face.

"That's right, I'm your best friend, the one man in the world who'd never do anything to hurt you." He pulls her into a sitting position, in which she promptly slumps forward, and gently rubs her back, patiently telling her to breathe in and out till her breathing finally returns to normal after what seems an eternity.

Ivan looks up when he hears footsteps. Instead of Eliisabet and Aleksey returning from the market, Kat and Nikolas returning from their walk, or Anastasiya and Katrin returning from sunbathing, it's the source of all Lyuba's trouble returning to the scene of his crime. Upon seeing Ginny starting to unlatch Tatyana's highchair, Ivan leaps up and moves menacingly towards him. In terror, Ginny starts for the stairwell.

Ivan grabs him. "You thought it was such a joke when you tricked Lyuba into getting drunk, didn't you? You're already trying again to hurt our dear little baby! How would you feel if someone ten times your size threw you down the stairs and tried to kill you? And you'd bleed and nearly die and the person ten times your size laughs and laughs and you're crying and hurt and—" Unable to control his flaring anger, he pushes Ginny down the stairs. Fighting back the graphic images flashing through his head, he rushes back to Lyuba and curses his father for doing such barbaric things to him when he was an innocent child. It was one thing to swear to himself he'd never harm any of his future children, but he wasn't counting on horrible things being visited on them by other family members.

***

An hour later, Aleksey and Eliisabet come in, carrying several baskets of food. They look in disgust at Ginny lying on the floor.

"I don't think I can move. Help me up, *pozhaluysta*!"

"Now what happened?" Aleksey notices Ginny's been talking at a very rapid pace, sweating and itching a lot, and having nervous tics, along with the dilated pupils, and wonders if that has anything to do with his even more antisocial and hoodlum behavior. He also hears Ginny's heart beating almost out of his chest, and his arms and legs look like they're shaking.

"Lyuba thought she was drinking water, but I really gave her vodka. She started having hysterics, and Ivan got so angry at me he pushed me down the stairs."

Ivan has carried Lyuba to the divan and is standing protective watch over her. He gives Ginny a murderous glare when he sees him coming back upstairs.

"Get him away from me now!"

"He's going away if he knows what's good for him." Ivan strokes her hair. "That awful scoundrel will leave you to recover, and by tomorrow you'll be as good as new. Here, I got you a glass of real water. The more water you drink, the more it'll help flush the vodka out of your system. Or you can go to sleep and get rid of it that way."

Anastasiya looks suspiciously at them for a minute. The way her alleged boyfriend is looking at Lyuba is the look of a man head over heels in love, and he's talking to her and treating her like she's more than just a close female friend. He certainly never looked at her like that or acted that way around her.

***

Lyuba finally comes to herself at night, after everyone has had supper. Eliisabet has volunteered as a wetnurse so Tatyana won't go hungry. After Ivan brings some light leftovers into Lyuba's room, she nibbles at them and then falls asleep. He sets the dirty plate and utensils on the nightstand, tucks Lyuba into bed, and kisses her on the forehead before tiptoeing out. He'd love nothing more than to crawl into bed beside her, but refrains for the sake of appearances and what Lyuba might think when she wakes up and finds him there.

Lyuba has a deep, peaceful sleep, dreaming about her wedding to Ivan, in a big cathedral in New York City, full of their friends and her remaining family. Her beautiful dream is broken by the sound of Pyotr's voice. When she reaches for the clock, she realizes in embarrassment it's one in the afternoon and she seriously overslept.

Pyotr is walking out by the time she puts on fresh clothes and comes into the living room. Ginny saunters up to her, his pupils dilated and his heartbeat rather audible.

"Pyotr's taking us to a new place tonight, near Tushino. We don't want to arouse suspicions by staying too long in the same place." Ginny starts scratching and leaves the room.

"You know what the best part is?" Ivan smiles. "It'll be just our ten-member band, the Stray Dogs, as we just christened ourselves, in honor of the Acmeists. By tomorrow evening, Anastasiya and Katrin will just be a memory!"

"The Stray Dogs." Lyuba smiles. "I like that name. We are a bunch of stray dogs who got thrown together for better or worse. We're a whole mishmash of partial families, and only together are we a complete unit."

"Would you like to come back and be my girlfriend again, now that we're moving on without Voroshilova?" Ivan whispers, taking her hand.

"I don't know if it's appropriate yet," Lyuba says sadly. "What will the others think of me jumping into your arms only seven months after Boris abandoned me?"

"Come on, you know you were thinking of it only days after Tanyechka was born! If you really wanted a respectable period to elapse first, why did you let me kiss you for five minutes instead of immediately pushing me away?"

"Maybe because it'd been awhile since I was kissed by someone who knows how to do it right. Boris was disgusting. It was like being inhaled or devoured by a crazed vacuum, and he always slobbered all over me."

"Just so you know, I've never kissed Anastasiya. You're still the only woman I've ever kissed, touched, or held. All I've done with her is hold hands, dance, and talk. The woman is so prim, proper, and Victorian, she'd probably be horrified if she knew what we did that week at the hotel and that we were only moments away from going all the way before you stopped me."

Lyuba abruptly releases his hand and looks at the floor guiltily when Ginny returns. She gasps when she spies a huge knife in his hands. Aleksey grabs him, and he feels Ginny violently trembling and sweating.

"Let me go right now! Or I'll drive this through your heart and kill you!"

Aleksey releases him, and Ginny continues on until he sees Ivan coming towards him with a possessed look in his eyes. Ginny drops the knife and starts running as fast as he can, screaming in terror, and dives into the cabinet under the kitchen sink. Ivan opens the cabinet door slowly. He grabs Ginny and begins to slam him against the wall until his teeth are chattering. Ginny wiggles away and starts running again, Ivan hot on his heels.

"Where were you when my cousin got pregnant against her will? Why are you always taking your anger out on me?" Ginny screams as Ivan punches him. He runs into the living room and ducks behind the divan.

"Why are you itching yourself again?" Lyuba demands. "Are you having an allergic reaction to something, or should I not want to know what's causing your strange behavior lately?"

"You know, I always suspected Boris had something to do with drugs when he had that shady job in the valley," Ivan says. "I wouldn't be surprised to find out Ginny's also using drugs. Their behavior is so similar it scares me."

Ginny glares at Lyuba when she starts to open her mouth. He rushes over to her as she leaves the room, and follows her into her bedroom.

"We're the only ones who know what really happened when Boris got you in trouble, and what he did to raise money for immigration. Do you want to ruin your reputation? They think you always preferred Malenkov to Konev, and that you willingly did that weird thing that makes babies. Can you imagine the pitiful looks everyone would give you, and how enraged Konev would be? He might try to kill Malenkov!"

"Friends don't keep secrets from friends, and Vanya has always told me all his secrets, even his most painful ones."

Ivan has followed them into the room. "What are we talking about?"

Ginny begins itching himself again, his hand shaking like a leaf. "Lyuba was just telling me how you've told her all your secrets, and she doesn't think she should keep secrets from you, even when some things are better-off secret."

"Are you referring to how my father, may he burn in Hell, used to beat the hell out of me when he was a drunk? Praise Christ that waste of life is dead. I've still got some scars from it. He pushed me down stairwells, clubbed me, whipped me, beat me, punched me, kicked me, slapped me, all sorts of horrible things. Lyuba told a teacher whose husband was in the Okhrana, and they arrested my father for public drunkenness. Unfortunately, it's not a crime to beat your wife or kids, so they had to find another reason. He sat in jail for a month, and was pretty good after that."

"Wow, that must've hurt a lot. People who beat their kids are jerks." Ginny pulls a strange bottle out of his back pocket. "I'm going to the bathroom to take some pills for a headache. You don't have to worry about me going after you again today."

Lyuba squeezes his hand after Ginny has gone. "Why would anyone want to hurt the sweetest person in the world? You were an innocent child, and didn't deserve to be abused so horribly."

"You were an innocent child too, and your father hurt and abused you in a different way. My scars are physical and yours are mental. Maybe that's why God chose us for each other, because we're both scarred, and normal people wouldn't understand."

"No one will ever hurt Tanyechka the way I was hurt. I'd kill anyone who tried to do such degenerate things to her."

"And I'd snap in half anyone who dared try to beat any future sons of ours. When we finally have our own blood children together, they'll be so loved, cherished, and protected. The thought of spanking a misbehaving child just once makes me sick to my stomach. I could never hurt any child of mine. I want him to get all the love I was denied from my own father. Perhaps the only advantage to being an abused child is that it makes the survivors willing to do anything to protect their future kids from the same fate." He reaches out for Tatyana and lifts her into the air. "Is it okay if I play with the baby while you're packing?"

"Of course, my *golubchik*. If you're so wonderful to a child who isn't your blood, I can only imagine what an incredible father you'll be to our blood children."

3

That night, Pyotr comes for Lyuba's and Eliisabet's families. Everyone smells a funny odor coming from Ginny as they're getting into the van, but they chalk it up to not bathing.

"Here we are," Pyotr says, stopping the van. "You're on the third floor."

After everyone goes in, Ginny begins jumping on the bed for Eliisabet's family. He ignores Eliisabet when she comes in, and starts jumping even harder.

"Get off that bed."

The slats slide from under the mattress.

"I said quit it, you *mudak*, or you'll poke holes in that bed!" Eliisabet screams, fed up by his antics.

Ginny stops after he pokes a huge hole in their mattress.

"You sleep there then. And don't you dare bother us because it's broken. If you have anything to say, say it now or shut up forever!"

Ginny takes his suitcase into the room and then goes over to Lyuba. Ivan listens at the door to Ginny yelling at Lyuba and saying the most horrible things about everyone in the band. He can't believe a twelve-year-old kid has the nerve to speak so meanly to an elder, let alone a lady or one of his relatives. His mother taught him real men don't raise their voices to women or say cruel things about them. Lyuba's *Tyotya* Margarita seemed like a sensible, intelligent, lovely woman. It's hard to imagine how such a monster as Ginny could've come from such a nice woman.

Ivan follows Ginny into his room and stands over him as he opens his suitcase.

"What? So what if I yell at her from time to time?"

"You smell funny, and your voice sounds very odd. You've never been this mean to her before, and I don't like how you think you can treat a lady like that! You don't show her any love! Do you know you're at least the fourth abusive guy she's had to suffer through?"

"If you love my cousin, why did you let Malenkov get his claws into her?"

"I don't know anymore. My only excuse is I'm a mouse and not a man if I let the woman I love go so easily. I thought she loved him, and had no idea my former best friend was capable of such evil things. I was too much of a gentleman to jilt Voroshilova, and played along with that stupid, childish charade. If Lyuba had known it was all a lie, she might've jilted Boris before the worst happened. I wish to God we were safe in America, and that Tatyana were my blood child."

"Well, it's too late now. It's too scandalous for her to be with you after having another man's baby. If you did it anyway, I'm sure you'd act exactly like Boris, running away because you can't handle the responsibility of fatherhood. Malenkov was such a *dryan*, he didn't marry her and make her a respectable woman."

"If I got your cousin pregnant, I'd never leave her! Do you not see me raising another man's baby as my own and taking on that responsibility when I don't have to accept it! Do you think I enjoy bathing her, sitting with her when she's sick, or dressing her? I'm twenty-one years old, and have no sane reason to give up my freedom as a bachelor to play father to someone else's baby!"

"I bet that's what Boris was thinking the night he rented that cabin and started drugging her up!"

"Out with it! You know something you're not telling me!"

"Boris wanted to become a man, and decided to rent a cabin. He went to one of his smuggler friends and bought a huge bottle of strong liquor and some kind of drugs. Lyuba told me the last thing she remembered was Boris forcing a glass of something down her throat. She woke up with a huge headache and guessed what happened when she saw they were both naked. I knew he was leaving. He told me he had no intentions of sticking around. But don't tell her I told you!"

Finally. Conclusive proof Tatyana wasn't conceived in love. He feels strangely vindicated, knowing Lyuba didn't take Boris as her lover. He can't wait to get his hands around Boris's pudgy little neck. Ivan goes into Lyuba's room and finds her sitting in a corner, Tatyana on her lap, both of them sobbing.

"Why does he have to be so mean to us, Vanya? It's one thing if he's mean to me because he resents me trying to be his substitute mother, but my baby has never done anything wrong to anyone! She's such a beautiful child! If I didn't have you to love me and stick by me, I don't know what I'd do!"

"Is it true what Ginny told me? About how Boris got you drunk so he could have his way with you? I always suspected Tanyechka wasn't conceived in love!"

"*Pozhaluysta*, don't think I'm a whore. That was the one and only time I ever had intercourse with Malenkov. That was not making love. It was a crude physical act he forced on me when I was too drunk to know what was going on. I wanted to stop, but he forced all this mixed liquor on me so I couldn't fight him off. In the morning, I woke with a terrible headache and blood running down my legs. Boris looks even chubbier naked. I felt so bad, like I'd cheated on you, even though we were both in other relationships. I felt robbed of something special, the first time I experienced that since you-know-what." Lyuba gets up with Tatyana and sits on the bed.

"My Lyuba is not a whore, no matter what happens to you. If Malenkov raped you, you didn't willingly have relations with him! Your first real time can still be with me!" He sits beside her and pulls her into his arms. "There, you can cry on my shoulder, and I'll stay with you till you feel better. Holy Mother of God, I can't believe Malenkov could be so degenerate. I respected you when you told me you wanted to stop, no matter how close we were to the physical act. If we had made love, I never would've been so brutal I caused you to bleed! Even physical virgins aren't supposed to bleed if they're with guys who care about not hurting them!"

"Rape is when you're held up at knifepoint in an alley or someone breaks into your room and holds you down on the bed. I was in a relationship with Boris, and he didn't have to use force after he got me drunk enough."

"If he did that to you against your will, no matter how he did it, he raped you! You're as blameless as you were when your father did his disturbed, deranged things to you. I know you haven't been as close to me as always these past seven months, but you're still recovering from what Boris did to you. I know you're not ready to reunite with me yet. As soon as you're ready, I'll be right here waiting for you, no matter how long it takes."

"But what about Anastasiya?"

"Forget her. Even if she comes back, I'm not going to fuel her delusions anymore. You're the only one I want. This is my family right here, you, me, and Tanyechka. Now, forever, and always."

4

The next morning, Kat and the Vishinskies arrive with Pyotr.

"What the hell happened to the bed, Liza?" Pyotr asks.

"Ginny jumped on it really hard, and right before he stopped, the slats broke and he poked a huge hole in the mattress," Eliisabet says. "Honestly, Petya, we're all fed up by this brat. Can't you find a home to stick him in, or better yet, a box for him to live in?"

Pyotr shakes his head in resignation. "What else can we do but keep him? His mother's such a good person, and she doesn't deserve to lose her only child. I've got enough younger siblings to know kids usually mature out of bad behavior."

A loud knock pounds on the door. Lyuba grabs Ivan's arm, shaking, when Pyotr opens the door to several police officers.

"If the worst happens, let me die in your arms," Ivan whispers.

"Has there been a problem, Officers?" Pyotr inquires cordially. "I wasn't aware my friends had broken the law."

"We've arrested several men for dealing cocaine to the tenants. You are to let me search your rooms and turn your pockets inside-out. If cocaine is discovered, consider this your first warning," the tallest officer says. "You'll be arrested if you're caught with drugs a second time. Any users among you, consider yourselves lucky we're not going to serve you the same fate as the drug traffickers we just arrested."

"Well, I never! Cocaine!" Ginny shakes his head. "What's the world coming to, with cocaine floating around a boardinghouse?"

Lyuba and her friends mutely stand by as their rooms are searched, and turn their pockets inside-out after the officers have rooted through every room, leaving a mess all over the floor in their wake. Ginny screams and begins cursing, jumping up and down, when asked to turn his pockets inside-out. Ivan pins Ginny down and forcibly turns the pockets inside-out. Quite a large supply of pills, powder, and bottles fall out. Lyuba can't find her tongue as the officers put all the drugs into a bag and storm out. Pyotr also is speechless as he takes his leave.

"So this is what this big mystery is all about!" Ivan thunders. "I knew there was a sinister reason for your most recent antisocial, hoodlum behavior beyond just feeling restless or being a normal kid who's gone too long without a parent to discipline him! You were using cocaine at least since you returned, correct? There's no other reason for why you were acting so violent, mean, and trying to kill everyone! Before you were just an annoying little *mudak*, but these drugs turned you into a monster!"

"I like cocaine," Ginny protests, starting to scratch again. "When I was running around on the streets right after you threw me out of the car, I was approached by a doctor who took pity on me and gave me free cocaine for pain relief for my broken arm. It felt so good, I've been doing it ever since."

"At least you're honest," Lyuba says.

Ivan drags Ginny all the way downstairs by his ear, then back upstairs again. No sooner have they reached their quarters than Ginny wrests free of Ivan's grip and runs down the fire escape.

"I wish this time he'd really stay away," Lyuba says. "As soon as we're in America, he can become my aunt's problem."

***

Ginny reappears during dinner, an extremely large mink squirming in his arms. Everyone stops eating to stare at him.

"Unless you intend that as a meal or a fur coat for my baby, you can take that right out of this house," Lyuba commands. "Where the hell did you find that?"

"I was walking around and saw it stuck in a trap. I thought it would make a nice pet." Ginny sets it on the floor, and it runs right into Lyuba's room, making itself at home on the bed where Tatyana is sleeping.

Lyuba pushes her chair back, runs into the room, and grabs her baby. The mink jumps onto the floor and runs back to the kitchen. Fuming, Lyuba puts Tatyana in her pram, stomps over to Ginny, and cuffs him on the ears.

"Stop it! Now I have to go and look for that mink."

"Thank you for completely ruining our appetites," Eliisabet snarls.

"You'd better get rid of that wild animal as fast as you can," Ivan says. "Knowing you, you didn't want a pet. I bet you were hoping it's rabid, and wanted it to bite somebody."

"He won't get rid of it on his own," Lyuba says. "Don't give him that much credit."

"There's nothing you can do about it," Ginny asserts. "It's my new pet, and lives here same as I do."

"Think again." Ivan gets up, grabs it, and throws it out the window.

"That was my mink! Just for that meanness toward my new pet, I'll do something worse tomorrow."

"Do and I'll kill you."

5

Ginny goes outside right after breakfast the next day. After coming back for lunch, he takes a large burlap sack out of his suitcase and promptly disappears again. He returns during supper, dumps the now-full bag in the closet, and pulls a chair up, putting his elbows on the table. Everyone smells a very odd odor coming from the closet, but they're far enough away from it that it's not overwhelming.

"Get your filthy elbows off the table," Eliisabet says. "This instant."

Ginny keeps them on as he grabs a piece of bread with his dirty hands, gobbles it with his mouth open, and reaches for the pitcher. When he reaches for the pitcher again, he bumps into Lyuba's bowl of borshcht, which splashes onto the floor and breaks. She kicks him as she leaves the table.

"See what you did to your cousin?" Ivan grabs Ginny's elbow and smashes it against the table until Ginny fears a broken bone or worse.

Ginny wriggles out of Ivan's grasp, runs off to his room, sinks down into the hole in the bed, and starts examining his elbow. It hasn't broken, but Ivan has given him one hell of a big bruise that's becoming a bump. Ginny bawls as he finds blood all over his elbow.

In the middle of the night, Lyuba is woken by Tatyana's screaming. In her half-asleep state, she smells a very bad odor. It smells like sewage commingled with ammonia and old sweat. When her eyes adjust to the dark, she sees dead squirrels on the bed. Resisting the urge to vomit, she leaves with Tatyana and her doll. She's so nauseated by what she saw, she doesn't wonder where in the world Ginny got all those dead animals.

The only unlocked bedroom is Ivan's. After setting Tatyana on the bed, Lyuba gets onto the floor. She wants with every fiber of her being to crawl into bed with Ivan and wrap her arms around him, but she knows how scandalous that'll look should they be discovered there in the morning. Even Kat doesn't sleep in the same bed as Nikolas, and they're engaged, not just opposite-sex friends.

Ginny comes to the door and starts giggling. "Lyuba, I won't have you sleep on the floor."

"I'm not a slut," she retorts, though she longs to fall asleep in Ivan's arms for the first time since March 1917, that wonderful week at Mr. Fyodotov's hotel.

"You'll have to get into the bed at some point. The kid isn't nearly weaned yet, and she'll probably get hungry during the night. What'll it be, the floor or the bed? Don't you pride yourself on being a good mother?"

Lyuba curses Ginny as she gets into the bed, lying as far away from Ivan as possible without fear of falling out.

***

When Ivan wakes in the morning, his first sight is Tatyana. "Good morning, *knyazhna*. To what do I owe the honor of seeing my baby girl first thing in the morning?"

Tatyana gives him a big smile.

"Where's your mother, *knyazhna*?"

Lyuba is furious at herself for waking after Ivan. Now she's stuck here to explain.

"Ginny put dead squirrels in our bed—"

"Do you think I care why you slept in my bed?" he whispers. "It's been so long since that week at the hotel, and that mattress in the hayloft wasn't even close. I can't wait till I can go to sleep holding you every single night again. I wish I'd woken up in the middle of the night so I would've known you were here. Tell me you wouldn't have loved waking up to feel my arms around you."

She leaves his room as quickly as possible, forcing herself not to respond. Ginny smirks at her when she comes into the kitchen. He continues dumping the squirrels into his bag, periodically stopping to scratch himself. She glares at him when he finally leaves after taking his good old time.

"You'd better dispose of those disgusting things. Wild animals, particularly dead ones, spread disease. Tanyechka's too little to have had any childhood diseases, and she's too young for a smallpox vaccine, even if we had access to a doctor."

"Take it easy. I'm going to visit my new friend the furrier, and won't bother you till I come back when it gets dark."

Ginny disappears down the fire escape with his bag and doesn't return till supper is almost over. Eliisabet winces when he takes a seat next to her, in the only available chair.

"Don't you dare start anything," she whispers violently.

Ginny reaches out and kicks Kittey repeatedly. After supper, he goes outside with his bag, Ivan hot on his heels.

"Why're you out there after dark?" Ivan asks. "To get drugs?"

He grabs Ginny by the ear and yanks him inside.

Ginny goes outside at two in the morning and retrieves his freshly-filled bag, along with getting more cocaine. After swallowing a few of the pills, he creeps back up the fire escape and checks to see the coast is clear before tiptoeing back into the third floor. Then, without further ado, he dumps the carcasses on Tatyana.

Lyuba wakes to Tatyana's screams and that same overpowering stench. Her stomach lurches when she sees more dead squirrels. The sole live squirrel bites her hand so badly, a huge patch of skin is ripped off and left hanging. She grabs Tatyana with her able arm, marches into Ivan's room, sits on his bed, and shakes him awake.

"Look what happened to my hand."

"You poor thing. Looks like you'll be an honorary *levsha* till it heals. Let me stitch it up for you." He takes her into the bathroom and puts her hand under scorching water as he washes the wound, then puts a needle under the same scorching water.

"Are you going to poke that in me?"

"I won't hurt you on purpose." He represses the urge to say something about wishing he could poke something else in her, since Lyuba would be so horribly offended she might never speak to him again. At the rate he's going, he'll probably turn twenty-two next year still a virgin.

"That really hurts," she gasps. "Can't you just cut off the torn skin and put gauze over the wound?"

"Be brave, Lyuba. You've been hurt far worse by your father and Boris, and they didn't love you like I do. I'll try to finish as soon as I can. You'll have less of a scar this way."

"I wish I had some of Ginny's cocaine to numb the pain!"

"I'm going as fast as I can. I bet you never thought you'd have the chance to have left-handed stitches put in you, did you? I don't think there are that many left-handed doctors or nurses. Most of us are artists, writers, and musicians. I wanted to be an artist till my father beat it out of me."

"Can't you give it a break for a little while and then start again?"

"You gave birth all by yourself, no doctor, midwife, hospital, medical equipment, or drugs! Not that I'll ever know, but I'm pretty sure that was more painful than some stitches in your hand."

After the final stitch is in, he pulls a bottle of iodine from the medicine cabinet and brushes it all over the wound. He squeezes her good hand with his right hand as she screams. Then he goes to the icebox, fills a small bag with ice cubes, and puts it on her hand.

"Now I can kill Ginny for doing this to you."

Ginny sits bold upright in his bed when Ivan begins whaling on the door. Ginny hears his door being broken down and screams.

"If you ever bring dead animals in here again, I'll break your neck."

Ginny crouches down into the hole and shudders.

"Get every last rabid animal out of here this instant, or I'll kill you."

Ginny finds himself stuck and screams. Ivan reaches down for him and yanks him out of the hole.

"I'm giving you a few more seconds to start. Go."

Ginny grabs his bag in split seconds and runs into Lyuba's room. He starts dropping squirrels into it and throws the live one out the window. Then he brings the bag back to Ivan.

"You expect me to get rid of this for you? Maybe you're okay with looking at and handling animal corpses, but the mere thought makes me want to vomit. I'm no hunter or furrier."

Ginny runs to the nearest window and opens the bag. Ivan grabs him by the shoulder and yanks him away.

"I don't think so. No one wants to come across a repulsive pile of dead animals. They'll also attract flies and maggots, which I'm sure even you know carry disease. Go deposit them a decent distance from our inn. Look, there's a shovel in the closet to help you."

Ginny groans as he picks up the shovel with his other hand and heads outside.

6

The next morning after breakfast, Lyuba hears a car driving up. When she goes to the window facing the front of the building, she recognizes Pyotr's new Russo-Baltique he got as a present for making all As his first year at Moskva University. She remembers how Ivan used to drive her around in his father's Russo-Baltique, and how they had their first kiss in that car. Now, in the span of only two years, she's been expelled from a world of private automobiles and higher education. As she waits for Pyotr to come up, she wonders if she'll ever be a part of the cultured world again.

"I wanted to invite you go to the Tretyakov Gallery with me. It's been so long since you've done anything cultured or fun, and you deserve to get out and see something beyond four walls and a roof. I should warn you, the gallery no longer has heat or electricity, but the paintings are still there, and as beautiful as ever."

"You're an angel!" Lyuba proclaims. "But an art gallery is no place for two babies, and dear Kittey has limited mobility."

"I've already worked all that out. I asked a woman downstairs if she'd mind watching three children and a baby for the day, and she happily agreed."

"I'm twelve," Ginny protests. "I don't need a nanny."

"You're delusional if you think anyone here trusts you alone, let alone in an art gallery. You'd steal something, run away, or harm the children. Now start walking."

***

The apartment downstairs is a shambles when they get back. Even worse, the nanny is tied up, her eyes red. When Pyotr calls for the children, Kittey and Nikolay come out of a closet and Ginny crawls out from under a bed.

"What in the hell happened here?" Lyuba asks.

"I didn't tie her up," Ginny insists. "Just because I've been guilty of misbehaving before doesn't mean I'm always to blame."

"Then who the hell did?" Ivan demands as Aleksey gets a butcher knife to cut the rope.

"Bolsheviks, who else? One of them was Pyotr's father. Kittey hobbled into the closet with Nikolay when we heard the shouting and banging at the door, and I ran to hide under the bed, but I recognized him from my hiding-place. Pyotr's father threatened her with a rifle and only left her alone when she insisted she doesn't follow politics. Two of his friends tied her up so they could search the place. Luckily, they couldn't open the closet door, and didn't suspect I was under the bed. They went upstairs briefly, but came back when they realized no one was home."

Lyuba goes from room to room looking for Tatyana and begins screaming when her baby doesn't turn up anywhere. Ivan grabs Ginny by his sore ear.

"I'm not lying. This time I had nothing to do with it. If I were you, I wouldn't try to find her. It's a trap to lure Whites to the police station. Zhora once told me about a campaign like this. Bolsheviks hold White children hostage until the parents come to find them, and they're arrested or killed. They don't send them to the orphanage right away all the time. I don't think you have nearly enough money to pay a ransom and get them to look the other way."

"Why the hell didn't you take Tanyechka when you hid?" Ivan pinches Ginny's ear even harder. "Kittey's crippled, so it was your responsibility. Thank God Kolya's old enough to walk, or we would've had two missing babies."

"I couldn't stop them," the nanny blubbers. "They had rifles."

Pyotr takes a 100,000-ruble note out of his pocket and unfolds it. "My father's behavior in no way represents my views. You deserve some money after the scare you went through, even if you didn't perform the babysitting services I hired you for."

Lyuba runs upstairs, goes into her room, and slams the door. Ivan grabs Ginny and squeezes every last ounce of circulation out of his ear before going back to their apartment to comfort Lyuba. It takes a good five minutes for all the blood to return.

"I want my baby. Can you get me her doll in place of her?"

He places the doll in her lap, remembering sadly how he braved the influenza and typhus epidemic to go into that toy store on Tverskaya Street. He was so happy about buying a present for the newborn he already considered his own child, even knowing she wouldn't be old enough for a doll for awhile. When he saw that ragdoll with a blue dress, dark brown braids, and deep brown eyes, he knew that was the one for Tatyana, more than an expensive porcelain doll with silk and velvet clothes, blue eyes, and corkscrew blonde hair.

"They're going to kill my only baby! Is this my punishment for never wanting kids until I actually had one?"

"I won't let them kill her. In my heart, she's my child too."

"I'll never have my daughter smile at me or give me the feeling of being wanted again. She was the only thing ever that was all mine."

"Say the word, and I'm all yours too."

"You're so sweet and gentle, my Ivan the Meek. You're my best friend in the whole world." Lyuba throws the doll back on the bed. "A doll isn't a baby. Our baby should be holding her doll right now, but instead she's in a diabolical baby prison without her parents to protect her."

"Don't cry. You've been so brave since we've left home!"

"You're my whole world, Vanya! My twin soul!" Lyuba breaks down crying and holds him tightly. "Whatever happens to Tatyana, I still love you!"

7

A week later, Ginny drops a note in Lyuba's lap during breakfast.

"When I used the lobby phone last night, Zhora told me the address of the prison. It's not one of the big ones like Lubyanka or Butyrki."

Lyuba pushes back her chair and leaves her food uneaten. She's barely been able to keep anything down the last week, but now she has even less of an appetite. Her knees buckling, she goes to put her shoes on, stuffing the note in her pocket.

"Praise Christ," Ivan says. "I thought we'd never see our daughter again."

Lyuba grasps Ivan's hand as they start the walk towards the indicated address. For the umpteenth time, she curses herself for not saying yes to his proposal.

****

Chapter 7: Lyuba's Time of Troubles

At the prison, Lyuba identifies herself, and presently Tatyana is brought out by a fat, homely, mean-looking female warden. Tatyana begins smiling and cooing the moment she's set back in her mother's arms, and Lyuba begins sobbing with relief.

"Are you sure it's the right baby?" Ivan asks.

"I'm her mother. Of course I know it's the right baby!" Lyuba holds Tatyana close to her heart. "There, you're back with your *mamashka* now, *knyazhna*, and your *papashka*. That must've been really scary when you were separated from everyone you know and love. Nothing bad can happen to you now!"

Ivan gingerly takes her little hand in his.

"She won't break, Vanya. When you have a child of your own, you won't be so inexperienced."

He thinks guiltily back to how he pumped Lyuba's head full of unrealistic expectations about having plenty more children. "I love her as much as I do you. If she dies today, my heart will break as much as if you were killed!"

After everyone has claimed their children, they're ordered into the basement. There are no windows, and the concrete floor is sloped, with several drains and hoses attached to the walls. Then the massacre starts. A policeman grabs a baby from its mother and throws it to the ground, ignoring the mother's screams. A second policeman shoots the husband, while several laughing officers come forward and gang-rape the mother. After this, it becomes a free-for-all. Lyuba looks away and clings to Ivan's arm so tightly he starts to lose circulation, and Tatyana begins screaming at all the noise. They may be at the back of the crowd now, but there's only so long they can hide unnoticed.

"They're going to rape you and kill our baby! I'll strangle them with my bare hands if they try to!"

"No, Vanya! You'll be dead first!"

"I'm so much stronger than those Bolshevik swine! I can bend a horseshoe with my bare hands!"

"They have guns! You always fought with your hands, not weapons! Besides, I'm not new to being raped. I just tune it out, and it goes faster."

A slight, fair-featured policeman taps Lyuba on the shoulder, blushing somewhat at encountering a woman taller than he is. "How old are you? You look like you could be the daughter of some of these women."

"Nineteen. My child's father is twenty-one." She's so terrified, she doesn't have the wherewithal to feel guilty for lying about Tatyana's paternity in front of a policeman.

The officer looks at her hands. "I admire an honest woman. You're not afraid to admit this man isn't your husband and your child is a bastard."

"Can you handle these roaches by yourself, Andrych?" someone calls. "We're on our way to lunch after this very productive morning."

He casts a glance back at the other officers, who are all on their way upstairs after leaving the floor littered with dead and dying bodies. "Yes, I'll be fine. I had my eye on this woman all morning, and wanted to enjoy her for myself."

Lyuba's stomach turns as the other police leer at her, while Ivan wonders if he can make a run for it and strangle this man with one of the hoses.

As soon as everyone else is gone, the man takes Tatyana and ties a thick strip of cloth around her mouth. "You can untie it as soon as the building is out of your line of sight," he whispers. "I don't want her making any noise and giving away the fact that I let her live. Now get out of my sight and don't let on I let you off so lightly. I'm an illegitimate child myself, and my mother wasn't even twenty when I was born, so I'm taking pity on you. Go!"

Lyuba takes Tatyana and walks out, in shock from the whole ordeal. There must be more decent Bolsheviks than just Pyotr, but she can't believe one in a position of authority, however local, would do something so kind. No matter how much her heart rends at Tatyana's muffled cries, she resists the urge to untie the cloth around her mouth.

Shortly after they reach Tushino, several Cheka men run by with guns, Kostroma Hounds, and Borzois. Without wasting a moment, Ivan drags Lyuba behind a bush. Lyuba thinks it must be a blessing in disguise that Tatyana can't give them away by crying. Ivan holds her tightly, Tatyana sandwiched in between.

By the time the men have finished searching the area, it's growing dusky. Lyuba shivers in her bone-thin clothes and cuddles Tatyana closer.

Ivan strokes her hair. "Had I known we'd be out so long, I'd have made you take a warmer change of clothes. I hate when it gets so cold at night, even when the weather's beautiful in daylight. There are only a few months of nice weather, and we should enjoy it all day, not just during daylight."

"Are we going to walk the rest of the way back in the dark? I'm scared we'll run into bad guys in the dark, and won't be able to see knives or guns."

"Don't you worry about a thing. We can sleep on the ground, and in the morning we'll start back. I'll watch over you to make sure no marauding rapists or thieves try to attack you. In the meantime, I think our baby needs to eat."

Lyuba slips the cloth off Tatyana's mouth and slides Tatyana under her blouse. Tatyana wriggles in protest when her mother ties the cloth around her mouth again as soon as she finishes nursing.

"Don't you worry, *knyazhna*, you'll soon have that nasty thing taken off your mouth, and you can make all the noise you want," Lyuba croons.

"We're far away from the police station," Ivan says. "She might choke if we leave it on much longer. I highly doubt those police were looking for us."

Lyuba unties the gag, then heads down to the banks of the Skhodnya River, unpins Tatyana's diaper, dips it into the water, wrings it out, and puts it back on her. Tatyana is indignant at being treated like this by the person she loves most, but soon falls asleep, tired out from the tantrum she's throwing.

"One day we'll live in America," Ivan whispers as Lyuba lies on the ground and falls asleep, Tatyana locked in her arms. "You'll have everything you can ask for, and you'll never have to be treated so horribly by bad guys. We'll live in our own house and won't have to run away ever, we'll have nice food, you'll wear pretty clothes, and best of all, your parents will be married and you'll hopefully have at least one little brother or sister." He brushes the hair out of Lyuba's eyes and kisses her on the forehead before taking his place next to her on the ground.

2

In the morning, Ivan wakes first and picks up Tatyana. "Good morning, *knyazhna*. Did you have a good sleep? It must've been really scary to sleep outside, but I watched over you and your *mamashka* to make sure no bad guys hurt you in the night."

Lyuba takes Tatyana and nurses her. Ivan turns away in embarrassment when this time she unbuttons her blouse instead of sliding Tatyana underneath. Afterwards, she heads down to the river for another makeshift diaper laundering.

"Here," she says as they're walking.

Ivan's whole face lights up when Lyuba hands Tatyana to him. The entire way home, he tells her a Krylov story.

When they get to the boardinghouse, Ginny runs up to them. Lyuba stiffens at the sight of her cousin, though relaxes somewhat when she sees he looks somewhat normal today, and isn't itching his skin off.

"We've got a very unwanted visitor," Ginny reports. "I think you can handle him yourself instead of getting our innkeeper involved."

Ivan's eyes narrow at the sight of Basil approaching.

"Hello, comrades!" Basil calls. "A pleasure to see you all, especially Lyuba!" He puts his hand on Lyuba's arm and licks his lips, leering.

"Keep the hell away from my cousin, filthy Georgian," Ginny snaps.

Ivan yanks Basil away from Lyuba and shoves him face-down into a huge mudpit. "That was your first warning. If you don't go quietly into the night, there will be far worse consequences."

Basil picks himself up and wipes off as much mud as he can, though he's still coated in it. Forcing a smile, he tags along inside and plants himself on one of the lobby davenports, instantly getting mud all over it. Aleksey, who's reading *Izvestiya* on a plush red chair, gives him the evil eye.

"Is Boris around? Maybe I can convince him to let me have Lyuba. While I was away in Tbilisi, Litvinov wrote me a few letters and said Lyuba and Boris were courting."

"Boris set sail for America the night Lyuba gave birth," Ivan says. "The only man my Lyuba will ever marry is me." He swats

Basil's hands away from *Pravda*. "That's for everyone to read. They won't be able to read much if it's coated in mud."

Lyuba runs upstairs to change Tatyana's diaper, then retires to her room, where she sees two letters on her bed, postmarked New York City. One is from her mother and the other is from Boris. She rips open her mother's letter first, wondering how in the world her address was discovered when they've had no contact in over two years.

Dear Lyubov Leontiyevna Zhukova:

Imagine my surprise when Boris Aleksandrovich Malenkov appeared on our doorstep this March!

Of course, we had no choice but to take him in and treat him as our own son. We were longing for any information he had about you and Ginny, but he didn't want to say anything until May, claiming the past was too painful. I almost died of shock to hear you and he had a bastard! I was furious my only child could do something so disgraceful as to have relations outside marriage!

I can hardly believe what a slut you became. I hope to God you gave this child to an orphanage so it can be raised properly, and so you can escape the shunning you deserve for being so whorish. The money enclosed is for you to come to America so you can marry Boris, as marrying any other man would be very scandalous. I took the liberty of changing American money into rubles for you. If you don't come by December, I'll assume you've chosen to give yourself over to being a slut.

A hope for forgiveness,

Yekaterina Iosifovna Zhukova.

Lyuba throws the letter into the rubbish bin but puts the money in her drawer. The second letter has a rather ugly diamond ring inside, with an unflattering, sharp rectangular cut and a hideous yellow gold band.

My lady Lyubov Leontiyevna Zhukova:

Here I am in America. You should've seen the look the postmaster gave me when I handed him an envelope in Russian. My night school teacher says my English is getting better every day. I'm free here. I can say anything I want, and I don't have to live in danger of fleeing whenever the Reds approach. Only criminals get sent to jail, and there are no labor camps to be afraid of. Your mother and Tyotya *Rita treat me as if I'm their son. We're in a neighborhood called Greenwich Village. Thankfully, they'd left the notoriously poor, crowded, filthy Lower East Side by the time I arrived. I'm always the center of attention when*

I talk about life in our dear home of Moskva, which strangely is referred to as "Moscow" in my history books.

I've got my eye on a nice townhouse across the street, which we can move into when you come to America and marry me. I've been a fool. I spent all my money from my bellboy job to buy you this engagement ring. Don't believe what your mother says, because I can hardly wait to see our child. You wouldn't believe the amount of people who think I'm stupid because I'm a Slav. I've gotten into quite a few fights to defend our homeland. Think whatever you want, but I still love you and can barely wait till you and the baby come to America to be with me. Your aunt misses Ginny badly.

With love from "the land of the free and the home of the brave,"

Your Borya.

Lyuba starts crying, barely believing Boris still thinks of her. She composes herself when Ivan knocks at her door.

"Come in, Vanya, I've gotten the nicest letter from Borisko!"

"Knowing him, it's a pack of lies to lure you back into his trap."

Lyuba holds out the American dollars. "Look, my mother sent me money so I can come to America to marry Boris!"

"Where's her letter?"

Lyuba points to the rubbish bin.

"Now what did that *suka* say? I love how she convinced you to jilt me and remain in Russia instead of fleeing to America, while she turned around and did just that only a week later!"

"She called me a whore."

Ivan reads the letter, shaking with rage. "The nerve of her! It's not your fault Boris abandoned you! How can he claim to want you back after everything he did to you?!"

"It took a few months for this letter to arrive. I'm sure he was tortured by the thought of leaving us all the way to America!"

"You know that's complete nonsense. Anyway, Basil left, thank God. Would you like to go downstairs? As long as we're here, we might as well enjoy the nice lobby. Neither of our other residences had such a nice lobby."

Lyuba follows him downstairs and for the first time really takes in the lobby. Whomever their innkeeper is, he certainly values culture and the written word. The walls are filled with artwork, and the coffeetables and side tables have classic novels as well as newspapers. A few sculptures are also scattered about.

"Alyoshenka, can you come here and help me?" Eliisabet asks as she comes downstairs. "Kolya just threw up, and it's all over our room and his clothes."

"Do you think he's coming down with something?" Lyuba asks. "I hope Tanyechka won't catch it, or that she didn't catch anything when she was in that horrid baby prison."

"No, I think he's just been out in the heat a bit too long. If he needs quarantining, we'll let you know."

Lyuba puts her hand on her head. "I'm not feeling so well myself. I'll be lying down here till my headache feels better."

"Of course," Ivan says. "After what you've just been through, you deserve to sleep for the rest of the month. I'll feed Tanya kasha, and if she's still hungry, I'll bring her back down to you for nursing."

"You're so sweet." She settles down on the largest davenport. "You'll make a good husband someday."

In the middle of her nap, she swears she hears footsteps coming from the front door, followed by the even more unnerving sensation of someone tying her up and putting something around her mouth. She writes it off as a strange nightmare brought on by the awful week she's had.

Ivan comes back downstairs with Tatyana several hours later and is struck by an eerie silence. Lyuba is no longer in the living room, and when he calls for her on each floor, there's no reply. His heart beating faster and faster, he tries to open the front door and finds it stuck, though the knob has no problems turning. When he goes to the windows and raises the curtains, he doesn't see her in the yard.

Ivan, full of a foretaste of dread, runs into the manager's office. Mr. Golitsyn looks up from a photo album and puts down a fork of pickled *selyodka*.

"I'm very sorry to disturb you, but I can't find my best friend. I'm positive she was abducted by an unwanted visitor we got today, a man who's long had delusions about her interest in him. I always feared he'd do something more than leering at her, touching her, and making inappropriate comments, and now I think he's finally done it. The front door is stuck. Can you go out the back door with me and help me find them? You'll know him by his reddish-brown hair, hazel eyes, and pathetic height. He's a Georgian. Not a drop of Russian blood in his body."

Mr. Golitsyn reaches into his desk and pulls out a gun. "It would be my pleasure. I saw the man you're describing earlier today, and had a very bad feeling about him. Now I know my instincts were right."

They go out the back door and look around the property for a good long while, not finding any traces of Basil or Lyuba. Ivan is about ready to give up and call the police when he sees rustling in bushes near the riverbank. He sets Tatyana on the ground and rushes up to the bushes, his heart in his throat. Mr. Golitsyn aims his gun as Ivan pulls the bushes back and finds Lyuba and Basil. Basil freezes when he sees the barrel of a gun pointed right at him.

Ivan immediately notices Lyuba's clothes are rumpled and torn, but doesn't have the heart to ask the obvious question. He feels her shaking like a leaf when he leans down to help her up, and notices her knees buckling as he leads her away from Basil. He wants to throw up when he realizes she's leaving a trail of blood.

"Get away from here right now," Mr. Golitsyn growls, keeping his gun aimed at Basil. "Don't think I'll hesitate to shoot you. If you dare come back to my boardinghouse, I'll have you arrested as a trespasser. As I understand it, you're not a Russian. You're a foreigner from Georgia. Who will the police believe, a native Russian or an outsider?"

Lyuba puts her arms around Ivan in an iron grip, still shaking violently, as Basil takes off. As soon as Basil disappears from view, Mr. Golitsyn puts his gun in his pocket and picks up Tatyana. The entire way back to the boardinghouse, Lyuba doesn't say a word. She only mutely nods when Mr. Golitsyn asks if he can take Tatyana inside and give her to Eliisabet to take care of till she feels well enough to go in. As soon as he's gone inside with her baby, she sinks down onto the veranda.

"I might be twenty-one and still a virgin, but I know what it means when I see a woman with torn, rumpled clothes and leaving a trail of blood. If you tell me what I suspect, Beriya is living on borrowed time."

She crumples over on her side and begins sobbing hysterically, her whole body violently shaking. Ivan is afraid to go near her when she begins uttering a series of primal screams.

"Why does it always have to be by force? What did I ever do so wrong I deserved to only experience that against my will? Maybe I don't deserve to know what it feels like to be with a nice guy like you. I'm a piece of trash, a whore, like my mother said. If I were a nice girl, I would've been your respectable wife, not the mother of another man's illegitimate baby."

"Did Basil do what I think he did?"

"Thrice. I tried to get him off me, I swear I did, but he did things you don't want to know about. I think I'll have marks and bruises tomorrow. *Pozhaluysta*, don't blame me for not trying harder to get him to stop or for not screaming when he took me. I swore I felt someone tying me up and putting a gag over my mouth when I was sleeping, but I thought it was just a nightmare. He said he'd come back later to do it again. Four men have had me by force now, but the only man I've ever wanted is you."

"Don't worry, *golubka*." He lies next to her and strokes her hair. "You're safe now. Basil is gone and I'm here. I failed you today, but I'll never fail you again. I took care of you when Malenkov beat you when you were pregnant, and I'll take care of you after Beriya did his disgusting things to you. If he comes back, he'll have to get through me, and I'll die before I let anyone hurt you."

He sits there holding her for two hours, Lyuba still shaking violently and refusing to let go of him. Finally, as the air starts getting chillier, he pulls Lyuba up and takes her inside.

When they're back on the third floor, Lyuba pulls Ginny aside and begins whispering. "I'm leaving tonight. If you want to come with me, pack and be ready by midnight. You're my only family besides Tanyechka, and I'd like to think you can behave decently when push comes to shove. You really surprised me when you defended me to Beriya today, and I hope things like that can continue."

Ginny grunts. "No one likes me here. I guess I'll go with you and try to start over."

"No cocaine. You have to promise me that."

"Yeah, I'll try to be good if it means we can go to America faster and I can see my mother again."

Lyuba tiptoes over to Aleksey and continues whispering. "I

know this is a very big favor to ask, but I'm leaving tonight, and I'd really appreciate if you or someone else in the band could help me with getting a horse. So many awful things have happened since day one at this boardinghouse, and I think it's a good idea to start over."

"By yourself?"

Lyuba's heart flutters. "I can't leave without Vanya. I love him much too much. Would you, *pozhaluysta*, slip into his room and pack his things? He only has that one tattered valise, and I'm sure you'll easily find all his clothes and the other things he unpacked. But don't tell him anything. I want this to be a romantic surprise."

"Of course I'll help you. You and Ivan will be Kolya's godparents when we're in America, and it's a wise idea to have male protection."

After Ivan goes into the kitchen to start making supper, Aleksey goes into Ivan's room and folds up his few clothes. As he's putting the clothes, Ivan's books, and the two small framed paintings into the valise, which wasn't fully unpacked, his eyes catch on a small purple box. Curious, he pulls it out and opens it. There sits a beautiful citrine bracelet and a folded-up note. When he unfolds it, he sees Ivan's smudged, slanted lefty writing and the date 10 April 1917. Aleksey realizes Ivan must've bought this as a present for Lyuba right after they left home, but for whatever reason didn't give it to her right away, and then couldn't give it to her because they both got involved with other people. He's probably forgotten about it by now. Feeling very sad for his dear friends because they haven't found their way back to one another yet, he refolds the note, closes the box, and puts it back at the bottom of the valise.

***

At midnight, Lyuba takes her lightest suitcase, picks up Tatyana, and creeps downstairs with Ginny, who's been given orders to alert Ivan as to what's going on. Lyuba has decided to surprise him with a declaration of her love and a desire for their reunion at the moment she's leaving, which seems more romantic than matter-of-factly telling him she's leaving and wants him to come along. Eliisabet carries her other two suitcases. Aleksey is waiting by the back door, standing beside a beautiful Kabardin. Lyuba instantly falls in love with him as she nuzzles his snout and scratches him behind the ears.

"This handsome fellow's about two years old. The stable manager threw in a cart for free, so you'll have somewhere to put your luggage. I already put Ivan's valise in the cart. Good luck and Godspeed!"

Lyuba puts her suitcases in the cart and makes a nest of blankets for Tatyana in a corner. Ginny dumps his luggage in next and climbs into the cart. No sooner has Aleksey gone back to bed than Basil saunters up, singing a song in Georgian.

"Hello, darling Lyuba. Ready for more? This afternoon was just a warm-up. Now that I'm a proper man, I'll be even better."

Lyuba, her black eyes flashing, stamps on his foot, punches him in the stomach, and spits in his eye. While Basil is still reeling from this surprise greeting, she climbs onto the horse, tightly holds the reins, and urges him on to a gallop. Ginny runs back inside and dashes upstairs, banging on Ivan's door.

"What the hell do you want at this hour?"

"Basil just came back, and he's not taking no for an answer. You're not one of my favorite people, but we have a common enemy. I don't want him to gain on her while she's making her getaway."

Ivan rushes to the fire escape door and sees Lyuba on a galloping horse, Basil running after her as fast as his little legs can carry him. "She's leaving without me?"

"She'll explain everything, but only if you go and take care of Basil!"

Ivan turns on the light and opens his closet, only to find all his clothes gone. He looks around the room and realizes all his belongings are gone, except one pair of day clothes and his shoes in the bottom drawer of the bureau. As soon as he's dressed and shoved his pajamas at Ginny, he runs into the kitchen, rummages around for the largest knife he can find, descends the fire escape, and runs as fast as he can in the direction of Basil and the horse.

Basil stops in his tracks when he sees his pursuer, a knife in his raised left hand. Lyuba yanks on the reins to get the horse to stop, slides off, and stands against his flank, praying Ivan isn't about to do something foolish. She certainly didn't expect him to come charging out with a knife.

Ivan grabs short little Basil by his collar. "Do you have any last words before I send you to Hell, filthy Georgian?"

Basil wriggles out of his iron grasp and runs back to the inn, Ivan racing after him. Ivan has never seen Basil run so fast before. After he catches up to Basil in the lobby, he grabs him again and plunges the knife into Basil's side. Once Basil is on the floor, Ivan grabs a lamp and smashes it over Basil's head. Basil starts moaning in agony. Still not satisfied, Ivan yanks Basil back to his feet and pushes him through the window into the bushes.

"What in the world is going on here?" Mr. Golitsyn demands.

Ivan drops to the floor and crawls to the back door, his heart in his throat. Though Mr. Golitsyn said he'd shoot Basil or report him to the police if he showed up again, Ivan isn't about to risk being discovered for taking the law into his own hands. The police might still be looking for him over two years later.

"Can someone get a doctor?" Basil moans.

Aleksey swings a lantern towards the broken window. Ivan knows he should go and see if Lyuba is still in the vicinity, but he doesn't want to leave until he knows if Basil is alive or dead.

Aleksey steps through the former window and nearly trips over Basil, who's removed his shirt and is now in the middle of bunching it up to act as a bandage and tightening his belt around his wound to try to stanch the bleeding.

"Oh, it's only Beriya. I assume Ivan did this. Good for him."

"Ivan Ivanovich should've come to me when he discovered the foreign trespasser had come back, no matter how late it was," Mr. Golitsyn ruminates. "I would've shot him on the spot for flouting my order to never return. I don't have any sympathy for people who trespass twice in the same day or abduct and rape women."

Aleksey kicks Basil right over his wound. "So that's why Lyuba felt the need to run away so suddenly and secretively! You deserve to be castrated!" He pushes the lantern at Mr. Golitsyn, pulls Basil upright, and delivers two strong punches, one to the nose and the other to the eye.

Basil screams as Aleksey drops him. "You can't leave a poor wounded comrade here to die!"

"Die you will, *mudak*. I'll burn you alive if you're not dead by dawn!"

"You seem rather cognizant," Mr. Golitsyn observes. "Ivan Ivanovich probably couldn't see well enough to stab you in a better spot. Since you don't appear to be dying, you can put yourself to your first good use all day and get the hell off my property."

As soon as Aleksey and Mr. Golitsyn have gone back upstairs, Ivan tiptoes out the door and starts following the hooves leading away from the boardinghouse. To his great relief, he finds Lyuba about where he last saw her, not already vanished in the nearby Khimki Forest.

"Now can you explain why you felt the need to leave in the middle of the night and not tell me? What if I'd never found you again?"

Lyuba longingly takes in Ivan's beautiful deep brown eyes, his sensuous mouth, and his gorgeous Slavic facial features. "Come here, Vanya. Alyosha packed your valise, and it's in the cart. I want you to come with me, because I love you. My stupid head always ruins what my heart knows, but maybe our relationship will stand a chance of surviving if we're together alone, turning over a fresh new leaf."

"You really mean that? After how many times you've pushed me away or gotten scared, you're finally giving yourself over to me?"

"On my word of honor." Lyuba stands on her toes and kisses him. "How could I leave without you?"

Ivan looks at her lovingly. "You really want me as your sweetheart again?"

"There's no other man in the world I want to be with, my handsome stallion."

Lyuba clings to Ivan as she savors the feeling of his arms locked around her and his soft, sweet mouth on hers. She wishes they could stand there all night just holding one another and making up for lost time.

"Never mind about anything else now," he whispers as he finally releases her. "We'll never be separated again, no matter what happens!"

"How I love you, Vanya."

Ivan mounts the horse and reaches down to help her up. "Let me take the reins. You've done enough taking the reins for awhile, and need to relax and let me do my manly duty as your protector."

After scouting the area for awhile, they find a little abandoned shack. Ginny hasn't put in an appearance since he deposited Ivan's pajamas in the cart, but Lyuba knows he'll show up again just as he always has. That boy is impossible to lose.

Lyuba collapses onto the thin mattress and wraps her arms around Ivan when he lies beside her, her soul crying from joy at finally being able to sleep beside the man she loves again. Tatyana crawls to the bottom of the mattress and picks up a piece of paper. Lyuba, curious, takes it from her when she sees handwriting.

"Thank God we found this and not our enemies. This is a message from someone in the underground, providing the addresses of several people willing to hide Whites in their homes. The nearest one is Ilya Petrovich Lebedev. Maybe we can stay there till we're able to go to America. But I fear there's many a slip 'twixt the cup and the lip. We might be stuck here for a long time."

"Who cares how much longer it takes to get to America? You're my sweetheart again, and that's all that matters."

***

When day breaks, Lyuba produces the victuals she packed, and they enjoy a breakfast of hard-boiled eggs, salted ham, and cold roasted potatoes, along with water from a canteen. She rolls her eyes when Ivan turns away as they change into day clothes. It's not as though they've never seen one another naked before. Once they're changed, and Tatyana has had a diaper change, they load up their cart and head out of Khimki Forest.

And no sooner have they re-entered civilization than Lyuba instantly longs for the safety of the forest.

****

Chapter 8: Trouble with the Godunov Cousins

A young man with sandy hair and sharp, icy-blue eyes blocks their way, flanked by Ginny and a young man with raven hair and eyes. The dark-haired man is clad in a loud purple shirt, a blue fedora, and red-and-white-checked trousers, and is smoking a cigarette in a jade holder. All he's missing is a monocle to complete his ridiculous foppish appearance. A somewhat baby-faced young man with brown hair and eyes is off to the side, astride a horse.

"Hello. I'm Mikhail Yakovlevich Godunov, this is my cousin Konstantin Mstislavovich Godunov, and that's Pavel Lavrentiyevich Teglyov on the horse. *Pozhaluysta*, call me Misha, and call my cousin Kostya. We're all comrades now, with no distinctions of formality between strangers." His eyes widen. "Hey, I remember you from school!"

"I remember you too," Ivan says sharply. "You must've just graduated university, though I can't vouch for a moron like Kostya being accepted into any university or even a technical school."

Misha snorts. "I dropped out of university as soon as I found out my father died in the war, and started my own business. Kostya joined me in the business after he graduated gymnasium last year, and never bothered with university. Anyway, we just met this fine young man, and over the course of our smalltalk, we discovered he has an unemployed female cousin. Being the smart businessman I am, I immediately saw the opportunity to recruit a new employee. Only parasites are unemployed. But a working woman never has a baby, and I'm not about to start employing unwed mothers or any women with brats."

Kostya pulls Tatyana out of Lyuba's arms faster than she or Ivan can react, laughing at Tatyana's screams of terror and how she's reaching her arms out for her mother.

Ivan looks back and forth between Kostya holding the screaming baby and Lyuba lifelessly lowering her face and covering her ears. "Ginny, how can you be such a traitor? Or don't you have all that cocaine out of your system yet?"

"I had nothing to do with this, the same way I had nothing to do with what happened last week. Just because I've been bad before doesn't mean I'm always to blame. They never told me Lyuba had to surrender her baby to work with them."

Kostya starts stroking Lyuba's hair, which she grew back after Ivan cut. "I can think of a lot of customers who'll love this long mane of hair. Too many women these days wear their hair short, like harlots. That's fine for moving picture actresses, but not real women."

Lyuba's skin crawls, while her heart still rends at being so close to Tatyana and yet unable to hold her. She already regrets her rash decision to leave her friends. "What are you talking about?"

"Prostitution, of course!" Misha laughs. "But don't think Kostya and I are pimps. We let our girls keep their money. Think of it as an upscale brothel we manage. We make all our clients use prophylactics, so there's no need to worry about popping out another bastard or catching syphilis. Kostya and I practice what we preach. I have a bastard son myself, and I certainly don't want anything like that happening ever again."

"My cousin is not a prostitute!" Ginny shouts. "I thought you meant a normal job like typing or waitressing!"

"She'll be working and living in our house. Aren't we good, exemplary Soviets for giving our employees a place to live rent-free, in addition to giving them work? We also live with our *babushka*, Pasha here, and a young boy named Aleksandr Sergeyevich Shepilov. The house used to belong to Sasha's family, until he turned them in. That boy is so smart to see socially dangerous elements! We're so grateful to our wonderful new government for giving us such a beautiful, generous housing upgrade. We've been there since this spring, and can't believe we put up with our old piece of junk as long as we did. Sasha wanted to be somewhere familiar, and we sure needed a housing upgrade. We run our business on the first floor; the hookers live on the middle three floors; and we live on the top floor."

"Sweet little Sasha informed on his own family?" Lyuba gasps.

"His parents, his three sisters, and his two brothers. We can't afford to let enemies of the people go unpunished just because they're flesh and blood. If left unchecked, they become a cancer, infesting everyone around them."

Kostya begins running, Tatyana still screaming and squirming in his arms. Lyuba screams and urges the horse into a gallop after

Kostya. Her stomach drops to her knees when she realizes he's headed right towards the Skhodnya River, Pavel's horse galloping ahead of him.

"Think about our generous offer," Misha says. "I fully expect you to come to us soon and announce your intentions to join our brothel. You're unmarried, so you shouldn't even have a child. I wish I had the nerve to dispatch Kostya to do the same to that bastard kid of mine."

"Maybe I wasn't meant to have a child in this lifetime," she says lifelessly as Misha walks off. "God must be trying to send me a message that that angelic baby wasn't supposed to be long for this Earth, the way her life's been in jeopardy so many times already. This is what I deserve for being so against the idea of marriage and children my whole life."

"I am so, so sorry." Ivan squeezes her hands. "I know you never wanted kids growing up, but you were such a good mother to our baby, and mothering came so naturally to you. You'll be a wonderful mother to the eight additional children I still hope we can have together."

"I'm really sorry if I caused any of this to happen," Ginny says. "I really mean that this time. I didn't realize those guys ran a brothel and that they were going to kill your baby."

Lyuba bursts into tears and wraps her arms around Ivan, sobbing against his shoulder. "I signed my own baby's death warrant when I ran away last night!"

"There's no need to cry," a soft, unfamiliar voice says. "Your baby is fine. Very shaken-up and cold, but otherwise fine."

Lyuba looks up and sees the baby-faced young man astride his horse, cuddling Tatyana, both of them soaking wet. He smiles at her as he extends Tatyana. Ivan's eyes light up at the sight of Lyuba cuddling and kissing Tatyana, and he hopes desperately Tatyana never has to go through another hardship or separation.

"What was your name again?" Ivan asks. "And what exactly are you doing with the Godunovs?"

"I'm Pavel Lavrentiyevich Teglyov. *Pozhaluysta*, call me Pasha and Pavlik. I'm seventeen. The Reds murdered my entire family last May, and the Godunovs moved me in with them just in time to save me from the same fate. I fell in love with their head prostitute, a beautiful girl named Nadya. The brothel doesn't do business over the winter, so Nadya gets a few months of reprieve. I'm such a lucky guy to get to spend the winters with her. They put her up in their old house, she's that trusted and important. She merits a house all to herself."

Ivan laughs. "Your girlfriend is a prostitute? How can you want to be with someone who sleeps with so many other men? For all you know, you've gotten syphilis from her."

"Nadya's not like that. She's a good girl, only seventeen, and has only been a prostitute since last June. Her parents and aunt were murdered by Bolsheviks two years ago, her little brother and sister are dead too, and all ten of her cousins were taken away. She barely escaped after the Reds stole her virginity and tried to murder her, and went to live with her uncle after she recovered. After he was taken away, she went to look for work and ran into the Godunovs. And for your information, I've never slept with her. I'm waiting for our wedding night, when she's not sharing herself with so many other men."

"However can we repay you for saving our baby's life?" Lyuba asks, grateful for the glaring sun that's rapidly evaporating the water on Tatyana. "You're a beautiful angel sent by God at just the right time."

"I don't want any special rewards for doing the right thing. All I did was get to the river ahead of Kostya and immediately jump in as soon as he threw in the baby and took off. They've done this to other children before, after offering work to every new woman who shows up in the neighborhood. This time I went along, since I couldn't bear to hear one more story about them murdering an innocent child just so they might have a new employee."

"God should bless you regardless. Will you accept our friendship in return? We could use a friendly face in this new neighborhood, while we're finding a place to stay."

"Yes, I'll be very happy to be your friend. Right now my only real friend in town is my Nadya."

"Could you take us to a place with a phone?" Ivan asks. "Our friends deserve to know we're safe and sound, after the clandestine way we left, and there's a certain unmentionable order of business I'd like to find out the result of. From what I overheard before I left, it didn't end the way I'd hoped."

"Sure thing. Why don't I take you to my place? Kostya will be out gallivanting for awhile, probably going to the moving pictures, and Misha generally stays holed up upstairs, drawing dirty pictures, reading the newspaper, and ordering filthy paraphernalia. He's very hands-off in his management."

***

As Pyotr drives up to the boardinghouse, he notices a human form lying on the ground in a pool of blood, shards of glass everywhere. Hoping it's not one of his friends, he stops the car, scrambles out, and rushes over to the wounded.

"Basil! What the hell are you doing here, and what happened to you?"

"Litvinov! How good to see a comrade who gives a damn about me after the horrible attempt on my life! I was beaten and attacked brutally by Konev and Tvardovskiy. All because I had a little fun with Lyuba and came back for more! Tvardovskiy said I deserve to be castrated!" Basil loosens his belt and pulls his blood-caked shirt off his wound. "This was able to stop the bleeding. Konev didn't stab me in a vital area, thankfully. So much for his claim about being such a good fighter. I want you to call a doctor, any doctor."

"If you said what I think you said, get the hell out of here and find a doctor yourself, you *mudak*!"

"But we're friends!"

"I cannot believe you actually did that! Little did anyone know how deep your obsession with Lyuba actually ran." Pyotr kicks Basil and heads inside.

Mr. Golitsyn comes out to greet him. "You have wonderful timing. I just received a phonecall from Ivan Ivanovich, wanting to talk to one of his friends. Would you like to take the call so I can go upstairs and alert his other friends?"

"Sure thing." Pyotr takes the outstretched phone. "Hello. I assume you're not here because of what you did to Basil. I can't believe you stabbed him instead of just beating him black and blue. The wound unfortunately wasn't fatal. He's cognizant and conscious, though he's still lying on the ground. Did you and Alyosha attack him together?"

"No, Alyoshka came upon the scene as I was leaving. It's a really long story I'm not interested in telling right now. All you need to know is Lyuba didn't feel safe there anymore, and decided to leave in the middle of the night. She also had a lot of other bad memories of that place. Basil reappeared as she was leaving, but I caught him before he could catch her. He ran back to the inn, and you saw the evidence of what happened next."

"I care less about what happens to him. I hope he dies of gangrene or sepsis. Where are you now? Are you safe, or should I come over to arrange a place for you to stay?"

"I don't know what neighborhood we're in, but it's close to Khimki Forest, and our old enemies Misha and Kostya Godunov live here with little Aleksandr Shepilov. Their young boarder Pasha saved Tanyechka's life and befriended us, and promised he'd help us with finding shelter."

"I could've gone the rest of my life without wondering what happened to those damn Godunov cousins. They're probably just as horrible as I remember them."

"You can sure say that again. Misha is a university dropout, and Kostya never started. They would've killed my baby if our new friend Pasha hadn't risked his life to save her. They run a brothel out of the old Shepilov house, since Sasha turned in his entire family. That's where we are now. Thank God, so far no business has been conducted in the main room, so I don't have to avert my eyes from all manner of sin and vice."

A pretty young lady with green eyes and orange-brown hair steps out of one of the rooms and smiles at Ivan. A small green bag embroidered with a swan is slung over her right shoulder. "Would you like some service when you get done using the phone, Comrade?"

"Sorry, I spoke too soon. I've just been solicited by a prostitute. Her answer is no."

"Why not? No one ever comes into a brothel just to use the phone. Hotels, general stores, and restaurants have phones too, but you chose to use a brothel's phone."

"That's a long story."

"Basil just walked inside," Pyotr reports. "I wish you'd told me as soon as you found out what he did to Lyuba, so you and Alyosha wouldn't have to take matters into your own hands. The last thing you want is trouble from the authorities, since you're not supposed to officially exist."

Basil staggers onto the muddied davenport and groans in pain. "Someone's getting me a doctor, and I'm not going anywhere till I'm guaranteed medical attention."

***

The prostitute sidles up to Ivan. "We haven't had such a good-looking customer in awhile. I normally charge nine million rubles and fifty kopeks, and the other girls go for anywhere between five to seven million rubles and fifty kopeks."

"I don't have nearly that much money, and I don't believe in prostitution. I really am here just to use the phone."

"It's hyperinflation, Comrade. Do you think we'd charge so much if the ruble hadn't become so worthless? You must be one of those men who never sets foot inside a store and leaves all the purchasing up to his wife or mother."

"I've only been to a few stores during the last few years. That's a long story."

Lyuba walks into the house and stiffens. "Vanya, hang up the phone and come with me. They know we arrived safely, and now we can get the hell out of this torrid den of sin. Clearly this hooker has no idea you're purer than a monk."

"I have to go, Petya. Tell the others we're safe and sound."

***

Basil fumes as Pyotr hangs up. "Someone still needs to find me a doctor. I never suspected you were so cruel as to ignore a wounded friend in favor of a stupid phonecall."

Pyotr fixes him with a steely expression. "You got exactly what you deserved. The only place you need to be going is the loonybin. I didn't witness any of your behavior yesterday, but it's more obvious than ever before you're touched in the head. I care too much about Lyuba to subject her to having her name dragged through the mud in a rape trial, so the loonybin is the next-best thing to keep you away from her."

***

"I see you've met my girlfriend," Pavel says. "This is Nadezhda Osipovna Lebedeva. Her family's from Pskov, but they moved to

Moskva a really long time ago."

"That's a very pretty swan on your bag," Ginny says. "Did you make it yourself"

"My *Tyotya* Zhenya made it, since our surname means 'swan.' The swan is the most beautiful animal in the world, and it's a symbol of so many good things, like eternal love and brotherly love. Nobody would kill a swan, not even sadistic Misha and Kostya!"

***

Basil throws his hands over his face when all of Lyuba's friends and Mr. Golitsyn come down the steps and stand in front of him with accusatory eyes. Pyotr joins the group and yanks Basil's hands away from his face.

"I can't believe what happened yesterday," Nikolas says. "I don't blame Lyuba for wanting to get far away from you."

"If you'd raped my wife too, I would've given you more than just some punches and kicks," Aleksey says.

Nikolas nods. "I'm glad you didn't get your hands on my sister or my fiancée either."

"I'm disgusted," Kat says. "I always knew you were disturbed in the head, but not that you were that disturbed."

Basil screams as Pyotr, Nikolas, Aleksey, and Mr. Golitsyn set upon him. He can only dodge their fists and kicks so long, until finally Mr. Golitsyn manages to take hold of his collar and drags him outside. He shoves Basil into Pyotr's car and drives to the Moskva River, while Aleksey and Pyotr hold him in place. When they reach the river, Mr. Golitsyn abruptly brakes, drags Basil out, bodily lifts him, and throws him into the river, Basil screaming all the while. After Basil lands with a loud splash, he crawls out and drags himself along in search of a public phone.

2

That night, Lyuba and Ivan sleep in Nadezhda's attic. They never set foot inside when it belonged to the Godunovs, or came anywhere near the house. Since Misha and Kostya were such bullies and full of themselves, it always seemed they'd have more than a modest house. After spending much of the last two years living in crowded boardinghouses and abandoned houses, though, it seems positively spacious. Lyuba would be very happy if she had a house like this for her American home with Ivan, and would never complain. It certainly beats the tenements she's heard about.

"The Godunovs won't miss me if I spend one night away," Pavel says as he gets into bed beside Nadezhda. "They won't send the bloodhounds after me. We have our own lives, and they don't bother me too much unless I somehow manage to offend them. They probably won't be that mad when they discover I saved your baby. It might teach them a lesson about acting rashly and thinking they can do whatever they want without any consequences."

"So I guess we're taking the other bed?" Lyuba blushes.

"We're all adults here," Nadezhda says. "There's no sin or scandal if an adult couple sleeps in the same bed, whether or not you have relations. Besides, it's nice to sleep cuddled up to the man you love. Pasha's company in bed is much nicer than the impersonal sexual company of all the guys I service."

"What a lucky guy I am," Ivan smiles. "It's been so long since I shared a bed with the beautiful future Mrs. Koneva. That mattress in the hayloft and that little pallet in the shack last night don't count, and I didn't know you'd crawled into my bed last week."

"So we all have surnames derived from animals. I'm a swan, Lyuba's a beetle, and Ivan's a horse. Though how terribly unenlightened to assume your woman wants to adopt your surname."

"*Kon* also can mean the knight on the chess board," Lyuba says. "Vanya's my knight. But as much as I'd like to shed my disgusting father's name, I was never fond of the old-fashioned assumption a girl must change her name. I was never a traditional type of girl, and I don't like the symbolism of passing from one owner to another. It's my name too, even if it also belonged to my horrid father. Women effectively disappear once they're married, and are never referred to under their given names again. I want more identity than someone's wife."

"For now all I want you to change is your clothes," Ivan says. "Put on your pajamas and join me in bed, Mrs. Koneva."

***

Ginny sneaks out of the loft at two in the morning, carrying a knife and heading for the brothel. As soon as he recognizes the five-story house, he creeps around back, scales the fire escape, and climbs in through an open window. The floor is carpeted, so he doesn't need to worry about his shoes squeaking and giving him away. Ginny lets his eyes adjust to the dark, then tiptoes from room to room till he finds his former best friend. He grimaces when he realizes Aleksandr has become much better-looking than he is.

"Hello, dearest Aleksandr. Mind if I join you?"

Thirteen-year-old Aleksandr looks up sleepily from his feather bed, his brown hair falling across his face and very, very dark brown eyes. "Hello, Comrade. Who are you?"

"I'm Ginny Kharzin. Remember me? We used to be best friends. Now I'm your worst nightmare!"

Aleksandr screams as Ginny starts punching him, too shocked to punch back at first. Old Mrs. Godunova comes running, followed by Misha and Kostya.

"Sasha, what is this boy doing to you?" Mrs. Godunova bellows.

Aleksandr slumps over groaning, crying from the pain. Before Ginny runs away, he stabs Aleksandr below the shoulder.

"Speak to us, Sasha!" Mrs. Godunova weeps.

"I'll find who did this to me and haul him off to Lubyanka by his neck, and damned if I don't break it on purpose on his way there!"

Misha stumbles downstairs for the phone and calls the hospital, begging for an ambulance, while Mrs. Godunova puts pressure on the wound. Ten minutes later, the vehicle speeds up, and Aleksandr is loaded inside. Misha orders Kostya and his grandmother to stay behind in case any more intruders come around. All the way to the hospital, Misha rants and raves about the young assailant who snuck in and cowardly ran away. He runs inside as Aleksandr is borne in on a stretcher, and stays by his side in the overflowing waiting room.

"Hello, little comrade. Looks like someone tried to kill you too!"

"I remember you from school," Misha says. "I can't believe how many old acquaintances I've run into today."

Basil begins ranting about what happened to him, and Misha chimes in with Aleksandr's story. Most egregiously offensive of all is the fact that the boy who did this is the same boy he had such a pleasant conversation with this morning.

Aleksandr is taken into the doctor's office after fifteen minutes, and Misha is barred from following him. Fuming, Misha grabs a match and cigarette from the receptionist's desk and begins puffing away for dear life.

"Konev and that little boy just earned a cell in Lubyanka," Basil growls.

***

At five in the morning, a police officer storms into Nadezhda's house, taking advantage of the unlocked master door, and picks the lock on the secondary entrance. He proceeds to pick the locks on all the other doors until finally he finds what he wants in the attic. Lyuba shrieks and pulls the bedsheets tightly around herself, horrified to be seen in pajamas by a strange man.

"My name is Officer Bulyakov, and I'm looking for Mikhail Mikhaylovich Kharzin. Last night, this boy brutally assaulted Aleksandr Sergeyevich Shepilov. You're damn lucky that boy's injuries aren't serious and that I'm willing to look the other way just this once. Boys will be boys, and sometimes horseplay takes an unexpected violent turn."

"Ginny!" Lyuba gasps. "Are you still using cocaine?"

"I beat him up really good and knifed him before I left."

"If I may proceed. Basil Yakovlevich Beriya wants to press charges against Ivan Ivanovich Konev for trying to kill him as well. Since Comrade Beriya's wound isn't life-threatening either, and his testimony was extremely garbled and contradictory, I'm willing to look the other way on that too. But only if you get the hell out of here and never show your faces again. I want you out in ten minutes, or you'll be thrown into prison and then off to corrective labor. I'm timing you!"

Officer Bulyakov steps out to give them privacy, and Lyuba, Ivan, and Ginny dress, get their luggage, and hurry outside with a few minutes to spare. Officer Bulyakov unties the horse.

"If I ever see you again, I'll throw you in prison. I'd advise you to get the hell out of this neighborhood and never violate the law again. Understood?"

Lyuba casts a glance back at the neighborhood as Ivan leads the horse towards Khimki Forest. This is hardly the romantic reunion she dreamt of. After less than two days, it's already more curse than blessing.

3

For the next few months, they eke out an existence in the woods, forage for food, and sleep on the ground, never staying in the same makeshift encampment longer than one day and night. Under the stress of living like hobos, Lyuba and Ivan's romantic relationship has quickly fizzled out in favor of more important priorities. Along with the stresses of this itinerant lifestyle, they also have to deal with Misha, Kostya, and their band of friends frequently passing through the woods to hunt and fornicate with women. It galls Lyuba to think about how people like the Godunovs and their friends are still living the life of Riley, while she and her friends have been displaced and now can only dream about the time they led such a comfortable, safe existence.

One day in November, as the air is starting to grow colder, Kostya, Misha, and Aleksandr appear with hunting rifles. Kostya is dressed as foppishly as ever, in a purple and green checked hunting outfit and a red beaver hat. By the time Lyuba sees them, it's too late to slip away unnoticed. Lyuba tenses up, and Ivan's eyes flash. Ginny, worn down after the last few months, no longer rushes to join forces with their enemies. His palms start sweating and his breath shortens. He now has more important priorities than acting up to get attention or make believe he's all grownup.

"What an interesting surprise. I thought you left the neighborhood to avoid more trouble with us. But now that we're here, I should enjoy this rare opportunity." Kostya leers at Lyuba. "I always wanted you back at gymnasium, and now that you're not a virginal schoolgirl anymore, you can't object to lying with me. I found out Konev isn't your child's father, so you doubly have no reasons to object to it. Once someone becomes a fallen woman, she's a whore forever and has no moral room to shun sexual offers. If you cared so much about your virtue, you wouldn't have fornicated outside of wedlock and not married the fellow."

Ivan growls. "I'll kill you if you touch her."

"Why don't you leave her alone?" Aleksandr asks. "I'm sure you can find plenty of women who'd love to sleep with you. Don't bother someone who already has a fellow. You can go to Lena if you're that desperate. We're here to hunt, not play. You have plenty of time to do that when we're not hunting."

Misha punches him. "You're only thirteen, and have no business lecturing us about how to live our lives. And you know damn well Lena is my woman, not Kostya's. Besides, I only sleep with Lena when the whore comes to me for food." He turns to Lyuba. "Lena's the mother of my bastard son Yuriy. Believe me, I learnt my lesson from that fiasco. I never sleep with anyone without prophylactics now. Don't you worry either of us will give you another brat."

"But rape is a crime," Aleksandr insists. "You have enough women willing to sleep with you, and don't need to force yourself on someone."

"Shut up!" Kostya shoves Aleksandr against a tree. "What does a child know of relations between the sexes?"

"Enough to know rape is a crime!"

Kostya thumps him on the head with his rifle. "You've just earned a good beating."

"I want my mother." Aleksandr starts crying. "It wasn't right to turn in my family!"

"We're going back to the house, and I'm giving you a good beating. *Bolshoye spasibo* for ruining both our hunting and our chance to enjoy a new woman."

Ivan crosses himself as they leave. "The boy hasn't gone completely rotten."

"We might not be so lucky next time," Lyuba says. "And we can't live in the woods much longer. Winter is coming, and I don't want Tatyana to get sick and die of the cold."

"We'll think of something soon," Ivan promises half-heartedly, squeezing her hands. "I'd never let our firstborn die. Maybe Petya knows a place we can go. If God's kept us alive and together this long, surely we can get through the winter."

4

The next day, as Lyuba and Ivan are settling in for the night, the silence is broken by many footsteps crackling against the dead leaves. Lyuba feels sick when she sees the Godunovs with their friends. She abruptly unlatches Tatyana, ignoring Tatyana's cries for more milk, rebuttons her blouse, and puts on her bone-thin coat.

"Aleksandr's at home, and won't trouble us this time," Kostya says. "The beating I gave him should teach him to stay the hell out of our business. And he ruined our hunting."

"What do you want?" Ginny asks.

"Your cousin, of course," Kostya sneers. "Only now I can have even more fun, since all my buddies are here. We're not stingy about our women, and often share them. But Misha promised me I could take my turn first, without anyone watching."

Misha nods. "We're going to the tavern down the road, but we'll be back shortly for our prize. Kostya, *pozhaluysta*, don't do anything stupider than usual. If I come back to find you've been just as buffoonish as always without me to help you, I'll never let you do this again."

Kostya puts his hands in his pockets and shuffles around after Misha and their friends have gone off. He looks nervously at Lyuba a few times, then at the ground.

"Will you, *pozhaluysta*, leave us alone?" Kostya snaps at Ivan and Ginny. "I don't need an audience, and that includes you."

"You're as much a buffoon as I remember you," Ivan says. "Your cousin's a scoundrel, but at least he's not a moron. But continue standing there not doing anything. In fact, I welcome it. If you touch my woman, I'll rip you in half."

Kostya sinks down on the ground and stares at the light breaking through the trees, twiddling his thumbs. Ivan is deciding whether they should pull up their encampment and move on, or if he should stay to take on Misha when he returns, when the decision is made for him in the form of rapidly approaching footsteps.

"Kostya! Are you done?" Misha calls.

"I haven't even started, to be perfectly honest!"

"What a baby! The hell not?"

"He wouldn't leave me alone, and he threatened to attack me if I tried anything."

Misha kicks a pile of leaves. "How did I know you'd act like a buffoon when left to your own devices? Leave him to me. I'll show you how to teach someone a lesson. You're such a baby, you've only ever beaten up Aleksandr, not someone your own size. Well, Konev? Care to make good on your threat with someone who actually knows how to fight? If you try to stab us like you stabbed Basil, I'm calling the police."

"I've lost my interest in fornication for tonight," one of the friends announces. "If we have to fight someone before we can enjoy this woman, I'm not going to bother. That's too much work just to stick my *khuy* in a hot body."

Misha kicks a tree as, one by one, his eighteen friends walk back to the tavern. After everyone is gone, he lunges at Kostya and delivers several strong punches and kicks, cursing up a blue streak. As soon as he's done with Kostya, he heads for Ivan and grabs his left arm, twisting it behind his back. Lyuba's stomach flips at the resulting, sickening crunch of bones. She closes her eyes so she doesn't have to see anything else.

"Maybe now you'll finally get the hell out of my neighborhood," Misha says. "The next time I come to enjoy your woman, you won't be able to do a damn thing to stop me. You can't live in the woods forever. If you have any sense, you'll come back to the main city before winter starts, so you won't freeze to death."

"Who cares if they freeze to death?" Kostya asks. "Four less people for Comrade Lenin to have to feed."

As they walk off, Lyuba can barely find her tongue, still in shock from everything that just happened. Most galling of all is how Ivan wasn't very proactive at all about defending her these past two nights. He more or less let the Godunovs do what they wanted, and they didn't leave because of anything he did. This pathetic passivity from a man who stabbed Basil a few months ago leaves her cold. Even if they're not exactly a couple at the moment, they're still supposed to be best friends, unless Ivan's heart has grown as cold as the coming winter towards her.

"I think that *svoloch* broke my arm," he gasps as soon as the Godunovs are out of sight.

"No kidding. Can you get your arm out of the sleeve so I can see it?"

"I don't think so." He grips her hand. "I'm useless without my left arm. *Pozhaluysta*, take my shirt off for me."

"I can tell you're lying to me, just so I can baby you. You always used both hands to button your shirts before, and there's no reason you suddenly can't use your one good hand. I can read you like a book, Vanya." She gently brushes a tear off his cheek. "I always wondered why you're so overly sensitive and cry so much.

Men aren't supposed to be like that."

"Because I love you. And I'm the most sensitive sign on the Zodiac, Cancer, the crab. Supposedly that's a horrible match with your Sagittarius, the centaur. Who knows, maybe that's why we can't just live happily ever after." He crinkles up his face. "Get my arm out of the sleeve. The pain is killing me."

"I should take you to a doctor if you're in that much pain."

"Just get it out of the sleeve. Don't rip my shirt. My mother made it."

Lyuba unbuttons his shirt and eases his arm out of the sleeve. "I don't see any bones sticking out. It can't be that bad."

"Don't move my arm. Do you know how to set the break?"

"No. I'll have to take you to a doctor."

"A lot of doctors give me a bad feeling. Only a few generations ago, it was indecent for a man to look at and touch a strange woman naked. And I can't imagine you'd want that for yourself, given what's happened to you at the hands of four abusive so-called men."

"You can't go around holding your arm in that same exact position until it heals! This isn't like when you gave me stitches and pulled them out a few days later. We need a professional for this."

Lyuba puts Tatyana and their luggage into the cart, helps Ivan into the remaining space, and pulls a blanket over him. She gets onto the horse with Ginny and leads them out of Khimki Forest, towards the main thoroughfare. The first building she sees in the gathering twilight is a hotel. Leaving the others in the courtyard, she steps inside to call Pyotr.

Lyuba is sitting in the cart, cuddled up to Ivan and trying to keep warm, Tatyana asleep on her lap, when she finally hears a car driving up and recognizes Pyotr's Russo-Baltique. Flooded with relief, she gets up and runs toward him when he stops the car.

Pyotr opens the door. "I'm going to take you to a Dr. Yavlinskiy. He's the closest doctor I could find, and he won't tell my father and older brothers I've been aiding Whites. Ginny, do you mind following after us? I'll drive slowly so you don't lose us."

"Sure," Ginny says. "We like our horse. He's like a member of our family now."

"We named him Branimir," Lyuba says. "He's our great protection."

Ivan grits his teeth as he gets into the car. As soon as Lyuba is inside, he grips her hand again and slumps against her.

"I'm very glad to see you," Pyotr says as he starts the car. "Basil was taken to a mental hospital last month, so he can never hurt you again. The day after, all of us beat the living daylights out of him, and the manager threw him into the river. I hope you didn't get pregnant from him."

"Thank God, no. The next time I get pregnant, I hope I'm a respectably married woman."

"That would've been the last thing we needed," Ivan says. He feels like a dog for keeping the secret of Lyuba's near-infertility from her, but forces himself to remember why he's doing it. Secrets kept with noble intentions are better than maliciously-kept secrets.

Lyuba and Pyotr sit in the waiting room when Ivan is called in. Lyuba smirks at how he insists on going by himself instead of begging her to hold his hand. Probably doesn't want to look like a pansy in front of the doctor.

"You were right to bring him along. A lady who travels by herself isn't safe from rapists and thieves."

"I love Vanya, but our relationship fell apart again. Every time we're together, something splits us apart! We were starting to get back together when we left, but we haven't really been acting like boyfriend and girlfriend. I think we're back to being best friends of the opposite sex."

"Tell him. As simply as that." Pyotr pulls a chocolate bar out of his pocket and lets Tatyana have a piece. "There's no reason to overcomplicate something as simple as love."

When Ivan comes out with his arm in a cast, Pyotr looks at Lyuba. She looks at the floor, then rises and walks towards Ivan.

"I'm sorry if this isn't the most romantic time or place, but I want to tell you I love you more than anyone in this world. I hate how we just let our relationship fizzle so quickly and easily when we were in the perfect position to start over. I want to be with you for always, and I don't want anything else to ruin it!"

Ivan brushes her cheek with his good hand. "Thank God. I thought you'd never say that."

"In the meantime, you need a place to stay," Pyotr interrupts.

"You can stay here for the meantime, but I'll come by soon to take you to safe winter lodgings in town."

For the next two weeks, Dr. Yavlinskiy lets them live in his office. During the day, they stay in his private medical library, the door locked and the windows shuttered, with food brought to them by Pyotr. At night, they sleep on beds in the post-surgical recovery suite, making sure to wake and go back to the library as soon as Dr. Yavlinskiy arrives at the start of the workday.

In late November, by which time they're already sick and tired of this existence, Pyotr drives up at night and knocks on the door. Lyuba slowly raises the curtain and breathes a sigh of relief when she sees their friend instead of an enemy. Without waiting to be asked, she gathers up their luggage and helps Pyotr to load it into their cart. Once again, Ginny rides Branimir while they ride in the car.

"I found you a place with a very nice young couple," Pyotr says as he stops the car. "They indicated they've already met you, and they're more than happy and willing to give you a place to stay."

Lyuba's eyes light up at the sight of Pavel and Nadezhda on the veranda. She and Ivan return their smiles as Pyotr transports their luggage inside.

"I'm glad to see you again!" Pavel cries.

"I should say so," Nadezhda agrees. "The off-season couldn't start soon enough for me. I just got through with vomiting after that pervert Kostya paid me fifty million rubles to kiss him. I washed my mouth out with Listerine as soon as it was over."

Pavel shows them into a large room with three beds, each covered by heavy blankets and a quilt. "That bed is for Nadya and myself, the trundle bed is for Ginny, and the other bed is for you, Ivan, and the baby."

"But we're not married," Lyuba protests.

"Neither are Nadya and I, and we're only seventeen!"

"This bed is too close to the wall," Ivan says. "I can't sleep like that."

Pavel moves it away, then pushes it back when a macabre stain reveals itself. "It isn't supposed to move from there."

"What was that on the wall behind it?"

"I don't know." Pavel pulls on his collar.

"It looked like blood. I'd like to think I'm not superstitious, but I don't think I'll feel safe or comfortable if this house were the site of a murder."

"It is blood," Nadezhda says. "It's the blood of my parents, who were murdered here. Some days, I wish I hadn't survived."

Lyuba crosses herself. "Why would you come back here if there are such horrible memories? And what's wrong with the Godunovs' old house? Did they make you give up that house and find a new one?"

"This is my old home, and someone has to keep it occupied. I spend winters here instead of at Misha's old house because I like being close to my parents' memories. Memories are all I have left to remind me of them, and are more precious than gold."

****

Chapter 9: Revisiting the Past

One day in early December, Pavel comes back from buying food and supplies with a big smile on his face. After he brushes the snow off his coat and removes his boots and winter wraps, he produces two letters from his large burlap sack.

"Can you believe I had to wait five hours in line? To say nothing of how I had to barter for everything instead of spending real money. I can't wait to go to America, where they don't have long lines, food is always guaranteed, and money's worth something."

"America must be a dream come true," Lyuba agrees. "I'm looking forward to going to church again and living without fear. I almost forget what it's like to go to sleep without worrying I'll have to wake up in the middle of the night to flee at a moment's notice."

"Well, first things first." Pavel hands Lyuba the letters. "After I got our supplies, I stopped at the post office and saw this letter addressed to you and Ginny."

Lyuba crosses herself. "That's my aunt's name. I can't imagine what it's like to have to address a letter to just a name and city, and pray it finds the recipient." She tears it open and finds two letters, one bound with purple ribbon and the other with azure ribbon. She scans them quickly and hands Ginny the letter with azure ribbon. As soon as Ginny unties the ribbon, he begins reading aloud.

My Dearest Ginny:

How I miss my little scalawag son! This is a picture of the new house where I live with your Tyotya *Katya and Boris Aleksandrovich. It's in a neighborhood called Greenwich Village. No more Lower East Side tenement for us! Boris has found work as a bellboy in a nearby hotel. It's very menial work, and many people make remarks about "the stupid little Russian spy boy" and "that dumb sub-Pollack." He's very upset by this, and many people make remarks about me and your* Tyotya *Katya also. Our accents make some people stare. I work as a cleaning lady at a Czech Catholic church, a cook at a Russian cathedral, and a sweeper at a Serbian cathedral.* Tyotya *Katya works as a maid for a very wealthy American man with an Italian father, a Hungarian mother, and a Greek wife. They've caught her stealing money more than once.*

It'll probably be winter by the time you get this letter. How I miss the lovely Russian and East Prussian winters! Make sure you, Lyuba, and her baby all stay warm! I want to believe you've all stayed together, and that Lyuba didn't give her baby to an orphanage. Having a child to live for is a powerful motivator to survive, and I would never be so un-Christian as to judge her for having and keeping a child out of wedlock. No matter what the law says, no child is illegitimate in the eyes of God or its loved ones, and there's no reason to declare a child "has no name" simply because it doesn't have its father's surname. A woman owns her surname as much as a man, no matter where it comes from, and I always want you to remember this.

I worry about your father. I haven't received any word from him since last spring, so I'm starting to worry he may have been killed or taken prisoner. If he survived the war, perhaps he found his way into the White Army and fears his letters being intercepted. Your Dyadya *Leontiy I could care less about. He's one of the most selfish, vulgar, tasteless, crude, evil, degenerate men I've ever met. If he survives and comes to America, I don't want you anywhere near him. As soon as you come to America, I'll get a new house for us. With God's will, maybe your father will join us.*

I'm upset you're missing so much school. You haven't even finished the fourth grade, and you're the age of a seventh grader now! There's a very sympathetic woman who teaches Boris at the high school; perhaps she can be your teacher too. The way things are going, you'll be high school-aged yourself by the time you come here. Don't worry if you're the oldest student; it's very important for you to get an education!

I'm also worried you haven't been to church for so long. Every Sunday, Tyotya *Katya, Boris, and I go to church, and we're very warmly welcomed. Thankfully, the services are in Russian, not English. I wish we'd brought you and Lyuba with us to America!*

Are you being a good boy? I hope you aren't acting out anymore, as you were when I last saw you. I hope you've grown up a lot since then.

I will always love my little boy Mikhail Mikhaylovich Kharzin, known lovingly to all as Ginny!

Your Loving Mother,

Margarita Iosifovna Kharzina.

"It's a very pretty house," Ginny says. "America must be a paradise, with freedom of worship, make-up education for older students, and jobs for women."

Lyuba unties the purple ribbon around her letter and begins reading it aloud.

My dear niece Lyuba:

How have you been getting along? Have you gotten word from your uncle?

I'm very ashamed of your mother's cruel letter to you. I thought she agreed to burn it, but she snuck it into the post anyway. I had no idea until our mailman told me she gave him that letter. I'm boiling over her behavior. She's become nearly as worse as your father. It's hard to believe this is the same person who was always so responsible and mature when we were growing up, who went to work young, did without, and helped to run the household after our dear father died in the 1889 influenza pandemic. Although God knows what being married to that degenerate for so many years did to her mind. That could be the only way she knows how to react and behave, in the absence of a normal life. Abnormal is normal for both of you.

I'm pretty mad at Boris as well, but he claims he's completely sorry and that he was drunk when it happened. Did you have a boy or a girl? I'm very much looking forward to seeing my first grandniece or grandnephew! What did you name it? Pozhaluysta, *tell me you kept your baby and didn't succumb to pressure to put it in an orphanage. Boris also wonders if his parents are still alive. Have you gotten any word from them?*

Do you really want to marry Boris? If you don't—and you have every right not to!—you can live with me and your uncle, if he's still alive. You'll always have a place with me, and I'll treat you like my own dear Ginny.

I didn't want Ginny to know the true extent of people's Russophobia, so I only mentioned the mildest insults. In reality, Boris was beaten up several times during his first month here. His assailants were American boys who called him "a dumb Slav," "a Commie spy," "a sub-Pollack," "a stupid Russian," "a bleeding-hearted Satanist," "a Slav atheist," and "a feeble-minded Ruskiy idiot." They beat him pretty severely, and he limped home with black eyes, a broken and bleeding nose, a broken leg, and strangle marks around his neck on the first occasion. At the hotel where he works, the customers sneer at him and laugh and point when he's talking, to mock his accent. Borya ran home crying every day for three months.

When I and your mother got here, it was July 1917. The boat rocked the whole way, and in June everyone got sick. Several people died and were tossed overboard. I was seasick every night, and your mother called in her sleep for Matushka Rus. *We both cried ourselves to sleep out of missing Moskva. We nearly lost our luggage when we were unboarding, because everyone was pushing and shoving at us. We could barely walk into the examining rooms of Ellis Island.*

Our English was very weak, so we had to have an interpreter. You're lucky you were taught English at gymnasium, and that you learnt it as well as a na-

tive, without the usual accent. They asked us so many questions and looked for so many diseases we know we don't have! We could barely keep from crying when they changed our kopeks and rubles into U.S. dollars and cents, so our young money-changer, Slava, let us keep them as one last keepsake from home. It was extremely crowded when we sat down to eat. A rude Polish man and his German wife sat in front of us and made rude comments about our food, black bread and borshcht. We felt very left out when we left the island to go to a new life, because everyone else was weeping, hugging, and kissing one another, while we had no one to greet us. Luckily, we were allowed to leave without a male escort, perhaps because we're older women and have husbands somewhere (dead or alive). It's not right that so many other women who immigrate alone, single or married, aren't allowed to enter the mainland alone, as though they'll get into trouble without a man around. No scandal is assumed when a man travels alone and enters the mainland without a wife or female relative. Well, this is the same country that erases a woman's name after she's married, and forever after identifies her under the aegis of her husband.

In spite of the xenophobia, nativism, and anti-woman attitudes, we're so thankful we're safe in America. Maybe someday Russia will be free again, and the monarchy will be returned to power. I go to sleep every night with the hope that someday, I'll be able to go back to Moskva.

This house is a dream come true after three months in a filthy tenement with ten other families in the Lower East Side. Thank God we were out of that overcrowded tenement by the influenza pandemic. We had to wear masks over our mouths everywhere we went, until it finally went away. I hope it didn't catch you, Ginny, or any of your friends! I was so sad when I heard it had claimed the lives of two of my favorite artists, Egon Schiele and Gustav Klimt. Schiele's wife Edith also succumbed.

Every night we labor over our English books. We're very much looking forward to becoming real Americans, but we were born Russians and will die Russians. Our walls are hung with pictures from home; framed Russian proverbs; paintings of scenes from various fairytales by Krylov, Pushkin, and earlier fables; pictures of the most important writers, poets, artists, dancers, and playwrights; and pictures of various Tsars and their families. Our secretary is filled with ikons, hollowed Easter eggs, and the family balalaika.

We cried ourselves to sleep the night after we discovered the Tsar and his family had fallen victims to regicide by godless child-killers, woman-killers, and unpatriotic thugs. I can hardly believe such people were made in the image of God as you and I. Only someone without a heart and soul could murder inno-

cents. Even if you disagree politically, there's no reason to murder someone, particularly not a child like our dear Tsesarevich. Children can't help the family they're born into. For all we know, Tsar Aleksey II could've been a wonderful Tsar who brought Russia into the 20th century with humane, enlightened rule.

You're going to love America, in spite of its imperfections and 19th century throwbacks. Your English is as good as your Russian, French, and German, so you'll get along fine. Pozhaluysta, *come soon, while it's still possible to immigrate, or I'll never see my son and niece again, and I'll never see my grandniece or grandnephew!*

With love and hope to come to America soon,

Tyotya *Margarita.*

"Now I know where you get your strong-mindedness and progressive views from," Nadezhda says.

"Yes, isn't she marvellous?" Lyuba asks. "She gave up her birth name and married fairly young, but she went to art college, postponed motherhood, and only had one child. And she cared more about the influenza deaths of artists than actors."

"It's so nice of her to offer us a place to stay when we come to America," Ivan says. "It's a good idea to leave while the borders are still fairly open. That money from your mother will hopefully cover ship fare, and most importantly, we've all got our passports."

Ginny looks at the floor. "Now, don't get mad at me for what I'm about to admit, since this happened a long time ago, when we lived in the valley. I sort of shoved Lyuba's passport into a vase my mother made. I tried to get it out later, but it's stuck."

"What were you thinking?" Lyuba shrieks.

Ivan grabs the decorative grey vase from a shelf and has a look inside. Sure enough, the darkness is broken by the telltale pale green of the Imperial Russian passport. He rifles around Nadezhda's sewing basket for the smallest-gauge knitting needle he can find, hoping for success with the technique his mother taught him to extricate objects trapped in small spaces. When the passport remains stuck after a good twenty minutes of trying, he throws the needle on the floor and roughly puts the vase back on the shelf.

"If my arm weren't broken, I'd beat you up." Ivan gives Ginny a good whack on the head with his right arm. "Hopefully I can extract it once I have my dominant arm back."

"I'm writing back to my aunt," Lyuba says. "It'll take my mind off Ginny's abhorrent mischief. At least he claims that didn't happen recently. I'd hate to think he's going backwards, after so long of being good."

"We've got plenty of paper and ink," Pavel says. "That's one thing we've always got plenty of, even when food is scarce and we're running low on fuel. Who are we going to write letters to when our families are gone?"

Lyuba has a seat at Nadezhda's desk and inhales the creamy stack of paper. "I always loved the smell of a good old book and paper. I'm glad you don't have a typewriter. Even if I knew how to type, typewritten letters are so impersonal and cold." She dips an orange and black fountain pen in a nearly-full inkwell and begins writing, using the old-style Cyrillic she grew up with instead of the new-fangled orthography reforms.

Dear Tyotya *Margarita:*

We just got your letters today. We're staying with some wonderful new friends, and our old friends are in another neighborhood. It's been a long, strange journey since you last saw me.

I had a little girl, and yes, I kept her. Her name is Tatyana Ivanovna Zhukova. I want nothing more to do with Boris, although I feel very terrible for the way people are treating him because he's Russian. She's named for the late Grand Duchess. I offered to name her Anna, after Vanya's mother, but he declined. She was born 23 January 1919, and will be one year old next month. She's the most beautiful baby I've ever seen. I hope Boris doesn't demand rights, because he doesn't deserve to be her father. Vanya is her father as far as any of us are concerned, most of all Tatyana herself. That's the man she recognizes as her papashka.

Do you remember my old school friend Aleksey Tvardovskiy? He married a lovely girl named Eliisabet Kutuzova last spring, and they have a little boy, Nikolay, who was born 7 November 1917, New Style. He's a very sweet little boy, and is two years old now. I was his mother's midwife, and can't believe that tiny baby who was born into my hands twelve weeks early has not only survived but thrived. You really would've approved of how a woman doctor from the women's medical school came to assess mother and son the next day.

My friend Nikolas Vishinskiy and his dear little sister Kittey survived a labor camp and came home, and Kolya is now engaged to my friend Kat Vrangel. Dear little Kittey caught polio in January 1919, but thank God, the paralysis wasn't permanent, and she's been gradually relearning how to walk.

We haven't heard from our friends Anya Furtseva or Aleksandra Minina for a long time, and can only hope they're safe. Petya's been looking out for everyone. He's a saint. Basil Beriya is in a mental hospital now, which is where he's belonged his whole life.

Tell my mother I don't intend to marry Boris. I don't ever wish to see my father again, if he's survived. Ginny has grown up quite a lot. It'll be forever until we're together again!

Your loving niece,

Lyuba Zhukova.

"I'll take it to the post office first thing tomorrow," Pavel promises. "I'll buy the nicest stamps I can afford. In another lifetime, I loved seeing foreign stamps on letters, as well as ordinary Russian stamps."

Lyuba shudders and huddles closer to Ivan as the wind howls, threatening to blow through the cracks of the house. Presently, thick snow starts plummeting to earth. Pavel jumps up and throws five more logs on the fire.

"Thank God I just got food and supplies. Looks like the infamous Russian winter will strand us for awhile. But I won't forget to mail your letter, even if it's a long trek to the post office in the snow."

"Why don't we amuse ourselves by telling stories?" Nadezhda asks. "My parents and I often whiled away the winters with storytelling. Maybe you don't believe me given my profession, but I'm a romantic at heart. I'd love to hear the story of Lyuba and Ivan's secret romance."

"You don't want to hear that story," Ivan insists. "It starts very darkly, and ends unhappily. All that matters is I'm back with my woman now."

"I don't care. The best, most realistic love stories aren't all sunshine and flowers. I don't want to hear about a boy and girl meeting, falling in love, and immediately living happily ever after. That's boring and unrealistic. The couple needs to earn their happy ending in a worthwhile story. I hate people who get happy endings on a silver platter, tied up in neat hospital corners."

Lyuba sighs. "Fine, you asked for it. I'm no storyteller, but I hope you enjoy it. It starts the night my dear uncle came home on furlough."

2
Early March 1917, Old Style

It's not unusual for Ivan's father to visit Lyuba's father, particularly at night, but this night is different from all other nights. Tonight, Ivan invites himself over after his father arrives. He's passively stood by long enough as Lyuba has been abused by Mr. Zhukov. It's now or never if he wants to take matters into his own hands and prove himself as Lyuba's hero.

Ivan sets down his English book, glad to have any excuse to abandon his worst subject, and goes upstairs to fetch his father at 9:00. That's usually the time Mr. Zhukov creeps into Lyuba's room to do his depraved things. What Ivan isn't expecting to find is his father's voice coming from behind Lyuba's door. He stands there, nauseated and paralyzed by fear, as he listens to their depraved speech and noises. Lyuba, as usual, doesn't make a sound. As soon as their fathers announce their intentions to go to the kitchen for more beer, he ducks into a closet. When the coast is clear, he timidly knocks on Lyuba's door.

"May I come in?"

"Have I ever not let you come in when you've come to comfort me afterwards?"

Ivan sits next to Lyuba, wincing at her rumpled clothes. When he puts his arms around her, he feels her violently trembling. "They have no decency or morals. I've half a mind to take you away from here and never return. Why don't you tell your uncle what's going on? Unlike your parents, your aunt and uncle have sense."

"The same reason you never told outsiders about your father beating you and drinking too much. No one believes a child against a parent, and police don't take cases like that. It's our dirty, shameful secret."

Ivan jumps a *versta* upon seeing their fathers stumbling into the room not five minutes later. He's never been caught sitting with Lyuba afterwards over all the years he's known Lyuba's secret and has snuck over to comfort her.

"What the hell are you doing in my daughter's room, you sinistral miscreant?" Mr. Zhukov shouts. "Do you intend to rape my daughter in my very own house?"

Ivan jumps up, fighting his urge to throw a punch. "Who the

hell are you to talk about raping Lyuba? You do it all the damn time like it's the most normal thing in the world! The only time you left her alone since I've known you was when she had diphtheria. While she was quarantined and you took off to the countryside to avoid dealing with it, I was the one taking care of her most of the time. I've known for a long time what you've been doing to Lyuba. Are you going to admit your degenerate, sinful actions?"

Lyuba pulls her arms around herself, shaking even more under her father's accusatory glare. "Vanka, our fathers were doing no such things!"

Ivan stares at Lyuba in cold horror and disbelief. "Why are you suddenly denying it?"

"Go on, get out of here," Mr. Konev orders. "I never should've let you come here if I'd known you'd make trouble."

"You don't deserve to be a father," Ivan growls as he stalks out of the room.

"You were right to deny it," Mr. Konev says once the door is closed. "He knows too much. If he weren't my only child, I'd kill him for knowing these things. I can't believe he thought it was decent to say all that to his elders." He sits down and then immediately jumps back up. "I forgot to bring more scotch. It's my very favorite. Come, Lyonya."

***

"Where's your son going?" Mr. Zhukov shouts when they're in the kitchen. "Look out that window, and you'll see him running away! I didn't even hear the back door open or hear footsteps!"

"What's happening?" Mikhail demands. "I just saw Ivan and Lyuba run through the door! Lyuba has a bag, like she were planning to run away!"

"And you didn't stop her?" Mr. Zhukov screams.

"I heard every last thing going on upstairs. I hope they get away from you. That's my niece you're abusing, a good girl!"

***

Lyuba grabs Ivan's arm. "Wait for me, Vanya!"

He spins around to face her. "You want me only when you know they won't tell you to deny how they treat you. I never knew *my* father was in on it too till tonight!"

"He isn't, well at least not normally. *Pozhaluysta*, you know what it's like to be abused by your father and too scared to do anything. But now I'm ready to escape. Take me away from here!"

"I can take you to my house, but I have no idea where you can go from there. If you really mean it, I'll find somewhere to hide you."

As they run to the Konev house, they hear Mikhail threatening to shoot Mr. Zhukov with his rifle. Lyuba prays her uncle makes good on his threat.

"Back without your father?" Mrs. Koneva asks.

"*Matushka*, do you know where Lyuba and I can go that's far away?" Ivan asks.

"Why would you want to go away? I hear screaming. Did you upset him?"

"No time for explaining. I need to get her away from her father, and I'm sure *Batya* has half a mind to beat me after what I said."

Mrs. Koneva sighs and pulls out her address book. "Here, this hotel is all the way on the other side of the city. Take your father's car. He probably won't notice it. Pretend you're married if you stay in the same room. Respectable hotels won't accept unmarried couples, even if nothing happens between them." She pulls off her wedding ring and shoves it at Lyuba. "You can make up a story about why Ivan isn't wearing his wedding ring."

Ivan grabs the keys to the Russo-Baltique and the pile of rubles his father got on his last bootlegging run, then quickly goes upstairs to throw some clothes and his school supplies into his valise. He opens the car door for Lyuba just as Mr. Zhukov runs out, his face inflamed. Mikhail raises his rifle and shoots him in the face, sending him to the ground.

"*Spasibo, Dyadya* Mishenka!" she calls before Ivan drives away.

"Are you okay?" he asks as he turns onto the road. "I mean, beyond the obvious wounds."

"I can't believe he shot my father. God willing, my father won't press charges."

"The *mudak* deserved it. I would've shot him myself if I had a gun."

They sit in silence during the drive, though Ivan looks over at Lyuba a number of times. She can tell he's looking at her even in the dark, and looks away each time, very uncomfortable under his gaze.

Ivan parks the car when they get there and refuses to get out. "Can you admit you love me?"

"I beg your pardon, Vanya?"

"I've seen the way you look at me, even if you pretend you prefer Boris. Now that we're finally alone, there should be no secrets between us. *Pozhaluysta*, make me the happiest guy in the world by telling me my dream girl loves me as much as I love her."

Lyuba looks at him longingly. "I've loved you since we became friends and I took back how mean I'd been to you!"

He takes her hand, his heart thumping. "Is it okay if I kiss you?"

"Of course! You don't need to ask permission, but it's nice you're such a gentleman and wanted to make sure I wanted it."

Ivan nervously leans over and quickly kisses Lyuba. He hopes he's doing it right, though he's always heard it comes naturally, no matter how scared one is about doing it for the first time. When he sees the exuberant smile on her face, he does it again. She wraps her arms around him on the third time, and doesn't flinch when he holds her in return. After having her body treated like a meat market or cheap circus for years, it feels wonderful to finally be treated gently and respectfully by a man.

Ivan is thrilled she's letting him embrace and kiss her, as if they're the only two people in the world today. Lyuba can feel him shaking. Ivan can feel her shivering, but this is a good kind of shivering, not the way she always shakes when he holds her after her nightly abuse by her father.

"Let's go inside. We don't want to arouse suspicions."

"No, Vanya, we can run away to America! We don't have to go inside just because we're here. You can drive us to the depot, and we can get a train to the coast. Then all our pain will be far behind forever."

"It's nearly one in the morning. The hotelier must be wondering why we've been in this car so long. We'll discuss further plans tomorrow."

Lyuba reluctantly gets out of the car and takes her bag, following Ivan to the door.

A man with brown hair and eyes, of average height, opens the door after they ring the bell. "You came here awfully late. I was just about to go to sleep. We can discuss payment and how long you'll be lodging tomorrow." He extends his hand. "I'm Vasiliy L'vovich Fyodotov."

Ivan accepts the handshake. "I'm Ivan Ivanovich Konev, and this is my beautiful new bride Lyuba. *Bolshoye spasibo* for your gracious hospitality."

Mr. Fyodotov leads them upstairs to a big room. "This room is free, and doesn't have any upcoming reservations. You'll find the candles and matches on the bureau."

"No gas or electric lights?" Lyuba asks.

"This isn't one of Bloody Nikolay's palaces. I surmise you're upper-class and out of touch with how most real Russians live, but it's too late to get into a political debate. Have a good night."

Lyuba sinks into a chair as Ivan lights the candles. As the room fills with light, she starts investigating her surroundings more closely. It's not a half-bad room, with several small tables, a double-sized mattress covered by a red quilt, and some books. As she peruses the humble bookshelf, she pulls out a slight volume called *What Is to Be Done?* When she sees who the author is, she drops it like a hotcake.

"Looks like our innkeeper is a godless Bolshevik." Ivan kicks the book into the closet. "Though beggars can't be choosers. This fellow might stock books by Ulyanov, but he's giving us a safe place to stay, and he never asked about my lack of a wedding ring."

Lyuba looks around nervously, twisting in place. "You can have the bed, and I'll sleep on the floor."

"Oh, come on, you know you can trust me. I'd never force myself on you or even touch you if you don't want it."

A nearby door slams, and two people begin a loud political argument. At first Ivan is tempted to go next door to tell them to shut up, then thinks better of putting his nose where it doesn't belong. Standing up to Lyuba's father earlier tonight was probably the boldest act he'll commit for a long time to come. He has a seat on the bed and looks at Lyuba, who sheepishly tiptoes over to sit beside him.

"How serious were you about running away to America? Think how much safer it would be for us...for a child..."

"Since when have I ever wanted children?"

"Wouldn't you love a little child we could call our own? And whether or not we have a child, we'd be far away from your degenerate father. I hate the fact that the law considers women their husbands' property, but that means your father would face serious charges if he came after you again."

"No, I don't want *any* child! I've never dreamt of having a child! I'm not that type of woman. I'm going to go to university and find a job that accepts women, like my mother's. I'd be bored stiff if I had to spend my days boiling diapers and darning socks."

"You can go to university in America too. They have a lot of nice schools that admit women, and some all-women schools. I assume their laws forbid married women to work most jobs, so you'd have to stay home anyway. If you really love me, you'll go anywhere with me."

"I wasn't thinking rationally when I suggested running away to America. It's a nice dream, but I don't want to drop out of gymnasium and start over in another country with barely any money. I don't want to follow in my mother's footsteps by marrying and having a baby before I'm even eighteen. Twentieth century women shouldn't do that. And I'd miss our homeland too much."

"I'd make everything worthwhile. You'd never regret anything. As long as you keep *Matushka Rus* in your heart, you'll never forget our homeland as long as you live." Ivan gets up to blow out the candles. "All that matters is we have each other." He edges closer to Lyuba and kisses her as the political argument behind the wall intensifies.

Lyuba wraps her arms around his neck and kisses him back. Though neither knows what they're doing, it's not that difficult to figure out. Before long, her whole body is tingling, particularly the part of her body she previously felt only shame about. Carried along only by instinct, she slips her trembling hands under his shirt and tenderly caresses him. Ivan unbuttons his shirt and throws it on the floor, then tentatively guides his hands under her blouse. She nods her consent, and he smiles an awestruck grin as his hands get acquainted with her voluptuous breasts. He nibbles at her neck as he fumbles with her buttons and gently removes her blouse. By now Lyuba's whole body is throbbing with electricity, and the abominable sensations she's known her whole life are replaced by the loving, gentle touch of a man who loves her. She lies down and pulls Ivan onto her, letting him kiss and touch her in that position. While they're tentatively getting acquainted with one another's bodies, Ivan slides his hand up her leg, excited to discover she's not wearing bloomers. He doesn't have time to reflect on why this might be. All he cares about is the lack of an additional layer of clothes between her skirt and the forbidden fruit. Lyuba instinctively gives him greater access, and softly moans as he delicately fondles her. She raises her hips for him to pull off her skirt, and closes her eyes as he continues exploring her forbidden fruit. No one has ever treated this part of her body with such respect and reverence before. He seems to care more about giving her pleasure than finding his own.

Lyuba's hand trembles as she reaches for the buttons on Ivan's trousers. He smiles at her as she slowly slips her hand inside.

"I won't make you do anything you're not ready for," he whispers. "You don't have to touch me back if you don't feel comfortable with that yet."

"*Ya tyebya lyublyu.* Of course I won't avoid touching all of you." She guides his trousers off his body and throws them onto the floor, then timidly begins to caress his most sensitive flesh.

Ivan gasps. "That feels so good, *golubka.* Just be careful not to tear my foreskin. It's more delicate than you'll ever know."

After a lifetime of unwanted experiences, Lyuba doesn't venture to look, and only applies a very light, tentative touch. From his almost-immediate reaction, she surmises he's so excited to be touched by a woman, it doesn't matter how intense her touch is. A feather would probably cause the flesh to awaken.

"Vanya, I don't want a child," Lyuba whispers as Ivan starts to climb on top of her. Her whole body is trembling with desire to have the most intimate physical connection possible, and she knows he won't be rough or brutal, but without a diaphragm or prophylactic, there's no guarantee he won't get her in trouble and bring disgrace to her as a young unwed mother.

"I'll separate from you before I reach the height of my ecstasy. Don't worry, I know there are other ways for a woman to reach ecstasy, so I can still provide you with full pleasure even if I deny it to myself." He swirls his fingertip around her shoulder. "Would you prefer my hand or mouth to bring you pleasure, or both?"

"No, I really can't do this so soon. It doesn't feel right so soon after what just happened."

Ivan's face falls. "Are you really, really sure?"

"I really want to be with you in that way, after how long I've loved you, but I just can't. I'm sorry I let myself get so carried away. *Pozhaluysta*, tell me you still respect me and aren't upset I led you on."

Ivan gets off her and kisses her shoulder. "Of course I still respect you, *golubka*. I wouldn't let a girl I didn't respect have such personal contact with me. I'll still be your sweetheart even if you don't want to go all the way. You've got a beautiful body, by the way."

Lyuba blushes. "*Spasibo*. I suppose you need a cold bath now. It must hurt when a man is left in that unsatisfied state."

Lyuba gets out of bed to get her travelling bag so she can put on pajamas. As she squints her way over, she knocks over the table where she and Ivan put their bags, and their neighbors shout at them behind the wall. Lyuba runs back to bed and hides under the covers when she hears footsteps approaching their door.

"What's going on over here?" their male neighbor asks, opening the door. He's very big and tall, and looks like a Roman gladiator. A little picture of Lenin is sewn on his shirt pocket.

"My wife knocked over a table," Ivan tries to explain, glad they're safe under the covers and weren't walked in on without any clothes. "She didn't do it on purpose to annoy you."

"Well, you're interrupting a fine fight! I finally seemed to be winning over that stupid cow Yefrosina, until I was so rudely interrupted."

"No one told you to come here because there was a noise," Ivan says. "Why don't you go back to fighting with your wife?"

Their neighbor grimaces. "She's only the aunt of five of my children. I'd never marry a peasant fool like Yefrosina. My paper wife Alla's in prison, not that I care. Her overly moral father forced us to marry when he discovered we'd had several children. All three bastards went right to the orphanage, so I don't know what his problem was. I hope my new woman isn't caught by her father, since I have no intentions of marrying again, even in name only." He slams the door and goes back to his fight.

"I can't believe what some people consider appropriate to share with strangers," Ivan mutters as he changes into pajamas. "Rest assured I'll never be anything like that. The only woman I want is you."

***

Lyuba wakes up at five in the morning and reaches out for Ivan, whom she sees is also half-awake. "Why did you have to stop? I wanted you so badly, even though my mind was telling me no."

"I'm a gentleman, and would never force myself on you. And you raised a valid point about not wanting a child right now."

"I hope you don't think I'm a tease because I got you all excited and made you stop moments away from intercourse."

"Of course I don't think you're a tease. Maybe I was too eager to make love to you right away. What was I thinking, only hours after our fathers raped you?"

"My sweet, gentle Vanyushka is not a rapist. Lying with you could erase all my bad memories and replace them with good associations."

"Someday soon, *golubka*. Right now all I want to do is go back to sleep."

***

They awake again at 8:00, when light is streaming in through the curtains. Lyuba rolls out of bed and goes to put on day clothes, shivering under Ivan's gaze.

"Holy Mother of God, you're a beautiful woman. God made no mistakes whatsoever when he created you."

"You're not so bad yourself," she says shyly, trying not to look too much at his unclothed body.

"We have to go to gymnasium unless we want to be busted for truancy. Don't worry, we'll be away from here soon, if I can figure out a plan by then."

They go down to the hotel dining room for a quick breakfast, putting extra hard-boiled eggs, bread, and apples in a small sack for lunch. Lyuba lowers her gaze from that of the other guests, knowing they must assume she and Ivan slept together last night. As soon as they're done eating, she follows him out to the car. The entire drive to school, she says nothing.

Ivan parks the car in the small parking lot allotted the teachers and older students lucky enough to have automobiles. "I know what you're thinking, that I don't respect you anymore after I've seen you naked and touched your body. Don't you know me better than that?"

"I know you respect me, but it's hard to look you in the eye after what happened. Even if we stopped just short of intercourse, we've seen each other naked and touched each other's bodies. We can't go back to just being best friends."

"Then you're in luck. I don't want to go back to just being best friends either. As soon as possible, I'll make you my wife." He gets out and goes around to open Lyuba's door. "Don't worry, I won't tell anyone. I don't want your reputation to suffer if people knew you did that with someone before marriage."

The entire day, they go about their normal routine and resist the urge to betray anything in their eyes or body language. Finally, at the end of the day, while everyone gets on the tram, they're able to be alone again. After looking both ways, they head to the music studio. No sooner have they sat down behind the piano and fallen into one another's arms than Aleksey and Nikolas come in.

"What are you doing here?" Ivan asks. "Go get the tram!"

"I knew it," Nikolas says.

"We won't tell," Aleksey promises. "Your secret is safe with me. I knew Lyuba always really preferred you over Malenkov!"

They stay at the hotel for a week, every night heavily making out but not going all the way, until they receive a phonecall from Mrs. Zhukova. Though Ivan refuses to believe it, Lyuba believes her mother's story about how Mr. Zhukov has repented and learnt his lesson. Ivan has a sick feeling in his stomach when he drops his new girlfriend off at her parents' house, but he has no legal authority to intervene. He counts himself lucky Mr. Zhukov doesn't come out to attack him for taking off with Lyuba. Still, leopards don't change their spots overnight, and it's a only a matter of time till he finds proof Mr. Zhukov is still as immoral and deviant as ever.

****

Chapter 10: The Swan Mates for Life

"You can't leave me hanging there," Nadezhda pleads when Lyuba finally stops talking. "You only told me about the first week of your affair, and it lasted a month. I want to know everything, bad and good. This isn't a moving picture serial like *The Perils of Pauline*. I shouldn't have to wait to hear how it ended. By the way, did you ever catch the name of your obnoxious neighbor? My cousin Alla has a paper husband under those exact circumstances. He raped her. There was no consensual intercourse. She was very young, and he's several decades older."

"I honestly don't remember his name after all this time, though I must've heard his roommate calling him by it," Lyuba says. "And I'd really prefer to end the story there, instead of taking it to its tragic conclusion."

"You must tell me how it ended. I'd never stop reading a book halfway through either."

"We have to eat dinner first," Pavel says. "Everyone, come to the table. We can continue the story later."

Lyuba heads to the table and gratefully accepts a plate of boiled potatoes, roasted chicken, carrot and turnip salad, and black bread. All too soon, the heavenly feast is over, and they retire to their places around the fireplace. At Nadezhda's urging, Lyuba sighs and continues telling her story.

"It was late March for us, though really April by the modern calendar, and my father had just received induction orders. The day he enlisted was unusually warm, so Vanya and I skipped gymnasium…"

2

"We're going to sit by the pond all day and forget your father ever existed. I hope he gets killed by the Huns. That's one Russian death I'd celebrate."

"We can't just sit here all day," Lyuba says. "That'd be boring. Why don't we do schoolwork first, and then enjoy the rest of the day. Let's start with English, since you're so keen to go to America."

"I finally learnt Roman letters!" Ivan beams like a little boy. "Staying after school with Miss Tolstaya for extra help has really been worth it. Watch me write their alphabet!" His sleeve picks up dirt as he writes with a stick.

Lyuba smiles along with him as he writes the letters. "Can you say anything in English?" She brushes the dirt off of his left sleeve. "My sweet *levsha*."

"I know five phrases. 'Please pass za plate,' 'Zank you very much,' 'You're velcome,' 'I vould like zat over zere,' and 'Please speak slowly, because I am Russian and don't know English very vell.'"

"I love how you sound when you talk English. I hope you never lose your beautiful accent when we go to America."

"Also I'm learning how to go shopping in America. Miss Tolstaya taught me how to change kopeks and rubles into American money."

"How would you ask for the price of something?"

"I'd read the label."

"How do you ask the price, Vanyechka?"

"Vat eez za price of zees?"

"You must learn English very well, or people will stare at you. Can you translate this into English?"

Ivan rolls his eyes at the length of the assignment. "Mrs. Kosygina gives too much homework. She's one of those lunatic radicals taking over the gymnasium. One day I walked past her house and saw her rip up a picture of the Tsar."

"I've heard talk about her husband having an affair and beating her when he's not with the other woman." Lyuba wrinkles her nose. "This passage is from that book by Ulyanov! Talk about ridiculous!"

"Let's start our arithmetic problems then."

Lyuba wrinkles her nose again. "I hate trigonometry."

"You and me both. Why don't we forget about our schoolwork for today? It's not like we're failing any classes and can't afford to neglect assignments or studying."

"Don't you want to go to university after you graduate?"

"I have to spend my money on ship fare to America. Then I'll have to work very hard so I can support you and the children we'll have."

"I never accepted your invitation to run away and have children with you, did I?"

"No, but you never rejected it either!"

"Just asking, but how many children would you like?"

"Oh, eight or nine. The house would always be full."

"You want me to have children until I'm dead of it?!"

"But you were 'just asking.' You could just as easily marry Boris and only have two or three children."

"Just asking again, where would we live?"

"We'd live in New York City first. I don't know if we'd have enough money to move to another immigrant city like Pittsburgh or Boston. When we have enough money, we'll move to the fertile American Midwest and start our own farm. We wouldn't have to answer to anybody!"

"But that'd mean starting all over from scratch several times!"

"I know you're not 'just asking,' Lyuba. Admit you'd love to marry me and run away to America!"

"Yes, I've thought of nothing else ever since I've known you! But how can I accept when you've never asked me?"

"You know me too well to think I don't intend to marry you. I'd never practically make love to a girl I didn't want to marry. We'd get married in St. Basil's and then sail to America. I'll take you away from the terrible things I see coming."

"I'm only seventeen. That's too young to get married nowadays, even if it's not a child's age."

"It isn't too young to know you love me!"

"No, it isn't." Lyuba cuddles up against him. "Now that we're on this subject, let's start working on geography. Show me where New York City is."

Ivan reaches for his geography book and flips it open, searching for the correct page. "Right there. It's on an island, right across from Italy, I believe. Those places in green are the Midwestern states. My father thinks I don't know the meaning of hard work, but I do! I'd break my back working to make sure you're taken care of and that we have a roof over our heads and food on the table."

"My Russian teacher gave me the Bunin story 'The Gentleman from San Francisco' to read. I've heard wonderful stories about California."

"Yes, but it's too far away, and it's too expensive to get train tickets from New York to California. I don't think there are many

Russians there. Most of their immigrants are Oriental. But maybe someday we can visit."

"What sort of boat would we take to New York City?"

"Probably an ocean liner. There's a lady in green who greets the people sailing into New York Harbor, Lady Liberty. She holds a torch."

"New York City is beautiful, my uncle says. But no one could ever find a city more beautiful than Moskva."

"When we move to the Midwest, we'll have a dog, a cat, and a lot of horses. I want to name one of our sons Igor, after my late uncle."

"I'll name one of our daughters Yekaterina, after my mother and *prababushka*. I know you're not very fond of my mother, but she's a strong person who's suffered a lot. You shouldn't judge her unless you know what she's really been through in her life."

Ivan ignores this comment, not wanting to start a fight. "I don't want a namesake. It's no fun having the most common male name in Russia. Even the equivalents in other languages are the most common male names in those countries. It's like announcing, 'Hi, my name is Yawn.'"

"They'll have your eyes and my face."

Ivan looks at a nearby pastry vendor. "Would you like some sweets? I'll let you decide if you want them before or after lunch. It's getting pretty late, and we need to eat something."

"You needn't bother. I can survive without pastries."

"No, you deserve everything nice in the world." He jumps up and heads towards the vendor.

"You can have all you like for free," the man says. "Anything for young lovers. It warms the heart to see young people in love, after so much bad news from the front, and all this turmoil in the government."

Ivan smiles and fills up a basket with *chak-chak*, *pastily*, *vatrushki*, *limonnik* slices, *beignets*, chocolate croissants, *canelés*, and *petit-fours*. Lyuba shakes her head when he returns with the overflowing basket of sweets.

"I haven't seen French pastries in years," Lyuba says. "When I lived in St. Petersburg, we sometimes went to French restaurants and bakeries. My uncle visited France ten years ago, and got to enjoy so many lovely desserts every single day. I'm rather jealous he got to travel the world. Besides attending boarding school in Saskatchewan, Canada, he's also visited America, Germany, France, Poland, Bulgaria, Greece, and Italy. And, of course, East Prussia."

"Hey, look at that. There are a couple of ducks who don't realize it's not time to migrate home yet. They must be crazy to come back so early, or to have never left."

Lyuba peels a hard-boiled egg. "Who could blame them? This is their home, and they don't want to abandon it just because of tough times." She smiles at a family of geese swimming up. "New life begins at the oddest times, even when logic says no."

"Very symbolic, wouldn't you agree? I think God's trying to send you a message it's your destiny to marry me and go to America."

"Or perhaps my destiny is to stay here and weather out the tough times, instead of cowardly escaping. Things could always get better instead of worse."

A baby swan and its mother swim up next. By this point, Lyuba wonders if she's dreaming, or if she and Ivan fell asleep and are just now waking up several months later.

"They say the swan mates for life," Ivan whispers. "When it selects a mate, the two swans swim together and their beaks form a heart shape. Do you catch my drift?"

"We're soulmates," Lyuba whispers back.

"And soulmates are bound together by God, destined to always be together, no matter what happens."

Taking courage from how it's growing dusky and that she won't be able to see the look on Ivan's face, Lyuba decides to make a confession. "Vanya, my father didn't live up to my mother's promise. He's been at it again."

"What?"

"Don't be angry! He's probably far away by now."

"Not if I catch him in time," Ivan snarls, leaping up and running down the road.

"Where are you going?"

"Off to get my hands around your father's neck and kill him, that's where!"

Lyuba runs after him until they reach a small wooden building where the new recruits are registering. Mr. Zhukov is at the desk, filling out paperwork.

"Here to say goodbye to me?" Mr. Zhukov beams at Lyuba. "I came three hours late and waited twelve hours in line. It's a wonder I didn't starve from eating your mother's lunch in the smallest pieces possible."

"You *mudak*, you've been at it again!" Ivan punches Lyuba's father right over the gunshot wound on his face.

"At what again?"

"You know exactly what! Only this time I'm going to kill you!"

"Stop this!" the recruiter bellows.

"I'll kill you before you reach the battlefield. I'll choke you to death and laugh at your pain. Then I'll shoot you right where it'll cause the most painful death imaginable."

Ivan rips out a piece of Mr. Zhukov's hair by the roots. Then he picks up a wooden stick and beats his knees until Mr. Zhukov is screaming for mercy. The recruiter notices in horror that Ivan is left-handed, and crosses himself.

"You want to cripple me?!"

"Yes, I do! Get the hell out of here and stay the hell away from Lyuba for the rest of your life, or I'll come back after you and *really* kill you, you *mudak*!"

The recruiter pulls Mr. Zhukov up off the floor. Mr. Zhukov spits in disgust.

"She's my daughter, and I can do what I like with her! It's a man's right to do whatever he pleases with any woman he wants to do it with!"

Ivan takes Lyuba's arm and leads her home, his stomach churning. He knew Mr. Zhukov would continue raping her as soon as she came home, and he knew it was against his own better judgment to believe Mrs. Zhukova's claim of his repentance, but he was as true to form as always and just passively rolled over. His one hope is that, since Mr. Zhukov is gone, Lyuba will finally feel safe and have no more reasons to reject his offer of moving to America.

***

On the first of April, Mrs. Zhukova pulls Lyuba aside when she gets home from spending Saturday with Ivan at the moving pictures.

"You're only seventeen and still in gymnasium. Ivan will be

nineteen in June. It's not such a big age difference, but I don't like it. It's not an equal disparity yet. He'll be away at university while you'll still be in gymnasium. Once he's at university, he'll lose interest in you. I expect you to finish gymnasium and do better than I did, but we're not a university family. That's a foolish pursuit and waste of money when you could immediately go to work. Never forget we're not upper-middle-class by birth and don't come from the same type of world as his people."

"Ivan says he'll marry me and take me to America."

"We've worked very, very hard to get where we are. Throwing it all away to start over in a foreign country is tantamount to spitting in my face after all I sacrificed my whole life. Do you think I wanted to marry at all of seventeen and be forced to leave school early, or to be robbed of my childhood and take on a woman's role when I was just seven years old? I had no choice when my dear father died during the influenza pandemic. I never complained about what was expected of me, and worked even harder to make something of myself."

"I'll be happy and loved with Vanya, even if our life might not be easy at first. I'm not trying to trivialize your sacrifices or disrespect you. If you want me to do better than you did, you should want me to go to university and find more meaningful work."

"Why can't you marry a boy with unlofty ambitions, like Boris?"

"Because I know I can do much, much better than waking up every day and going off to be exploited in a factory. In America, everyone can become rich, even if they arrive with just a dollar."

"I learnt the hard way. When I was your age, I was in love with a very nice young man, Andrey Grigoriyevich Fyodorov. He wanted to take me to America too, but my mother reasoned with me just as I'm trying to reason with you now. I jilted the dreamer and settled for your father. A drunk with coarse manners who earns money is better than a romantic dreamer with his head in the clouds. I was sick to my stomach when I discovered what he was doing to you, but I couldn't do anything about it. Better a financially comfortable life with a degenerate than the poverty and shame which come from being a divorcée or a runaway with a small child. Truth be known, America doesn't have golden streets and rivers of milk and honey. Those are stories told to make us feel good about leaving our homelands, but in reality, there are many poor people struggling to survive. You need to think long and hard about what you're going to do, but for the sake of your future, I urge you to end this dalliance with the neighbor boy."

(Skip to 3 April 1917 on the old Julian calendar, when our story began.)

Ivan catches up with Lyuba as she's leaving gymnasium at the end of the day.

"Let me know right now. You're my soulmate. I'll marry none other than you. You're going to be my wife, the mother of my children! I have enough money saved up for us to get married and sail to America today. Tell me right now. Are you going to marry me or not?"

"*Ya tyebya lyublyu*, Vanya," Lyuba whispers. "But I'm too young to marry, and my future lies in *Matushka Rus*. We must pretend this past month never happened."

"What are you trying to tell me?"

"I'm sorry. I cannot marry you and go to America. Russia is my destiny, for better or worse. It's as simple as that."

She starts for the door, and Ivan runs into a nearby closet to cry.

3

"That's so sad!" Nadezhda says. "Whyever did you have to listen to your mother and ruin your chances of going to America to be safe?"

"I was too weak-willed. I still am. I should've said yes. But then I never would've had Tatyana. I cannot imagine life without my precious little daughter!"

"As much as I wish you'd never gotten ensnared by Malenkov, we never would've had our dear baby otherwise," Ivan agrees. "But we'll have even more children together."

"I hope you do," Nadezhda says. "It would be too sad if you ended up like my parents, with so many years between children, and not by choice."

"You have siblings?" Lyuba asks. "May I ask where they are, or if they're still alive?"

Nadezhda crosses herself. "I was nine when Gennadiy was born. Our sister Platonida came a year later. God must've needed them more than we did, since they weren't long for this world.

Platosha starved to death in 1915, when she was only three. Her fragile body couldn't survive, no matter how much of our food we gave up to her. Five-year-old Genna died in 1917, a week after the February Revolution. On our way home from school, a sniper bullet hit him in the forehead. I carried him all the way home, where he died ten hours later. Their little graves are in the front yard." She rubs her fists over her eyes. "Only a few months after I lost Genna, my parents were taken too, and ever since I've been alone in this world. I stayed with my dear *Dyadya* Ilyushka for awhile, but then he was taken away too. He pushed me into a closet to save me from the same fate. Now all I have to remember the past are this house, the dried blood behind the bed, and those tiny graves. God willing, you'll have a much happier life than I've had so far."

4

Lyuba's twentieth birthday is the eleventh of December. Though they're still snowed in, for lunch Ivan and Pavel have prepared her a veritable feast of gingerbread cake, mushrooms stuffed with breadcrumbs and walnuts, roasted potatoes, chicken dumpling soup, rye bread, and beet salad. She tries to protest when Ginny and Ivan produce presents, but to no avail.

"You shouldn't have gone out in this weather just to get me meaningless birthday presents."

"Of course we should've," Ivan says. "You deserve everything nice in this world."

Lyuba reluctantly takes Ginny's parcel, wrapped in light green tissue paper. Inside is a large glass pendant. On the front, the word *Freedom* is written in all the Slavic languages. On the back, it's written in the Germanic and Romance languages.

"That was very thoughtful of you. I imagine this was a holdover from before the Revolution, perhaps intended as a Christmas ornament."

"To make up for how I couldn't give you a present last year, this year I got you two presents," Ivan smiles. "A rabbit fur hat for this year and a book of Turgenev stories for last year. I know he's one of your favorites."

"Yes, he had such a beautiful, sensitive soul, just like you, my belovèd."

Though they're not in permanent housing, the country is still racked by civil war, and they're apart from their friends, Lyuba thinks this is possibly her nicest birthday ever. It took a long time to realize it, but she now knows her aunt, Pyotr, and Eliisabet were right when they urged her to choose the man she loves, no matter how scared she is or how much easier it'd be to choose a socially safer alternative. With any luck, her pair bond with Ivan won't be torn asunder again.

5

Meanwhile, Basil is whiling away his time in a mental hospital run by Vladimir Maksimovich Gorshchenko and his unmarried daughter Mariya. He's chained to the wall between a man claiming he's Karl Marx and a woman who screams out the Nicene Creed nonstop. Though Basil is a little touched in his head, he's the sanest person in this place by far.

"Am I in here for life?" he asks Miss Gorshchenko.

"Without a doubt. Is Comrade Beriya ready for his breakfast?"

Mr. Gorshchenko puts a bib on him, and Miss Gorshchenko feeds Basil porridge.

"I'm not crazy! I'm not crazy!"

"That's what they all say," Mr. Gorshchenko sighs.

"But I'm special. Why couldn't I have been taken to a place in my homeland at least?"

"Where is Comrade Beriya from?"

"Quit talking to me as if I'm a third person not in the room! I was born in Moskva, but my five-greats-grandparents came from Georgia."

"That's a funny name, Beriya. It sounds like the name of a crazy person, doesn't it, Manya?"

"Indeed, Papa. Is Comrade Beriya ready to drink some water?"

"I always have wine with my food!"

"Exploiter of the proletariat," the man who thinks he's Marx mutters.

"Is Comrade Popov ready for his breakfast too? What about Comrade Nemova?"

"It isn't right," Basil cries, tears rolling down his cheeks. "This is no way to treat people, even people who deserve it!"

****

Chapter 11: The Plot Thickens

"Where are you going, Borya?" Mrs. Kharzina demands. "Don't try to tell me sneaking out with suitcases is a run-of-the-mill occasion!"

"I'm just going for a walk."

"Why are you bringing suitcases if it's just a walk? And who goes for a walk after midnight, and in winter?"

"Fine, you've caught me! I'm going home so I can be happy again!"

"How can you be unhappy here? If you can no longer handle the disrespect at the hotel, I can help you find a better job. Returning to Russia is a horrible short-term solution to current heartache."

Boris starts crying. "I don't love America! You don't understand! I miss Russia! I want to see Moskva again before I die! I miss my home!"

"This is our home now. I miss Matushka Rus *too, but I have to learn to live in a new country."*

"I want to see my child! I'm a horrible father. I don't deserve to be a father! I want to know what my child looks like! I want to beg Lyuba for another chance! I miss Moskva!"

*"*Pozhaluysta, *Borya, think of your future. You're building a new life for yourself here. There's no life for you back home, only suffering and insecurity."*

Boris grunts. "Maybe you have a point. I'll go back to sleep and think about this more carefully tomorrow."

Mrs. Kharzina returns to her room, believing Boris is doing the same and thinking about what a horrible mistake he almost made. She doesn't hear his footsteps softly padding through the door.

***

Mrs. Kharzina awakes at nine the next morning and starts dressing. The house is eerily silent, when ordinarily Boris is banging about at this hour as he gets ready to go to work. Normally, she'd be hearing noise from the kitchen right about now, as Boris indulges one of his favorite pastimes.

"Borya, it's getting late. Don't you want to get to work on time?"

When there's no answer, she goes into his room.

"Boris? Have you left for work already?"

His suitcases are on the floor, and the bed is made, so she assumes he went to work. However, when he doesn't come home by midnight, she begins to get worried, and goes to the police station. Since her English isn't perfect yet, she asks for a Russian translator.

"Have you seen a young man, nineteen years of age, named Boris Alek-

sandrovich Malenkov? He has black hair and black eyes, is about five foot eight in the boots he normally wears, is rather pudgy, and was wearing an old fur coat, boots, and hat the last time I saw him. His unenhanced height is five foot three."

"Is the boy any relation to you?"

"He's been living with me and my sister since he came to America this spring. Our families were friends in Russia."

"Where does Boris work? Maybe he's working overtime, or stopped at a bar on the way home. You know how men that age are. Or perhaps he visited a friend and decided to stay the night."

"Last night I caught him about to creep out of our house with suitcases. He said he misses Russia and isn't happy here. He left the suitcases behind, but perhaps that means he left with just the clothes on his back."

"Maybe he's been killed."

"Don't say that! Although I hope he didn't get into a fight at the hotel where he works. The people there have been quite cruel to him. Knowing how impulsive and childish this boy is, I'm sure the more likely explanation is he did exactly what I caught him about to do. He may have left the suitcases as part of a ruse to make me believe he didn't run away."

The police officer motions to someone. "Randolf, this woman is looking for a missing young man. Give her the papers to file a report."

***

"Are we ready to leave yet?" Boris asks. "The sooner this ship pulls up anchor, the better."

"All the Ellis Island rejects seem to be accounted for. The authorities always make sure they're deported as soon as possible. If anyone so much as suspects I'm illegally smuggling you into Russia, we're both in trouble. Hide under the boat over there. This journey may take awhile. Remember, you must hide again as soon as I give the signal. That may be often."

2

It's two hours past bedtime in an orphanage in Minsk. The two oldest girls, Anya and Vera, are on the top bunk talking, while two little girls are asleep below. The head warden's niece, a week away from her tenth birthday, is also on the bottom bunk, wide awake and not even trying to fall asleep. The five of them just recently arrived, though the first four are no strangers to orphanage life.

"How many orphanages have you been in now?" Anya asks.

"Ten," Vera says. "It's hard to believe our older sister Alla was still with

us when we started this terrible journey. I miss her so much. And my dear parents, of course, my other older sisters, my dear aunt and uncle, and my cousin Nadya. Sometimes I wonder how many Lebedevas are still left in this world."

"This is my fifth. My little brother Leontiy and I have been in Arkhangelsk, Yaroslavl, Brest, Tsaritsyn, and Minsk. I'm going to organize a riot one of these days, before these cows in charge get any ideas about sending me to prison. They're delusional if they think we don't know where the oldest hostages go." She stops talking as the oldest, fattest, nastiest warden comes in.

The warden slams a club against the wall, sending reverberations throughout the room. "I heard talking after lights-out, so I decided to hold a roll call as punishment. If anybody refuses to answer, the whole room will get beaten. Then the guilty party or parties will be beaten again. Just for extra punishment, I'm not going in alphabetical or age order."

"I can't understand Russian," a little three-year-old girl on the opposite side of the room says, rubbing the sleep from her brown eyes. "I only know Ukrainian."

The warden hits her over the head with a club. "Nina Ignatiyevna Medvedeva."

"Here."

"I always hated that surname. And here come some more surnames I never liked. Yelena Vasiliyevna Klykachëva."

"Here."

"Svetlana Yuriyevna Khrushchëva."

"Here."

"The stupid Ukrainian mistake, Valentina L'vovna Kuchma."

"I'm not stupid," Valentina protests in her little voice after one of the older girls translates for her. "My mama and tata *love me."*

"Your parents aren't here now, are they, you little suka*? Moving on. Inna Aleksandrovna Zhirinovskaya."*

"Here."

"My own niece who refused to squeal on her traitor parents, Inessa Andreyevna Zyuganova."

"Here, Tyotya *Dasha, and my parents aren't traitors."*

"Yes they are. I'll beat you later for that treasonous sass. Now where's the most unruly girl in these quarters, Anna Rudolfovna Godimova?"

"Here."

"Vera Ilyinichna Lebedeva."

"Here."

"Natalya Ilyinichna Lebedeva."

"Here."

"Fyodora Ilyinichna Lebedeva."

Fyodora is sound asleep. Vera nudges her with her leg to wake up before Mrs. Zyuganova finds out, but it's too late.

"Asleep during roll call? This will teach you to disobey the orders of our fine orphanages built for children of enemies of the people!"

The other girls keep their mouths shut as Mrs. Zyuganova beats Fyodora with her club. Fyodora doesn't scream, wanting to avoid being beaten even harder.

"I hope that taught you a lesson, you stupid little suka. *Don't you dare think I'll take pity on you because you're young. I don't give a damn if it hurt. You deserved it." Mrs. Zyuganova throws the five-year-old back onto the bottom bunk with Natalya and Inessa, and Natalya immediately enfolds her terrified baby sister in her arms. "Olga Leonidovna Kerenskaya."*

"Here."

"Dinara Olegovna Nikolayeva, whose parents couldn't be bothered to give her a normal name. Talk about uppity ideas."

"Here."

"The Jew, Larisa Adolfovna Dietermann."

"Here."

"Klara Mikhaylovna Nadleshina."

"Here."

"And the half-breed Jew-Russian, Irina Samuelovna Brodskaya."

"Here."

"Everyone is to go to sleep. Anyone not dressed, washed, and out at the breakfast table by six will get a beating. Is this clear, Fyodora Ilyinichna Lebedeva?"

Fyodora nods, still clinging to Natalya. Mrs. Zyuganova spits on the floor and staggers into her room across the hall. Presently, the strong smell of cigarette smoke wafts into the room. Fyodora begins coughing.

"Hey! Who's coughing? If you don't shut up immediately, I'm coming back there to beat you!"

Fyodora turns toward the wall and closes her eyes, trying to get fresh air. She barely remembers a time before entering the orphanage system, but she does vaguely remember the rest of her family and being happy. She has to believe her sisters when they say someday they'll be happy again and back with the rest of their family.

***

In the morning, they quickly wash, put on their ugly uniforms, and troop out to the dining hall. Mrs. Zyuganova brusquely calls roll, then begins smoking another cigarette. Her four oldest daughters go around dumping sickly-looking porridge onto plates.

"Some new rodents are coming tomorrow, so we need to get rid of some of you in return. I decided to eliminate Larisa Adolfovna Dietermann, Anna Rudolfovna Godimova, and Vera Ilyinichna Lebedeva, since they're too old for this orphanage. The train will come to take you away tomorrow at noon. Don't you other vermin dare think you can remain here safely. I can easily find plenty more rats I'd like to get rid of, both boys and girls."

"Where are we going?" Larisa asks.

"None of your business, Yid. You should know better than to question anything I say. You're damn lucky I'm enjoying a cigarette now and don't have two free hands to beat you."

"I know exactly where we're going," Vera says. "You're sending us to prison. My older sister Alla was sent to prison shortly after we arrived at our first orphanage, since she was sixteen. They told her she was too old to be there, and needed to be in prison."

Fyodora starts crying, which in turn sets off Svetlana and Valentina. Mrs. Zyuganova throws her cigarette down, pulls a belt off the wall, and starts beating them. Valentina starts crying, which only makes Mrs. Zyuganova beat her even harder.

"I think that's enough belting for now, Matushka,*" one of the Zyuganova daughters sneers. "Let the little* suki *think about what they've done wrong. They can't reflect on their misbehavior if you keep beating them."*

Mrs. Zyuganova drops the belt. "Breakfast is over early, thanks to those insolent little rodents. I don't give a damn if you're still hungry. You are all to report to the courtyard now for the morning devotional songs and readings. Come on, go."

They grab their regulation coats, line up, and troop outdoors like prisoners in a chain gang. Mrs. Zyuganova's oldest daughter, twenty-seven-year-old Lyudmila, sits down at a piano and begins playing "The Internationale." One of her other daughters, Rufina, distributes lyric sheets in case anyone doesn't know the words. Many of the girls only mouth the words, and Valentina just looks at the paper in confusion. At barely three years old, she doesn't know how to read, either Russian or her native Ukrainian.

"Not everyone is singing, Matushka,*" Lyudmila says.*

The girls sing at the top of their lungs as Mrs. Zyuganova waddles into the crowd, while Valentina aimlessly begins singing nonsense syllables. When Mrs. Zyuganova cannot find the original guilty parties, she picks on Inessa, cursing at her and beating her with her fists.

"Thanks to my traitor niece, there will be no more singing. Instead we will now do a dance around the image of Our Leader, Vladimir Ilyich Lenin!"

She forces the children to join hands and dance around a huge statue. Vera spits at it.

"Praise be to Our Leader, the savior of our people, the one who has led us the proletariat to triumph...." Mrs. Zyuganova starts.

A strange man strides into the courtyard and hands Mrs. Zyuganova a telegram. She turns white as she reads it, and shoves it at her four daughters, who've gathered around her. The telegram flutters to the earth, and they run inside crying.

"Good riddance," Inessa sniffs.

Several of the girls gather around her after she grabs the telegram, though they're confronted by a language which looks like Russian on the surface, but contains many strange words.

"What is that, Ukrainian?" nine-year-old Olga asks, brushing her long dirty blonde curls out of her face.

"It's Belarusian, my people's long-repressed national language," Inessa says. "My parents were modern enough to teach it to me, though my school only used Russian. This isn't good news. My Dyadya *Dima was in an accident in his coal mine."*

"I hope he dies, so that mean old witch can leave," Olga sneers.

"Don't say that about Dyadya *Dima! He's the nicest man on the face of this Earth. I've tried to write to him, but* Tyotya *Dasha forbids me. He has no idea I'm in this orphanage and that my parents were arrested for accidentally using a newspaper with Lenin's picture as firewood. I hope he adopts me."*

"But wouldn't he live with your aunt, if he's her husband?" thirteen-year-old Inna asks. "You'd have to put up with that ugly fat suka *too, even if your uncle's as nice as you say he is. I can tell who wears the pants in that family."*

"They haven't lived together since Tyotya *Dasha started this house of horrors. He has no clue how that evil* suka *really lives her life. While he's been working in a coal mine since he was ten years old, she's been living one of the most traitorous lives ever. He's not smart, but he's very kind-hearted. He can't read or write, and barely managed to graduate from elementary school, but that shouldn't be the measure of worthiness."*

"How would he support you if he adopted you?" Natalya asks. "I don't imagine coal mining makes him rich. And I've heard that vile woman mention younger kids, besides the older girls helping her enslave us."

"They have twenty-seven, who amazingly have all survived so far. Tyotya *Dasha also had seventeen miscarriages and three abortions."*

Many of the girls instinctively clutch their midsections.

"And I thought I had a big family!" Vera says. "I'm only the eighth of ten. I'd want to kill myself if I had to be pregnant forty-seven times."

"Comrade Lenin loves people like my uncle and cousins. After this stupid war is over, I'm positive he'll start helping us. Isn't that why we overthrew the Tsar, so the common people could have better lives?"

"I hope we start having better lives soon," Natalya says. "I can't wait much longer."

***

The next morning, a few hours earlier than promised, a train pulls up to take away the children Mrs. Zyuganova has decided to trade in exchange for the fresh blood. Though Mrs. Zyuganova and her daughters have spent the rest of yesterday and this morning weeping and cursing, the news of the accident hasn't slowed down the official plans.

"Where's the Jew Larisa?" Mrs. Zyuganova asks, blinking away tears. "Not that I give a damn about any of you or remember names with faces, but I know she's one of the newer ones, and one of the older ones."

Inna raises her hand. "Yesterday she found out from your daughter Ivana that she indeed would go to prison, so she ran away to the lace factory down the road. You might get in trouble if you march over there to try to steal one of their employees."

Mrs. Zyuganova breathes fire. "I cannot believe my own flesh and blood betrayed me and let you imbeciles know official secrets. Now I'll look completely incompetent if I only transport two girls when I promised three. Just this once, you vermin will go on the transport to the new orphanage. But don't get any ideas. Your new warden may immediately send you to prison when she sees how old you are. The next warden could make me seem like a loving maternal figure."

The children unboarding the train march through the snow and stand in line by the gates. The Zyuganova sisters herd them inside, shouting at them to move quickly and wait for room assignments. Mrs. Zyuganova grimaces when she realizes all but three of the new arrivals are boys. Her daughters Ivana and Ksyusha are in charge of the boys, so she won't have many chances to terrorize and dominate these fresh victims.

Mrs. Zyuganova stands in front of the three new girls and crosses her arms. "You're not following the boys. Girls are on one side of the building, boys are on the other, and never the twain shall meet. If you have any brothers or cousins in that group, you'll be lucky if you manage glimpses of them during orphanage-wide events and master roll calls. Give your particulars to me, and then I'll take you to your quarters. It's too bad if you don't like them."

Lyudmila pulls the heavy girls' register off a shelf and blows off the dust. Since her mother can't read or write cursive, she's the one responsible for recording intake information.

"Names, ages, and nationalities?" Mrs. Zyuganova barks.

The dark blonde girl in the middle steps forward. "Naina Antonovna Yezhova, age eight, from Petrograd."

"Nice necklace. It's mine now." She grabs a citrine necklace hanging around Naina's neck.

Naina slaps her hands away, reaches under her dress, and pulls a gun on Mrs. Zyuganova. "No it's not. My mother gave it to me when I was four. It's my birthstone, and the only thing I have to remember her by except an old family photo. Steal it and I shoot you. My papa gave me one of his handguns before I was taken away, and I'm not afraid to use it."

Mrs. Zyuganova steps back, her heart pounding and her eyes wide. "Next?"

The oldest girl, with dark hair and eyes, steps forward. "Yekaterina Karlovna Chernomyrdina, age twelve, from L'viv."

"L'vov," Mrs. Zyuganova growls.

"No, it's really L'viv. I might be a native Russian who was born in Ukraine, but that doesn't mean I enforce Russianized names on their cities. I'm not an imperialist. As a Belarusian, you should really know better than to use the language of the oppressor. It's taken how many years again for your native language to become widely-used and the official national language?"

The littlest girl, with sable hair and eyes, steps forth. The chain for her ID has to be tripled over so it won't drag on the ground. "Karla."

"Surname and patronymic?"

"I'm two and from Yaroslavl."

"Surname and patronymic?"

"I don't know."

Mrs. Zyuganova picks Karla up, throws her into a wall, and begins beating her. The other girls stand by in cold horror. They're used to getting beaten, but it's shocking for Mrs. Zyuganova to beat such a tiny child. Karla is even littler than Valentina.

"Stop beating her!" Naina grabs Mrs. Zyuganova's left arm and bites it. "She's only two years old! My cousin's name is Karla Maksimovna Gorbachëva, and if you hurt her again, I'll kill you. Remember, I've got a gun, and I know how to shoot. It's not just for show."

"Quiet that tiny one down!" Mrs. Zyuganova screams. "I'll deal with your insubordination later. You're dreaming if you think you can keep a gun in my orphanage, or that I won't be back to steal that beautiful necklace."

Naina scoops up the hysterical Karla, cuddling and kissing her. Mrs. Zyuganova spits as the new girls walk down the hall.

"You can't pick your own quarters! I'm the only one who gets to assign rooms."

Naina turns around to face her, giving her a steely-eyed look. "I am well accustomed to the rules of orphanages by now. I don't like you. In fact, I don't think we'll be sticking around much longer. Just try to stop us. You know you can always get three fresh victims where you found us."

Mrs. Zyuganova spits in disgust. "Enough wasting time. We're lining up outside now, and everyone whose name is called must get on that train." She pulls a dirty paper out of her pocket and unfolds it. "Lyuda, you read the names."

Ten boys are called, including some of the girls' brothers. Their sisters hold their breath as the girls' names are called. Anya, Inna, Irina, Yelena, and Svetlana breath a collective sigh of relief when they too are called. The train is filled out by all three Lebedevas, Valentina, and Olga. As the chosen ones troop onto the waiting train, dark-haired nine-year-old Klara realizes no further names are being read and screams.

"My brother is on that transport!" Klara howls.

"Tough luck. If you sneak on, I'll beat you." A cruel smile appears on Mrs. Zyuganova's lips. "Oh. I'd love to get rid of my traitor niece Inessa. Off you go!" She seizes Inessa and throws her into the girls' car.

"Fedya! Fedya!" Klara screams, running toward the train.

Mrs. Zyuganova pushes Klara into the snow. "Would anybody like to sell her place to little Klara Mikhaylovna Nadleshina?"

"I would! I would!" Inessa screams.

"Stay on that train, Inessa! I want to get rid of you!"

Inessa's eyes light up when she sees a man clad in an old fur coat approaching. As he comes closer, she definitively recognizes his red-brown hair, grey eyes, and ram-like forehead. She leaps off the train, runs for him, and flings *herself into his arms. "*Dyadya *Dima! Take me away and adopt me! I've been in this orphanage since my parents got arrested, and* Tyotya *Dasha beats me!"*

He hugs Inessa tightly, then turns to face his wife. "Dasha, what's the meaning of all this? You told me you were living and working at a hospital, and I had no idea my brother and sister-in-law were arrested. Had I known, I would've come immediately and adopted Inessa."

"I thought you were hurt in a mining accident," Olga says. "Did you have a miracle recovery?"

"I was never injured. They had me mixed up with another fellow, and I came to tell my wife the happy news. Little did I know I'd find her leading a secret double life and abusing my darling niece, my dear brother's only child."

Mrs. Zyuganova yanks Inessa from her uncle's arms, throws her back into the girls' cattlecar, slams the door shut, and puts a metal lock in place. "Goodbye, my traitor niece. I hope they treat you even worse at the new place. Comrade Conductor, start the train!"

Inessa screams as the train begins to move.

"Someone help me!" Klara screams, grabbing the window. "I ran to the other side of the train while Inessa was stalling for time. I can't be separated from my big brother."

Vera and Anya jump up and pull her inside.

"You're really brave for such a young girl," Vera marvels. "Though I bet you'd want to escape even if your brother weren't here. That woman was a nightmare."

"You can sure say that again," Naina says. "We hid in the baggage holds until the coast was clear. We're very sneaky. After seeing how she treated Karla, I had to say no and move on to another orphanage!"

"Let's just hope the new orphanage is a step up from the hellhole we're leaving," Anya says.

***

9 February 1920, the train finally comes to a stop. Due to all the fighting in the area, the train has been rerouted numerous times, and the children have been brought into the actual train, out of the frigid cattlecars. Many of the children can't remember the last time they've had real beds or such decent food, and aren't looking forward to the inevitable arrival at a new orphanage.

The woman who greets them stands painfully straight and has beady little eyes, funny-looking ears, a hat too small for her head, and a terrible haircut. "Welcome to Kiyev," she says in a voice like a police sergeant. "I'm Mrs. Brezhneva, your new orphanage mother. I like to think of myself and my assis-

tants as stern but fair. I only beat people who get out of line. If you mind your business and behave, I'll leave you alone. Now we're going inside to take roll. The boys will go first, and then they're going with some of my assistants to their side of the building. I don't allow much mingling, but I allow brothers and sisters to meet every so often."

The children line up in the main hall and recite their names, ages, and cities of origin, as Mrs. Brezhneva records them in a large register. When the boys are finished, several assistants step forward and lead them away. Then the girls begin reciting their particulars. The last girl in line, tiny Karla, once again only provides the information she understands.

"Karla, two, from Yaroslavl."

"Surname and patronymic?"

"I don't know."

"How could you not know?"

"She's only two," Naina explains.

"Little Valentina Kuchma is only three and she knows who she is!"

"There's a big difference between two and three. You must not have any children if you don't know this."

For a moment, Mrs. Brezhneva's eyes mist over, but then she blinks and resumes tapping her pen against the register. "Someone has to give me her particulars, or she can't enter the orphanage."

"She's my cousin. Her patronymic's Maksimovna, and her surname's Gorbachëva."

Mrs. Brezhneva shuts the register and puts it back on the shelf. "Everyone, follow me. You may find your room changing often, as children come and go, but for now, it's everyone for herself. Don't try to claim rooms marked as maximum occupancy. The last thing I want is for my orphanage to become a breeding-ground for disease and death. We have quarantine rooms for anyone who gets sick, and I'm very careful to only put children in the quarantine room corresponding to their disease. Believe me, I know better than you might imagine how devastating disease can be, particularly in children."

An ominous chorus of loud whooping coughs serenades them as they proceed down the hall towards their new rooms. And yet, in spite of the foreboding atmosphere, Mrs. Brezhneva doesn't seem half-bad. Taking courage from this, Inessa goes in search of Mrs. Brezhneva's office as soon as she's claimed a place in a bedroom. She shudders as she sees quarantine signs advertising the presence of not only whooping cough, but also diphtheria, measles, scarlet fever, typhus, and influenza. At least here sick children are quarantined instead of allowed to mingle freely and infect everyone else.

"What do you want, Comrade Zyuganova? You're a bold one, daring to come into my office without permission or advance notice."

"I don't belong here. My uncle wants to adopt me, but my suka *aunt forcibly separated us. You'd better not send me away or let anyone else adopt me. He has to be waiting for me to return to Minsk."*

Mrs. Brezhneva furrows her brows. "Is this the truth? I don't want to release a child only to discover she's going back to enemies of the people, or, worse yet, to live on the streets with the besprizorniki.*"*

"I'm a very honest person. Just send a telegram or letter to Dmitriy L'vovich Zyuganov of Minsk. If you send it to my fat suka *aunt, he'll never receive it."*

Mrs. Brezhneva sighs. "I'll see what I can do. But remember, you're no better than anyone else just because you have adoption prospects. While we're waiting for word from your uncle, you'd better be on your best behavior."

"I promise, Comrade Brezhneva."

Such go the lives of the orphaned or presumed-to-be orphaned children of the enemies of the people.

3

"There's a visitor for Comrade Beriya," Miss Gorshchenko announces. "Does Comrade Beriya know Comrade Malenkov?"

Basil just about drops dead of shock. "Boris! I thought you went to America!"

"I did, but now I'm back. What the hell put you in this place?"

"The rantings and delusions of Pyotr Litvinov and Aleksey Tvardovskiy, that's what! Have you seen Lyuba? I'm trying to run away to see her, only I'm chained to the wall, as you can see!"

"Have you seen my child? I cannot describe the feeling I have, knowing soon I shall see my child—*my child!* I cannot believe I'm a father."

"It's a girl, and I don't remember if I caught her name. Did you come back to marry Lyuba?"

"I most want to see my child, though I also need to beg Lyuba for forgiveness. Hopefully she'll be a good girl and give me a second chance."

"When you find Lyuba, let me know. I've been itching to see her since our memorable last encounter!"

"You and Lyuba?" Boris's eyes narrow.

"I know Lyuba had a good time, but Konev, Litvinov, Tvardovskiy, and Vishinskiy all called it rape. You know how a woman really means yes when she says no, particularly after she's made you desire her."

"You *what?*"

"No, not you too!"

Boris grabs Basil by his throat and pins him to the wall. "Knowing you, I tend to believe what everyone else says! How could you do such a thing to the mother of my child?"

"Nurse! Malenkov is trying to kill me!"

The nurse comes running, and her jaw drops to see what's going on. "Comrade Malenkov, what are you doing to Comrade Beriya?"

"I just found out he's here for raping the mother of my daughter! I hope they castrate you!"

Boris grabs his coat and stalks out. He pulls his muskrat hat around his ears as he slams the door.

4

On 25 March, Lyuba's party arrives at a Garden Ring boardinghouse Pavel recommended before they parted ways. Hyperinflation is still going strong, the ruble worthless, so they must perform housework to earn their keep. Lyuba can't help but wonder if the money her mother sent will do anything but make an ocean liner company laugh, and if she'll have to barter in exchange for a ticket. At least money was still worth something when Ivan wanted to elope.

"Nothing will keep us apart again," Ivan whispers to Lyuba as Ginny knocks on the door. "If we can find a priest, we'll get married as soon as possible, and I'll adopt Tatyana."

An average-sized man opens the door and extends his hand. "Greetings. I'm Andrey Vitaliyevich Andropov. You're just in luck, I have some rooms upstairs. Will you need one or two?"

"Two, of course," Ginny says. "I'm not sharing my room if I can help it."

"Three rooms," a vaguely familiar voice calls. "The lady will stay with me, if you'll allow an unmarried couple to share a room. That other man isn't her husband, unless I'm very much mistaken and they betrayed me while I was away. I can't believe what a beautiful coincidence this is. Now I don't have to go looking all over for you."

Lyuba lets go of Ivan's arm and shrieks. Ivan steps back, stunned, amazed, and furious, as Lyuba throws herself into Boris's arms crying.

"What in the hell are you doing here?" Ivan demands. "Why would you leave America to come back to this? Do you have any idea we have a typhus epidemic? I hope to God you're not infected. Lyuba, you're not thinking straight right now. Once you process this shock, I expect you'll push that fat, short man away. He doesn't deserve your sympathy."

Lyuba is sobbing onto Boris's shoulder. "Oh, Borya, you're back where you belong! Have you thought about us often?"

"Every single second. Why do you think I came back? I arrived a few weeks ago and started making inquiries into your whereabouts. I didn't remember Litvinov's address, so I went to see the Beriyas. They said Basil was in an insane asylum, but that he might have some information. I couldn't believe what he admitted when I visited him. Is it true he was sent there for raping you?"

She nods. "I'm so glad you came back. I've felt so ashamed of being an unwed mother, even if I almost never go out in public. I know what I am, even if other people don't. But I adore my baby and couldn't imagine life without her, even if she is illegitimate." Lyuba sinks into a chair and buries her face in her hands.

"And we both know what Malenkov is, even if he wants to pretend he's reformed and wants you back," Ivan says. "Lyuba, *pozhaluysta*, don't tell me you're seriously considering reuniting with him. You never loved him, and only let him court you because we all got our signals so badly crossed. You're my woman now, and I won't let this slovenly slug steal you again so easily."

Boris wrests Tatyana out of Ivan's arms. "Cute kid. She looks like a tiny version of Lyuba. She must be over a year old now."

"She's fourteen months," Lyuba says. "Her name's Tatyana Ivanovna Zhukova."

Boris's face falls. "You gave her your surname and Konev's name as a patronymic? If you're so ashamed of unwed motherhood, why wouldn't you give her my name? And if you wanted to pretend you were married to Konev to fake respectability, why not temporarily call her Koneva?"

"Oh, believe me, her surname will eventually be Koneva, and so will Lyuba's," Ivan says. "Why the hell are you here? I don't want to know what kind of shady dealings you had to undertake to come here. I refuse to believe you came here normally."

"Excuse me for giving a damn about the child I abandoned before she took her first breath! I cannot believe I'm a father. Tanyechka, I'm your father!"

Boris slings her onto his back and gets down on all fours to give her a horseback ride, while Ivan stands by clenching his fists and Lyuba continues softly weeping.

"I bought something for you in Petrograd." Boris reaches into a shopping bag and hands Tatyana a book. "Tales by Krylov and Pushkin! I can't wait to read it to you. I'll sing to you too."

Tatyana wiggles away and toddles over to Ivan, holding up her arms.

"You see, Malenkov?" Ivan smirks as he picks her up. "Emotionally, I'm her father. You abandoned her before she was born."

"But Borya's back now!" Lyuba says. "He made a very bad mistake, but now he's here to take care of me and Tatyana. Christians are supposed to forgive each other, not hold grudges for past mistakes. Borya wasn't thinking straight before."

Boris reaches back into the bag and ties an orange hairbow in Tatyana's hair. "She looks even prettier now. Orange is my favorite color, and I hope she'll love it too. I bought this after I found out I have a daughter." He gazes at Tatyana. "You're my little *knyazhna*. How about changing her name to Tatyana Borisovna Malenkova? It's so damn emasculating my child doesn't have my name."

"She doesn't have a birth certificate. If you're sincere about wanting to stay with us, we could change her name when we register her."

"Perfect. I love the sound of that name. Why don't we take my baby out for a stroll?" Boris slings Tatyana onto his shoulders and takes Lyuba by the arm.

"If you keep slinging her around, you'll kill her!" Ivan yells.

"She's mine and not yours, unless I'm extremely mistaken. You haven't really been sleeping with Lyuba while I was away, have you?"

"Konev's still a virgin," Ginny reports.

Boris bursts out laughing. "At almost twenty-two? What's wrong with you?"

Ivan storms upstairs with his valise, while Boris starts out the door with Lyuba and Tatyana.

"Hey, Malenkov, what's wrong with your right leg?" Ginny asks. "Since when did you get a limp?"

"My leg's asleep, and that's the last question I want about my personal business." Boris hops through the door.

Lyuba can't help noticing the limp too. While she walks at a normal, leisurely pace, Boris lags behind and drags his right leg more than walking on it normally. When they come to a crowd of people, Boris shouts, "Cripple with wife and baby coming through!"

"You're not crippled," Lyuba chastises him.

"Yes, I am. The first time I got beaten up in America, I had my leg broken. It was so severe it didn't heal for seventeen weeks. I had to go to work with my leg in a splint so I wouldn't get fired. I learnt quickly how to hide the fact that I couldn't bear any weight through that leg. Even now I can barely walk on it. It gives me excruciating pain every time I bear weight on it. In November, I was beaten up by Scottish thugs who called me a sub-Pollack, a Ruskiy idiot, and a Bolshevik spy. I couldn't bear the Russophobia, which is another reason I had myself illegally smuggled home."

"Silly Borya, why did you ever leave? Are you going to marry me now?"

"That's supposed to be my line. Don't make me feel even more emasculated. Say, why aren't you wearing the ring I sent you?"

Lyuba looks at her hands. "I threw it into the Skhodnya River. It was an ugly reminder of what you did to me, and I didn't care how much it might be worth now that the banks have collapsed."

"I worked really hard to afford that ring. You just threw all that hard-earned money into the river. God knows how long it'll take me to save up for another one. But all is forgiven now. I wasn't thinking straight when I abandoned you, and you weren't thinking straight when you threw away my ring. How soon would you like another child? I'd love nothing more than a little boy in my own image."

"How can I be sure you won't abandon this one too? I'm willing to forgive you for what you did to me and Tanya, but I can't be so sure what your future intentions might be."

"Trust me, I never would've left had I seen that beautiful child. You must hate me now, even if you say you forgive me."

"I could never hate my sweet, gentle Borisko."

"So sweet and gentle I beat you, threatened you, got you drunk, left you and the baby to the Bolsheviks, in a sense raped you, and beat you till you nearly started to miscarry my child!"

"Don't be so selfish. She's my child too. I've been with her all her fourteen months on Earth. You just met her today. Don't tell me now you're her real father. Ivan has been with Tanyechka her whole life and loves her like his child. In fact, I hoped to marry Vanya till you came back! Now I don't know what to think anymore. I love Vanya, but you're the father of my child, and it's not right to refuse to marry the father of one's illegitimate child if he's willing to take responsibility. As unconventional as I am, I still care about what people think."

"You're just as beautiful as I remember you. I can't tell you've had a baby." Boris sets Tatyana on a park bench and kisses Lyuba. "It may seem hard to believe, but deep in my heart, I love you like none other. I'm a coward, a bully, a loser, and selfish, but I know what I want. If you give me a second chance, eventually I'll grow up and prove to the world I'm a nice guy."

Lyuba grabs his arm. "I feel someone staring at us, Borya."

"Aw, go. I've just seen a much more appealing woman than you." Misha pushes a redhaired girl with a baby in her arms into a mudpit.

"Can I have some food, Misha?" the girl asks. "I don't care what you want in exchange. Yura and I are hungry, and so are my mother and Zina. Would you really let your own baby starve?"

Misha runs up to Lyuba. "I prefer you over Lena anyday! And what a surprise, another old face from school I never thought I'd see again. What happened to Konev?"

Boris waves his hand. "Ivan was only standing in for me while I was away. Now I'm back to reclaim my woman and baby."

Misha grunts. "One of these days, I swear I'll finally get to enjoy your body. If this man left you without marrying you, who's to say he won't leave again? And Konev didn't act like much of a man the last time I saw him, so I wouldn't count on him standing in my way either." He stalks back to Lena.

Lyuba cringes against the bench, holding Tatyana tightly, as she realizes this must be the bastard son and his mother whom Misha has referred to. She's horrified to realize how young Lena is, significantly younger than Misha, and prays she never becomes such a fallen woman she'd beg a brute for food in exchange for dignity.

"Aw, get out of here. I'll give you tickets to the circus. It's a show starring clowns dressed up like the leaders. It'll be real, real fun. Go!" He throws the baby into a puddle of waste, shoves Lena into his car, and starts driving like a madman.

"First let me have some food. I can live without the circus, but I can't live without food."

Misha grabs her by her flowing red hair. "I don't feel like giving you any food today, you damn whore. You and your family can starve for all I care. There's the circus tent now. Go!" He shoves her out of his car into another mudpit.

"I haven't eaten in three days!"

"That's not my problem." He digs a dirty, crumpled 100,000-ruble note out of his pocket. "Decent circuses always have concession stands. You can buy sausages or *shashlyk* during the intermission."

Lena picks herself up out of the mud as Misha speeds away. Her stomach rumbles as she buys a ticket and finds a seat.

A young clown dressed like Lenin approaches her as she's taking her seat. "You're pretty cute. I love red hair. How old are you?"

"Thirteen. How old are you?"

"Fifteen. I've been in the circus all my life. Today I'll perform just for you."

During the show, the clown makes several faces at Lena, and she makes a few back. As she's making one of these faces, she feels a heavy hand on her shoulder.

"Under arrest for making fun of Our Leader."

"I'm only thirteen! And we were just having fun!"

"Then you're going to an orphanage."

***

After the circus is over, Misha drives back up and calls for Lena. When she doesn't appear after thirty minutes, he storms into the manager's office to inquire after her.

"Oh, that one. She was taken away by the police halfway into the show."

"I have more money than just about anyone in this bankrupt country. I can get her out." Misha shoves several 100,000-ruble notes at the manager.

"Not that I know from personal experience, but I assume you can't trace someone once she's in an orphanage. If the local orphanages are too crowded, they could take the child to another city. And what does a man your age want with such a young girl? What are you, a pervert?"

Misha is seething as he climbs back into his car and races home. After he parks behind the brothel, he runs through the streets aimlessly until he bumps into Lyuba and Boris, on their way home.

"That young whore was taken away, not that I really give a damn, but where am I supposed to get such a lovely young body from now? I liked having such a young conquest and controlling her."

"You should be ashamed of yourself," Lyuba says. "A girl that young should be a virgin, not a grown man's sexual plaything. And not that I think you give a damn about your son either, but a fat woman came by and picked him up after you left. She identified herself as his aunt, and had some very choice words for you when I told her what I observed."

Misha turns away and kicks a stone. He bangs his hands against a wall and screams curses.

Lyuba begins walking faster and huddles closer to Boris. "At least you're more of a man than Misha. If you know what's good for you, you won't ruin your second chance."

"Of course I won't. I've repented, and shouldn't have my past offenses held against me for the rest of my life."

"You don't know your own biological child, Borya. You missed her first steps, crawling, words, rolling over, everything. There's no way you can relive or make up for missing fourteen months."

"But I'm here now. Don't you agree we belong together? If not for you, there'd be no me. I often think of that day my parents were taken away. If I hadn't been at your house, I might've ended up in prison too. Had you not come along the day we left Moskva,

I might've been picked up off the street. You saved my life twice. Don't you ever think about that?"

"What about Vanya? I saved him too."

"But you saved me twice."

"Do you really think you deserved saving when you didn't do much to earn it? You stumbled into being saved, whereas I actively saved Vanya. I was the one who went to look for him when his house was on fire. What worthwhile things have you done with yourself since I saved you?"

"I'm a loser, true, but that doesn't mean I'm a horrible father. Haven't I spent the day proving I'm a good father to my child?"

"You're selfish if you can't see her as my child too! I'm the one who carried her in my body and gave birth to her, the one who's taken care of her for fourteen months. All you've done to be a father so far is contribute seed and give her some presents."

"Come on." Boris swings Tatyana onto his shoulders and takes Lyuba by the arm. His hand is on his injured leg as he limps.

"Sit down. You're in pain."

"It's pain I've gotten used to. The doctor told me this leg is crippled for life."

"That's only if you let it be crippled! You think it's crippled, so you're not bothering to help it get any better!" Lyuba starts massaging it. "Does that feel any better?"

"Immensely. So long since you've touched me."

"I was helping your leg, not trying to arouse you!"

***

"What took you so long?" Ivan growls when they return at 5:00.

"We ran into Misha, and then Borya needed help with his crippled leg."

"Better watch out, or I'll cripple your other leg," Ivan snarls.

"Don't be so possessive," Boris snarls back.

Tatyana toddles over to Ivan and holds up her arms. "Bed."

"No, *I'm* going to put you to bed." Boris grabs her and starts upstairs, ignoring her screams. "Then I'll read you a story from your new book."

"*Nyet, nyet, nyet!*" Tatyana howls, beating him with her tiny fists.

5

Lena is led to the front door of an orphanage at 8:00, a guard on either side of her. The building is permeated by an air of agony and hopelessness. A stern-looking woman smoking a cigarette curses as she turns on the outside lights and opens the door.

"What's the meaning of dropping a new brat on my doorstep this late at night? This is my personal time, after spending an entire day tending those roaches."

"This is Yelena Vadimovna Yeltsina. She's thirteen and from Moskva. We felt taking her to Petrograd would put her far enough away from any family stupid enough to try to look for her. This was the first orphanage we passed. The little upstart thought it would be funny to make faces at a young clown dressed like Comrade Lenin."

The warden grunts and grabs Lena as the officers walk away. "I'm Comrade Voznesenskaya, and I'm your worst nightmare. As you've arrived an hour after bedtime for the older girls, you'll have to take the bed with Mikhaila. You'll be given your uniform, coat, and nightgown in the morning." She drags Lena down the hall and shoves her into a bedroom full of unnaturally cold air. "Over there, Comrade Yeltsina. My Mikhaila is the one with the beautiful long sable tresses."

Mikhaila is as still as a stone. There are no noises coming from her. Lena shrugs and gets into bed, assuming Mikhaila is an old-timer and has gotten used to sleeping in such a frightfully cold room.

"Where are you from?" the girl across the way whispers. "I'm from Kiyev. My name's Antonina Borisovna Petrova."

"I'm from Moskva. I'm so hungry—I haven't eaten anything in three days!"

"Have this." Antonina throws Lena a loaf of bread. "There's something you should know about Mikhaila—"

"What's the meaning of talking after hours, Comrade Petrova?" Mrs. Voznesenskaya demands. "Do you want to end up like Mikhaila?"

"No, Comrade Voznesenskaya."

"Good."

***

In the morning, Lena glimpses a piece of paper lying across Mikhaila's chest.

"Get up, Mikhaila." Lena takes her by the hand. "Your hands are awfully cold."

"I should think so!" Antonina says. "She's dead! Haven't you seen her epitaph?" She picks up the paper. "I wrote this the night she died. 'Here lies five-year-old Mikhaila Maksimovna Gorbachëva, from Yaroslavl. She's survived

by a sister, Karla, twenty-three months; a cousin, Naina Antonovna Yezhova, seven; and a close friend of the family, Yekaterina Karlovna Chernomyrdina, eleven. Cause of death: beaten to death by Mrs. Voznesenskaya for demanding food upon arrival. The last word out of her petrified little mouth was: 'Freedom!' She stopped breathing three days after the beating, 12 September 1919, in Petrograd, Russia.'"

"I just slept in a bed with a dead person!" Lena screams.

"So you have," Mrs. Voznesenskaya says. "Isn't Comrade Gorbachëva well-preserved? She was so pretty, I had to keep her like this. Before I abandoned religion, I would've called her an incorruptible. Now I attribute it to a not-yet understood scientific phenomenon. Sometimes I brush her long black hair. I'm barren, so I like to pretend she's my daughter."

"That's disgusting!"

"And your treasonous behavior at the circus wasn't disgusting, Comrade Yeltsina?"

"I'm not your Comrade."

"This is the future of 1920, not the dormant land of Bloody Nikolay." Mrs. Voznesenskaya looks down and frowns. "I see lice on Comrade Gorbachëva. We'll have to cut off her hair and use someone else's until it grows back."

"Mrs. Voznesenskaya's crazy," Antonina whispers. "Acting as though she's alive!"

"Mikhaila and I are going for a ride. Comrade Baryshnikova, watch the children." Mrs. Voznesenskaya puts a coat around the dead child. "And you, Comrade Yeltsina, I trust you'll think about your actions while I'm out. I don't tolerate sass in this orphanage. This is why Mikhaila was beaten, because she didn't know her place. But now she's my child, so I forgive her."

6

Tatyana picks up a jar of dried oats and toddles over to Lyuba. "Eat."

"Let me feed her." Boris grabs her and starts preparing the oatmeal. "Stop yelling, Tanyechka. I'm your father. He was only standing in for me while I was away in America."

"*Nyet, nyet, nyet!*" Tatyana screams with all her heart.

"I think we all know by now who's really her father," Ivan says. "Emotionally, she's my child. Tell him, Lyuba. Tell him to leave or else!"

"After last night?" Boris asks.

"What about last night?" Ivan clenches his spoon in his fist. He knows Lyuba slept in Boris's room, but wants to believe their sleeping arrangements were as chaste as when he's shared a bed with Lyuba.

Boris sets the bowl of oatmeal in front of Tatyana and begins feeding it to her. "Lyuba and I are grown adults. Even you can't possibly be that damn naïve. Just because you live like a monk doesn't mean I do too."

"You *mudak*!" Ivan grabs Boris by his throat. "This is what had Lyuba so confused for so long, you and your feigned love for her! If she gets pregnant by you again, I'll make her get an abortion!"

"I wasn't raped, Vanya," Lyuba protests. "It was consent."

"I'll believe that when Hell freezes over. You'd better leave us alone, Malenkov. Just when Lyuba was finally mine again, you perfectly time an intrusion into our lives! I could kill you!"

Boris picks Tatyana up and tosses her up and down in the air.

"You might kill her!" Ivan snarls.

"She's my daughter, and I can treat her however I want!" Boris glares at Ginny. "What do you want? I can't believe you're still hanging around when you were always running away to do your own thing before. Last night, I told Lyuba to kick you out. We don't need you."

"I'm never going to kick my cousin out," Lyuba says firmly. "He's done more for Tanya than you've ever done, believe it or not, mostly thanks to his association with Georgiya Savvina."

"Yes, Ginny's a valuable member of our group," Ivan says. "We have more right to kick you out for showing up fourteen months after you split."

Boris tries to play with Tatyana later in the day by ducking behind a davenport and then jumping up again. He doesn't get it when she screams and cries in terror. Then, when it comes time to put her to bed, he rocks her so forcefully she starts to get sick to her stomach. He ignores the queasy look on her face when he puts her into the trundle bed.

"Now that she's asleep, we can work on trying to conceive a son," Boris whispers.

7

On the first of April, Boris gets a professional photographer to take everyone's picture. He goes all out for Tatyana, even giving her a bath and washing her hair. Ivan is furious Tatyana is starting to become more friendly towards Boris, and is still shocked Lyuba can go back to Boris after everything that's happened in the last year. Even if she's just humoring him and doesn't want to make him angry, that's still going too far. She should have absolutely nothing to do with Boris after the inhuman way he treated her.

"Is something bothering you?" Lyuba asks. "You're normally never nearly this affectionate. Are you using this show of extravagance as a way to mask something deeper?"

"If only you knew," he whispers, blinking away tears.

***

"Poor, sweet Lyuba. You deserve so much better," Boris whispers in the middle of the night, kissing his child's sleeping mother. "As much as I love you, I don't love you the way Ivan always has. Sleep on, my love. I'm a coward. Goodbye, my precious little Tanyechka. *Ya tyebya lyublyu*, but I have to leave. I'm sorry, but I don't deserve either of you, and have no choice but to leave you." He brushes Lyuba's long hair out of her eyes. "I deserve to be shot. I'm pondscum. Take good care of yourselves." He drops a note on the pillow as he tiptoes out of the room.

On his way to the nearest depot, he sees Misha's and Lena's baby on the ground, covered in filth, with a note pinned to him:

Dear whomever may find this baby. This is Yuriy Mikhaylovich Yeltsin, the 13-month-old bastard my sister, Yelena V. Yeltsina, had with Mikhail Ya. Godunov. His birthday is 18 February 1919. Lena was taken to an orphanage last week, and Misha doesn't want this baby. My mother and I are poor, so pozhaluysta, *whomever finds him,* pozhaluysta, *take him in and take good care of him. May God be with you both and save my little nephew from this tragic life!—Zinaida V. Yeltsina, 2 April 1920.*

Boris considers the matter. He's on his way back to America and doesn't know if he'll ever see Tatyana again. Another baby, and a boy at that, has been delivered to him at just the right moment. Now he has another chance to be a father, to a child who won't care how they came to be father and son.

From the corner of her eye, Zina sees her nephew being picked up by a pudgy man with a limp. Wanting to make sure this potential adoptive father is on the level, she creeps over to him.

"Where are you going?"

Boris jumps. "Are you a spy?"

"No, don't be afraid. I'm Zina, the one who wrote the note. Are you going to take care of Yuriy like he deserves?"

"I'm on my way back to America. I've got a really nice home, plenty of food, and more money than this bankrupt country could hope for. America's just as bountiful as you think it is."

"God will be with you. I can only dream of going to America. My mother's ill, my older sister Valya's in prison, my baby sister Natasha's in an orphanage, my father took a bullet in my place, my fiancé was murdered, and now Lena's gone as well. May God be with you!" She pats Yuriy on the head. "Remember your *Tyotya* Zina loves you, Yura!"

***

"Good morning, Borya," Lyuba mumbles. "Borya?"

She reaches over and finds the note. *Dear Lyuba and Tanyechka—I can no longer pretend I belong with you. I love you, but goodbye.—Boris.*

Feeling like the biggest fool who ever lived, Lyuba mutely gets dressed and changes Tatyana's diaper. She must've been dreaming if she thought Boris were serious about reforming his character and becoming a real father. As if she could forget so easily how much she loves Ivan and that she was never willingly in a relationship with Boris before.

"Where's Boris?" Ginny asks when Lyuba enters the kitchen.

"He left us." Lyuba puts Tatyana in her highchair. "Again!"

Ivan is overjoyed to read the note Lyuba hands him. "Finally gone! Now you're all mine again!"

"What am I, a whore? I was just sleeping with another man, and now you immediately want to be my fellow again?"

"I was your beau till a week ago, when you flung yourself into Malenkov's chubby arms after fourteen months of absence. But I forgive you for your moment of weakness. God knows, he's played so many head games with you before. I don't blame you for falling victim to him again. You were just confused. But now that he's gone, I'll see to it you're never confused again."

****

Chapter 12: Another Time of Troubles

"Who's that in the garden, Alyoshenka?" Eliisabet asks as she and her husband go for a walk around the property. Her eyes widen. "Oh my God, that's Basil!"

"What?"

"Oh my God! Look what he's doing to my rosebush!"

"Oh my God! How dare he do that to your roses? As if he couldn't find the outhouse!"

Basil hears them talking and waves.

"Are you blind, or couldn't you find the outhouse?" Eliisabet yells.

"I had to go so badly, I went right to the flowers!"

"Hey!" Aleksey remembers where Basil is supposed to be. "Why aren't you at the Marx Center for the Crazies? How did you escape?"

"I slipped out of my chains last night." Basil takes his clothes off and lies in the sun. "I love sunbathing."

"In the presence of a lady?"

"Tell your wife to avert her eyes!"

Aleksey gets a gleam in his eye and begins softly speaking to Eliisabet in Estonian. "I just thought of the perfect revenge for this *mudak*. Remember what I threatened to do the night I found him lying in the bushes?"

"Oh, my God!" Eliisabet nearly turns green in disgust.

"Yes, that's exactly what I'm going to do." Aleksey notices Basil's eyes are closed. "Big lazy *mudak*'s already asleep. I'll get some sedatives from the medicine cabinet and find a good-sized knife in the kitchen. Think of it as doing a public service."

Eliisabet sighs, but does nothing to prevent him. Knowing Basil's history, he escaped to try to find Lyuba. If he's castrated, he won't be able to assault her again.

During dinner, the entire boardinghouse is disturbed by Basil's screams. Mr. Golitsyn storms outside to find the intruder he thought he got rid of months ago. He breaks into a laugh when he sees what happened to Basil.

"How can you laugh! I need medical attention! One of your boarders must've assaulted me while I was asleep, and did something to me that made me sleep through the pain!"

"You raped one of my boarders, remember? I made it clear in no uncertain terms I'd have you arrested if you ever showed your face around here again. Have fun explaining to a doctor why you've been castrated."

"Hey, that's not fair! I know it was Aleksey Tvardovskiy, and I want him arrested!"

"As I understand it, you're an escapee from a mental home. Not only that, you're a foreigner. No one will take your side. Now get off of my property or I'll have you arrested."

2

The next morning, Aleksey rolls out of bed, very pleased with himself for what he did to Basil yesterday, and starts getting dressed. He stops in his tracks when he sees the date 3 April on the calendar.

"I'm going to town after breakfast," he announces when he sits down at the table. "Hopefully I'll be back within an hour."

"What are you going into town for?" Eliisabet asks. "What if they find you and take you away? I don't want to be a widow so young, and Kolya needs his father."

"I'll get some money or bartering goods from Mr. Golitsyn before I leave."

"Tell Petya to get it for you. I need you. What if you're exposed to someone with typhus?"

"Don't worry about what might happen to me. Things are a bit more settled now, and I've got a hearty constitution."

"It feels so empty without Lyuba, Ivan, and Tatyana," Kat says. "Don't shrink our band even more."

"This isn't up for discussion. I'm a grown man and can handle myself. Besides, it's not healthy to stay cooped up in a boardinghouse for so many months. I haven't been out in ages."

Eliisabet shakes her head, but knows she can't prevent him from doing what he wants to do. It's not like they're in the middle of a warzone, and things have started to calm down a bit recently.

Aleksey goes into Mr. Golitsyn's office after breakfast. "I need some money or barter goods to buy a present for Liza. It's our second anniversary. She'll kill me if I don't get her anything."

"Here." Mr. Golitsyn reaches under his desk and produces a

bag of 100,000-ruble notes. "Don't let yourself be killed, Tvardovskiy. You have a child who needs you and a wife who loves you. My own wife was killed in August 1917, and my three-year-old son Vitya was beaten to death in April 1918."

"I'm very sorry to hear that." Aleksey steals a glance at the open photo album on his desk. "Is that a picture of you with some of the Imperial Family?"

Mr. Golitsyn shuts the album. "I'm a prince," he whispers. "Don't tell anyone my secret. Those godless Reds might try to kill me if they knew a deposed noble is walking around freely. Now be off with you, with God's blessing, and come home in one piece."

Aleksey heads toward Strastnaya Square, remembering it's one of the busiest areas of the city. He enjoys the feeling of freedom as he browses the various kiosks and stores.

"What are you looking to buy, Comrade?" a florist asks.

"What should I get my wife for our second anniversary?"

"Flowers, of course. I have them at very good prices. If you don't have rubles, I accept jewels, precious metals, food, clothes, and carvings. Whatever you have to pay with."

"Buy her chocolates," the next vendor shouts. "I bet she hasn't tasted chocolate in a long time."

Aleksey smiles. "I know. I'll buy her a wedding ring. We couldn't afford rings, and could barely afford a real ceremony."

"Jewelry's expensive, Comrade. Do you have several million rubles or a thousand pounds of gold or rubies?"

"Afraid not. I'll keep trying." Aleksey has no idea exactly how much money Mr. Golitsyn gave him, but doesn't want to count it in public or admit he's got more money than the average person. That might raise questions about exactly where he got it from, after he said he couldn't afford wedding rings.

"Here, take mine," an old man says. "My wife and I need all the money we can get to go to America."

"That's a very generous offer, but I could never take someone else's wedding rings. Those are symbols of your love, and it'd feel wrong to take them."

"Are you up to waiting hours in line at any store?" the woman selling chocolate inquires. "I don't think there are that many jewelry stores still in business. The people have more pressing priorities these days than acquiring jewelry."

A young woman wrapped head to toe in thick blankets is slouched against the brick wall of a bakery. "Would you like some service, Comrade?"

"Not if it's prostitution. I'm looking for a gift to give my wife on our second anniversary."

A man coming up the street taps him on the shoulder. "I happened to overhear your conversation. I'm a jeweler, and I'm on my way back to work after my lunch break. Follow me. It'll be a bit of a wait, but we'll be glad to give you what you want."

Aleksey takes his place at the back of a fairly long line. His legs and feet are aching by the time he finally hears the words "Next?" and finds himself at the head of the line. It's been three years since he used the famous legs of iron many Orthodox faithful boast of, developed from standing so long during services.

"Yes, I'd like a pair of wedding rings. Nothing fancy, just plain gold bands. I want them engraved with our initials, E.M.K. and A.V.T., and our wedding date, 3 April 1918. Today makes it two years."

"That'll be five million rubles, Comrade. I'll call you when they're ready."

Aleksey takes a seat in the lobby and begins reading a magazine. The propaganda annoys him, but it's the only reading material available. Half-heartedly he wonders what would happen to him if any of these people he's seen and spoken with today knew he lives at a boardinghouse run by a deposed prince.

"Comrade, wake up! Your rings have been done for an hour!"

Aleksey jumps up and drops the magazine. "Here's your money. May I have a box for them?"

"Certainly. Don't lose this. I know she'll give you Hell if you forget your anniversary!"

Aleksey gets home at 11:00 and first gives Mr. Golitsyn back his leftover money, marveling at how much is still left.

"I was worried sick about you!" Eliisabet runs to him and hugs him, tears rolling down her face. "Where have you been? Did you see Petya about what you wanted to get?"

Aleksey extends the box.

"What is it?"

"Happy second anniversary, Liza."

"Is it our anniversary?"

"I thought you'd give me Hell if you found I'd forgotten!"

"I was the one who forget, Alyosha. What's in this box?"

"Open it."

Eliisabet opens it. "Golden rings."

"Wedding rings. I had them engraved with our initials and wedding date."

"We can't afford these. I don't want to know how you convinced a jeweler to make these, or what kind of payment plan you agreed to."

"I got the money from Mr. Golitsyn. I gave him back the money I didn't spend."

"You took money from the manager?"

"It was for a good cause, and he gave his blessing. Now why don't you put the ring on?"

"Do it for me," Eliisabet whispers. "I'll put yours on for you." She puts the box on the nightstand. "I'll always remember our second anniversary now."

3

Lyuba's party sets out from Mr. Andropov's boardinghouse on 5 April, heading right back into Khimki Forest. After so long of living indoors, Ginny is indignant to once more have to live in the woods, sleep on the ground, and wash in the Skhodnya River.

"Did we really have to go back into these damned woods? Even when I was living on the streets, I never lived in the woods."

"We'll be in a house again soon," Lyuba promises emptily.

"It's nearing sundown," Ivan says. "I'm going to chop firewood." He slings the axe over his shoulder and heads off.

Ginny's ears perk up. "I hear footsteps. We'd better take off. I don't want more trouble with the Godunovs."

"You told us that yesterday too," Lyuba scoffs. "It was just your overactive imagination."

"I really think I hear footsteps! I'll be taking my bath in the river. If you're smart, you'll get out of here until we know the coast is clear." Ginny runs off and climbs down the riverbank.

As she's listening to her cousin splashing about during his makeshift bath, Lyuba freezes. Now she hears footsteps too, and she's all alone but for Tatyana. She jerks her head up when she sees whom the footsteps belong to.

"Hello, Lyuba. I nearly had a nervous breakdown looking for you!"

"How did you escape from the loonybin?" She backs away from Basil and pulls her arms around herself.

"By the brute force of a desperate man in love, I slipped out of my chains!"

"You don't love me. You're sick in the head. Don't you dare go after me again."

"How could I? Tvardovskiy castrated me!"

Lyuba scoops up Tatyana and runs until she hears the sound of an axe chopping wood through the blood rushing and pounding in her ears. She prays she doesn't trip on anything in the gathering twilight.

"Did you miss me?"

Lyuba points, her throat too dry to speak.

Ivan advances towards him with the axe. "What the hell are you doing out of the loonybin! I'm warning you right now, Beriya, I'll kill you if you so much as touch a hair on my Lyubochka's head or go anywhere near our baby. You're damn lucky I didn't murder you after you raped her."

Basil gives Lyuba his usual creepy leer before turning on his heel and walking away. Her skin crawls as she huddles close to Ivan.

"I know that *dryan* too well. That's not the last we'll see of him. He's stupid if he thinks we believe he's leaving us alone forever." Ivan drops the axe and takes Tatyana from Lyuba. "Isn't that right, *knyazhna*? Your *papashka* will snap that awful creature in half if he dares come back."

Ginny ascends the riverbank. "Did I just hear Basil?"

Lyuba nods. "If he has any mental capacity, he'll know to stay away for good."

During the night, Lyuba has the strangest feeling Basil is lying right beside her. Thinking it a nightmare, she turns over, but the feeling is so strong, she can't distinguish dream from waking state. In her dream, it's 1917, and the Reds have found them on the street where they once lived. Lyuba can't understand anything the

Bolsheviks are screaming at them. With a nightmarish feeling, she realizes she's forgotten her mother tongue. She jerks awake at seven in the morning and sees Basil standing before her, a sick smile on his face.

"Have you been here all night?" she asks in English. Once again blood pounds and rushes in her ears, amid a wave of nausea.

Ivan jolts awake and leaps up. "What the hell are you doing here, Beriya!"

"Having fun with Lyuba, of course. I cast one of the magic spells I learnt back in Georgia."

"Lyuba, did he rape you?"

"I can't understand you, Vanya."

"Why are you talking to me in English?"

"Why are you talking to me in Russian?"

"I'll try my best to speak English to you until Basil's little voodoo spell or whatever the hell he did wears off." He speaks slowly, so he won't make mistakes with his heavy accent and fairly limited English. "What did Basil do to you?"

"I could've sworn he raped me repeatedly while I slept."

"Do not talk so fast."

"I dreamt they found us the day we left home, and I couldn't understand what the Bolsheviks were saying, because I've forgotten our language!"

"I am going to kill Basil."

"No, Vanya. We can forget Basil ever existed and flee Moskva. I don't want you to be a killer. You're too gentle to kill someone."

"Not if that someone is Basil Yakovlevich Beriya!"

"You don't *mean* that, Konev." Basil starts to run away, but Ivan grabs him by his throat. "Let go of me. I can't breathe!"

"You won't breathe anyway once I kill you!"

"They'll arrest you, take you to prison, and kill you!" Lyuba shouts. "I need you to protect me!"

While Basil is still purple in his face and gasping for air so frantically he's starting to scare himself to death, Ivan grabs the axe and slams the blade over Basil's head. Blood oozes out.

"How will you hide the blood?"

Basil screams as the axe hits his head again. "Stop that, Konev! I want to go back to school in Tbilisi and get away from you! I'll take Lyuba with me!"

Brain matter starts sliding out. Lyuba is getting sick to her stomach, and Ginny shuts his eyes. Tatyana is screaming at all the commotion and the fact that her mother won't hold her like she always does when she cries.

"*Pozhaluysta*, Konev. I'm begging you. I'm desperate. I won't go after Lyuba again. I've learnt my lesson. I'm sorry! I'll go back to the Marx Center for the Crazies! Don't kill me! My mother will be so sad! Even if you hate me, I'm someone's son, brother, cousin, nephew, and grandson! I'm begging! Let me live! I'm only twenty-two! I haven't lived yet! I'll get treatment, marry the girl my mother picked for me when I was eighteen, and live out the rest of my life being obedient to Lenin. I swear I'll never go after Lyuba again! I'm begging you! Don't kill me! *Pozhaluysta*!" Basil is crying hysterically. "I don't want to go so young! I'm afraid of Death! *Pozhaluysta, pozhaluysta, pozhaluysta*! I love life! I haven't lived yet! Spare me, Konev! *Pozhaluysta*! You'll never ever hear from me again! *Pozhaluysta*!"

And then Basil screams no more, as Ivan delivers the final blow. Brain matter oozes out. Ivan grabs his hand and checks for a pulse. There is none, nor does any breath come from his mouth anymore. Basil Yakovlevich Beriya is dead.

"You killed him!" Lyuba screams in Russian.

"Thank God you can speak our language again." Ivan starts digging earth to make a grave for Basil. "I'll bury him deep in the earth of our homeland, so no body is ever found. You're safe now, Lyuba. He's gone."

"You killed a man! Now you're damned by God. You're going to Hell! You disobeyed a Commandment, went against all which is good and right in the world, and took someone else's life in your own hands! How could you have played God?!"

"Do you still love me?"

"I'm shocked by my answer, but I still love none other than you!"

"Help me, Lyuba. Wipe the blood off the ground with his shirt."

Ginny jumps when he hears a little noise. "Did anyone else hear rustling?"

"It's just your imagination," Ivan says as he pushes the shovel deeper into the ground. "At least the earth's no longer frozen."

Lyuba turns her head and vomits when Ivan rolls the mangled

corpse into the deep pit and tears off Basil's pants to wipe up the remaining blood. While he's cleaning up, Ivan notices what's missing from Basil's anatomy.

"That was recent," Lyuba says when she notices him staring. "Last night he said Alyosha castrated him. I never knew eunuchs could do that."

"Eunuch or not, he'll never do that to you again." He begins pushing the dirt back into the pit.

"We need to get out of here as soon as possible," Ginny says as he looks around for spies. "We should try to find an inn, not live like hobos in the woods forever."

"I killed a man." Ivan starts crying. "But I had no choice. I'm going to Hell. I can't be with you when we die. I'm a sinner. I have to confess to a priest."

"Over time, I'll forgive you." Lyuba spreads the earth around to make it look as though it's an ordinary piece of ground. "And I still love you."

4

In late April, a policeman carrying a club enters their latest encampment. Lyuba grabs Ivan's hand and begins shaking.

"Are you Ivan Ivanovich Konev, date of birth July fifth, 1898?"

"Why?" Ivan asks suspiciously.

"Answer him, Vanya," Lyuba whispers.

"Yes, I am. Why ask, Officer?"

"About two weeks ago, Yelena Liparitovna Beriya went to visit her oldest son, Basil Yakovlevich, and was told he'd gone missing. Several days later, the local police visited her. They'd gotten word from Aleksandr Sergeyevich Shepilov that you murdered her son. You're under arrest."

"Arrest me too," Lyuba says. "I refuse to let you take him from me."

"Then follow me. Let's go, enemies of the people."

"Take good care of yourself," Lyuba whispers to Ginny before she shifts Tatyana to her other hip and takes Ivan's arm.

Ginny, in a daze, climbs onto Branimir and heads for the only house that won't turn him away.

***

"Grigoriy! What a surprise!" Georgiya squeals when she sees

her visitor riding across the expansive lawn.

Ginny dismounts Branimir and runs to the front door, dropping to a whisper. "Lyuba and Ivan were just arrested. Can I stay here until they get out?"

"Arrested? What for?"

"It wasn't a political crime, I can tell you that much. The person Ivan did it to deserved it so much."

Georgiya looks around. "Sure, come in. You're always welcome here. My, that's a beautiful horse you've got. You're so lucky you've still got a horse. I think the authorities look the other way at my family having so many horses because we're so important, and there'd be trouble if we were forced to give them up to the Red Army or to feed the masses. I love riding. Why don't we go riding right now?" Georgiya runs inside. "*Papashka*! Grigoriy's here for a long visit!"

Mr. Savvin comes down the hall smiling. "What a surprise. Come into the kitchen and have some cookies. I'll get a servant to bring in your luggage."

Ginny follows Georgiya into the kitchen and practically inhales the luxurious scents pervading every last molecule of the air. He can't remember the last time he had so much wonderful food, and doesn't think to question this devout Communist family matter-of-factly maintaining servants, living in an ancestral estate, and having so much money and food while the common people struggle to survive.

"That's our new cook, Miss Goldmann," Georgiya says as she reaches for a thick honey cookie. "Our old cook, Miss Guseva, was an enemy of the people who dared to still go to church."

"What kind of name is Goldmann?"

"She's Jewish. Haven't you ever heard a Jewish surname before? Most of them don't follow Russian forms."

Ginny stuffs his face on cookies, until the overflowing platter is finally gone, and then follows Georgiya to the stables. A host of Orlov Trotters and Russian Dons are feasting on apples, hay, carrots, and grass, while Mr. Savvin walks among them and scratches their ears and necks.

"This is my new saddle," Georgiya announces. "I told my *papashka* I really wanted blue velvet, so he got it for me."

Ginny gapes as Mr. Savvin boosts Georgiya onto her horse non-sidesaddle. "It's awfully wicked for a woman to ride like a man. It leads to impure thoughts."

"Welcome to the Twenties, Comrade Kharzin." Mr. Savvin laughs. "Russia is changing for the better, like it or not."

5

Lyuba holds onto Ivan's arm as they walk down the dreary Lubyanka entrance hall, glad they've been unhandcuffed. For Tatyana's sake, she tries to hold in any outward signs of terror or nervousness as they pass cells on either side and hear people being tortured.

"There's your holding cell. Once you're formally sentenced and have confessed, you'll move to a different cell."

"Now that we're in prison, I want to see a priest," Ivan says. "Now."

"Get in your cell first. I'll bring one by later if you're lucky. Wait your turn, enemy of the people."

"A lady in our cell?" one of the prisoners gapes. "I'm so lucky."

"Too bad for you, she's mine." Ivan pushes him off the bench to sit down.

"What are you in here for?"

"I killed a man."

"Wow. At least you have a reason. Me, I wrapped up some food for a customer in a newspaper with Lenin's picture. It was an honest accident!"

"Liar," the officer sneers. "You enemies of the people have plotted against us for years!"

"When are we going to eat?" Lyuba asks.

"When we feel like it."

"Can I have some food to give my little girl?"

"She's just an ordinary prisoner too. I don't care if she starves to death. You're damn stupid for bringing your child along, but there's nothing we can do about it now."

Ivan reads *Izvestiya* while waiting for the priest. The prisoner who's finally led in several hours later looks nothing like the priests he remembers, but the guard insists this is a real priest.

"What do you want, my son?"

"I have a sin to confess."

The priest looks around. "Step this way. There's no privacy here, but that corner is empty. Obviously, you won't be able to venerate the Gospel and cross, and I won't be able to cover your head with a stole when we're done."

Ivan crosses himself after he kneels in the corner. "I haven't confessed since January 1917 Old Style—I think it's February 1917 New Style. I have sinned and damned myself to Hell."

"Did you commit adultery?"

"No, she isn't my wife, and I'd never be unfaithful to her, married or not."

"Did you have a child out of wedlock?"

"No, that's not my blood child. I killed a man. He went after her repeatedly, and I warned him, but he raped her again. I had no choice. I've stained my soul with blood. I'm a bad man. I'm going to Hell."

"Is the lady your fiancée?"

"Not yet, but I love her like nothing else. If you're wondering, the child was conceived under duress. My sweetheart's not a slut."

"Only criminal murder is forbidden by the Bible. You're allowed to kill in warfare, as punishment for a serious crime, in self-defense, and when someone breaks into your home at night. God understands you did it to protect your lady and that it wasn't cold-blooded. Think of all the moral men who killed our enemies in the war. I doubt they're going to Hell because they had to kill as part of their military duties. It's the intent that matters."

The next room over, an interrogation is going on. Ivan hears a woman screaming and sobbing. The names Nureyev, Sergeyev, and Lebedeva are being shouted all over the room. Nureyev and Sergeyev appear to be the interrogators.

"What's going on in there?"

"That young woman arrived an hour ago. They're forcing her to confess to God knows what."

Shortly after the priest recites the prayer of absolution, Nureyev and Sergeyev shove the woman into the cell. Her red-brown hair is matted with blood. Though all the light seems to have gone out of her green eyes, she nevertheless becomes somewhat animated when she sees Lyuba, the only other woman in the cell.

"You have a pretty daughter," she says softly. "I'm Alla Ilyinichna Lebedeva. You don't look much older than I am. I'm nineteen." She rubs one of the bruises on her face. "My parents never spanked me or my nine sisters growing up. It's a rude awakening to grow up surrounded by so much love and then get into the hands of cruel people who don't care you can feel pain. I still have nightmares about my two youngest sisters Natasha and Dora being brutally beaten after we arrived at an orphanage with my other little sister Vera."

Lyuba puts her arm around Alla. "My boyfriend was beaten by his father all the time growing up, and I was constantly beaten by the blood father of my darling child when I was pregnant." She gasps. "Did you just say your name is Alla Ilyinichna Lebedeva?"

"Have we met?"

"I know your cousin Nadya! I stayed with her over the winter, and she told me stories about her family. It can't be a coincidence you share the same surname and that her *Dyadya* Ilyushka had ten daughters, the youngest four of whom had the same names as you and your sisters. She believes you're all dead."

"Right now I feel more alive than dead, but for whatever reason, I'm still briefly alive. They're trying to charge me with having three illegitimate children and giving them away, yet I don't see that rapist Yatsenko, my paper husband, among these prisoners. Men get away with everything in this world, and women are punished for daring to not be Madonnas every single second of their lives. I thought the Bolsheviks were supposed to be so modern and desperate to move Russia into the twentieth century."

***

Stale black bread, burnt sausage, and watery borshcht come around at eight at night. Tatyana starts whining at the sight of the food.

"Eat this, *knyazhna*. It's our only food since we got arrested," Ivan says. "Your mother and I are eating it, and you're old enough to eat substantial food instead of only mother's milk."

Tatyana starts to cry into her borshcht.

"No crying," the guard growls.

"That's Gruzin, Sergey Osipovich," Alla says. "He's very sadistic."

"Why is there a small child in the prison cell? Why wasn't she taken to an orphanage?"

Lyuba clutches Tatyana. "Don't take my baby."

"Don't you dare take my child to an orphanage," Ivan growls. "If you take her from us, we'll never see her again."

"The child must go into protective custody at once." Gruzin opens the cell door and wrests her out of Lyuba's arms. "If you're lucky, we won't kill her."

"Goodbye, my little *knyazhna*." Ivan takes the orange bow out of her hair. "I won't let you steal this from her."

Lyuba turns away to avoid looking at her screaming child in the jailer's arms. Perhaps it was impulsive and foolish to insist on going with Ivan, but she doesn't regret going with the man she loves, the same way Boris's mother insisted on going with her husband.

After everyone has eaten, Gruzin collects the dishes and bowls and throws them into a box. Lyuba barely has any appetite, and is barely able to keep down what little she's eaten. She can't get the image of her precious only child out of her head, and starts sobbing at the thought of Tatyana being abused by orphanage wardens or adoptive parents. Her stomach is in knots at the thought of Tatyana falling into the hands of a degenerate like Mr. Zhukov.

When bedtime is called, Gruzin brings around blankets.

"It's cold in here. May I have another blanket?" Lyuba asks.

"No. You have what you're given. No hands inside the blankets. We get up at six on the dot. Goodnight, enemies of the people."

"You and Tatyana could've gone with Ginny," Ivan says. "Why did you choose to be arrested with me?"

"So we could still be together. And, I suppose, we'll be here for many, many years."

"You're lucky we let two ladies into the cell," Gruzin snarls. "Don't expect to have female company once you're sentenced and moved to a real cell."

***

They're awoken at six the next morning. Breakfast is stale bread and tea.

"I like sugar in my tea," Alla says. "This is too bitter. Do you at least have honey?"

"You're not getting sugar in your tea, you shameful whore!"

Gruzin snarls.

They eat stale black bread and oatmeal with wine at noon. Then, at five, they're called into the courtyard to walk around a bit.

"How long am I in here for?" Ivan asks the guard.

"How the hell should I know? You haven't been sentenced yet."

"Then I'll be in here indefinitely too!" Lyuba declares.

"You only came because you insisted on following your lover. They'll probably let you go in a week or two, since you haven't done anything wrong."

***

The next day, Gruzin comes up with Tatyana and shoves her at Lyuba, who bursts into tears and greedily clutches her baby.

"What made you change your mind?" she asks as she cuddles and kisses Tatyana.

"We're letting you go. You did nothing. But if anyone ever finds out..."

"Is it legal?" Alla asks, looking up from her overcooked porridge.

"I don't know myself, shameful whore."

"I have a name, Comrade Gruzin. I'm Alla Lebedeva."

"We're all comrades now, shameful whore."

"I want to leave too. My only crime was being raped by a monster thrice and bearing children each time. If that act is so illegal, that excuse for a man should be here too, with an even harsher sentence. I was an innocent young girl, and he was an adult who couldn't keep his worthless *khuy* in his pants."

"Try to sneak out and I smash your head in with a rock!"

Alla goes back to her porridge.

"You—Comrade Konev. Get in that line. They're going to read your sentence to you. Time to leave, Comrade Zhukova!"

"Goodbye," Alla says. "You're very nice people. Most of my cellmates have been mean and cruel."

"I will not leave," Lyuba says. "Either allow him to leave too or I'll stay right here."

"I said go. I meant it." Gruzin grabs her arm.

"I bet Ginny went to Georgiya's house," Ivan says. "Go there and get him right away. Take care of yourself." He makes the sign of the cross over Lyuba. "*Ya tyebya lyublyu.*"

"Goodbye!" Alla says.

Once Lyuba and Tatyana are out on the street, Gruzin walks back to his prisoners.

"We're going to Georgiya Savvina's house," Lyuba tells Tatyana. "You never met her, but she's a very brave young girl who saved our lives when you were only a few days old."

Since she doesn't know Georgiya's address, she asks the nearest person for directions. Georgiya is too young to be well-known, so she says she's looking for Leonid Yuriyevich Savvin's house. Leonid is actively involved in local politics. The stranger, recognizing Leonid's name, draws her a map.

"*Spasibo*, Comrade," she says. The word "Comrade" sticks on her tongue.

The estate looms before her at seven in the evening, after walking around quite awhile in search of it. The Savvin estate is technically outside city limits, on the outskirts of Moskva, not in the heart of the city. Though Lyuba has lived here for twelve years, she hasn't freely walked around in three years, and it's such a large city.

"Yuriy Ignatiyevich Savvin?"

"Yes, that's right. Who are you?"

"I'm Ginny's cousin. I've come to pick him up."

"Step inside, Comrade Zhukova. Grigoriy is playing chess with Zhora and Lyonya."

"Lyuba!" Ginny cries when she steps into the parlor. "Did you escape from prison?"

"They let me go. You were wise to come here."

"Where's Ivan?"

"He's still in prison, but I hope he'll join us soon."

"What prison?" Leonid asks.

"They were in Lubyanka," Ginny says.

"So your cousin is an enemy of the people!"

"No! Ivan went to prison because he killed a man, and she went with him."

"Good. If anything else had been the case, I wouldn't have let you into my house!" Mr. Savvin laughs.

"*Papashka* laughs a lot," Georgiya says. "He's always happy, especially now that we're winning the Civil War."

"I must insist you stay the night. It isn't safe for a woman with two children to travel at night."

"You've been very kind, to have housed Ginny so many times," Lyuba says. "I'll never forget how much you've helped him."

"My wife will show you to a spare bedroom. I hope the bed will be to your liking."

"You look hungry," Georgiya says. "*Pozhaluysta*, have some left-over potato soup."

"Yes, Tatyana and I are very hungry. *Bolshoye spasibo*." Lyuba smiles at Georgiya and follows her into the kitchen.

"Your little girl is quite a beauty," Georgiya says as Miss Goldmann heats up the leftover soup. "How old is she?"

"Fifteen months. Before I knew it, she was using simple words and walking!" Lyuba snuggles against Tatyana's face.

"Take good care of her. My *papashka* says children are the future of the Soviet State. As Comrade Lenin says, 'Give me a child for eight years, and he will be a Bolshevik forever.' That's why it's wrong to have an abortion, because you'd be killing our future. You must also never commit suicide while you're pregnant, either. Our Leader encourages large families. My *papashka* only has me and Leonid to be his future."

"You're a regular rulebook, aren't you?" Lyuba tries to laugh.

"Oh, yes, Comrade Zhukova. At school I learn everything Our Leader, Marx, and Engels have ever written. I'm still top pupil, and in the eighth grade. I was skipped to eighth from seventh because I know my lessons so well. If I didn't know my lessons so well, I'd be ignorant and almost as good as an enemy of the people!"

"Russian education today must be so different from when I was in school."

"It certainly is. I'm sorry you were expelled from gymnasium just because you were born into the wrong kind of family. I trust you know better now. You'd love what Aleksandrovskiy Gymnasium has become. We even get to sing and dance! The songs are all in honor of Comrade Lenin, and we dance around a huge statue of him. Leonid helped to make the statue my class uses. There are also pictures, busts, and paintings of him like crazy. I love him like my own father. He's like my own father. I want to scream the name of Vladimir Ilyich Lenin to the heavens, jump into his lap, and hug and kiss him. I could never feel such love for another. He's our savior. I can't imagine what it'd be like were Bloody Nikolay still in charge, can you?" She checks Lyuba's face. "Don't you also love Comrade Lenin more than your own father?"

"Yes." Lyuba can answer that honestly and immediately. "Why don't you put your new education to good use and tell this last-generation woman what constitutes being an enemy of the people?"

"Why, plotting against Comrade Lenin in all sorts of sly and underhanded ways, of course. Some woman tried to kill him two years ago. I was glad when they killed the traitor. I love none other more than Comrade Lenin. He must be the kindest man in the world. He must be the kindest human being in the world, too. He'd never hurt anybody. His heart is full of love for everyone, except for enemies of the people. He's like a little *dedushka,* looking out for everyone with love in his heart. I want to run to him and hug him until I've nearly squeezed him to death! I never loved Bloody Nikolay. He was the greatest enemy of them all, let me tell you! I was overjoyed the day he was executed, and rightly so!"

"Food is ready," Miss Goldmann says.

Lyuba looks at her strangely. "Russian isn't your first language, is it?"

"No, Miss Goldmann speaks Yiddish," Georgiya says. "I also wondered about the accent at first. I thought it was German, until she set us straight."

Lyuba and Tatyana eat the potato soup while Georgiya sings a song praising Lenin. On the kitchen wall, where a photo of the Tsar once hung, is now a picture of Lenin. A picture of Trotskiy hangs next to it.

"Here's your bed," Georgiya says after she leads Lyuba to a spare bedroom. "Our old cook Miss Guseva used to sleep here. It's a feather mattress. To celebrate the death of Bloody Nikolay, my *papashka* ripped apart all the mattresses and burnt the cornhusks. My mother sent our maid, Miss Primakova, to buy many pounds of feathers. Now we all have feather beds!"

"No picture of Our Leader on the wall?" Lyuba asks.

"Miss Guseva really was an enemy of the people, wasn't she? I'll get a spare from my drawer." Georgiya runs back in an instant. "Right where he belongs, watching over his loyal servants the Russian people."

Lyuba falls asleep holding Tatyana, while rain pounds on the roof and Comrade Lenin watches over them "like a little *dedushka*." If Ivan were released from prison, they could get married, join the Party, buy a nice house in Moskva, and all would be safe again. They wouldn't be forever fleeing from the Reds...

"Wake up!" Ginny shouts at eight the next morning. "Zhora has a lovely house, but I think we should try to find that safe house you found the address for last year. To prevent people from finding out his address, I ate it after you were arrested. But I memorized the route. I think it's good luck his name is Lebedev. Even if he's no relation to Nadya, it's a good sign."

Lyuba dresses herself and Tatyana, then goes down to breakfast. Several servants transport their luggage into the cart, and Ginny leads Branimir out from the stable.

"Goodbye, Yuriy Ignatiyevich. *Spasibo* for your kindness." She shakes Mr. Savvin's hand before mounting Branimir. "With any luck, my Vanya will soon be with me again."

6

Alla's sentence has been read to her, and she has twelve years in prison to look forward to. She's been moved to a cell with an older woman looking at a picture hidden under her coat.

"Is that you and a sister? I wish I had one of mine now. I have nine."

"I have one, but this isn't a picture of us a long time ago. They're my two little girls, Misha and Karla. Misha's six and Karla's two. I miss my babies."

"Misha's a girl?"

"Her full name's Mikhaila. I know it's a very unusual name in our language, but my husband really wanted his brother Mikhail to have a namesake."

"Sofya Mitrofanovna, I said no talking to the new inmate," the guard growls.

"My Misha's beautiful and my Karla's kind. They were with my niece Naina and my best friend's daughter Katya when they were taken away. Misha had a way of saying the wrong things at the wrong times. I worry about her."

"Cell check." A warden walks in to take the guard's place for the night. "Alla Ilyinichna Lebedeva, age nineteen, twelve-year sentence, confessed to being a whore with three abandoned bastards."

"Yes, that's me."

"Sofya Mitrofanovna Gorbachëva, birth name Bulgakova, age thirty, twenty-year sentence, confessed to being an agent of the Whites."

"Yes, that's right."

"Filippa Yakovlevna Aleksandrova, age fifty, thirteen-year sentence, confessed to aiding the Germans."

"Yes," the older woman the next cell over says.

"I confessed to anything after they beat me senseless," Sonya says. "Are you really a whore?"

"No, but the part about the three bastards I gave to homes is correct. Just because I'm not a virgin doesn't mean I'm a whore. When something is done to a woman against her will, she's as innocent as a holy martyr."

7

As dark approaches, Misha and Kostya walk up to Lyuba and Ginny. Lyuba gulps and holds onto Branimir's neck tightly, desperately wishing Ivan were there to protect her.

"Where's her father?" Misha asks, pointing to Tatyana. "I mean Malenkov, her real father, not Konev, the pretend father. Although I'm also curious where Konev is."

"Boris left," Lyuba says vaguely. "Ivan is in the city."

"Where's Malenkov now?"

"I don't know."

"Tell me where he is right now or I'll break the neck of that brat!"

Lyuba's eyes widen and her heart begins beating wildly. "If he told me the truth in his goodbye note, he's probably on a ship right now."

"Where might this ship be going?"

"I think he went back to America."

"So a double-traitor is the father of your bastard!" Misha sidles up closer to her. "Those clothes can't be warm enough in this weather."

"I manage. Spring is here, and it'll get warmer very soon."

"What are you doing about food?"

"The forest is always full of food to forage."

"When was the last time you ate real meat?"

"I don't need meat to survive. I've learnt to subsist on very basic food."

"So you must be starving."

"We manage without meat. Many other people are also doing without meat, since food shortages affect everyone." Lyuba hopes Misha can't see how she's shaking.

"Would you like meat and candy for your cousin? Maybe you're stupid enough to accept a starvation diet, but a boy that age deserves real food."

"My cousin eats what I eat and no longer complains."

"Then would you like some water?"

"We get it from the river."

Misha shoves Ginny out of the cart and picks up Tatyana. "Look how skinny this brat is. Would you like some food for her? It's your right to be stupid and eat roots, leaves, and berries, but I thought you cared about this brat. I have medicine, in case she gets sick." He holds Tatyana over a rock. "What would you prefer, me smashing your illegitimate child's head over a rock or letting me enjoy your luscious body in exchange for food and medicine for her? You've obviously already had relations, so it's not like you're an ignorant virgin who thinks it's immoral to do that outside marriage."

Lyuba leaps off Branimir and runs towards Misha. "You win, you big bully. But this is only for my little girl. Let's go."

Misha lends her his arm and leads her behind a bush. Lyuba wants to vomit as they lie down and Misha does what he wants to her. She closes her eyes and digs her hands into the ground, praying it'll be over soon. At least he's not making it personal by kissing or caressing her. As soon as he finishes up, he pulls his pants back on and stands up. Before he leaves, he tosses her a bag of hard-boiled eggs and bread.

"Here's your food, baby." Lyuba peels one of the eggs. "Eat it all, my precious little Tanyechka."

Without Ivan, Lyuba has lost her self-respect. He's the only person who's ever respected her fully and completely. The next night, she gives herself to Kostya for sausages; on all the nights following, for several weeks, she'll give herself to any of their friends for meat, blankets, fish, or fruit. She's become as good as a whore by the time they see a small house standing in the distance in mid-June, at the address Ginny memorized, a short walk from the fairly new Novodevichye Cemetery.

"Is anybody home?" Ginny asks, knocking on the door. "Is this smallpox quarantine sign on the level, or a ruse to evade authorities?"

"Wait a minute!" a male voice screams. "I'm in the bathtub!"

Ginny barges in a minute later. The man hasn't finished buttoning his shirt, revealing a big purple scar across his chest. He has one blue eye and one brown eye, and his hair is brown with copper highlights. Lyuba has never seen anyone with two different-colored eyes before, and shies away from looking directly at him.

"Had you come in any earlier, I would've been indecent!" He continues buttoning his shirt, his hands shaking. "Thank God I always put my trousers on before my shirt, or I'd never be able to look that woman in the face!"

"Where did that scar come from?" Ginny asks.

"Never seen a man who was nearly beaten dead? Are you spies?"

"Are you Ilya Petrovich Lebedev?"

"No, my patronymic is Nikolayevich. Why?"

"But do we have your first and last names correct? My cousin found a message someone in the underground wrote, providing your address as a safe house for Whites."

"Yes, I've sheltered Whites several times before, and yes, you do have my other two names correct. Close the door, people might see us and kill me! I escaped from prison and amn't about to get thrown back in. My niece Nadya left a letter, explaining she put up that phony smallpox quarantine sign to protect our house, but one can never be too careful."

Lyuba shuts the door and steps inside, trembling. This man's bitterness and anger belie his kind face. His introductory behavior doesn't bode well at all for even a short-term stay.

"Are you by any chance the same Ilya Lebedev who had ten daughters and a niece named Nadya? And are you from Pskov?"

He grunts. "'Had' is the operative word there. Even if my daughters are still alive, I'll never see them again in this lifetime.

My family moved from Pskov a long time ago, before I dreamt my beautiful wife and ten daughters would be taken away from me like they never mattered. Don't step on my little dog!"

Lyuba looks down and for the first time notices a golden ball of fluff with a very happy face. "Cute dog."

"She belonged to my Svetlana. Don't touch her!" Mr. Lebedev points upstairs. "Pay me in the morning, either rubles or goods. It's late."

"I have no money."

"Then out you all go! I don't put my hide on the line for free when I'm an escaped convict!"

"No!" Ginny yells. "Why do you yell so much?"

"If you'd seen your wife killed in front of you and your ten children all taken away, wouldn't you be a bit angry too?!"

Lyuba leads Ginny upstairs. She cannot believe Nadezhda's uncle is so mean. It's obvious this is one and the same as Alla's father and Nadezhda's uncle, though his curt, rage-filled behavior doesn't match at all with their descriptions of him as a loving, kind, gentle person who loved his family.

"I like this bed," she says as she reads the name carved on the headboard. "This was Matryona's bed."

"I'll sleep in Fyodora and Natalya's bed," Ginny says.

"He may be mean, but at least he didn't turn us away." Lyuba goes downstairs. "*Spasibo* for your kindness, Ilya Nikolayevich!"

Mr. Lebedev growls and goes back to playing solitaire. "So what? Stay quiet or they'll arrest me! If they discover I've been a free man for this long, I might take a bullet in my brain this time, not just constant beatings."

"I like your dog. What's her name?"

"Svetlana named her Kroshka, because she was as tiny as a crumb." He picks her up and puts her on his lap. "She's twelve years old. You probably don't care unless you're interested in dogs, but she's a Pomeranian. I have no idea how she survived while the house was unoccupied, but God was good to me and gave me one loved one to return to. Perhaps kind neighbors fed her, or she found feral dogs. Do you play écarté?"

"I don't know cards."

"My seventh daughter Alla loved cards. Now go away and leave me to mourn for my family. All I have left now is this little dog."

"Nadya's alive and well. I know her. She lives and works in the city."

He crosses himself. "Why didn't you immediately tell me?"

"I wasn't sure if it was just a coincidence you share your name with her uncle, and that you're also from Pskov and had ten daughters. She says you pushed her into a closet to save her when you were arrested."

"Well, I can't do anything about reuniting with her now. If I leave this house, I'm a dead man. It's a special kind of torture to live so close to Chekhov's grave and not be able to regularly pay my respects as I used to. Would you like a drink?"

"No, I don't drink. My name's Lyubov Leontiyevna Zhukova, by the way. The boy's my cousin and the little girl's my daughter."

"Where's your husband?"

"I have none."

"Then how did you have a child?"

"That's none of your business. But speaking of illegitimate children, I met your daughter Alla when I was in prison."

"Really?" He pushes his cards away.

"They're charging her with abandoning three bastards. She says she was raped all three times, and that the father was a paper husband. Now that I think of it, I can't help but wonder if I met her husband a few years ago at a hotel. The particulars of their stories are so similar. She's very pretty."

"Naturally. My Zhenyushka and I never produced anything less than a beauty. I would've liked a son, but God must know better than I what sex I was meant to have. Perhaps I'm being punished for how I forced Allochka to marry that brute. I didn't have all the facts. All I cared about was lessening her shame, not knowing she was raped all three times. I thought I was doing my job as her loving father."

8

The roof over the cell is leaking. Alla and Sonya have put blankets over their heads, but to no great avail. Tonight's the night they've dreaded, and the leaking roof is eerily symbolic.

"Lebedeva, Alla Ilyinichna, and Gorbachëva, Sofya Mitrofanovna, collect your things. Ask no questions along the way."

"I'm cold," Alla says.

"I know you're taking them to be shot," a new inmate says.

"Liar," the warden sneers. "They're only going to a new cell."

As they're walking down a hall lined with thick carpets, Alla grabs a piece of bread from a tray and splits it into two.

"Why did you steal that bread? Wait right here while I go to see the head warden about this theft from the workers of the world."

Ivan has ended up in a cell with, of all people, Rudolf Godimov. Rudolf has gone half-insane since his arrest in 1917, and spends much of the day talking to himself.

"Alla Ilyinichna."

"Who's there?"

"Don't you remember me? I don't look that much different with facial hair, do I? It's not like I've been in here long enough to look like a mountain man just yet."

"Konev. Yes, I remember you. Are you waiting to be shot also?"

"I'm starting to go insane in here!"

She leans against the cold metal bars. "How would you like to break out of here? While we're still alone, we can make a run for it. You, me, and Sonya."

Ivan stands up. "Are you crazy?"

Alla pulls a keyring out of her blouse. "Look what I stole when my jailer was drunk this morning." She starts going through the keys and unlocks the cell on the fifth try. "Coming or not, Konev?"

He looks back at Rudolf, rocking in a corner and blathering nonsense, then down the darkened hallways. Without wasting another moment, he puts his hand into Alla's.

"Thank God we're not on one of the higher floors," Alla says as they walk quickly and purposefully down the hall. "Just act naturally."

As they approach the exit door, several Cheka officers playing cards and drinking look up. Alla continues to walk straight ahead, not making eye contact, as though she's been sent on an errand and her presence here is nothing out of the ordinary.

"Who are you, and where are you going unattended?"

"We're going to the outhouse," Alla asserts. "Our jailer gave us permission and sent him as our escort, to make sure we came back on time."

"You think we were born yesterday? How did you manage to get so far without being sent back to your cells for such egregious behavior? If you're really going to the outhouse, you can turn around and go right back where you came from. You enemies of the people really are pampered, expecting to use an outhouse instead of the pail in your cell."

"It's now or never," Alla whispers as she breaks into a run.

Ivan wonders what he got himself into as he runs after her and Sonya. Over the pounding of his heart, he barely hears the thudding footsteps of the officers following them. He doesn't look back to see if they're drawing guns, though he has no doubt they are.

Alla makes it out the door first and begins running across Lubyanka Square, faster than he's ever seen a woman run. Sonya follows her, with Ivan not far behind. He's already lost sight of Alla as he and Sonya near the large fountain in the center of the square, across the street from a large shopping plaza. The next thing he's aware of, a gunshot rings out and Sonya crashes to the ground. Blood starts gushing from her upper right arm. Ivan's heart is in his throat as one of the officers comes up to them.

"Damn, I just missed. What a lousy shot. I say you should be the one to drag her back to the prison. We'll beat her until she's dead. If you make a false move, you're a dead man. You're damn lucky you're not already a dead man after that outrageous attempted escape." The jailer walks off.

Thinking only of preserving his life so he can be released and be together again with Lyuba, he bends down to pick up Sonya, struggling under her weight and fighting the urge to vomit at the sight of all the blood.

"I have two little girls! I don't want to die and leave them orphans!"

Ivan looks around furtively. "Maybe your life is more valuable than mine. If my Lyuba had been shot during an escape attempt, I'd want someone to take pity on her and help her." He pulls off part of his sleeve and tightly wraps it around the wound.

"You use that hand?"

"Yes, that's how God wanted to create me. Not all of us gave in to people trying to bully and shame us out of our natural inclination."

"God bless you. I'll never forget you." Sonya turns and runs.

The jailer reappears moments later, tapping a club against his hand. "I knew it. You were in on their escape from the start. We should've shot you all in the back instead of letting you run this far."

Ivan looks down at the jailer, holding back the urge to strangle him and take advantage of his height and physical strength. "She ran away too fast for me to catch up with her."

"Liar. Either you let her escape, or you weren't paying attention and let her get away. Come, back to your cell. You'll be shot in the morning."

He mutely follows the jailer back to his cell. His heart rings in his ears the entire walk back. The jailer raises his eyebrow at the sight of the opened door, with no evidence of sawed bars. Ivan holds his arms up and lets the jailer frisk him, feeling triumphant when no keys are discovered. As soon as he's inside and the door is shut, he pulls off his shirt, soaked with Sonya's blood, and divests Rudolf of his shirt. Rudolf is so out of it, he barely notices what Ivan is doing and doesn't protest. If he's going to die in the morning, at least he can spend his final night in a clean shirt.

While Ivan is waiting on the cold floor that night, waiting to go to Hell for killing Basil, he falls asleep and has a dream about his mother. She's standing in a field, holding out her arms to him. Her voice comes back to him without a minute's hesitation. When he wakes, he feels as though she's waiting for him outside. Deserting Rudolf to his lonely seventeen years in prison, Ivan stands up and tries the door. It instantly gives way, and he realizes the jailer must've been so distracted by his anger and humiliation he forgot to lock it. Taking this as a good omen, he walks quietly outside. A very peaceful feeling pervades his soul, and he feels no fear as he continues to walk, unnoticed and unmolested, out of the prison. Perhaps his mother is watching over her precious only child from the other side. Once in Lubyanka Square, he bumps into an older woman behind the fountain.

"Matushka?"

She bites her lip. "I have no living children. My only child died seven years ago. You have me mistaken for someone else, I'm afraid."

"I'm terribly sorry." He looks around just to make sure no one is coming out of the prison to apprehend him. "I thought you were my dear mother, Anna Afanasiyevna Koneva. You look so much like her, and I just had a beautiful dream about my mother and how she was waiting for me."

She looks at him closely. "My name is Valeriya Afanasiyevna Koneva. Anna was my sister. We married brothers, so our new names were the same."

He squints at her in the dark. "*Tyotya* Lera, it's you!" He bursts into tears. "I thought I was all alone in the world!"

She throws her arms around him. "You don't have to cry, Ivanok. I'm here now, and I'll take care of you as though you were my dear Lizochka. Thank God someone else from our family is still alive. I found you just in time. I'm fleeing for America while I still have a chance, and I'm sure there'll be a place for you on the ship too."

"I'd love to go to the land of freedom, but I can't go without Lyuba, Ginny, and Tatyana."

"Who are Ginny and Tatyana?"

"Ginny is Lyuba's cousin, and Tatyana's her baby."

"Your baby too, Ivanko?"

"Boris is the blood father. I know it's embarrassing, but I've never known a woman. It's more embarrassing for a man than a woman above a certain age to admit one's virginity. Society expects women to remain virginal and modest, but a man is expected to have experience."

"Don't worry about that. Good things come to those who wait." Valeriya smiles. "If you can get them and meet me at Nikolayevskiy Station before dawn, I'll take you. Do you know where they are?"

"No idea, but I'll find them. Trust me, I'll find them no matter how long I have to search. Lyuba's my twin soul, and I'd never dream of leaving that precious piece of my soul behind."

"I can't afford to wait that long. Every second is a matter of life or death, and I'm not taking any chances. I hope you understand this isn't personal. But I'm glad you won't go anywhere without Lyuba. I'd think less of you if you wanted to leave alone and fling her to the wolves." She laughs slightly. "You look different with facial hair. I hope you get rid of it as soon as you're in a safe place. You never had the type of face suited to a beard."

He nods, still blinking away tears. "I hope the next time I see you is in America, where we're all safe and sound. Have a safe journey."

"Don't you worry, my dear boy. You'll find your Lyuba and bring her to America with you eventually. When two people are meant to be together, they always find their way back to each other. I always believed you and the neighbor girl had a special pair bond and that God wanted you to be together." Valeriya hugs him again. "Goodbye. May God guard your coming and going and see you safely back to your sweet Lyuba's arms."

9

The next day, Lyuba decides to give Tatyana a bath.

"May I have some hot water to bathe my little girl, Ilya Nikolayevich?"

"Get your own."

"It's your house!"

Mr. Lebedev growls and fills a metal tub with water, then hoists it onto the wood-burning stove. As soon as steam starts rising, he sets it on the floor and pours cold water in. Then he goes back to playing solitaire and drinking vodka.

"May I have some vodka?" Ginny asks.

"Find your own black market contact and buy your own. I only have a limited amount of supplies in this house, with the occasional friend bringing necessities I've run out of. I'm not about to waste my precious vodka on a thirteen-year-old, particularly not when the entire alcohol industry is underground."

Ginny starts looking at the pictures in an opened trunk. "Are these your girls and your wife?"

"Leave my things alone!" Mr. Lebedev slams the trunk. "Go read one of my books on the shelf! I've got Chekhov, Tolstoy, Turgenev, Pushkin, Krylov, Gogol, Dostoyevskiy, Lermontov, the works!"

"Kroshka's a cute dog." Ginny starts petting her.

"Leave her alone! I only have this dog now!"

"Ilya Nikolayevich, stop yelling at my cousin!" Lyuba scolds.

Ginny spends the rest of the day playing with a set of checkers that belonged to Vera. Lyuba sits downstairs and reads Turgenev's

On the Eve.

"Want some vodka? Unlike Ginny, you're an adult."

"I told you, I don't drink. And the last time I drank vodka, it was because of a dirty trick of Ginny's, and I had a horrible reaction."

"Drinking makes you forget your misery, Lyubov Leontiyevna. Here, have the rest of my bottle. Don't drink too much the first time, though. After you learn how to hold your liquor and get used to the taste, you can slowly start drinking more. I'll teach you écarté, so we can spend the evening doing something besides dwelling on the past."

Lyuba drinks herself nearly drunk on Mr. Lebedev's vodka and plays écarté with him for hours. By the time she starts upstairs to put Tatyana to bed, she's so weighed down by drink she can barely walk. He watches her stumble up the steps, smelling of vodka.

The next day, Lyuba and Ginny write a letter to Pavel and Nadezhda.

"Ilya Nikolayevich, where's the post office?" Lyuba asks.

"Up the road."

"Will you take me there?"

"Whatever for? You can't get lost just going up the road!"

"I need a male escort."

"Let Ginny be the escort!"

"He's only thirteen."

Mr. Lebedev growls his routine growl and gets his shoes and hat. "Just a minute. I suppose it's not too dangerous if I'm just outside for a very brief while, and don't make any eye contact."

Lyuba gets their letter and climbs onto Branimir.

"Why aren't you riding sidesaddle?"

"I might fall off. If a man doesn't ride sidesaddle, why should I?"

Mr. Lebedev drags Branimir to the post office and rushes him back to the house in record time. Lyuba is still mounting Branimir after depositing her letter when Mr. Lebedev yanks on the mecate rein, almost causing her to fall off.

"I have to give Kroshka a bath today," he announces as soon as they're safely inside. "Thank God no one saw me."

"Can I do it for you? I like feeling useful, and maybe you'll like me more if I earn my keep through chores."

"It's enough I'm letting you stay here for free and eat up my food!"

"I have money, Ilya Nikolayevich. My friend Petya gave it to me. Emergency money, just in case we ever ran out. It's finally time to use it, though I imagine it's worthless given the hyperinflation." Lyuba reaches into her pocket and takes out four envelopes bulging with bills. "Now I have no more."

"How long have you been wearing that jacket?"

"Four years. Everyone always bothers me to get a new one, but I don't mind wearing it. Besides, it's so bone-thin, it's perfect as a light outer wrap in warmer weather."

He goes into a closet and pulls out a lovely dark blue wool coat with filigreed silver buttons, a silver fox lining, and a shearling collar and cuffs. "Take this coat. It was Lyolya's."

"No. It's much too nice."

"Lyolya only got a few chances to wear it before she was taken with Sveta, Fima, and Dina to God knows where. Someone must wear it. They didn't let her grab her coat." He puts the coat around her shoulders. "It's a perfect fit, though you're a lot taller than my Lyolya. It goes below the knees, and won't leave you with cold legs. Maybe I was rash to be so uncivil to you initially, but it's the only way I know how to react after all the pain I've lived through. *Pozhaluysta*, forgive me. I wouldn't want someone to treat any of my daughters that way. I don't want you to think I'm a bad, mean person without a heart or emotions."

"Yes, I forgive you. I know exactly what you mean about not being normal, in ways you'll never fathom. It's nice to find someone besides my Vanya to be abnormal with."

"God willing, life won't be abnormal forever. It never is. Hopefully, we'll still be alive to see the end of this modern-day *Smutnoye Vremya*."

****

Chapter 13: Red Shadows

"I've come to inquire about helping with the children." Alla steps into Mrs. Brezhneva's office. "I saw your ad in the paper shortly after I moved to Kiyev."

"Come in, Comrade. What are your credentials?"

Alla has a seat. "I got my childcare experience the old-fashioned, hands-on way. I'm the seventh of ten daughters, and helped a lot with raising my three little sisters. There are big age gaps between the last four of us, given how my parents were getting older, so I was more than old enough to truly care for babies and small children. I wasn't a child myself, just pretending to help or doing minor things like folding diapers."

"Have you any children of your own?"

"I happen to have three sons, but they were given to orphanages. My paper husband deserted me after I was arrested for the crime of having children out of wedlock. As though I'd tried to assassinate Comrade Lenin, hidden one of the Romanovs, or another heinous crime. I'm a woman wronged."

"Are your sons at this orphanage? This orphanage is for children of enemies of the people! If someone comes here to see a relative or the child of a friend, it's quickly found out, and it puts the whole orphanage at risk!"

"No idea where my sons are, and I don't ever want to know. They're children created from rape."

"And your name is?"

"Alla Ilyinichna Lebedeva."

"Three of the girls here are Lebedevas. Is that your married or single name?"

"I never took my husband's name. We're husband and wife in name only, and never lived together. Lebedeva's a fairly common surname. I'm sure you have children here who aren't related just because they share a surname."

"Did you have prior knowledge of this fact, Comrade Lebedeva?" Mrs. Brezhneva looks at her closely, trying to read any cues in her face.

"No, I didn't." Alla keeps the same poker face she came in with. "What am I, an idiot to jeopardize a potential job or get your orphanage in trouble?"

Mrs. Brezhneva looks her up and down again. "Unpack your things, and start to work this afternoon. This coming weekend, you may take a small holiday. Perhaps you have family you'd like to visit. But only this once. I expect you to be a loyal worker and live on orphanage grounds, in the dormitory for workers. If you're still here and a loyal worker after a year, we'll talk again about holidays."

Alla knows there are spies everywhere, and every harmless slip of the tongue may be construed as an act trying to undermine Comrade Lenin. "My mother had a faint heart, and died after hearing of the attempt on Comrade Lenin's life by that deranged madwoman Fanya Kaplan. My father remains."

"Where are your sisters?"

"The older ones turned out to be enemies of the people! They're in places where they're being taught to love Our Leader as much as I do! Why if he were in this room, I'd run to him to hug him!"

"And your husband?"

"Anton Alekseyevich Yatsenko. He cavorted around with a woman for twenty years, had five children with her, and never married her. Then he raped me on three different occasions. When my father found out, he made me marry him. We never divorced, but now he has a third woman. He's breaking the law."

"And your father?"

"I peered in on him after I was released from prison. I saw him playing cards and drinking. My release so early from prison would've shocked him, so I decided to wait awhile before coming in the house."

"Go to the bathhouse, Comrade Lebedeva. The ones we were saddled with this morning are more traumatized than any of the other ones already here."

Mrs. Brezhneva leads Alla into the large marble-walled bathhouse. The boys run away quickly before Mrs. Brezhneva can punish them for sneaking over to see their sisters, girlfriends, and cousins. The girls stand at straight attention.

"Are all these new ones orphans, or children of enemies of the people?"

"Most of them are orphans. Or half-orphans. Like that poor girl over there, she and her mother just got out of prison together. The mother had her at age fourteen. She'll be one of the cooks. And that older girl. One of many who fled, newly-orphaned, after the Ukrainian attempt for independence backfired violently. Those five sisters, they were victims of another failed revolution in Belarus, those came from Moldavia, that one's Polish, and I feel sorry for the ones who aren't Slavic!"

Alla has been raised a staunch Slavic nationalist. She looks with suspicion at the girls who aren't Ukrainian, Russian, or Belarusian. As she helps to bathe each one, she hears story after story of horror. Parents taken away in the night and the children spared because the enemy didn't search in the back room; a house set on fire and the child escaped through the back door; a terrible train wreck going to the coast to sail to Finland; a circus stampede caused by Bolshe-

vik police shooting at clowns putting on a skit making fun of Comrade Lenin; beatings by soldiers; a knock at the door always causing fear; several stories about pogroms; being taken forcefully from one of the bands of besprizorniki*; being caught homeless; and every story of horror imaginable. A number of the girls carry scars, burns, and scratches sustained from rapes, beatings, or attacks during one of the nationalist revolutions. Now, nationalism is forbidden. Everyone is to become a Soviet.*

"What's your name, little comrade, and what's your story?" Alla asks the last girl who comes into the bath.

"My mother was raped at thirteen. Then we lost everyone five years ago. We fled into Russia, and everything went well until the Tsar was overthrown."

"Where did you get those scars on your back?"

"I was whipped."

"By a Red officer?"

"By a Turk."

"These last girls are Caucasians," Mrs. Brezhneva says with disgust. "Chechens, Ingushis, Dagestanis, Azerbaijanis, Georgians, Armenians, Basmachis."

"I haven't heard of most of those nationalities."

"Join the club. They didn't even have patronymics in their nations. We had to ask what their fathers' names are."

"I'm Comrade Izabella Vartanovna Nahigian," the girl with whiplash scars says. "My father was a Turkish rapist, so my mama assigned me the patronymic Vartanovna after one of the most important Armenian saints."

"What's a patronymic?" a Chechen girl asks.

"What's a saint?" an Ingushi girl asks.

"They're as worse as the Baltic children," Mrs. Brezhneva sneers. "They don't know Russian Cyrillic. At least the ones from Ukraine and Belarus know Cyrillic in some form!"

"I'm Kyrgyz," a little girl announces proudly.

"You're a Soviet now," Mrs. Brezhneva corrects her. "Before, I just had to deal with Slavs and Yids. Now I'm being swamped with refugees from places I never knew existed. Russian names are long enough, but some of their names I still can't pronounce! Like Comrade Georgia over there and her cousin. One's name ends in 'ashvili,' and the other's name ends in 'adze.' Comrade Nahigian has a tamer surname. Those other three girls of various former nationalities have even more long-winded names! I call them Comrade K., Comrade P., and Comrade Z. for short."

"I'm Comrade Zouranjian."

"I'm Comrade Petropashvili."

"I'm Comrade Kwaśniewska."

"Whatever. Wear nametags."

"But I can't write in your alphabet yet," Comrade Zouranjian says.

"I only know Russian Cyrillic cursive," Comrade Kwaśniewska says.

"There's nothing 'former' about my nationality," Comrade Petropashvili says. "I'm still Georgian, even if your people have designs on crushing my people yet again. As we speak, Georgia is still a free country, and so is Armenia. Some of us just got caught in the crosshairs, and were deported to your foreign, enemy land."

Alla looks at this group of girls in quiet horror. The oldest of the bunch, Comrade Petropashvili, looks to be only about twelve, and already all of them are calling one another and themselves Comrade. It frightens her to death. Surely Vera, Natalya, and Fyodora haven't succumbed to such mind-numbing indoctrination yet.

"Comrades, we'll all get dressed now and march right back to our quarters! There's a bag with three pairs of the regulation uniform on your new beds for each of you. There are lots of new children, so there are now five to a bed, twenty to a room, and smaller portions for everyone at meals. The daily study will begin in fifteen minutes!"

Alla seats herself next to Mrs. Brezhneva at a table with fifteen girls, from Moldavia, Chechnya, and Georgia. She pretends to be fascinated with the lessons in the political indoctrination workbook about Marx, Lenin, Engels, class struggles, and the Tsar. The girls who can't read yet are being told a story about Comrade Trotskiy by a plump young woman.

"That's my mama," Izabella says proudly.

"Be quiet, Comrade Nahigian. All talk and no study makes a poor offering for the bright future of the triumph of Soviet Socialism!"

Karla Gorbachëva gets up with Valentina Kuchma during storytime. Both have to be escorted to the outhouse by Comrade Nahigian, Senior. The older girls who cannot read consider this an outrage, and begin to shout curses at Mrs. Brezhneva, making the dulya *sign, spitting at her, and kicking her.*

"I didn't teach them such coarse manners, Comrade Lebedeva. They learnt it all from former orphanages. I only beat a child if she gets out of line. But right now, there are too many to beat all at once. They'll have even smaller portions tonight at supper as punishment."

"You have awful hair, Mrs. Brezhneva," one girl sneers. "Like an ape cut

it."

"That hat is a man's hat! And also too small for your pathetic head."

"You have beady little eyes!"

"Where is Mr. *Brezhnev, pray tell?"*

"Your ears are pointy."

"You smile and laugh at inappropriate times."

"I think you're mentally sick."

Comrade Nahigian, Senior, returns with Karla and Valentina. The girls who acted up get only a quarter scoop of gruel during supper. After the meal, Mrs. Brezhneva goes up to the girls who dared say grace.

"We always said grace at home," Izabella says in a small voice.

"Hey! That one's saying grace again!"

"That's Sarah," Klara Nadleshina volunteers.

"Why are you praying, Comrade Sarah?"

"Her full name is Sarah Mendelovna Katz."

"Comrades Katz and Nahigian will never pray here again."

"I'm supposed to pray before and after I eat, Comrade Brezhneva."

"Maybe you did before the great Leader led our people to triumph!"

"There's a civil war going on, Mrs. Brezhneva," Katya Chernomyrdina points out. "One day a city or county is in Red hands; the very next day the Whites reclaim it. Our Kyiv has changed hands at least ten times."

"I wish you'd stop oppositionally using Ukrainian names for this republic's cities. As a proud Russian, you should want to use our names. And I'm no longer Mrs. I'm Comrade now."

"Then why don't we call you Mrs. Comrade or Comrade Mrs.?" Naina Yezhova asks.

"The same reason we're all Soviets now. The Whites may have victories, but they're becoming less frequent every day. Western support is dwindling. Their army is disorganized and falling apart as we speak. Loyalist Whites long ago fled abroad. For the remaining ones to stay here is beyond suicidal."

Alla sees her three little sisters marching off to their room after the dishes have been washed and Mrs. Brezhneva has given the nightly lecture on Socialism. They glance her and stop moving.

"Vera, Natalya, and Fyodora Ilyinichna Lebedeva! Is there a problem?" one of the lead orderlies, Miss Nevskaya, asks.

"I thought I saw that picture of Our Leader hanging askew," Vera claims.

Alla raises a finger to her lips and goes on to her section of the building. The three of them go quietly to their room.

"What's this?" Mrs. Brezhneva storms over to Zouranjian. "You just made a cross over yourself, you enemy of the people!"

"I do that before I say my bedtime prayers. I'm still a good Communist, you old dingbat!"

"Comrade Kwaśniewska is wearing a crucifix necklace!"

"My mother gave it to me. I'm a devout Catholic and *Communist."*

"You'd think that after three years of living under Comrade Lenin, you'd all have changed your evil ways!"

"Ever hear of Christian Socialism?" Zouranjian challenges her.

"Go reread the Manifesto *until you realize 'religion is the opiate of the masses.' Didn't you do your lesson properly today in the Socialist workbook?"*

"I told you I can't read Russian Cyrillic."

"The orphanages are strapped enough for money as it already is. Don't dare beg me for reading and writing lessons, enemy of the people."

"Too many things are forbidden, Mrs. Brezhneva. Open display of religion, reading books by certain authors, going to circuses with clowns dressed like Red leaders, getting married in a church, having a baby baptized, and now it's moved up to nationalism!" Ohanna Aramovna Zouranjian makes another cross over herself in defiance.

2

Lyuba sits looking at Mr. Lebedev's book about the lives of the Russian saints. She never had Tatyana baptized, and hasn't gone to church, confessed, or had Communion since April 1917. Yet she can still recite every prayer like she did as a Sunday school student sitting between Ivan and Boris. Ginny proudly boasts he's long forgotten the prayers he learnt a lifetime ago. Before Lyuba and he knew what it feels like to be in the position the peasants were in for centuries, constantly fearing for their lives and subject to violent overlords. There are a number of White strongholds and victories in Southern Russia and Western Siberia, but that doesn't matter up in Moskva. At least they're not in Petrograd. The Red Terror and the Cheka have been the worst and bloodiest there, Lyuba keeps hearing. A ring of the phone, a cryptic letter in the mail, a knock at the door, a soldier with a gun, being awoken in the middle of the night, all are possibilities in Lyuba's nightmares.

A knock at the door sounds. Ginny looks through the window and sees a small group of Red Army officers holding guns. Kroshka begins barking hysterically as the soldiers pound on the door.

"Can't you read the sign?" Ginny asks after he opens a window. "There's a smallpox quarantine in effect here. Five of my relatives are very sick."

The leader immediately steps back. "I'm sorry, but we can't read very well. We're former peasants. Hopefully we'll learn to read and write after this damn war is over. We didn't need to be asked twice when the Bolsheviks promised us an education and better jobs if we joined the Red Army."

"I'm so glad to see friendly faces." Mr. Lebedev forces a smile. "My daughter's husband was taken hostage by Whites a few months ago, and she's been living in terror of a similar fate ever since. Some unruly people complain about the Red Terror, but what about the White Terror? I don't want Lyubov, Mikhail, or Tatyana to be taken prisoners like my son-in-law. Mikhail's father was forced into the White Army and his mother held hostage to ensure her husband wouldn't desert."

"Things are going to get better. The White cause is doomed. Within the year, we'll push our way into the South and drive them out."

3

In the morning, Mrs. Brezhneva roots through the suitcases of the new arrivals. She rips up magazines, throws ikons against the wall, tosses forbidden books into the fireplace, snorts at family pictures, and takes money.

"Are we going to be adopted?" Ohanna demands.

"You wish, Comrade Zouranjian."

"The Whites control the South. Therefore, Armenia, Georgia, and Azerbaijan are free. Tell me again just why the hell there are so many of us from Transcaucasia in this hellhole in Kiyev."

"It's called War."

"Give me back my book," Sarah pleads.

"It's not written in Russian."

"The Yiddish press is free now."

"Not in my place! Besides, that's not a real language. It's just a Jewish dialect of German. There's also no need to keep using that ghetto language in the twentieth century. Your native language should be the national language of your birthland, not an invented minority dialect."

Vera finishes making their bed. "There are four of us," she whispers.

"At least four," Natalya says.

4

"There are supposed to be four of us." Lyuba picks up seventeen-month-old Tatyana and sits her at the table. "I'll never see Vanya again, and now have only memories to live on."

"There might've been *none* of you if I hadn't come up with that quick, clever lie yesterday!" Mr. Lebedev says. "Thank God none of them recognized me."

"Yes, *spasibo*, Ilya Nikolayevich. Your kindness means the world to me."

He smiles at Tatyana and gives her a small piece of chocolate. "Is your Vanya her father? I haven't heard you speaking about any other man so lovingly."

"He was her father every way but in blood. She only was with her real father for one week this spring."

"Is her blood father in prison?"

"He's going back to America as we speak. He came back here illegally."

"Do you care to share the story of how you came to be an unwed mother? Surely we like and trust each other enough by now. I won't judge you. My own Allochka was an unwed mother thrice over, and I discovered it wasn't at all what I assumed. She was an innocent, blameless victim, but I was too busy rushing to lessen her shame to care what really happened."

"Vanya thinks it was rape, even if it didn't involve being held at knifepoint or assaulted by a stranger. We were a couple. He rented a cabin one night when everyone was away, so he could sleep with me. But I didn't want to, so he got me drunk and mixed some kind of drugs in the liquor. And out of that unwanted union came my precious Tanyechka!" Lyuba cuddles Tatyana.

"He fled to America to escape responsibility," Ginny chimes in. "The second he left, she went into hard labor."

"Our friend Eliisabet was so scared by the approaching Bolsheviks she went into labor twelve weeks early. Vanya had to carry her as we escaped. The look of love she and Aleksey exchanged after I presented them with their baby son brought tears to my eyes also. That baby was conceived in love and is being raised by two married parents. More than Tanyechka has. If I had it to do all over again, I never would've consented to go to that stupid cabin, and Tanyechka would be Vanya's blood child."

5

"Boris Aleksandrovich Malenkov! We were worried sick about you!" Mrs. Kharzina slaps him across his face.

"Oh my God, it's my bastard grandson!" Mrs. Zhukova runs over to take the baby. "I wonder who he got this red hair from. This baby is a boy, Rita. You told me Lyuba wrote to you saying she had a girl."

"She did." Boris gulps. "I found this one on the ground with a note pinned to him. The aunt wanted a better life for him. His name's Yuriy Yeltsin."

"The child I hold in my arms isn't my flesh and blood?"

"He's an illegitimate child too. His father is Mikhail Godunov, a bully who was a few years ahead of me at gymnasium. Misha grew up to run a brothel with his cousin Kostya, who was in my class."

"Another bastard!"

"I'm going to raise him. He'll take the place of my Tanyechka. He'll be like my own son, and I'll be his adoptive father, like Iosif was the adoptive father of Christ."

"You compare yourself to the adoptive father of Jesus! From one disgrace to another you went!"

"Already Yura's quite attached to me. He's no longer Yuriy Mikhaylovich Yeltsin. He's Yuriy Borisovich Malenkov. Since Tanyechka's full name is Tatyana Ivanovna Zhukova, not Borisovna Malenkova, I need some way to pass my name on."

"Oh, my shameful daughter and the just as shameful father of her bastard!" Mrs. Zhukova starts crying.

"I loved my baby girl the minute I set eyes on her. She looks just like Lyuba. I'll always be there for her when she and Lyuba come to America, but I forfeited my right to be called her real father the night she was born, when I ran away to escape responsibility."

"You've lost your job at the hotel, Borya," Mrs. Kharzina says gently.

"Just as well. I was treated like dirt there anyway."

"Let's see. I work three jobs, but the positions I fill are women's work. You wouldn't want to cook, sweep, or clean, would you?"

"The couple I work for could use a butler," Mrs. Zhukova says, looking at Yuriy in disgust.

"You still work there after you've been caught stealing so many times?"

"I'll do what any responsible man should do when he arrives in this coun-

try," Boris says. "Work with my own people instead of exposing myself to abuse from outsiders. In the morning, I'll start working in a factory."

"They'll work you sun to sun, Borya. You'll get five minutes to eat lunch. Fires are often. They aren't very clean. They'll exploit you and pay you dirt. Come work with me at one of the churches."

"As what, a cook?"

"You can type papers for the priest or teach the children their lessons. Anything is better than mindless factory work."

In the morning, Boris warms up milk for Yuriy and sets out a little plate of mashed carrots and crackers for him. He's sixteen months old, a month younger than Tatyana. After feeding Yuriy, he wraps him in swaddling clothes, sets him in the perambulator he bought when the ship stopped in Finland, and walks to the nearest Russian Orthodox church. He leaves three hours later, happy as a little clam, and writes to Lyuba once home.

"Now you've really *turned your life around, Boris Aleksandrovich," Mrs. Zhukova says approvingly.*

6

Tatyana awoke from her afternoon nap crying for her father, and now Lyuba is crying for Ivan too. While Tatyana sits on the floor playing with little Kroshka, Lyuba drowns her sorrow with Mr. Lebedev's liquor. She passes out before supper is served. Ginny stares in amazement as he piles his plate with hard-boiled eggs, sourdough rolls, pickled beets, dill pickles, and sausages.

"Before she only got drunk if someone did it to her. Now she did it all on her own. She falls apart so easily. All she has left are me and Tatyana."

"Are you really the same boy who couldn't stop throwing temper tantrums and behaving childishly?" Mr. Lebedev asks.

"I'm truly a changed boy."

"There's the door. Go see if it's another group of Reds. I'm not going to risk showing my face twice in the same short timespan."

Ginny peeks through the window. "It's a woman alone, carrying a valise in each hand. Her face is very scarred, and her hair is rather short for a woman."

"Another boarder. Lucky me. You open the door, and I'll take your cousin upstairs. My new boarder might not want to lodge here if she thinks I have a habit of sheltering drunks and letting ladies drink."

"The man who should be taking care of her is Ivan."

"Complaining about what happened won't suddenly make it change. She needs someone to take care of her while her sweetheart is gone." Mr. Lebedev lifts Lyuba out of her chair, making sure to keep his arms around her knees and shoulders, and staggers upstairs. As soon as they're in the attic, he deposits her on her bed.

Ginny opens the door and steps back at the up-close and personal sight of the scars all over the woman's face.

"Is this where Ilya Nikolayevich Lebedev lives?"

"Yes it is. Are you seeking a safe house?" Ginny averts his eyes from the scars, which are also all over her hands.

"I'll be here for awhile. Can you lead me in the direction of the washroom? I'm dusty from my long flight from Siberia."

"It's right over there." Ginny points.

"Over where?"

"I just pointed it out to you."

"I'm sorry, but I'm blind. It wasn't always this way. I was blinded by a fire three years ago, when the Reds tried to kill me. They used me as a freak in the labor camp circus, since I couldn't do normal work."

Ginny leads her there. "I can't imagine being blind."

"I'd just turned twenty-seven when I was trapped in eternal darkness. I never even got to marry and have children. I thought I was being a modern woman by waiting a few years after graduating university, little dreaming most of the men my age would soon be taken for the war." She removes a gold chain from her neck and hands it to Ginny. "*Pozhaluysta*, give this to the proprietor so he can put it with the valuables."

Mr. Lebedev comes back downstairs after the washroom door is closed. "Where did she go?"

"I took her to the washroom. She's blind."

He crosses himself. "How tragic. I won't charge her, on account of her disability."

Ginny pushes the chain at him. "She thinks you have a place for valuables. If you really do have a safe, you should make Lyuba use it. She's got a lot of jewelry, and refuses to sell any of it, since Ivan gave it to her."

Mr. Lebedev stares at the necklace. It's a long gold link chain, of twenty-carat gold, with a flat gold oval pendant, inscribed "Galina Ilyinichna Lebedeva, 10 May 1890. First child of proud happy parents, Ilya Nikolayevich Lebedev and Yevgeniya Yermolayevna Lebedeva." His whole body shakes as he crosses himself.

"Praise God you found your way back home in spite of your blindness," he says when she makes her way over to the table. "Thank God you're alive." He takes her right hand. "I'm over here, Galya."

Galya steps into his arms, and Mr. Lebedev breaks down crying. Lyuba and Ginny look away, not quite sure how to react to witnessing what should be a personal, private moment. At least this means Mr. Lebedev still has human emotions, in spite of his gruff exterior.

"Many people took sympathy on a blind woman, and helped me along the way. My camp had to evacuate because our troops were on their way. I made sure to be last in line, and kept walking slower and slower until eventually I was left behind. Where's Mama?"

"Your mother is dead. The month after you were seized, she was murdered. I've been in prison. God was good to me and allowed me to escape and find my way home. Nadya kept our house safe with a phony smallpox quarantine sign."

She gasps and crosses herself. "I came to you, Papa, because I was on my way to America. I'm useless as a blind woman, but America has doctors who can perform sight restoration operations. A great number of people took pity on me and gave me money. I had a priest count it for me. He told me I had three hundred million rubles and five thousand kopeks. Enough for ship fare to America, even with hyperinflation, and an operation."

Mr. Lebedev leads her over to a chair and puts the knife and fork in her hands. "Eat my supper. Pickled beets, eggs, sourdough rolls, dill pickles, and sausages."

"No, you've suffered enough. I'll eat my own food."

"I insist. God has been very good to me and given me a second chance to be a father and have a family. Nothing in this world is more important to me than my family. It's the one thing we can count on when we've lost everything else."

7

Boris leaves Yuriy with Mrs. Zhukova and goes to the job he found teach-

ing in the church school. He kneels and crosses himself before he enters the church, then sees the priest.

"Am I a bit too early, Batyushka*?"*

"I changed my mind. The babushka *of your daughter came last night to thank me for what I did for you, saying how many mistakes you made, but instead of serving to make me help you in your attempt to reform your shameful life, it only made me want to have you nowhere near impressionable young children!"*

"But, Batyushka*, I've made mistakes, and Mrs. Zhukova acknowledges I'm turning my old life around now!"*

"I had to hear of these sins from the babushka *of your daughter, who should rightfully be your mother-in-law! I should've heard them straight from your mouth in confession! Then I would've assigned you your penance! In your case, I'd suggest about fifty fasts to start off, and then only after I hear you acknowledge you have indeed sinned!"*

"I go to church every Sunday now I'm in America. There was only a brief respite when I was confused and went back to Russia, and then came back to America after acknowledging my mistake."

"Sin number one: Quite a number of years ago, you caused a young girl to take her own life. Number two: Living in sin with the mother of your child."

"But Ivan was there too, and Lyuba and I didn't start our sexual relationship until April 1918, about six months after we became a couple. Actually, five months, going by the new Russian calendar. It was the twenty-seventh of October, shortly after the second Revolution, and that night there was a ball to celebrate. That's when we got together."

"It was the ninth of November, my son, when you started on your disgraceful path away from goodness and towards evil."

"I still go by the Russian calendar in my heart and mind."

"Your third sin: Luring your girlfriend away from goodness and taking her to a deserted cabin, getting her drunk, taking her virginity, and getting her pregnant out of wedlock."

"I apologize for that completely! Even for yelling at her and beating her all during the pregnancy!"

"Mrs. Zhukova mentioned none of that."

"I never told her, that's why!"

"Number four: Engaging in illegal activities to raise the money to get a ship ticket to America. Your daughter's babushka *told me you told her it was drug trafficking!"*

"Yes, and it paid very well. We also served as village toughs on and off,

roughing up the Bolsheviks who dared trespass into our White stronghold. Up till the Tsar was murdered by godless regicidal mudaki, *it looked like we were going to win the Civil War, so we were relatively secure in our little corner of Mitino."*

"Number five: Leaving your daughter's mother the night she gave birth. She easily could've died delivering your daughter, without a doctor or midwife. An eleven-year-old boy was the only one there as she brought your bastard into this world!"

"I love my daughter. She looks like a miniature version of Lyuba."

"Number six: Illegally leaving America to go back into Russia."

"That's hardly a sin."

"Seven: Deserting your daughter and her mother once again."

"I had to do it."

"Eight: Leaving Russia again, this time illegally."

"No one questioned me."

"Nine: Getting back into America illegally."

"Here I am, untouched by the authorities!"

"Ten: Taking a bastard back to America with you."

"Yuriy's like my own son at this point. I'm adopting him as soon as possible."

"Why don't you go manage a whorehouse if you're so unrepentant about all your sinning?"

"I love the Church. I love Lyuba. I love my little Tanyechka. I love Matushka Rus. *I love Yura now. Come to think of it, all those things are where I'm not. I can take Yuriy with me and go back to Russia right this minute!"*

"You dare take that child into danger to do more sinning!"

"The priest I grew up with was a forgiving man! I never met a priest who was so judgmental." Boris gets up and walks back home.

Mrs. Zhukova and Mrs. Kharzina are gone when he gets back, and Yuriy is nowhere to be found either. Today is Thursday, so Mrs. Kharzina will be sweeping at the Serbian cathedral. He runs over there and bursts inside.

"What have you done with my son?"

Mrs. Kharzina drops her broom and approaches him. "I came home because I forgot my handbag, and Katya had already left for work. Yuriy she left on the floor. He was crying, and she hadn't changed his diaper! I quickly saw this was no way to live, so I took him to the nearest orphanage." She pulls a folded stack of papers out of her handbag and pushes it in Boris's face. "And this letter you wrote Lyuba! My heart broke when I found out you were forced off your ship in Denmark when your papers weren't in order! You poor boy, walking and taking crowded trains all the way into Belgium and then held for two weeks in quarantine! Thank God you and that dear little boy were given a clean bill of health."

"You took my son to an orphanage?"

"You have a daughter, Borya, not a son. In time, you'll realize it's better for him to be adopted into a stable two-parent family. Now go to work and think about the next child you'll have, this time a child conceived in love, with a woman you love for the right reasons."

Boris doesn't tell her he's lost his job. Steaming mad, he takes a subway and a ferry to New York Harbor and asks about the next ship leaving for Russia.

"Over there. A handful of undesirables are being sent back on that one. What a pity. Are you looking for one of them?"

"I want to go back myself. I have to bring my daughter out of the country."

"You don't want to wait here for her to join you?"

"She isn't even two years old yet. It isn't safe for a child."

"Was she taken from you when you left?"

"Her mother's raising her. I want us to raise her together, as a married couple. No child should grow up with the stigma of having an unwed mother."

"Get on that boat. Sounds like a real emergency. Better to save your child's mother from more shame."

Beaming, Boris gets on the ship, his passport in his rucksack.

8

Early Saturday morning, Alla arrives at her father's house. At first she hesitates when she sees the smallpox quarantine sign, then peeks through the window and sees quite healthy people around the table. She opens the door slowly and peeks in. Everyone is eating *blinchiki*, no frightening pustules in sight. Ginny is feeding Kroshka scraps from the table.

"May I join you, Papa?"

Mr. Lebedev looks up and crosses himself. "Alla!"

Alla climbs into her father's lap and hugs him. "Thank God you're still alive. After I escaped from prison, I had to come home to see our dear old house again. Lyuba told me Nadya said you were arrested two years ago, so imagine my surprise when I saw you behind a window. Since it was so late, and I didn't want you to die of shock, I decided to get out of the city and come back at a later date. I don't work nearby, but my new boss gave me permission to visit family, to prove what a good boss she is."

"You escaped Lubyanka!" Lyuba gasps. "What happened to Vanya?"

Alla bows her head and crosses herself. "He helped me and my cellmate Sonya escape. When Sonya caught up to me, she told me he'd been caught. He was shot the next morning, according to what she overheard one of the officers saying. He was supposed to drag her back to prison as proof he hadn't been in on our prison break, but he took pity on her. Thank God the bleeding tapered off and the wound was able to be treated, because he used part of his sleeve as a tourniquet. Because he let her escape, he was given a death sentence."

"My sweet, gentle Vanyechka has been dead the past week!" Lyuba starts crying.

"I'm sorry to break the sad news. Even if the prison break was my idea, he saved Sonya's life before he left this Earth. That trumps the sin of murder, if God considers justifiable murder a sin."

"Now Tanyechka has lost both her fathers." Lyuba wrings her fists across her eyes. "Aren't you scared to come back here so soon after you escaped from prison?"

"I work in Kiyev, at an orphanage. God led me to exactly the right city and orphanage, because I found Verushka, Natasha, and Dora there."

"Praise God!" Mr. Lebedev says. "Since you were wily enough to escape from prison, I assume you can get your little sisters out of the orphanage. Praise Christ I have five daughters left."

"Who's the fifth?"

He motions to Galya. "I take it you didn't recognize your oldest sister because of all the scars. Galya's blind now."

Alla jumps off her father's lap and hugs Galya tightly. "I'm so sorry I didn't recognize you!" She reaches for her father's hand. "Do you know the whereabouts of any of my other sisters?"

"Dina, Fima, Lyolya, and Sveta were taken the night after you and the three little ones. A week later, Motya was taken, and then came Galya. Your mother is dead."

"I know about *Matushka*, Papa. One of my jailers told me in a sick little sneer how he was one of the sick excuses for life who killed her."

"And I've lost the only person who ever loved me completely!" Lyuba wails. "Poor Vanya didn't get to experience sexual intimacy with a woman once in his life, and now the Konev name has died out!"

Lyuba sits the rest of the weekend with a blank stare on her face. When Alla takes the train back to Kyiv on Sunday night, Lyuba goes to bid Alla goodbye at the depot and then goes back to the house to cry herself to sleep. On Monday morning, she sits on the bench in front of the house to take in the sun. If her heart and soul can't be warmed up, at least the merciful warmth will assist her physically.

9

"Where the hell is my cousin?" Naina is screaming at Mrs. Brezhneva. "Katya and I came back after the morning exercise break to see if she was up yet, and found several beds in her section of the room empty!"

"How should I know? These children aren't under lock and key. You shouldn't assume the worst just because you've had bad experiences with previous orphanages."

"A group of people came in during the morning and took twenty girls, including Inessa and Karla," Olga volunteers.

"People? What people, relatives of the girls?"

"No, they all wore some sort of uniform," Klara says.

"They were going around examining the place and told us you should fix the leaky lavatory, and that the new uniforms are wonderful, but yet you go above and beyond the call of duty by having the children call themselves 'Comrade,' instead of just their names," Inna says.

"So these were Reds and not Whites?"

"I half-forget which side has control of Kiyev right now," Ohanna says. "It's changed hands so many times. I want to go back to Armenia, and Alina wants to go back to Georgia."

"Who's Alina?"

"Comrade Petropashvili. If you'd taken the time to learn our first names, you'd know these sorts of things."

"They took children without my knowledge or permission!"

"This was rather early in the morning, and you'd beat anyone who disturbs your sleep," Fyodora says.

"Can I still catch these burglars who dared go behind my back to try to run my own orphanage, or is it already too late?"

"The train left a few hours ago," Sarah says in a small voice.

Alla comes into the building.

"Comrade Lebedeva, agents of the Reds or the Whites, or whoever's got control of Kiyev right now, came here this morning while I was sound asleep, never once bothering to wake me to tell me they were here to inspect the place, and took twenty girls!"

"You weren't expecting any people?"

"No! I always got a phonecall alerting me to prepare before!"

*"Now my cousin is gone!" Naina howls. "*Tyotya *Sonya will kill me! It's bad enough Mikhaila was murdered!"*

Karla screams when she wakes up in a dirty cattlecar with nineteen other girls. Naina and Katya are nowhere to be seen.

"Likely we're being sent back to Minsk," Inessa says. "Mrs. Brezhneva was in the final stages of closing Dyadya *Dima's adoption of me. He's probably waiting there right now for me! Boy, I can't wait to finally live in a real house again, go to school, eat nice food, catch up with my cousins, and wear my own clothes. I hope he takes me to see a moving picture as a reward for my ordeal, and buys me pretty jewelry."*

One girl peeks out the window and howls. "It's a sign in Russian Cyrillic, not Ukrainian or Belarusian Cyrillic!"

"We're going to Yaroslavl," the driver shouts back to them.

"But that's a long way from Minsk!" Inessa begins sobbing. "I want to go to Dyadya *Dima!"*

"I don't remember my surname and patronymic!" Karla sobs.

Inessa carries Karla off the train when it stops very late the next evening, and takes Valentina by the hand. Everyone begins weeping at how dirty the new place is.

10

"Look at my cousin wasting like that." Ginny slurps down the morning celery stew. "She's barely eaten the last few days, and just sits on the bench outside and sleeps."

There are rings under Lyuba's eyes, her whole face has turned red and puffy from crying, and her skin has grown pale. "Remember when you slurped your borshcht and made such a scene right after Tatyana was born, and that nosy old *babushka* made me feel so humiliated in front of so many people?" Lyuba begins sobbing again. "Who will I have for male protection now? Vanya was my next door neighbor for nine years, my best friend, and we loved each other so, so much, yet something always kept getting in the way of our being together permanently. And now he's dead, probably burnt in a mass grave, after being shot for doing what he did best—kindness!" Lyuba starts crying even harder. "If only I could've been carrying Vanya's child. There'd always be a part of him with me, instead of only memories. Now Tanya is fatherless twice over."

Lyuba finishes her celery stew and goes to sit on the bench again. Ginny takes down a book of Lermontov's poetry and begins reading it. Tatyana falls asleep beside Kroshka.

"Your dog is very attached to Tatyana," Ginny observes. "She might be crumb-sized, but she's as protective as a huge breed. Will you take her with you when you go to America?"

"Of course. Now I have two daughters to take as well. Five, if Allochka gets my three youngest daughters out of that orphanage."

"If Petya weren't so devoted to the Bolshevik cause, I'd ask him to go with us to America and marry her to put her out of her misery. At least one of her suitors is left."

"She could always find a husband in America."

"Ivan treated Tatyana like his own child. He was going to adopt her. It's a wonder no authorities ever tracked Lyuba down and tore Tatyana out of her arms. She wouldn't be a widow or divorcée with a justifiable cause for divorce. She'd be on her first marriage, with an illegitimate child. No man wants to marry such a woman. Guys like Ivan are rare."

"Lyuba strikes me as an intelligent woman. I'm sure she could find an understanding, modern husband in America. If my Allochka ever has the freedom to remarry, I hope no one would hold her own blameless past against her."

"Our band is in tatters now, strewn all over the place. We lost Alya and Anya last January, and Katrin and Anastasiya remained behind when we moved last August. No one wanted Anastasiya in our band to begin with, but at least Katrin was kind of useful, and we could have intelligent conversations with her. Bands inevitably lose members as time goes on."

"A band? That's what you considered yourselves?"

"We did what bands do, moving on all the time to safer places, stealing to get food, living under the noses of the authorities, camping on the ground, fleeing all the time, packing at a moment's notice, you know. Aleksey and Ivan were the leaders, after that coward Boris Aleksandrovich Malenkov walked out on us. We called ourselves the Stray Dogs."

Mr. Lebedev smiles. "There was a group of Acmeist poets who called themselves the Stray Dogs. They named a café in Petrograd after themselves. Where are the rest of your Stray Dogs now?"

"Last we heard, still at the boardinghouse we left in August."

"You've lost six people now?"

"These things happen in any band. We'll always have Petya to fall back on. Basil is gone, not that he ever did anything useful when he was one of our pretended helpers. He only tagged along with Petya because he was obsessed with Lyuba."

"Was he really so evil?"

"He was a foreigner." Ginny's nose wrinkles. "And a rapist."

***

Lyuba's head jerks up. "You're from the Godunovs' band. Misha and Kostya sent you here. What are you offering today, money, meat, potatoes, fish, bread, blankets? It'll be cold before long, and I need more blankets for my little girl."

"Lyuba, don't you know me?"

"Oh, what man in your band haven't I known by now. Are you the one who gave me the pork after that fifteen-minute feel I gave you?"

"The Godunovs forced you into prostitution?"

"Oh, no, I became a shameless whore on my own. Not like I got any pleasure out of it. I've never gotten any pleasure out of a sexual experience. It was all for food, water, and blankets."

"I know it's been awhile, but not more than two months!" He looks straight into her eyes. "Don't you recognize me with a beard?"

Lyuba shrieks, leaps off the bench, and throws her arms around him, her whole body violently shaking. She breaks down sobbing for the umpteenth time recently when she feels his arms locked around her. "It's you, Vanyechka, love of my life! You escaped before they could shoot you because you love me! Oh, I've been such a whore with that band the Godunovs have, all because you weren't there! I sold my body for food, money, and blankets for

Tatyana! I've been with so many men, while you've never gotten a turn at it!"

"I'm a wanted criminal, Lyuba my love. I escaped Lubyanka and found my *Tyotya* Lera. She was going to America. I didn't find you in time to go with her. But we must get out of Moskva, the sooner the better!"

"Shall we go south to the White strongholds?"

"No. That's too far a journey. We'll go up toward Estonia. I want us to be out of Russia by next year at this time!"

"Only if I leave with you, Vanyechka."

"You know I wouldn't dream of leaving you behind to the Bolsheviks."

"And you'll adopt Tatyana."

"She's my daughter, and you'll be my wife by next year." He reaches into his pocket. "Look what I stole. Two wedding rings. From now on, we'll pretend what we should've pretended all along."

"Come right inside. You haven't changed clothes since you broke out of prison?"

"No. Leave that alone. I'm fine. All I need to do is shave."

"Ilya Nikolayevich will surely give you a change of clothing. He gave me a new coat without being asked."

"Yes, but don't look. You might not like what you see."

Ginny looks up from Lermontov. "Ivan, you're alive!"

"I escaped to avoid being shot. I'm a wanted criminal. We're leaving Moskva as soon as possible. From now on, you're Lyuba's brother. Better get used to using your real name, Mikhail."

"I prefer Grigoriy, my middle name. Zhora calls me that. I bet I'm the only Russian with a real middle name, and I like making the most of it."

"Whatever you call yourself, you're her brother. You and Lyuba were orphaned quite young and raised by a doting Cossack family. When she married me at fifteen, you both took my name." He turns to Mr. Lebedev. "What's a good assumed surname? Privately, we'll be the Konevs, but I'm not dumb enough to just change my patronymic and keep using my same surname."

"Bodrov. Short, simple, and to the point."

Ginny pulls on his sleeve. "Can I still visit Zhora?"

"I'm afraid not. We have to get out of here as soon as possible, and not do anything that arouses suspicions or puts anyone at risk."

"Do as Ivan says, Ginny," Lyuba says. "We've come this far, and I don't want us to be split up again so close to freedom in America."

Ginny shrugs, picks up a book, and goes upstairs to read. Tatyana is still asleep with Kroshka. Lyuba goes upstairs with Mr. Lebedev, who goes into his room and returns with a medium blue shirt, pale brown trousers, white cotton stockings, and a well-laundered union suit. He puts the clothing in Lyuba's arms, trying not to look at her during this somewhat personal exchange. For her part, Lyuba is relieved the union suit is safely tucked into the middle, not on display. She hurries back downstairs after muttering a thank-you.

"Here you are—" Lyuba drops the clothes and stops in her tracks.

Ivan turns around, his eyes dilated. "I told you not to look!"

"I've seen you shirtless before. And have you forgotten that week at the hotel? I've seen you with *all* your clothes off!"

"Oh, so you didn't notice what I was afraid of you noticing."

"Yes I did. Those are wounds on your back!"

"They're from bramble patches I had to wade through on my way to finding you. They'll go away."

"Those are whiplashes, Vanya. They did that to you after I left prison!"

"You weren't supposed to find out!"

"I should've been there. I never should've consented to leave without you."

"If you'd stayed, Tatyana would've been taken away, and we never would've seen her again!"

Lyuba touches the wounds gingerly. "Have you treated them yet?"

"I'm still on the run from the law! First I killed a man to save you, then I get thrown into Lubyanka, then I help two women prisoners escape, then I'm told I'll be shot in the morning, and then I escaped prison myself and just now found you!"

Lyuba leaves and comes back with soap, a washcloth, and a basin of water. "Sit still."

Ivan winces at the soapy water on the still-fresh wounds on his back. "Can you knock me out with chloroform?"

She smirks. "If only all our friends knew how sensitive you really are."

"Do you have to dig so far into those wounds? It's not like I spent the last few months in a cesspool of diseases or slept on blood and rust."

"I'm getting any infections out so you don't catch something. You didn't let me get off when you put that iodine on my hand. I hope you didn't get tetanus or hepatitis."

Halfway through the cleaning, the washcloth slips out of her hands as she starts sobbing. When she tries to pick it up, she falls onto her knees and knocks over the basin, sending dirty water and soapy residue spilling in a puddle on the floor.

"Come here, *golubka*," Ivan says softly. "What are you thinking? I'm safe and we're together again. We'll never be apart again if I can help it." He pulls her onto his lap and puts his arms around her, stroking her long sable hair.

"My sweet, gentle, darling Vanyushenka was tortured and hurt by those jailers for no reason! It's been years since your father laid hands on you, and now you were beaten all over again! I'll have nightmares tonight, seeing you being whipped by those savages! How dare they treat you like you couldn't feel any pain and had no feelings!"

"Well, it's over now. It only happened once. I grit my teeth and got through it. I had to take it like a man so I wouldn't look like a pansy to anyone."

"What did you do to deserve being whipped!"

"They don't need reasons for anything there. I was a model prisoner up till my escape. They decided I needed some torture like all the other prisoners, and pushed me against a wall in one of the torture chambers. At least they beat me and not you. I would've strangled them with their own whip had they seized you and tried to give you thirty whiplashes."

"Thirty! That's not human behavior! How dare they hurt you so badly! You didn't do anything wrong!"

"Like I said, it's over now. God willing, we'll be out of here soon and will be in a land that doesn't torture people and hunt them down for having different opinions."

Lyuba sits on his lap holding him for the next twenty minutes, as he whispers in her ear about the farm he wants to have in the American Midwest, and all the children they're going to have. When she's finally collected herself and calmed down, she resumes cleaning out the wounds on his back and then goes for iodine. After she's done applying the iodine, she puts dressing on his back and secures it with strips of gauze going around his chest.

"You're a good nurse, Lyubashka. Now that you're finally done, can I see my daughter?"

"She missed you too. I wasn't the only one. She cried all the time for her *papashka*, and Kroshka, the little dog, tried to cheer her up. But first, you need to rest and eat. You also need to shave. She probably won't know who you are with a beard!"

Lyuba has Ivan lie in bed upstairs after he gets rid of his facial hair. She hands him Mr. Lebedev's clothes and disappears until lunchtime, when she comes back upstairs to give him a bowl of borshcht. At supper, she comes upstairs with two bowls of *rassolnik* on a tray, Tatyana toddling behind her.

"She's already eaten. I told her you were upstairs taking a nap. She couldn't wait to see her father!"

"Papa!" Tatyana squeals.

Lyuba's eyes brim with tears as she watches Tatyana pull herself onto the bed and toddle over to hug her father. Ivan reaches into his pocket and pulls out the orange hair ribbon, which he lovingly ties in Tatyana's hair. It's the family she never wanted, crystallizing before her eyes. The love she sees in Ivan's eyes for Tatyana is real. He has become her real father. Her destiny lies with the love of her life. She wants nothing more to do with the Zhukova name and all the pain the man she got it from caused her. From now on, she will engage in the charade of being Mrs. Koneva.

****

Chapter 14: Sorting Things Out

That evening, Pyotr comes to Mr. Golitsyn's boardinghouse in a large wagon with a false bottom. The top is covered in newspapers and dead fish.

"Has there been any trouble?" Kat asks. "Everything here has been so peaceful since that awful first week."

"I just received a phonecall from Lyuba. In April, she and Ivan went to prison because Ivan killed Basil—"

"What!" Eliisabet shrieks. "He killed a man!"

"What did Lyuba go to prison for?" Nikolas asks, white-faced.

"She didn't want to be separated from him. Ginny stayed at Georgiya's house till she got out. Ivan helped two women escape earlier this month, and was going to be shot in the morning for it. He escaped and just today found Lyuba, Ginny, and Tatyana."

"I'm glad he killed Basil," Aleksey says.

"How did they find out?" Kittey gasps.

"Aleksandr Sergeyevich Shepilov was spying on them. I can't believe what that boy turned into."

"Why did he kill Basil?" Kat asks.

"He raped Lyuba again."

"That's impossible," Aleksey asserts. "After what I did to him!"

"I can't believe it either, but apparently it's possible. Now enough catching up. You need to start packing. You're moving to the outskirts of Moskva tonight. I promise you, by March, you'll be leaving for America."

"March?" Kittey asks. "Less than a year?"

"I have the plan all memorized in my head. I burnt the papers last week, after committing it to memory. Remember, I could be charged with being a double agent."

"Are you coming with us?" Eliisabet asks.

"I can't. My father is an important man in the Communist Party, and he'd send thugs to kill me if I defected. I also believe in Bolshevism, yet lately it's not exactly following the teachings of Marx down to the letter. Like seizing land from the peasants. That's nowhere in anything Marx or Engels ever wrote. You didn't hear this political heresy from me."

"But you'll go with us as far as the coast?" Nikolas asks.

"I lied to my father and his important bureaucratic friends about taking a trip to see how different cities are adjusting to Bolshevik rule. I'm supposed to gather information to publish in an important journal of political critique, written by several different camps of Bolsheviks. I'm deferring my third year of university for this. The plan is for you to set sail on the fourteenth of March, 1921."

"What's special about that date?" Nikolas asks.

"It's the thirty-eighth anniversary of the death of Marx. Estonia is free, but if the Bolsheviks crush the Baltic states like they crushed other independent republics, there's a distraction built into that date. With all the memorial speeches and parades I expect to be held, no one will much care what's going on at the harbor."

"And then we're free," Kittey says incredulously.

"There are still a bit over nine months yet to go. Don't count your chickens before they're hatched."

They leave the boardinghouse at midnight, carrying their suitcases and wearing layers of clothing in the hot summer night. Pyotr drives them in the wagon for an hour, occasionally stopping to chat with Party members guarding the roads. The wagon he explains away as his transportation during his coming tour of the cities west of Moskva. It's one in the morning when they get to the house, which looks more like a large, imposing hotel.

"Get inside as fast as possible. Even one of Comrade Litvinov's sons can be followed." Pyotr herds them out of the wagon at the speed of light and flings open the door. "Look back one last time. During autumn, I'll move you to Tver, unless something goes wrong and I need to come up with an emergency plan and another place to keep you."

"We won't do a thing to stir up suspicions," Kat promises.

Two women come running in the door, their clothes ripped and covered in grey smoke residue, their hair black from soot, their hands full of bags.

"Oh, Petya, we found you just in time!"

"Our boardinghouse was torched, and we got away with our lives and everything we own!"

"They were shooting everyone and throwing grenades and raping old women and grabbing children and there was blood everywhere and they stole things and we got out through the back window with our things!"

"They made us watch the slow, painful torture of an eighty-seven-year-old man with burning coals on his eyeballs and a red-hot fire poker up his nose, and they poked pins and needles into his face and sodomized his dead body, and everyone was screaming, and people who screamed were knifed!"

"We'd been there over a year, and now ruins!"

Pyotr looks at the one with short hair. "Katrin?"

"We nearly got burnt alive while we were saving our things!" Anastasiya blubbers.

"I showed all my papers proving me a member of the Party, and they told me to take part in the pillaging, but I refused to leave Stasya!"

"Thank God I saved my cosmetics."

Aleksey looks at them with disgust. "Your boardinghouse burnt down, and all you could think about was saving material things over your own lives?"

"I can't live without my cosmetics, shampoo, furs, expensive clothes, pictures of handsome men, and magazines."

"The reappearance of these two harebrains just threw a major kink in your great plan, Petya!" Kittey shouts.

"They were with the Cheka," Katrin shudders.

Pyotr throws his hands up. "You two find a room, and don't dare do anything more to ruin my plans! So now I have a dozen people to smuggle out, not just ten."

"I don't want to leave, unless it's to go home to Estonia. I belong to the Party. This is just temporary craziness. They'll settle down to live the best Socialist ideals eventually."

"But I *am* leaving," Anastasiya asserts. "I don't want to live like this, my existence practically illegal, with the constant fear of having to run at a moment's notice. I want to go to America and live my dream of becoming a fashion designer."

"If you join the Party, you can become a famous fashion designer here. Even proud Bolshevik women should care about looking nice. Maybe someday you could design clothes for Comrade Krupskaya, my hero."

"I cannot become part of something which is morally reprehensible to me."

"The Bolsheviks are on the march. If anyone does anything to arouse suspicions here, I'll be arrested along with you." Pyotr walks through the front door and goes back to his wagon.

2

Lyuba wakes up in the middle of the night and finds Ivan lying next to her. Her eyes widen, and she looks around to make sure Ginny is still sound asleep.

"I hope I didn't scare you. I just couldn't help myself when it's been so long since we shared a bed. That's all I wanted to do. You know me better than to think I came here to have my way with you."

"You're a good boy, Vanya. You've never forced yourself on me to satisfy your own selfish pleasure. Most men don't listen to a woman when she tells them to stop moments away from the actual act."

"I'm not a boy. I'll be twenty-two in a week!"

"You don't do things grown men do, like drink, womanize, and tell dirty stories. You're as pure as a choirboy."

"Guilty as charged. I can't argue with you there." He brushes his hand against her face. "When I was on the run from prison, all I could think about was you."

"No one wants to marry such a slut. I'm fine to lie down with, but not respectable enough to marry. Deep down, I suspect even you have reservations about marrying someone with so many previous men."

"Those other excuses for men only wanted your body, and never had you by consent. When you offered yourself to the Godunovs and their friends, that was under duress, not desire. I want your heart and soul, not just your body. After I discovered what your father did to you, I didn't think you were damaged, a slut, unworthy of an honorable husband." He squeezes her hand. "I always felt so helpless as I watched through my bedroom window as your father came in and pulled the drapes shut. I heard everything. I probably don't want to know the answer, but was it going on for a long time before you moved next door, or just recent?"

"You won't like this very much, Vanyechka. He started three days after my second birthday. I was damaged merchandise very young. I was too young to remember the exact starting time, but I can't remember a time when he wasn't raping me. He later felt the need to tell me the day he started."

Ivan drops her hand and clenches his fists. "If he's still alive, I'm going to hunt him down and strangle him!"

"No! I felt what it was like to be without the only person who's ever loved me completely, and if you killed another man, you'd go to prison again!"

"Neither Basil or your father deserve to be called men! I'm the only man who's ever treated you like a human being, not like a dog or a prostitute!"

"Do you really still love me, after how many times I've thrown your selfless love back in your face or not fought harder to be together? I don't do it because I'm a heartless *suka* who enjoys playing games with you, I swear. I don't know what to do with a nice guy who wants me for more than sex."

"Soon you'll be mine permanently, and won't feel the need to keep running away from what's in your heart." He takes her hands and strokes them.

"Why don't we go to a clerk's office and get it over with? Becoming your wife would do wonders for my mind, just as becoming a mother when I never wanted a child forced me to adapt to that other role I was so afraid of. For better or worse, a woman has to stay faithful to her husband and take care of her child."

"I want us to be married in a church, not an office. That's not a real marriage. Such a marriage isn't valid under Orthodoxy, so we'd be living in sin. Besides, you deserve a wedding worthy of a Tsaritsa."

"We had that chance, and I ruined it. I thought I was making the best decision by choosing to stay in Russia and finish gymnasium, but little did I know my world was about to fall apart."

"It doesn't matter anymore. The money I saved for us to sail to America and have a stately reception at St. Basil's was squandered on presents for that vain little witch Anastasiya Voroshilova to make you jealous. Even if I still had that money, it'd be useless."

"I forgive you. I just wish you could forgive me for listening to my mother and not coming back to you sooner. She's been in America for over three years, and I've had so much time to marry you. I had no parental supervision to get in my way. I could've easily married you the very day she left, but I'm too weak-willed, damaged, and stupid." Lyuba starts to cry. "She left me behind. Ginny and Tatyana are my only family left. Our friends aren't family, as much as they feel like family. Although perhaps someday little Kolya will be our son-in-law."

"Our little girl is only seventeen months old. It's far too early to think about that!"

"*Our* little girl, Vanya?"

"She's always been my child, even if I didn't make her. I loved her before she was born, and I was the who took care of you while that *mudak* was off doing God knows what with his shady friends. Every time I felt Tanyechka moving after Malenkov beat you, my heart flooded with relief."

"Why couldn't you come while I was in labor? Petya could've found a doctor or midwife by himself, and didn't need you. You came in with that shallow snob Anastasiya Voroshilova. Thank God Ginny kicked her out right that very minute."

"I can never be sorry enough for how I pretended to be in love with her to try to get you to leave Boris. I regret so much not going right into that house and being there while Ginny fetched the doctor. I should've been there. But the moment I saw Tanyechka, she became my baby."

"I pictured Boris holding my hands as I gave birth, both of us crying, and getting married as soon as possible. Even if I never loved him, it was the right thing to do. I never contemplated returning to you, since that would cause too much scandal and make Borya angry."

"That was my child you gave birth to, even if I'm not the blood father. Of course, your other children will be mine biologically too. We have the first already, so there's eight more to go. All your other pregnancies will go much more smoothly. You'll never have to worry I'll beat you."

"He didn't beat me that often."

"He pushed you down the stairs, beat you right over the baby with an iron crowbar, tried to squash her to death, and slammed you into walls! Not to mention all those bruises, scratches, and strangle marks, or all those times he beat you with a belt or stick."

"I was trained to expect that kind of behavior in a man. Not beatings necessarily, but abuse and disrespect. Part of me is afraid of being loved forever by a sweet, nice man like you. It doesn't feel normal."

Ivan kisses her for the first time in months. Lyuba purrs her approval as he runs his left hand along her face and down her neck. She takes his hand in hers and pulls it towards her breasts, but he doesn't take the hint.

"We're not *really* married. We only have to pretend in public."

"We'll be married one day, love. Don't you want a lesson?"

"You said it yourself. I'm a good boy. And I want it to be special, like that night at the hotel when we almost went all the way. We don't have enough privacy here."

Lyuba falls back asleep in his arms, her head against his shoulder. The only man attracted to her who can withstand the temptation of such a situation, she thinks before she falls back asleep.

Lyuba decides to see if she can persuade him. The next day, she looks on approvingly after breakfast as Ivan reads to Tatyana from one of Mr. Lebedev's books and then puts her down for a nap after lunch. She can't help smiling when he feeds Tatyana mashed vegetables for supper. *Like a real father*, she thinks. He puts Tatyana to bed that night in the crib upstairs, then spends the next few hours discussing the news with Lyuba, Galya, and Mr. Lebedev. After Ivan retires to bed a few hours later, she puts down *Notes from Underground* and creeps upstairs. While he lovingly watches Tatyana sleeping, Lyuba steals into a closet and divests herself of her blouse.

Ivan turns around when he feels Lyuba's hand on his shoulder, then instantly looks away. "What are you doing!"

"Get your hand away from your eyes, Vanya, and look at me."

"What if Mr. Lebedev comes up here right this minute and sees you topless!"

"Look at me, my good little choirboy. For the love of Christ, you've seen me completely naked before, and now I only have my blouse off."

He looks right at her face. "I thought I told you yesterday."

"Oh, even *now* you're looking me right in my eyes! You're almost twenty-two and a virgin!"

"My mother raised me to respect women!"

"At times like this, I doubt you were named for Ivan the Great. Might as well have been named for Ivan the Meek!"

"I'm anything but meek."

"Oh, right, you have it out with anyone who gets you mad, but around me you turn into a little polite schoolboy."

"Did either of you want some crumb cake before bed?"

"Here comes Mr. Lebedev! Go hide in the closet!"

"Tell me which Tsar you were named for again, the Great or the Meek."

"He's coming up the stairs!"

"After the life I've lived, I'm hardly modest."

Ivan unbuttons his shirt, throws it around Lyuba, and starts buttoning it up just before Mr. Lebedev enters the attic.

"What in the world was going on up here?"

"I was trying to get the man I love to lighten up!"

"My daughters slept here. I don't want anything scandalous to happen in their room and soil their sleeping quarters." Mr. Lebedev sets the plate of crumb cake on a table and goes back downstairs.

"Yes, you *were* named for Ivan the Second, the Meek."

"No I wasn't. You should know that."

"Although sometimes I swear you were named for Ivan Grozniy, with the violent temper you have. And you killed a man."

"I was completely in the right! And because I killed him to protect the love of my life, I'm now an escaped criminal!"

Lyuba looks down at her unexpected change of clothes. "Now I know why some women say it's exciting to wear a lover's clothes. Your manly scent is all over this, making me want you even more." She leans in and kisses him. "When I thought you were dead, I cried myself to sleep. I thought, if only I'd been carrying your child, there would always be a part of you in the world."

"I don't want you to bring another child into a war-torn country. Bad enough Tatyana was born during this modern *Smutnoye Vremya*."

"I'm dying to become a respectable woman."

"I've always respected you. No matter what society says about you."

3

Lena and Antonina tiptoe around Mrs. Voznesenskaya as she's sleeping. Mrs. Voznesenskaya's favorite girl in the orphanage besides the dead Mikhaila is fifteen-year-old Klarisa Mstislavovna Baryshnikova. Klarisa is indeed a baryshnitsa, *a lucky woman. She uses her position of trust and authority to sneak extra food to the girls in her quarters; drug Mrs. Voznesenskaya's nightly vodka so they can stay up late and plan an orphanage break; smuggle packages to their recipients; arrange secret meetings with boyfriends, brothers, and male cousins; let the girls write letters home; and set up lists of chores for the most hated girls. Klarisa is also an expert forger. She always wears gloves when she puts together fake documents, and sometimes uses her left hand to give the forgery an added look of authenticity.*

"Why did tonight's cook keep those five girls extra?" Lena is shuddering.

"Miss Kaganova let the five Jewish girls stay behind because they're her own. Last week, Mrs. Kirkorian kept behind the three Armenian girls, and whenever there's a Russian cook, a selected group of us get to stay for extra portions," Antonina says.

"Mrs. Voznesenskaya will sleep for hours," Klarisa smirks. "You'll be long gone by the time she's awake. I forged papers to make it seem like a governmental agency came in the night to take you away to avoid overcrowding."

"I can't get very far if I go tonight," Lena says. "My hair's barely begun to grow back." She shudders even more when she looks at the dead, incorruptible Mikhaila. Mrs. Voznesenskaya shaved Mikhaila's head to get rid of the lice, and took away Lena's long, flowing red hair to make a wig.

"'I'm barren, so I like to pretend she's my daughter,'" Antonina mimics.

Klarisa extends a red French human hair wig. "Ask and you shall receive. I trust you won't miss this godawful new uniform. I wish I could've found you slightly nicer street clothes to change into."

"I hope my mother and remaining sister haven't given me up for dead. As soon as I get home, we should move somewhere safer."

"Did you really think you were going back to Moskva? I've gotten you travel papers for Canada. As to your mother and Zina, I made inquiries, and found out they moved to Tver shortly after you came here. I suppose they had the same thought you did, avoiding trouble. I'm sure your little boy is safe with them."

"Canada? Not America? And how are Tonya and I supposed to travel so far without an adult escort?"

"America has a number of immigration restrictions, while Canada's more open. I'd feel terrible if you were immediately deported after I went to so much trouble to smuggle you to safety."

4

Ivan looks up the next night and immediately looks away when he sees Lyuba casually standing there without a stitch of clothing. As much as he longs to look, he can't let himself get tempted.

"You tried this last night, and I told you your answer."

"I'm giving you one minute to look at me before I take matters into my own hands. Didn't you ever look at art in school?"

"But this is *you!*"

"You're not looking at me, Vanya. And you said you wanted nine children."

"Did you really miss me that much?"

"Look at me, Vanya."

He slowly turns to look at her, his gaze travelling up and down her body several times. "You're beautiful."

"I bet Anastasiya Voroshilova never took all her clothes off for you, did she?"

"Why do you have to bring that dull-headed woman up? I'm back with you now, and I never loved that harebrain. But I can't do that. You know how sickeningly pure and moral I am. I've never even smoked a cigarette."

"Because you're a good boy, my Vanyechka." Lyuba starts unbuttoning his shirt and is pleased when he throws it onto the floor. "Now show me you really are almost twenty-two instead of a meek twelve-year-old Sunday school boy."

"You've been with so many other men..."

"What's there to be compared to, love? It was all rape or prostitution. But maybe that's your way of trying to tell me why you're so hesitant to be my lover. You think I'll compare you to other men, or you'll never measure up, or you don't want the stigma of bedding used merchandise. It's hard to believe you're the same person who was so eager to do that the first night at the hotel. You couldn't keep your hands off my body."

"That was a different time and place. Everything's different now, more complicated."

Lyuba gets into Matryona's bed. "Aren't you coming, Vanya?"

Like an obedient puppy, Ivan lies next to her and begins to kiss and caress her. Lyuba gasps in delight when she feels his hands exploring her body, treating her like gourmet chocolate to be slowly savored instead of a cheap cookie to be quickly gobbled. As he nibbles at her neck, Lyuba gently touches the wounds on his back.

"They're not so deep. They'll go away. You can do whatever you want to me, and I won't complain." He gently pulls on her knee for improved access to her most erogenous area, and she buries her face in the pillow to stifle her ensuing moans as he stumbles across the most sensitive part of her body.

Lyuba has just undone the top button of Ivan's pants when Mr. Lebedev comes into the room. He stops in his tracks.

"I thought I told you my rules yesterday! My daughters slept here! This was Matryona's bed!"

"We're under the covers, Ilya Nikolayevich. You didn't see anything."

"You know my rules. Matryona slept there." Mr. Lebedev turns around and goes back downstairs.

Ivan gently pushes her hands away.

"You're so damn lucky I love you so much. If I were any other type of woman, I probably would find someone who doesn't care when and where we lie together. A man your age should be eager to do this, not find excuses to stop. At least you don't need a cold bath this time."

5

Pyotr comes down to breakfast the next morning with a tattered valise stuffed with official-looking pamphlets and notepads, covering his false passports for Ivan, Lyuba, and Ginny, and the passports he forged for Nikolas and Kittey. All the other Stray Dogs have their original passports. His father is at the table with four of his important Party friends and five of Pyotr's brothers.

"Dobroye utro, moy syn," Mr. Litvinov beams. "So eager to start on your journey?"

"You know me, I've been passionate about spreading the word about Communism since I was a young boy!"

"Are you also passionate about turning in enemies of the people?"

"I don't associate with people who try to undermine the Bolshevik cause. I cheered loudest of all when Fanya Kaplan was shot for trying to murder Comrade Lenin!"

"I've taught you well, my boy." Mr. Litvinov sips his tea. "Weren't you good friends with Ivan Ivanovich Konev?"

"Yes, even though he and his family supported Bloody Nikolay."

"Are you aware he was in Lubyanka and was supposed to be shot earlier this month, because he killed one of your good friends, Basil Yakovlevich Beriya?"

"I know Basil is dead, *Batya*. How could I not? It was in the newspaper!"

"So then you know about how innocent Basil was taking an early morning walk by Konev one morning and set the man off. I remember the stories from your school days, Petrushka. Konev had a big temper. The slightest thing could set him off. He should've been named for Ivan Grozniy!"

"But Ivan has a big heart. As big as his bad temper."

"For no sane reason at all, Konev grabbed an axe and slammed it over poor Basil's head repeatedly, completely ignoring his pleas to live."

"Basil was no saint. Decent people are never thrown into nut-houses like the Marx Center for the Crazies."

"His brain oozed out of his head, my boy. That's cruel and inhumane death!"

"Basil raped Lyubov Leontiyevna Zhukova multiple times. He wasn't attacked for no reason."

Mr. Litvinov smiles. "She's a beautiful woman. What man could help himself?"

"So you condone rape!"

"He's a man possessed by Satan, that Konev. Even as he was killing your friend Basil, he insulted him by using the axe with the hand of Satan!"

"Ivan's left-handed. That doesn't mean he's possessed by Satan. That's an old wives' tale! I cheered him on every year when he refused the new teacher's orders to start writing with his right hand. That's how he came into this world, left-handed. Perhaps it's a special mark of greatness, since so few people have that trait."

"Kuzma was originally left-handed, and *he* was purged of Satan by his first grade teacher!"

Pyotr's oldest brother Kuzma smirks. "*Batya* was wondering if you're still in contact with Konev the murderer and Satan-possessed left-handed demon."

"I haven't seen Ivan in months. Not since last year, if I remember correctly."

"You're admitting to being in contact with a defector to the new Soviet State!" the next-oldest brother, Venedikt, shouts.

"I see him when I see him. He's changed location numerous times since the triumphant Revolution, so it's not like he has a permanent address I can visit whenever I feel the need to chat."

"Konev escaped from prison," the third-oldest, Viktor, says. "That means he's a wanted criminal."

"Before you start on your journey, dear brother Pyotr, you have to prove your loyalty to Communism," says the brother a year his junior, Fredrikh.

"Yes, by helping us track down this terrible enemy of the state. We'll find out where he's being a fugitive and burn the place down," eighteen-year-old Rikhard says. "That's what happens when you run away from the law."

"I'm a loyal Communist and am completely insulted by the mere notion I'm trying to undermine its strong foundation. Don't you know I read Marx, Engels, and Comrade Lenin every day like enemies of the people read the Bible? I'd never cross you, *Batya*."

"Answer his goddamn question, Pyotr," his oldest sister, fat twenty-eight-year-old Leonida, snorts. "Are you or aren't you going to help *Batya* and his important Party friends catch this left-handed criminal?"

Pyotr knows what double-crossing he's about to undertake will be greater than any of the double-crossing he's done over the past three years. "Yes. I'll do it, *Batya*. I'll throw the first grenade or torch."

Pyotr gets into his car and discovers three of his father's Party friends are following him. Hoping he won't waste too much precious gasoline, he drives around the city desperately, going down every side street and into every small neighborhood and nearby town he can think of to throw them off. Finally, three hours after he set out, he loses them near Nikolayevskiy Station.

***

Lyuba starts up at the sound of a car pulling up outside, and tiptoes to the window to slowly raise the thick, medium blue curtain. "Praise Christ. That's our friend Petya, the Bolshevik saint I told you about. I imagine he has a safer place for us to hide in. You've been so good to take us in without advance notice, and have treated us so nicely. I'll never forget you, and I pray you find the rest of your daughters."

"About the money you gave me to pay your rent. Take it." Mr. Lebedev pushes the bills into her hands. "I don't need it. Lyolya's coat is yours to keep too. You need a new one. If I find my Lyolya anytime soon, I'm sure she'll agree giving you her coat was the right thing to do. Someone needs to wear it, even if that person can't be the original owner. It's too nice to gather dust in a closet."

"You've been so kind to us, Ilya Nikolayevich. If you ever escape to America, I'd be delighted to see you again." Lyuba opens the door.

Pyotr hands them each a fake passport. "Get in the car and pull the black blinds down. My father wants me to track you down, Ivan, and torch the house the others are at. This is the gravest act of double-crossing I've ever taken part in."

They run into the car with their suitcases. Once Lyuba takes a seat, she looks at the names on their phony passports. Lyubov Mikhaylovna Bodrova. Ivan Igorovich Bodrov. Grigoriy Mikhaylovich Bodrov. Tatyana Ivanovna Bodrova. Perfect.

"I took away your patronymics, Lyuba and Ivan, and replaced them with patronymics from your uncles. I hope you approve."

"Does your father know what you've been doing these past three years?" Ginny whispers. "How you've been helping Whites?"

"He knows of no such thing, and never will. I'll take part in destroying the residence I sent the others to, but only after I smuggle you all out. I'll try to stall my father and his friends until at least September. That's when I plan to sneak you into Tver." He looks at Ivan, shaking his head. "You should've seen how much hate my father had in his eyes, saying *levsha*, as though you're possessed by Satan."

"God made me a *levsha*," Ivan says. "Who am I to argue with Divine will?"

"Why you?" Lyuba asks. "You have six brothers and four brothers-in-law who could easily help your father as well."

"I saw the looks in their eyes, Viktor, Fredrikh, Rikhard, Kuzma, Leonida, Venedikt, and the four Party friends he brought over to the house. Like they all suspected me of something terrible, but didn't want to let on just what. I think my father is on to me, with all my trips around the city, and now this supposed journey to report back on Communism in Western Russia for a scholarly Party publication next spring."

"You're going to do research so as not to give yourself away. I don't want you to be thrown in prison or killed. You're our only hope to go to America."

"Of course I'll do the research! That's my whole cover for getting you twelve on that ship in Tallinn."

"Twelve?" Ginny asks. "Have you found Alya and Anya?"

"Katrin and Anastasiya. Their boardinghouse was torched and looted a few days ago. They left by a back window after almost dying in the fire, because they just had to save all their cosmetics, furs, clothes, vanity items, celebrity pictures, and magazines. Unbelievable how shallow those two are! And Katrin an alleged committed Socialist! There are to be no more trips into town from now on, do you hear me? I have plans for you to get on that ship in March. Any little thing could totally destroy your chances of leaving."

"What's the itinerary?" Ginny asks.

"One thing at a time. Now keep quiet, and when I stop the car, rush right into that house and go into the room I'll show you. I have enough trouble already with this double-crossing I'm about to undertake with my father."

6

Lena gets on the ship, carrying her bags, followed by Antonina. They show their passports and tickets to the captain, and he waves them on.

"No male guardian or relative?" an older woman asks. "You're awfully brave to travel alone at your age."

"Are you volunteering your husband as our chaperone?" Antonina asks.

"My husband's gone. Dead, probably. My two little girls are gone as well, and my niece and my best friend's daughter. I almost joined them in the other world, but a very kind young man helped me to escape Lubyanka after I was shot in the arm."

"Maybe you can pretend to be our aunt," Lena says. "We just escaped an awful orphanage and are pretending to be cousins. As soon as I'm in Canada,

I'll write to my mother and remaining sister, Zina. I'll do whatever it takes to bring them to safety. I miss my little boy Yuriy so much. I hope he doesn't treat me like a scary stranger when I finally see him again."

The woman's eyes widen. "You're a mother? I won't judge you, but I can't believe someone who looks so young already has a child. At your age, I have to assume this wasn't a child created through choice."

Lena nods. "I got pregnant at eleven and gave birth at twelve. I'm thirteen now. At least my mother and sisters never called me a slut or forced me to give him to an orphanage, since they know what Misha's really all about."

"My father was created out of wedlock too, and not through choice either. Though his mother, unlike you, gave him to a married couple to raise. You're very brave to keep a bastard."

"Our orphanage matron was a sick woman." Antonina shudders. "She's kept a poor dead girl in a bed for almost a year. Lena had to sleep with her. Mrs. Voznesenskaya, that sick devil, is barren, so she likes to pretend the dead girl is her daughter, like brushing her long black hair, putting a coat over her, and carrying the corpse out for walks. That's deranged."

"I made faces at a clown dressed like Lenin at a circus," Lena says. "The clown made faces flirtatiously first, so I made them back. For that, I was arrested and thrown into an orphanage, starving."

The woman looks at them hopefully. "Did you by any chance run into my two girls, my niece, or my best friend's daughter? Do the names Katya Chernomyrdina, Naina Yezhova, or Mikhaila and Karla Gorbachëva ring a bell? My Mikhaila is probably the only girl with that name in the entire empire."

Antonina turns white. "Are you Mrs. Gorbachëva?"

"Call me Sonya, pozhaluysta. *I'm only thirty. I don't feel old enough to be called Mrs. or Widow yet!"*

"If you're Mrs. Gorbachëva, your older girl is the dead girl I had to sleep with!" Lena shudders.

"Mrs. Voznesenskaya got very enraged at Misha upon their arrival." Antonina puts her hand on Sonya's arm. "Misha demanded food almost as soon as they were processed, and Mrs. Voznesenskaya started beating her. She was petrified, but not too terrified to have a courageous last word, 'Freedom.' Three days after the beating, Mikhaila stopped breathing."

"One of my babies is dead!" Sonya lowers her head to her hands and starts weeping. "Forty-two weeks of pregnancy and forty hours of labor, all for nothing! Who murders an innocent child? She was too young to do anything wrong!"

Antonina puts her arm around her. "Karla left with the other two girls a short time later. She was saved. Your niece Naina seemed as tough as nails, as young as she was. She even had a handgun. I'm sure she's looking out for Karla, wherever they are now."

"I'm leaving behind the dead body of my firstborn child!"

"Our friend Klarisa will probably do some work to get people over to the orphanage and have them discover the dead body Mrs. Voznesenskaya covers with a sheet whenever authorities inspect the place. She may manage to ship it overseas in a coffin. Thanks to Klarisa's position of trust, Lena and I are going to Canada!"

"I'm sorry, we didn't introduce ourselves. I'm Yelena Vadimovna Yeltsina, and that's Antonina Borisovna Petrova. If it helps you feel any better, I know how torturous it feels to be far away from your child and not know if you'll ever meet again in this lifetime. I miss my darling little Yura so, so very much."

"Oh, look, a steamship. They can get people across the Atlantic in as little as two weeks." Antonina points. "Meanwhile we're stuck taking a huge ocean liner."

"Who's that man pushing everyone else in line aside?" Sonya asks. "Why is he in such hurry to unboard? And why do some of those people have an X on their clothes?"

Boris comes roaring onto the ship leaving for Canada. "Has anyone here seen my daughter and her mother?"

"I remember you," Lena says. "You're the fat man with the limp."

"I remember you too. You had a baby named Yuriy."

Lena's eyes narrow. "How did you find out my son's name?"

"Your sister Zina left him on the ground with a note pinned to him in April. She wanted someone to take him and give him a better life, since she and your mother could no longer care for him. I took him back to America with me."

"You took my son?"

"At the time, it seemed like a great idea, taking another baby to replace my own baby! Your sister saw, approached me, and gave her full approval."

"I love my baby! How dare you take him to America and then leave him to come back here!"

"That's not the worst of it. My daughter's great-aunt took him to an orphanage because my daughter's babushka *left him on the floor crying and without changing his diaper. She claimed it'd be impossible to take care of a baby when we all worked."*

"My son! An orphanage! Do you know I'll probably never see him again!

Who'd let an unwed mother reclaim her child from an orphanage! I'll never get my son back!"

"My daughter's mother was in the exact same situation, and nobody ever came to take my daughter away. You must remember her too, since she was with me the last time you saw me."

"She's old enough to pass for a married woman! I'm only thirteen! How dare you take my son away from me!"

"Blame your sister or my daughter's great-aunt and babushka!"

"You'd better hope to God Yura hasn't been adopted, you irresponsible cripple!" Antonina shouts. "Lena might never see him again!"

"Don't call me a cripple. Just my right leg is crippled. I was beaten up by Russophobes who broke my leg really badly, and was forced to keep working with a splint. I can still barely walk on my right leg without excruciating pain. It didn't heal for seventeen weeks."

"Oh, like a crippled leg is more serious than never seeing my baby again?"

Boris, infuriated, limps off the ocean liner and goes to get a train to Moskva. After travelling all day, he finally unboards at the mental home.

"Yes?" Miss Gorshchenko asks. "Are you here to visit anyone?"

"Tell me if Basil Yakovlevich Beriya is still safely imprisoned here. I want him coming nowhere near my little girl's mother. You remember me. I visited him this March, and got into an argument with him after finding out he's here for raping my daughter's mother. Where is he? Still safely chained to the wall?"

"Comrade Malenkov. Yes, I remember you. Comrade Beriya escaped one night that month. We were making the rounds and feeding people their breakfasts, and we saw he'd gone. Comrade Popov, a nut who thinks he's Karl Marx, and Comrade Nemova, who screams out the Nicene Creed nonstop, his neighbors against the wall we chained them to, told me and my father he slipped out of his chains after trying to bite them off. We were all speechless. But then my father looked closely, and actually did see bite marks! Go figure!"

"Did you catch him?"

"Sit down. Were you good friends with Comrade Beriya before he was put in the nuthouse for raping your child's mother?"

Boris drops into the indicated chair. "Not exactly good, but we got along better than my other friends got along with him. I tolerated him to a greater degree."

"So you felt sympathy for him."

"I feel no more sympathy for that sick, sick mudak. *He truly believed my child's mother enjoyed being raped!"*

"I know. That's why he got punished even more severely the next time he did it."

"He raped her again!"

"It was all over the local papers, about a young spy catching sight of the murder during an early morning walk. This wasn't a regular spying mission, just something he innocently happened upon! There were blood and brain fluid everywhere, all over the ground. Comrade Beriya was screaming and crying, and the murderer showed no remorse as he banged the rapist over the head time after time with an axe. The murderer was a levsha, *the boy reported. The man was rather tall, and his face was full of fury, like he'd die of rage if Comrade Beriya didn't shut up and die instantly. The murderer was arrested shortly afterwards and thrown into Lubyanka with his female companion and your daughter."*

"Ivan killed Basil! I can't believe it! He could get really furious at people when they set him off, but I never once guessed he'd actually go through with it and kill someone! He killed a man! Basil is dead. I can't believe it."

"Nobody ever found the body. We know the murder took place in Khimki Forest, but the authorities have better things to do with their time than to dig up the entire forest to find the exact location. After the boy ran away to report to police, they didn't do anything about it for a few days, until they got tired of dealing with the frantic mother hassling them with phonecalls every other hour about where her son had disappeared to. They told her then."

"Ivan is in prison. And Basil is dead, Lyuba's in prison, and my little girl is in prison too, if they haven't taken her away and stuffed her in an orphanage! Everyone I care about is gone!" Boris starts crying like a little child.

"Your friend, the levsha *who killed your other friend, Comrade Beriya the rapist, escaped from prison. He was supposed to be shot in the morning after helping two women prisoners escape. Now he's a wanted criminal. The woman and baby were set free shortly after the arrest."*

"This is so hard to digest, Comrade Gorshchenko!"

"Indeed."

"How dare he kill Basil. I wanted him to be punished in a nuthouse, not by being murdered!"

"I doubt you have another chance to win back your daughter's mother. The paper reported she was adamant about being arrested with the murderer, and only after being ordered to leave several times did she actually leave him."

"Lyuba and Ivan were best friends and next door neighbors. She loves me, not him. In fact, for all Ivan's talk about how much he adores my daughter's

mother, he's never slept with her, and he'll be twenty-two in a few days. I wonder if he's really attracted to women at all."

"Now, now. Konev said he killed Comrade Beriya out of his love for her."

"He doesn't love her. He was furious at me when I came back earlier this year, but if she'd really loved Ivan all these years, she never would've rushed into my arms like that the moment she saw me, nor would she have slept with me every night that week." Boris gets up and starts for the door. "I'll have proof soon enough Lyuba loves only one man—myself!"

7

Ivan is looking numbly at Lyuba. He cannot believe what she's just told him.

"I told you, I went to visit Nadya and Pavlik last night, and there were a lot of Nadya's clients hanging around. One of them was quite taken with me, and we both were having a lot to drink. He took me outside, and he—"

"He raped you! I'm going to hunt him down and kill him! I can't stand to see you go through yet another trauma!"

"Well, I figured, maybe I'd be safer from future rapes if I sold sex. Then I'd be the one in control, and no one would need to rape me ever again, since I'd be offering it of my own free will. I'm hardly a virgin, so why not join Nadya in her business and start making money off it? I can make so much money, we can go to America sooner than planned. I told Nadya I'll start work this afternoon."

"So you're going to be a prostitute! Treating yourself like a piece of meat!"

"There's good money in it for us, and I still love you."

"Petya told us not to go into town anymore. I'm a wanted criminal, and he's in danger of having his cover blown because of his latest act of deception."

"I'll live at the brothel. Nadya's the only hooker who doesn't live there."

"What about Tatyana?"

"She'll stay with you, of course. I'll miss her so much, but I don't want my little girl to see what her mother's doing to make the money to get us to America." She picks up Tatyana and cuddles her. "You'll be a good girl for your *papashka*, won't you, and do everything he and the other adults tell you?" She turns back to

Ivan, still cuddling Tatyana. "I know this looks bad on paper, but you have to believe I'm doing this for positive reasons and that you're the only man in my heart. If you were more worldly, you'd understand how one can have love without sexual acts and sexual acts without love."

"How could you? Just last week we practically made love to each other, and now you're going off to degrade yourself like that!"

"I still love you." Lyuba sets Tatyana down, picks up her valises, and kisses Ivan very briefly on the lips. "Goodbye, Vanya."

Ivan watches her leaving the house and going back to the neighborhood they had so much trouble in, the neighborhood where he killed Basil. He watches his heart go walking away from him for the umpteenth time and curses himself for being such a passive, submissive, obedient wimp of a man who's starting his twenty-second year of life. What a rotten birthday.

****

Chapter 15: Paternity Warfare

"Don't you want any of the birthday cake Kat and I made?" Eliisabet asks that afternoon. "I'm surprised Lyuba hasn't come to join us yet. I hope she's not ill."

"How can I want anything to eat when the woman I've loved since I was nine years old is right now letting a strange man have her body? She's become a prostitute, Liza. And just last week we practically made love to each other."

"A prostitute?" Kat demands. "Did I just hear you correctly?"

"Now you can have me again," Anastasiya grins. "I can't believe what a whore she is. I never suspected she was such a slut, not even when she got pregnant out of wedlock."

"Go away, you shallow, brainless excuse of a woman. I love only Lyuba."

"Give it up, Konev," Nikolas agrees. "She keeps walking away from you. That should tell you something loud and clear."

"She's been used by men her entire life! Boris and the Godunovs are hardly the first who exploited her!"

"What, you mean she was with men before Boris?" Kat gasps. "That's sure news to me!"

"Could it be Petya?" Aleksey asks. "If it was, that was sure a well-kept secret!"

"No, not Petya. She's never been with Petya."

"What other boy is there?" Eliisabet asks.

"Not a boy. Two grown men who should've known better. I'm only telling you this because we're such good friends, and I know you'll believe me and won't blame or judge Lyuba. I trust you'll never reveal this to anyone. Three days after her second birthday, her father destroyed her. Sometimes my father joined in too. Not that often, but sometimes. They should both go to Hell."

"Ivan, what exactly are you saying?" Aleksey asks.

"I'm saying Lyuba grew up being raped every night by her father!"

"She told you this?" Kat asks. "Was she drunk?"

"I witnessed this through my window. We were neighbors. I even listened outside the door the night we ran away to the hotel. I was such a *durak* for taking her home after a week and believing her father would suddenly keep his hands and *khuy* off her."

Kat turns green. "That man always gave me a bad feeling, but I never dreamt what was really wrong with him."

Eliisabet drops her fork. "Holy Mother of God, I knew there was a secret reason why she kept insisting she couldn't be with you and had to stay with Boris! She talked in vague generalities about being afraid of staying with a nice guy, but I never dreamt it was anywhere in that perverted league! No wonder she feels more familiar with being abused and disrespected by men!"

"And for being the only man who's ever treated her like a human being instead of an outlet for sexual desires, I keep having my love thrown back in my face!"

"Give her time, maybe a week," Nikolas says. "You want to look like a hero to her, rescuing her from the life of exploitation she's been forced into. You should rush right in there, grab her into your arms, propose marriage, and carry her away."

"She said she was doing it only for the money, though that doesn't make me feel any better."

"Do you or don't you want to look like a hero to her?" Eliisabet asks.

"Fine, I'll go to her in a week, but I don't expect a miracle. She's done this to me so damn many times before. If I were a man and not a mouse, I'd never have let her leave me or get away so many times."

2

That evening, Tatyana wakes him up with a loud cough. Ivan turns over and tries to go back to sleep, but the cough continues. *Lyuba would know what to do*, he thinks darkly.

"Okay, I'm coming, my little *knyazhna*." He picks her up and starts tapping her on the back. "Did some food go down the wrong way?"

"You're not very good at the fathering thing, are you, Ivan?" Eliisabet stops at the doorway. "It's croup. Kolya had the exact same thing last week. The best remedy is a room full of steam. What you're doing only works if you're burping a baby or if she's choking."

He runs down the hall into the only bathroom with a shower, turns it on full blast at the hottest temperature possible, and stands there with Tatyana till the cough goes away.

"Damn her. How dare she leave me with a child when she knows I have no idea how to take care of one by myself! I only did the easy stuff before, like bathing her."

"I thought you loved Lyuba!" Eliisabet chides.

"Don't mistake me, I love Tanyechka as though she's my own child, but I was an only child. I don't know how to`take care of a baby. That's an instinct the mother has, not the father."

"You'd better hope to God she comes back here. And you said you wanted nine children."

"I can find my way around the kitchen. I know how to cook. I can operate first aid and do elementary sewing. I'm not that stuck in the Dark Ages. I just don't know how to care for babies single-handedly."

3

Lyuba always was the one to give Tatyana her morning feeding. The next morning, Ivan has to get up early to warm milk and mash vegetables, then comes upstairs, carries her down to the table, and sits her in a highchair.

"What?" Kat asks in horror. "You're not going to change her diaper? She stinks!"

"What for? That's women's work!"

"Don't look at me to do that," Eliisabet says. "I just finished toilet training Kolya last month, and amn't about to do it all over again so soon."

"I don't know how to do that!" Ivan carries her outside to the outhouse, unpins the diaper, and sets her down on the hole in the ground.

Tatyana looks at him with a puzzled expression. Eliisabet comes up and starts giggling.

"She doesn't make a connection. She's only seventeen months old. Most children aren't out of diapers till their second birthday, and aren't dry through the night until their third birthday."

"I'll make her make the connection."

"Oh, for the love of God. I'll show you one time, and then you'll have to do it yourself." Eliisabet picks Tatyana up. "Do you know how to take a diaper off?"

"I just did!"

"You can't just take it off and be done with. You have to clean it, get a fresh diaper, and pin it in place."

Ivan watches her changing Tatyana. "You expect me to do this."

"You're her father, aren't you?"

"That's damn right I am."

"Don't you ever want to give up and find another woman to love, one who won't keep rejecting your love?" Eliisabet uncaps the powder. "I have no doubt you love each other, but it doesn't seem likely you'll live happily ever after."

"I won't rest easy till Lyuba is Mrs. Koneva."

"I'm not Mrs. Tvardovskaya. Don't assume a twentieth century woman will automatically follow that old custom and give up her identity."

"Lyuba wants nothing more to do with her evil father. I admit I get my own name from an evil father too, but what are we supposed to do, both change our names to something new?"

"She told me something before that first victory ball, about how the only reason she wasn't with you was because she was scared to be with a nice guy, and I didn't want to know the reason why. I said I'd never judge her if something horrible were done to her and that I hoped she might trust me enough to tell me eventually, but I never dreamt it was something as diabolical as incest! I wondered if she might've been raped, but never in my wildest dreams did I imagine the rapist were her father!"

"Okay, you're done. How soon will she need to have this done again?"

"It all depends. You can tell by checking for leaks or odor. Even you can't be that clueless about childcare."

"Now can I feed her breakfast?"

"Now she's ready."

***

Ivan fails miserably that afternoon as he tries to copy what Eliisabet did earlier. Kat, Kittey, and Eliisabet come up and giggle.

"You don't need to wear winter gloves. It's not like you'll get Bubonic Plague from changing a diaper!" Kat laughs.

"Watch where you put that pin!" Eliisabet shouts.

Tatyana howls.

"You just stuck the pin in her skin!" Eliisabet censures.

"Aren't you an enlightened man," Kittey smirks.

"Well, this is women's work!" He picks up Tatyana to cuddle and kiss her. "You know your *papashka* would never hurt you on purpose, *knyazhna*. After what my diabolical father did to me, the last thing I'd ever do would be to deliberately hurt any child of mine."

It is all falling apart. Ivan has never gone long without a woman to take care of him. He suffers through two more diaper changes, three naps, and two more feedings before he sets Tatyana down in the crib for the night, only to be jerked awake at two in the morning by her croup. Cursing to himself, he grabs her and dashes into the bathroom to turn the shower on. He's hardly thrilled when it comes back again the next night. He sits on the floor with her and cries for two hours.

"Hello, murderer. Do you mind if I take back my little girl?"

Ivan turns white in fury. ***"You! Who gave you permission to enter this house! You dared to come back here illegally a second time! This is my child! You abandoned her before she was born! Get the hell out!"*** He sets Tatyana down on the floor as soon as she starts breathing normally again and storms toward Boris, hitting him with the back of his hand.

"Were you this furious as you killed Basil?"

"Get out! How dare you claim she's your daughter! I'm the man who's raised her all her going on eighteen months on Earth!"

"What's going on?" Ginny asks, running into the hallway.

"This *mudak* Boris has come back to wreck more havoc in our lives!" Ivan gives his former best friend a push backwards down the stairs. "Get the hell out of this house before I kill you, you *dryan*, you *sukin syn*, you worthless piece of *govno!*"

Tatyana starts crying at the loud noise.

"You see what you did?" Ivan scoops her up and rocks her back and forth. "It'll all be over soon, my precious little *knyazhna*. Just as soon as that man gets out of this house. He wants to take you away from me, but there's no way in the world I would ever give my angelic little girl away to anybody!"

"I was the one who got Lyuba pregnant," Boris growls from

the bottom of the stairs. "She's mine."

Ivan hands Tatyana to Ginny and jumps down the stairs, scaring his former best friend to death. ***"Her surname is Koneva, and her patronymic is Ivanovna! Her surname is not Malenkova, and her patronymic is not Borisovna! Get the hell out! I will never let you take my child away from me! I've adopted her in my heart! You abandoned her and almost caused her mother to miscarry her at least five times! I was the one who took care of her after you beat her up, to make sure the baby was still moving! You, I wouldn't even trust you to be her godfather!"***

"What in the world is all this screaming?" Eliisabet demands. "Ivan, you woke up Kolya, and he won't go back to sleep now!"

Ivan grabs Boris by the throat and bangs his head against the floor, ignoring his gasps for breath. The other people in the band come running from their beds to see what the noise is all about, and crowd all along the stairwell.

"Is that an intruder?" Aleksey asks.

"Is he a Bolshevik?" Kittey asks.

Boris is five feet three inches in stocking feet. He's petrified of Ivan, who stands six feet three in stocking feet. He gives a sigh of relief as his former best friend releases him from the stranglehold.

"Look who's come crawling back to Russia illegally a second time."

"Oh my God, that's Boris!" Kittey gasps.

"Our friendship is *really* over now, as far as I'm concerned! He wants to take my child!"

"She's *my* child! *I* slept with Lyuba! You never did!"

"You told me you wanted me to take care of Lyuba and to tell the child I'm her father!"

"I changed my mind once I saw her in March."

"I'll never change *my* mind. Tatyana's my daughter."

"I love my little girl! I truly repented."

"If you had really repented, you would've confessed to a priest, done your penance, and been waiting safe in America so you could play a role in her life! You wouldn't have decided repenting on your own was good enough and

come illegally into Russia twice to try to ruin my life!" Ivan begins to punch Boris, like an unrestrained wild animal.

"*Your* life? I beg your pardon, Konev?"

"My life is with Lyuba and our daughter!"

"You've never slept with her. Admit she wants me and not you."

"Lyuba and I have loved each other since we met, and you know it!"

"Then why haven't you ever slept together? Are you homosexual?"

"What's a homosexual?" Kittey asks.

"A deviant who prefers his own sex," Nikolas says.

"What's going on down here?" the manager demands. "Who's raising such a riot in the middle of the night?"

"This *mudak* who used to be my best friend has come back to ruin my life and take my daughter! I hope he rots in Hell!" Ivan starts strangling Boris again as he reaches for a knife in his pocket.

"Who is this man Ivan Igorovich is attacking? He didn't check in at my office."

"That's because he snuck in here without permission! If he takes my child, I'll murder him!" Ivan raises the knife above Boris's throat.

Aleksey and Nikolas grab him and are barely able to restrain him from lunging for Boris, who's gasping for breath.

"She's *my* daughter," Boris informs the manager.

"The Bodrovs came here with Madame Bodrova's brother and their young daughter Tatyana. In fact, Ivan Igorovich was carrying the child, and for the past few days, since his wife has been in town working, he's taken care of their daughter full-time. Being a man, he isn't as good at it as she is, but he's improving every day."

"Madame Bodrova my left foot! She's Miss Zhukova, and *I'm* the father of that child!"

"Ivan Igorovich has been under a lot of stress these last few days, what with his wife being away, and taking care of his daughter all by himself. Are you contesting the paternity of this child?"

"There's no contest. I know the child is mine."

"You had relations with her before she was married to him?"

"There *is* no marriage to Ivan! She and I slept together one night at a cabin, I got her drunk, and that's how Tatyana came about."

"I don't care to hear the personal details, you intruder. Even if the girl isn't biologically his child, he's her father in every other way."

"She's *mine!* I made her!"

"And *I've* been with her all her going on eighteen months on this Earth. I do the things fathers do. You showed up to ruin my life."

"I want my child back."

"She's been *my* child since she was born, you *mudak*!"

"Do any of you really trust Ivan to raise my daughter? Look how he violently attacked me! He started screaming at me in the bathroom, so loudly my child began to cry. Then he left her with Ginny and went after me! He pushed me down the steps and jumped down all thirty steps, like a devil flying after a good little child in a fairytale! He didn't fall, he just landed and started attacking me, first with strangulation as he banged my head against the floor, and then he started to punch me! You saw how he came after me with that knife! And you know this is a man who's killed before."

"He killed the man who raped his wife. That's justifiable," the manager says. "And he was trying to protect his daughter from being kidnapped by you!"

"Ivan *has* no wife!"

"Then who was that woman who came in with him and the two children, his mistress?"

"His female best friend."

"Why were both wearing wedding rings?"

"You really are naïve, aren't you?"

"He strikes me as a very noble man. He killed a man to avenge the rape of his wife, and would've killed you to protect his daughter from you."

"Look at him! Look how he went after me after I innocently requested he give me back my daughter! He and his father were named for Tsar Ivan the Third, the Great, but both have violent personalities, or, should I say, his father had a violent personality and Ivan has a violent personality. He attacked me and would've killed me if you hadn't come in just then! He should've been named after Ivan Grozniy! He attacked me! And he woke up the whole house with his screaming fit in the bathroom and then down here while he was attacking me within an inch of my life! All I want is my little girl, and I'll be on my merry way!"

"Like hell you'll take my daughter," Ivan snarls.

"Leave this house at once. The girl belongs to Ivan Igorovich, as he so eloquently proved tonight."

"Eloquently! He attacked me, Sir!"

Ivan goes over to Ginny and takes Tatyana. "Look one last time, you *dryan*. You had every chance in the world to be her father. I've been her father for almost a year and a half. She's been mine since I saw her right after she was born. This will always be my child, one of two loves of my life, the other being her mother, the woman you abandoned the night she gave birth!"

"This child doesn't biologically belong to you?" the manager asks.

"I adopted her, and I don't love her any less just because she's not blood."

Boris looks at Tatyana with tears in his eyes. "You can always go to bed with Lyuba and get her pregnant, and then you'll have a child of your own! Let me have *my* child! You can have five or six kids with her, just give me back my child!"

"Interesting you should mention having more children, you *zhopa*. Several days after my child was born, I found a midwife to make sure there were no complications. Lyuba doesn't know this because I don't want her to die of grief, but she told me there was serious internal damage. Guess who brought it on! You, beating her up during her entire pregnancy! The midwife said it'd be a miracle if she has another child, and, even more miraculous, if the child doesn't miscarry or die at birth! If Lyuba's unable to give me the son I want, it'll be all *your* fault!"

"So Lyuba will give you a boy and I'll have my girl. We're even."

"*Any* child she gives me I'll want! I want a son to carry on my name, but if she gives me another girl, I won't love her any less than I'd love a son."

"This fight is over," the manager announces. "The girl clearly belongs to Ivan Igorovich. And you, I want you out of this house right now. Go."

Ivan takes Tatyana back upstairs, Boris seething with rage.

"He came back," Kat finally manages to say. "I thought we'd never see him again after his first two cowardly disappearing acts."

"Where does Lyuba work, by the way?" Boris calls. "And what exactly is she doing for a living?"

"Wouldn't you like to know," Ginny sneers.

"She's become a part of the oldest profession in the world," Eliisabet says. "Ivan's heart is broken, though she swore she still loves him and is only doing this to raise money to buy ship tickets for America. Lay the hell off the man, okay?"

"Sure she loves him. As a friend."

"You know Lyuba and I are soulmates, you *chyort*, you *zhopa*, you *durak!*" Ivan glares at him before turning around and taking Tatyana back to her crib. "I adopted your daughter, and someday I'll be her stepfather."

"I made that child out of my love for Lyuba. I've been totally monogamous my whole life. That girl you all claim I caused the suicide of, I never slept with her. But only with my Lyuba."

"Wait a minute," Katrin says, finally finding courage to speak. "Malenkov caused a girl to commit suicide? When was this?"

"A long time ago, and the particulars aren't important. I never gave her the rope or knew what she was planning." Boris slams the door.

4

Boris shows up again two days later as everyone is eating breakfast. He comes up to the kitchen window and leans in.

"Oh, look, that man is back again," Eliisabet says.

"Liza, wasn't Kolya's birth the most powerful thing we ever went through together?" Aleksey asks, loudly enough for Boris to hear.

"It sure was, my darling, attentive, responsible husband. The circumstances were very scary, but we were together."

Ginny smirks in the direction of the window. "Alyosha was right there, holding her hands as she labored, even if he hadn't planned on fatherhood so soon."

"And your wedding was so sweet," Kat coos.

"Alyoshka didn't need to be forced to make me a respectable woman," Eliisabet goes on. "Meanwhile Boris thought it was appropriate to abandon his pregnant girlfriend."

Blushing, Boris turns away and heads back to the abandoned resort where he's been staying. He chokes ahead of time on the stench of beer, wine, vomit, urine, *govno*, and blood that'll be sure to greet him once he enters the old resort where bands of *besprizorniki* and their older counterparts are staying, stacked up like sardines, and always afraid to leave anything unattended, for fear of it being stolen by an unscrupulous bandmember.

"What's wrong? You get too old for your band, or were you thrown in prison and couldn't find your band after you escaped?"

"My band kicked me out! This is my second time back in Russia since I left home last January. I was living in America."

"So you were safe in America, and you came back into danger. How utterly stupid," a fat thirteen-year-old girl says.

"To add insult to injury, last night I was brutally attacked by the reincarnation of Ivan Grozniy, all because I wanted to take my daughter to America with me! How dare he claim to be her father! He never even slept with her mother!"

"You abandoned your child?" an old man asks.

"I made some really bad mistakes last year!"

"Including leaving your child?" a skinny fifteen-year-old girl asks.

"Leave me alone. That child will be mine, and the courts will agree with me, come Hell or high water!"

"The mother, did you get to see her?" an old woman asks.

"She's become a prostitute, apparently!"

"So help you God." A seventeen-year-old crosses herself. "You brought her misery all on yourself, you dirty *mudak*. She needed your love and didn't get it, so now she's turned to strange men."

"You don't even know me!"

5

Three days later, Ivan goes into town with his fake passport and Tatyana. He storms over to the house where the Shepilovs used to live before backstabbing Aleksandr turned them in, where the Godunovs now live with Aleksandr and their grandmother.

"Are you here for service?" a young girl asks.

"I want to speak with Lyuba."

"Hello, Ivan." Lyuba appears in the doorway of the front room, wrapped in a blue silk shawl. "Today the customers are entering and exiting so fast, none of us have any time to keep dressing and undressing. A lot of us are wearing just shawls or robes to keep business moving."

"I'd never rush you, my love. Come back home, and I'll treat you like a human being again."

"You brought Tatyana." Lyuba breaks into a smile. "Does my baby want some milk?"

Ivan looks away as Lyuba drops the front of the shawl to nurse her.

"I didn't know mothers could give milk so long," a prostitute says.

"She's a year and a half old. How I love my baby!"

"If you loved her, you'd come home!" Ivan pleads. "Do you know, just days after you walked out on me, her unworthy biological father broke into the house at four in the morning and tried to take her! Of course, being the strong guy I am, I lunged at him and attacked him to protect my little girl!"

"I told you I still love you, Vanya. That should always be enough."

Ivan drops to his knees after Lyuba pulls the shawl back up and passes Tatyana to one of the other prostitutes, taking her hands in his. "You rejected me when I first asked you this. I've come back to try again."

"I told you, we'll go to America together. You know I want to go to America with you now!"

His hands begin trembling. *"Ya tyebya lyublyu. Khotish byt moyey zhenoy?"*

Lyuba begins to cry. "That was so beautiful, and so sweet. But you know I'm in no position to accept such a proposal right now, just as my new career is taking off!"

"I just asked you if you wanted to become my wife, and you say you prefer to be a prostitute! Why not put a real dagger through my heart too!"

"Look, unless you've come here for service, you're wasting everyone's time. I could've made a lot more money by now if you hadn't come charging in here like a man possessed!"

"I asked you to marry me, and you just put another knife through my heart!"

"Goodbye, Ivan." Lyuba puts Tatyana back in his arms. "I'll be done with work in September. Then you can ask me again."

"I don't have the heart to put my heart back on my sleeve after this latest cruel rejection!" He stalks away, fighting back tears.

"You could've told him you're getting practice, so when you finally sleep together, you'll give him the best sexual experience of his life," one of the prostitutes smiles.

"Pasha wishes I weren't a hooker, yet he never acts like this," Nadezhda says. "He supports me in my career. Better watch out, or maybe your Vanya won't be so submissive about rejection the next time. One more rejection might be all it takes to throw him over the edge."

****

Chapter 16: Trying Times

Four of the Lebedeva sisters wake up in their tent in the makeshift labor camp they've been at for the past three months. They're in Bulun, right on the Lena River, up in the Arctic Circle. Even in the middle of July, it's starting to get colder. Lyolya, age twenty-one, was severely beaten with iron bars right over her knees three weeks after they arrived at the first makeshift camp, in warmer Uralic Omsk. Her three sisters have mastered discrete ways of holding her up as they march to and fro, so she doesn't give her limp away.

Svetlana, twenty, is one of the more higher-ranking zeki, *thanks to working in the excuse of a hospital. Svetlana's lifelong dream is to be a nurse, specializing in newborns. Lyolya's dream is to be a dancer, if she ever regains the use of her knees. Dinara wants to be a traditional housewife, go to America, and raise a big family like her mother did. At twenty-three, she feels her marriage marketability running out. Serafima, age twenty-two, wants to be a businesswoman.*

"We've mined so much, we've just about used up the natural resources," the lead guard announces. "Start forming lines. You'll march in groups of five until we get to the nearest place with an abundance of ore. Leave the shelters you made. They'll go to the next group who comes this way."

"Can't we go down in boats along the river?" someone asks.

"We have no boats, enemies of the people. Let's start marching."

"We're going to Tiksi." The camp leader opens up a map. "This journey will involve wading across the Lena River. If you take off your shoes and don't put them back on once we're on dry land, you'll be shot for not moving fast enough!"

Svetlana takes out a roll of heavy cloth dressing she snitched from the makeshift hospital and wraps it around their shoes, securing it with twine after she finishes rolling it around each shoe and cuts the roll with her jackknife. Once the dressing is cleaned and dried, it can easily be reused on wounds. After they're all suited up, they strap their knapsacks to their backs and move down to the river.

"Up the steps to the bridge. Anyone who pushes or shoves other comrades will have to wade the entire way across the river!"

Halfway across the bridge, several guards notice Lyolya limping. The lead guard blows a whistle and makes everyone stop in their tracks.

"Who is this person limping? Why hasn't anyone pointed out this person who's dragging down our level of productivity?"

"This is Yelena Ilyinichna Lebedeva," an older man says. "She's in

charge of measuring out the gypsum at the end of each day and making sure nobody cheats during the mining."

"So she purposely deceived us about her crippledness to get a work position in which she could very well hide being crippled? Did she come into the camp crippled?"

"I became crippled three weeks after I arrived at the first camp, Comrade Karakozov." Lyolya forces herself to maintain direct eye contact and a steady tone of voice. "I've been an industrial worker in spite of my injuries."

"But all our injured zeki *are shot so they won't drag down productivity!"*

Lyolya thinks quickly when she sees him pulling out a gun. "There are too many people here. You may accidentally hit one of them if you shoot at me, and then productivity would be even worse."

"You're right. Get on top of the guard rail to the right."

Lyolya is boosted up by Svetlana and Dinara, clutching her knees. She can barely stand straight on top of the guard rail. Her sisters stand by, their hearts in their throats.

"Should I jump and wade the rest of the way as a punishment for hiding being crippled?"

He gives her a push, sending her toppling face-forward down into the river and on top of a large rock. "The rest of us, let's move on."

Dinara looks down at her.

"Yes, Comrade Lebedeva? Would you like to join your sister? Looks like you've still got two left where she came from!"

The three of them move on with the others without a word.

2

"No, *knyazhna*! Haven't I had enough troubles since your mother left me?" Ivan stumbles out of bed at five in the morning and picks up Tatyana. "At least you didn't decide to wake me up with croup this time!"

Tatyana stops crying and starts to itch herself. Ivan is ready to give up and send her off to Lyuba at this point.

"Tell me that's not what I think it is!"

"Want my mama!"

"So do I, but do you see me crying?"

"Need her!"

"I'll get salve and bandages to cover this rash, and then I'll put you back to bed. In the morning, I'll get you warm milk and mashed fruit." He walks down the hallway with her and goes into the medicine cabinet.

"Oh, Ivan, you really don't know anything about children, do you?" Eliisabet asks. "You don't put bandages over measles!"

"Measles! That's what killed my cousin Liza!"

"Kolya woke me up at midnight, crying and scratching himself furiously. I instantly knew that could only be measles when I turned on the light and got a good look at that rash. Don't you recognize measles anymore? It's been awhile since I've been around children, but it's hard to forget the signs of the most common childhood diseases!"

"Why has she forsaken me!"

"Perhaps because you're too timid? You tackled Boris to prevent him from running off with your precious adopted daughter, but when you're around Lyuba, all you do is look at the ground and mumble!"

"I'm rather shy. You'd never guess it, would you?"

"Shy? This from the man who jumped down thirty steps in a single bound and then began to strangle Boris?"

"I asked her to marry me, and she told me she's still going to be a prostitute!"

"Want my mama!" Tatyana repeats.

"Neither of us are going to have our wish fulfilled, I'm afraid."

Ivan spends the day hovering over Tatyana in a back room designated for quarantine, where Nikolay has also been moved. He breathes a sigh of relief when Nikolas walks by.

"Thank God. Where are the two competent women in this band? I can bear changing diapers and preparing meals, but sick children is too much!"

"Kat and Liza have been helping Kittey."

"With what, that new cane? She can almost walk on her own; I don't think that requires much help!"

"My sister is thirteen, not such a young girl anymore."

"What's that supposed to mean?"

"It means I could be an uncle if Kittey had premarital relations with a beau."

"Oh, spare me if that happens to me! And I didn't need to know such personal information! You should've made up a story instead of telling me such indelicate news, even if you didn't bluntly spell it out."

"Your Lyuba will come back before Tatyana's old enough to be a mother. Not to worry."

"Then send for the other two women in this band. I'm that desperate!"

Katrin and Anastasiya come trotting into the room, draped in their fancy clothing and glossy makeup.

"Ladies, Ivan needs help in caring for his daughter."

"*His* daughter?" Anastasiya asks. "That child belongs to Boris. I admit you've been raising her like your own daughter the past year and a half, but Boris obviously cares enough about her to come back illegally twice. That's true paternal devotion."

Boris pokes his head through the window. "I climbed up the trellis. Now that Ivan's calmed down from his mad fury, can we talk like civilized people about my child?"

"Lyuba wants what we all want," Katrin says. "To become a respectable woman. Liza got pregnant out of wedlock too, but Alyosha married her five months after their son was born. You, you took off to America the night Lyuba gave birth! Are you going to marry Lyuba to prove you really did repent?"

"I don't want to be tied down by marriage just yet. I love Lyuba, but I care more about my child right now."

"And just what do you intend to do once you've gotten your child?"

"Raise her on my own till Lyuba decides to marry me."

"What if she decides she'd rather marry *me?*" Ivan snarls.

"I'll be a great father!"

"*I'm* the man who's taken care of her since she was born! I learnt how to change diapers for her! Do you even know one end of a child from the other?"

"I gave her a bath and washed her hair."

"Yes, and as I recall, the next morning you left again. Deserted twice."

"I want my child. And I want her back now."

"A family is a man, a woman, and their child," Katrin says. "Lyuba herself considers Ivan to be Tatyana's true father."

"They're not married, and never will be. Konev knows it's a lost cause. He and Lyuba may have romantic fantasies about a life together, but Lyuba has no chemistry with him. I'm the only man she's ever slept with!"

"If you only knew," Ivan snarls.

"What? You mean you've slept with her and never told me about it? Or is it Petya?"

"I think he means Basil," Katrin says, feeling it's not her place to tell Boris the secret Ivan recently told them about what Lyuba's father did to her.

"Oh, that was rape, Konev! And all her antics with being a prostitute, that doesn't count for anything either. Only with me did she have the real thing."

"Then prove to her you really love her," Ivan says. "Ask her to marry you. I did just a few days ago, and she said she wanted to continue giving her body away to strange men. Try for yourself and see what she says."

"Okay. When she says yes to me, I'll be back here to collect my daughter and take Lyuba to America with me."

"She never *was* your daughter. I'm her real father."

"Stop this paternity warfare!" Nikolas shouts. "Love makes a family, not blood alone. And Ivan is willing to die for Tatyana, like he proved to you when you came here to try to take her."

"Her name is Tatyana Ivanovna Koneva, you *mudak* unworthy of life, not Borisovna Malenkova."

Boris lights a cigarette. "I'm going off to find Lyuba. At least *she'll* recognize me as the father of our child instead of saying any old person can fill the role!"

3

"Is she dead?"

"She's still warm except for being partially submerged in water."

"Is there any identification on her?"

"Let's take her home. She looks like a Russian, not a native Siberian. I'd help a native Siberian too, but this one will understand our language, and it's nice to see other Russians in town."

The next thing Lyolya is aware of, she's lying on a bed in a small three-room log house in Bulun. Four children, two girls and two boys, are sitting looking at her.

"I think you broke your knees," the oldest, a girl, says. "They made a frightening crunching sound when we moved your legs, and when I gently

touched them, it didn't feel like the entire kneecaps were connected."

"What, again?" Lyolya shouts. "My kneecaps were already broken three years ago and didn't have a chance to heal properly. Now I'm even more of a cripple."

"Do you remember how you ended up on that rock?"

"I was pushed off a bridge and left for dead as my mining group started to march to Tiksi. They discovered I was a cripple, and I somehow persuaded them not to shoot me in the crowd. I'm surprised they didn't check to make sure I was dead before moving on. Zeki *never get away that easily. Aren't you going to turn me in to the authorities to let them know I survived and should be shot?"*

"We aren't like that out here," the younger boy says. "So long as you're in our home, you'll be safe. We'll never let any bad guys hurt you."

"Our family fled here several centuries ago to escape from Ivan Grozniy," the older boy says. "Now we're safe from Lenin as well."

"Oh, heretics. My family moved from Pskov to Moskva, but we never once denounced the Tsar. No matter how bad a Tsar might be, there might be a better one next time. How could anybody slander God's anointed?"

"Out here we don't keep up with politics. All we care about is our daily bread. We love the land, and don't care about the particulars of who's ruling it, so long as we're left alone."

"I see our houseguest from the river has regained consciousness." The mother comes bustling into the room. "I'm Beatrisa Zakharovna Smirnova, and these are my brave children who dragged you in here this morning—Bella, fifteen; Vsevolod, thirteen; Mariya, twelve; and Rostislav, ten."

Lyolya gently feels her knees, and cries out at the immediate, sharp pain. "At least here I won't be a prisoner. But as soon as I can walk on my own again, I want to go to America. I always wanted to be a dancer in California, and damned if I'll be a cripple the rest of my life. I can't let those godless Bolshevik mudaki *win."*

4

"I asked you to please look after Tatyana, and I come back to find you drawing in notepads? What a waste of money."

"It's Stasya's dream to be a fashion designer," Katrin says. "And don't assume I was doing that the entire time. I like drawing my own designs from time to time, for fun, but it's not something I see my career in. I want to be a public intellectual, maybe write for the left-wing presses. Unlike *Knyazhna* Stasya, I fetched Tatyana water and food, put cold compresses on her, and talked to the kid. Just because I'm a woman of the world doesn't mean I'm one-tracked. It's pretty insulting to assume I spent the entire time drawing merely because I happened to be doing it as you walked in. I only started drawing when the kid fell asleep."

"Don't be so rude to Katya," Anastasiya chides. "She's our safety net. If anyone bothers us, she can pull out her Party membership card and we'll be on our merry way. It also won't cast suspicions on Petya by his father and paranoid brothers."

Ivan waves his hand at her. "Since the two competent women in this band have been busy all day, I thought I'd give them a break and make supper."

"You made supper? This is a surprise."

"Oh, yes, Konev loves to cook," Katrin laughs. "His mother taught him. I think it's because she was disappointed she got a boy instead of a girl, and wanted to do all the girl stuff anyway. Whatever the reason, he can cook very well. I like that about you, Konev. You might be unenlightened in certain ways, but you're a modern man in others. What did you make us?"

"*Shashlyk.*"

Their mouths begin to water.

"It's on the table right now, if you're interested."

Anastasiya and Katrin put down their sketchpads and rush downstairs. The grilled lamb is on a platter in the center of the table. Meat again, after so long of nothing but vegetables, fruits, and breads.

"Where'd you get the lamb?" Ginny asks.

"A young girl brought it to the back of the house this afternoon, wrapped in plain brown paper, saying it was a gift from Lyuba for taking such good care of Tatyana. Lyuba bought a large lamb from the butcher this morning, after she'd had ten clients. She bought it with the money she's made in the past week." Ivan tries desperately not to think about how his belovèd gave her body to strange men in exchange for the feast he's about to enjoy.

"So instead of giving you her hand in marriage, she buys us a lamb."

Ivan looks again at the note Lyuba scribbled, the note that was pinned to the wrapping paper. *My belovèd Vanyechka*—Bolshoye spasibo *for being so understanding about my latest rejection of your love and for taking care of our little girl. You'll always be her father, even though you didn't biologically help me to create her. Take this lamb and cook it for everyone tonight, and give large portions to Ginny and Tatyana. The other two little ones, Kittey and Kolya, also deserve the taste of meat again. I'm imagining when we're finally in America and have those nine children you want, sitting at our own table and eating* shashlyk *I bought at the butcher shop, with the money you made at a respectable job to support your loved ones, not with money I'm making from letting strange men have my body. You'll always be the only man in my heart, no matter how many men have known me.* Ya tyebya lyublyu, *Lyuba.*

"You're putting your elbow in my face!" Anastasiya shouts.

"Then stand at my right side or get away from me."

"Ivan's a *levsha*, don't you remember?" Ginny asks.

"I thought they teach children like that to use the proper hand. My older brother was one too, but he was untaught early."

"Seems to me someone doesn't know her own so-called former beau all that well, or she's forgotten everything about him in the year she's been away."

"Here." Ivan stands up and carves a big piece which he deposits on Ginny's plate. "Lyuba mentioned in her note that you and Tanya should have the largest portions."

"Unlike everyone else here, *I* remember what real meat tastes like."

"You don't have to rub it in," Kat says.

Ginny chews with his mouth wide open. "I ate lots of meat when I stayed with the Savvins. They're important people, and get access to lots of nice things."

"They're nobodies outside this city," Katrin says. "The important people of the Revolution are Comrades Lenin, Trotskiy, Zinovyev, Bukharin, Kamenev, Bubnov, Sokolnikov, and the women who supported them, not local bigwigs. I guarantee you nobody in power has ever heard of these people, or doesn't remember them if they've indeed met."

"Katrin, when we go to America, will you drop your association with Communism?" Eliisabet asks.

"Why would I do a crazy thing like that? It's what I believe in. All my life, I wondered why we Estonians should be under the rule of a foreign power, and why my parents and siblings would support a foreign ruler. I finally put my foot down and said no more. My Party membership is the real deal, not something I did out of convenience to continue my education."

"You might be denied entrance to America!" Kat warns. "I've heard they have rules about not admitting political radicals."

"In the land of the free?" Katrin laughs. "I don't think so!"

5

As July drags on, Ivan notices Lyuba hasn't sent any more letters, notes, or gifts. He occasionally leaves Tatyana in the quarantine room and goes to watch the Godunov house from a back window. One of the regulars by now, Lyuba looks as though she's having a grand time. She and Nadezhda have lunch under a tree in the backyard with four or five other women and laugh about the day's customers, then join arms and skip back to work, laughing. Boris has also started to show up, and Lyuba always greets him with a big hug. Unbelievable.

"Tell me," Nadezhda says toward the end of the month, "do you really think you're doing yourself a favor by constantly going back and forth between those two men? Which one do you really love the most?"

"Boris promises a future. He knows the meaning of hard work, and we also have a child together, though I consider Ivan her real father. Ivan is a dreamer with his head in the clouds, and while I have no doubts he loves me and would never leave me over something trivial, love alone can't build a stable future for a family."

"My Pasha's also a dreamer, yet we believe love can conquer anything."

"Look what I found floating in the river!" one of the hookers sings. "A diamond ring! This could sell for more money than any of us, even Nadya, makes in a day!"

"That's *my* ring," Lyuba gasps. "Boris sent it to me in a letter, and I flung it into the Skhodnya River last autumn. I wasn't about to keep another man's ring when I was with Vanya at the time, and that ring isn't exactly my idea of pretty."

"Will you let us sell it and get enough money right now for ship tickets for you, your cousin, your angelic daughter, and the man you love?" Nadezhda begs. "Or will you wear it and pretend Boris is the man you truly love?"

Lyuba slides it onto her finger, hoping Ivan sees it and becomes just as jealous as she was when she saw Anastasiya wearing his ring. If he were a real man, she would've been wearing his ring. At least Boris was proactive enough to buy her a ring, even if it's not her style at all. Perhaps it was meant to be, if the ring were found floating in the river so much time later.

"I have a more important question." Misha storms into the room, with Kostya hanging on his heels like a leech. "Have any of you ladies ever had unnatural sexual relations?"

"No, Misha," Nadezhda says. "I draw the line at any of us taking a female customer. She can always go to you if she wants it."

"I don't mean woman homosexuals. I mean different *types* of sexual relations."

"Talk sense, Misha," Kostya snaps. "Even *I* don't know what you're getting at!"

"You're also the one who's such a baby he doesn't know how to begin a sex act on his own! I well remember that night I came back from the tavern and asked if you were done, and you said you hadn't even started yet, with all the time you had."

"And we paid Konev back good for refusing to let me start it! We broke his arm!"

"Like *he* was standing in your way. A real man takes what he wants and damns the consequences, you wimp!"

"Oh, Misha, even you're afraid to do it with me," Nadezhda laughs.

"Here's a picture I've drawn to help you," he growls in her face. "I've got five very anxious men waiting outside the door to do just this, and they want ten volunteers signed up."

"What's the meaning of this picture?" Mariya Dmitriyevna Berdyayeva asks. "I know what the drawing shows, but what are these people doing?"

"And I thought Kostya was a naïve little buffoon!"

"It's a man and a woman," Nadezhda says. "But the woman is dressed, and the man is only dressed from the waist up."

"How can a woman have sexual relations if she isn't undressed?" Lyuba asks.

"For the love of the Revolution!" Misha drops his pants and storms over to Nadezhda.

"We have a deal. I'll give it to any men but you and Kostya. And if I were you, I wouldn't display that pathetic thing in public. It's never a good thing when your foreskin is longer than your ugly *khuy*."

"Don't you ever read erotic novels?" Misha is practically crying.

Kostya finally interprets the picture his brutish older cousin has drawn. "If I wanted to have that done to me, I'd go to a man, not a woman! And that's only for homosexuals, Misha! Are you telling me you're a homosexual?"

Misha turns red in fury. "Is everybody here really so stupid as to not understand the meaning of this picture I've drawn for their convenience?!"

"I just figured it out. Did you mean to draw another man instead of that woman?"

"I meant to drawn exactly what I meant to draw, you blathering fool! I thought I might like this stuff with a hooker, not another man!" Misha swats his cousin over the head with a brick.

Mrs. Godunova comes downstairs. "Boys, what's the meaning of this loud argument? Has there been a rowdy customer? Tell him you'll see about the mistake right away. Did you charge too much for his groceries?"

"What groceries?" Kostya laughs. "Is that code for a woman?"

"Keep quiet!" Misha snarls into his left ear, quickly pulling his pants back up. "*Babushka* thinks we're running a little grocery store, not a brothel!"

"Oh my goodness!" Mrs. Godunova sees Misha's drawing and faints.

The five new customers come into the room.

"There'll be a little wait, I'm afraid," Misha growls. "None of the ladies understood what you wanted, believe it or not! Even our most seasoned prostitutes hadn't the foggiest!"

Lyuba and Nadezhda laugh about it after their workday is over.

"Can you imagine, a normal man wanting a woman to give him homosexual sexual relations?" Nadezhda cries in glee.

"Even *he* called it unnatural at first, then swore up and down it *was* natural!"

"I draw the line at having a *khuy* in my mouth!"

"Exactly. We're not that kind of women, to do such vilely unnatural acts even with a member of the opposite sex!"

"Well, there are some who'd argue our insistence upon all our customers using prophylactics is unnatural too. But who wants a baby in such a life? Me, I wouldn't know who the father was if none of them used anything to prevent it. After Misha's little episode today, I don't know if I can take much more of this career of mine. Doesn't every woman, deep down, just want to be taken care of by the man she loves instead of being so independent?"

"I never did. Even if I did, in vague sorts of ways, I never let the fantasies drift that far away from my known realities."

"Well, you've got that ring on your finger. I guess you decided on marrying Boris."

6

Ivan comes home early after he goes to watch Lyuba again at the beginning of August. It's all like a sick nightmare. The lamb is almost all gone, Lyuba is off being a prostitute, Tatyana has recovered from measles only to almost immediately come down with rubella, and Boris has talked his way into Lyuba's heart again. He sits down at the table and pours himself a drink. Though the retail sale of alcohol has been illegal since 1914, their innkeeper has quite a large stash of the precious contraband.

"Aren't you a teetotaler?" Anastasiya asks.

"We're engaged, since Lyuba is back together with Boris. I had a good time with you when they were together before, and it sure made her jealous."

"So we're not really engaged, just pretending to be?"

"For as long as it takes. You're temporary fun while I'm waiting on Lyuba to come back to me."

"I can win you over again. I'm positive. Soon our engagement will be for real and no longer just to make Lyuba jealous."

7

"What the hell happened to my house?"

"You never lived in that house. Three years ago, all the houses on this block were Tsarist houses. We solved that problem for sure, Comrade. We killed everyone, if they hadn't already fled on their own before we got to them. We arrested some people, and killed others. The enemy of our enemy was not our friend in

that case. Since this entire block and a few side-streets were on record as housing an inordinate amount of Tsarists who'd made their anti-Bolshevik and anti-provisional government views public, we worked with the law to nip the problem in the bud. These people were just as much a threat to the modern Russia as those damn Romanovs. The glorious new marble homes which you see were built specially for more deserving Soviet citizens. That garden over there, we planted it right over where we burnt a great deal of the bodies."

"My son, my only child, he would've been old enough to go to prison. He'd be twenty-two now. And what about my wife?"

"Are you one of those Tsarists we had to execute? The house that stood there belonged to an Ivan Vasiliyevich Konev."

"That would be me."

"You must be a different one. That man died in prison in April 1917. The body was dumped into the prison graveyard."

"The young man, the only child, was he among the people you found living in this house?"

"The woman we killed. Foolish amateurs. They dragged the woman off and killed her, leaving the son free to run away from justice. They burnt the house, but no body, not even remains, ever turned up. They even searched the sub-cellar, and still no body. It was probably burnt so severely it melted in the heat."

"I really, truly loved my son. I had problems with the bottle, Comrade, but I never stopped loving my only child. Pozhaluysta, *can you tell me if you ever arrested any man by the name of Konev, a young man, a bit over six feet tall, dark brown hair and eyes, as strong as ten men, a terrific temper?"*

"There was a man by that name in his early twenties who was in prison from April until June. He killed a man. He escaped and is now a wanted criminal."

"Oh, my boy and I, we were really named after the wrong Tsar with our temper problems!"

"Ivan Ivanovich Konev went to prison with a woman and a baby girl."

"My son wasn't married the last time I saw him, but I bet you anything that was the neighbor girl. Little did I know I'm now a dedushka.*"*

"If you really have changed, like you claim, you can find your son and turn him in to the authorities so he can be shot for escaping prison, Comrade Konev. We'll spare your daughter-in-law and granddaughter, but your son must die."

8

After the lamb runs out, Pyotr comes by with two boxes of

canned goods.

"We're back to this stuff?" Ginny whines.

"Yeah, I liked lamb!" Katrin says.

"I have a secret treat I got from the cook." Pyotr lifts up a cloth over a silver platter. "Lox!"

"They're not yet on to us?" Kat asks.

"I convinced my father Ivan would never be stupid enough to stay in Moskva. And next month, you will really leave Moskva."

"I made my decision, and I'm sticking by it," Katrin says. "Where Stasya goes, I go."

Anastasiya greedily sticks a fork into the smoked salmon.

"Wait your turn. You're hardly the youngest person in this band," Aleksey says.

"Oh, shut up. I'm engaged to Ivan, so I have authority to get larger portions, since I—"

"Only in your delusional world are you engaged!" Eliisabet laughs.

"No, I told her we're engaged," Ivan says.

Anastasiya nods. "To make Lyuba jealous initially, but now I'm getting him to come around to me. Lyuba is back together with Boris, so why not?"

"If you think this time you really have a chance with him, you'll only hurt yourself," Aleksey says. "Everyone except you knows Ivan's been in love with Lyuba since they met as children. She's been mistreated her whole life, and Ivan's the only one who knows how to give her real love and respect."

"She's clearly chosen to be mistreated."

"Come, now. Does anyone know what day it is?" Eliisabet tries to stop the impending fight. "It's the twelfth of August, and today our Tsesarevich would've been sixteen years old. If our Tsar had abdicated properly and given him the throne under a Regency, our Tsesarevich would've taken power in his own right today."

***

Lyuba and Nadezhda bow their heads over their supper of *rassolnik* with sour cream and wine.

"I was four and a half years old when I heard the cannon fire three hundred one times, to announce the birth of Tsesarevich Aleksey. It's hard to believe one of my happiest memories has become one of my saddest memories" Lyuba's eyes well up. "All those years of prayer were in vain. Instead of praying for a Tsesarevich, the entire empire should've prayed for our Tsar and that damned German woman to become better leaders. I can't speak ill of our dear *Batyushka*, but I don't understand why, after waiting so long for a boy, he'd turn around and deny his precious only son his rightful throne twelve and a half years later. Our heir should be celebrating his sixteenth birthday today, even taking official power, not already in the other world!"

"Russia cannot function without a Tsar," Nadezhda agrees. "Does nobody remember what happened last time this happened?"

"I've heard stories about some of them surviving and popping up all across Europe, but not all of them can be telling the truth. Maybe none of them are telling the truth, and people believe them because it's too abominable to think all of them really were murdered. Surely at least one had to survive."

"God protects the Tsesarevich. He's alive and well somewhere out there. When the time is right, the truth will come out."

Misha stands in the corner, doodling more of his pornographic pictures. "All of them are dead, dogs. Even the servants they did away with. The only Romanovs left in this country are descended from the one who got in trouble and was exiled to Central Asia in the last century. We'll never be ruled by a Tsar again."

***

Ivan spends the rest of the day drinking. By now even Ginny is concerned about this.

"He got his temper from his father," Nikolas says. "Why not drinking too?"

"We'll have to start hiding the drink from him," Kat agrees.

"That might make him even angrier," Eliisabet says.

"He was at his angriest in ages when Boris returned," Aleksey says. "I don't think hiding the liquor from him will possibly make him even angrier."

"And for all his talk about being engaged to Anastasiya, they sure don't act engaged," Ginny says. "They don't even kiss. All they do is hold hands."

"I've seen him drink in bed," Nikolas says.

"I found empty bottles under it one morning while I was cleaning," Kat says.

"He's really losing it," Eliisabet agrees.

They watch him drink away the rest of August. The only times he's sober are when he attends to Tatyana. Therefore, everyone is relieved to hear he's going back into town for Lyuba and won't leave until he wins her back.

****

Chapter 17: Ivan Grozniy Dva

"Are you a lucky woman, Lyuba!" one of the newer prostitutes, Ida, sings. "There's a very handsome, tall man asking just for you! Is he ever handsome! Brown hair, brown eyes, and he said he only wanted you!"

"Damn him. Send the man away right now. He can't just show up when he knows full well I have appointments!"

"You can forget about appointments." Ivan grabs her right arm, struggling to stand straight. "You're coming home with me. Tatyana has been sick for almost two months, and I can't bear Anastasiya! If you don't leave with me, you might regret it."

"Look at all my money." Lyuba points to a sack. "Hundreds of millions of rubles and kopeks! I'm fast becoming one of the top prostitutes!"

"I asked you to leave with me. I really am unable to get by without a woman to take care of me, I mean really take care of me, including to love me!"

"It's my body, my decision, and I can do what I please. I'm not your little slave!" Lyuba pulls away from his hold, recoiling from the overpowering smell of alcohol on his breath.

"*Pozhaluysta*, I told you, I'm not feeling myself lately. You're not doing me any favors by treating me like this."

"I'm staying right here!"

"I told you you're coming home with me!"

"And I said I want to stay right here for a few more weeks. Just a few more."

"How can you say you love only me but give your body to strangers every day for money?!"

Lyuba snaps. ***"For the love of God, Ivan! Leave me alone!"***

She instantly regrets it. The one person who's never raised a hand against her suddenly pounces on her like a wild animal, knocks her to the floor, and begins to shake and hit her.

"What are you doing!" Nadezhda comes running into the room.

"I'm sorry, Nadya, he was just so handsome and he was asking only for Lyuba, and I thought she was the luckiest woman in this place to get such a handsome customer!" Ida blubbers like a lost child.

Lyuba regains her speech. "You're drunk! You've been drinking! You've turned into your father!"

"I wouldn't have turned to drinking if you hadn't become a prostitute, a common piece of trash in the street, living here with all these sluts and whores!" He yanks on her hair. "Just look what you've done to me, you trollop!"

"Somebody stop him!" Nadezhda screams.

"He's a wanted criminal, and Misha and Kostya will only be too happy to turn him in!" Lyuba reminds her. "Leave the room and let him beat me! He might attack you too, and I'm the only one he wanted to see!"

"Do you think I like having to take care of my child all by myself, cook meals, change diapers, nurse measles, drink all day long, cry myself to sleep if I'm not drunk enough to numb the pain, and live each day knowing the woman I once loved is a prostitute?! You thought I could go through my whole life never once asserting myself?"

"You've changed into a drunken monster like your father!"

Nadezhda and Ida clear away and watch from behind the door of the back rooms where they work, as he continues to shake and hit her.

"What is going on?" Masha gasps.

"A scorned lover seeks his revenge," Ida weeps.

"Everybody, that man is extremely angry right now, and if anybody tries to save Lyuba, he'll go after you too. Nobody go into the front room!" Nadezhda commands them.

"Do you think I like living with the knowledge you've rejected my love whenever we get close to becoming engaged, and have chosen to live here and be a slut and whore?"

"You're drunk! You don't know what you're doing!"

"For the first time in my life, I'm asserting myself, not standing back and letting people walk all over me like a little meek boy!"

Misha and Kostya come downstairs and glare in unison at the prostitutes.

"What's this screaming?" Misha asks. "Another request you can't translate into plain Russian?"

"You mean like doing homosexual acts with members of the opposite sex?" Nadezhda giggles. "I draw the line at having a *khuy* in my mouth, Misha!"

"There's an argument going on in the main room," Ida informs him. "We're waiting it out over here, until he gets done beating her."

"Our prostitutes are to be treated very well!" Misha shouts. "We can't very well market you all off if you're black and blue!"

"I ordered them to wait back here, boys," Nadezhda says. "And wait we all will, till the angry customer finishes his business."

"You'd better listen to Nadya," Masha says. "She's our leader. The head prostitute, you two excuses of men who can't sleep with her!"

"Do you think I like knowing my belovèd has been had by several hundred men, while I've stood back and waited like a meek child?! Don't you think a twenty-two-year-old man wants to know what it's really like to be with a woman?"

"You're drunk! If you were sober, we'd be talking this out like adults, not this! Stop it!"

Misha and Kostya go back upstairs and listen for the screaming to subside. Nadezhda and the other prostitutes wait for two hours behind the door, as the screaming and sickening sounds of pummeling continue unabated.

"You never treated a woman like this before, Konev!"

"Perhaps because I'm finally acting like a grown man, not a meek little boy who keeps taking rejection after rejection! You know, you don't distinguish anymore from your customers, so you probably won't feel any differently about *me!* Are you now such a slut you'll take them for free?"

"You're drunk! You don't know what you're doing!"

"I've taken enough of your rejections!" He undoes his belt buckle.

"Oh, my God," Nadezhda gasps. "I think he's going to rape her!"

"You don't know what you're doing!"

"What did he do to her?" Ida wails. "There's a huge gash on her left cheek!"

"Snap out of this, Konev! You're supposed to love me unconditionally!"

"I think it's time *I* had a turn with you!" He starts unbuttoning his pants. "And then you're coming right home with me! I don't care I've been drinking!"

"His whole face is clouded with fury!" Masha whispers.

"She's black and blue!" Ida weeps. "She'll be out of commission for at least a month!"

"You were named after Tsar Ivan the Great, not his grandson! I won't be able to make any money if you don't stop it!" With her waning strength, she manages to deliver a well-placed knee. If he retaliates, at least she attempted to defend herself.

Ivan yelps from the sudden, unexpected pain. As he's curled up, waiting for the ache to subside, he notices blood under his fingernails, and what looks like actual flesh under several of his right fingernails. Then he looks around the room, and fills with cold horror when he sees the left side of Lyuba's face bleeding, her hair frazzled, fresh bruises and scratches all over her visible flesh.

"My love! What have I been doing!"

"Let go of me, you brute," Lyuba snarls, slapping away his hand when he tries to touch one of the bruises on her face.

"I can never be sorry enough! I was drunk out of my mind!" He rebuttons his pants and puts his belt back on. "*Pozhaluysta, pozhaluysta*, forgive me! The Devil made me do it! You know I've never done anything like this! I had a moment of weakness!"

"You beat me within an inch of my life. You're as strong as ten men. You easily could've killed me with your bare hands, you beast! You were getting ready to rape me!"

"I'll never raise my hands against you again! *Pozhaluysta, pozhaluysta*, believe me, I'll spend the rest of my life making this up to you and proving this was a one-time abomination! I still love you more than anyone!"

"I'm sure your father said that to your mother!"

"I sinned. I nearly killed you. You have every right to never want to see me again!" Ivan stands up and walks through the door, shaking and nauseous.

"What was the big holdup in there for?" a customer asks. "Did they throw a big party and not invite the newer customers?"

"Some women have to be taught a lesson the hard way," Ivan mumbles.

The customer comes into the house. Nadezhda flings back the

door and begins to cry.

"I thought he would've raped you," Ida bawls.

"I don't want to see him ever again!" Lyuba shouts. "He could've killed me!"

"He knocked you to the floor so fast I couldn't blink!" Nadezhda wails.

Misha comes downstairs and halts in his tracks. "What happened to her?"

"An angry customer," Masha says.

"Lyuba, you're out of commission for the rest of the month. Anyone who tries to do business with you will be given to one of the other seasoned prostitutes. While you're recovering, you'll have complete bed rest."

"That man is going to come back again for me, I just know it! After I recover, I want to get as far away from Moskva as I possibly can!"

"Wonderful. I've been transferring some of the more experienced girls to an encampment in Podolsk, where soldiers, both Red and White, stop by when they get lonely. Already fifteen of our girls have elected to go there at the beginning of next month."

"Perfect. Sign me up to be a camp prostitute. The sooner I get the hell away from that man, the better!"

"What about your daughter?" Masha asks.

"I'll go back for her, then get on that train to the soldiers' camp."

2

The others in the band are alarmed when Ivan returns without Lyuba. His face is a deathly shade of white, his eyes are lifeless, and he's visibly shaking.

"So you see?" Anastasiya smirks. "He was meant for me."

"Now you're going to drink even more, after her latest rejection!" Kat shouts. "You'd better hope no one saw you or followed you. Every time you go to that damned brothel, even if you're just looking in a window, you put your life on the line."

"Petya came by to tell us his father's going on a terror-spree at every place you've ever stayed at," Kittey says. "He got the records of their boarders. Mr. Golitsyn told the truth and said he didn't know where you'd gone, and he was arrested. A man claiming to be your father also showed up at Petya's house, demanding to know what happened to you. Though your father is dead and they had a body to prove it, Petya's father believed the man."

Ivan sinks into a chair and buries his head in his hands. "I'll never drink again. I'm back to being a teetotaler."

"Did you and Lyuba have a fight?" Eliisabet demands.

"A rather violent fight."

"Well, it couldn't possibly be as violent as when you went after Boris last month," Nikolas laughs.

Ivan falls deathly silent.

"You attacked Lyuba!" Ginny yells. "I thought you loved her more than anyone and never raised your hand against a woman!"

"These things happen. I was super-drunk and livid."

"You don't beat the love of your life by accident," Aleksey says. "You were always so protective and gentle with her, and suddenly you beat her?"

"I apologized as soon as I realized what I was doing! The Devil made me do it!"

"Did she accept your apology?" Kittey asks.

"I don't think so. I'll have to go back again in a few days to tell her just how sorry I am."

"You don't beat a woman and then beg for her forgiveness," Nikolas says. "Some things are beyond forgiveness. Lyuba isn't the old-fashioned type of woman to stoically accept a man beating her."

"Boris sure got her forgiveness, and he beat her a lot more than just once. If she can forgive him, she can forgive me. At least I'm sorry, and that was a one-time abomination."

3

Boris shows up at the Godunov house two days later with a box of chocolates and an emerald bracelet.

"Any particular prostitute you wish to do business with?" Misha asks at the doorway.

"My usual. The mother of my daughter, of course!"

"Your daughter's mother was beaten within an inch of her life two days ago. She won't be able to do any business for the rest of the month."

"Beaten? By whom?"

"An angry customer, apparently."

***

Lyuba gingerly takes a small bite of the *selyodka* on the plate. "Nadya, have you ever had a scare?"

"Yes, I was shot at by an angry customer, but Misha quickly disposed of the *mudak*. He's good to us, though he doesn't respect us as human beings."

"I'm five days late."

"I missed two months last year, and it turned out I was just worried about all my responsibilities as the head prostitute."

"I never missed before, except when I conceived Tatyana."

"Well, now you're an important woman. That's enough to make anyone miss."

Lyuba glances out the window. "Oh, look, there goes Boris. I guess he wanted to see me today."

"Let him wait to see you until you're safe in America. Soon enough you'll be far away from here. Although I do think your Vanya was sincere in his apology."

"I never saw him that angry in the twelve years I've known him. Not even when he got into fights in the schoolyard or went after Boris or Basil."

"Pasha never blew up like that at me, and he's also not exactly happy the woman he loves is a hooker. He understands this is all just sex, not about love at all. My Pasha's the only man in my heart, and I can't wait to someday make love to him and only him, no other men ever again."

"Do you know when you and Pasha are going to America?"

"Misha would be very angry if I left. I'll have to slide my head out of the lion's mouth."

A knock sounds on the door. Nadezhda goes to open it and jumps back. "You! Don't you know that thanks to you, Lyuba is out of commission? Look what you did to her, you beast!"

Lyuba shrinks into a corner of the bed. "Nadya, get him out of here!"

Nadezhda goes back to Lyuba, and they cling to one another. "You could've easily killed her. You're as strong as ten men, Ivan, and half a foot taller than she is. And you said you loved her more than anybody. Fat chance."

Ivan bows his head. "I came back to apologize, my love."

"Don't you dare ever call me that again, Konev. If you loved me, you wouldn't have nearly killed me."

He feels yet another dagger tearing into his heart to hear her using *vy* with him. "I was drunk and angry!"

"You turned out to be just as much a user as every other man I've ever been with. My God, you almost killed me!"

"If you really loved me, you wouldn't be here! You'd be with me!"

"How dare you use *ty* with me after what you did to me. Nadya, I want him to get out of here now."

He ventures a glance at her, then immediately casts his head downward again. "I can only imagine how much that horrific wound on your face must hurt."

"Guess who put it there, you brute! Would you like me to take all my clothes off so you can see all the other bruises, bumps, gashes, and scratches you put on me? Or to feel the huge goose eggs on the back of my head, from how hard you kept thumping me against the floor? Leave here now! As soon as I recover, I'm going to take my little girl, and will never see you again!"

His eyes well up with tears. "I did that to you. I do not deserve to be called a man."

"Get him out of here, Nadya! His crocodile tears are worthless after what he did to me! His actions are beyond forgiveness!"

"I'll go have a word with him alone, and then I'll be back to sit with you. Doesn't he know he could've killed you?"

Lyuba sends Ivan a look of pure hate as she makes the *dulya* sign.

Nadezhda storms into the hallway with him. "You nearly killed her."

"I'm going to be sorry every day for the rest of my life! I feel like a monster for what I did, after how I've always protected her and been so gentle. Thank God I came back to my senses before I could rape her. I could never forgive myself if my first time doing that was through rape."

"You have no chance in Hell of ever getting her back."

"You and Lyuba are pretty close. Can't you tell her how sorry I am, and keep telling her till she finally believes me? I'd sit on hot coals outside the door for a month or stand in icy water for a week as my penance! There's no life for me without Lyuba."

"I want to believe you're sincere and that this was a one-time aberration caused by extreme extenuating circumstances, but this is hardly the time to try to get her to forgive you. You nearly killed her!"

"Lyuba and I had similar childhoods. We understand each other in ways other people could never. We're soulmates. All is right in the world when Lyuba and I are together. And Tatyana and I both need Lyuba. That's the only family we have left."

"Once you've lost someone's trust, you can't just wave a magic wand and earn it back overnight. You have to prove you're sincere over a long time."

He bows his head again. "I'm dying of a broken heart, Nadya. I need Lyuba or I'll die."

"It was almost she who died recently. Metaphorical death doesn't compare to near-physical death. And given how you're a wanted criminal, you're risking your life to come here, no matter what Lyuba thinks."

"Fine, I'll leave, but I can't go on much longer without my love. She just has to forgive me sometime, and remember the special bond we have. I won't be happy again till my beautiful swan is back where she belongs."

4

Boris shows up that night at the house to rant and rave. Ginny glares at Boris when he sees him at the door.

"Lyuba was beaten within an inch of her life two days ago, and can't do any business now!"

"She's a prostitute. Customers get angry," Anastasiya says. "It shouldn't surprise you to learn your whore was knocked around as part of her job."

"I'd like to know just who beat her, so I can give him a piece of my mind."

"Oh, nice. Too bad you didn't show this much concern for her the night you left her right before she went into labor with your child," Kat says. "You're also forgetting how you beat her many times when she was pregnant. Are you one of those 'Do as I say and not as I do' hypocrites?"

His eyes light up. "Is that my child? Is she better?"

"Yes, my child is feeling better now, thanks for asking." Ivan smirks at his former best friend and continues rocking Tatyana. "Her rubella broke just last night. Not that I wish any suffering on my child, but it's too bad she only got measles and rubella this summer, not chickenpox. I'd love for your pride to be smashed by finally getting the one childhood disease you somehow avoided for twenty years. You don't deserve miraculous immunity."

"Say what you will, but she's biologically mine."

"And emotionally *mine!*"

5

Misha and Kostya don't like Boris hanging around their house without doing business. He hangs around for the next five days, refusing all the prostitutes they bring out to him, even refusing to watch them having their transactions.

"I'm a one-woman man, sorry."

"Well, the one you're asking after, your child's mother, is out of commission until her injuries go away!" Misha snarls.

"I don't care what you say, Godunov. I'm going to see her right now."

"You do and we'll ban you from ever coming here again!"

While the Godunovs are out having lunch with their grandmother in Sokolniki Park, Boris sneaks upstairs to see Lyuba and knocks on the door.

"Nadya, is it Konev again?"

Boris flings the door open. "We're going to do it right now! I'm tired of waiting on you to recover!"

"Lyuba is too bruised to do anything sexually, I'm afraid."

Boris goes over, drags Lyuba out of bed, and pulls her downstairs to the main business room, giving the evil eye to everyone else there.

"Don't you know Lyuba can't do business for at least another week?" Masha demands. "Are you that impatient you can't use your own two hands in the meantime?"

"Everyone out! We're going to do it right here, right now!"

The other prostitutes leave the room and shut the door.

"Borya, you see how bruised I am!" Lyuba pleads. "You'll enjoy me much more when I'm healthy again."

"It isn't very nice to keep yourself away from the father of your child!"

"I'm out of commission!"

"Well, I'm putting you back *in* commission!"

***

Nadezhda descends the steps fifteen minutes later to see Boris beating Lyuba, alternating fists and a belt. "What are you doing!"

"Perhaps she lost her sense when that customer beat her! I'm beating the sense back into her!"

"Do you know who beat her?"

"Are you going to tell me?"

"Your best friend."

"Liar!" Boris continues to pulverize his daughter's mother.

Nadezhda runs outside and is grateful to see the car pulling up. "Stop the car! You'll never believe what's happening!"

"Is Lyuba in any mood to see me now?" Ivan begs.

"Your best friend showed up and dragged her downstairs. He was really mad at her because she hasn't been working the past week since you beat her, and now he's beating her too!"

"I can't believe I'm saying this, but he'll probably slap her around for a bit and then turn his mind to another prostitute, or, more likely, his favorite subject, food. He gets pudgier every time I see him. I don't think he's a real danger to her, though I wish I could intervene right now and not have to sit helplessly on the sidelines yet again. She might be even madder at me if I intervene now, or he might beat her harder if I try to rescue her as he's doing it."

Sure enough, Boris presently emerges from the brothel, dusting off his clothes. Ivan crosses his arms and blocks the path.

"So I understand you beat Lyuba."

"I had a right to! I wanted her, and she wasn't giving it to me, so I had to take matters into my own hands! So I had to knock her around for awhile until she let me. Oh, don't give me that look, it wasn't rape! We share a child together! So anything we do is allowable, including me beating her from time to time! She's as good as my property, and needs to obey me!"

"Nadya, step away."

Nadezhda takes several steps back, praying no one sees Ivan and reports him to the police or shoots him.

Ivan grabs Boris and slams his head against a rock, then

throws him onto the ground and punches him. ***"You abandoned Lyuba and your unborn child! And this is your second time coming back here illegally! All our problems are your fault! I want you to go back to America and let me live in peace!"***

"We used to be best friends, Konev!"

Ivan seizes Boris by the neck and slams his head against the rock again and again, until his teeth are chattering, then begins to choke him. "After we go to America the legal way, we'll settle into our own apartment, I'll get a job, and as soon as possible, I'll marry Lyuba! Then we'll set a court date and have it in writing I'm Tatyana's true father, you *dryan!*"

***

Nadezhda runs back inside. "The man who beat up Lyuba came back."

"She should be glad she's going to the soldiers' camp to advance her career," Masha says. "She'll be away from him once she moves on."

"We'll all work in the rooms over to that side today. Lyuba's having trouble with her two feuding lovers. I don't know why some people believe it's romantic when two men fight over a woman."

***

Boris leaves the yard shaken and angry. "Oh, thank God, a police officer. Officer, that man who just went into the house tried to kill me, all because I had a disagreement with the mother of my child!"

"What was his name?"

"Ivan Ivanovich Konev."

Officer Bulyakov's eyes narrow. "Brown hair, brown eyes, very tall, a *levsha*, a terrible temper, as strong as ten men?"

"That's my former best friend alright!"

"We'll have him followed. Thanks for informing on him. That man is a wanted criminal. Do you know, he escaped from prison!"

"I'm glad to be of service." Boris limps away.

***

Lyuba screams when Ivan enters the back room. "Don't you touch me!"

"I just gave Boris a beating for doing this to you." He drops to his knees and tenderly touches the fresh bruises on her face.

"You nearly killed me last week! Get your hands off me!"

"I was drunk and angry! Oh, you look awful. I know *I* didn't put so many bruises on you." He falls onto all fours in prostration. "*Pozhaluysta, pozhaluysta*, forgive me. I still love only you, and I'm sick to my stomach thinking about what I did to you. I let the Devil control me during a moment of extreme weakness, and didn't fight hard enough against this evil inclination. For the rest of my life, I'm going to be tortured knowing what I did to my soulmate."

"Do you promise you'll never raise a hand against me again?"

His heart leaps in joy to hear her using *ty* again. "I swear to it before God, my love."

"Then you can start making it up to me right now." Lyuba rubs a bruise forming over her shoulder. "He really knocked the breath out of me. Misha brought me a cloth and a pail of heated water after you beat me. I know you can do a much better job of taking care of me than Misha."

Ivan lifts her onto one of the mattresses. "I'll get you hot water, and then I'm taking you home. Our little girl needs her mother, and I need you." He starts for the door.

"Where are you going?"

"I'll be right back."

***

Officer Bulyakov takes down the number on the license plate, then goes off.

"Has there been a problem?" Misha asks as he returns from his afternoon in Sokolniki Park.

"We can always get you a woman from our brothel as a bribe!" Kostya winks.

"What brothel?" Mrs. Godunova asks.

"Stay quiet in front of *Babushka*, you *zhopa*!"

"A wanted criminal was just here, beating one of your clients. Does the name Konev ring a bell?"

"Konev! He's been here! I want wolfhounds over to his house, or grenades, or police, as long as he doesn't escape justice twice!"

***

"Here you go. Heated water." Ivan takes one of the rags on the floor, puts it into the basin, and presses it against the bruises on her face.

"He really pounded me hard right over the collarbone."

He unbuttons her first five buttons and presses the rag against her worst batch of bruises. "So you forgive me."

"I've known you for twelve years, Vanyechka. In all that time, you never got angry at me or did anything like that. I know you're sorry. That was a one-time abomination. I forgive you."

"You forgive me for nearly killing you?"

"Now you're back to being my Ivan the Meek, not Ivan Grozniy."

Ivan cleans the blood off her face. "Do you feel better now?"

"I won't feel better till I'm out of this infernal place."

"I'll take you home. Now you're really out of commission."

"Don't forget my money. That was the only thing I did any of this for."

Ivan picks her up and carries her out to the car he borrowed from one of the boarders. "Stay right there while I get your belongings."

"No! What if Boris comes back!"

"You'll be fine for a few minutes."

Nadezhda sees him coming and passes Lyuba's packed valises and her sack of earnings through a window. "They know you're in town," she whispers. "Take Lyuba and get the hell out of Moskva, unless you want to be shot for escaping prison."

He walks back to the car and puts the valises and the money in the backseat, then opens Lyuba's door and sets her in the seat.

"Now I really know you're sorry."

"We're leaving Moskva together. The police know I was here."

***

As soon as they reach the house, Ivan opens the door and carries Lyuba upstairs, ordering Ginny to carry in her things.

"Oh my God, you really did a number on her," Aleksey says. "She's totally black and blue and bleeding!"

"Not all of it came from me. Boris just beat and raped her."

"The police know Vanya was there," Lyuba whispers. "Alyoshka, you alert the others in the band. Go on to Tver ahead of us. Only my Vanyechka is the wanted criminal."

"I put that scar on your face." Ivan begins to cry over her face. "I've been tall and strong since I was a boy, but I never dreamt I'd use that to attack the woman I love more than my own life! You're going to lie down the rest of the day. Now I'm going to ask you again. *Khotish byt moyey zhenoy?*"

"If you buy me a nice ring, I'll consider us pre-engaged."

"That's the best thing you've ever said to me!"

"But right now, I'm too bruised to do much of anything."

"Here we go." Ivan sets her on the bed. "You lie down the rest of the day."

"That really was a one-time abomination. After all we've been through together, particularly over the last three years, I know that's not how you normally act at all."

"Enough talk. Try to get some sleep. When we're able to locate a priest, I'll confess how brutish I was to you last week. You're going to try to take a nap, and then I'll be back with something for you to eat." Ivan kisses her on the forehead and leaves the room.

Aleksey, Eliisabet, and Nikolay are getting into a van. Pyotr is lifting Kittey into the front seat, while Nikolas and Kat load the luggage.

"A fine fix you've gotten everyone into! I had to concoct such a lame excuse to leave my house! And that man my father is having as our houseguest is really adamant he's your father! I'm driving these six to Tver, and will take the other two tomorrow. You, Lyuba, Ginny, and Tatyana will have to walk by means of this circuitous route I've sketched out on this map. You'd better all pray to your God you're not robbed in the hills and mountains I've got you travelling along!"

Kat and Nikolas finish loading the van.

"Well, goodbye," Aleksey says. "See you in Tver."

Pyotr drives off.

***

Boris comes to the back door ten minutes later, knocks, and creeps up behind his former best friend.

"I came to warn you the police are looking for you, Konev. I told them you beat me up. Guess I sort of turned your whereabouts in. Well, good luck in running from the law again."

"You dare come back here! Lyuba is black and blue

and bleeding thanks to you! Within two weeks, Lyuba, Tatyana, Ginny, and I will be in Tver! You go back to America and let us alone!"

"You beat her first."

"Lyuba forgave me. Know why? Because she knows I love her more than my own life and will never do such a thing ever again. And how dare you claim I beat her first when you beat her over and over again when she was pregnant!"

"I'm going to apologize to Lyuba and take my daughter."

"My daughter is asleep, and so is her mother."

"Well, then there'll be less of a fight. She'll wake up in my lap in the train or on the ship. I only came back here to get my child."

"Tatyana considers *me* her father. Now stop goading me, or you'll really regret it."

"Lyuba's wearing the ring I got her. By a miracle, one of the other prostitutes found it floating in the Skhodnya River."

"I pulled it off her finger right after I set her in the car. She told me I have to buy her a nice ring, and then she'll consent to being pre-engaged."

"Come now, Konev. Lyuba always comes back to me, no matter how badly I treat her."

Ivan sees red. ***"And she always chooses me because I treat her like a lady, like a Tsaritsa, not a punching bag or a toy! You fill her head with garbage, and I talk sense back into her every time! She'll be Mrs. Koneva soon, and you know it as well as I do!"*** He picks up the pot of boiling water on the stove and pours it onto Boris's head, which results in hysterical screams.

"Vanya, what are you yelling about?" Lyuba asks.

"I told you to lie down and get some sleep, my love. I'm just getting rid of the disgusting excuse for life who fathered Tatyana."

"Are you making supper for me? Let me do that."

"You lie down and rest, and I'll have a wonderful meal for you as soon as I can manage. But you'll have to wait awhile, since I just spilled the water for the soup. Do you mind chicken soup?"

"Lyuba." Boris is gritting his teeth in pain, his face and neck lobster-red, steam rising from his skin and hair. "So glad to see you're up and about again."

"You covered me in bruises, and Vanya came for me and brought me back here, where I belong, you animal. He apologized for beating me last week, and his first apology was right after he stopped beating me. He knows how to treat a woman. It's a shame you never took any hints from your own best friend in how to respect women." Lyuba turns and goes back upstairs.

Boris runs up the steps, but Ivan grabs him from behind. "Just where do you think you're going, you *svoloch*?"

"To run ice water over my head, idiot!"

"There's some right here in the icebox." Ivan throws a chunk of ice at him. "Now take it and be gone."

***

Lyuba wakes up two hours later to the sight of Tatyana, who's been moved from her crib into the bed. Smiling as best she can in spite of her sore face, Lyuba sets Tatyana on her lap.

"Here, I made you chicken soup." Ivan has a seat to her right. "Your hands are too bruised. I'll hold the spoon."

"Oh, you really are my best friend in the world. What did I ever do to deserve such a loyal, unselfish man to be both my best friend and future husband?"

"What did *I* ever do to deserve someone like *you* for my best friend and future wife?"

After she finishes the bowl of soup, Ivan goes back downstairs for a dish of rice pudding with maple syrup on top. Lyuba begins to cry.

"I don't mind cooking, I told you. I don't feel lessened by it. I also learnt how to change diapers."

After she finishes the pudding, Ivan goes downstairs to clean the kitchen. Feeling terrible for how she treated her best friend in the world for the past two months, Lyuba goes into the medicine cabinet, writes a quick note and puts it under her pillow, then uncaps a bottle of sleeping pills and swallows them all with the glass of ginger ale Ivan left at the bedside. She's sound asleep when Ivan comes back into the room.

"Sound asleep, my belovèd. When you wake up in the morning, I'll bring you breakfast. You don't need to worry. If Boris comes back here, I won't let him lay a finger on you or Tatyana. I'll be sleeping here right beside you, and you know I'd die to protect you and our little girl."

6

Boris limps, wounded and angry, into the abandoned resort to the smells of wine, beer, liquor, blood, and human waste. He reaches for his belongings and begins to pack.

"Have a fight with that man who's raising your daughter?" the religious seventeen-year-old girl asks. "Was it more confrontational than the first one you had when you came to his house right after you got here?"

"This time he poured a pot of boiling water right over my head! Thank God I found a pump in time to prevent more serious injuries."

"That man was your best friend?" an old man asks.

"Not anymore! We're finished! He can take Lyuba and my child, just as long as he leaves me alone!"

"Are you going back to America now?"

"So I beat her and had relations with her by force! She's the mother of my daughter, and I wanted her so badly I was in pain!"

"You've got two perfectly good hands," one of the bandleaders from across the room laughs. "Use them, Comrade."

"And engage in a sin?"

"As much a sin as leaving your pregnant girlfriend to give birth alone?"

"Shut up! You barely know me!"

"You've been here two months, Comrade," the skinny fifteen-year-old says. "Each day you prove yourself more and more of a nuisance."

"Take the other man's advice and find a priest to confess to," an old woman says.

"I think Ivan should go and be a priest if he's so damn religious, and let me have Lyuba and my child back! Ruining his life my left foot!"

"You did seem to perfectly time both intrusions into his life."

"The man is twenty-two and a virgin! He's a perfect candidate for the priesthood already!"

"Perhaps you're the reason he's afraid to sleep with your child's mother," another bandleader says.

"You all barely know me! I'm leaving Russia, this time for good. I won't return till a Tsar is put back on the throne."

"Then you'll never be back," the fat thirteen-year-old girl says. "At least half of the Imperial Family is no more, and the women aren't considered because they're women, thanks to that worthless Tsar Pavel trying to get back at his mother and feeling threatened by a powerful woman. So there will never be another Tsar."

"Shut up, everyone! Then they'll go to the grand dukes and princes who came next in the order of succession."

"Even I stopped dreaming such fantastic dreams," a middle-aged woman says. "Nobody wants a Tsar back, you raving lunatic."

"When I get back to America, I'll get a job at another church, teach Russian nationalism to the children at the Sunday school, and join a monarchist society. I won't have left *Matushka Rus* in vain. Goodbye, everyone." Boris picks up his bags and limps through the door. "Maybe I'll see some of you in Manhattan sometime."

7

In the morning, Ivan tries to nudge Lyuba awake, but she won't move. She flops over on her side, taking her pillow with her. He sees the note she's written and grows pale.

My dear Vanyechka—You're so good to me after I've put daggers through your gentle heart so many times, time after time rejecting your love because I'm afraid of being in a relationship with a man who loves me completely and not just for physical reasons. I'll probably only end up breaking your heart even more in the coming months. I never did anything to deserve your kind, unselfish love. Goodbye, my love. I took an entire bottle of sleeping pills last night. I want to be buried in the soil of our homeland. Don't cry for me. There will be other women who won't be afraid of your love for them. Your wife will be such a lucky, loved woman. I'm already jealous of her. Always yours, Lyuba.

Anastasiya and Katrin come into the room, fuming, with valises and suitcases in their hands.

"You put everyone in this band in danger," Katrin says. "By going into town and pulverizing Boris. Do you know, he informed on you to the police, and now Petya's father has men out searching the city with a vengeance!"

"Flee with us, Ivan," Anastasiya says. "We'll join the others in Tver. You're only one of many possible 'enemies of the people' whom Mr. Litvinov could be interested in tracking down, but he knows you and Petya were friends, and he's testing Petya's devotion to the greater Communist cause."

"I've just read a note Lyuba wrote last night, saying she took an entire bottle of sleeping pills, and you want me to leave her!"

"Let Ginny take Tatyana. The police sent by Mr. Litvinov are already out searching the outskirts of Moskva, right where we're staying! You must leave right now, or you may be killed!" Katrin begs.

"I'm not leaving Lyuba. Or Tatyana, or Ginny for that matter. My whole world is with the three of them."

"But you just said she wrote a note saying she took an entire bottle of sleeping pills!" Anastasiya whimpers.

"Do you understand, she's my best friend and the woman I love, and I've never abandoned her since we left home!"

"Well, Katya and I are leaving right now. I guess we'll read about you in the papers, after the police set fire to this house and drag you out, burnt alive, with the tiny corpse of Tatyana and the corpses of Lyuba and that annoying cousin of hers."

Anastasiya and Katrin turn and walk towards the train station.

"You said it yourself, Nastya. Never look back. We're leaving Moskva forever. America, here we eventually come."

8

"So I understand my son is indeed not married?"

"It's all a great big forgery designed to protect himself from the long arm of the law," Mr. Litvinov says. "Look. I listed every residence at which he's stayed. The first record I have dates from January 1919. The manager was a Mrs. Utyosova. She died in the blaze that destroyed the place two months later, but we managed to get the records out safely. A man fitting your son's description, with the same name, stayed at this hotel. Our next record is from a boardinghouse here in Moskva, March of that same year, run by a Gumilyov. He left there last August with a group of others. Gumilyov has since died. In late June, Bolshevik forces overran the house and burnt and looted it. We also saved those records. The next manager, Golitsyn, was arrested. Your son only stayed there for a week last August and then disappeared one night. Golitsyn swore he didn't know what had become of him. Nobody knew, in fact, until he killed Basil Yakovlevich Beriya this April. Our last known whereabouts of your son are from when he escaped Lubyanka this June."

"Here's a new collaborator we hunted down, Batya,*" Viktor says proud-*

ly. "Bring the sukin syn *in, Kuzma, Venedikt!"*

Kuzma and Venedikt drag in Mr. Andropov by his arms.

"Very good work, boys. Who is he?"

"I'm Andrey Vitaliyevich Andropov, originally from Gorkiy. I run a boardinghouse. This April, the man you spoke of stayed there with a woman, two children, and another man. Honestly, I'm just a humble innkeeper who minds his own business. I don't know anything about enemies of the people or escaped criminals."

"Start talking! We want names! Names of collaborators who are hiding this very dangerous escaped criminal!" Viktor rages.

"The second man, rather short for a man, might I add, and a bit portly, arrived first, and insisted the lady stay with him. She was very glad to see him, and he was ecstatically happy to see the little girl in their party. He's her father, and was meeting her for the first time. Normally I don't let unmarried couples room together, but with the horse already out of the barn, it seemed pointless to intervene. I need to stay in business more than I need to enforce old-fashioned morality."

"He was Boris Aleksandrovich Malenkov," Mr. Litvinov says.

"Whoever he was, he left after a week, and the others left not so long after that. I have no idea where they went."

"They've obviously stayed in the area!"

"The tall man became enraged upon seeing the short man. I don't intervene in my boarders' private lives, but I could make out that the fat, short man had abandoned the woman and that she took up with the tall man some time after that. The tall man felt he should still be with her and raise the child, even after the runaway lover reappeared, ready to take responsibility."

"Oh, my Ivanko is still trying to win the heart of the neighbor girl." Mr. Konev smiles. "But she has a child with Boris. It's indecent to get involved with another man's woman unless he's left her for good. Ivanko shouldn't have assumed Boris was gone forever."

*Pyotr comes in the door and warily regards Mr. Andropov. "*Batya, *who is this man?"*

"Andropov. Another dead end. Ivan Vasiliyevich is frantic to find his son and make sure no harm comes to him, but that'll only happen if he turns himself in! I have a dozen children, so I have no idea what it must feel like to know your only child is in danger of being killed by the authorities if he doesn't turn himself in of his own accord. We're going to find him within the week, and if we don't, I'll issue an order to whomever finds him to shoot him on the spot."

9

Lyuba comes out of her pill-induced sleep at 9:00 at night, racked by a terrific stomach ache. She immediately crawls to the bathroom to vomit all those barbiturates in her system, too sick to wonder how she survived. The entire house is deserted except for Ivan and Tatyana. The feeling is too eerie to shake off. Lyuba peers through the bedroom window and sees a circle of men wearing Cheka uniforms in the bushes, holding guns. She recognizes that uniform even in the dark. Mr. Litvinov is standing behind them, with a man who looks exactly like Ivan's father, towering over everyone else. She turns white in terror.

"Ivan, where's my cousin?"

He runs into the room and pulls her into his arms, holding her tightly. "Thank God you're alive. There were thirty sleeping pills in that bottle! Petya took our friends to Tver the evening I brought you home, and Anastasiya and Katrin left this morning. Ginny became afraid when he heard rustling in the bushes and boots pounding against the cobblestones, so he packed quickly and ran, leaving through a large water pipe and getting quite dirty. We'll have to leave by the water pipe also."

"Vanya, there are Cheka men outside in the bushes. Petya's father and a man who looks just like your father are with them!" Lyuba puts her arms around him and begins to cry. "I'm leaving tomorrow morning bright and early to go to Podolsk. I promised Misha. I'm taking Tatyana with me. We're going to a soldiers' encampment, where I'll service the soldiers, both Red and White. At least there I can be temporarily safe. And you, I want you to get out and join the others! I'll be with you as soon as I've made some more money. Maybe it'll help to throw off suspicions."

"I wish you weren't immediately running back to more exploitation almost as soon as I rescued you, but I'm in no mood to argue with you after what's happened between us. As much as I detest how you treat yourself like a piece of meat and a sexual playtoy for strange men, *Ya tyebya lyublyu*, and I'll drive you there. You'll change your mind sooner or later, when you miss being treated like a human being."

***

"Look, here comes the manager," Mr. Litvinov says. "Pardon

me, Comrade. Where might you be going at this hour?"

"Out to walk in my garden. Has there been a disturbance to necessitate the Cheka's coming here? All my boarders are law-abiding citizens."

"Do you have a boarder named Ivan Ivanovich Konev, staying with a woman, a thirteen-year-old boy, and a girl not yet two?"

"The only man who fits that description is Ivan Igorovich Bodrov."

"Is this man six feet three inches tall, dark brown hair and eyes, a *levsha*, a terrible temper, as strong as ten men, very possessive about the woman, a bit shy around her?"

"Bodrov fits your physical description, but I don't know why you're asking about him."

"Because he's a wanted criminal who escaped from prison!"

"He killed the man who raped his wife. I would've done the same if it were my wife!"

"What are the names of the other people in his party?"

"His wife Lyubov Mikhaylovna, her brother Grigoriy, and their daughter Tatyana."

"He's the one," Mr. Konev says. "Igor was my brother's name. Ivanko would've picked his uncle's name to use as a false patronymic. The woman's name is Lyubov, and her cousin's middle name is Grigoriy. The boy lived in East Prussia till the war broke out, and his parents were so Prussianized they gave him a real middle name. Her uncle's name is Mikhail. They're all using fake names!"

"But why would Bodrov lie to me?"

"Perhaps because he's a wanted criminal hiding from justice!" Mr. Litvinov explodes in rage.

"I don't like insinuations against my boarders. Bodrov was defending his wife's honor, Comrade. It's not as if he killed the other man in cold blood!"

"Aim through the top story window," Mr. Litvinov commands the Cheka men. "I saw movement behind the curtain."

"My only child may have killed a man, but he's my hope for the future! He'll carry on the family name!"

***

Ivan sets Tatyana on the floor. "Lyuba, I just heard rifles. Get down on the floor."

"And what? You'll let yourself get shot to protect me, yet again? Stop being such a gentleman."

Ivan pushes on her shoulders and forces her onto the floor. "I won't leave you and Tatyana until we hear them all leaving. We've survived together for almost three and a half years, and I refuse to let a bullet separate us now!"

Mr. Litvinov's private Cheka corps shoots up into the window until they run out of bullets. After everything Lyuba's already gone through, this only seems a minor terror. Seeing them there in the bushes was the most terrifying part of all.

"Okay, arrest this man. We'll be back to find your son, Comrade Konev." Mr. Litvinov grabs the manager.

Ivan tentatively stands up after the voices have trailed off, shuts the window, and pulls the linens off the bed. "We'll have to sleep on the floor. I'll lock all the windows and doors. I'll drive you to Podolsk first thing tomorrow, my love, though I still hope you change your mind between now and then."

"You have a beautiful heart, Vanya. I do know how awful this looks on paper, but you must keep believing you're the only man in my heart. I'm not doing these things on purpose to hurt you, though I can't imagine how it'll make you feel to have to take me back into prostitution."

"I'd sit in hot coals if you asked me to, *lyubimaya.*"

10

In the morning, they go out to the car Ivan borrowed a few days ago, and reach Podolsk within the hour. Neither of them says anything during the ride, and neither makes the first move to get out of the car when Ivan parks a discreet distance from the camp.

"Tanyechka, be a very good girl for your mother. You're the two loves of my life." Ivan cuddles and kisses her. "I already miss you more than you'll ever know."

Lyuba rubs his shoulder. "One day I'll give you blood children, as many as you want. You should feel honored you're the only man I love and trust enough to consider procreating with. These men are just money, not love and an honorable home."

"Well, are you getting out or not?"

Lyuba starts crying again. "This is when you're supposed to beg me not to go because you'll die of a broken heart without me!"

"I'm a big boy. Twenty-two years old. I can survive without you."

"You're supposed to persuade me not to leave you again, take me back, and go with me to Tver!"

"Then don't go! Just make your decision so I can get out of here before Misha sees me!"

Lyuba picks up Tatyana and her luggage and gets out of the car. "Why didn't you beg me not to go?"

"I can't stop you from doing what you want to do. I already know I have your heart."

Lyuba leans through the door and hugs and kisses him good-bye, then walks up the hill with Tatyana and the luggage. Ivan starts driving away as soon as he sees the Godunovs out of the corner of his eye.

"Hello," Misha greets her. "You have the best work ethic of any hooker I've ever employed. I can easily think of many other women who'd use such injuries to get out of work, instead of still coming on time when they're black and blue. I won't make you service too many men till you completely recover. Go in that tent, and the soldiers will be brought in as they come. The head prostitute will explain about housing and food after you get settled in. Just give it some time, and before long, that nasty business in Moskva will seem like a distant nightmare."

****

Chapter 18: Repentance

Lyuba has been in the camp now for four days, each time feeling sorrier and sorrier for the lonely, women-deprived soldiers. At mealtimes, she and Tatyana go to the designated eating area and eat mostly mush. No real food. She kicks herself for not being with Ivan. She's thinking about him for the umpteenth time on the morning of the fourth day, when the tent flap opens and another soldier comes in.

"I'm sorry, I've never been to a prostitute before, but I'm so lonely I had to do something about it. My wife would be upset if she found I'd been unfaithful to her, but she probably thinks I'm dead, since I haven't written to her in the longest time."

"You won't be the first married man I've serviced. It's normal and natural to feel lonely. Just remember, this is only sex, not love. What would you like me to do?"

The soldier looks into her eyes. "You look strangely familiar, though I have no idea where I would've ever met a prostitute."

Lyuba shrieks. "*Dyadya* Mishenka!" She throws her arms around him.

"Lyuba? What in the world are you doing here? Don't tell me your evil father sold you into prostitution."

"You don't want to know what brought me here. It's not a pleasant or short story."

"I don't mind hearing it, and I'm sure you won't mind avoiding that filthy business as long as I'm here. As far as I know, there are no time limits. Perhaps God sent you here to prevent me from committing adultery."

Lyuba bursts into tears as she starts telling the entire story of the last three and a half years. Every time she mentions Ivan, she feels her heart shattering, and she has to take several minutes to compose herself before continuing. Finally, her uncle gently lays his hand on hers.

"Do you really love Ivan as much as you say you do?"

"I'd die for him. He's the only man who's ever treated me like I'm worth something, not a piece of meat or a sexual object."

"Then why are you here instead of with him? Your actions speak louder than words. Someday he may finally declare enough is enough, and find a woman who's not afraid to be with him."

"Whenever we start to get close, I become frightened and run away from his love. I'm scared of his unconditional love. I'm not a heartless tease who enjoys leading him on so many times. It kills me to be apart from him, but I don't know what to do with a good man who loves me. My whole life, the abnormal has been normal. I don't know how to be normal, even if I know what normal is supposed to be like."

"Do the right thing. Go back to Ivan right this very day and tell him you really love him. I remember him as very forgiving and kind, but a person can only take so many rejections. You don't want to wake up one day when you're fifty and regret how you let the love of your life get away. If you can't get out of Russia, your lives may be short, but at least you can die knowing you're with the person you love most of all in this world."

2

"Okay, Petya, we've found the final piece of the puzzle. Here's your chance to prove to me you really are a devoted Communist."

"*Batya*, I could quote you Comrade Lenin backwards and forwards!"

"That's all abstract," Kuzma snorts in utter derision of his little brother. "*Batya* means like putting those fine teachings to good use!"

"But you just said you searched the house the morning after you shot into the top story window, and no body turned up!"

"He must've gone into town. I don't know. Now are you going to do yourself the great honor of starting the blaze that'll kill or help along the surrender of this most grave enemy of the people?" Mr. Litvinov asks.

"I'll do it, *Batya*."

3

It's late afternoon, and the entire house is deserted. After Ivan finished packing, a number of dead bodies showed up when he went for a walk around the house, under beds, stuffed into wardrobes, lying on the floor, in a grand piano, even in the outhouse. Still reeling from shock, he goes back downstairs and sits in a chair, then jumps up at the sound of the doorbell. He slowly creeps up to the door and looks through the curtains and the peephole. Tatyana is standing there with Lyuba's three suitcases, alone.

"Did your mother send you back here, my little *knyazhna*?" He doesn't think to question how such a small child could've transported heavy luggage all by herself. "Now there'll be two of us going to Tver."

"Make that three of us."

Lyuba steps into the house, and what happens next is what she's always been afraid of. She rushes into Ivan's arms and breaks down crying. After they've cried and embraced for ten minutes, she runs her hands through his dark brown hair, and they start to kiss and cannot stop. She doesn't mind standing on her toes to reach her belovèd, who stands half a foot taller than she. They only pause for a few moments before they start to kiss again. Lyuba isn't afraid when she feels his hands move across her face and down her neck, across her back, over her ribcage, and through her hair. Prompting him along, she runs her hands over his back and then onto his chest, and she feels, for the first time, not just a physical sensation, but a spiritual one borne out of love as he begins to caress her breasts. *Like a man and woman should be*, she thinks in ecstasy.

"That's enough for now," Ivan finally gasps as he pulls away. "There's such a thing as too much of a good thing."

"It'll never be enough for the time being, my love," Lyuba whispers. "We'll never get enough of this good thing. We've fought so hard, against each other, and other people, to truly give in to our hearts!"

"Don't get me wrong, I've long dreamt of this moment, but we have to get out of here. I found dead bodies all through this house!"

"I've been dreaming of this even longer than you, *golubchik*!"

"I went back into town yesterday and obeyed your orders, my love. I'll be off to find the ring I bought, and then we'll be on our way."

Mr. Litvinov comes up to the house with twelve of his important Party friends; his seven sons, Kuzma, Viktor, Venedikt, Fredrikh, Rikhard, Pyotr, and fifteen-year-old Mitya; and twenty specially-selected Cheka men. He passes out unlit torches.

"You said you killed everyone in the house."

"Quit stalling for time, Pyotr!" Kuzma grunts. "Prove your

loyalty!"

Pyotr tries to hide his thumping heart as Mr. Litvinov goes around lighting everyone's torch.

"Now, Petrushka, my favorite son, you do the honors. Throw the first torch in. Your former friend will come out like a scared animal, and we'll arrest him and take him back to Lubyanka, where he'll await his sentencing. If he comes out and doesn't talk back to us, he'll only get twenty years in a hard labor camp. He'll still be forty-two when he gets out."

Pyotr gulps and throws the first torch against the frame of the house. His six brothers and the others follow suit.

Tatyana comes running to her mother and begins whimpering.

"Your father's just off looking for something. The three of us will never be apart again." Lyuba tries to pick her up, but Tatyana runs away.

"I can't find it, my love. I won't leave this house till I do."

Tatyana runs up to Ivan. *"Dom gorit!"*

"Don't be ridiculous. They think everyone's dead. We can make a clean getaway and join the others in Tver."

"Dom gorit!"

Lyuba's heart thumps. "Vanya, do you smell burning wood? That scent is imprinted in my brain!"

A blazing rafter comes down and lands on the floor. Lyuba looks down the hall and sees almost the entire downstairs consumed by flames.

"We have to get out right now! Forget about the ring, and we'll flee!"

Ivan glances through a window. "Too late for any of that. I just counted forty people in the bushes, including Petya!"

"Petya would never betray us."

"This time he was being observed by his father, and if he didn't do it, he'd never be able to help us get to America. Go out by the side door, run away, and I'll catch up to you as soon as possible."

"I'll never leave you again!"

"This is no time to be stubborn. Take our daughter and run for your life!"

"I have no map."

"Petya will be waiting for you, I'm sure of it. I'll find you. Not to worry, *golubka.*"

"I cannot leave knowing you may die!"

Ivan takes her by the arm and marches her over to the side door. "This is the only door where you can leave without getting noticed by all those people! Run!"

Lyuba stays there waiting for him for another fifteen minutes, as the increasingly hot air is permeated by the sounds of shattering glass and groaning timbers. When Ivan returns, he picks up their luggage and throws it through the door, then puts Tatyana in her arms.

"I told you to run, and I meant it! You'll die of smoke inhalation if you stay here much longer!"

"Can't you just leave the ring and come with me?"

"I told you, I'll be right with you!"

4

The next thing Lyuba is aware of, it's morning, and she's lying in the front yard, Tatyana in her arms, luggage on one side of her, a charred ruins on the other, Pyotr standing above her, not a living being in sight.

"You passed out pretty bad from all those fumes you inhaled yesterday."

"Yesterday? The fire went on so long?"

"I found you passed out, and Tatyana was struggling for breath. My father, his henchmen, and my evil brothers had just left to get water to put out the blazes. I took my chance, and saw you lying there passed out with your little girl! I quickly carried you to the front of the house and put up the luggage to shield you from their view from that direction. Luckily, they never went around to the front of the house. Ivan didn't turn up. He either died in the fire or ran away."

"Look again. He can't be dead."

"The first time he was lucky, the second time even luckier, but the third time? One can only elude Death so long."

"I'm sure he'll show up sooner or later. He always does. But what am I supposed to do in the meantime, tag along with you? I have no male protection now."

"I'm taking a train into Tver, but I can't risk taking you with me, as much as I'd love to. If you're lucky, you might catch up with Ginny before he gets any farther."

"A thirteen-year-old boy as compared to Vanya, a twenty-two-year-old man who's as strong as ten men? That's your idea of male protection?"

"I agree it's important to have male protection, but it makes no sense for such a tomboy and advocate of women's rights to be so insistent on always travelling with a man. You're taller than a lot of men, and could probably defend yourself just as well." He hands her a map. "I outlined the safest route possible into Tver. This is your knapsack. I packed a tent, tent equipment, canned food, a can opener, some firewood, and clothes. I'll take your luggage on the train with me."

Lyuba fumbles with the clasp on one of her suitcases and pulls out Lyolya's coat. "I'll need my nice new coat, in case it gets colder at night."

"Yes, that's a good idea. Now get going and never look back."

"You're asking me to leave Moskva! This has been my home for twelve years!"

"Look one last time. One day you'll be back, maybe as a tourist, if this régime gets overthrown or voted out, or if the régime makes it safer for people who don't subscribe to the official state ideology to live freely. But you *will* be back. Trust me on this."

Lyuba puts on the knapsack and takes Tatyana. "I guess this is goodbye."

"Not to me. And not to Moskva. Moskva will always be in your heart, forever. Better to leave now with a lot of happy memories than after a nasty confrontation with the authorities." Pyotr starts tying the luggage together. "You'll see me again in Tver, and we won't part ways till March, when I'll put the twelve of you on a ship to America. We'll always be friends, forever. I'll write to you regularly when you're in America. If I can do it legally, I'll also come visit you once in awhile." He hugs her. "Goodbye, Lyubov Mikhaylovna Bodrova. Don't forget your false name."

Lyuba trudges up the hill and looks back at Moskva until she can see it no more. St. Basil's. The Kreml. Clean Ponds. Patriarch's Pond. The Tretyakov Gallery. The Russian State Library. The Museum of the History of Moskva. The Rumyantsev Museum. The

Triumphal Arch. So much beautiful architecture, so much history steeped in every stone. Her home for the past twelve years. The city where Tatyana was born. Out of sight, but never out of her heart.

5

Lyuba finds Ginny hiding out in the high part of the hills in the evening. She shakes her head when Ginny starts to ask the obvious question, and Ginny doesn't press the subject. They pitch the tent after they've trudged on for two more hours.

"How far do we have until we reach the others?" Lyuba asks after she maneuvers herself into her purple pajamas underneath a blanket.

"A little over one hundred *vyorsty*. If we walk quickly, we might get there in two weeks. Hopefully, the nice weather will last, and we won't have a sudden cold spell during summer's last gasp." Ginny blows out the lantern.

"Petya's risking everything to take us to America. Have you ever thanked him?"

"I have an idea. The night before we get on the ship, we'll give him a present in gratitude for all he's done for us."

"Like what?"

"Perhaps something that depicts true friendship. Are there any famous friends in Russian history?"

"That's a good idea. While we're in Tver, you can get back to your studies. You'd be going into the eighth grade this month. I want you to study Russian history, English, German, literature, arithmetic, and science. You must get a good job in America, and that can only happen if you're properly educated."

"I already know German and English quite well. And wherever will we get the books?"

"Petya can arrange for their delivery."

"Sure, if you insist. I want my mother to be proud of me. It would mean a lot to me if you keep mum about how bad I was before. I don't deserve to have my past held against me, same as how you don't deserve to have your own recent past held against you. No one can ever understand another person's mind."

6

Lyuba, Ginny, and Tatyana trek along over the next week, trudging up hills, wading across creeks, walking over rocks, each day leaving Moskva farther and farther behind. Sometimes they hear battles going on down below. They don't care anymore which side is winning, because the White cause is doomed. A few bands of *besprizorniki* are also in the hills. Ginny is still a clever thief, and manages occasionally to take food from them. He produces fish, fresh bread, and pickles. Each day the weather grows colder and colder, though a typical Russian September is much warmer than the famous brutal winter. Lyuba slips on Lyolya's coat and wraps Tatyana in blankets at night, while Ginny has made off with a new coat and pair of boots for himself.

"You're turning into Boris, stealing instead of doing things honestly."

"Desperate times call for desperate measures. Anyway, we just passed Klin. Maybe another week of travelling?"

"We always had male protection before. I feel so open to attack, with my only reliable protection gone. Vanya could've killed a man twice his size with his bare hands. I once saw him bend a horseshoe with his bare hands! He even bragged he could wrestle bears and panthers. He was five feet one when I met him, and he was only nine. You're taller than average too, but your growth is slower."

"Consider him coming to meet us. Look how many times all of us in the band have eluded certain Death!"

"His father was six feet seven inches tall. Vanya was only four inches shy of his father's height. Imagine what his sons would be like." She closes her eyes as Ginny blows out the lantern. "If only I were carrying his child, I'd always have a part of him no matter what. I wouldn't even care I'd court scandal with unwed motherhood all over again."

7

"I understand you're Margarita Kharzina." Lena stands in the doorway. "Tonya, Sonya, and I arrived in Canada two weeks ago, and we travelled into New York City today. We looked up Boris Aleksandrovich Malenkov in the phonebook, and this is the address which turned up. A man we talked to on the street told us Mrs. Zhukova was at work and Mrs. Kharzina was the only one home."

"Am I supposed to know you?"

"I'm Yelena Vadimovna Yeltsina. Malenkov took my baby son Yuriy in

April, and in June you took him to an orphanage. I want my son back, and I'll have to engage in a bit of deception before they'll give him to me. I'm a thirteen-year-old mother, not a situation which is exactly encouraged anywhere."

"Oh, the baby! But Yuriy's probably been adopted by now. I feel for your predicament, but babies tend to be adopted much quicker than older children."

"I was horrified when I got pregnant at only eleven. As you can imagine, it wasn't by choice, to say the least. But as soon as Yuriy was born, I fell in love with him on the spot."

"I understand how that maternal feeling can be. My only child, also a son, is now thirteen, and I haven't seen him since April 1917. Perhaps we may get lucky and the baby hasn't yet been adopted. I'll lie and say there was a mistake, and Yuriy's mother was stunned and horrified to learn her son was taken overseas by an irresponsible man who doesn't know how to be a father to either Yuriy or his natural daughter."

"You'll pretend to be the mother?"

"They already know I'm not his mother. Who's the older woman standing behind you?"

"That's Sonya Gorbachëva. She's thirty."

"Sonya, can you pretend to be Yuriy's mother?"

"Of course. I'm already pretending to be Lena and Tonya's aunt, and they're pretending to be cousins. I lost my two children, and doubt I'll have the chance to be a mother again. My firstborn is dead, and the second is in an orphanage."

Mrs. Kharzina squeezes Sonya's hand. "You never know if you may see your surviving child again in this lifetime, or if you'll someday find a new husband to have more children with. In the meantime, there's no time like the present. I have today off from my job as the cook at a Russian cathedral." Mrs. Kharzina gets her handbag.

Twenty minutes later, they're escorted into the orphanage. Lena looks around hopefully for Yuriy.

"I'm Mrs. Kharzina. Remember me?"

"You brought the baby boy here at the end of June, yes."

"You remember the story I told you, about him being left by his aunt for someone to take? And the young man who took him thought he was doing a good deed, but it turned out we couldn't possibly raise a child given our hectic work schedules?"

"Now are you able to take the baby on? This orphanage isn't a halfway house for children while their guardians or parents figure out how to provide a

better home life. These children can't handle so much uprooting."

"I understand that, but his mother, sister, and cousin have come to America and are furious Yuriy was taken by a man who can't even be a father to his own child! These are his mother, Sofya Mitrofanovna Yeltsina; his sister, Yelena Mikhaylovna Yeltsina; and his cousin, Antonina Borisovna Petrova. Mrs. Yeltsina is naturally furious at what happened to her only son, after already losing two other children. Has Yuriy been adopted yet?"

"Most of our children don't get adopted right away, though babies tend to go quicker. Wait one moment, and I'll see if he's still here."

The man comes back a moment later carrying Yuriy, now going on nineteen months old. Lena bites her tongue to repress a smile, though her heartrate quickens.

"Was Mr. Yeltsin a redhead?"

Sonya looks at Yuriy, who has the same red hair and aquamarine eyes as Lena. "Yes, my oldest and my youngest child both take after Mikhail."

"Sign here, Mrs. Yeltsina."

"In Russian or Roman script?"

"Whatever you can write better."

Sonya scrawls her name in Cyrillic script, using the pre-Revolutionary letters. She doesn't need to stop to remind herself she's using a false surname in order to get Yuriy back to Lena. The plan has become etched in her brain.

"Your baby must be very happy to see you again, Mrs. Yeltsina. That kidnapper ought to be ashamed of himself."

8

"So there you are. I can't believe I finally found you after how long I searched."

Lyuba stands up from the rock she's sitting on. Three projected days from the end of her journey, she almost expects the worst.

"What's wrong, don't you recognize me? It wasn't even two weeks ago we reunited and held each other and told each other we'll always be together!"

"Oh, Vanya, how dare you not come immediately to find me! I thought you'd died for sure that time!"

"You're not happy to see me?"

"Of course I am! But how dare you come up behind me like that and not join us right away!"

"I had to take a different route, *golubka*. I didn't want to put you at risk."

"I miss Branimir. Petya sent him to Tver ahead of us, in a train. Branimir would get us there a bit faster."

"You're not glad to see me?"

"You know I am!"

"No hug or kiss hello for me?"

"You really like to push your luck, don't you?" But Lyuba kisses him just the same. "There, are you happy now?"

"You know I won't really be happy until we're safe in America, you're Mrs. Koneva, and you've given me my son."

"Lucky Tatyana. She gets to be carried instead of walking. My back aches so much from carrying this heavy knapsack. Petya took all our luggage on the train with him. And I thought I was in pain when I was pregnant."

"Here, let me." Ivan takes off her knapsack. "I'll carry it for you."

"You won't be seeing much of Ginny until the evening. He likes to go on ahead and search out the area for any unfriendly bands."

"You don't need to worry now. As soon as we get to the new place, we'll never be apart again. Now Boris will never be able to find us."

"Can you promise me that when we get to America, he'll never interfere in our lives again?"

"As soon as we're in America, we'll find a nice little house for our family, which I hope will soon include our own child."

"If you're so eager to have a child, why don't you do something about it right now?" She runs her fingertip along his neck.

"It's not right to bring another child into a war-torn land." Ivan looks guiltily at the bruises on her face and the scar he put there. "It serves me right to have to constantly see the evidence of what I did to you when the Devil was controlling me. That's a punishment I deserve."

9

Lena is now back in the house, rocking Yuriy to sleep and periodically leaning down to kiss his red hair. Mrs. Zhukova comes in and looks with surprise at the three visitors.

"They came from Toronto. They arrived there two weeks ago and today came to get the baby back. The little redheaded girl is his mother."

"For shame! You did the right thing by giving that bastard to an orphanage!"

"Look how happy little Yurka is now. Lena may be only thirteen, but she's a wonderful mother. He seemed to immediately recognize her, after all those months apart."

"What kind of whore has a child so young?"

"I'm not a whore," Lena says, holding Yuriy tightly. "I met the father a week before the February Revolution. I wasn't yet twelve when I got pregnant. He'd been giving me food for awhile before then."

"For absolute shame!"

"Yes, shame on me, shame I was hungry and my mother and three sisters were going hungry also. Just pure shame!"

"Misha gave her cabbages and sausages," Antonina says. "It wasn't much, but it was enough to feed her shrinking family. When you're starving, you don't care how the food comes to you or what it is."

"Whenever I needed more food, I gave him my body. He used guile and deception. The first time was May 1918. He was almost twenty-two then. He promised me food for my sisters. Then he dragged me out to his car, raped me, beat me, and threw an apple into my face. We split the apple five ways, for me, my mother, and my three sisters. Thankfully, my family never called me a slut after I discovered I was expecting."

"Whatever is the world coming to!"

"Surprised someone can genuinely love and want a child conceived out of wedlock instead of feeling ashamed, giving him away, or having an abortion? Thank God my mother was a kind, understanding, loving woman who knew I was an innocent victim who'd been cruelly, barbarically abused."

"Worse yet, you have no father for this child!"

The doorbell rings very loudly and obnoxiously, followed by insistent knocking.

"Get the door, Katya, and shut up," Mrs. Kharzina chides.

Mrs. Zhukova almost faints. "It's Boris!"

Lena gives him a dirty look and clutches Yuriy tighter. "So it's the one who almost made me lose my baby forever."

"Is that Yuriy? Thank God my baby has returned safe and sound."

"Yes, my baby is safely back in his mother's arms, thanks for inquiring. Your daughter's great-aunt showed me how to start lactating again, since it's been some months since I was last with my baby. My companions and I are going back to Toronto tomorrow morning."

"You scoundrel!" Mrs. Kharzina slaps him. "You were insulted by a priest, and you decided to soothe your hurt feelings by going back into Russia illegally a second time?!"

"How do you know what that awful priest said to me?"

"I asked him! How dare he call himself a priest! Surely you've sinned, but not as much as he thinks you have!"

"Spasibo *for getting Yuriy back for me, little girl. I'll take him and be on my way."*

Lena makes the dulya *sign. "I'm no little girl. I'm a mother, you arrogant little swine-head."*

"March into the nearest factory, church, or store offering employment, and you stay there no matter what anyone says to you!" Mrs. Zhukova rages in his face. "How dare you give up on finding work so easily!"

"Show me some sympathy, pozhaluysta! *The first day I was back in Moskva, I found out one of my friends was murdered, and then the murderer himself went after me! That man should've been named for a different Tsar!"*

"Who was murdered?" Mrs. Kharzina asks.

"Basil Yakovlevich Beriya."

"By whom?" Mrs. Zhukova asks.

"Guess. Which one of my friends had a volatile temper?"

"Is it Pyotr?" Mrs. Kharzina asks.

"There was no sane reason to do it! He should've been sent back to the mental home, not murdered!"

"Beriya was in a mental home?"

"Guess why he got there! In his twisted mind, he truly believed Lyuba enjoyed being raped and that she'd gladly do it again!"

"She must've done something to warrant it," Mrs. Zhukova says. "A normal woman walking down the street dressed modestly won't be raped. I thought I raised her better."

"That is not true! I should know. It makes you feel powerful, like you're really in control. But then he was murdered by one of my very best friends!"

"I thought Pyotr and Basil were good friends."

"It was Ivan. Or, should I say, Ivan Grozniy Dva, the way he went after me after I innocently requested my daughter! The man is dangerous. He was so loud he made my little girl cry. His screaming fit in the bathroom woke up the whole damn house! Then he hit me with the back of his hand, pushed me backwards down a flight of thirty stairs, actually jumped down all thirty steps, began to choke me and bang my head against the floor at the same time, punched

me, began to choke me again, and pulled a knife on me! Let's not even start discussing how he went after me after I last saw Lyuba late last month! The man slammed my head against a huge rock so many times, I'm surprised I wasn't knocked into amnesia!"

"Oh, that Konev boy." Mrs. Kharzina smiles. "He's so strong, he can bend a horseshoe with his bare hands!"

"You dare smile about his strength when he practically killed me! He can bend a hundred horseshoes with his bare hands, and it won't make funny his vicious attack upon my life!"

"I really think Lyuba would be better-off if she marries Ivan."

"Lyuba can only marry Boris," Mrs. Zhukova insists. "She's used goods, and a woman can only marry the man who took her virginity. Besides, Boris is the baby's father. The only man who could become her husband now is Boris. I taught Lyuba to stay in a marriage for better or worse. Even if you don't love your husband, you're bound to him and must put up with his bad behavior."

"Tanyechka's surname is no longer Zhukova," Boris says. "It became Koneva just recently, after Lyuba promised she'd change her name to Tatyana Borisovna Malenkova. Lyuba herself has also begun pretending to be a Koneva. Ivan is well on his way to taking Lyuba away from me!"

"Perhaps that's for the better, at least temporarily. Lyuba wants to give an image of being a proper married woman, not an unwed mother. Pretending Ivan is her husband lessens her shame."

"She could've bought a wedding ring and pretended her husband went to America, which I really did, instead of using Ivan to pretend she's a married woman with the husband still in Russia! And why wait so damn long to start pretending they're married? Seems to me she still loves me."

"I'd prefer the Konev boy for my nephew-in-law over you any day, Borya," Mrs. Kharzina says. "He's more responsible than you."

"Responsible! By almost killing me!"

"He's never deserted my niece like you so cavalierly did when she most needed you. A man who really loves a woman doesn't abandon her."

10

"Lyuba, Lyuba, tell me what you dreamt about that made you scream in your sleep. You know you're safe with me." Ivan cradles her in his arms and strokes her hair. "But don't tell me if you're having nightmares about what I did to you. I wish I could forget that ever happened."

"What haven't I had nightmares about while I've been walking in these hills. Ginny doesn't always sleep in the tent, so he doesn't know I have nightmares. I dreamt the Cheka broke into my house, killed my mother and aunt, and took me and Ginny to a labor camp."

"I would've found you and killed your captors. You know that."

"You were almost killed yourself, Vanya. I found you just in time. If only you'd been man enough to run away with me then and there."

"I had no choice, *golubka*. With all those Reds on the street, we couldn't very well have made a run for it. We had to go with Boris and Ginny. You yourself insisted you weren't ready to marry me."

"But what about the time we almost did get away together?"

"I should've punched Basil and killed him then and there, instead of waiting so long to kill him."

"It's still hard to imagine, my gentle-hearted Vanyechka being a murderer, with blood upon his hands. And the way you went after Boris during his latest visit!"

"You're truly the only one who really knows about my sensitive side. Everyone else thinks I'm this cold-hearted brute with a *groznik* temper, but you know the real me. Now go back to sleep. We only have roughly one more day of travel. Then we'll see the others, and Branimir, again. Don't you feel happy about having less than a year left before we set sail for America?"

"The thought of leaving our Motherland makes me sad, not happy."

"We'll always have *Matushka Rus* in our hearts, love. One day when it's safe to come back, we'll return."

Lyuba goes back to sleep in his arms, Tatyana still sound asleep on her other side. Ginny is sleeping in a cave.

11

They finally reach Tver the next evening. When Lyuba walks through the door, she sees everyone, including Pyotr, having supper at the communal table. A rather fat woman is continually serving food, while her mother is busy at the coal-burning stove. It gives the picture of home.

"These women know what it's like to abandon their home," Katrin says, her mouth stuffed full of mushroom *pelmeni*. "They fled

Moskva after one of the daughters was taken by authorities to an orphanage. They opened a new boardinghouse here in Tver."

"We're serving everything you can imagine. My favorites are the *pelmeni*; it doesn't matter what it's stuffed or topped with!" Zina Yeltsina slaps down a huge ladleful of pickled beets onto Kittey's plate.

"Excuse our manners," Aleksey says. "These are Viktoriya L'vovna Yeltsina and her only remaining daughter, Zinaida Vadimovna."

"Zina and I have already met, very briefly," Lyuba says. "I'm glad to see she and her mother are still alive. It's too bad about her sister Lena disappearing."

"I have four daughters," Mrs. Yeltsina says. "And a grandson. Now only my second child is left. Moving to Tver was absolute murder, Comrades. I had typhus, and only recovered two weeks ago. Zina thought I was going to die."

"My little sisters Natasha and Lena are in orphanages, and my older sister Valya's in prison," Zina says.

"Zina's lover was murdered by the Bolsheviks," Kat says. "After she finished her studies abroad in Stockholm, she came back to Moskva with a master's degree in chemistry, worked as a student teacher for several years, and then came her valiant, noble lover. He didn't care she's a bit plump. They were together two years and planning to get married. Then she lost him so cruelly. She was forced to watch it. Now she's a thirty-one-year-old spinster, and no men are interested in her since she's fat. She says she was always fat, but not this big when she was with her fiancé."

Ginny inspects Zina's handwritten menu. "How about *selyodka* with onions and borshcht with sour cream?"

Mrs. Yeltsina takes several *selyodki* out of the icebox and begins to chop the onions. "The sour cream is entirely self-serve, Comrade."

"We had the mashed potatoes," Eliisabet says. "They're quite good."

"Don't give my cousin that much *selyodka*," Lyuba says. "He's been eating a lot of fish over the past two weeks, all stolen from rival bands in the hills."

"I didn't give you any fish," Pyotr says in surprise. "I thought

Ginny was learning to live without."

Anastasiya stuffs a huge hunk of boiled meat into her mouth. "Why don't you come and join us, Lyuba? Ivan, you can sit next to me."

"No he won't, Voroshilova. He loves only me. Mrs. Yeltsina, I'll have boiled chicken."

"You have caviar!" Ginny pushes aside the bowl of borshcht drowning in sour cream Zina has just set before him. "Change my order to caviar!"

"You'll do no such thing as long as I'm paying your bills," Pyotr says. "Not even Katrin and Anastasiya requested caviar."

"There are rich boarders here," Katrin announces. "Nastya and I are going to the ball they're giving this evening."

"Yes, God knows we're the only ones in the entire band with real clothes to wear to a ball," Anastasiya says.

"I'll wear my mink stole, my green silk tango shoes, and my black satin evening gown. I hope I catch the eye of a man as handsome as Wallace Reid or Douglas Fairbanks."

"I'll wear my baby blue silk dress with ten petticoats stitched underneath, my matching straw hat with peacock feathers, and my white leather tango shoes."

"Um, Anastasiya, if you came home from the labor camp with only the clothes on your back, how exactly did you reacquire so much finery?" Ginny asks, almost gagging on the sea of sour cream in his borshcht. "Money is worthless these days, unless you've secretly had one of those rare well-paying jobs."

"Katya gave it to me, little urchin. She was kind enough to sneak over to my house after my seizure, and gathered up all my stuff. At least I can enjoy an extravagant, comfortable lifestyle with one person in this band."

"I can't figure you out, Katrin," Lyuba says. "You claim to be such a committed Communist, yet you're still lugging around cosmetics, ridiculous clothes, pictures of celebrities, and vanity items. And after how you've been made homeless by the Reds, you still support them."

"All is forgiven now," Katrin says. "I've been profusely apologized to for that unfortunate incident last March. Those idiots who evicted me on account of Stasya weren't acting on Comrade

Lenin's orders. I'm sure he'd be horrified if he knew what some of his so-called followers are doing in his name."

Katrin and Anastasiya disappear from the table and go to change into their finery. When they return, they waltz down the stairwell into the room servicing the richer boarders as a ballroom. Though Lyuba never cared for balls and only went out of social obligation and to look normal, she can't help but be curious about the first ball she isn't expected to attend. As she stands at the door, longingly looking at the people who belong to a world which is now but a distant memory, she spies Anastasiya's dance partner and sees red. Uncaring she's not dressed for a ball and hasn't properly bathed in two weeks, she storms into the room.

"Ivan Ivanovich Konev, what do you think you're doing?"

"I came to steal some of the *zakuski* on the table, and Anastasiya came up to me. Before long, we were dancing. Would you like to dance now?" He holds his arms open and smiles.

"How dare you. After everything we've been through, you go and start flirting with this brainless excuse of a woman all over again! I don't think I'll talk to you for the rest of the evening."

"What, you don't want to dance with me? It's been too long since we danced. You're much prettier than all these other women with their expensive gowns and cosmetics. Your beauty is all natural."

Lyuba bristles at his touch. "Don't touch me. Not after you were just dancing with that shallow, empty-headed creature!"

"I'm apologizing for my behavior right now. It was against my better judgment."

"Why should I believe you?"

"Because I love you. How many times do I have to prove how much I love you? *Pozhaluysta*, don't say you're still angry at me for what I did to you in August, though I don't deserve your love and forgiveness after my grotesque behavior."

"How many times have you been with her?"

"Lyuba, you're the only woman I've ever done anything with. Anastasiya has always been just pretend. I'm going to give my virginity to you, as a special gift I can give you only once."

"Lyuba's no virgin," Anastasiya says. "You'll be getting used merchandise. Why not save yourself for me? I'm as virgin as I was the day I was born."

Ivan glares at her. "This must be too hard for you to grasp, but Lyuba's still a virgin in her heart. She didn't love any of those excuses for men who had her body."

"You can't really want a woman with a child. That's another man's bastard."

"Tatyana is my child, and always has been. Are you so indecent you see nothing wrong with insulting the love of my life while she's standing right here?"

"The Devil take you." Lyuba goes storming off to find Pyotr.

***

Pyotr looks up from reading *Izvestiya* when he hears a knock at his door. "What can I do for you?"

Lyuba steps inside his room. "I'm going to make Ivan jealous of you, so he'll swear never to cavort around with that Voroshilova woman ever again!"

"How are you going to make him jealous?"

"He dances with that brainless woman, I can sleep with you!"

Pyotr's eyes widen.

****

Chapter 19: Tver

In the morning, Ivan knocks on Pyotr's door. "Petya, do you know where Lyuba disappeared? I'm coming to apologize to her. I swear I'll never do anything so stupid ever again, just tell me if you know where she is!"

Lyuba answers the door, wearing a peach silk robe. Ivan looks at her, then sees Pyotr sitting up in the bed.

"What are you doing in Petya's room?"

"We're very good friends, and he *really* comforted me last night. I spent the night with him. I think I'll stay here until we leave."

"I felt so lonely last night without you asleep in my arms, my love."

"You mean you didn't take Anastasiya back up to what was supposed to be *our* room?"

"Of course not! Now what is Petya doing with you in such a scandalous situation? You don't mean to tell me he slept in the same bed as you!"

"Did he ever." Lyuba begins smiling. "Petya told me he was a virgin, can you believe that, Ivan, at almost twenty-one years old? I was the first woman he ever slept with. He told me it was the best experience of his life!"

"You were angry at me for dancing with Anastasiya, so you slept with Petya? What was that supposed to prove?!"

"If you're ready to apologize now, I can accept it. If not, I'll continue to sleep with Petya until you make me a sincere apology."

Ivan runs out of the house and into the garden, reeling in shock at what he just saw and heard. Lyuba runs after him, not bothering to put on slippers.

"Just what were you trying to prove, *golubka*?"

"I wanted to make you jealous."

"So you slept with Petya!"

"He was pretty good for someone who'd never been with a woman before."

"You just threw another dagger into my heart!"

"You're not numb to the pain yet, after so many rejections?"

"You slept with Petya!"

"Think of it as gaining great experience for when I finally become your lover."

"You slept with Petya!"

"Is that the only thing you're going to say to me, Vanya?"

"I might as well betroth myself to Anastasiya."

"Fine. Then you won't object to Petya and I being lovers. I guess Petya was my first real lover. Every other man was just for money, food, or rape."

Ivan shudders when he sees Lyuba and Pyotr together that night at the supper table. Even worse, Pyotr has his arm around her.

2

"Let me tell you, Natasha, Mrs. Voznesenskaya is a real nutjob," Klarisa tells the new arrival. "See that girl in the bed over there? She's been dead for over a year. 'I'm barren, so I like to pretend she's my daughter.' Talk about sick!"

"I want to go home." Six-year-old Natalya Yeltsina looks at the ground. "I forget what my parents look like, and my three big sisters."

"Don't cry, Natasha. I'll get you out of here soon enough."

"I haven't seen my parents or big sisters in so long. The bad guys came for me one night after the Revolution. They wanted to take me away from my Tsarist family."

"Mrs. Voznesenskaya is out like a light, after the drugs I mixed into her nightly vodka. In two weeks, I'll have another list of twenty girls I'm going to get out of here. Do you want to go too?"

"I want to go home."

"Most of them don't have any homes left to go to anymore. A bunch of our last girls went to Sweden, and two went to Canada." Klarisa looks at Natalya's ID card. "You're a Yeltsina? One of the girls I sent to Canada was named Lena Yeltsina, and she had red hair and aquamarine eyes just like you."

Natalya stops crying. "One of my sisters is named Lena. I don't remember her very much, but I remember she looks just like me."

"I'll put three of the older girls in charge of taking you safely to your big sister in Canada. Manya, Lyuda, Grushenka!"

Three girls between the ages of thirteen and sixteen march over.

"This is little Natalya Vadimovna Yeltsina. You're to take care of her, for you'll be taking her to Canada with you in two weeks. Lena Yeltsina is her big sister, the redhead who left with Tonya in July."

"Yes, Klarisa," fourteen-year-old Lyuda says.

"These are Lyudmila Igorovna Shulgina, Mariya Filippovna Yermilova, and Agrafena Mikhaylovna Surikova. They're your new best friends. Lyuda knows her way around the kitchen quite well, almost as well as I do; Grushenka's an expert seamstress and is always sewing forbidden objects into the mattresses; and Manya's a thief. Do you have any special talents?"

"I can steal extra portions from the kitchen."

"Good. The cook tonight is Miss Kaganova, so none of us will be the girls she keeps after. But when there's a Russian cook, we sure will get to stay behind for the better portions, and you, I, and Lyuda will all take a little something extra, to line our hungry stomachs with. I'm Mrs. Voznesenskaya the Mad's favorite hostage in this hellhole, so she never suspects a thing from me!"

3

"I never once thought you'd actually sleep with Petya!"

"Shut up, Ivan, Petya's trying to give me a lesson."

"A lesson in what, how to break my heart even more?"

"No, a lesson in Communism."

"It's one thing for you to sleep with him to make me jealous, but really!"

"Petya wanted a constitutional monarchy. To have Communism become the law of the land, of course, but not to kill the Tsar! He was horrified at how the Tsar was murdered in cold blood after being tricked into abdicating. Petya wanted him to live out his days in peace. Right now we're working on *What Is to Be Done?* Do you remember that book, Vanya?"

"It was on the shelf in our hotel room, *golubka*. How could I forget any part of that beautiful time?"

"Now Lyuba, I think Comrade Lenin's a genius." Pyotr's whole being is one giant smile. "Only I do so hope after things calm down a bit, he'll get back to real Marxist teachings. Seizing land from the peasants is so anti-Marxist I can't believe my father and brothers are defending it! Emergency wartime measures my left foot!"

"*I'm* a *levsha*," Ivan scowls. "There's nothing wrong with my left hand, my left eye, my left ear, or my left foot!"

"Don't be so overly sensitive," Lyuba says. "It's only an expression."

"An expression which hurts my feelings!"

"Oh, learn to write like everyone else," Katrin says. "Try copying this sentence from *Izvestiya*."

Ivan picks up a pencil and tries to write right-handed. He can barely hold the pencil straight. It wobbles all over the piece of paper Katrin has ripped out of her notepad. The end result is totally illegible.

"I can't read a word of this writing!" Katrin declares. "This handwriting is totally illegible!"

"Told you I can't write with my right hand."

"Now, back to *What Is to Be Done?* In this rather difficult passage here, I believe Comrade Lenin was trying to say..."

Ivan storms away and goes to join the others in the garden, taking in the mid-September sun. Even the lilies, roses, and daisies do nothing to warm his soul, though at least the sun warms him physically.

"Did Lyuba really do something so bad?" Eliisabet asks. "Tanya and Kolya look so cute, sound asleep together. I hope they grow up to be childhood sweethearts."

"She slept with Petya to make me jealous, and now he's busy indoctrinating her into being a lunatic Bolshevik!"

"When are you going to give that woman a rest?" Anastasiya asks. "I thought you were engaged to me now, not her."

"Perhaps she's trying to expand her worldview, understand where the other side's coming from," Kat suggests. "If she's caught and interrogated, she'll be able to pretend she's a knowledgeable Bolshevik."

"How can she just stamp on my heart like that!"

"She's frightened of your love for her, you told me." Aleksey is sitting on a rock. "Whenever you start to get really close, she runs."

"She can't keep running forever!"

"Looks like this time she ran right into the arms of Petya," Anastasiya says.

"You shut up, you brainless excuse of a woman! I adore Lyuba, and have since I first laid eyes on her!"

"It's time to move on to a more promising project. Me."

"You're delusional if you think I ever loved you! I gave my heart to one woman, and that's Lyuba!"

"Your namesake loved his first wife passionately, but he moved on and had six more wives after that."

"You're confusing me with someone else. I was named for Tsar Ivan the Great, not his grandson."

"Oh, really. Even after you went after poor innocent Boris?"

"Why don't *you* adopt a child, raise her for a year and a half, have her blood mother show up and demand her back, and see how *you'll* react! I'd die for my little girl!"

Tatyana wakes up and begins to cry for her lunch.

"Isn't that right, love of my life?" Ivan picks her up and looks at her with love in his eyes. "I'd die for you and your beautiful mother."

"You have brown eyes and hair, Ivan. The girl has black eyes and hair. Sort of like her father, didn't you ever notice that?"

"Didn't you ever notice Boris walked out on the love of my life and treated her absolutely horribly? I'm the man who's been her true father all her twenty months on Earth! And she looks everything like Lyuba and nothing like Boris."

"You're still not her real father."

"Moses and Jesus were also adopted."

"And that means what to me?"

"She's just as beautiful as her namesake. Aren't you, my sweet little Tanyechka? Pretty soon we'll be in America, and you'll have a little brother or sister."

"This is really getting frightening," Anastasiya shudders. "I don't see Aleksey pouring so much affection on little Kolya as you are on Tatyana! Men aren't supposed to show so much love and affection for children. That's a woman's job."

"Oh, right, I'm supposed to hide my feelings for my darling daughter and pretend I don't love her?" Ivan lifts Tatyana into the air. "Who's the most beautiful little girl in Russia?"

"This is really disgusting me." Anastasiya gets up and parades back into the Yeltsina boardinghouse.

4

Lyuba cuddles up to Pyotr after they've finished a lunch of cold kvass soup over *What Is to Be Done?* "I only told one other person this, and this was last month. Now I'm really getting scared."

"Is someone following you?"

"No. I'm late."

"Late for what?"

"I'm two months late, and I'm truly frightened. The only other time this happened was when I got pregnant with Tatyana. But I haven't had any of the same symptoms I did before, so this is really puzzling me."

"You think you're pregnant?"

"I don't know who it could possibly be this time. All the men I serviced used prophylactics, and the only other man who possibly didn't was Boris."

"Now, you never know. You've been under so much anxiety these past few months. Chalk it up to that."

"I know it can't possibly be Misha, since he learnt his lesson from getting the eleven-year-old pregnant. None of the customers are allowed to do business in his brothel unless they show a prophylactic that hasn't been tampered with. They've only ever had three pregnancies, and they all ended in abortions. I pray to God it isn't Boris again."

"You're in a fine fix if it is Boris again!"

"Yes, I know. But how can I find out now? There were other men with black hair and eyes I did business with, not just him."

"Will they come after you if they find out where you are?"

"No, they only want to capture Vanya. For all they know, I took sick or was offered work at a rival brothel. I never signed a contract, and wasn't expected to give advance notice. I'm not the first woman to just up and quit working for them."

"Then call right now."

***

Misha is awoken from his late afternoon nap by the ringing phone. "Yes, who is this?"

"It's me, Lyubov Leontiyevna Zhukova."

"You left Podolsk. Did something happen to you in the soldiers' camp?"

"I'm sorry for not alerting you as to my departure, but you'll soon understand I couldn't possibly have continued work in my condition. I'm two months late."

"You know it couldn't possibly be me. And I never let a man in unless he's shown me his prophylactic at the door. The soldiers were under the exact same orders."

"That's why I think it's my baby's father again."

"Hold on. I'll get Kostya. Maybe he's been letting unprepared men into my brothel. It's just the kind of thing he'd do!" Misha puts down the phone. "Kostya, my stupid, irritable cousin, come in here!"

"Yes, Misha?" Kostya is holding an open scrapbook of pictures of his favorite moving picture actresses. "You interrupted me at a terrible time. I have so many loose pictures I need to glue into these pages, and it takes awhile for the glue to dry. This is an all-day project."

"One of our former prostitutes is on the phone, saying she thinks she may be pregnant. Have you been letting in customers without the proper equipment, or with damaged equipment?"

"Is this supposed to be about men who can't perform sexually? I don't exactly check for that sort of thing!"

"Prophylactics, you genius!"

"I follow your rules right down to the very last letter, but I don't believe they apply to me."

"That's so typical of you, though I can't imagine any women would sleep with you willingly. You're too stupid and cowardly to even enjoy a lady by force. Anyway, do you know Lyubov Leontiyevna Zhukova?"

"Yes, I've been with her quite a number of times. What a voluptuous, womanly body."

"Did you come prepared?"

"I went to see a doctor in Klin about a problem I'd been having. He advised me to stop wearing prophylactics, because I was just about dying of hives."

"Durak!" Misha swats him over the head with *Izvestiya*. "So it's either you or her daughter's father!"

"I didn't want to worsen my hives, Misha!"

"Yes, Miss Zhukova. It's either Malenkov or my irresponsible cousin Kostya. The nerve of that cousin of mine!" Misha slams the phone hard.

***

"It's either Kostya Godunov or Boris."

"What are you going to do about it?"

"I don't know."

5

At midnight, Anya slips out of Mrs. Brezhneva's orphanage with nine-

year-old Leontiy by the hand. Fyodora, Natalya, and Vera follow them, suitcases in hand.

"Mrs. Brezhneva's becoming more tolerable day by day," Fyodora begs. "She would've let Alla take us home with her if we'd asked."

Alla is waiting for them in a car she stole from one of the teachers. She'll be taking them to Pskov.

"I think the city changed hands again," Vera says. "But from who to whom, I'm not sure anymore."

"We only have little Lyonya for male protection," Natalya says. "What are we going to do?"

"Fanya Kaplan shot Comrade Lenin all by herself," Alla says. "She didn't get a man to do it for her. Now let's all forget our pasts and move on to a shining new day."

6

It's now early October. Pyotr is closing up his research on how the townspeople are reacting to the Bolshevik rule, and mapping out the route the band will take to their new dwellings in the city.

"Lyuba, I don't like what you're doing to Ivan." Pyotr slips off his pajama pants and pulls on red button-front undershorts.

"He danced with Anastasiya, and I made him turn green with jealousy."

"I love being your lover, but give the man a break! He wants only you."

"Then why did he dance with that vain blonde woman the first night we were here?"

"Why did *you* sleep with me?" Pyotr pulls on brown corduroy trousers.

"To make Ivan jealous of you. And maybe I was a little curious about what it'd be like to be your lover and sleep with a man who wasn't afraid of going all the way. It's really nice to finally know what it's like to enjoy consensual sexual relations, not force or prostitution."

"He apologized the very next morning, and you continued to sleep with me."

"You sure haven't been unhappy about that arrangement."

"Well, now I *am* getting unhappy. You've given me a wonderful few weeks, but now I'm telling you to go to the man you love."

"*You're* the man I love now, silly. It's hardly unheard-of for a person to have more than one love in a lifetime."

"You know exactly what I mean. I've seen him. He looks dead. He only looks happy when he's with Tatyana. But a child needs two loving parents, not just one. And she needs to see them together. When you go to America, he'll marry you and adopt her, and you'll have no more reason to feel ashamed of your unwed motherhood. Ivan has gone above and beyond the call of duty in being a real father to her the past twenty months. Now go back to him and become a real family."

"I love being your lover." Lyuba slips her hand into his pants and fondles him.

"You don't love me. Our relationship went from deep friendship to a purely sexual one. With Ivan, you have everything. You're soulmates." Pyotr gently pulls her hand out of his pants, throws his pajama shirt on the floor, and slips on a fresh white-and-blue-striped shirt.

"If he were my soulmate, he never would've danced with Voroshilova. My soulmate wouldn't keep finding an excuse not to sleep with me every time we're a couple. Now he knows what happens to men who hesitate too long on staking their claim."

"You think about this." Pyotr drops his notes on the bed and goes downstairs after dressing.

Lyuba pictures every time she and Ivan have been split apart by something stupid. This is time number eight, she thinks darkly.

***

"You don't love Anastasiya. You love Lyuba."

"You know what, Pyotr? You're only the latest thing that's ruined my relationship with Lyuba! She ran right into your arms!"

"You know she loves you."

"She loves me so much she runs each time we start to get really close!"

"Maybe she has issues. Nothing a little psychoanalysis can't cure."

"What kind of a fancy word is that?"

"Haven't you ever read Freud? You're not *that* backward, are you?"

"I was two months away from graduating gymnasium when that crazy raving lunatic Lenin returned to the Motherland, overthrew God's anointed, and killed him a year later! I'd be in my last year of university now if he hadn't come back and ruined everything! Sort of like how *you've* ruined everything!"

"I told Lyuba we're finished. I want her to be with you, for always."

"How do I know you're not going to pull crazy stunts like Boris did?"

"I'm not Boris."

"Yes, but you *are* one of many people who've ruined my chances for happiness and a future with Lyuba!"

"Listen, Konev. I have the map right here. Tomorrow morning you'll go to four different houses in Tver. One for you, Lyuba, Ginny, and Tatyana; one for Aleksey, Liza, and Kolya; one for Nikolas, Kat, and Kittey; and one for Katrin and Anastasiya."

Ivan cringes at Anastasiya's name. "I led her on again. I'm sorry."

"Lyuba is truly the one who deserves an apology. She thought you loved her, and you danced with Anastasiya."

"It wasn't my fault! It just sort of happened, and Lyuba would never have seen it if she weren't looking into that stupid ballroom at right that moment."

"She forgave you for beating her up but not for dancing with another woman. A woman's heart is a strange thing to understand!"

7

That evening, Anastasiya parades around in the ballroom wearing a pink feather dress and white mink boa. She smiles at Ivan, who's come to steal *zakuski* again. He's not exactly starving with the food provided by Mrs. Yeltsina and Zina, but he can only find treats like *canapés* and hard cheeses in the ballroom. Not to mention the caviar, which is available at dinner every night, but which he's refrained from ordering so the other Stray Dogs won't accuse him of living like a prince while they eat more basic food.

"Get away from me. You look like a chicken."

"Now, there. Would Lyuba get all dressed up like this for you?"

"Lyuba understands modesty and sensible clothes."

"She's so modest she was a prostitute! And Boris, Pyotr, Basil—"

"You dare pass judgment on the love of my life!" Ivan stalks upstairs.

"He certainly wasn't like this when we were together before," she says to Katrin, who's wearing a green silk dress with straps and a pink muskrat boa. "I never once suspected back then he was secretly in love with Lyuba."

"A man's heart is a hard thing to understand."

Lyuba has left a note for him on a table in the hallway. *I'm very sorry for what I've been doing with Petya. I hope you'll forgive me yet again, Vanya, for you know I love only you. All the other men are only distractions when I become afraid of how much you love me. And I don't know how to react normally when you hurt or disappoint me. The only way I know how to react is to run away or strike back to give you a taste of your own medicine. I'm waiting in the room that was supposed to be ours. Come quickly.*

Lyuba looks up as he enters the room. "Coming to apologize?"

"Is Pyotr hiding in here?"

"You can check." Lyuba gets out of bed and yanks back the covers. "Now look under the bed and see if Petya isn't hiding."

He searches the whole room. No Pyotr. Then his eyes fall upon Lyuba, who's slipped into a black silk nightgown that clings to her body and stops three inches above her knees. He takes in her body with lustful eyes.

"Yes? You're going to look at me all evening?"

"This time we'll be together forever. No interruptions. I really mean that this time."

"Yes, no interruptions whatsoever." Lyuba goes back to the bed. "You must've felt so lonely without me."

"A part of my heart, my soul, is missing whenever you're not with me!"

"You're the most romantic Russian man I know. You always speak to me in such poetic, sweet language, my Ivan the Meek."

"I'm hardly meek."

"Then show me you were named for his great-great-grandson, the first ruler to ever be called Tsar."

Ivan goes to lie beside her and draws her into his arms, kissing her and running his hands along her back and through her hair. Lyuba has never felt like this with any of the other men she's been with. Only one lights a fire in her heart and soul, makes her heart stop beating or beat even faster and melt at the same time, who makes her light-headed, with a stomach full of butterflies, her great dreadsome meek one.

"You know, I never even kissed Anastasiya."

"Shut up and continue what we've started!"

"What did you like Pyotr, Boris, or the others to do?"

"It doesn't matter. What do *you* want to do?"

"To make you happy."

"Then anything you do *will* make me happy!"

"You have so much experience already."

"When will you stop comparing yourself to other men?" Lyuba unbuttons his shirt and runs one hand along his back and the other across his chest.

"Don't touch my back. It still hurts. But feel free to touch anything else you'd like."

Lyuba purrs in approval as he continues to kiss and caress her for the next twenty minutes, until she suddenly pushes him away.

"What did I do?" Ivan looks like a hurt little child. "Did I touch you the wrong way?"

"It's not what you did, my love. I just remembered something."

"About your father?"

"Vanya, I almost decided not to reunite with you that night we escaped from Mr. Golitsyn's boardinghouse. I didn't want to tell you because it would break your heart. You would've done more than stab Basil if you knew what he did to me. I pictured me telling you to leave me, and you crying and looking deep into my eyes with that sad heartbroken look you get, begging me with your eyes, '*Pozhaluysta*, tell me what's wrong and how can I fix it?,' and me turning away, and you trying your hardest not to cry, and blaming my latest rejection of your selfless love on God knows what or who, and I was scared of Basil's ghost coming after me if I told you, since he ordered me in a very low whisper never to tell anyone, and—"

"Lyuba, *moya golubka*, can you just tell me what's gotten you so upset just now?"

"His ghost will come after me and kill you, my belovèd!"

"I don't believe in ghosts. Only the Holy Ghost, and that's not really a ghost like you're imagining."

"Okay. But you must promise not to get too mad, because I know too well you can go from Ivan the Meek to Ivan Grozniy in a matter of seconds if something really ruffles your feathers."

"I can tell already I'm going to get mad!"

"So I won't tell you."

"You're going to tell me exactly what Basil said that made you remember it just now."

"It wasn't what he said so much as what he did to me."

"What else did he do, beat you?" He gently touches the wound on her face.

"No, no beating. I can't tell you, because I know you'll get really mad."

"You can't keep this a secret forever. It'll all come out sooner or later."

"Okay, but promise not to go over the deep end. While he was raping me, he threatened me over and over. If I tried to move or push him away, he squeezed my waist until there were red marks. He said he'd kill me if I pushed him away one more time—"

Ivan leaps out of bed, puts his shirt back on, and opens the window.

"Where are you going, Vanyechka?"

"You should've told me that very afternoon! I could've taken a gun and blown his brains out then and there! He threatened to kill you!"

"What more can you do to him? He's already dead!"

"Not dead enough," Ivan growls, climbing down the trellis.

"Where are you going, *golubchik*?"

"Back to Moskva to dig him up and cut his corpse into pieces with the axe I used to murder the *mudak*, that's where! I'll take a train and get it over with as soon as possible!" He grabs the axe and shovel from a trunk of tools the band keeps on the front veranda, and shoves them into a large burlap sack. "I'll be back in your arms by tomorrow!"

"Don't go!" Lyuba screams. "You're a wanted criminal!"

Ginny comes into the room. "Did I just see Ivan climbing down the wall?"

"He says he's going back to Moskva!"

"He's crazy!"

Ivan goes back into the house to grab one of the guns Mrs. Yeltsina keeps for protection. As he's putting the safety on, he spies Katrin's Party ID lying on a table, and grabs that too. He storms into the office and finds a jar of white paint used for typewriter errors. After he whites out her surname, first name, and patronymic, he writes a fake name, Dmitriy Pavlovich Kuznetsov, over the still-drying white paint, and changes the date of birth, place of birth, and sex, never minding the white paint and ink smudging onto his hand. Ivan finds a small jar of paste near the typewriter, rips off Katrin's picture, and affixes a random male picture in its place. He makes it to the train station at 11:00 and buys his ticket with a silver figurine from the supply of small goods Pyotr gave them for bartering. When asked for identification, he pulls the red book out of his pocket. He also complies with the order to show what's in his bag.

"What do you need with a shovel and axe, Comrade Kuznetsov?" the conductor asks suspiciously.

"I'm an undertaker. There was a problem back in Moskva. The family thinks a tombstone is marking the wrong grave. I have to exhume the body to find out if some enemy of the people didn't switch coffins while my back was turned."

"You can never trust anybody these days!"

8

Katrin finds her Party ID missing when she's packing up her things the next morning. She tears apart her room to try to find it, and it's nowhere. When she remembers she left it on a table downstairs, she throws a lilac silk robe over her pale green cotton pajamas, steps into blue silk slippers embroidered with silver thread, made in the style of lotus shoes, and rushes downstairs. Katrin begins to cry when the belovèd red book still doesn't materialize. All she finds is the small picture she was so proud to pose for at age seventeen, when she realized her longtime dream of officially becoming a Communist.

"Crying because you're leaving?" Mrs. Yeltsina asks. "For the love of God, go put on day clothes before you take breakfast. I don't allow nightclothes at my table. At least you put on a robe before you came downstairs."

"I lost my Party ID!"

"This is a great incentive to abandon Communism," Nikolas says. "Now you don't have any excuses to stay behind in Russia!"

Ivan comes through the door two hours later, just as everyone is loading their baggage onto the wagon, hitched up with Branimir and three horses Pyotr has just bought.

"Oh, thank God!" Lyuba runs to Ivan and hugs him and kisses him. "How dare you go back to Moskva!"

"Katrin is having a personal crisis," Ginny giggles. "She lost her Party ID."

"It's right here." Ivan pulls it out of his pocket.

Katrin turns white in rage when she flips it open. "My name isn't Dmitriy Pavlovich Kuznetsov! I'm not a man, nor was I born July eighteenth of 1895 in Omsk! How dare you ruin my most important possession! This is useless now!"

He waves his hand at her dismissively, then turns back to Lyuba. "I got there very late at night, with owls hooting loudly. I remembered the exact spot where we buried Basil, and found it easily. Thankfully, no one else was lurking about as I dug the *mudak* up and axed the moldy, decomposing body into little pieces. I was so blinded by rage, I didn't have the presence of mind to feel even slightly nauseated as I divested the skeleton of the rotting flesh and muscles with a knife or cut his head off. I was about to start smashing the bones into smithereens when I hit upon the idea of selling the remains. That way, this dangerous trip would be about more than just revenge. I'm no scientist, but I know decomposing remains are useless for medical studies. Bones, however, can be quite useful. I loaded the entire skeleton into my bag and took a train to Petrograd, where I got directions to the Imperial Academy of Sciences. I sold Basil to a rich professor for quite a hefty price. He'll take the bones to Kunstkamera for further study and possible display."

Several of the Stray Dogs, particularly Anastasiya, are vomiting.

"Three hundred million rubles." Ivan hands the bag of money to Lyuba. "Count it. It's all there."

"With three hundred million rubles, we could go straight to America instead of fooling around in this city for another five months!" Lyuba exclaims. "Coupled with all my money, we could easily go right to the Midwest and buy our farm too! My mother will be so proud of me when she learns I chose a rich man after all."

"You'll all do exactly as I bade you," Pyotr says. "One wrong move and my cover is blown."

"But we're rich now. Surely the ruble exchange rate isn't so pathetic as to mean our hundreds of millions of rubles are worth only a few hundred dollars."

"Your riches will still be there in March, when I get you on that ship. Thirteen of our lives are hanging in the balance, and one wrong move will mean the deaths of all of us. I'm sorry, but this is how it must be."

Pyotr drives the wagon away as soon as everyone boards. They've ridden for about an hour when suddenly Lyuba gasps. She looks desperately around the wagon, and her suspicion is confirmed.

"Vanya, we forget someone back at the house!"

"I think you're imagining things."

"We forget Tatyana! We must've been so distracted by your horrific story, we didn't think to make sure she was loaded into the wagon."

He looks around the wagon again. "Pyotr, turn back. We forget our little girl. I can't believe how careless and unobservant we were."

Pyotr turns around and glares back at Ivan. "You're so enamored of risk-taking, Konev. You walk back, if you remember the way, and pick her up yourself! Otherwise I'll go back myself when you're settled into your new lodgings."

Ivan jumps off the moving wagon and walks back. Lyuba crosses herself and silently prays nothing bad has befallen her precious only child in this short time.

9

Ivan arrives back at the Yeltsina boardinghouse two hours later. Zina gets the door, her face as white as a sheet.

"Your party left just in time, Ivan Ivanovich. Fifteen minutes later, the Reds broke in and starting shooting everyone. My mother's under the table with a bullet to her chest, but she's still breathing, praise God. I ran and hid in a back room. Everyone except my mother and I are dead. Even small children weren't spared. They were asking for you, since they somehow found out you were staying here."

Ivan grabs the door frame, violently shaking. "Where's my little girl? Give me my daughter! Even if she's dead, Lyuba and I can still bury her in the soil of our homeland!" He resists the urge to burst into tears in front of Zina, imagining the tiny, bloody corpse of the child he loves so much.

Zina walks swiftly to the outhouse and comes back with Tatyana, who's clutching her doll. "No one would ever think to look in the privy. They went in and looked around, but not down. I just cleaned it yesterday, so I wrapped her in a blanket and lowered her down as soon as I heard the footsteps and shouts."

He crosses himself. "I am so sorry, *knyazhna*, that we forgot you. You could've been killed!" Ivan takes her from Zina and hugs and kisses her. "God will bless you, Zinaida Vadimovna, for saving the life of my child."

"Your daughter is so cute, like a little kitten. I wish I'd had a baby."

"She's not mine biologically, like you probably heard. You can adopt like I did. I won't love my future biological children any more than I love Tatyana."

"I'm fat. I had one too many *pelmeni* as a girl. And my fiancé was murdered by the Bolsheviks. Now I'm an old maid at thirty-one. *Pozhaluysta*, my three sisters and my father are gone. I'll have no one left if my mother dies."

"My mother was murdered by the Bolsheviks too. I memorized their dirty faces. I've seen the ringleader a few times, the one who hit her in the head with a rifle. I wish desperately I could inflict the same pain upon him as he did to my mother!"

"Will you help me rescue my mother? I taught chemistry, and I have a first aid kit."

Tatyana begins whimpering.

"You must be hungry, *knyazhna*. I hate to do this, but I have to ask you to go without me. Follow the ruts in the mud. I hope they stopped to wait for us. The faster you run, the faster you'll see your *mamashka*, and I bet she'll give you a present for being such a good girl."

10

Lyuba sees Tatyana walking alone as dusk gathers that evening. She jumps off and grabs Tatyana into her arms, frantically hugging and kissing her.

"Where's your father, *knyazhna*?"

"With Zina."

"He didn't come with you?"

"No."

"Oh, that irresponsible, foolhardy Konev!" Pyotr shouts.

"You're talking about the man I love," Lyuba chides.

"Ivan has gotten your entire band into so much trouble over the past few months! It's like he wants to be caught by the authorities and sent back to prison!"

"Stop the wagon. He might yet catch up to us."

"I have emergency plans in case anybody finds out I've taken you to Tver. You'd better all hope to your God I don't have to use them. You won't like very much where you'll have to go if Tver falls through."

"Where?" Ginny asks.

"You'll find out if it has to happen."

Pyotr leaves the wagon and unties his biped. He rides back to the Yeltsina boardinghouse and makes it there at midnight, when it's pitch black. As he steps inside, he slips and lands very hard on his left knee. He immediately slips again when he gets up. Not wanting to slip a third time, Pyotr crawls over to the nearest gas light and feels up the wall for the switch. He freezes when he sees the floor covered in blood and dead bodies. Pyotr's clothes are now covered in blood as well.

"Ivan Ivanovich Konev, do you have a death wish?!"

"I came back for my little girl. Didn't she make it there safely?"

"Yes, she's safe with us now. You're damn lucky she's used to walking fairly far distances at her age. I stopped the wagon for the others to go to sleep. You're getting your band into so much trouble!"

"There was a massacre fifteen minutes after we left. Zina and I removed bullet shards from her mother and stanched the bleeding. Zina went to sleep on the floor with a blanket, so no one would see movement behind any windows. They know I was here. Thankfully, Zina managed to hide Tatyana from the Bolsheviks, so they didn't see her. Mrs. Yeltsina needs a doctor."

Pyotr fumes in rage as he grabs the telephone. "Yes, Operator. Put me on the line with the nearest doctor. An older woman was shot in the chest."

Ivan sits in a chair until Pyotr gets off the telephone. Pyotr points to the biped.

"I can't ride that with only myself!"

"You'll have to! I can't risk both our lives!"

"So you'll stay here until the doctor arrives?"

"I have to. Of course, I'll have to change clothes so the doctor doesn't see me like this. I trust I'll find a change of clothes in one of the rooms. Our original plan can't do now. You won't stay in Tver."

"Where are we going?"

"Oh, you'll find out." Pyotr stands the biped upright. "I rode it by myself just fine."

11

Pyotr has stopped the wagon under a thick grove of trees up in the hills. Ivan reaches the others at 3:00, and crosses himself when he sees they're all still there, unharmed. He ties the bicycle back up and lies beside Lyuba.

"Are you back, Petya?"

"Go back to sleep, love. It's me. We'll both go to sleep, and in the morning we'll find out just where Petya will be taking us."

"I feel safe with you, Vanya. I'm so glad we agreed not to keep letting stupid trivialities break us up." Lyuba goes back to sleep in his arms.

***

Pyotr returns in the morning, fuming mad, grabs the reins, and jerks the four horses awake. He hits the wagon with a stick to wake everyone up.

"There's been a change of plans. We're going to Novgorod."

"Where?" Eliisabet asks. "You can't be serious! Novgorod's hundreds of *vyorsty* away! We'll never get there before it starts to snow. It probably already is snowing there."

"I can't go to Novgorod," Ginny says. "I already told Zhora to order her parents to buy a second home in Tver."

"Who cares about your stupid girlfriend!" Anastasiya howls. "Not Novgorod!"

"Yes, Novgorod. Blame Konev. There was a massacre at the house fifteen minutes after we left. The police know Ivan's in Tver. We'll be so much safer in Novgorod. I'm taking a train there to do my research for the article my father thinks I'm working on. You'll split up into teams. Alyosha, Liza, and Kolya will continue on in the wagon; Katrin and Anastasiya will take a train; Kittey, Kat, and Nikolas will meet a man with another wagon halfway through the day; and the other four will have to get out and walk."

"Don't you dare make Lyuba walk! She could barely walk from Moskva to Tver without going crazy or dropping dead!" Ivan shouts.

"It's your fault, Konev. You're walking to Novgorod, and that's the last word of complaint I'm going to hear out of anybody."

"Leave us Branimir. And get us a cart, so we won't have to walk."

"I can't possibly walk all that way with winter coming so soon!" Lyuba sobs. "It won't be good for my health. I think I'm pregnant."

Ivan turns to stone. "You've suspected this for how long?"

"I'm three months late. I called Misha to inquire about any possible fathers, and the only two men who could possibly have done it are Boris and Kostya."

"Novgorod it is," Pyotr repeats. "No cart, no nothing, just your own two legs to carry you there."

"You'll never make my Lyuba walk that far starting in October!" Ivan shouts. "Didn't you just hear her?"

"I'll drop dead if I even walk as far as I did from Moskva to Tver, a hundred simple *vyorsty*!" Lyuba agrees.

"Even I don't think I could walk that far. And how will we keep warm, stay safe from the police, sleep at night, or lodge?"

"Fine." Pyotr throws a sack of money and small goods at Ginny. "There should be enough there for four train tickets. I'll take this wagon as far as the next town over, and then you'll get on the next train to Novgorod."

Halfway through the day, Pyotr unloads the luggage belonging to Kat and the Vishinskies, and they carry it over to a man with a new wagon. This wagon is powered by a motor, not horses.

"It's almost two hundred fifty *vyorsty* into Novgorod!" Katrin howls. "And my Party ID is ruined!"

"This time you won't stay at any boardinghouses along the way," Pyotr says solemnly. "My father has linked the names of everyone in your party to Ivan. He'll be after blood. The next city will be Torzhok. See that river? There'll be a ferry to take Kat and the Vishinskies in their wagon. I arranged it all. Then the driver will take them by way of Vyshniy Volochyok, Bologoye, Valday, and then on to Novgorod. Lyuba, Ivan, and Ginny will have to take a raft on the Volga and hike through the Valday Hills. In Valday, they'll take a train like I promised. The two unwanted people in your party will take the train with me. Liza, Alyosha, and Kolya will cut through to Ostashkov, take their wagon up through the Valday Hills, and continue on to Novgorod. Are there any questions?"

"This is really goodbye to *Matushka Rus*," Kat says.

"You won't get to Novgorod any later than the middle of November, I expect. And there is to be minimal contact, do you understand this, Konev, between your groups. Bad enough to be responsible for three others besides yourself, but do you really want the deaths of all twelve of you to be your fault?"

"He'll be a good boy, Petya. Vanya usually obeys my orders," Lyuba says.

"Yes, Lyuba," he says in a tone of voice he used to take with his mother. "I'll be your Ivan the Meek."

"I don't want to ride on a raft," Ginny grumbles.

"We've all done worse," Aleksey says. "How about that time we walked all that way through Khimki Forest?"

"Or the time we had to flee the valley," Kat says.

"And the time the deserters visited and I was roped into Boris's stupid charade of feigning labor and having a stillbirth!" Lyuba says.

"The nights we slept in the forest, with nothing but leaves and a blanket or two for warmth," Eliisabet says.

"It was even worse for me to flee as a cripple," Kittey says.

"Katya and I watched an old man being tortured with hot coals and fire pokers, and then they sodomized his dead body," Anastasiya says.

"I was ordered out of my beautiful mansion, all because they discovered a White living with me, told to collect my most important possessions, temporarily thrown out of the Party, and herded onto a wagon with Nastya and my maid," Katrin says.

"Kittey and I dug trenches and chopped trees in a labor

camp," Nikolas says.

"I had to mine for gypsum in my labor camp," Anastasiya says. "I watched people fall down from fatigue. They were shot and left to die."

"How about *me* being forced to lie to my father and brothers!" Pyotr shouts. "If I were still an Orthodox Christian, I'd be praying every night that I'm never found out!"

"You're still Russian Orthodox," Aleksey says. "Your baptism was never revoked just because your family became Bolsheviks."

"I revoked it in my heart. I'm an atheist now."

"Oh, but the most terrifying time of all was when I gave birth to Nikolay!" Eliisabet says. "There was no midwife, I was twelve weeks early, and I didn't want to scream and give us away as we walked to my Alyoshenka, so I just breathed faster and faster, and it seemed like an eternity before we reached him, and then out came my little Kolya!"

"At least you had me," Lyuba says. "When Tatyana came into this world, I only had my eleven-year-old male cousin."

"It wasn't time yet, and I nearly fell dead of shock when I saw Liza in full-blown labor!" Aleksey says.

Pyotr smiles. "So then we agree going to Novgorod is the least of our troubles."

"I hope after Novgorod, everything's smooth sailing," Eliisabet says. "By the time we get there, it'll probably be November, like you said, and then we'll have only four months left in Russia."

"Does anyone have any objections to leaving the country? Speak now or forever hold your peace."

"They don't want us here," Anastasiya sighs. "And they already recognized me once."

"I won't be back until the Bolsheviks are overthrown," Lyuba says.

"I don't want to come back till the monarchy is restored," Kat says.

She, Nikolas, and Kittey get into the new wagon. Pyotr hands the reins of the first wagon to Aleksey, and then he, Katrin, and Anastasiya unboard with their luggage and start walking. Katrin mutters curses in Estonian as her heavy luggage rack bangs against her legs, while Anastasiya complains about what an inconvenience this is. Lyuba shakes her head at how quickly they've forgotten this is the least of their troubles.

"You heard Petya," Eliisabet says. "Minimal contact at best."

Nikolay begins to cry.

"They're not leaving us for very long," his mother tells him.

"I want Tatyana!"

"Your little friend will be going with her parents, like you're going with your parents," she tries to soothe him.

"Ivan, where have you disappeared to?" Lyuba demands.

"Pyotr said we'd be taking a raft. He didn't tell us we'd have a prefabricated one ready," Ginny says. "We have to build our own."

They've put together a raft an hour before dusk. As they sail up the Volga toward Torzhok, Lyuba looks back at Tver and watches it disappear too quickly before her eyes. The old way of life is really gone forever, and only in America, with her fellow expatriates, can she ever hope to rebuild what was snatched from her. Nothing remains of the old way of life anymore, just a few secret pictures of various Tsars and Empresses, some coins and stamps with the images of those dynasts, the official Tercentenary photograph of the final Imperial Family, and the textbook Lyuba learnt French from, with the image of the Tsesarevich pasted into the front to show the students their future Tsar had used the same book to learn French. Even the alphabet is no longer quite the same.

"Look back, Ginny, Tanyechka. We have not even half a year left in our Motherland. You will never see Russia again, only in your dreams, until some day when the people grow brave and strong and overthrow the Bolsheviks, like we eventually overthrew the Mongols, Napoléon, the Swedes, the Poles, and the Lithuanians. Don't be sad. It may take awhile, but the Russian people are never content to sit around being imprisoned by cruel conquering tribes!"

****

Chapter 20: Novgorod

They finally reach the cabin Pyotr bought for them in the middle of November. After the raft, they hiked through the Valday Hills, and then, in the city of Valday, got on a train taking them to Novgorod. It's already snowing when they stumble through the door.

"How long do we have here?" Ginny asks.

"Until Petya comes for us, I suppose," Lyuba says. "Vanya, you're not a pack horse. I could've carried some of the luggage."

"You have that stupid knapsack Petya saddled you with. For all your talk about the inherent equality of the sexes, you sure didn't look like you're equal to my strength while we were hiking through the hills."

"Well, you're an aberration. You're stronger than most men."

"Aren't you glad we've almost never been apart for the past twelve and a half years? I'm equal to a whole unit of bodyguards!"

"Now, now. Don't get so full of yourself you forget whom you're named for, my meek one."

"I was named for his great-great-grandson!" Ivan comes in the main room and drops the luggage onto the floor. "Do you find it too cold? If you do, I can go out and get firewood."

"Let Ginny do that. You never know if we weren't followed."

"Ginny doesn't know how to use an axe. You poor thing, you're shuddering. Take that dumb knapsack off, and I'll start a fire."

"I was just thinking about what you've done with that axe."

Ivan bows his head. "I have blood on my soul. I don't know if I have the right to enter a church after what I did, no matter what that priest said. But I had to kill him. One lifetime with you will keep me full of good memories to remember when I'm suffering for an eternity in Hell."

"My gentle Vanyechka is *not* going to Hell! Sometimes murder is justifiable. I once hated the thought of having my life revolve around a man who'd open doors for me, pull out my chair, and protect me from reality, but now I sort of feel honored you killed the scum to defend my honor—at least, what little honor I still have left."

"You have nothing *but* honor in my eyes, *golubka*. It's society that thinks you have none left."

Lyuba slides off the knapsack at last. "My back hurts. I think I'll take my first sound sleep in months to help get rid of the pain."

"You should've let me carry that. Why don't you lie down, and I'll see to it that your back doesn't hurt much longer."

"Ginny's staying here. I don't think we'll be able to do that."

"Just lie down, and I'll be right there."

Lyuba waits impatiently for him to return with the firewood, chopped with the same axe that killed Basil and then chopped up his rotting body six months later. Ginny starts unpacking and then, wonder of wonders, sits down with one of the books Lyuba ordered Pyotr to get.

"What is that, German?"

"I haven't had occasion to use my German in a good long while. I think I need to brush up on it. I haven't spoken anything but Russian for too long."

"Good boy."

"I'm no boy. I'm coming up on fourteen, and becoming a man."

"To your mother and to me, you'll always be a little boy."

Ivan comes back into the cabin and smiles his beautiful smile. "Lie down and roll over on your stomach. I'll see to it that I take away your back pain." He unbuttons the back of her blouse and begins to massage her back.

"That feels wonderful, Vanya. I love how your hands are so gentle with me and Tanya, and so strong and powerful with villains like Basil."

"I get my strength from my father, I must admit. It sounds kind of odd, but I learnt how not to behave from him."

"Are you afraid of him coming back and hurting us again?"

"He's dead. The man who came to stay with the Litvinovs is truly deranged. Didn't Mr. Litvinov ever read about our *Smutnoye Vremya*?"

"The man I saw in the bushes looked exactly like your father. Not like how the first False Dmitriy looked nothing like the dead prince!"

"My father is dead. We overheard the jailer say so ourselves."

"The man in the bushes was even taller than you are, too!"

"So what? I thought we'd be getting away from all possible interruptions up here. And by next year—next year!—we'll be safe in America and saving up money for our wedding."

"I'll finally be a respectable woman."

"Does your back still hurt?"

"No. You fixed it."

"From now on, I'll carry all your luggage." Ivan buttons her back up. "Remember what I went to save the day the house burnt down? Here it is." He reaches into one of the bags and hands her a black box.

Lyuba opens it and finds a sapphire ring. "Oh, Vanya, this is so beautiful. It's the most beautiful, perfect ring I could've asked for."

"Look forward to an even more beautiful ring later. I insist on buying you an official ring when I ask you to marry me again. You didn't say you'd marry me, only that you wanted me to buy you a nice ring and then you'd consider us pre-engaged."

"This isn't a real engagement ring?"

"If you'd told me you wanted to be engaged with no stop beforehand, I would've gotten you the biggest, most expensive stone in the world!" He slides it on her finger. "I can't wait till you're wearing my wedding ring too."

2

They settle into the cabin smoothly. Ginny attends to his studies; Lyuba sweeps the floor, washes and irons her clothes, and gives Tatyana little lessons; and Ivan cooks most of the meals and makes sure there's enough firewood and that no draft gets in.

"Why don't you wash my clothes?" Ginny asks about a week after they've settled in. "I've got a big heap of laundry with your name on it."

"That's improper. You're the one who's so dead-set against a woman riding a horse like a man."

"Of course that's improper! It leads to impure thoughts!" Ginny tries to block out the memory of Mr. Savvin's humiliating laughter.

"Well, would *you* like to wash a camisole or nightgown? To say nothing of unmentionable items for women above a certain age."

"You've broken so many laws of so-called respectable society already, so why bother to be so Victorian about things like washing men's clothes?"

"I'll wash all the clothes if you're so offended," Ivan volunteers. "But when we're in America, I won't be able to do it much longer. I'll be off working to support you and our two children."

"We only have one," Lyuba says. "Don't count your chickens before they're hatched and expect us to immediately have a new baby after we're married."

"I mean the one that's on the way now, the one fathered by either Boris or Kostya."

"I should've told you this three days ago, but that was quite improper too. It was a scare. I'm positive it wasn't a miscarriage. If it were, I would've been four months along, and there's a big difference between a miscarriage and a normal cycle."

"That's sort of too bad."

"You wanted me to disgrace myself yet again by having a second child out of wedlock, this time with no knowledge of who's really the father?"

"I'm longing to be a real father. As much as I adore Tatyana, she's not my blood. I won't love my blood children more than her, but I really want to know that feeling of holding a newborn and being humbled at how I created that life."

"You'll get a blood child soon enough. Don't worry." Lyuba sits up at a knock sounds at the door. "You go answer that, love. If it's a Bolshevik, you can attack him, but if I get the door, I can't possibly fend for myself."

"That's one of the things I love about you. One moment you're presenting yourself to the world as a—is there a Russian word for it?—woman who wants to be treated like a man, or who wants more rights, and the next you're back in a traditional role, demanding I protect you from attackers."

"Are you going to get the door?"

"I've already given away my soul to the Devil for you." Ivan gets up and unlocks the door.

The next thing Lyuba knows, he's punched the man standing at the door and is grabbing him by the throat, slamming him against a rock outside the door. "Ivan Ivanovich Konev, what are you doing to this helpless man?!"

"How does it feel to be pounced upon by someone who could

kill you if he got just a bit angrier? I had that feeling often. I was scared, and frightened, and I felt unloved every day of my life except by my mother and Lyuba, and you drank and drank and drank and beat the living daylights out of me! I watched with sickened eyes from the tree that night as you murdered your own brother. I killed Basil to avenge his raping Lyuba, not in cold blood like when you went after *Dyadya* Igor in a drunken rage! You're supposed to be dead, you *mudak*! Talk to me! What, you're not going to beat me, crying and scared to death, until I'm almost dead?! I've been dreaming of this for a long time. Oh, and then you had to add rape to your list of sins against God and humanity! You were a grown man, *Batya*, and I use the term 'man' loosely, and you and Lyuba's father raped her and used the coarsest language possible! How dare you call yourself a man! Don't you dare go into that house and get your hands on Lyuba and my daughter! Why couldn't you stay dead, you *svoloch*! You've been dead three and a half years! You never apologized to me! Get away from this house right this very instant or I'll break your neck!"

Mr. Konev pulls away from his livid son. "Glad to see you're still safe from the authorities, Ivanok."

"Don't you dare call me that name! You never felt any affection for me! Were you miraculously resurrected?!"

"Here's the story, Ivanok. There was a man who'd just died, who looked a lot like me, with black hair and brown eyes, just two inches shorter than I am, so it was an easy body switch. We wore the prison regulation clothes, so I didn't need to switch my outfit. I tore off his nametag and replaced it with mine, then left his lying around. They assumed he escaped and I died." Mr. Konev looks meaningfully at his son. "So, is my dear wife really dead?"

"I watched terrified as they broke down the door and dragged her away. We never figured out if all these arrests and vigilante attacks in our area of the neighborhood were carried out by Bolsheviks, Kerenskiy's thugs, or a combination of both. Lyuba says they hit her in the head with a rifle, threw her in a ditch with dead bodies, and burnt her. I ran away as quick as I could. She gave her life to protect me, her belovèd only child."

"She was a weak sort of woman. That's just the sort of thing she'd do, try to be a damn martyr instead of saving her own hide."

"I cried my eyes out that night because my mother was dead!"

"I loved Anyechka, Ivanok. She was the love of my life. She gave me my son, you! I began to drink because I was depressed she wasn't giving me more children."

"You did not love my mother!"

"I just told you, she was the love of my life. She was my wife, Vanyushenka. Not just your mother. My sweet little Anyechka. She was so beautiful on our wedding day, and she was the only one who could talk sense into my head and make me not beat you as often."

"You never wanted any children."

"That's a damn lie you told yourself to feel better about why I was getting drunk and beating you."

"Where's Mr. Litvinov?"

"I came to Novgorod on my own."

"Oh, really. To turn me in, or to rape Lyuba? Or both?"

"I'm a changed man. I'll stay here for a few days, and then I'm leaving for America. I think I've overstayed my welcome. Maybe I can fake another death to stop goading Mr. Litvinov on. He wants you dead, but I can't live if my only child dies and discontinues the Konev line!"

"I'll be keeping my eye on you." Ivan drags his father into the house by his ear. "Look, you three. It's the real Dmitriy."

Ginny's right ear twinges in remembrance of pain. Being dragged up the stairs by his ear was the worst.

Ivan drops his father on the floor and stands in front of Lyuba, twisting his left arm around her. "This is a warning to you. I would kill again to protect her."

"I no longer drink. You don't need to worry."

"That's your granddaughter. If I catch you alone with her, I'll strangle you."

"She's not your child. I heard from numerous contacts Mr. Litvinov tracked down that she really belongs to Boris."

"Do you see Boris? I've raised Tatyana for twenty-two months. Boris has only seen her a few times."

"She's an illegitimate child. Whyever wasn't she taken to an orphanage?"

"Because Lyuba and I love our daughter, and she was never detected because we're still on the run from the Bolsheviks. Who knows what would've happened if we'd been living normally."

"What kind of life is that, bringing a child into a war-shattered world?"

"This life isn't forever. We're going to America next year, and then our daughter will have the life of a normal little girl."

"America's streets aren't lined with gold, my boy. You'll be poor. At least I know I'll be poor when I arrive."

"Lyuba, Tatyana, and I will find an apartment quickly, and I'll finish my schooling and get a job after I get my diploma. Then we'll save up enough money to have a fancy wedding, and survive hard times together because we all love each other."

"You're still a romantic dreamer with his head in the clouds, Ivanok."

"I'll make Tatyana my legal daughter. I'll take it to the courts if need be, just to have it in writing, finally, that she's my child in every way but blood. No one in his right mind would award custody to that irresponsible *mudak* Boris. After I marry Lyuba, Tatyana will become legitimate in society's eyes."

"I'm hungry. Do you have anything for lunch?"

"We have *rassolnik*. Sit down, Mr. Konev." Ginny gets up to fetch the pot banking in the ashes in the fireplace.

"I want sour cream in my *rassolnik*, little boy. And pour it out for me. I never was able to order my Ivanok around, because it'd just be a repeat of what my stupid, incompetent brother did at the table. But I see you're right-handed, unlike my clumsy son and late brother."

"Do you have a problem with me being a *levsha*?" Ivan challenges him.

"I was depressed enough when a year went by and then another, and my Anyechka wasn't getting pregnant with a second child, but then we discovered you were a child of Satan. I tried so hard to make you enter into the way of goodness and right, but you refused."

"God made me like that. I'm hardly one to argue."

"I like how Ivan is left-handed," Lyuba says. "He's different from everyone else. Don't we all need to be unique? He looks at the world with different eyes because his left side is more dexterous than the right side."

Ginny spills the *rassolnik* on Mr. Konev's lap. He snickers as Mr. Konev leaps up and begins screaming. Then he flips a spoonful of the sour cream onto Mr. Konev's shirt. For the first time in his life, Ivan isn't afraid of his father, and begins laughing at him. Lyuba soon regains her tongue and starts laughing too, as Mr. Konev dashes outdoors and begins rolling around in the snow. She's thrilled to see the mirthful smile back on Ivan's face and to hear the joyful laughter coming from his throat.

"You won't be laughing much longer when I come back in the house!"

"Well, one can have too much of a good thing," Ivan says, composing himself. "Come back inside, old man. I'll keep my eyes on you."

"It's not very nice to threaten your father."

"It's not very nice to help an enemy of your only child in his quest to find me and kill me!"

"It was my way of finding you, Junior."

"Well, now you've found me, and can scram."

"I plan to spend a few days here."

"I heard you the first time, *mudak*. That doesn't mean I accept it."

"I know you don't believe me, Ivanok, but I would've volunteered to be thrown in prison for twenty years in your place. You're my only child! And you remind me so much of Anyechka, with her dark brown hair and eyes."

"The same woman you seemed to take so much delight in slapping around until I got old enough to defend her against your drunken attacks?"

"I had a disease, son. I was sick. But I'm better now."

Ivan keeps an eagle eye watch on his father as the day progresses. At supper, he orders him to sit on the floor and eat his bowl of *solyanka* like a dog, seated in a corner. Mr. Konev is humiliated at the laughter issuing from his hosts as he gets the soup all over his face. Several times, the bowl slips off his knees.

"That's right, you're just a dirty old dog," Ginny sneers.

"Can I have a spoon?"

"You can use your hands," Ivan says. "Remember when you lashed out at *Dyadya* Igor because he always spilled something?"

"He was a clumsy fool, that damn brother of mine."

"The world isn't designed for a *levsha*. Naturally, he was more clumsy than a right-handed person might be. You made it worse with your temper tantrums."

Lyuba looks over at Ivan, and her heart aches for him, remembering how abusive and violent his father was, a hole in his heart because his mother was murdered and he could do nothing to stop it, and how she and Tatyana are the only people left in the world who truly love him. She takes his hand in hers and smiles at him with her eyes. After he returns the mutual feeling of love, he goes on.

"Remember that night you forced *Dyadya* Igor to eat on the floor? Now *you're* eating on the floor."

"People make mistakes, Ivanok. I wasn't very patient with my clumsy brother."

"Oh, look, he's got a big piece of fish stuck to his nose!" Ginny giggles.

Mr. Konev dives back into the bowl with his face to try to shake it off, and comes back up with a large piece of cabbage there instead. Laughter fills the room.

"When Lyuba and I get married, I hope you provide even more entertainment. Maybe we can dress you up in a jester's costume."

Thoroughly humiliated, Mr. Konev tries to finish the *solyanka* as quickly as possible and goes back outside to wash his face in the snow. He reads old issues of *Izvestiya* for two hours before announcing he's going to bed.

"You didn't bring luggage," Ivan says caustically. "I hope you're not planning to take my nightclothes."

"It's too cold to sleep naked. I'll stay in my day clothes."

"And where will you sleep, old man, on the floor?"

"There are two beds. I'll take the one you have."

"No way in Hell will you ever do such a thing! You can share with Ginny."

"Talk about scandalous. Lyuba's cousin and daughter are young and impressionable, Ivanok, and you're not married. Do you mean to tell me you're having premarital relations with this woman, this scorned whore, in the same room with her cousin and illegitimate daughter? In my day, it was a social disgrace to do such a thing!"

"Lyuba's no whore. And I'm old-fashioned. All we do is sleep in the same bed. Get your mind out of the gutter."

"Come on, my boy, you're twenty-two!"

"There's something called self-control."

"I married your mother at eighteen, so I didn't need to resort to whores to satisfy my natural urges. But you're twenty-two!"

"Yes, amazing I have morals and principles. And I told you not to call me Ivanok."

Ivan doesn't sleep a bit that night. Every little sound jerks him awake from near-sleep, and he every time sits up, convinced it's his father coming to rape Lyuba.

"Stop that, Vanya, you're holding me too tightly," Lyuba growls halfway through the night. "And I don't like sleeping facing the wall."

"This way you're better protected."

"And Tatyana barely has room to turn around!"

"It'll all be over soon. As soon as my father leaves like he said he would."

It was one thing to make a laughingstock out of Mr. Konev, but now it becomes a different story. Lyuba is more than annoyed at breakfast when Ivan sits next to her and puts his arms around her so tightly she can barely move her arms to eat. Mr. Konev sits across the table from them, eating *blinchiki* and hard-boiled eggs.

"Stop that, Ivan. I feel like you're following me everywhere," she snaps when she ventures outside after lunch to watch the rabbits eating the carrots she set out for them the week before.

"I should've followed you everywhere a long time ago. Then your father would've known I'd kill for you. I have to tolerate my father because, awful as his past behavior is, he genuinely could've reformed. But your father could never reform himself. He's a very sick person, my love, and if I run into him again, I'll strangle him."

"My father set me on the path to becoming a whore."

"You've never been a whore in my eyes, *lyubimaya*." Ivan draws her close and kisses her eyelids. "It takes two to create a bad reputation, not one. You were always a victim, never a willing participant. Even if no one else realizes that, I always will."

"They'll call you all sorts of names too, for living with this slut who had a child out of wedlock, was a prostitute, and—"

"They can throw as much mud as they like, as long as they throw it on us together."

"What makes you still love me so much, after how much I've continually disgraced myself?"

He touches the scar on her face gently. "Your heart is still pure, *golubka*. I'm the only man in your heart."

"You always will be. If you ever died, I'd die of grief. Even if I managed not to die of sadness, I'd never fall in love again. I hope you make me a respectable woman after we go to America. I don't want to drag you down into my life of shame. I couldn't handle the shame if I were to have a second child out of wedlock."

"If that happens, so be it. I've waited so long to become a blood father, I no longer care that much about the particulars. Next year at this time, we'll be in America, and possibly expecting our first child."

"Oh, look, a mink. Remember that awful mink Ginny dragged in?"

"You're laughing about it now. I was furious at him!"

"That boy was a handful, wasn't he? But you really straightened him out. Now he listens to me when I tell him to do something. You've got your father obeying you too." Lyuba glares at him when she almost trips over his boots. "You don't need to keep monitoring my every step!"

"I'll monitor your every step as long as my father's here."

3

Mr. Konev stays two more nights. Lyuba is relieved when he leaves the fourth evening. Now she won't have a constant bodyguard anymore.

"How do we know he won't creep back in tonight and do terrible things?"

"Oh, come off it, my *groznik*, and take a nap. You haven't had any sleep since your father came here. There are rings under your eyes."

"Will you bring me a blanket and get me some tea, like my mother would've?"

Lyuba bristles. "You think of me as a substitute for your mother?"

"Not in that way. But will you?"

"Anything for my sweet *groznik*," she says adoringly.

She and Tatyana go outdoors to watch the rabbits and birds feeding.

"One day we'll watch the wild animals come to eat outside our house when your father has taken us to the Midwest. After he makes enough money in New York City, we'll take a train to start again in the fertile American Midwest, where we'll farm for a living, and you'll have eight little brothers and sisters, a dog, a cat, a bunny, lots of horses and ponies, and a little coat made out of wool we shore from our own sheep. We'll milk our own goats, we'll always be happy, and you won't have to live in terror anymore. You'll get to learn all the things I did in school." Lyuba begins to draw the old Russian Cyrillic alphabet on a notepad. "Do you remember these letters, my little *knyazhna*?"

"Ah, beh, veh, geh, deh," Tatyana recites.

How could I not have had this sweet little girl? Lyuba thinks lovingly.

4

"So that girl, that girl who just turned fourteen a short time ago, got to come to Canada and then go skipping down into Manhattan to take back her bastard baby son, with help from a woman pretending to be the real mother, but I, a twenty-year-old man, don't get to bring back my daughter from Russia?" Boris stands up and brushes off his pants. "Unbelievable!"

"Mr. Malenkov, you'll set a very bad example to the children if you continue to tell these scandalous stories about your shameful personal life," Father Spiridon says. "You said you were religious. What's so religious about all these stories you've spent the past five hours telling me?"

"I'm only being perfectly honest, Batyushka. *The other priest was furious I hadn't told him everything."*

"Your daughter's babushka *thought she was doing a good thing by telling him how you've reformed yourself after so many mistakes."*

"It was so good it got me fired! Now, what to do for penance?"

"You'll teach in the religious school as part of your penance. You must also spend three hours a day praying to any saints of your choosing, kneeling on rocks. You've sinned that terribly."

"How about Ivan? He attacked me and told me I have no rights whatsoever to my little girl! The man is dangerous. I won't feel safe when he comes to America. He'll want to get the courts to give him full custody of my daughter,

I'm sure of it!"

"Now, now. What judge would let a woman raise a child born out of wedlock with a man who isn't the natural father when they're not married?"

"I'll have to get Lyuba to marry me."

"But Ivan could make the case you abandoned Lyuba and your child thrice, and weren't very fatherly or humane towards either."

"How was I not humane! I love Tatyana more than my own life! I'm a father, but unfortunately for me, I made some mistakes, and now my child is being raised by that bully who should've been named for Ivan Grozniy!"

"You beat her multiple times during her pregnancy, and on your second illegal trip home, you did it again."

"I can find justification for beating your wife in the Bible. Plenty of men do it."

"Then you're misinterpreting God's word, my son. Miss Zhukova also isn't your wife."

"If Ivan has his way, she'll be his *wife after they get to America!"*

"What's so wrong with that?"

"Wrong! He's not Tanyechka's real father!"

"Then she'll grow up with two fathers, like Christ did."

"Wrong! I am her only father! How dare you compare Ivan Ivanovich Konev to God Almighty?!"

"You do realize you're being rather insulting towards a priest."

"I'll start my penance right now." Boris kneels and raises his hand to cross himself.

"I told you, you must pray on rocks. You've sinned that severely."

Boris mumbles an obscenity and kneels over the rocks.

5

"Look, we've got visitors," Ginny calls one day in early December. "An older man and woman."

"You never know these days if they could be spies," Lyuba says warningly.

"Yes, Zhora tells me in all her letters that there are all sorts of enemies who hate Comrade Lenin."

Ginny opens the door to the older couple. Both have greying black hair. The woman has blue eyes, and the man has black eyes tinged with tiny little hints of blue.

"Are you spies?" Ginny asks, as Lyuba hangs her head at his bluntness.

"We were just released from a labor camp. I don't think we could've become spies so quickly," the man says.

"We found out there are Whites in this part of the city," the woman says. "We've been searching desperately to find our child, our only child. He'd be twenty now. Do you know Boris Aleksandrovich Malenkov?"

Ivan smiles and extends his hand. "I'm very glad to see you're still alive, but all I can tell you about Boris is that our friendship is over. You have no idea what kind of deplorable, inhuman behavior he's engaged in, and I won't burden your hearts by sharing the horrific details."

Mrs. Malenkova shakes his hand after her husband and returns the smile. "Yes, now I recognize you. You must be Ivan Ivanovich Konev, and that must be Lyubov Leontiyevna Zhukova. Who's the boy?"

"That's my thirteen-year-old cousin Mikhail, called Ginny," Lyuba says. "He looks a lot different than he did last time you saw him, doesn't he?"

"Oh, yes, the East Prussian boy. Anyway, we've been so isolated we don't know what's happening in the outside world. Are we winning the Civil War?"

"Sadly, we're losing. The West has pulled most of its financial support. The White Army is falling apart as we speak."

"Have they let the Tsar flee the country for somewhere safe?" Mr. Malenkov asks.

"They didn't tell you?" Ginny asks. "The Imperial Family was killed almost two and a half years ago, and we've heard reports of eleven other Romanovs being murdered. All the others fled into exile. Some of them very narrowly escaped Bolshevik custody."

"That's not possible," Mrs. Malenkova says. "That's a wild rumor."

"The Bolsheviks murdered at least eighteen Romanovs, and the survivors are no longer in Russia," Ginny repeats. "Only Grand Duke Nikolay Konstantinovich and his descendants were spared, but even they might not be safe in Tashkent forever."

Tatyana toddles up and looks curiously at the visitors, then at her parents.

"I assume this is your child, Lyuba and Ivan?" Mr. Malenkov

asks. "When did you get married? I always knew you preferred him over my son, though Borya seemed blind to your true feelings."

Lyuba picks her up and holds her out to them. "It's a very long story, but Vanya isn't her blood father. Meet your granddaughter."

"We have a granddaughter?" Mr. Malenkov smiles at Tatyana as he holds her.

"She's twenty-two months old. Boris abandoned her. By the time he came back to try to be a father, it was too late, and he ran away again."

"He's blessed with a child and he runs out on her?"

"Look, Sanya, how beautiful she is," Mrs. Malenkova says. "She looks just like Lyuba."

"Once we're in America, I'm going to adopt Tatyana," Ivan says. "You don't want to know the half of what Boris did. But I'd never keep you away from her. You're really nice people, and you deserve to enjoy your only grandchild."

"Can I serve you something?" Ginny volunteers.

"Yes, *pozhaluysta*." Mrs. Malenkova takes Tatyana from her husband. "What a beautiful blessing to discover. I can't believe I was a *babushka* for so long and never knew. Sanya and I would be more than happy to act as grandparents to your blood children with Ivan as well. There shouldn't be any inequality between Tanya and her siblings."

"That's a lovely offer," Lyuba says. "Vanya wants nine children, so we've got eight more to go."

Ivan tries to smile, full well knowing a miracle must take place for Lyuba to have even one more child. If he tells her before she gives him his own biological child, she'll probably feel inadequate and run even further away from his love than ever.

Mr. Malenkov and Mrs. Malenkova stay the night and leave in the morning. One more link to their past, gone. Every night, Lyuba dreams about rebuilding the old life in America, with all her old friends and neighbors settling in on the same streets of the neighborhood, as if their entire section of Moskva, where most people always supported the Tsar, right or wrong, has been transplanted across a great wide ocean.

6

Lyuba's twenty-first birthday is 11 December. After she wakes up and dresses, she heads for the kitchen and makes breakfast, the same as always, never having felt a birthday is anything special or out of the ordinary.

"What do you want, Ivan, eggs or *blinchiki*?"

"Go back to bed and sleep a little longer. I'll make you a birthday breakfast fit for a Tsaritsa."

"No, I insist, you go back to bed, and I'll bring you breakfast."

"You're the birthday girl, and you deserve to spend the day relaxing. This is your last birthday in Russia, love, and I want you to always remember it as nicely as possible."

Lyuba reluctantly returns to bed and goes back to sleep, dreaming of spending her next birthday in America as Ivan's wife and expecting their first blood child. This dream has eluded her for so long, and she's actively thwarted it several times, but sometimes dreams come true. Real life is never as perfect as a dream, but in the meantime, it's nice to dream.

****

Chapter 21: Goodbye to the Motherland

The year has turned into 1921, and it's now Orthodox Christmas. Aleksey, Eliisabet, and Nikolay came to visit a few days ago, which did wonders for Lyuba and Ivan's spirits.

"I would've brought in a tree, but cutting down trees might be illegal now," Ivan says. "We'll settle for doing something else."

"It's been so long since I had a Christmas tree," Lyuba says longingly. "I hope our first American home isn't one of those tiny, cramped tenements. I don't think we could fit a tree in there, and I don't know where they get trees in New York. It's a huge city, not near the countryside. We might have to make do with an artificial tree."

"Artificial or real, we'll make it the nicest tree possible. I can't wait to see the look on Tanyechka's face when she sees her first Christmas tree, with so many presents underneath waiting for her. Dyed Moroz will get you lots of presents too."

Lyuba snickers. "You know I'm too old to believe in Dyed Moroz, and that I never liked the idea of lying to children. Anyway, I wish we could have even a humble Christmas feast. It won't feel like Christmas with just potatoes, bread, turnips, and fish."

"Why don't we go ice-skating? I found a pair of ice-skates in one of your bags last night."

Lyuba sends him a sharp look. "What were you going through my bags for?"

"You hadn't unpacked this one yet. I thought they were things you hadn't used since we left home, and that I could sell or barter them."

"I've got a staggering amount of money, and you're newly-rich as well. Anything in that bag could never earn nearly as much money as we've got now. I never unpacked that bag because those things are useless now. I started unpacking it in Ryazan, a lifetime ago, but it was too painful to look at them. They remind me of happier times, before Russia went up in flames."

"Why don't you put on your coat, hat, scarf, and mittens? We can find a frozen patch of water around here somewhere."

"And we'll take Tatyana with us?"

"I'd like to take her on a walk," Ginny pipes up. "I'm meeting my girlfriend down the road. Her family's visiting Novgorod, and she really wanted to see me one last time. Zhora wants to pretend she's got a baby sister."

"Can I trust you to bring her back in one piece?" Ivan asks in a serious tone.

"Of course. How long will it take for you to stop holding the past against me? I know I acted up a lot, but I'm behaving nicely now."

"Georgiya's a lovely, intelligent girl," Lyuba says. "I don't see why not." She points to Ginny's coat. "I do wish you'd pick up your clothes instead of flinging them on the floor."

"Tatyana will be back in one piece. If she isn't, Ivan may kill me."

Ginny throws on his winter clothes and boots while Lyuba dresses Tatyana in her tiny coat, mittens, scarf, and boots. When they're both wrapped up, he picks Tatyana up, waves goodbye, and heads off. Ten minutes later, Lyuba steps out the door wrapped in winter clothes, wearing ice-skates.

"You're not wearing ice-skates, Vanya. You'll slip and fall."

"I can break my fall. Need I remind you we taller people have more time to stop a fall?"

"I'm not as short as some people we knew. I'm tall for a woman. Five feet nine. I'm much taller than that pathetic Voroshilova."

"Now, be humble."

"As humble as the man who repeatedly brags about how strong he is and how he could strangle someone twice his size with his bare hands? Who told me as a boy how he could wrestle with bears and panthers, and win? That humble person?"

"It's good to know you think I'm so brave."

"Now you're just flattering yourself, my Vanyechka."

"I've seen you smile more since we've been in Novgorod. You were so unhappy in Moskva."

"I'll be even happier in America, love. Then I'll become a respectable woman, and I'll be able to make you happier too. I hope you love me even more after I give you a blood child."

Ivan changes the subject. "There's a nice patch of ice."

"I'd die of grief if I didn't give you a son. Imagine if Boris had damaged my ability to have children because he beat me so much when I was carrying Tatyana!"

Trying not to give away the dirty secret, Ivan just nods mutely.

Lyuba steps out onto the ice. "Why do you look so forlorn? Do you know something you're not telling me?"

"Why do you think that?" he asks defensively. "Whatever gave you that idea?"

"Don't get so snappy. I didn't accuse you of anything."

He follows her onto the ice. "I'd never keep a secret from you. But I hope you know I'll still love you more than anyone even if you never give me any blood children."

"You're leading me to believe you do know something. What exactly were you whispering about with that midwife?"

Ivan comes up with a quick lie. "She said you're a perfect candidate for having lots of children. You're in perfect health to carry as many as a dozen more children. You passed your first delivery with flying colors." *What a dog you are, Konev*, he tells himself bitterly. *You're a dog to tell such a lie to the woman you love.* "Give me your hand."

Lyuba holds onto him as tightly as possible. "I last wore these that February, before our whole world fell apart from under us."

Ivan pulls free of her grip, and she slips backwards.

"You did that on purpose, so you could come to my rescue. I know how your mind works."

"You're not very humble." He slides over to her.

Lyuba seizes his hand and pulls him down next to her. As the afternoon progresses, they do more falling than ice-skating.

2

"That was not my fault, Grigoriy. She dashed ahead and slipped on the ice all by herself." Georgiya hauls Tatyana out of a snowbank and briskly brushes the snow off her coat. "Now I'm glad I only have Leonid the pain as a sibling."

"How long was she in the snowbank?"

"I was in no rush. She stayed put after she fell into the snow. It wasn't like we lost her."

Tatyana turns to her cousin with a pleading look. "Carry me."

"See, she talks a little," Ginny says. "She'll be two in a few weeks."

"Now she wants to be carried. Before, she couldn't stand how I wanted to carry her."

"A small child isn't a pet to be cooed at. It's a small human being who depends on people to care for it. Maybe she didn't like it because she only met you once before, nine months ago. You're a very new person to her."

"And to think you were once like a child from a Grimms' fairytale."

"I've changed, Zhora. I have better self-control now, and I'm more mature, if I can say that without sounding haughty."

"Our Leader knows a lot about self-control. He's the hero of everyone in my class. Can you believe, some people in my classes said their heroes were people who are now declared enemies of the people! Can you imagine that, Grigoriy, or that before my school became edified by truth, most people, including, amazingly enough!, myself, didn't know Bloody Nikolay had so little Russian blood it was laughable? We discussed this at length in mathematics when we did percentages. We calculated he had point zero zero six percent of Russian blood in his traitorous body. I was shocked!"

"Then why was his family on the throne so long if they didn't have the right kind of blood?"

"They kept the people ignorant, silly! But now we're free. For my history class last year, we had to write a paper on the Tsar whom we hated most. Most of us chose Bloody Nikolay, of course, but others spoke out against his equally bloody father; Tsar Aleksey the Meek for suppressing the rightful revolts of the exploited proletarian peasants; and the Tatar trying to pass as one of us, Boris Godunov."

"I wish I still went to school. I'd be in the eighth grade now."

"I bet you'll be the smartest person in your class in America. Maybe you'll make up for lost time so well, you'll skip ahead to your real grade and won't have to graduate when you're over eighteen."

"Don't look. I just saw someone who could turn my cousin and her boyfriend in to the authorities. Shepilov." Ginny's voice drops to a whisper.

"That little sneak! And who in his right mind hires a boy to do the work of a man? The slick *mudak*'s been working as a spy since two months before his eleventh birthday. Explain that to me."

"Hello, Georgiya, traitorous *sukin syn* who tried to murder me."

Aleksandr comes right up to them. "I was very interested in knowing why the Savvins went to Novgorod, and then I remembered, Zhora is Ginny Kharzin's girlfriend. And who does Ginny Kharzin live with? His cousin and her boyfriend, Ivan Ivanovich Konev, the man who murdered Basil Yakovlevich Beriya in pure cold blood and escaped from his just desserts. I explained to my gracious hosts what I thought was going down, so we took a train here. Mrs. Godunova's staying at a fancy hotel while Misha and Kostya are out scouring the area for Konev. Don't look so damn alarmed. They don't suspect you're staying in these hills, and the weather's too bad to warrant much active searching. But do be warned. You may want to leave the city by the end of the month unless you want your cousin's boyfriend to be dragged back into Moskva to face punishment for his crime. Like I said, be warned. I didn't see you, you got that, as long as you tell your cousin to split the hell out of Novgorod before the end of January."

3

Lyuba looks up from her religious book when Ginny and Georgiya return with Tatyana an hour later.

"We ran into Aleksandr Shepilov," Ginny begins. "Misha and Kostya are in the city, looking for Ivan. We have to call Petya."

"I feel bad," Tatyana says.

"She ran ahead, Comrade Zhukova, slipped on ice, and fell into a snowbank," Georgiya says. "She needs to be warmed up."

Lyuba takes Tatyana and cuddles her. "Georgiya, you're from an important Muscovite family. Don't drag yourself down into the White plight my cousin and I are involved in. Say nothing at all to the Godunovs, should they come calling, and don't contact my cousin again until we're in America. We're immigrating for political asylum, and the Soviet authorities can't make the American government deport us. Stay safe."

Ginny sees her to the door. Lyuba looks on and nods in approval.

4

Several days later, however, Lyuba becomes very aware they'll need to get in touch with an outside contact when Tatyana becomes very sick. Pyotr is wrapping up his supposed research for the article in the cities nearest Novgorod, so she doesn't bother him.

However, Pyotr left her a map of the area, including a doctor's office.

"Which one of us should take her to the doctor?" Lyuba asks. "It's either that or getting her to swallow these two pills."

"I can't let you go," Ivan says. "You'd never be able to defend yourself."

"And you're a wanted criminal. Misha and Kostya are searching the area for you, and no doubt Mr. Litvinov won't be far behind."

"I have a fake passport, remember. Too bad Katrin took back her Party ID, so I can't pass as Dmitriy Pavlovich Kuznetsov again. I don't know why in the world she'd still want that thing when she herself said I made it useless. She's desperately clinging to Communism no matter what."

"God is keeping us alive for one another, my love. By now I know you'll never end up dead. We'll die on the same day, in the same hour, because soulmates aren't meant to be apart for very long. But take these two pills just in case. You'd better be back with her in time for her birthday."

"That's right. Our little *knyazhna* will be two years old soon!"

"I'm cold," Tatyana says in her little voice.

Ivan fashions a baby-carrying device with a long, heavy scarf, then buttons her inside his coat, leaving her head hanging out. "Now you'll be nice and warm, little *knyazhna*."

The doctor's office is a five-hour walk from the cabin nestled safely in the hills. It's twilight by the time the building appears in the distance. A crowd of angry people are gathered in front.

"The doctor said he won't be back for two more days."

"He had to testify in a court about a patient who expressed subversive thoughts."

"I'm glad the Civil War seems to be almost over. The doctor's only tying up some loose ends."

"Are you sure it's almost over?" Ivan asks. "You can't confidently predict the end of a war. We all thought the war in Europe would end by Christmas, and it dragged on for over four years. Nothing's really over until the official surrender."

"The White cause collapsed this autumn! Their pathetic army and a huge group of refugees were driven down to the Black Sea, where they sailed to France. All we have left to do is take over the places that set up anti-Bolshevik governments, like Georgia and Armenia; put down ridiculous rebellions; and conquer holdouts in the Far East. Haven't you been following the news at all?"

"Not really. So I guess the Bolsheviks won."

"Yes, we won. Russia can finally start moving into the twentieth century now."

He dares not pray or cross himself in the midst of this pro-Red crowd. Instead he sits on the snow with Tatyana and waits for the doctor to return. Not wanting to provoke the already angry crowd, he whispers to Tatyana in his broken, heavily-accented English.

"No worry. Soon we will be in land that welcomes everyone. No more suffering for you, *knyazhna*."

"There were men asking about a tall man whom you seem very much to resemble." An old, fat woman comes up to them. "Are you by any chance wanted for murder in Moskva?"

"That's an extremely forward question, but to set your mind at ease, I'm no murderer. It so happens I killed the lowlife who raped my wife, but I'm not wanted for that killing. The authorities applauded me for taking care of that public menace."

"You're very honest, Comrade. These men said their criminal suspect killed in cold blood, not to avenge a woman being raped."

"*Spasite*," Tatyana says. "I'm cold."

"She's cute," a thirty-year-old woman comments. "How old is she?"

"She'll be two years old in two weeks. Does anybody have any water? I only have two pills, and she needs to swallow them."

"Is she your first child?"

"She could very well be my only child. My wife doesn't know this, but it's a miracle our daughter was born alive. If she gets pregnant again, it'll be an even greater miracle."

"I have a canteen," someone volunteers.

"Here we go. Swallow them both."

Tatyana gulps the pills down with the water instinctively, the way she and Nikolay have always instinctively known to not cry when they've been on the run, the same way she was able to walk so far to the wagon in Tver. Ivan's heart aches for this child who's never known a normal life or had typical baby or toddler behavior.

"Good girl. Now we sit and wait for the doctor to arrive."

5

Back at the cabin, Lyuba is just now realizing she'll have to present her true passport to American customs, not the fake one Pyotr made for her. He's gotten passports for everyone in the band who didn't have one, but she has a real passport, lodged in that vase. She's been trying in vain to remove it for the past two days. By the time she sees Ivan return, carrying Tatyana in his coat, she's given up hope. The idea of smashing the vase isn't an option, since her aunt loves that vase.

"What took you so long? I was starting to assume the worst."

"I had to wait for two days, since the doctor was in court. Don't worry, we got food every so often."

"And then? Is my baby feeling better?"

"Just a slight cold. Everything's fine now. Good thing she didn't get sick on the ship."

"About that ship. I just remembered I can't go to America with you. My passport is stuck inside my aunt's vase."

"I'll get it out for you. Not to worry. I have my stronger hand back, unlike the last time I tried to pull it out."

"Believe me, I've tried everything. I guess I'll be staying behind."

"This isn't about your passport. I know you too well. You're just saying this because you're getting scared of my love again. When are you ever going to relax and trust that a nice guy really does want to be with you for the rest of your life?"

"Nice job putting words in my mouth. That wasn't what I was thinking at all. You'll take Tatyana with you, of course. Keep her as a memory of me. If you never marry and have natural children of your own, at least you'll have Tanyechka. She'll be declared legally yours, I'm sure of it."

"This is a bunch of *govno* you're telling me! I'll get the passport out for you, or all four of us will stay behind! I told you I'd never leave without you!"

"Ivan Ivanovich Konev, you should watch your language. Tatyana will be getting impressionable ears soon!"

"Sorry," he mumbles. "Give me the vase. I'll get it out for you."

He sits down with the vase, a pair of tweezers, and a knitting needle. Lyuba rocks with Tatyana as he tries in vain for two hours. Nothing is happening.

"Here's a great excuse to stop driving yourself insane," Ginny reports. "I see Petya at the door, with all the others, in a wagon."

Pyotr doesn't knock, he just comes right in. "Georgiya Savvina just came to me and told me. The Godunovs and now my father are in the city looking for you. Pack up right now. We're going to Pskov. You'll stay in a house I'm paying for. We have to leave as quickly as possible."

"Yes, Petya," Lyuba whispers. "You're our patron saint. Nobody else has protected us like you. I'll never forget how kind, noble, and selfless you've been."

"It's Branimir!" Ginny exclaims. "I never had a real pet before. Branimir is the closest I've ever come."

Lyuba grabs Ivan's arm when she hears barking. She looks around, half-expecting their enemies to be there with a pack of scent hounds, but instead only finds a medium-sized ball of fluff on the wagon seat, with a bright red collar.

"He's Kittey's," Pyotr explains. "She's able to walk without her cane and calipers now, but she's scared to try walking completely on her own. I bought her a purebred Samoyed for her final security blanket. She named it Andryusha, after her father."

Pyotr makes everyone hide under the wagon's false bottom. On the top, there are several layers of bloody sheep and cow carcasses. The bitter cold prevents them from reeking to high heaven.

"Petya's pretending to be a butcher," Kat tells them.

"Last time he made us hide under a wagon, he posed as a fishmonger," Eliisabet says.

"Everyone be extra quiet," Pyotr warns. "Misha and Kostya are in the city."

6

A week and a half and one hundred fifty *vyorsty* later, they arrive in Pskov. There's no time to take in the beauty of the last Russian city they'll set foot in before they cross the border to Estonia and the coast. Pyotr shuttles them quickly into a large, imposing-looking house under cover of darkness. He orders them not to leave or make any noise. All the shades are pulled and drawn. The floors are padded with extra-thick carpets. No sunlight is allowed in. Lyuba already wants to scream after two weeks of this locked-up existence. They hear boots in the night, every night, and the sounds of riots and strikes going on, but they cannot peer out to see what's going on. Pyotr has to come in and out by an airvent covered with slush.

"Will this be over soon?" Ginny demands irately in the middle of February.

"Soon," Lyuba promises. "Next month we'll go to America."

"I hear knocking at the door," Nikolay whimpers.

"Petya always comes in by the airvent," Eliisabet says. "It can only be bad news."

"I know just how to handle this." Katrin gets up and answers the door to several Cheka officers. "Hello, good comrades. I've been a member of the Party since April 1917, and was Communist long before it became official. I'm one of your most ardent adherents."

"Why hasn't anyone been going in and out of this house?"

Katrin waves her hand. "Our landlord is paranoid."

"I've seen a young man with blonde hair and blue eyes going in and out of this house by a back entranceway. We have reason to believe this young man's helping a convicted criminal. You wouldn't happen to be sheltering a rather tall young man with brown hair and eyes, would you?"

"All three of the men in our party have brown hair and eyes. Just look."

"I only see one man, and he isn't the exact description we're looking for. He's not tall enough, and his hair is wavy. I guess we can arrest him, and he can fill us in on the details. If he's good and obedient during our interrogation, we'll make him a sergeant. Come on."

Eliisabet and Nikolay look on, numb, as the Cheka men take Aleksey away. Aleksey meekly goes along with them, his head held high. After the door slams, Eliisabet crosses herself.

"When Vanya was arrested, I ordered them to arrest me too," Lyuba reminds her. "Run after them and tell them to take you too."

"I would, but it's not good for my health!" Eliisabet whispers. "It's a good thing I didn't tell Alyosha yet, or he'd be worried sick about me right now. Alyosha and I are expecting our second child."

"You know this for certain?" Kat asks.

"All the same symptoms are there. Of all the times to bring new life into this world. I thought my second child wouldn't be created till we were out of this madhouse."

"Petya will get Alyoshka out of prison," Lyuba says. "Your second child will be born in America, a citizen from birth. You want that future American citizen to be healthy, so you should try not to worry too much about Alyosha."

"I knew Kolya was a boy. And I feel this one is a girl."

"I have an idea," Kittey says. "Since she'll be born in America, you can honor our new home by naming her Novomira."

"New world." Eliisabet smiles. "There's an unusual name."

"You must stay healthy for little Novomira," Kat says. "Think good, and it will be good."

7

That evening, Lyuba goes upstairs to put Tatyana to bed and notices Ivan and Nikolas are nowhere to be seen. Then she sees one of the windows broken, the curtains flying in the breeze, and two sets of footprints in the snow. Quickly she plugs the window with a pillow and waits for the nightly visit from Pyotr.

"So you took them to a different location after what happened to Alyosha?" Kat asks. "I have no idea how you smuggled yourself into the house and snuck off with them without any of us knowing."

"What happened to Aleksey?" Pyotr asks.

"I opened the door because I thought I could solve the problem, but they took him!" Katrin says. "They led him to a police wagon and arrested him, and said they'd interrogate him until he gave up the whereabouts of Konev."

"You idiot," Pyotr snarls. "Now my cover will be blown if I make one wrong move in getting Aleksey out of prison and at the very same time getting the other eleven of you safely over the border to Estonia! We'll have to leave this house tonight!"

"Where did Nikolas go?" Lyuba asks. "Nobody suspected anything of *him*."

"I'll investigate as soon as I get you moved over the border tonight."

"I can't leave without Ivan."

"I'm Stepan Litvinov's favorite son. I'll definitely be able to get all three back here within a few days. Now, start packing, everyone. We're crossing the border to Estonia tonight."

"Hooray!" Anastasiya jumps up and claps her hands. "I'll get to see my old neighborhood and my house again!"

"This is no happy little walk down memory lane. We're all going straight ahead. No questions asked."

"I refuse to leave without my husband," Eliisabet says.

"I can't leave without my fiancé," Kat says. "Kittey needs Kolya too. He's the only relative she's got left in this world."

"Her new dog will keep her fine company while you're waiting," Pyotr says.

"You're behaving like the wrong namesake," Lyuba says. "Be a good, understanding man like Saint Pyotr, not a boorish lout like Pyotr the Great."

"Yes, Petya, I don't like your bad manners and brusque comments lately," Eliisabet agrees. "We're all under stress, but we don't behave uncivilly."

"Kittey, Ginny, put on as many layers of clothing as possible," Pyotr orders. "Then come back down here with all your luggage. I'll sedate the dog."

"Where are you taking my cousin?" Lyuba asks.

"Over the border into Estonia. It's only about twenty *vyorsty* away."

Ginny and Kittey are ready in fifteen minutes. As Pyotr leads them outdoors under cover of darkness, dragging Kittey's sedated Samoyed in a large wooden trunk, he points out visible historic markers in Pskov. Many old churches, mansions, and monasteries dot the snowy landscape, as well as the frozen Velikaya River. Kittey holds Ginny's hand so she won't have to entirely walk on her own.

"This is the last Russian city you'll see for a long time," Pyotr whispers as they climb up into a cattlecar of a train he's gotten an Azerbaijani émigré to operate. "Look back and remember it."

Kittey reaches down and scrapes away the snow until she reaches dirt. She scoops a handful of dirt into a miniature porcelain teacup. "I'll keep this Russian soil until I'm old and grey."

"You're going to Tartu. The next people to join you will be Katrin and Anastasiya."

"Oh, joy," Ginny says as Pyotr pushes the panel shut.

8

Lyuba watches from a tiny crack in the wall to see who's coming and going. After Pyotr leaves the next evening with Katrin and Anastasiya, she sees Nikolas approaching the house. He's alone.

"Where were you?" Kat demands.

"We fled after we heard what was going on downstairs, but since a riot broke out, nobody, not even the authorities, cares who's coming and going. We thought it'd be safest if we split up, even if it meant leaving unannounced. Where's Kittey?"

"She, Ginny, and the harebrains went to Estonia with Petya," Eliisabet reports.

"Thank God. I hope Estonia's independence holds, and that the Reds don't crush them like they've crushed other republics."

"Didn't you go with Ivan?" Lyuba demands, pouncing on him.

"There was a shooting during the riot. We had to hide in a trench full of dead bodies. It took forever for the murderers to go away."

"So my Vanya is in a trench full of dead people!"

"He'll come back. I'm sure of it. When has he ever not come back?"

***

Pyotr comes back the next evening for Kat and Nikolas. Eliisabet hands Nikolay to Pyotr too.

"At least one of my children is guaranteed passage to America. I'm not leaving till you bring back Alyosha."

"You're expecting?"

"I didn't exactly plan to bring another child into this war-scarred land, but it is what it is. If I die, at least I'll die knowing one of my children is safe."

9

Now only Lyuba, Eliisabet, and Tatyana are left in the house. Lyuba's last memories of her homeland are watching a riot merged with a rather bloody strike through a tiny crack in a wall, not a glorious Christmas or Easter pageant, the Tercentenary celebration, the centennial of the Battle of Borodino, catching sight of the Imperial Family in St. Petersburg, or an elaborate church service.

"You know what I'm thinking about?" Eliisabet smiles before they go to bed. "My Kolya and your Tanyechka are only fourteen months apart, and best friends. Who knows? Maybe they'll grow up to get married."

"Yes, I've thought about that possibility many times."

"I feel in my heart and soul the child I'm carrying is a girl, and when you get to America, I know Ivan won't waste any time in putting a wedding band on your hand, so you'll have a second child too. If it's a boy, maybe he and Novomira can get married too, and we'll share two sets of grandchildren! She'll be a little older than your potential son, but I don't care about that. Who says only the man can be older? Shakespeare married a woman eight years his senior."

Lyuba jumps. "There's the door. We can plan our children's futures plenty when we're sailing to America. Right now we have more pressing concerns." She goes downstairs and peeks through the crack.

"Let me in. I just escaped from prison."

Lyuba opens the door for Aleksey, who's white-faced and shaking. "Go upstairs to your wife. She refused to leave until you came back."

"A very nice man helped me break out of prison. He said he's also on his way to America. Mikhail, his name was. He was a soldier in the White Army."

"I'd like to believe that could've been my uncle. Where is he now?"

"He hopes to go to France, and then America."

"More importantly, where's Ivan?"

"I don't know. Where's everyone else?"

"They're in Estonia with Petya. Only Liza, Tatyana, and I are left."

"When's Petya coming back?"

"Tomorrow evening, so you'd better be ready to leave with your wife."

10

Pyotr comes the next evening without fail. He looks pleadingly at Lyuba as Aleksey and Eliisabet put their coats and boots on.

"I told you, I'm staying right here with my daughter until my one true love has come back."

"You are in danger," Pyotr hisses. "I'll take your luggage, and if Ivan still hasn't returned in five days, I'm ordering you to take Tatyana, run across the border, never look back, and never stop running!"

Pyotr goes out the door with Eliisabet, Aleksey, and the rest of the luggage. Eliisabet has covered her rosebush with thick burlap. Every year, these beautiful peach roses have bloomed without fail, in spite of being uprooted so many times. Everyone finds them very symbolic of how life blooms with enough hope and determination.

"Remember what I said," Pyotr reminds Lyuba sternly. "Your life may depend on it. This is no time for romantic fantasies."

"I understand I need to leave as soon as possible, but I'm not going to abandon my best friend."

Lyuba watches her luggage going out the door, being carried by Pyotr. All the things she packed when she and Ginny left home, she thinks sadly. And yet she cannot help but remember all the things she didn't think to pack, the things that just wouldn't fit no matter how hard she tried. No pictures of her father, thankfully. She and Ivan went through their luggage about a week after they reached Novgorod, and he ordered her to rip her father out of all her pictures. And so she had. Perverted bastard scumbag, trying to control his only child, stealing her virginity at the age of two, traumatizing her away from giving her heart to the man she truly loves, leading her to believe she'll be better-off in a relationship with a man who only appreciates her for her body instead of her mind, heart, and soul!

The smell of blood is in the air the next morning. Rotting bodies are everywhere when she peeks through the crack. Fires are spreading. And to top it all off, Pyotr comes into the house to inform her the Azerbaijani émigré operating the train has been arrested, and that he himself was being watched late at night by the awful Godunov cousins.

"So you want me to walk over the border tonight."

"Not walk, run! Flee for your life, and don't let go of Tatyana! Don't stop running till you reach Estonia! You can look back once you've crossed over."

"I cannot leave without him!"

"If the worst happened, you can find a new love in America."

"What man wants to marry a woman who's not a virgin, who

kept the daughter she bore out of wedlock? They all think I'm a slut. Only Ivan never passed judgment on how society treats me, like a sexual plaything. It's different with you and my other male friends, since you've known me since I was a girl, and don't see me as a potential wife. Well, you still have feelings for me, but you know what I mean."

"You can find a man who also lost his love and marry him."

"I am nothing without Ivan! I lose my self-respect without him! And you dare ask me to leave the Motherland without him! I'll fall back into prostitution and self-degradation if he's gone! He's the only one who was with me the entire time we've been running from the Reds!"

11

After Pyotr has left, Lyuba sits the rest of the day, nothing to do but wait. The only thing left in the house for entertainment is a piano, and Pyotr absolutely forbade them to play on it. He stuffed it up with thick skeins of yellow yarn to prevent it.

"Lyuba, let me in. I haven't eaten anything in days."

"Vanya, are you there?"

"I've told you, I can't leave the Motherland without you!"

Lyuba opens the door quickly.

"Where are the others?"

"Petya took them to Estonia on a train, two at a time, and he took our luggage last night with Alyoshka and Liza. We have to run for our lives! The man operating the train was arrested, and Petya's falling under suspicion as well! Do you know, the Godunovs are in the city now, and they were watching Petya last night, and I told Petya over and over again I'll never leave without you! You are my life, my heart, my soul!"

"You really mean that?"

"You treat me like a human being, Vanya! And we've almost never been apart in all this time, my love!"

"Then why haven't you given me a proper greeting yet?"

"There's no time! When we're in Estonia, you can kiss me to your heart's content! Today is our last day in *Matushka Rus*, do you understand!"

"Our last day?"

"Yes, our last day, my love."

"I was in a trench of dead bodies for the past few days. And I was followed here. I want you to take Tatyana and hide upstairs until I know for sure we won't be followed over the border."

"We're going to leave by the airvent. Right now."

"Go upstairs, and I'll be right there."

Lyuba goes up the stairs carrying Tatyana and sits down with her in the nearest closet. She freezes when she hears someone coming into the house.

"You know, I would've assumed you were just another refugee, but then I heard the reports about an escaped criminal. This criminal was a Muscovite. You're a native Muscovite. This criminal is six feet three inches tall. You are too. The criminal has dark brown hair and eyes. So do you. Well, that could be a description fitting any man in his early twenties. But then I saw you signing your name to a document in the train station in Valday several months back. You have the same name as the criminal. Granted, that also might've been a coincidence. But you were using the patronymic Igorovich and the surname Bodrov, and I also had heard the criminal was using those as false names. And how many people write with the left hand? You did. You know, it's sort of funny. One evening in autumn 1917, several of my fellow officers and I paid a friendly housecall to a group of young people."

"What's the point of this?" Ivan demands.

"There was a man there fitting your exact description. Including two pregnant women. One woman really was pregnant. The other woman, my men and I concluded quickly, was only pretending to be pregnant. She and her supposed husband weren't even wearing wedding rings! Now, granted, perhaps they'd been sold. But I could tell full well she wasn't truly pregnant. She didn't act pregnant. She appeared surprised when her 'husband' told us she was in labor. You, the other man, and the falsely pregnant woman left the room. There were no screams or cries of a woman in natural labor. Those were the phoniest labor noises I ever heard. Not five minutes after you left the room, the man with black hair announced it was a stillbirth! We found very little blood on the floor. It was human blood, not afterbirth. No weeping inconsolably or anything. We right away smelled a rat."

"Why did it take you so long to turn us in?"

"There was a little boy in the house. He threw a temper tantrum because he didn't want to eat the food the true pregnant woman was serving. You hauled him off the floor. With your left hand. You opened a closet and pushed him in. With your left hand. You slammed the closet door shut. With your left hand. When you returned to the table, you pulled out your chair and were dragging the little boy by his ear. Both actions completed with your left hand. You picked up a fork. With your left hand. You drank from your glass. With your left hand. You took a pickle from the large pickle jar on the table. With your left hand. You—"

"Okay, you've fully established the fact that I'm left-handed," Ivan snarls. "So what?"

"Well, you see, the criminal we're after is also a *levsha.* How many coincidences did I need to realize you're the criminal who escaped from Lubyanka? I also discovered your whore has an illegitimate child. You'll be arrested, and probably will end up with forty years of hard labor. As for the illegitimate child, she'll be sent to an orphanage."

"You can have my daughter when you pry her from my cold dead hands!"

"Oh, but we also found out this bastardess isn't your biological child, Comrade Konev. We know all this because we've been in contact with two very concerned young men, Mikhail and Konstantin Godunov."

"The Godunov cousins can rot in Hell!"

"There is no Hell anymore. Religion was disproved along with the idea of a monarchy."

"One day the people will demand a restoration of the monarchy!"

"I also found out you were supposed to have died in a fire in April 1917."

"God protected me, and I'm alive today."

"God is dead."

"You will not take me to any prison. My daughter will stay with her mother. I'll do what you want me to do, leave the country and never return."

"That should've happened a long time ago. But if you insist neither you or the bastardess will be taken away, I know a solution.

Kill you."

"I'll kill you first."

"You can't run faster than a bullet, Comrade Konev."

"Fine. Kill me and send me straight to Hell! I know I'm going to Hell. I killed a man."

"Don't you dare do anything to him!"

The man slumps onto the floor. Lyuba drops the fire poker.

"I told you to stay upstairs!"

"He would've killed you, Vanya! I could never let that happen!"

"He'll wake up, remember everything, and track me down again!"

The man starts to move. Lyuba sticks him in the chest with the fire poker, and blood gushes out. He almost immediately goes limp.

"You killed Basil to protect me. Now I killed this man to protect you."

"I can't find words to describe my shock! You just killed a man!"

"So now you know how I felt."

"The second we're in America, we'll find a priest to confess to. I never confessed after I beat you. Now you have a sin to confess too."

"We'll go to Hell together now."

"Enough stalling for time. We have to leave this house."

"It's probably swarmed by Cheka agents and the Godunov cousins!"

"Not out in back. They won't suspect a thing out back."

"By the airvent, the way Petya went in and out?"

"No. Keep holding Tatyana. You'll see. You may want to close your eyes, *golubka*." Ivan picks Lyuba up and starts upstairs.

"Where are you taking me?"

"You'll have to trust me," he says as he opens an upstairs window. "Don't let go of me or Tatyana!"

"You're going onto the roof! Look how much ice is here!"

"Don't look back. You cannot make a single noise. I'll carry you, you'll carry Tatyana, Tatyana will carry her doll, and this is how we'll leave *Matushka Rus*."

Lyuba holds back a scream as he leaps off the roof. And then she holds onto both of them for dear life. This is how Lyuba, Ivan, and Tatyana finally leave Russia, running for their lives across the border in the ice and snow, a riot in Pskov, Cheka agents searching for Ivan, no looking back allowed, no crying. Lyuba will remember this day for the rest of her life, the day she left her Motherland and wasn't allowed to look back, scream, or cry. Ivan doesn't stop running until he sees a train station coming into view in the dark.

"What city are we in?" he asks the nearest person.

"Orava."

"Are we in Estonia? You have no idea how long we've been dreaming of getting out of our homeland and into your country."

"You've come to the right place. Welcome to my beautiful country."

"*Slava Bogu*," Lyuba whispers to Tatyana. "We're finally free. You'll never have to live in fear ever again."

"Put us on a train to Tartu," Ivan tells the man at the ticket booth. He pulls some rubles out of his pockets. "Thank God I'm finally in a country where money is worth something."

Lyuba crosses herself at the sight of the train steaming into the station. "I hope we can find our friends easily. Tartu is a big city."

"I'm sure we'll find them. We always find each other again." He puts his arm around her. "I told you I wouldn't leave without you."

"Didn't you get tired of running so far?"

"Because you and Tanyechka were with me, it didn't seem so far at all."

She picks Tatyana up and takes Ivan's arm as they board the train. It's not going to be a very long trip, but she makes herself comfortable in her seat and tries to relax, watching the snow-covered landscape going by. As soon as they've unboarded in Tartu, she scans the announcement board, desperately searching for any notes from their friends. Finally, her eyes light on a note in Pyotr's handwriting, begging her to come to the address he's listed. Just to be safe, she tears down the note so it can't be seen by the wrong people, who for all she knows could be soon to follow. Then she asks after the nearest restaurant.

"What do we need to eat for? I'm sure we'll have food when we join the others."

"You must be starving, Vanya. You haven't eaten in days!"

"I can live without food for a little while. The only thing I can't live without is you."

12

"Get her to stop coughing!" Vera commands. "Otherwise the building will be torched, and we'll be sent back to Mrs. Brezhneva!"

Fyodora has contracted whooping cough since they've finally arrived back in Pskov. Now the six of them are in an old abandoned building, holed up in a back room, with a bookcase jammed against the wall.

"I called Papa at the post office," Alla says. "When he comes here, there will be six of us."

"There are *six of us," Vera says.*

"I mean Papa and Galya. Anya and Lyonya aren't our true family."

"And then? Where will we go then?"

"To America. I took our passports when I went to see Papa last year. Thank God Nadya was smart enough to put a phony smallpox quarantine sign on the house before she left. We'll be free soon. We're just waiting for Papa to come."

Alla stops talking at the knock on the door. She opens it and in steps Galya, followed by Mr. Lebedev, walking solemnly, Kroshka cradled in his arms and trying to jump down to the floor.

"He's really here!" Natalya shouts, running over to her father.

Mr. Lebedev lets Kroshka down on the floor and begins to cry. He, Vera, and Natalya hug and kiss and cry for the longest time.

"Four of my daughters are alive. I can't believe it."

"Five, Papa, five," Natalya says. "Dora's on the mattress over there. She's got whooping cough."

Mr. Lebedev strides over on shaking legs and picks his youngest daughter up. Fyodora stops her coughing and recognizes the father she hasn't seen in almost four years. She only vaguely remembers what he looks like, but she's never forgotten he has two different-colored eyes.

"Papa, you finally came back."

"Praise God we're together again," he says, his voice shaking. "Now that our family's back together, we'll never be separated ever again, and I'll spend the rest of my life smothering you with all the love and protection you were denied while we were apart. No one will ever hurt a hair on your head again."

"Why are you stumbling around, Galya?" Natalya asks.

"Didn't Alla tell you? I'm blind now."

"You can tell us the story on the ship to America. The three of us also have plenty of horror stories to tell."

"Where's Mama?" Fyodora asks.

"She's in a very nice place where there's no more suffering," Mr. Lebedev tells her, holding back tears. "We'll see her again someday."

"Where are my other five sisters?"

"I don't know. Some of them may be with your mother."

"Pozhaluysta, *Papa, we have to go to America. Take* us *to a place where there's no suffering," Natalya pleads.*

"So then Mama went to America?" Fyodora asks.

"She went to a magical place with angels, harps, fountains, gold, eternal youth, and love," Mr. Lebedev elucidates.

"Look, Dora, here's Kroshka," Vera quickly jumps in. "Dogs are like elephants, they never forget."

Mr. Lebedev carries Fyodora back to her mattress and tucks her in. Almost as soon as she's been tucked in, Fyodora starts violently coughing again. Kroshka jumps onto the bed and snuggles against Fyodora, frantically wagging her tail and licking Fyodora's face. Though Fyodora is still racked by whooping cough spasms, she manages to put her little arms around Kroshka, and the severity of the coughing gradually subsides.

"She's so young to have gone through this," Mr. Lebedev muses. "God willing, her heart will start to heal and she'll have a chance to enjoy a normal, happy childhood now."

13

Not much of historic Tartu is left, due to a preponderance of fires in the eighteenth century, particularly the Great Fire of Tartu in 1775. However, Pyotr has managed to get a decent rental property in the Old Town, a stately fifty-year-old brick house with three stories and six bedrooms. Though Estonia in February and March is just about as cold as Russia, they venture out for short walks or rides on Branimir when the weather is slightly more forgiving. Katrin has taken them to Town Hall Square; the old, venerable University of Tartu, where she once dreamt of studying; the ruins of Tartu Cathedral; Jaani Kirik, a beautiful Brick Gothic church; the Orthodox Uspenskiy Church; Peetri Kirik, another lovely brick church in Gothic Revival style; Telleri Kapel, a small chapel built of white stone; and the university's library. Lyuba can barely understand a word of the books and newspapers Katrin has been borrowing and buying, but every so often she recognizes a Russian or German cognate. Now that Estonia is independent, and Russia has signed a treaty renouncing all rights to the land in perpetuity, it seems as though Katrin wants to remain in her hometown instead of following the others to America. As lovely as Tartu is, it's far too close to Ivan's pursuers, and Lyuba isn't so sure she could master a language with fourteen cases, so much agglutination, and so many double vowels in those already tongue-twisting words. The language sounds beautiful, but seems a nightmare to learn.

Almost two weeks into March, on the very day they're supposed to leave for Tallinn, Katrin storms into the first floor living room during lunch, brandishing a newspaper. She throws it at Pyotr, who understands fairly good Finnish and can therefore understand enough of its sister language.

"Is there a story in particular you want me to read, or am I supposed to guess? You're supposed to be packing, not wasting your time with a temper tantrum. You can read the paper all you want in Tallinn, but right now, we have to get ready to leave."

"Those stories!" She points to them. "Those *mudaki* I faithfully supported for almost four years are violating the Treaty of Tartu! How dare they prevent my people from returning home! Thank God I came back illegally, or I might've been trapped too. And why the hell do the Estonian Bolsheviks want us to become part of the Soviet Union? Our patriots fought so hard for us to finally win our freedom, and they want us to fall under occupation again immediately?"

"What you need to do is have lunch and pack, not pontificate about politics. Of all the times you could've chosen to rant about politics. We get on the ship in two days, do you hear me! Just two days! We're leaving by the back door. I've already got the dog sedated."

"What about Branimir?" Lyuba asks. "I don't want to leave him after he's been so loyal and helpful. His new owners might not treat him so nicely."

"You and that stupid horse!"

"Ships allow animals as long as they've got the proper papers," Eliisabet says. "There were dogs, cats, and birds on *Titanic*."

"Where will you stick a horse in the big city?"

"We can put him up in a stable," Ginny says. "I'm sure plenty of New York's millionaires have horses, even if there's not enough room in the city. Lyuba and Ivan have more than enough money to foot the bill."

"So you're going to spend good money on keeping a horse in a blasted stable. An excellent use of your windfall of riches. Are you planning to visit and ride every week?"

"When I have enough money, I'll take Lyuba and our children to the Midwest," Ivan says. "We'll take Branimir in one of the animal cars. It's not right to abandon our friend."

"Yes, *pozhaluysta*, Petya, we've grown really attached to Branimir," Lyuba says. "I'm sure you'd take excellent care of him in our place, but he doesn't know you as his rider."

"Fine. The horse goes. But we're still leaving Tartu as soon as we finish lunch."

"How are we leaving?" Aleksey asks.

"We're going to walk to a peasant driver I hired. All of us this time will be hiding underneath dead fish! My life is also in danger! I'll have him hitch Branimir to the wagon."

"My fellow Estonians—" Katrin starts to blubber again.

"You keep quiet, you damned traitor! Finally you're seeing just how wrong you were, two days before we leave for America!" Aleksey snarls.

"I still support the ideals of Communism, but this is a pure hate crime! I thought Communism would free my fellow Estonians from the awful yoke of Tsarist oppression, but now they're turning around and oppressing us all over again!" Katrin begins to cry the first real tears of her life. "Why did we bother fighting so hard for freedom if the Estonian Bolsheviks want to turn around and join the Soviet Union? This isn't a political party I want to support. You were all right about how Bolsheviks aren't the right side to support, but I didn't want to listen. I found a reason to excuse everything I found distasteful, thought it was just an emergency wartime measure or certain people weren't acting on Comrade Lenin's wishes."

"We can't take you if you'll give us away by crying!" Pyotr shouts.

"I thought we could be free, make our own government and nation, but now they're trying to suppress us as soon as that dream came true! I've lost my appetite. I'll pack and eat in Tallinn."

Katrin is still blubbering when she comes back with her luggage. Everyone is clustered around the back door waiting for her, and Pyotr is pacing back and forth like a caged animal.

"We can't take her if she's crying," he announces. "Even if Estonia is free, we can't be sure we haven't been followed and aren't being watched as we speak. My ruse with the dead fish will be worthless if there are noises coming from underneath it. Speaking of worthless, I'm sure your luggage is a whole lot of dead weight. You and Anastasiya have been living like pampered princesses while the rest of my friends have lived like paupers. Even Lyuba, Kat, and Ginny, who were able to pack as much as they wanted before they left home, haven't had reason or want to use a lot of their non-necessary items. Need I remind you that you almost got killed in a fire because you insisted on packing all your nonsense first? I expect this sort of silliness from Anastasiya, but you're intelligent and politically-minded. It makes absolutely no sense for a woman with your mind to lug around finery and luxury items. Lyuba told me about how wonderful you were in Khimki Forest, like foraging for food and pitching a tent, so you know how to survive without the lap of luxury."

Pyotr picks up Katrin's luggage and yanks it apart. Ridiculous feather boas. Fur coats. Tango shoes. Clothes and shawls made of silk, satin, velvet, velveteen, taffeta, chiffon, leather, suede, wool, and lace. Hand-held fans with exquisite designs, both European and imported from the Orient. Hats so ridiculous even Anastasiya laughs. Bottle after bottle of hair care products and makeup. Pictures of Grand Duke Dmitriy, Douglas Fairbanks, Thomas Meighan, John Barrymore, and Wallace Reid. Three stupid-looking wigs everyone bursts out laughing at. Katrin buries her face in her hands, her cheeks flushing.

"Tell me again, Empress Katariina, what will you do with all these things once you get off the boat?" Pyotr laughs in glee. "How do you reconcile this silliness with your fervent Communist beliefs?"

"I can't go to America empty-handed!" Katrin screams. "Repack my luggage right *now*, Pyotr Stepanovich Litvinov!"

"When did you ever need a wig?" Eliisabet laughs.

"For costume balls! I never wore them anywhere else!"

"Are these playing cards on this hat?" Nikolas laughs.

"This one has stuffed birds on it!" Kat says.

Pyotr repacks the luggage, unable to contain his laughter as he handles each item. "Fine. Take your worthless possessions to America. Can I bet how long it'll take before you start selling them to make money?"

"Who'd buy this stuff?" Ginny laughs in glee.

"*I* bought this stuff, little urchin!"

"You're hardly a paragon of fashion," Nikolas says.

"Yeah, what other woman besides you has hair cut like a man's?" Kat asks. "Even women daring enough to cut most of their hair off style it femininely instead of cropping it."

"I like having short hair! It's modern and convenient."

"Okay, now." Pyotr opens the door. *"Odin, dva, tri, chetyre, pyat, shest, sem, vosem, devyat, desyat!"*

They set off for the peasant's wagon.

14

Mr. Lebedev, his five daughters, Anya, Leontiy, and Kroshka are waiting overnight in a hotel overlooking the coast. They picked up a small companion on the way. Natalya Yeltsina. Klarisa's great plot to send her to join Lena in Canada totally fell through, and Lyuda, Grushenka, and Manya were sent to prison by Mrs. Voznesenskaya after she discovered them unrolling her cigarettes and taking out the tobacco, replacing it with a brown powdery poison. Furious, stunned, and angry, Klarisa stabbed her deranged "mother hen" in the back by drugging her out cold a day before a team came by to inspect the orphanage. When the team got there, they saw the orphanage arrayed in all its filthy glory and majesty, with Mrs. Voznesenskaya passed out in the outhouse, a pornographic picture book open to a particularly scandalous page, plenty of human waste shoveled out of the hole in the ground and around Mrs. Voznesenskaya the Mad, a dozen drained bottles of vodka in her lap. Then Klarisa had pulled the sheet off the dead Mikhaila and the team had been even more shocked. When Mrs. Voznesenskaya came to herself, she was sitting in a jail cell. Ha ha ha.

15

Pyotr hitches Branimir to the peasant's wagon and climbs under the dead fish. Anastasiya whimpers as Nikolas shoves her into the fish. Aleksey stuffs everyone's luggage under the fish as well. The last person to get there is Ivan, dragging a young boy by the hand.

"Who the hell is that?" Nikolas asks.

"I'm Fedir Yosypovych Mazepa. My family and I fled here from Ukraine, and now we want to go to America. Ivan helped me up when he saw me trip."

"Fedir's nine," Ivan says. "Here comes his little brother Dmytro."

"No!" Pyotr shouts from underneath the fish. "I have twelve of you already! I can't take fourteen!"

"Our parents are coming too. We're travelling on my father's passport."

"No!" Pyotr shouts, turning red in rage. "Not sixteen!"

"Oh, come on, Petya," Lyuba begs. "Your namesake Saint Pyotr would've taken on sixteen hundred people to save from being persecuted."

"I was also named after Pyotr the Great, who didn't really give a damn about other people's misery all the time!"

"Will the wagon break if four more come in?" Ginny asks.

Pyotr grunts. "Get in. These are the last stray people we're going to pick up, I'm warning you right now!"

16

Pyotr, the Stray Dogs, and the Mazepas arrive in Tallinn on the thirteenth of March, smelling like dead fish. As soon as the wagon stops, he herds everyone into a small house by the gulf.

"There it is. The Gulf of Finland, gateway to the North Sea and the Atlantic Ocean."

"Look, Kittey, if you strain your eyes hard enough, you can pretend you see America!" Nikolas says.

"The boat will dock here tomorrow bright and early. Be here, or you might never have another chance to leave."

"Petya, I don't have my passport," Lyuba says.

"Sure you do. Break that vase, and it'll fall out. A stupid vase isn't more important than your safety."

"But my aunt loves that vase. She made it in the women's art college in East Prussia."

"If you don't break that vase or manage to get that passport out another way, you'll never go to America."

"I can always get a new one. In the meantime, I can stay behind with you. I can't imagine it'll take long to acquire a replacement."

"You're just getting cold feet. Now, the ship will have about two hundred other passengers. You'll be travelling second-class."

"Second-class?" Katrin shrieks. "First-class doesn't have to wade through all the creepy, diseased, lower-class scumballs from dirty, premodern, mud-hovel villages no one's ever heard of! The doctors come right on the ship to examine them, and they don't have to go through the hassles of customs or filthy strangers!"

"Welcome to real life, Empress Katariina," Pyotr chuckles. "And you claim to be a committed Communist."

"If we strike an iceberg, at least we'll be second-class," Aleksey says. "Though I suppose only our women will be lucky. I'd have to stay behind and drown, or never live down my unmanly actions."

"This ship isn't like *Titanic*. That was a once in a blue moon tragedy, and modern ships are required to have enough lifeboats and safety watches."

"The second I get to America, I'm going to join forces with other Estonians," Katrin declares. "When it really boils down, I love my people and progressive politics more than fashion and celebrities. I'm going to write for the Estonian press, if they have any, and become a public intellectual. I certainly won't join the Communist Party after their traitorous actions. I'll become a Socialist." Katrin rips out the pages in her Party ID, tears them up, and throws the pieces into the Gulf of Finland. "I feel so ashamed."

"Tomorrow is the thirty-eighth anniversary of the death of Marx," Pyotr reminds them. "While other people may be marking the occasion with speeches and parades, you'll board the ship. And then it's goodbye."

17

That evening, while the others are busy looking over their memories in their suitcases and thinking about what they'll be doing early tomorrow morning, Ivan takes Lyuba out by the water, where they sit down on a small wooden bench.

"Lyuba, you've been my best friend for thirteen years, and we've only been apart a few times. All the horrible things we've lived through, we lived through together. I know you're no longer scared of your love for me or my love for you. After everything you went through, you decided to trust me, and not push me away for another round of sexual exploitation with someone who doesn't care about you as a human being."

"Of course, you're my dearest and best friend."

"You've always been more than a friend to me. You got rid of that stupid ring Malenkov got you, not once, but twice! Now you're wearing the ring I got you. We'll face some tough times in America, but we'll get through them just like we've gotten through the past four years. You're so beautiful, like a work of art or a Greek or Roman goddess, and all the men want you, and you've given your body to so many of them, but only to me have you given your heart and soul."

She rubs his arm. "We can retire to our lodgings if you'd like my body, finally."

"I keep telling you, it's not the right time. We need a place of our own, with complete privacy, at a special time, and I don't want to risk creating a child before I know we can afford it."

"Then I'll take a job too. I know how much you want a child of your own."

"I won't have you work. All the men look at you, and I can feel them wanting you, wanting to be with such a beautiful woman. I want you to stay safe at home, taking care of our children."

"Now, now. Don't be so old-fashioned."

"I'm not trying to sound old-fashioned. I just would feel very uneasy if you worked with men. You wouldn't be safe from their leering glances."

"So you brought me out here to tell me you won't let me work in America?"

"Perish the thought. Why don't you close your eyes?"

Lyuba closes her eyes. She opens them uneasily when she feels Ivan's shaking hands taking hers.

"I tried this thrice before. I hope I finally get a positive answer the fourth time! *Ya tyebya lyublyu. Khotish byt moyey zhenoy?*"

Lyuba freezes, not knowing what to do. She wants to scream yes, but she also wants to think about what this will mean, cementing their undying love, meaning she won't be allowed to get scared and run from Ivan's love and into the arms of another man, since adultery is forbidden by the Church. All during her pregnancy with Tatyana, she was afraid for her life and her unborn daughter's life. She would feel the fetus moving and know it belonged to a man she only slept with because of a sick, manipulative trap that pulled her away from the man she's always truly loved. Boris never gave a damn and never once felt Tatyana moving or kicking. With Ivan, he'd never let her leave the house, and would never be able to stop feeling for fetal movements. Lyuba also knows he'll provide for her and not throw her away when he gets tired or decides to take a break from adult responsibilities. She finally regains her speech and opens her mouth.

"This is a surprise, but my answer—"

"I should've known your answer would be a fourth resounding no! You will never stop getting frightened of my love! Are you planning to run back into the arms of Pyotr, or maybe you're planning on going back to Boris, or, better yet, going back to Moskva to resume prostitution, or maybe even try a married man this time? I should've known! Go on, tell me a fourth time you're afraid to marry me because you can't handle being with someone who truly loves you!"

"If you'd shut up long enough for me to finish speaking, your answer would've been yes, yes, yes!"

"It would?"

"Yes, it would."

"I'm so sorry. But you were silent for so long—"

"Your answer isn't yes anymore, though! Your problem is that you never know just when you're supposed to shut up or speak up! And you have a heavy Russian accent! Your English is miserable, and you're supposed to leave for America tomorrow morning! You also have problems with their alphabet, you're afraid of my body, and you're passive, submissive, and totally the opposite of the image you project to other people! And look at this scar you put on my face! Just look at it! And you really have a violent temper! You should've been named after Ivan Grozniy, not the Great! You think you're such a real man when you're beating the life out of someone who makes you angry! You never try to settle a dispute with words! You settle it with fists! Well, I'm not going to America, since I don't have my passport, so you can marry that shallow snob Anastasiya Voroshilova! I'll stay behind and marry Petya, the only man left in this world who really loves me!" Lyuba storms off.

Ivan is shocked at her outburst. She's never before given him such a tongue-lashing. He goes back to the lodgings to try to find her, but she's not there. Everyone else is asleep. Then he sees a note in her handwriting, the ink still wet.

I went to stay with Petya. He's a good, honorable, decent man. He'll take care of me until I get a new passport. By then, we'll be married, and we'll come to America together.

Ivan storms over to one of the more vacant rooms, grabs the nearest object off the rickety old shelf, and flings it to the floor with such violent rage it breaks into pieces. He starts to throw around the suitcases lying on the ground, and then goes into Katrin's hilarious possessions. He begins to throw her wigs, hats, and shoes around the room, using so much swearing and less than polite expressions he shocks even himself. The loud noise wakes up Aleksey.

"What the hell are you doing, Konev?"

"I'm not drunk. Lyuba rejected my fourth marriage proposal, after she was ready to say yes! She paused too long, and I interpreted it as another rejection. I told her I wasn't surprised, and she began to scream at me and tell me several things she hates about me, and told me her answer had swiftly changed to no. Look at this awful note she wrote me! She's going to marry Pyotr!"

"You broke this vase. Was it the one that belonged to your mother?"

"No, that one I didn't unpack. It's special." Ivan picks up the broken pieces. "My mother's vase is glass, and this one's clay. It's the vase that belonged to Lyuba's aunt—"

"Now she'll *really* hate you!"

"Look! Ginny put her passport into this vase, and I just broke it! This is Lyuba's passport!"

"Well, this certainly is a plus side of her latest rejection! We'll glue the vase back together, and you can tell Lyuba the happy news in the morning when she comes back here with Petya. Speaking of good news, Liza told me she has good news she's going to tell me in the morning. I can't wait to find out what it is."

18

Pyotr is on his knees trying to persuade Lyuba to go back to Ivan and take back her harsh words. Lyuba refuses to believe it.

"I like this hotel. I hope we get to stay here until I get my passport. Such opulence I haven't seen since before the Revolution."

"Listen, as much as I like you and think happily of how you took my virginity, I know you belong with Ivan. I want you to go to him in the morning and apologize."

"I want to marry you, Petya."

"I'd love to marry you, but I'm man enough to recognize you need to marry Ivan."

"Ivan is a bizarre cross between a *gromyko* and a mute. He talks too much at the wrong times, and doesn't say anything at all when it behooves him to speak up."

"You sleep on this matter. In the morning, we'll rejoin the others, you'll say yes to Ivan, and you'll board the ship on his arm. The next time I'll see you will be at your wedding."

Lyuba and Pyotr sleep in separate beds that night. In the morning, Pyotr calls for room service, and they partake of a traditional Estonian breakfast of cottage cheese, fried eggs with ham, porridge, and black bread with butter. Pyotr teaches her a few words of Estonian, and she smiles at him. Then he orders room service to clear the plates away. Lyuba waits in the rental car as Pyotr pays the bill.

"Are your papers all here?" she asks when he gets in the car with his two suitcases.

"Of course. If I don't have a lengthy article to show for my supposed research, my father will know for certain I two-timed him, the family, and all his Party friends."

Pyotr drives the twenty minutes to the harbor in silence. There sits the ship, tied up in Tallinn Bay. Scores of people are milling around waiting to board.

"What was that good news you had for me?" Aleksey asks his wife as they move up in the line.

"I'll tell you when we get on the ship."

Nikolas nudges Ivan. "Look, Lyuba came to apologize."

Ivan shakes his head. "She just came to rub more salt in my wounds."

Lyuba runs over and throws her arms around Ivan. "Petya persuaded me to apologize to you. I'm really sorry, not just apologizing because I was guilted into it or forced to do this."

"You told me you can't stand my heavy accent when I speak English. You said you detest my violent temper. You said you can't bear how much I talk. You told me I should've been named for—"

"Hush. I was only frustrated at your reaction to what you thought was another rejection. You know I love everything about you, my sweet *groznik*."

"So then I can try again a fifth time?"

"Look, Lyuba, it's Pasha and Nadya!" Ginny points.

"Oh my Lord." Lyuba turns around and sees Pavel and Nadezhda standing there.

"We made our way up to Tallinn too!" Pavel says. "Nadya finally got away from the Godunovs, and I went with her. But we don't have tickets for this ship, so we'll have to take a raft and find a sympathetic ship to pick us up."

"A raft?" Lyuba asks. "Won't it capsize?"

"I'm no dummy. I know full well how to build a good raft, and it's not intended to take us all the way to America. The next ship going by will have to pick us up, and I doubt we'll have to wait long. I want to get out of here as soon as possible."

"Holy Mother of God, those are my uncle and five of my cousins!" Nadezhda runs off to greet them.

"Well, isn't this one happy reunion after another," Pyotr says.

"That's Maksim Gromyko," Ginny shudders. "I almost forgot he existed, and could've gone the rest of my life without wondering what became of him."

"The ship will only have two hundred other passengers. It's becoming harder and harder to immigrate to the United States, to say nothing of how hard it's becoming to leave Russia. Everyone who could came here for one last chance to go to the land of freedom."

"This ship is not going to leave without the two of us!"

Everyone looks over at the two women dragging a trunk. Each has a knapsack strapped to her back. Pyotr turns white.

"Yes, we're alive and well, thanks for asking!" Alya shouts.

"They're alive!" Lyuba almost faints.

"We can have our happy reunions on the ship," Ivan says. "For now, we're going back to the bench."

He steps out of line and leads Lyuba over. This time, when he gets down on his knees and repeats "*Ya tyebya lyublyu. Khotish byt moyey zhenoy?*" Lyuba nods yes with tears in her eyes. They hold one another and cry.

"This is one of the happiest days of my life!" Ivan pulls her even closer and kisses her face, then slips a large emerald ring with small accent diamonds onto her finger.

"Everyone, the ship will be leaving in three minutes!" Pyotr shouts.

"Where's Branimir?" Ginny asks.

"He's with Andryusha, Kittey's dog, down in the kennels."

"Goodbye, Petya. You're one of the best friends I've ever had." Kat hugs Pyotr.

Pyotr himself is crying by the time he's said goodbye to everyone in the band. Ginny presents him with a fairly large, heavy coin.

"It's a present from everyone. We want you to have it to remember us by. We tried to think of something that would represent friendship, but when we saw this, we knew it was the perfect farewell gift."

"It's a coin with my two namesakes on either side."

Eliisabet nods, tears in her eyes. "You're our Saint Pyotr and our Pyotr the Great."

The captain lets the last person on board, and then the anchor is pulled up. Lyuba stands and watches the ship slowly moving away, her eyes growing cloudy. So close to freedom, and now she must watch her dear ones leaving without her, all because her passport is stuck inside a vase she refuses to break. She wonders if this is yet another subconscious way of pushing Ivan away.

"Lyuba, get out of here. I hear boots." Pavel takes Nadezhda by the arm and runs away.

"Why didn't you board the ship?" Pyotr demands. "You have a valid passport. I can't understand why you didn't just smash it the moment Ginny confessed what he did. Your freedom is far more important than a stupid vase." He stiffens, and his ears prick up. "I hear boots too."

Pyotr yanks on her arm, and they begin running as fast as they can back towards Tallinn's Medieval Old Town and away from the waterfront. Nadezhda and Pavel have already disappeared from view. Then Lyuba trips, and the next thing she knows, she's lost sight of Pyotr too, and thudding footsteps are rapidly approaching behind her.

Lyuba looks over her shoulder, barely less terrified when she sees he's not an enemy. "Vanya, you're supposed to be going to America! Don't be noble and try to stay behind with me. Your life's still in danger."

"I couldn't find you anywhere on the ship, and then I saw you back on shore. I wanted to hang myself when I realized I'd completely forgotten to tell you I accidentally broke that vase and freed your passport last night. It's there on the ship waiting for you. I rowed back to shore in a collapsible. Don't you know by now I'd never abandon you?"

"What?"

"I'm sorry I didn't tell you as soon as I saw you, but I was too preoccupied with finally getting a positive response to my marriage proposal. I couldn't think of anything else. *Pozhaluysta, pozhaluysta,* forgive me." Ivan leans down and pulls her up. "The captain was so generous as to agree to stop and let me go back for you."

Lyuba hugs him. "Praise Christ. I never thought there could be a positive side to that violent temper of yours."

As they're walking towards the water, Lyuba suddenly hears footsteps. Small footsteps.

"Just where might *you* be going?"

"Shut up." Ivan gives Aleksandr a push. "See that boat? It's taking us to America, and you'll never hear from us again."

"You think you can push me around because I'm only fourteen. Well, Misha's twenty-three and Kostya's twenty-one. Very much grown men. Not to mention all the Cheka men they've got with them. These Cheka agents are very much looking forward to bringing you back to Moskva to face justice for your cold-blooded crime of murder."

"I saved you from a well when you were a boy," Lyuba says. "And one good turn deserves another."

"That was before I became a Communist."

"Sasha, where are they?" the voice of Misha demands through the trees.

"I should tell him where you are. I felt absolutely no qualms whatsoever about turning in my family. Okay, once or twice I felt a bit bad, but then I realized my life is now, not living in the past longing for enemies of the people."

"Sasha, who are you talking to?" Kostya demands.

"*Pozhaluysta*, Aleksandr, I promise you we'll get on that boat and you'll never hear from us again!" Ivan pleads. "They'll stop looking for me once I've left the country, and they can't get me when I'm in the United States!"

"*Pozhaluysta*, Sasha," Lyuba begs. "I saved your life once, so you ought to save mine now!"

Aleksandr grunts. "Continue down Ahtri Street and run into that wooden Orthodox church. Don't venture outside until you can no longer hear us." He watches them obey his orders and is pleased adults listen authoritatively to a fourteen-year-old.

Misha and Kostya come rushing up with the Cheka agents moments after Ivan has pulled Lyuba inside the humble waterfront church.

"Where did they go?" Kostya shouts.

Aleksandr points to the right. "That way!"

Aleksandr, the Godunovs, and the Cheka agents take off. After the sounds of the boots trail off, Ivan and Lyuba slowly emerge from the Church of Saint Simeon and Hanna the Prophet. They're both shaking violently, and haven't had the cognizance to look around inside this beautiful historic landmark of Tallinn, built by their own people in the eighteenth century.

"He saved us," Lyuba says numbly. "The boy who spied on you killing Basil saved the very criminal he turned in."

"No more talk about that. We're going to a new life together!" Ivan leads her back to the nearby waterfront.

Lyuba cringes at the sight of the collapsible. "Running across the border was frightening enough, but now we're rowing out to a ship? What if we capsize?"

But every moment of the swaying collapsible journey is worth it, as is the steep slope into Tallinn Bay after the initial shallow water. Her arms don't get the least tired as she rows, because after so many secret vans and wagons in the night, she's now going to a final mode of transportation away from danger.

As soon as they reach the side of the ship, several of the officers rush to pull up the lifeboat. Lyuba keeps her eyes closed to avoid feeling seasick, and has to be pulled onto deck by Ivan. All their friends breathe a collective sigh of relief, and the ship soon begins moving again.

"You don't want to know what kind of trouble we just barely escaped," Ivan says. "Suffice it to say, we were all within spitting distance of the Cheka, Mr. Litvinov, and the Godunovs as we were boarding. Thank God you escaped just in time. Two people can evade capture better than a huge group."

"Thank God indeed," Mr. Lebedev gasps as he crosses himself. "I would've been a dead man, and would've lost my surviving children and Kroshka all over again. Those goons were searching for me too." He gently puts his hand on Lyuba's arm. "Lyubov Leontiyevna, if you're not offended by this suggestion, I'd be very much honored to once again assume a fatherly role in your life. I'll look out for you as though you were one of my own children, and regard you as unofficial family. I'd also like to invite you to use *ty*, in spite of our age difference. If we're going to have a close relationship, it doesn't seem right to keep using *vy*."

Lyuba smiles at him. "Yes, Ilya Nikolayevich, I'd like that very much. It means a lot to me that you're offering to become my surrogate father."

Tatyana excitedly runs over to them. "I missed you, Mama, Papa."

"I missed you too, my little *knyazhna*." Ivan lifts her up and cuddles her. "Once we're in America, your mother and I are going to work hard on giving you a dear little brother to play with."

"Can I have a brother in America too?" Nikolay asks.

Eliisabet smiles. "You'll get a little sibling later this year, sweetheart. I think it's a girl, but there's always a next time when you might get a brother."

"That was your surprise?" Aleksey asks. "That's the best surprise ever!"

"Speaking of surprises." Ivan gives Lyuba his arm. "I'll give you a tour of the ship, and give you your passport back."

***

Two hours later, they emerge from below deck to the most beautiful symbol of safety, water on all sides. Land is no longer in sight. Soon they'll land in Helsinki for a brief stop, and then continue on to America, with a few more brief stops in major ports along the way. Their long Russian nightmare is over.

"God has been so good to nobodies like us," Lyuba says. "So many miracles have been worked for us, but I think the best miracle of all is that we're finally engaged to be married and I'm no longer afraid of your love."

The lights are starting to disappear from the sky. Lyuba stands at the guardrail and holds onto it, leaning forward into the heavy wind. Her long sable tresses billow out around her, and as he catches her profile in the sunset, Ivan thinks to himself just how beautiful Lyubov Leontiyevna Zhukova is and what an *udachnik* he is to have finally won her heart.

But for how long, once they're in America, will they go until Lyuba may get scared and run again? *How long?*

Part II: America (May 1921–March 1924)

Part Two Characters

In order of appearance:

Lyubov Leontiyevna Zhukova (Lyuba)
Ivan Ivanovich Konev
Tatyana Ivanovna Koneva
Mikhail Grigoriy Mikhaylovich Kharzin (Ginny)
Eliisabet Martovna Kutuzova
Aleksey Vladimirovich Tvardovskiy
Nikolay Alekseyevich Kutuzov-Tvardovskiy
Katriyana Dmitriyevna Vrangel (Kat)
Nikolay Andreyevich Vishinskiy (Nikolas)
Katerina Andreyevna Vishinskaya (Kittey)
Natalya Vadimovna Yeltsina
Anna Pavlovna Furtseva (Anya)
Aleksandra L'vovna Minina (Alya)
Anastasiya Viktorovna Voroshilova
Katariina Kaarelovna Nikonova (Katrin)
Kroshka
Ilya Nikolayevich Lebedev (Mr. Lebedev)
Galina Ilyinichna Lebedeva (Galya)
Alla Ilyinichna Lebedeva
Vera Ilyinichna Lebedeva
Natalya Ilyinichna Lebedeva
Fyodora Ilyinichna Lebedeva
Anna Rudolfovna Godimova (Anya)
Leontiy Rudolfovich Godimov
Maksim Petrovich Gromyko
Branimir
Aleksander Kalvik (Sandro), one of the Ellis Island workers, later Katrin's husband, born April 15, 1898
Priest who marries Kat and Nikolas and baptizes Nikolay at the Kissing Post at Ellis Island
Woman in charge of Lower East Side boardinghouse Lyuba and her friends stay at
Pavel Lavrentiyevich Teglyov
Nadezhda Osipovna Lebedeva

Father Yakim, the priest of Lyuba and her friends' new church in Manhattan
Teachers and administrators at American school
Valeriya Afanasiyevna Golitsyna, Ivan's aunt, now remarried
Grigoriy Vasiliyevich Golitsyn (Mr. Golitsyn)
Vasiliy Grigoriyevich Golitsyn (Vasya), their son, born April 14, 1921
Ivan Vasiliyevich Konev (Mr. Konev)
Potapovskiy and other guards and overlords of Nadezhda's first labor camp
Svetlana Ilyinichna Lebedeva
Boris Aleksandrovich Malenkov
Police officer
Margarita Iosifovna Kharzina (Mrs. Kharzina)
Yekaterina Iosifovna Zhukova (Katya) (Mrs. Zhukova)
Aleksandr Timofeyevich Malenkov (Mr. Malenkov)
Aleksandriya Nikiforovna Malenkova (Mrs. Malenkova)
Yelena Vadimovna Yeltsina (Lena)
Antonina Borisovna Petrova
Sofya Mitrofanovna Gorbachëva (Sonya)
Yuriy Mikhaylovich Yeltsin
Novomira Alekseyevna Kutuzova-Tvardovskaya, the secondborn child of Eliisabet and Aleksey, born August 5, 1921
Mrs. Kuzmitch, a midwife
Leontiy Leonidovich Zhukov (Mr. Zhukov)
Mrs. Ptitsyna, a social worker on Ellis Island
Mrs. Kharzina and Mrs. Zhukova's Thanksgiving guests
Mikhail Mikhaylovich Kharzin (Mr. Kharzin)
Proprietor of an Upper East Side baby shop
Russian translator on Canadian train
Father Morodenko, a priest who refuses to assign Mr. Zhukov penance after hearing his repulsive, unrepentant final confession
Lyudmila and Raisa Nikolayevna Vishinskaya, firstborn children of Kat and Nikolas, born April 7, 1922
Fyodor Ivanovich Konev (Fedya), Lyuba and Ivan's son, born May 16, 1922
Dr. Ferdinand Alexander Scholl, a radical, nonjudgmental doctor

Matryona Ilyinichna Lebedeva, Nadezhda's cousin, the second of ten sisters, born March 13, 1892
Matryona's housemates
Agrafena Spiridonovna Proshchenikova (Granyechka) (later Likachëva), Boris's once-fiancée, born May 6, 1902
Father Spiridon Proshchenikov, Boris's employer and Granyechka's father
Boris's urologist
Viktoriya Kaarelovna Nikonova
Mrs. Hattie Samson, Katrin's maid
Mrs. Barbara Oswald, Katrin's cook
Mr. Frederick Rhodes, Katrin's butler
Karl (Kaarel) Osipovich Nikonov, Katrin's father, born 1881
Martina Leonidovna Nikonova, Katrin's mother, born 1881
Zakhar Lavrentiyevich Lazhenitsyn (Mr. Lazhenitsyn), Mr. Konev's partner at his liquor store
Officer Harry Baron and two other alcohol-friendly cops
Boris's students in the religious school
Georgiy Valeriyevich Likachëv (Gosha), the man who does end up marrying Granyechka, born 1900
Parents of religious school students
Russian-American mobsters
Mr. Glazov, the Russian-born manager of an iron factory
Daniil Gavriilovich Karmov, the vice-president of the union Aleksey starts at work, born December 5, 1897
Anna Afanasiyevna Koneva (Mrs. Koneva)
Pyotr Stepanovich Litvinov
Georgiya Yuriyevna Savvina
Yaroslava Stepanovna Litvinova, Pyotr's baby sister, born August 1, 1910
Oliivia Asta Kalvik, Katrin's firstborn, born December 16, 1923
Osip Ilyich Lebedev (Osyenka), Mrs. Zhukova and Mr. Lebedev's son, Lyuba's baby halfbrother, born January 9, 1924
Vasilisa Grigoriyevna Golitsyna, Valeriya's secondborn child by her second marriage, born January 9, 1924
Viktoriya L'vovna Yeltsina (Mrs. Yeltsina)
Zinaida Vadimovna Yeltsina (Zina)

Valentina Vadimovna Yeltsina (Valya), born July 20, 1886
Dinara Ilyinichna Sheltsova-Lebedeva
Yaroslav Markovich Sheltsov (Yarik), her husband, born January 2, 1896
Yevgeniya Yaroslavovna Sheltsova, their baby, born October 20, 1923
Sister Serena, a nun at Lyuba's church
Mariya Georgiyevna Likachëva (Manya), Granyechka's firstborn, born February 1924
Lawyers and judge
Serafima Ilyinichna Lebedeva
Yelena Ilyinichna Lebedeva (Lyolya)

Chapter 22: Ellis Island

"Look, it's the green lady!"

Lyuba looks up. Everyone has gathered on deck to try to be the first to glimpse the new land. Tatyana tugs at her mother's sleeve and points.

"So it is," Lyuba says, starting to cry.

It's May 2, 1921. After not quite two months at sea, they've finally glimpsed sight of America. They've survived bad food, ocean sickness, bad sanitation, rampant diseases they tried their best to avoid, bad water, listening to horror stories about the Red Terror over and over again, and most of all heartache for the Motherland. Now here America looms, after so long.

"I don't think I've ever seen anything so beautiful, except for you and Tatyana, of course." Ivan crosses himself. "Now we can go to church again, find a priest to confess to, and have Tatyana baptized."

Lyuba smiles at him with happy tears of joy in her eyes. She remembers all the nights they snuck up on deck to watch the Moon and the stars shining over the water. If nobody else was on deck, they laid on a cushioned lounge chair to kiss and caress one another. For the first time, Lyuba feels truly confident of herself as a woman. She stands up and strains her eyes as Lady Liberty comes into closer view.

"This day should've come four years ago," she muses.

"If it *had* come four years ago, we never would've had Tatyana!"

Lyuba watches ecstatically as land comes closer and closer. Everyone else is praying and gathering their luggage. Vera picks up Kroshka and sets her into the carrying case. Kittey hobbles over to Andryusha and herds him into a much larger carrying case.

"Look at all these tall buildings!" Ginny shouts.

"I'll remember this day forever!" Kat weeps.

"Think of all we went through to get here!" Eliisabet says with happy tears in her eyes.

"This must be the most beautiful city in the world," Nikolas says.

"Look, we could jump off the boat right now and swim just a few feet to shore!" Natalya Lebedeva says.

Natalya Yeltsina squeals in delight as the sun catches on her flaming red hair. Lyuba has grown quite attached to this little girl, and has agreed to care for her until Lena can be found. Natalya has also grown very attached to Lyuba, constantly spending time with her and calling her Lyubochka. Lyuba was a bit taken aback to be called a superdiminutive instead of her forename and patronymic, by someone almost fifteen years her junior no less, but Natalya explained she'd called her three big sisters superdiminutives too. Lyuba's heart had melted at the thought of little Natalya idolizing her as though she's Zina, Lena, or Valya.

The ship stops. At an order, the passengers slowly begin to disembark and get on board a ferry. Lyuba takes Branimir's mecate rein and leads him onto the ferry.

Katrin stiffens when she's handed a numbered tag. "We're not third-class slobs! *We* are second-class travellers!"

"You're going to be examined and questioned just like the third-class passengers." The man gives Katrin a dirty look.

Eliisabet waddles out, by now visibly pregnant. Nikolas helps Kittey hobble off. After the ferry arrives at Ellis Island, they're led into the buildings where they'll be examined and tested. Before Lyuba joins the others, she leads Branimir over to one of the immigration officials and explains, in her perfect English, her horse needs to be boarded at a stable. The officials smile at Branimir and scratch his ears. After Lyuba looks over a list of stables in all five boroughs and Long Island, she selects a stable on Long Island for $20 a month. Having no idea if that's a normal price, she obligingly produces some of her rubles to be converted and accepts the paperwork, to be filled in when she has a permanent address to be billed at every month. She prays Branimir will be in good hands as the officials attach an ID tag to the mecate rein and lead him onto another ferry.

"My aunt said she and my mother held tightly onto their luggage," Lyuba says when she rejoins the others. "I wouldn't leave it in that room if I were you."

"This is the most beautiful day of my life," Alla breathes.

Ginny tries to get out of line, but Lyuba grabs him by the arm. "I was only going to get some American soil," he whines.

"You can get American soil after we're finished in this building!"

"Look." Kittey proudly holds up the miniature teacup. "My Russian soil from Pskov."

"Put it back in your suitcase, or it might spill, and you'd be crushed," Nikolas says.

"We're all here!" Kat is crying in joy.

"Excuse me." Katrin pokes one of the men in charge of escorting the immigrants, a fairly tall man with blonde hair and green eyes matching her own. "I happen to be a very rich woman. I would've travelled first-class, only the man who got our tickets made us travel lousy second-class. We're special and demand to go to the head of the line!"

"I can speak your language, but I detect a foreign accent of some sort."

"Russian is my second language. I'm actually Estonian. So is my best friend and that other woman over there, the pregnant one. I was a very important person back home."

"Even you have to wait your turn in line, Miss."

"Miss Katariina Nikonova. I was named for Yekaterina the Great, and I certainly command as much respect as she did. I go by Katrin. Nobody ever calls me Yekaterina. I'm a whole sight better than some of those other women who just unboarded. Sniveling for their homelands, rags tied over their heads, hair all full of rats' nests, bad taste in clothes, totally illiterate, yet here I am, short hair, fashionable clothing, I've read all the most important minds, and I had my own maid!"

Katrin has chosen to unboard wearing a new outfit she bought in Tartu and hasn't gotten the chance to wear yet, a green velvet blouse, black leather tango shoes, blue silk stockings, and a white silk skirt. The man takes in voluptuous Katrin with her piercing green eyes and vixeny short haircut, and his heart begins to race.

"It just so happens, I also am Estonian, although I never learnt the language and was raised in Tver. I've been here since I was fifteen. I'm twenty-three now. My name's Aleksander Kalvik, but everyone calls me Sandro. Not the most Estonian-sounding name, but believe me, I really am entirely of Estonian blood."

She flashes him a flirtatious smile. "Yes, now that you mention it, you do look like one of my people. I'd be more than happy to teach you our language. That is, if you let my group go up ahead in the line!"

He's already quite taken with brash Katrin, so he lets her group go on ahead. Before Katrin has a chance to slip away, he writes his name, address, and telephone number on a notepad, tears the page out, and hands it to her, smiling a lovestruck grin. Katrin proudly shows off his contact information to the others.

"You just got here, and you've already met an Estonian man who's got a crush on you," Anastasiya smiles. "Way to go Katya!"

"What if one of us gets an X marked on our clothing?" Vera asks. "Like Galya, because she's blind?"

"Blindness isn't contagious, and I was blinded by fire, not disease."

"The American government is racist," Katrin proclaims. "Don't you remember what Petya said? They send back people with a little birthmark on the neck if it looks like it's contagious. I heard they sent an old woman back because one of her fingernails was black, though it wasn't from disease."

"They'll have me to deal with if they want to send back Kittey," Nikolas asserts.

Kat laughs. "You're not tall and strong like Ivan. You're no one to take on big, burly immigration officials. You spent the entire journey reading your precious philosophy books and debating ideas with intellectual passengers."

They're at the head of the line now, but made to stay three hours in a waiting hall. To pass the time, Mr. Lebedev takes out a book of poetry by Lermontov and begins to read aloud.

"You know, Ivan," Lyuba whispers, "Ilya Nikolayevich is a widower, and it could very well turn out my mother's a widow. Ilya Nikolayevich has been very kind to me. He'd be a perfect stepfather."

"If your mother isn't already a widow, I'll make her one," he growls. "If your father *is* here, and he does one thing to harm you or Tatyana, he's an automatic dead man."

"Does anybody have relatives to take them in?" Katrin asks. "I heard they routinely send people back if they don't furnish proof of employment or family waiting for them."

"I have my mother and aunt," Lyuba says. "Ginny, Tatyana,

and I will have a place to stay."

"I'm rich, so I don't need to worry. Stasya and I will rent the best penthouse suite money can afford. With all the money Lyuba and Ivan earned, they could also buy a nice home uptown instead of wasting time downtown with all the other immigrants. I hear all the city's millionaires live on Fifth Avenue."

"My aunt is here," Ivan says. "At least, I hope she made it. My father also may have come over, though there's no way in Hell I want that brute coming anywhere near my family."

"So you see? You have no leg to stand on criticizing me for hating my parents and younger siblings except Vika, and how I turned them in. You hate your own father, and Lyuba hates her father. It's not a crime to hate your relatives if they've done terrible things which go against your morals. Some things are beyond forgiveness."

2

"Time to be checked by customs," Sandro tells them after the three hours are up. "Don't say anything incriminating. Be warned, single women aren't allowed to leave the island without male escorts, and they don't let unmarried couples leave together."

"My mother and aunt came alone, and they were allowed to leave without men," Lyuba says.

"Who knows, maybe they found a gentleman to pretend was their brother, or perhaps it's different for women with husbands somewhere. Remember, it's not a lie if you don't have to prove it and no one gets caught."

"I'll pass myself off as your uncle," Mr. Lebedev reassures her. "I suppose I'll have to pretend to be the uncle of those blonde Estonian women too, and your redheaded friends. Although you and Kat could marry your fiancés here and immediately solve the problem of no related male escort."

"I remember what my mother said." Ginny shudders. "They're going to paw all over me looking for diseases I don't have."

"What if I don't remember all the American history I studied on the ship?" Aleksey asks.

"I heard they pry back eyelids with a buttonhook," Kittey says.

"I don't want to give up my Russian money," Kat says. "It might be worthless there, but it's priceless to me."

"I can't speak English," Vera says.

"I hear they ask about political leaders and our political views," Katrin says. "I don't wish to lie about belonging to the Party and my wish to join the Socialist Party once I'm a citizen."

"Their doctors don't even wash their hands," Ginny says.

They begin to move towards the staircase. Anastasiya is weeping over being treated like a third-class passenger, and already her eyes are red and bloodshot from the tears. Nikolas observes a number of officials looking at them ascending the stairwell.

"What do they need to look at us climbing stairs for?"

"Probably another sly tactic of the government to send back the useless people who travelled third-class," Katrin says. "Look at these people! I bet half the barbarians who travelled third-class are carrying venereal disease, goiter, and other uncivilized illnesses!"

"Get away from me, you dirty, unclean old man!" Anastasiya screams, almost falling down the stairs in her attempt to push an old man away.

"Don't cry, Nastya. It'll make your eyes all red, and that won't look good when they flip up your eyelids."

"Petya said first-class and second-class got interviewed on the ship! I understand second-class passengers might need to be treated a bit more in-depth than the slobs who travelled third-class, but this is obscene!"

Ginny reaches the top of the stairs first and presents his card. Anastasiya gives him a grimace that could freeze raw meat in July.

"I can feel their eyes all over us," she sobs. "They're just waiting for any excuse in the book to send us back."

"They'll think you have glaucoma if you don't stop crying!" Katrin warns her again.

Katrin glares at the man who stamps her card. She feels his eyes on her hair, probably wondering why it's so short, and then on her outfit, wondering why she's wearing such "immodest" clothes.

"I was told second-class passengers are treated almost as well as first-class passengers. *Pozhaluysta*, explain why we have to go through this barbaric, inhumane cattle drive with the dirtballs who came from mud hovels in places nobody's ever heard of."

The man mutters an insult in Russian and stamps the next card.

"Everyone walk slowly. Each group must walk about ten to fifteen feet apart."

"Look at these metal guard rails!" Anastasiya is weeping. "This is how they drive cattle! I feel like an animal!"

"Just think, soon we'll be renting a lovely penthouse suite, with no barbaric scumbags from mud hovels to bother us."

Katrin is ready to spit nails as her card is checked. The first doctor looks at Anastasiya's bloodshot eyes and says something to the doctor he's working with.

"What are you doing?" Lyuba demands in English. "You can't take my little girl away from us!"

"All children over the age of two must walk. You just told me she's twenty-seven months old."

"She's so tiny she'll be crushed!"

"And that child. He must walk too." The man walks behind them and takes Nikolay from Aleksey.

"You see?" Katrin shrills. "I knew we should've gone first-class and fought tooth and nail against Petya's stupid decision!"

"Stop poking me, filthy pervert!" Anastasiya weeps.

"Why are they taking so long?" Vera demands.

The next group up is Kat and the Vishinskies. Kat and Kittey are trundled off to another line.

"Why can't we be with my brother?" Kittey shouts.

"What's in that large package? There are noises coming from it."

"It's my dog Andryusha."

"Do you have a permit to bring an animal into this country?"

"Of course I do. Our friend back home saw to getting one."

Anastasiya sobs as she approaches the eye doctor, who's standing with his back to a window. She's outraged when he begins talking to her.

"Listen, I don't want to be here, so let's just get this over with."

"You don't speak English?"

"I don't care about English right now! I want to go find my penthouse suite and get away from these dirtbag lepers we're being forced to commingle with!"

"Why are you separating the men from the women?" Katrin shouts. "It's not right."

"I don't got no lice!" Ginny shouts in English in the examining rooms for men and boys. "I'm not dirty like the third-class kids!"

"I want my hat back!" Nikolay says.

"Have any of you been promiscuous?" one of the doctors asks.

"You're going to check us for venereal disease!" Ginny starts crying.

"It's a waste of time," Nikolas agrees. "Do that to the third-class men coming up behind us."

Anastasiya screams as the eye doctor flips her eyelids back with a buttonhook. Katrin whimpers when her turn comes. That indignity, however, is soon overtaken when various jigsaw puzzles are set before everyone.

"I'm twenty-one, not five," Katrin huffs. "If you're giving us these puzzles for us to pass our time, you could give us puzzles with a thousand or more pieces."

"They're to test your mental acuity, not for you to play with," a doctor informs her.

Katrin fumes as she begins assembling a puzzle of a human face as several doctors hover over her. Anastasiya can barely see through her bloodshot eyes as she tries to piece together a steamship.

Ivan has torn through the puzzles set before him after being declared as healthy as a horse and as strong as ten men. The final task given in this room is copying a geometric figure. Though the doctors are hovering over the other men in his group, he knows why they're staring the most at him as he begins drawing the diamond.

"Did you injure your hand?" a doctor asks through a translator.

"No, this is the hand God gave me my strength and dexterity in. Unlike other people, I never let anyone shame or bully me out of my natural inclination." He gives the evil eye to the men and boys in the room gaping at him for drawing left-handed. "Yes, believe it or not, we exist. The entire world is not right-handed, as much as you'd like to force everyone to be."

The doctor shuts up, too impressed with Ivan's health and strength to put anything negative in his record.

"Now are we all done?" Ginny asks when the last one in his

group, Aleksey, comes out of the examining rooms. "Those are the women right now."

"These ones are going directly over there." A doctor points to the ones with chalk marks on their shoulders.

"Where are you taking us?" Katrin screams.

"Look, Katrin and Stasya got an X on their clothes!" Ginny starts to giggle.

"This is not funny! This is an outrage! Now everyone will be held up for hours! We're not morons!" Katrin is weeping. "Just because we were very loud and angry about the way the doctors were treating us, they think we're crazy!"

"I got an E on my shoulder too," Anastasiya howls. "Just because of stupid bloodshot eyes I got from crying!"

Eliisabet has a Pg on her shoulder, for pregnancy. She obediently goes into the wire compartment with Galya, who also has an E, on account of being blind. Katrin and Anastasiya follow them.

"Where do we wait till they're done?" Kat asks.

"I have to go too," Kittey says. "They know I had polio."

"They marked me too," Lyuba says. "An F for face."

Ivan wants to jump out of a window when he sees the chalk mark on Lyuba's shoulder.

"They think this scar is malignant. I'll see you soon." Lyuba hands Tatyana to Ivan and smiles at Ginny.

"It's my fault you have that scar! If they send you back, you'd better believe I'm coming with you!"

"Don't start a scene here, my sweet *groznik*." Lyuba turns and joins the others with chalk marks.

3

"They gave us an X!" Katrin is weeping to the head nurse.

"All because we talked too much and were angry!" Anastasiya says.

"Your eyes are bloodshot," one of the nurses says in Russian.

"We're both Estonian. So is the pregnant one. She's got a husband and a sweet little boy who are being held up just because she's pregnant, so you'd better hurry the hell up and decide she's very healthy and isn't going to become a public ward like some of these strange creatures." Anastasiya points at an old woman talking to herself.

They sit and wait their turn at being examined. Anastasiya is brought a glass of ginger ale and a plate of crackers. Three hours later, when her turn is called, her eyes are noticeably improved.

"You see, all she needed was a nice rest and something to drink," Katrin says as the E is dusted off of Anastasiya's shoulder.

"About the X."

"We're both very opinionated women, Nurse, and were shocked at how second-class passengers could be treated so shabbily, as if we were third-class. I'll put my opinions to good use. I'm planning on writing for the Estonian press, if they have a large enough Estonian population. What's so wrong with a woman who gets a bit upset over the way she's been treated? Nastya and I will definitely prove ourselves far from insane."

"Why is your hair so short? Were you ill recently?"

"No, I like having short hair. Modern, empowered women don't wear their hair long. I'm also a big believer in the inherent equality of men and women. I'm very glad America finally gave women the vote."

"How about this woman, the other woman who got an E?"

"I'm blind, Nurse," Galya says. "I lost my vision in a fire when I was twenty-seven. It wasn't the result of any contagious diseases."

***

"What's the holdup?" Ivan demands of an official. "How much longer do we have to wait for my—my *nevesta?*"

"There are waiting rooms downstairs, or you can go on ahead and wait for her in the room behind the final stage of processing."

"Processing is for *myaso*—meat. Not people."

4

Galya comes out, followed by Eliisabet two hours later. Kittey comes out fifteen minutes after Eliisabet. Lyuba doesn't come back for five hours. By now it's almost evening, and nobody's eaten yet.

"Did you tell them it's just a scar, my love?"

"They still think it's a malignant growth, and want to send me back."

The others begin walking to the final stage of processing, carrying their luggage. Ginny looks at the other three, then catches up to the others. Ivan runs back into the room Lyuba was just in and grabs the head doctor by his throat.

"There has been mistake. This woman is very healthy. Her only problem is that scar. If you send her back, you must send me and our daughter back too."

"Mr. Konev, you're as strong as ten men. There's no way anyone here would dream of sending you back. You're worth ten native-born American workers. We could find nothing wrong with you."

"I can think of something that can send me back."

"We found not a blemish on you. You're staying."

"He's right, Doctor," Lyuba says. "I cannot go back unless he goes with me. Besides, think of our little girl. She needs her mother. You have to deport them with me. My cousin can stay in America. His mother will find him. She lives in the city."

"Look." Ivan picks up the doctor's pen and a piece of paper and begins to write, in rapid old-style Cyrillic cursive, a passage from the Bible that springs to mind. "I am a *levsha*. Many people do not like that trait. Think I am possessed by *Chyort*—Devil. And my English, very bad."

"Miss Zhukova, come back into the room. Mr. Konev, you and the little girl can go on ahead. We'll see what happens."

"I made promise to Lyuba, that I never leave her."

"If we decide to deport her, you, the little girl, and your fiancée's cousin can come say goodbye to her at the dock. Right now she'll be interrogated again by more doctors."

"It is scar. Not disease."

"Go along, Mr. Konev. It'll be awhile. If you want, we have rooms where you can wait overnight."

Ivan picks up his luggage and cradles Tatyana in the crook of his right arm. He walks dejectedly to the main floor area of the Registry Room and hands over his card to be checked, then waits in line behind Aleksey to be interviewed.

"Didn't Lyuba come?"

"No. She'll be checked one last time and then probably sent back. Ginny, get over here."

"I'm old enough to be interviewed myself," Ginny declares.

"No you're not. You have to be at least eighteen. Until we find your mother, I'm your legal guardian."

5

They wait in line for three more hours. By now it's dark, and everyone is starving but Nikolay and Tatyana. Until they're admitted to the mainland, Ivan and Aleksey are still the leaders of the Stray Dogs, and they decided the littlest ones would be the only ones allowed to eat. They took enough fresh food from their last meal on the ship to tide the children over for a little while. Everyone else can suck it up and go hungry for a little while, though right now Ivan's stomach is growling and making him regret this decision.

"Can you give me some of that cucumber, *knyazhna*?" Ivan begs.

"I want some too," Ginny moans in agony.

"We'll be out of here soon. You think I got good food when I was in prison?"

"Next?"

Ivan goes up to the available desk. "Hello."

"Can you speak English?"

"Not very well."

The interviewer gets the Russian interpreter and begins the interview. Ginny stands around whining, trying to annoy the officials with his rumbling stomach.

"What is your full name?"

"Ivan Ivanovich Konev."

"Your age?"

"Twenty-two. I'll be twenty-three in July."

"What is your marital status?"

"I'm engaged, but unfortunately my fiancée can't be here, since they want to deport her on account of a scar on her face!"

"What relation are the boy and the girl to you, Mr. Konev?"

"The boy is fourteen. He's my fiancée's cousin. The little girl is my fiancée's child, and as soon as we're married, I'm going to legally adopt her. We don't want the disgusting excuse for life who fathered her to have anything to do with her. He snuck into Russia twice illegally after his legal immigration to this country, and that included sneaking back out illegally! Thanks to that *svoloch*, the love of my life was left with a very slim chance of ever giving me a son to carry on my family name! That man is not going to come anywhere near my little girl or her mother! I'll spend the rest of my life in court just to put it on paper that the girl is mine!"

"That can all be taken care of once you're a citizen. What is your occupation?"

"I'm a laborer," he lies, not wanting to admit he's never worked.

"Can you read or write?"

"Of course."

"What is your nationality?"

"I'm Russian. More specifically, I'm a Muscovite."

"So your last residence was Moskva?"

"The last place where I lived in my own house, yes. The last place I stayed before I boarded the ship was Tallinn, Estonia."

"Where is your final destination?"

"Manhattan."

"Do you have a ticket to take the ferry into the mainland?"

"Not yet."

"Who paid your passage to America?"

"A very good friend of ours, Pyotr Stepanovich Litvinov."

"Do you have any money?"

"Yes."

"Is it more than thirty U.S. dollars?"

"Almost three hundred million rubles."

The interviewer turns grey. "That's a lot more than we can change currencies for, Mr. Konev. Are you going to live with relatives here?"

"My father and *Tyotya* Valeriya may be here, but I don't know where either lives."

"Have you ever been in this country before?"

"No, never."

"Have you ever been in an almshouse or supported by charity?"

"No." He hopes it's not a sin to tell white lies like this, though he never considered himself a charity case in the traditional sense.

"Have you ever been in prison?"

"I was a political prisoner," he lies, not wanting to tell the real story and give these people any reason to detain him overnight or deport him. "I escaped to save myself from a planned execution."

"Are you a polygamist?"

"I've only loved one woman ever, my fiancée."

"Are you under a contract to work in the U.S.?"

"No."

"What is your condition of health?"

"The doctors told me I'm as strong as ten men. They couldn't find a single thing wrong with me."

The man stamps "Admitted" onto their three cards. "Next?"

"Now we can wait for Lyuba!" Ginny says. "I'll carry Tatyana."

"You'd better not drop her."

"Of course not! I sort of like her now."

Their whole group walks back downstairs. Ivan sits on a bench and waits for Lyuba.

"Don't you know how lucky you are, Konev?" Aleksey asks. "Look at all the things we can do here! We can buy tickets for a ferry or a train, and they've got immigrant aid societies to help us. Liza just went to see someone about finding a midwife. You can look up your aunt, Ginny can find his mother, and we can all go to a boardinghouse."

"It's too dark to go anywhere. We'll get robbed. We're staying the night no matter what."

"I just send a telegram to my mother!" Ginny says. "You can telegram your aunt once you find where she's staying."

6

Their group spends two hours getting their currency changed. Ivan doesn't get all his money changed because there's so much of it, and is told to get the rest changed and immediately put into the bank once he enters the mainland. Katrin hasn't gotten all her money changed either.

"You have far in excess of one million dollars, Miss Nikonova! We can't change all that into American money without risking robbery! Particularly since you're an immigrant, and a woman who'll be living alone with the lady biting her nails."

Anastasiya has switched from crying to her old bad habit of biting her nails since she's gotten discharged by the doctors. She's biting them harder and more desperately than ever before, because she's afraid of spending the night here, on Ellis Island, surrounded by strangers.

"Have you any idea how I can find my aunt?" Ivan asks one of the ladies from a Russian immigrant aid society.

"We can look in the phonebook. What's her name?"

"Valeriya Afanasiyevna Koneva."

She looks through the phonebook. "No Valeriya Koneva listed. Perhaps she's listed with her husband or changed her name?"

"Her husband's been dead since September 1914. She was never the type to hide under a husband's identity, even to give the impression she wasn't living alone. I also can't imagine her Americanizing her name."

"Maybe she remarried. Would you know anything about her new husband?"

"I don't think she could ever remarry after how brutally her husband was murdered. Maybe she's living at a boardinghouse until she gets established. I can't imagine she went back to her birth name, Akimova. Holy Mother of God, I hope she safely arrived and wasn't murdered on her way out of Russia, or didn't meet bad news in another country along the way."

"Come on, Konev, it's time for us to eat!" Ginny yowls. "Mr. Lebedev just asked the way to the dining hall."

Ivan goes into the dining hall with the others, still furious over how Lyuba is being detained. He wants to collapse of heartache when Tatyana doesn't appear anywhere.

"Don't stall, or your luggage might get snatched," Ginny says.

"There she is. I didn't see her." Ivan runs over and grabs her up. "You must never walk away from us. There are bad people in this building. We don't know if Boris might be here too!"

There are barely any other people at the table, since it's so late. Ginny slurps his beef stew greedily and gobbles his bread and vegetables. The Lebedevas and Natalya Yeltsina eat almost as quickly as Ginny and then start on the tapioca pudding. Leontiy and Anya are more interested in the milk and pudding than anything else.

"I don't think we've had dairy since we had to butcher our cows!" Anya exclaims.

"Why did we have to kill the cows?" Leontiy asks.

"We didn't want Kerenskiy's thugs or deserting soldiers to get their grimy hands on our cows. That was the last real meat meal we had for a long time." Anya crosses herself. "I can't imagine what kind of horrible rations our dear parents and grandparents are getting, if they're still alive. Perhaps someday they'll join us."

"I hear they have priests here." Kat links her arm through Nikolas's. "They've nicknamed this place the Kissing Post because there are so many weddings."

"As romantic as that seems, don't you want a church wedding more? You don't have a wedding dress, and we don't have our own crowns."

"Why not? We can tell our grandkids and great-grandkids how we were married on Ellis Island our first full day in America, and they'll love and cherish the story for years to come. All our friends are here, and darling Kittey can almost walk on her own. We'll wear our best clothes, and get married tomorrow after breakfast. Besides, you heard Katrin's new friend. Single women can't leave here alone."

Nikolas grimaces as he swallows the last spoonful of tapioca. "Fine. You win. And it's only right to get married as soon as we can, after three and a half years. I've never known anyone else who had such a ridiculously long engagement."

"Ivan and Lyuba can have Tatyana baptized too! We'll have *two* things to celebrate tomorrow!"

"What if Lyuba isn't allowed to enter the mainland?" Ivan asks.

"We'll fight tooth and nail for her," Ginny says. "I don't like you when you're apart from my cousin. You and Lyuba can be married too, and it'll be a double wedding ceremony."

"I want to give her a big fancy church wedding. She's had such a hard life, with so many disappointments and traumas. I want to make her the happiest woman in the world by giving her an expensive wedding, to show her how much I love her."

"You have enough money." Katrin begins gobbling a large slice of cake. "You can easily afford that expensive wedding."

"First I have to find an apartment, get furniture, secure a job, get my diploma, and most importantly settle down in America. It should be in a church we're established members of, not one we just picked out of the phonebook. I want our wedding to be the happiest day of Lyuba's life, and I want to buy her an expensive wedding band with diamonds and an engraving. Our hearts are married already. We live together like husband and wife, only we're not lovers. I don't see why she'd object to waiting just a little bit more."

"At least get Tatyana baptized," Eliisabet says. "Alyoshka and I are having Kolya baptized."

"That's different. Tatyana can't be baptized, and I don't want to deceive a priest. She was born out of wedlock, and even if Lyuba and I married tomorrow, I'm not her natural father. The Church doesn't recognize her as legitimate. Only after I marry Lyuba and adopt Tatyana will she be considered legitimate."

7

At 11:00, they pick up their luggage and make their way toward the sleeping quarters. Vera places Kroshka beside her on the pillow. Anastasiya and Katrin find themselves below a Pole. Anya is horrified the family above her and Leontiy are Germans.

"Not to worry," Katrin says. "First thing tomorrow, we grab breakfast and get our tickets for the ferry to the mainland. This sick, twisted nightmare of being treated like third-class scum will be behind us forever."

They all sleep very lightly that night. They haven't had such bad sleep since they were hiding from the Reds, constantly afraid of what might happen. The Germans have set an alarm clock to go off at five in the morning, which annoys Katrin and Anastasiya to no end. Most of the new immigrants start drifting out about two hours later, which means it isn't a good idea to try to get more sleep.

"Come on. We'll eat our breakfast and then find a priest." Kat grabs her luggage and heads to the dressing rooms.

In fifteen minutes, they're gathered around the table again, having breakfast. Ginny picks at his porridge and moans for solid food.

"You'd better get used to this food," Ivan warns. "Unless you'd like to live with Katrin and Anastasiya in their fantasy penthouse suite?"

"That sounds like quite a marvellous idea."

"You belong with me, Lyuba, and Tatyana till we find your mother. You tried to stay with Katrin and Anastasiya several times before, and each time they promptly threw you out or made you stay in the garage. They don't want you."

"Ginny's now fourteen," Katrin says. "He was a ten-year-old brat when I met him. Now he's a fine young man with morals and convictions, and is very mature. Ginny, if you come with me and Nastya, you can sleep in a feather bed with silk sheets and pillows;

have tea, cookies, cakes, and pies from the most expensive bakery in Manhattan; go to a fancy private school; and take summer holidays to Long Island. But you must earn your keep. It would be a great help if you edited my articles for the finest Estonian immigrants' newspapers and magazines. Maybe I can teach you my native language."

"It's a deal!"

"No, Ginny, you're going to live with me," Ivan says. "You must stay with your family. Get Tatyana and bring her to me. She needs to be boosted up on a chair. Get a book for her to sit on."

"Tatyana didn't come to the dining hall. She's still asleep."

Ivan goes back into the sleeping quarters. His heart pounds when he realizes Tatyana isn't there. Shaking, he comes back out and grabs Ginny by his ear. Ginny groans.

"Where did your cousin go?"

"How should I know? Maybe Boris came during the night to greet us and was directed to his daughter."

"You'd better pray that's the worst that's happened to my daughter!"

Ivan storms off to search all the rooms, and doesn't find her anywhere. Then he goes outside to the docks and sees her in the arms of her mother. He runs over, grateful Boris isn't the reason for the disappearance, pulls Lyuba into his arms, and begins to cry.

"Are you waiting for the boat home? I'll smuggle myself and Tatyana aboard so we'll never be apart, and we'll start our family in a remote Siberian village where the Cheka can never find me."

"You don't need to cry, Vanya. The doctors and the board of immigrant appeals finally found in my favor and decided to let me be admitted to America. We're going to find an apartment and be married, and when we have enough money, we'll resettle in the Midwest, just like you always told me."

He looks closely at her. "What happened to the scar?"

"The doctor who looked at me last decided to be nice and perform a little operation. He put a numbing agent on my face and cut off the scar tissue, then stitched the skin closed. I can take the bandage off and pull the stitches out in about a week, and use aloe vera and honey to help the surgical scar fade away. Now we really *are* starting over. You don't need to have your heart break whenever you see the scar."

"I promise you yet again I'll never ever raise my hands against you. I didn't locate my aunt, so we'll take Ginny and our little girl to a boardinghouse. We'll have such a happy life from now on, and your disgusting father or Boris can't ever ruin that for us."

He takes Tatyana in the crook of his right arm and takes Lyuba on his left arm. They go back into the downstairs rooms and find the others.

"Is she being deported now?" Ginny asks.

"They're letting her enter. As soon as we finish with the wedding and baptism, we can get on the ferry going to the mainland."

"Who's getting married?" Lyuba asks. "Did you find a priest to marry us?"

"Kat and Kolya. They're already starting to move to the room for marriage ceremonies." Ivan kisses her on the forehead and leads her over.

"They have a proper priest here to marry them?"

Ginny nods. "Nikolay will also be getting baptized."

Lyuba watches with tears in her eyes as the priest marries Kat and Nikolas. Kat is wearing a purple silk gown and holding a nosegay of flowers she bought from one of the vendors. Nikolas is wearing the only suit in his possession. Kittey, the maid of honor, is wearing a pink velvet dress and holding a second nosegay. Aleksey, the best man, wears a cornflower-blue button down shirt and tweed trousers. The wedding crowns are borrowed, not theirs to keep, but that's a minor concern after all they've been through. For the first time since the Revolution, everyone takes Communion.

"Not all of us have made confession since our last time taking Communion," Kittey says.

"God will understand you were unable to do your duties to the Church because of very evil men who want to destroy religion and morals," the priest says.

"I forget how to make the sign of the cross," Fyodora confesses.

"Forehead, collarbone, right shoulder, left shoulder," Mr. Lebedev reminds his youngest child. "And put your first three fingers into a point."

The wedding proceeds. Kat and Nikolas exchange the rings provided by the priest, and they're pronounced husband and wife.

"Are you going to change your name here, or take care of it later?"

"No, *Batyushka*, we're both staying with the surnames we got at birth." Kat puts her arm around her new husband. "I can't believe I'm a married woman!"

"Now it's Kolya's turn!" Eliisabet says. "We want you to baptize our son. I must be honest, he was born out of wedlock, but we married when he was five months old and made him legitimate."

After the priest baptizes Nikolay, Lyuba looks at Ivan.

"Why don't we let the priest marry us too? Nothing would make us happier than to leave this horrible building finally married."

"Of course, but I want to give you an expensive wedding ceremony that'll be the happiest day of your life."

"Marrying you anywhere would be the happiest day of my life, Vanya!"

"You'll be even happier if the banquet boasts lots of wine, champagne, caviar, meat, and fish, and the most expensive wedding gown made by the priciest seamstress we can find."

"Yes?" the priest asks. "Can I be of service to you too?"

"Yes, *Batyushka*, I'm dying to be made a respectable woman by the only man I'll ever love. I want to leave this building as a respectable woman. I want to be Mrs. Koneva."

Ivan shakes his head. "I'm sorry if my fiancée is upset, but I really want to make her happy with a fancy wedding that'll be the happiest day of her life."

"And I told you, marrying you right here and now *will* be the happiest day of my life! Make me Mrs. Koneva. I can't bear to go on much longer having society throw mud on me."

"Whatever mud they throw at you, they can throw at me too. No wedding, *Batyushka*. Don't think I'm making an excuse. I never break a promise. Lyuba will have a fancy wedding, no matter how long it takes."

The priest moves on.

****

Chapter 23: American Reality

It's now midday on the third of May. They've left Ellis Island and are walking up the steps to the boardinghouse they've been referred to in the Lower East Side. It's a five-story brick building on Rivington Street, with several broken windows, not the well-cultivated boardinghouses they've grown accustomed to. Outside the building, several prams are parked unattended, presumably to allow the babies to get fresh air and sunlight. A number of dirty-faced children are playing and running in the streets and all along the sidewalk, while several peddlers stroll by, hawking delicious-smelling, foreign-looking food, rags, spices, and costume jewelry. The language many of these street urchins and peddlers are speaking sounds vaguely like German. This isn't exactly the majority Russian neighborhood Lyuba envisioned starting American life in.

Katrin opens the rotting door and bursts into tears as they filter into the lobby and peer into the empty rooms with open doors. The wooden floors are caked with dirt, soot covers the lobby walls, there are barely any windows, there isn't much room to unpack anything, and there's an old-fashioned wood-burning stove in the background. The air is also full of thick cigarette smoke.

"I'm going to be poring over the papers with Stasya. If we don't find a suitable penthouse suite by nightfall, we'll look again tomorrow."

"How many people to a room here?" Ginny asks.

"This apartment is awfully dirty," Fyodora moans.

A stout, short woman with disheveled hair, flour sack clothes covered in patches, mismatched wooden clogs, and a sooty face approaches them. "How many people?" she asks in the strange quasi-German language.

"Do you speak Russian, French, or English?" Ginny asks in German. "I'm bilingual in German and Russian, but your language doesn't sound like any German I ever heard."

The woman sighs. "Every so often I do get Gentile boarders. I was forced to learn Russian as a girl, and I suppose I could use it again if I absolutely have to. By the way, don't insult any of my boarders who try to talk to you by calling their language German. It's called Yiddish."

"We've got twenty-four people and two dogs," Nikolas says, relieved she speaks Russian. "That fellow back there with spectacles isn't really with us, but we know him from childhood. It's our duty to let him tag along until he finds permanent lodgings."

"We can put five in each room. I have no problems with pets, as long as the two dogs don't bother the other animals my boarders have. We have a communal dining room, and you eat what you're served. There's also the option of buying your own food and using the communal cookware and stove on each floor. Out of respect for my few religious boarders, please don't bring in any unkosher meat or fish, and don't cook dairy products with meat. If you don't know what is or isn't kosher, just ask."

"My friend and I want the real estate sections of every newspaper in the city," Katrin says.

"But neither of you speak much English," Eliisabet says.

"I'll translate for them just to get them away from us as soon as possible," Lyuba volunteers. "Anastasiya still has designs on Ivan."

"I want lunch first," Ginny says.

"First we have to pick out rooms. Aren't you thankful we're finally safe in America? You sent a telegram to your mother, so she'll find us and take us in."

"Only if she's got her own house and no longer lives with your mother," Ivan says. "It would be even more catastrophic if your father were alive and living with them. I don't want you to be mistreated anymore, and Ginny doesn't deserve that sort of influence. We'll find my aunt and live with her."

Lyuba takes Natalya Yeltsina into the first empty room, which is equipped with two small beds, a nightstand, a small table, a worn dresser with three drawers and barely attached handles, and a filthy broom. Mr. Lebedev and his five daughters take the room next door, which boasts two bunkbeds. To the other side of Lyuba's room, Nikolas, Kat, Kittey, Alya, and Anya Furtseva take up residence. Across the way, Anya and Leontiy go with Eliisabet, Aleksey, and Nikolay. Katrin and Anastasiya are forced to room on the uppermost floor, since all the other rooms are taken. Maksim also takes a room on the fifth floor, muttering about what an indignity it is to have to climb all those rickety stairs.

"Kat and Kolya can't have a typical wedding night now," Lyuba says. "There's no privacy, and this isn't their own home or a nice honeymoon hotel."

"Why don't we take a walk, get to know our new neighborhood? We might find something to buy. Now we can begin to rebuild what the Bolsheviks stole from us." Ivan opens his valise. "We're finally going to display these things, after so long of them gathering dust. Now no one can arrest us!"

Lyuba gazes lovingly at the coins and stamps depicting the Tsar and his family. Then there are the ikon of St. Vladimir and all the other ikons.

"Saint Vladimir is our special saint," Ivan whispers. "My mother and I were praying to him as the Bolsheviks broke the door down and dragged her off. I grabbed the ikon before I ran to the sub-cellar."

"Light a candle by your painting of the Tsar. In July, we can attend a memorial service in honor of him and his family. It'll be three years since they were murdered."

Lyuba and Ivan go outside, leaving Ginny in charge of Natalya and Tatyana. From the looks of many of the stores, restaurants, and houses of worship they're passing, they quickly realize this is a majority Jewish neighborhood, with many Italians, Irish, and Poles as well. However, there are still more than a few markers of a Russian presence. On many streets are reminders of the world that was destroyed. Bakeries. Bookstores. Newsstands. Churches. Grocery stores. Food stands. Schools.

Ivan crosses himself. "Look, another church. We'll have to go into one sooner or later. I still haven't confessed to a priest about what I did to you last year."

"I need to confess too, about how I was a prostitute, just for a lot of money. It almost cost me your love."

Ivan turns around after feeling a tap on his shoulder. "Pasha!"

"Is that really Pavlik?" Lyuba asks excitedly.

"Pasha, when did you get here?"

"And where's Nadya?"

Pavel's eyes take on a sad look. "I got away on the raft, found a sympathetic ship to take me on, and was okayed by the examining committee at Ellis Island yesterday. Nadya was too late. Misha and Kostya found her. Aleksandr may have saved you by pointing them in the wrong direction, but that path led right up to me and Nadya instead! I quickly got onto the raft and pushed off, but Nadya didn't make it. Misha was furious at how she'd run away. He waded into the gulf and grabbed her while she was still in shallow water."

Nadezhda languished in Lubyanka for two horrific weeks after she was dragged back to Moskva by Misha. Now she's on her way to Siberia in a Stolypin car, crying herself sick every waking moment, cursing Misha for turning her in, all because he was angry she left his brothel. She's too broken in the proud spirit she once bragged about freely to think of escape plans just yet. But she knows one cannot kill a swan.

"Do you have a place to stay yet?"

"I'm currently renting an apartment with Nadya's money. I got away with her money too. Now it can never be seized by Misha."

Misha went to Mr. Lebedev's house and found it deserted and striped bare of everything. Fuming, he discovered Mr. Lebedev already left the country. Everyone he wanted to turn in has gone. He's also threatened to denounce anyone who complains his favorite prostitute has stopped working at the Godunov brothel. The customers are keeping their mouths shut. In addition, he's been approached by Mr. Litvinov and told several of his prime suspects who might've known the whereabouts of Ivan have also vanished. Mr. Litvinov came back into Moskva to the news his sons let Mr. Andropov and Mr. Golitsyn escape because they really didn't seem to have any clues. "Don't you know Golitsyn is a noble name?" he demanded. "That man was from a princely family, or, worse yet, a prince himself! Nobles and royals are enemies of the people, boys, and you let one escape! You bring shame to the Revolution!" Worse yet, Mr. Litvinov found out Mr. Golitsyn left Russia on a ship bound for America. Perfect.

"We were just going to go into this church to confess to a priest," Lyuba says. "You must come too, and pray to God and your patron saint Nadya's safe wherever she is. She'll come to you sooner than you know it!"

Nadezhda has been sentenced to ten years in Siberia. Her crime is leaving her place of work without any notice she was quitting her job. Misha claimed to the Cheka to be her employer, and that he'd marked her down as a negligent worker who never came to work for the longest time. He claimed she was the third-most important person in the business after himself and Kostya, and that the level of productivity and customer satisfaction had dropped dramatically since Nadezhda's sudden disappearance without any notification. The Cheka bought it, hook, line, and sinker. Nadezhda is already losing weight from crying so much and eating so little. She sleeps very little in the Stolypin car, but her swan bag from her murdered aunt is always her pillow.

Lyuba and Pavel kneel by the candles inside the church. Pavel lights some for his parents, Nadezhda's aunt and parents, Platosha, Genna, and his eleven siblings.

"I would light forty-nine to honor everyone in my family, but I don't want to use up all the candles."

A priest who looks to be about thirty-five comes up to them. "Welcome to the Church of the Lifegiving Font. I'm Father Yakim. *Pozhaluysta*, excuse the pews. This used to be a Catholic church, but everything that happens here is fully Orthodox. Are you just passing through, or would you like information on Divine Liturgy times?"

"We all need to make confession," Lyuba says. "My fiancé wants to go first, since his sin is the most serious."

"No matter what you've done, it can't be beyond the pale of absolution. Follow me to the chapel, and you can start unburdening your heavy soul."

Ivan follows Father Yakim down the hall. Once inside the modestly-sized chapel, he crosses himself and kneels before the *analogion* by the ikonostasis. Father Yakim takes the blessing cross and Gospel from the *analogion* and extends them to Ivan for veneration. Ivan then puts the first three fingers of his left hand on the foot of Jesus in a large golden ikon of the Crucifixion.

"I entreat you, manservant of God, to make a full confession and hold nothing back."

"Forgive me, *Batyushka*, for I have committed the greatest sin of my life since my last confession thirteen months ago. I gave in to my dark side and almost killed the woman I love more than my own life. This sin was brought on by the fact that I'd been drinking for about a month and a half. I haven't touched alcohol since. I also lied to a woman so my true love might be jealous and come back to me. I'd used this other woman once before, pretending I had a relationship with her. I have a very bad temper, but I never ever struck, much less beat, any woman before this happened! It only happened once. She forgave me the next week when she saw how contrite and deeply sorry I was, but I want God to forgive me too."

***

Lyuba starts to pick up the lighting stick, then stops. "Vanya should light the candles for his own deceased relatives."

Pavel crosses himself. "My entire family is dead. I'm the only one left. As soon as Nadya gets out of Siberia, my family can begin again." His eyes grow bright. "I can't wait till we have a little Teglyov-Lebedev or Teglyova-Lebedeva."

"Vanya wants so much for our first child to be a boy, so he can pass on the Konev name. I want more than anything to make him happy and give him that firstborn son. He adores Tatyana like his own daughter, but I want to give him the joy of seeing me carrying his blood child and giving birth to that little boy he wants so badly. He doesn't care what the rest are. He so wants us have a big family. I never wanted even one child till I had Tanya, but since the man I love wants lots of children, I want them too."

***

"I've also been keeping a secret from my fiancée," Ivan continues in a whisper. "My fiancée has a child from a previous relationship, but it wasn't love at all. It was a tragic mistake. This disgusting excuse for life beat her during her entire pregnancy. The love of my life repeatedly refused my offers to take her away from the baby's undeserving father. She almost miscarried at least five times. A few days after the birth, a midwife examined her and told me there was serious internal damage that would make conceiving another baby, much less carrying it to term and delivering it alive, nothing short of a miracle. I've filled her head full of ideas that we're going to have a big family."

"That doesn't sound like a sin. You've done this out of love. If she doesn't know, she won't be burdened by the knowledge."

"Yes, that's what the midwife told me. She said my Lyubochka probably could conceive at least one more child if she doesn't know she's practically unable to do so."

***

"I was the oldest of twelve," Pavel says. "Five boys, seven girls. I can still see Yakov's foot and Dorofeya's arm. I was spared from that mass grave for the same reason Nadya managed to crawl naked through the woods to escape being eaten alive by dogs. God has a purpose for our lives, and I won't take my second chance at life for granted. I'm going to a garment factory tomorrow to inquire. I really want to be in business, like Misha and Kostya. They took me in and made sure I had everything. Their field of business wasn't exactly ethical, but mine will be. I hope poor little Sasha realizes his providers are snakes."

"Sasha still has a heart. He saved me and Vanya. He's a good boy."

"Hope springs eternal."

Ivan comes back with Father Yakim, a look of peace on his face. "I wasn't as bad as I thought I was, my love. He pronounced absolution."

"Now you can light candles for your relatives," Pavel says. "Lyuba was about to do it, but she realized you should light."

Ivan lights three candles. "For *Dyadya* Igor, my cousin Liza, and my mother. *Dyadya* Igor and Liza got proper burials, but my mother was denied that dignity."

"We can name our next daughter after your mother," Lyuba says.

"That really is a nice gesture, but nobody can replace my mother, ever. I also don't want a child to have the next-most common female name in history. Bad enough I have the most common male name ever, in every culture."

Lyuba follows Father Yakim to the chapel, kneels before the *analogion*, and crosses herself. It's been four years and two months since her last confession, so Father Yakim has to gently prompt her through everything. His voice remains very kindly, and his face shows only friendliness and compassion instead of annoyance and judgment.

"Forgive me, *Batyushka*, for all the many sins I've committed. Last year, from early July until late August, I worked as a prostitute, broke the heart of the man I love, and deprived my little girl of her mother. I had brief bed rest for a little over a week, then went to Podolsk to work as a camp prostitute. That only lasted four days, until I ran into my uncle and saved him from the grave sin of adultery. I had my little girl with me those four awful days. I also killed a man to protect the man I love from being killed himself. I haven't treated myself with respect for much of my life."

The others are filtering into the church. Kittey ties Andryusha's leash to the wrought-iron stoop handrail and runs inside, the first time she's moved so quickly since being stricken by polio. She runs back out, grabs Nikolas by his arm, and drags him in, Kat close behind them.

"I lit candles for your brother, wife, and sister-in-law, and for Genna and Platosha," Pavel tells Mr. Lebedev. "You remember me, don't you? We met very briefly in Tallinn. I'm Nadya's sweetheart, Pavel Lavrentiyevich Teglyov. She wasn't as lucky as I was, but God willing, she'll soon come to join me and we'll live happily ever after."

Nikolas and Kittey light candles for their parents. Ginny comes up with Tatyana tagging behind.

"Is this church to your liking?" Ginny asks Ivan. "My cousin's dying to become a respectable woman. This may not be an expensive cathedral, but it *is* a church. My parents taught me the size of the church doesn't matter if people aren't worshipping with happy hearts."

"Our second child will be baptized here!" Aleksey gushes to his wife. "Unless, of course, you want to join an Estonian church."

"It's the same religion, only in slightly different forms. Whether we worship in an Estonian or Russian church doesn't matter, as long as we're sincere. Besides, I doubt there are that many Estonian Orthodox churches here. My family was somewhat unusual for following Orthodoxy instead of Lutheranism."

By the time they arrive back at the boardinghouse, they've decided Lifegiving Font will indeed be their church. Ginny has also confessed to Father Yakim about every last rotten thing he's done. He was crying when he finished unburdening his heavy soul.

"Pasha's safe in America, and it's only a matter of time till we find your aunt and my uncle," Lyuba says over lunch. "Nadya will be here too before we know it, not a moment too soon. America is starting to close its doors. We came just in the nick of time."

Nadezhda counts herself damn lucky she was seized by Misha and thrown into prison in mid-March. Now, even though it's May, she still has her coat, fairly warm clothes, boots, and heavy brown wool stockings. She won't freeze to death in Siberia.

2

Katrin and Anastasiya are still poring over the newspapers the next day. Katrin used the phone in the lobby to call her new admirer, Sandro Kalvik, for help with translation, and he arrived less than twenty minutes later. Ever since his arrival, he's been gazing at

Katrin with moony eyes, and can't stop smiling at her.

"Many of our fellow Russians work in garment factories," Lyuba tells Ivan at lunch. "You can sew rather well, though you'd never admit it to most people. You sooner brag about how well you can cook than knowing how to sew."

"I have to go back to school before I start to work."

"Will a factory job only be temporary after you get an equivalency diploma?"

"Of course. I'll only work in a factory until we have enough money to move to the Midwest. By that time, we'll have three or four children, I hope." Ivan kicks himself for telling her such lies.

"You don't want to go to university and become a doctor, an engineer, or a businessman? We've got more than enough money for it."

"That landfall of money is for necessities, not things which aren't completely necessary. As soon as possible, I'll get the rest of it changed and put into a bank so we won't get robbed blind."

"Maybe I could work as an English teacher or in a garment factory."

"All the other men would want you for their own, and there are always sick excuses for life like Basil and your father. You're going to be safe at home, taking care of our children. Besides, I never wanted to be a doctor or engineer."

"You could be a cook in a fancy mansion. My mother works as a maid in a mansion."

"Don't you want to take care of me after I get home from a tiresome day at the factory, make me supper, and pamper me?"

"Sounds like you want a substitute for your mother, not a wife," Katrin giggles from behind the real estate section.

"Vanya's just old-fashioned, and very protective of me. It's not as if he wants to keep me under lock and key. It makes sense for me to stay home if we're going to have a new baby after we're married. I hope our little boy looks just like his father. Maybe he'll even be a *levsha* like his father."

Ivan smiles at her. "If Liza and Alyosha have a girl, and we have our son soon enough after they have their daughter, maybe they can get married, just like Tanyechka and Kolya might become sweethearts."

Eliisabet remembers all too well Ivan's mad rage at Boris the night he turned into Ivan Grozniy Dva, and how he told Boris that thanks to him, Lyuba is practically unable to conceive or give birth to a second child. And here he is, filling Lyuba's head with fantasies of being able to have at least four more children. But she also knows how much Ivan wants Lyuba to give him a child who's flesh of his flesh and blood of his blood, and that he desperately wants a son to carry on the Konev name, so she stays quiet.

3

After lunch, Lyuba and Ivan take Tatyana and Ginny and walk to the nearest school listed in the phonebook. Ginny whines and drags his feet. Coming along behind them are Anya with Leontiy, Kat and Nikolas with Kittey, and Mr. Lebedev with Fyodora and both Natalyas. Sixteen-year-old Vera would rather earn an equivalency diploma through continuing education classes, instead of suffering through the humiliation of being the oldest student in class.

"I'm old enough to work," Ginny complains. "I can get work at any factory. No one slagged Vera for choosing not to come."

"It's too late," Lyuba says. "Ilya Nikolayevich already called the school and told office administration six prospective new students will be enrolled. There's a lot of difference between thirteen and sixteen. Vera got a half-hearted education in the orphanage system, so her education wasn't completely interrupted."

"*Blyakha-mukha.*"

"Watch your language."

The school is a seventeen-block walk from the boardinghouse. The building which presents itself is a large, imposing brick structure ringed by a tall wrought-iron fence, with numerous fire escapes spiraling all along the walls. Lyuba and Kat grimace when they see separate doors for boys and girls, along with a third door for teachers. Ginny opens the blue door for teachers and lets everyone inside, then drags behind them all the way to the principal's office.

"Can any of these children speak English?"

"Only Ginny. He also knows German." Lyuba drags her cousin in by the arm.

"Is this your brother?"

"He's my cousin. He would've been going into the ninth grade this autumn if his education hadn't been interrupted."

"Are you Ginny's guardian? I can't say I've ever heard of a boy with that name before."

"His real name is Mikhail Grigoriy Mikhaylovich Kharzin. His baby nickname was Genie, but he couldn't pronounce it when he started to talk, and the name stuck. I've been his guardian since April 1917, but his mother is here in New York. We'll find her after we get more settled down."

"How about the other boy?"

"Leontiy never started school," Anya says. "I'm eighteen, and he's nine. We're brother and sister. We were half-heartedly educated by orphanages for about three years. He's going to live with me, and I'll get a job shortly. They taught him to read and write and lots of political propaganda."

Lyuba translates for the principal.

"Are your parents dead?"

"They're in prison with our grandparents. They were arrested for hiding peasants from government thugs putting down rebellions against landowners."

As the principal administers tests to Ginny, Fyodora, Leontiy, Kittey, and the two Natalyas, Lyuba and Ivan go off to look at the school with Tatyana.

"How long can this last, I wonder. Before I get scared again and run away from you." Lyuba says this very matter-of-factly, as though oblivious to what she's said to her fiancé.

"I'll see to it you're not scared. The sooner we're married, the better. A lot of men throw their wives away after they get older and treat them like dirt, but I'll treat you like a bride even when we're ninety years old. You'll never have to live the life of an ignorant peasant wife whose only purposes are being a slave to the mud hovel and having a child every year."

"I'll never get scared so long as we're married. I'd never commit adultery. Why did you have to refuse the priest yesterday? I'm dying to become respectable. The longer you put it off, the more likely it might be I'll get other ideas again."

"I don't care what other people think of you. As though they're of spotless moral character themselves."

"Before too long, Tatyana will be old enough to know the true story of her parents and would-be stepfather. People will fling mud at her too. She's already seen so much, and felt pain before she was even born. Unborn children can feel pain when they're developed enough. She doesn't remember, thank God, her unworthy natural father trying to kill us."

"I should've packed all our belongings and had Petya take them and Ginny to a safe location, then carried you to safety while you were asleep."

"I always thought Boris would get better and eventually come around, even when I began losing tissue in the last two months."

"Look at this nice artwork." Ivan pauses before a glass display case of student paintings and drawings. "Before long, Tatyana will be going to school too, and the children we'll have together. I once wanted to be an artist. I secretly found and read a book about the whole *levsha* experience. We're prone to being artists and musicians instead of doctors and lawyers."

"And you want to work in a factory and on a farm? What'll happen to your hands? They won't be able to be artistic anymore!" Lyuba sets Tatyana down and takes Ivan's hands in hers. "You only have a writing callus on your left hand. If you work in a factory or on a farm, you'll have calluses all over both your hands. Why don't you start painting pictures again?"

"My father beat it out of me."

"We're safe from both our fathers now. A grown man shouldn't be afraid of his father or use that as an excuse."

"You don't deserve to be supported by a poor, starving artist."

Kat and Nikolas come up. Lyuba looks enviously at their wedding rings.

"That principal was absolutely scandalized when he called me Mrs. Vishinskaya, and I said it's still Vrangel. He recorded Kittey's guardians as 'brother Nikolay and wife, Katriyana Vrangel.' As though I need to be identified as someone's wife instead of Kittey's sister-in-law. I guess I'll have to be identified as 'wife of Nikolay Vishinskiy' on my legal documents. How ancient."

"It's the way the world works. Respectable women are supposed to have husbands, and the ones like you and Eliisabet who opt to keep your family names need to have their husband's name clarified, so it won't falsely look like you're promiscuous or uncivilized."

"You used to want to stay a Zhukova your whole life. How come you suddenly want to take Ivan's family name?"

"My father did so many awful things to me. I want nothing more to do with his family name. Vanya had *better* make me Mrs. Koneva by next year at this time!"

"You'll be absorbed into his identity, as if you never existed under your real name. I've been looking at the American papers, and I don't see any married women identified under their own names. They're all 'Mrs. William Smith' and 'Mrs. Robert Jones.'"

"That isn't how married women are called back home."

"It's how they're referred to here! And I don't like it one bit."

They go back to the principal's office two hours later. Leontiy has been placed at the level of an advanced second grader; Fyodora and Natalya Yeltsina are at the level of kindergarteners; Kittey is at the level of an advanced seventh grader; Natalya Lebedeva is at the level of an intermediate eighth grader; and Ginny is at the level of an advanced sixth grader in every subject except German. In that, he's at the same level as a senior in high school, he gloats to Lyuba.

"Now all we have to do is get you enrolled in religious school," Lyuba says.

"I'm too old for that nonsense. Isn't it enough I'll go to church on Sundays, festivals, and fasts?"

"Do you remember more than twenty saints?" Kittey laughs. "I remember, and I was just ten years old the last time I went to church."

"Why don't you say some prayers?" Lyuba suggests.

Ginny proudly recites the Our Father in Old Church Slavonic. Even Kittey is impressed.

"Now we can go back to the boardinghouse and look for our own place to stay. You'll be going to an American school and attending church again, and before long you'll be an American boy. Your mother will be so proud of you."

4

Katrin and Anastasiya are still poring over the real estate section when the others come in. Sandro is counting Katrin's money in amazement.

"It would be even more, but customs refused to change all of it into American money for me," Katrin sulks. "Just because it was more than a million dollars. How am I supposed to live if I don't have all my money accessible? I'm used to having lots of cash, not writing checks. Hopefully I'll be able to have my own checking account as a single woman."

"Are you and Anastasiya planning to attend school?"

"Nastya wants to go to fashion school, but she needs an equivalency diploma first. I want to get to work right away, and not take time out to go to university. I want to be a newspaper intellectual, and also might do a little business on the side, like owning dressmaking companies and hotels."

"Oh, Katya, business is only for men," Anastasiya scoffs. "There's only one word for someone in business, a businessman. Not a businesswoman!"

"Until last year in our new country, women weren't allowed to vote either. Change will come if you let it. Look how much respect and power Comrade Krupskaya has. I can't think of a single other woman who's that high up in the new government."

"She's only that powerful because her husband's the boss."

"Comrade Lenin's wife is my hero! Besides all the Estonian nationalists, martyrs, and patriots. Who could be more inspiring than our own heroes except a woman who's the most powerful woman in the Soviet Union?"

"America's just getting over a Red Scare," Eliisabet says. "I wouldn't say much more on this subject, especially since we're recent arrivals. What if they've planted spies here? You never know."

"Don't worry about me getting arrested, Liza. Worry about your baby. If I decide to have children, I'll have them late, after I'm famous and well-established." Katrin leans over to feel the baby kicking. "What a pity I missed out on feeling your Kolya kicking before he was born. You poor thing, all alone except for Alyosha during most of your pregnancy, and then scared into premature labor."

"Do you ever think there might be something wrong with Kolya?" Anastasiya asks. "Since he was born so early?"

"The doctor said he checked out fine, and so did all the doctors on Ellis Island," Eliisabet says. "He talked and walked on time, and he no longer uses diapers. I had him at twenty-eight weeks, not twenty weeks."

"All the important men in the Party are secretly jealous of Comrade Krupskaya," Katrin continues. "Because *she's* Comrade Lenin's best friend and closest confidante. Even Comrade Trotskiy doesn't hold a candle to her. So what if he had a mistress at one time. Miss Armand wasn't the real thing, as much power as she had. Did he tell all his special top secrets to *her*, to that woman?"

"Okay, you've said your piece about how much you love and admire Lenin's wife," Kat says. "But we're in America now."

"As soon as I become a citizen, I'm joining the Socialist Party. I may have been betrayed by Communism back home, but those were Party nobodies. They were all disobeying Comrade Lenin's orders. Just because a very beautiful idea was misinterpreted by selfish people doesn't mean the idea and its leaders are wrong. I only abandoned the bastardized version of Communism, not real, pure, true Socialism."

5

The next day, Lyuba wakes up with a stomach complaint. She gets Tatyana dressed and then gets back into bed, waiting for the pain to pass.

"Don't you feel well, Lyuba?" Natalya Yeltsina asks.

"You, Ginny, and Tanyechka can go on without me. I'll be up later."

"If you've got stomach pain, you're going to stay in bed the rest of the day," Ivan says. "I'll bring you a light breakfast you can keep down."

"Don't do that, Vanya. We'll get crumbs all over the sheets, and the landlady will yell at us."

"I insist. Your health is the most important thing."

Ivan brings her a plate of eggs and a glass of water, then takes some of the American money from the dresser and goes out to buy groceries.

"Are you leaving me?"

"Not for long, love. I hope to be out of here by tomorrow. There are too many people here, and no privacy. I'll pick up some food."

He looks at the designs on the new coins. Not like Russian

coins. Only one coin, the shiny cent piece, depicts a national hero. The two figures on the nickel are a mystery.

Three blocks down, the market begins. Most of the people shopping are women and girls, many chattering away in the quasi-German language used by so many of the other boarders. Every so often, he catches snatches of conversation in Russian and similar-sounding languages, which he guesses could be Polish and Ukrainian, as well as some Italian and English. To Ivan's delight, he discovers fruit stands displaying all kinds of exotic fruits he's only seen in books, like pineapples, bananas, and mangos. There are also tomatoes, potatoes, herbs, freshly-slaughtered meat, oranges, tangerines, and berries of all kinds. He wishes he'd brought Tatyana along to see it all.

"Is your wife at work, or ill?" a woman asks in Muscovite Russian. "I'm sorry, I don't mean to pry, but I so rarely see any men in the market. I'm always curious about the stories behind the few lone men."

"No, I'm not married. My fiancée isn't feeling well this morning."

The woman looks up at him and freezes. "Ivanok!"

"*Tyotya* Lera!"

Valeriya hugs him tightly. "Yes, here I am, safe and sound. Have you been here long, my dear boy?"

"Just a few days. I looked for your telephone number in the books, but there was no Valeriya Koneva listed."

"That's because I remarried since you last saw me. My promise still stands. I'll happily take you into my home and care for you as though you're my dear Lizochka. You won't owe me a penny, and I'll never force you to move out until you're ready. I live in a two-story townhouse with a cellar, in the northern part of the neighborhood, near Tompkins Square Park. There's plenty of room for a few guests."

"This is too good to be true! I'll go back to the boardinghouse, collect Lyuba, her cousin, my daughter, and our belongings, and then we'll be off to your new house. There's also a little redhaired girl we're taking care of till she can join her sister in Canada."

"So you finally won the Zhukova girl's heart. I'm proud of you."

"I hope we won't be torn apart by misunderstandings and other people again. Back in Russia, it was like an American roller-coaster. One day we were madly in love, the next she was in another man's arms, being a prostitute, trying to make me jealous, or—"

"You have your belovèd's heart now, Ivanok. She'll make you happy instead of sad and depressed. Tell me your address, and I'll be there in twenty minutes with my car."

"You have a car!"

"Wait'll you see what else I have."

Ivan obediently goes back to the boardinghouse and starts to pack. Lyuba weakly smiles when he tells her where they're going.

"Look, there's her car now! Soon we'll have our own car, our own apartment, and a houseful of kids!" Overjoyed, he picks her up and carries her out to the waiting dark blue Rochet-Schneider. "Ginny, you carry the luggage."

****

Chapter 24: Family Reunion

The first thing Lyuba sees upon entering Valeriya's house is the baby in the pram.

"That's my little boy, Vasiliy Grigoriyevich Golitsyn. He's three weeks old."

"You had another baby at your age, *Tyotya* Lera?" Ivan asks. "What a beautiful miracle. You deserve a second chance to be a mother."

"I'm forty-three. That's not too old. God must've really wanted my husband and I to be parents, if he gave us another baby as soon as we remarried. My new husband also lost his first child, a dear little boy named Vitya."

"Did you say his surname is Golitsyn?" Ginny asks in shock.

Valeriya indicates the man coming up to greet them. "This is my new husband Grisha."

Ginny recognizes the barrel-chested boardinghouse manager. "Mr. Golitsyn!"

"You know my husband?"

"He ran one of our boardinghouses!"

"I never dreamt we'd share blood," Ivan manages to say. "He was always very nice to us, so I'm not worried your new husband will do anything untoward. I'm quite happy to welcome him into our shrunken family."

Mr. Golitsyn puts his hands on Ivan's shoulders. "Now that we're family, I must invite you to use *ty*. Lyuba, Ginny, and all your friends are also welcome to use *ty*. Our relationship is no longer that of an innkeeper and his tenants."

"*Bolshoye spasibo* for such a lovely invitation," Lyuba says. "I'll make an effort to switch to *ty*, and tell our friends they're welcome to do it too. You'll be my uncle-in-law soon, and an uncle and niece shouldn't use *vy* with each other. I always used *ty* with Valeriya, and it'd be too strange if I used *ty* with her but *vy* with her husband."

"That means a lot to me," Ivan agrees. "I'll try never to use *vy* with you again."

Valeriya picks up little Vasya. "He was born a bit early, because of my age, but he's normal, not Mongoloid. I take it that's your child?"

"This is my little Tanyechka. Doesn't she look just like her beautiful mother?"

Valeriya kneels and smiles at Tatyana. "I'm your aunt, and I'm going to have so much fun spoiling you."

"Did you know my father is alive?" Ivan asks in disgust.

"Do I ever. I didn't want that drunken murderer in my house, but he cajoled so much, I finally agreed to stick him in a back room when he came earlier this year. I made him go out and get a job. He found work as a businessman again, working at another liquor store. His experience with being arrested for bootlegging in the Motherland made absolutely no impression upon him, since he started doing it all over again. I make a thorough search of his room every day, and if I happen to find any beer, liquor, or wine, I take it downstairs and lock it away from him. Drunken monster. He claims he no longer drinks and that I won't let him have an occasional alcoholic beverage, but I don't want my second husband to be murdered by him too. He says he'd do anything if my sister came back to him from the dead. I can't believe he teamed up with people who wanted you dead, Ivanok, and worked with them to help to find your location."

"Thanks to his miraculous resurrection, I had to flee Moskva, and we left Tver just in the nick of time! A miracle we were able to go to Novgorod and the other cities we stayed at without being found out."

"They were going to kill Vanya in Pskov, but I snuck downstairs and killed the man," Lyuba says. "And then we ran into Estonia, the whole length on foot, without ever looking back at the Motherland."

"You aren't feeling well. Go lie down, and my aunt will take care of you."

Lyuba goes into a spare bedroom with a feather mattress and white satin sheets. There's a small bookcase in the room, with religious books, poetry, and a few works of literature. Some of the books belonged to Liza and have her name written in them. Lyuba's heart aches as she remembers Ivan's beautiful, delicate cousin, her life snuffed out at just thirteen years old thanks to measles pneumonia. Next to the bookcase is a mahogany table set with pictures of Valeriya's family and Mr. Golitsyn's family. Lyuba recognizes some of the people in the latter pictures as nobles from her textbooks and seeing them as a girl in St. Petersburg.

Lyuba opens one of the books in bed. It's a register of nobility, with many extra handwritten pages stuffed in, detailing which nobles are still alive and what happened to all of them. Grigoriy Vasiliyevich Golitsyn is listed among their ranks. His wife was Valentina Denisovna Trubetskaya, and their child was Vitaliy.

***

"Why don't you take Tanyechka out for ice-cream, and I can stay here with Lyuba?" Ivan asks. "You can take Natasha too."

"Your father comes home at five in the afternoon. Don't let him take any bottles up to his room." Valeriya hands Vasya to her nephew. "It's a miracle I reproduced again past forty. God knew I was meant to be a mother and to marry again."

Valeriya heads out with Natalya and Tatyana, while Ginny goes upstairs to snoop through Mr. Konev's room.

"You do know your new uncle is a prince, and that your little cousin is a prince also, albeit a displaced prince who'll never get to know his noble relatives?" Mr. Golitsyn comments to Ivan. "Granted, your aunt and I have a morganatic marriage, but I still consider Vasya a rightful prince by birth."

"You're a real prince?"

"Golitsyn is a princely name. I'm a noble. A poor noble now, but a noble regardless."

"A miracle happened for you when Vasya was born, after you lost your first son. Now your family name and bloodline can carry on after all."

Mr. Golitsyn crosses himself. "Vitka was only three, and my only child. I'm so blessed to be given another one, even if I'm the age when most people start having grandchildren. I was already so old when Vitka was born, after so many years of childless marriage."

"He has the same brown eyes my mother had." Ivan walks over to the bedroom to see if Lyuba's asleep, then walks back to Mr. Golitsyn. "I always wondered if *Tyotya* Lera had problems with having children, since she only had Liza when she was married to my uncle, but I wouldn't put it past a modern woman like that to deliberately only have one child. If she had a baby so easily as soon as she remarried, she obviously doesn't have any health issues. Lyuba's lucky she even has the one. Malenkov knocked her around so much, it's a miracle Tanyechka was born alive and never miscarried. A midwife told me if she conceives again, it'll be a miracle. I'd die for Lyuba or Tanyechka, but Tanyechka isn't mine biologically. She also won't be able to be baptized till I marry Lyuba, but even then a priest might rule she hasn't been made 'legitimate' because I'm not the natural father."

"Christ was adopted, and an only child."

"Tatyana's a human being, not a goddess. Lyuba will feel more secure in my love for her as soon as we have a child together."

"What if it really is impossible for her to have another baby, or if she miscarries?"

"I'll watch her like a hawk. I should've taken her away from Boris as soon as she told me she was scared for her life." Ivan sits down with his cousin. "But, of course, we won't know till we try. You can laugh at me, Mr. Golitsyn. I'm almost twenty-three and have never been with a woman."

"You've got remarkable self-control. That's an admirable virtue, not something to be laughed at and mocked."

Ivan sets Vasya back in the pram. "At this rate, I don't care if Lyuba has our first natural child out of wedlock too. I want to be a biological father so badly, it doesn't matter when that child is created."

***

Valeriya comes back at three in the afternoon. Tatyana is walking behind her great-aunt very slowly.

"We saw Boris on the way back home. I never noticed how pudgy his face is. What did Lyuba ever see in him?"

"It was just to make me jealous." Ivan picks up Tatyana and cradles her close to his heart. "I'll murder him if he tries to take my daughter."

"She slept with him to make you jealous? I should hope she didn't get pregnant out of wedlock on purpose just to make you jealous too."

"That's a long, twisted story. Needless to say, I consider it rape, even if Lyuba doesn't want to think of it like that. Malenkov got her drunk and drugged, and engaged in all sorts of deplorable, abominable behavior after that. You don't want to know the half of it."

"I recently went to a different church when my priest was away for two weeks on vacation. I was shocked to read in the newsletter that your former best friend is a teacher in their religious school."

"As long as he's not with my child." Ivan carries Tatyana over to the davenport and sets her down. "What does my little girl want for supper?"

"*Shashlyk.*"

"Your father will be eating with us," Valeriya says. "I hope I'm not made nauseous when he pretends to be overjoyed to see you."

Ginny comes downstairs with his arms stuffed full of things he deposits on the nearest table. "Look, Ivan. Your father is keeping a diary."

"I read that every day when I'm cleaning," Valeriya scoffs. "At least now he has a new outlet for his feelings of despair. He also has a picture of my sister with a candle by it. He tells me he felt a knife in his heart after he was pounced upon by his 'belovèd only child,' then promptly told my sister had been killed."

"He didn't even cry when he found out," Ivan says. "'She was a weak sort of woman.' If he was heartbroken, he sure didn't show it. He was very calm and analytical about the whole thing, and mocked her, in rather crude language, for supposedly being a martyr instead of saving herself. He even called her Anyechka, as though he'd loved her so much as to call her that."

"He did love her at first, until he realized they weren't having any further children. I knew him before you did, so I can honestly tell you he wasn't always a monster."

Ivan goes into the spare bedroom and comes back with the glass vase and tablecloth. "Tomorrow you can buy flowers and put them in my mother's vase. Tonight at supper, we can use this tablecloth. She'll be with us in spirit."

Valeriya pulls the mended section of the tablecloth into her hand and rubs her fingers along the red stitches. "I don't recall that tablecloth ripping. What in the world happened to it?"

"Basil started to cut it, but I stopped him before he got too far. I had to sew the tear to make it whole again. Regrettably, I didn't grab any pictures of our family while I was frantically throwing things into a valise. All I have are memories."

"You can take some of mine. Now tell the little boy to put your father's things back where he found them. I don't want that drunk to commit another murder."

2

Mr. Konev comes in two hours later, wearing a grey tweed suit, black bowler, brown leather shoes, brown silk socks, and a shiny yellow satin necktie. He walks over to his nephew and starts to pick him up.

"You don't touch my son, Ivan. He's no blood relation of yours."

"Sure he is." Mr. Konev lifts Vasya into the air. "You're my dead Anyechka's sister, and Vasya's your child. I'm his uncle."

"Your claim is shaky, considering my sister is dead."

"It's better than nothing like I'd otherwise have. Now my wife's bloodline can carry on through her sister."

"What about your own son, your namesake, your real hope to carry on the Konev family name? This morning I found him in the marketplace. He's staying here with us for the time being."

Mr. Konev puts Vasya back, crosses himself, and begins to pray. Valeriya rolls her eyes.

"What a false show of piety," Ginny says.

Ivan comes in with Natalya and Tatyana and glares at his father as soon as he sees him.

"My nephew went out to buy lamb. My true nephew, my sister's only child. You can go up to your room and wait till I finish making supper. You can pray there to your heart's content."

Natalya hands the wrapped lamb to Valeriya and goes over to the stack of books Ivan unpacked earlier. "Can you read me and your little girl a story? Vera and Alla read me lots of stories on the ship, and when we were in Estonia."

"That child isn't my Ivanok's flesh and blood, Valeriya," Mr. Konev rambles on. "I have a better claim on Vasya being my nephew that he does on claiming the little girl as his own."

"I've never seen a hat like that before." Ginny gapes at the bowler.

"That kind of hat is common in the vaudeville moving pictures," Valeriya says. "My former brother-in-law was dying to get one of his own after seeing so many of them in the moving pictures we go to on the weekends."

"I'm overjoyed to see you alive, Ivanok," Mr. Konev says. "I didn't know if you'd be able to make it out of the Motherland undetected by the authorities."

"I was almost killed in Pskov! If Lyuba hadn't killed the man with a fire poker, I wouldn't be alive today! I also almost got turned in to the authorities by a band of arrogants who like to take the law into their own hands when we were at the port of Tallinn! If you hadn't decided to casually make your survival known to Mr. Litvinov, everyone in my band would've been a lot better-off! We had to flee so many times because you got involved in my enemies' search for me!"

"I did it for all the right reasons. I wanted to save you from them!"

"So you got involved with the people who wanted to kill me. That makes a lot of sense." Ivan carries Tatyana to the davenport and picks up one of the books by Pushkin. "This was my favorite Pushkin fairytale when I was a little boy. It's called 'The Prince Who Became a Hero.' My mother used to read to me, back before that man you see over there decided to start beating me."

"Where's Lyuba?"

"Why do you want to know, so you can take advantage of her when she's not feeling well? She thinks she caught stomach flu."

"Are you going to join me at the liquor store, Ivanok? I don't want you to be exploited at a factory like so many others."

"I'm a teetotaler. Now I was about to read my daughter a story. It's what fathers do, love their children. Unlike someone we know."

"I'll buy you a nice present in two months for your birthday." Mr. Konev hangs up his bowler and opens a Russian-language newspaper.

3

Ivan tries to avoid his father for the rest of the evening. He glares at him at the table as they're eating the *shashlyk*. Ginny kicks Mr. Konev under the table.

"Your meat is sliding across the plate."

"That happens when you carve left-handed. Will you kill me like you killed your brother for spilling something?"

"I confessed to a priest for the first time in about ten years when I came to America. I'm in the midst of doing my penance. I sincerely want to repent."

"Try apologizing to your brother whom you killed."

"I will when I join him by the right hand of the Lord!"

"Is that a stab at me and *Dyadya* Igor for being *levshi?*"

"It's expressed like that in Scriptures. You do still read the Bible, don't you?"

"Then the people who wrote the Bible were just as mean-spirited towards *levshi* as you are."

"Do you cross yourself with the hand of Satan too?"

"I've always crossed myself left-handed, and it's not the hand of Satan. Ginny, do that thing you do at the table."

"You mean slurping my borshcht loudly?"

"No, when you used to put your elbows on the table to make someone spill or break something."

"I'm already kicking your father."

"*Tyotya* Lera, is he going to be moving out soon?"

"I doubt it. He has no wife to take care of him. But he could always remarry."

"It'd be pointless," Mr. Konev says. "She'd be too old to have children. I'm not going to marry a co-ed just to reproduce again."

"I finally had a second child at my age. It's not impossible."

"Besides, I wouldn't love a second wife fully. I'd want a remarriage more for children than love reasons."

"What about the one child you do have?"

Ivan sneers at him. "Would you still claim me as your own if you weren't my natural father?"

"You can't imagine my delight when Anyechka named you after me. I didn't know what I was doing after I realized we'd have no more children. I was possessed of the demon drink. We're all Christians here. Aren't we supposed to forgive one another for all our past sins?"

"Some things are unforgivable."

"I'm doing my penance faithfully. All so my only child might one day truly forgive me and love me again. Do you remember how you'd run to me and your mother as a small boy to show us what Dyed Moroz got you?"

"Spare me. You're making me mildly nauseous. Are you going to mention how you carried me piggyback in an Easter parade next, or how you cried when I was baptized?"

"I never would've harmed you if I hadn't been drunk out of my senses."

"I hope they beat you during your short stay in prison." Ivan stands up and takes off his shirt. "Look at those scars on my back. The remains of thirty whiplashes. You were only in Lefortovo for a few days. I was in Lubyanka for two months. You cannot put your arms under your blanket. You get only one blanket. You sleep on a board. You get terrible excuses for meals. You have to parade around outside for the entertainment of the guards, though they claim you're only exercising. Where were you when I was living in the lowest reaches of Hell in Lubyanka, *Batya*? Oh, this was before you decided to resurface and let the authorities know you survived and were trying to find me! I would've gotten at least twenty years of hard labor in Siberia if you people found me! Do you have an apology for that? I was a prisoner! They have thieves in some of the cells! At least some prisoners have people trying to get them out. You tried in earnest to throw me back in!"

4

Nadezhda is now a zechka *like Dinara, Serafima, and Svetlana. She's been put to work her first week of hard labor cutting the hair of* zeki. *As she shaves the heads of the men and finishes it off with nail clippers, she plots how to get back at Misha for doing this to her.*

"I have a complaint. I don't belong here. I was getting away from a bad boss, and he sent me to Siberia to die."

"Be quiet, Zh-50. You don't speak unless spoken to by a superior. If you were a man, you'd already be packing up your meager things and waiting for a transport to start working on the construction of a canal or dam for that insubordination."

"I also don't like how poorly some of the zeki *are dressed. They'll die in the winter if they don't have proper clothes."*

"So let them die. It's called survival of the fittest, Zh-50."

"I didn't escape certain Death when I was fifteen just to end up here waiting to freeze or be worked to death!"

"If you don't be quiet, you'll lose your comfortable job cutting hair, and we'll stuff you in the cooler for a week."

"Yes, Sir, Comrade Potapovskiy, Sir." Nadezhda throws a shabby tablecloth around the shoulders of the next zek *who sits down to get his head shaved.*

5

Ivan comes into his father's room at night and sees him sitting at the edge of the bed, weeping over an old framed family photo from 1898, holding an ikon in his other hand.

"I can't believe it. You really meant it."

"Meant what, my apology or how much I love you?"

"Everything you said today."

"June twenty-third of the year of our Lord eighteen hundred ninety-eight was the happiest day of my life. The love of my life gave me my only child."

"My birthday is now twelve days later, July fifth."

"When are you and Miss Zhukova going to be married?"

"As soon as I have enough money to give her an expensive wedding. By this point, it doesn't matter if our first child is born out of wedlock too."

"Doesn't your fiancée have a history of constantly leaving you for other men, particularly your best friend?"

"He doesn't know we're in America yet. By the time he does, it'll be too late for him to move in again and seize Lyuba and my little girl."

"You don't think he has any right to have contact with his own firstborn child?"

"He's no different than any other blood father who relinquished his child through adoption."

"Are you going to reconsider working with me?"

"I have to go back to school and get an equivalency diploma first."

"If you do come to work with me, you must know my business is sort of illegal now."

"Why, do you sell the liquor to minors?"

"No, we sell liquor period. About a year ago, it became illegal in America to make, sell, and drink any kind of alcohol. It's a black market store, just as my old liquor store was forced into becoming after that stupid ban on retail sale of hard liquor. No run-ins with the law yet, praise God."

"My experience in Lubyanka was just the tip of the iceberg. I won't try to find out what the American criminal justice system is all about."

Nadezhda has just suffered through a night of standing next to the latrine barrel. Shuddering in anticipation of the chilly winds that'll begin to blow in a few months, she walks towards the building where she now cuts hair. On her way there, she trips into another latrine barrel, and it tips over and spills onto the ground.

"Zh-50. You're going to clean this up with your hands and then spend three days in the cooler as punishment. You may start to work now."

Nadezhda curses Misha as she sets to work.

"All they'll give you is a fine and some time in jail. I don't think they've whipped, starved, or beaten prisoners in America for at least fifty years."

"Still, I don't want to take any chances."

"Did you already put Lyuba's child to sleep?"

"I put my daughter to bed with Natalya in the spare bedroom. Ginny's sleeping on the floor with a blanket underneath. You can't really believe Boris qualifies as her father after all he's done. Plenty of women throughout the ages have been raped and left behind. I don't think any of those scum turned up later and demanded to be granted full paternal rights."

"But Lyuba wasn't raped."

"Of course she was. The way you raped Lyuba isn't the only way to rape someone. I feel sick looking at you, knowing what you did to her."

"I was drunk, and it only happened maybe ten times total. I didn't have control of my senses. Tomorrow before I go to work, I can walk you down to the school. Maybe one day you can do more than just get an equivalency diploma. You can be a doctor, lawyer, or university professor. I only have my one child to pin my hopes for the future on."

"In the meantime, you have a granddaughter too. You've been a lousy father, but now you have a granddaughter to redeem yourself through. But I'm warning you, if you ever even look at Lyuba the wrong way or mistreat my child, I'm cutting you out of my life again."

6

Mr. Konev lives up to his word. In the morning, he says his prayers and goes downstairs to have a piece of bread with lard on it. Ivan gets up, goes downstairs for Tatyana, and carries her to the table.

"That's a breakfast? I ate better food than that during all those food shortages in the Motherland."

"Your aunt would rather eat poisonous mushrooms than make me a decent meal. You should see how much she hates me. That fancy prince second husband of hers, she makes him lunches of caviar sandwiches. She had a cherry custard once. I had to sneak downstairs at midnight to have some, because she told me she didn't make it for me."

"I'll make you something. Do you still like poached eggs with tea?"

Mr. Konev sits and reads the early morning pro-monarchy newspaper. Tatyana climbs into his lap and looks at it with him, sounding out some of the words.

"She can read already?"

"Lyuba taught her the letters, but she can't read words just yet. Isn't she precocious. Maybe she'll end up graduating first in her class." Ivan sets his father's breakfast before him.

"You made six eggs. Why am I only getting two?"

"Two are for Lyuba, one's for me, and one's for Tanyechka." He goes into Lyuba's room.

They leave the house at nine in the morning. Mr. Konev passes some of his coworkers on the way to the school and proudly introduces his son and Tatyana.

7

Nadezhda falls off the wide iron poles her captors have her balancing on as punishment and tries to get back up before someone sees her. The head guard has seen and walks into the punishment cell, brandishing a belt with spikes.

"You can't beat me. My old employers didn't respect me either, but they never beat me. If I were beaten, I would never have been able to be a productive worker. I was the head prostitute at my workplace. I can do the same here."

"Wrong. Prostitutes are enemies of the people. Just for that unforced confession, you're getting two more years onto your sentence."

"But most of the people here have only three!"

"We were looking for your uncle for a long time. He escaped from prison, and just as he was finally tracked down, it was too late and he'd already left for America. I can't believe he was merrily living under everyone's noses all that time and no one suspected it, because of a phony smallpox quarantine sign. So you're being punished for your crimes, your uncle's crimes, and the crimes of your cousin who also escaped from prison."

"Who do you think I am, Christ?"

"God is dead. But if you insist."

Nadezhda forgoes a beating in exchange for getting a log fastened to her back and rolled down four hundred steep stone steps. She lands in a dirty pond and floats there until she's found by another zechka *five hours later.*

"Most people rolled down those steps are dead or dying by the time they hit the pond. You're the first woman I've seen who was subjected to that."

"I have twelve years of this to look forward to."

The other zechka *unties her and pulls her out of the pond, then gasps. "Are you who I think you are?"*

"I've never seen you before."

"Are you Nadezhda Osipovna Lebedeva?"

"Yes I am, but now I go by Zh-50."

"I'm your cousin Svetlana!"

Nadezhda sees the familiar green eyes and russet hair in the twilight. "You are *Sveta! I can't believe I found someone from my family!"*

"Lyolya was pushed off a bridge and left as the rest of us moved on. Hopefully she was found before the blood loss or cold water overtook her. Two months ago, I was put on a work transport away from Fima and Dina. Now there are two of us." Svetlana puts her arms around Nadezhda and begins weeping. "I work with the hospital staff, so I'm higher up on the zechka *hierarchy. I'll take you in and take care of you, we'll escape or run out our terms together, and we'll go to America together."*

8

"This is my son and namesake, Ivan Ivanovich Konev. He'd like to get an equivalency diploma. He was two months away from graduation when he was thrown out of school because he supported the Tsar."

"Is that your daughter?"

"No, this is my granddaughter. Her mother's ill, so her father's taking care of her until she recovers."

"Will Mrs. Koneva be attending classes also?"

"No," Ivan says quickly. "I want her home with me."

"My son's very jealous," Mr. Konev says. "He thinks other men will all want to steal his woman away from him. My son is very respectable and is working toward creating a good life for his family."

"Your son lives with you?"

"He was taken in by my sister-in-law and her new husband, where I also live. She's my late wife's sister and my late brother's former widow. My brother and I married sisters."

"Is your son planning to go to college?"

"I want him to, but he insists he's just getting a diploma and going to look for work in a factory."

"When's his date of birth?"

"June twenty-third, 1898. He told me now it's July fifth due to the change in the calendar."

"Where did he go to school?"

"Aleksandrovskiy Gymnasium, it was called."

"Did he have a concentration?"

"Just general subjects, what everyone takes. Algebra, geometry, logic, trigonometry, English, Russian, German, French, history, biology, chemistry, whatever else schools taught back then."

"Your son needs to take preliminary tests first. Don't you have a job to go to?"

"Yes, but they understand if a worker can't always be there on time."

"What kind of job do you have that lets workers show up whenever they feel like it?"

"I work in a store that sells beverages."

"What kind of store sells beverages?"

"A liquor store," Mr. Konev whispers. "In other words, I work with the black market. If the police find out, we're all going to jail, and I'm not a citizen yet. I could be going back to Russia if I'm caught."

"Oh, who doesn't have a secret stash of alcohol in his house. I won't tell."

Tatyana sits on a rug next to Ivan as he takes the tests. She occasionally gets up from scribbling on the notebook and goes to sit on Ivan's lap, reading the words aloud.

"You haven't done this one."

"I'm saving this for last. The ancient Greeks called this mathematics, but your mother and I called it cruel and unusual punishment."

"Like the scars on your back?"

"That's just cruel punishment. I'm glad I didn't stick around to see what kinds of both cruel and unusual punishments those jailers had in store for me. I saw torture racks hanging on the wall. That was only the tip of the iceberg."

Three hours later, the teacher comes back in and collects the tests. Ivan has left most of the questions on the math and science sections blank.

"Papa calls this cruel and unusual punishment," Tatyana says.

"You'd say that about academic subjects, Mr. Konev? After what you went through in Russia?"

"That was just plain cruel. I didn't stick around long enough for them to get around to the unusual part too." Ivan scoops up Tatyana and starts toward the door.

"You don't want to wait for your tests to be graded?"

"You can call my aunt's house when you get my scores." He writes down Valeriya's number and hands it to the teacher, ignoring her stunned look at his left-handedness.

Halfway back to Valeriya's house, they pass a church letting out its religious school students. Ivan is about to cross himself when he sees who the teacher coming out with the students is.

"Is that Boris?" Tatyana asks.

"Yes it is. We're going to walk away as fast as we can, *knyazhna*."

Boris's eyes have already lit up. He pushes past his students and Father Spiridon and begins running to catch up with Ivan.

"Wait up, Konev. I've been waiting so long for you to come to America."

"I didn't come to America for you, you *mudak*. I came to be safe from the Bolsheviks. Right now, I'm on my way back to my aunt's house."

"First give me my daughter."

"Over my dead body. You can have her when you pry her from my cold dead hands, *svoloch*."

"A man can change his mind, can't he?"

"Too late. She's my child now."

"I'm willing to take responsibility now. Tanyechka, do you remember me? Your real father who loves you more than anybody?"

"You're not my papa."

"Then I'll have to take you and train you into realizing you're mine, all mine, and that I made a very big mistake."

"My child will be yours when you pry her from my cold dead hands. Even then, you'll still have Lyuba to deal with. She won't let you have her child so you can beat her too."

"I'm a changed man!" Boris reaches out to take Tatyana, but Ivan transfers Tatyana to his right arm and lunges at Boris.

"We used to be best friends! We're letting a woman come between us!"

"No, you're being a bad loser and wanting to get the child you abandoned before she was born. You lose, Malenkov. Face up to it." Ivan strikes him with the back of his hand and knocks Boris on his back.

"You're about to turn into Ivan Grozniy again! In front of a church and my little girl!"

"She's *my* child, you worthless piece of *govno*! You abandoned her!"

"What's this fight all about?" a police officer demands.

"This man is trying to take my daughter!" Ivan shouts, his accent suddenly even heavier. "I told him, he can take her when he pries her from my cold dead hands!"

"This man teaches at this church. Are you saying such a moral, decent man could try to kidnap someone?"

"He's been after her for a long time!"

"She's *my* child, Officer!" Boris yells, getting up and dusting his clothes off. "Is it a crime to make a mistake and lose my firstborn child because of it?"

"Did this other man take your child?"

"Malenkov abandoned her the night she was born! He could've killed her mother when she was pregnant! He didn't see her till she had fourteen months! He was with her for one week, then he goes back to America! The next time he came back, I showed him who was really the father!"

"Guilty as charged, Officer, but I made and corrected some major mistakes!"

"You admit to wholesale abandonment of a wife and child?"

"Oh, no, she isn't my wife."

"And never will be," Ivan snarls in Russian. "Trying to show off for the police officer with your flawless, unaccented English, you sadistic woman-beater?"

"You see, I got her drunk one night and sort of raped her, only she was drunk and there wasn't a struggle, and I didn't have to force myself, so it wasn't really true rape. I had problems when she was pregnant, like beating her a lot, but I've changed! I could've killed my own child before she was born!"

"Why don't you let this other man raise your child? You think a man who abandons his family can get to rejoin them after the fact, like nothing ever happened?"

"Ask her! Ask her which of us is her father!"

"You're Boris, the evil bad man. You're not my papa." Tatyana clings to Ivan's neck.

"Have your own children by Lyuba! Let me have my daughter!"

"I adopted her. You can go have your *own* children, Malenkov. With another woman, if you can find one who'll actually love you after she finds out about your shameful life of sinning. Does the name Lyudmila Denisovna Zubova ring a bell, you self-centered piece of scum?"

"She killed herself. I didn't hand her the rope, now did I? No!"

"You missed the wonderful moment I experienced when I saw her for the first time. You told me yourself to tell the baby I was her father."

"I'll be there from the start when Lyuba has my second child."

"Not on your life you won't be there when Lyuba gives birth to *my* first child! Oh, I should've said 'if,' not 'when,' because you gave her such serious damage she may never have a second child!"

"That's not my problem!"

"You're pushing me, Malenkov. As soon as I marry Lyuba, Tatyana will be mine legally. And then you can't touch her, ever." Ivan walks on.

****

Chapter 25: More Contentious Reunions

"Your aunt, Mr. Golitsyn, and Vasya are on a walk in the park, your father's at work, and Ginny and Natasha are at school," Lyuba whispers to Ivan. "And Tatyana's asleep."

"I have mathematics to study. I have to pretend I care why the two sides of this rhombus are congruent."

"Put that off until later. Don't you ever think about all those times we almost crossed the point of no return?"

"It's not what I'm thinking about now. These schoolbooks are all in English. Can you teach me what these words mean? Everything's so over my head. My French is far better than my English ever will be."

"It's not what I'd like to teach you." Lyuba throws the book onto the floor and runs her hands along Ivan's back. "You yourself see nothing wrong with having relations before marriage as long as you're not just looking for a cheap thrill."

"I saw Boris on my way back from the school my first time there."

"Did he see you?"

"Did he ever. But don't worry, I took care of him."

"Why didn't you tell me?"

"You were still suffering with stomach flu, *golubka*. I didn't want to burden you."

"You keep stopping what we start. You're as afraid of becoming my lover as I've been afraid of having a permanent relationship with you. Although in your case, I have no idea what's holding you back in your mind. At least I know why I've been so scared to be with you longterm. Are you afraid I'll leave you again after we've done that, and that you'll have wasted your virginity?"

"This isn't our house. Aren't we supposed to be picking Ginny and Natasha up from school?"

"For a man who wants nine children, you sure have a lot of excuses."

"We'll have the first one in no time. The sooner I get my diploma, the sooner we can start trying to have the first. You need to stop putting words in my mouth based on your own fears."

"Wouldn't it be awful if we don't have our first child right away?

You might not love me as much if I can't give you blood children."

"No such thing is ever going to happen." Ivan strokes her hair and curses himself for filling her head full of lies and hopeful half-truths.

Lyuba smiles. "Sounds like our first child is up already."

"How can you tell? I didn't hear her."

"I'm her mother. I sense these things, since we were the same person for nine long months." Lyuba gets up and walks to Tatyana and Natalya's room. "And to think I never wanted any children once."

"What would you have done if she'd been a boy?"

"I would've loved a son just the same, although I gave thanks she was a girl. A son would've reminded me of Boris. Mothers usually want daughters and fathers want sons. Even if boys are more valued, mothers usually get to keep their daughters longer. A son's only a son till he takes a wife, but a daughter's a daughter for life. Isn't that right, Tanyechka?" Lyuba picks her up and cradles her in her arms. "When I began having all those problems near the end, I seriously thought about dying in childbirth, and leaving behind one child of mine for you to raise as your own. I knew you'd never marry and have children if I were to die. Would you get an annulment if I failed to give you children?"

"God hears the prayers of those who can't have children. But we haven't even tried to have children yet."

"There's no shame in having an only child. We're only children, and so are Ginny, Alyoshka, and Boris. Your cousin Liza was an only child too."

"I hope that's not your way of telling me you support family planning. I didn't think you were that hopelessly modern. The Church forbids birth control, and I'm uncomfortable with the idea of natural methods. It's wrong to try to prevent having a baby. And a prophylactic might cut off my circulation or injure me, and I don't want an emergency circumcision. Russians don't do that."

Lyuba fixes him with a sharp look. "You're speaking to someone who was protected from venereal disease and more unplanned, unwanted pregnancies thanks to prophylactics. What would you have done if I'd contracted advanced syphilis and were dying now? But to turn the conversation back to a more pleasant direction, I can't wait till we baptize Tanya. Can you imagine what might've happened if I'd been arrested like poor Lena? She lost her out of wedlock baby just like that. Now she's lost him forever, most likely."

2

"You see that building? That's where the children of the zechki *are born and nursed. I consider myself lucky to be working here." Svetlana points the way inside.*

"What about the guards, trusties, and directors from the place up the hill?"

"The ones in charge here have made it perfectly clear you're now a part of this camp. The camp up the hill gave up a claim to you as a worker the second they rolled you down the stairs tied to that godawful log and didn't come after you."

"What if I had a baby here? The Godunovs wouldn't allow any men to do business if they didn't have a prophylactic, but I doubt many of the men here have them."

"You'd most likely never see the child again. Isn't this one precious?" Svetlana picks up a baby boy. "Yakov Mitrofanovich Kuznetsov-Rodionov. Six weeks old. Child of two ordinary zeki, *Mitrofan Yevgeniyevich Rodionov and Dina Yakovlevna Kuznetsova. The father took part in a demonstration against Lenin, and the mother was a thief. Most likely the child will be transferred to the nearest orphanage as soon as the indifferent mother finishes nursing."*

"I wanted so much to have Pasha's children, Sveta. But now I have to serve twelve years because of the sins of Alla, your father, and myself."

"Praise Christ Galya, Allochka, Verochka, Dora, Natasha, and my father are safe in America with your Pasha."

"How could a mother abandon her own child, even if she knows it'll be taken away to an orphanage? There's always hope someday she may see it again, or she might be permitted to collect it after her term expires. That's part of her, and she doesn't care."

"Some of the mothers here compare new life to fecal matter."

"Not seriously."

"One said it was like trying to defecate a watermelon."

"Who's this little girl?"

"That's a triplet. The mother, Rufina Alekseyevna Lenartova, is a thief too. The husband is one of the higher-ups in the camp infrastructure. By sleeping with him, she gets special privileges. Her triplets are five months old. They're going to stay in the camp to be observed like lab rats, being identical triplets. Even after she's freed, she cannot collect the girls and be done with this

Hell. They must stay here to be continually observed."

"Why aren't they allowed to use preventative measures to prevent having these poor, unwanted babies? How can anyone bear having a part of her walking around in the world and not seeing them mature?"

"Alla did just that with the three boys she had by that horrible rapist she was forced into marrying."

"But that was rape. These babies are mostly born out of consent."

"I'm the best nurse here. They wouldn't dare try to have relations with me. If I got pregnant, they'd lose me for quite some time."

3

"Come on, Ginny. Ivan's aunt expects us home by a certain time each day. You're slowing us down by always stopping."

"That woman walking behind us looks familiar."

"Maybe she was on the ship with us."

Ginny stops again, breaks into a smile, and runs to the woman. Lyuba shrieks when she gets a better look at the woman. Margarita Iosifovna Kharzina has put down a basket of groceries and is now hugging Ginny tightly.

"Vanya, that's my *Tyotya* Rita!" She tugs on his sleeve and runs to her aunt. "*Tyotya* Rita, you haven't aged a day since we last saw you!"

Mrs. Kharzina hugs Lyuba. "*Bolshoye spasibo* for taking care of my only child. What would've become of him if it weren't for you?"

"Lyuba's the best cousin ever," Ginny says. "I didn't always behave nicely, but she got me into line with lots of tough love."

Ivan suppresses a laugh at this blatant misrepresentation of Ginny's true behavior and how it finally ended, but doesn't want to upset Mrs. Kharzina by telling her the real truth. She'd probably be horrified if she knew about the half of Ginny's behavioral problems.

"This must be my grandniece. Thank God you kept her instead of giving her away. I hope you didn't let anyone make you feel ashamed for loving and keeping her, or daring to go out in public with her. These things happen, and innocent children and wronged women shouldn't be punished because a worthless man couldn't be bothered to do the right thing."

"Isn't she the most precious child ever?" Lyuba croons.

Mrs. Kharzina takes Tatyana in her arms. "Did you have her

baptized at Ellis Island, or are you waiting to do it in a proper church with family?"

"Ivan didn't let the priest baptize her after he baptized our godson Nikolay and married Kat and Kolya. He also shot down my pleas to get married."

"This doesn't sound like the Ivan Konev I knew." Mrs. Kharzina fixes him with a hard look. "My niece is dying to become a respectable woman. It'd do my heart good to see my grandniece baptized, finally."

"She isn't legitimate, Mrs. Kharzina," Ivan wheedles. "Even after I marry Lyuba, she still may never be able to be baptized unless Lyuba marries my worst enemy. He wants my child, and has tried to kidnap her several times! Don't you think I wanted to baptize her? I couldn't even perform an emergency baptism when she was so sick with measles and rubella. We have to follow what the Church says, not our own selfish inclinations."

Natalya looks curiously at Mrs. Kharzina. "You're Lyuba's aunt?"

"*Tyotya* Rita, this is Natalya Vadimovna Yeltsina. Her mother and two oldest sisters are still in Russia, but she says the older sister closest to her age is in Canada."

Mrs. Kharzina smiles at Natalya. "A young girl came to see me last year, accompanied by two friends, begging me to help her to get her son back from an orphanage. Her name was Yelena Vadimovna Yeltsina."

"That's my sister's name," Natalya says softly. "But Lena didn't have a son." She counts out her age on her fingers, then adds the age difference between herself and Lena. Natalya does this several more times to make sure she's calculated Lena's age correctly. "She's only fourteen, and didn't have a fiancé."

"That's a long story not suit for your sweet ears. Suffice it to say, this young woman looked exactly like you, and she had a beautiful baby boy who also has that same red hair and aquamarine eyes. Don't worry, I'll contact your sister and see to it you're reunited. I'm sure you'll love Toronto. But in the meantime, Ginny's coming home with me. Katya never should've convinced me to leave without you and Lyuba. Just look what happened to you because you stayed behind, so much suffering and uncertainty that could've easily been prevented by waiting a little while for a ship with four available tickets."

"Yes, and look *who* happened." Lyuba takes back Tatyana.

"Boris does seem to love her. He hung a picture of you in his room at our house when he lived with us. He moved out about a month ago, finally. Katya treated him as though he were her child. Why didn't she just adopt that slacker of a man, I said over and over again."

"Is Boris the only one who was living with you?"

"Nobody else lived with us after we got our own house, no."

"Have you received letters or packages from anyone in Russia?"

"Only your uncle. He told me in his first letter in ages, which I got in October, that he was about to commit adultery when his camp prostitute turned out to be you! He also sent a picture in the letter. Boris of course tried to get me to have it copied at a studio so he could have a copy too, as a second picture of his undeserved daughter and you."

Lyuba crosses herself. "Thank God. My father's probably dead or in prison."

"Speaking of prison, Boris told me you and Ivan were in prison, though I can't imagine what in the world you did to end up there. If that story is true, praise Christ you got out."

"You can sure say that again," Ivan says. "Are Malenkov's parents here? They met Tatyana in December, and said they were trying to go to America."

"Not that I'm aware of. It's a miracle you came when you did, since it's getting harder to immigrate. You'd think this weren't a nation of immigrants. Even the Indians' ancestors weren't born here."

They walk twenty blocks to the modest Greenwich Village house where Mrs. Zhukova and Mrs. Kharzina now live. It's just like it looked in the picture, only now there are roses in the front yard and a little grotto around back.

"I bought the miniature statue of *Matushka* Mariya at the store I now work at full-time," Mrs. Kharzina says. "As much as I'd grown used to my three part-time jobs, I couldn't say no to a full-time job. They said I was a perfect prospect when I told them I'd been a missionary. It's a Russian Orthodox store, with mostly books and religious articles. There are also paintings and plaques with inspirational sayings. They gave me the little grotto for free."

"And my mother still works as a maid in a mansion?"

"She still does more stealing than working. I don't know what's gotten into her, after how she always worked honestly before."

Mrs. Zhukova comes out of the house. Ivan starts to move towards her, but Lyuba pulls him back. She overheard enough of his outburst the night after the ball to understand he was about to go over to her house with a knife to stab her mother. If his mother hadn't restrained him, he might've gone to prison for murder three years earlier.

"How long has Lyuba been here? I expected her to come straight here. Boris will be overjoyed to learn his bride is finally here with their child. We can easily arrange a wedding in a month if we start planning immediately. I'd love to have my only child wear my wedding dress, but she should probably wear a color other than white. You won't want to lie in a church and before God about your virginity. Then we'll quickly baptize the child, and her godparents will be your aunt and uncle, if he's still alive. If not, the godfather can be one of your friends, so long as he's got spotless moral character. Better start filing the papers this afternoon."

"*Nyet, Matushka.*" Lyuba holds onto Tatyana. "Her godparents will be Eliisabet Kutuzova and Alyosha Tvardovskiy, since Ivan and I are the godparents of their little boy. We're only leaving Ginny here and coming back later with his belongings. I won't leave Ivan's aunt. When we have our own apartment and Vanka has a job, we'll be married. I wouldn't get married in your bridal gown if it were the only wedding dress left. It was your prelude to your awful marriage to a monster."

"Do you want directions to Boris's house? That boy became like a son to me, so I'll naturally be delighted when he becomes my son-in-law."

"Ivan will be your son-in-law. Didn't you hear me the first time? If you take me by force to Boris's house, Vanya will call the police. You'll have kidnapped his fiancée and forced me into an unwanted marriage to the man who abandoned me and my daughter. Vanyechka loves Tanyechka like his blood child. He'll die of grief."

"He's filled your head with his lies again, like the lies that almost made you desert the Motherland to go to America and marry him. After all I went through to assure you had a better life than I did, you're choosing to marry a poor man?"

"You set me against Vanya, and I started to believe it. That's why Boris was able to manipulate me into our relationship. If I'd listened to my heart, I would've been married and in America four years ago. I understand and respect why you feel it's important to marry for financial security, but a marriage is worthless if you don't love your husband. Vanya might be a romantic dreamer, but he loves me. Oh, and by the way, we've both got quite a bit of money now, so the man I love did turn out to be rich."

Mrs. Zhukova laughs. "If the neighbor boy has indeed come into money, I know it wasn't through honest, industrious work. It must've come through a lottery or inheritance. If you truly were rich now, you wouldn't waste any time in the city and would already be on your way to the Midwest to start that mythical farm. Money has a way of disappearing if you're not constantly working to replenish it." She holds her arms out. "I want to hold my granddaughter."

"Why, so you can take her to her biological father?"

"If you marry this man, I won't acknowledge the marriage or any children you have with him. You won't be in my will either."

"I always preferred Ivan," Mrs. Kharzina interjects. "Shouldn't it be enough you share blood with the man you wish were your son?"

Mrs. Zhukova sucks in her breath sharply. "Wait till your father comes home and finds out what his only child has done. He raised you to be a good girl, not a prostitute or someone who has a child out of wedlock. Marry Boris or repent of your sins and go to a nunnery."

"You're going to be a widow, Mrs. Zhukova." Ivan goes toward her menacingly. "If I catch your husband on American soil, he's a dead man. I'll have the honor of sending that vile child rapist to the lowest circle of Hell."

"You're going to Hell already, so adding another murder to your record must not be a big deal to you. But you won't be able to escape from jail again. What other country are you going to run to after this?"

"I don't care what the law says. What your husband did to Lyuba was monstrous, and needs an appropriate punishment. Even if it's not considered a crime, I can mete out justice privately. I hope you've grown used to being away from your husband, because he'll be dead right after he comes here, if he comes at all."

"You think I won't go to the police and say my daughter's partner in her life of sin threatened to kill my husband?"

"Vanya and I only live together. We've never slept together," Lyuba jumps in. "I'm not the whore you want to believe I am."

Mrs. Kharzina steps between them and waves her arms. "Can you please stop arguing so soon after we've finally been reunited? Ginny, you can come in and get settled. Someone can come back with your belongings."

"It'd be safest if my uncle brings Ginny's belongings," Ivan says.

"Your aunt remarried?"

"Yes. She has a month-old little boy, Vasya. My new uncle was the manager of one of the boardinghouses we stayed at back home."

Ginny pokes around the house while waiting for his belongings to be delivered. He recognizes the books, ikons, pictures, paintings, artwork, and his old toys.

"A fourteen-year-old doesn't play with tops, stuffed animals, and hobby horses."

"I put out all your toys because I knew someday my little boy would come to America. I kept this room like this for just that reason."

"You know," Mrs. Zhukova interjects, "Boris also is keeping a room set up for Tatyana in his new house."

"It'll serve just as well for the children he'll have with his wife," Mrs. Kharzina says.

"Yes, the other children he and Lyuba have will also use it."

"He can meet a nice woman at church, marry her, and send Tatyana presents for holidays."

"*Tyotya* Katya, any idiot can see Lyuba and Ivan are meant to be together," Ginny says. "Lyuba always comes back to him. She wasn't exactly jumping at your plans."

"Maybe my granddaughter can wear my wedding gown someday," Mrs. Zhukova blazes on. "I don't want my daughter to pretend to God and the priest she's a virgin by wearing white, even if it'll save money."

"Are you deaf? Lyuba isn't marrying Boris, and you can't legally force her to do anything. If you love Boris so much, why don't you adopt him?"

4

Mr. Golitsyn comes by two hours later with Ginny's things. Mrs. Zhukova sizes him up.

"So you're Valeriya Koneva's new husband. Do you actually approve of your nephew's relationship with my daughter?"

"You must be the woman who let her husband rape their daughter since she was two years old. Ivan takes very good care of her. Even his father is happy about their engagement."

"Let he who is without sin cast the first stone. Your wife isn't spotless either. She married her brother-in-law, which the Church considers spiritual incest. Although I don't remember which Akimova sister married which Konev brother first."

"Don't you talk to Mr. Golitsyn like that," Ginny chides. "He's a prince. Ivan's new cousin is also a prince by inheritance. It's treason to talk like that."

Mr. Golitsyn sets Ginny's suitcases down. "You'd never guess this is the same boy who almost got kicked out of my boardinghouse."

"What did he do?" Mrs. Kharzina asks nervously, as Ginny buries his face in his hands.

"Several men were arrested for dealing cocaine to my boarders. The entire building was searched, and everyone had to turn their pockets inside-out. Your son began pitching a fit when asked to comply. Ivan pinned him to the ground and turned his pockets inside-out. There was a lot of cocaine in that boy's pockets."

Mrs. Kharzina crosses herself. "You dealt drugs like Boris!"

"No, I *used* drugs. I never dealt them. It started out as pain relief for a broken arm. A doctor approached me, took pity on me, and gave me a lot of free cocaine. It continued from there. You don't want to know any of the things I did while I was using cocaine." Ginny sends a warning look to Mr. Golitsyn.

"Can we please get back to the more important, relevant matter?" Mrs. Zhukova asks. "I refuse to let my daughter leave me and that poor man whom I love like a son."

"If you're so in love with Malenkov, why don't you marry him?"

Ginny asks.

5

Boris is gobbling peach, strawberry, raspberry, and vanilla truffles on his new black leather davenport when his front door opens. He looks up at the people entering his house, wipes his mouth on his sleeve, and stands up, trying to decide if they're coming to evict him, to panhandle, or to see him about a child he teaches.

"I just paid my rent last week. Are you the parents of one of the kids I teach in religious school?"

"You teach religious school? With a soiled moral record like yours?" Mr. Malenkov demands. "Can you imagine the surprise your mother and I felt when we came to Novgorod after our release and discovered we have a granddaughter?"

"I'm so ashamed of you, Borya," Mrs. Malenkova says. "How could you abandon your own child before she was born?"

"I told Ivan to tell Lyuba's baby he was the father. So glad to see both of you alive and well." Boris gingerly hugs his mother.

"We heard from Lyuba, Ivan, and Ginny that's not how it was! You snuck back into Russia twice illegally! You can't make up your mind!" Aleksandr Timofeyevich Malenkov stands threateningly over his son.

"I've tried to be as nice as possible about it, *Batya*. But every time I try to peacefully get back my little girl, Ivan attacks me! He must've left out how he nearly killed me twice, once by jumping down thirty steps at once and choking me and almost knifing me, and another time by bashing my head against a rock!"

"Ivan told us you beat Lyuba the entire time she was pregnant. That's not love by any stretch." Mr. Malenkov picks up one of Boris's pictures. "Is this from the first time you were in Russia illegally?"

"With much pleading, I got Mrs. Kharzina to make me a copy of a picture of my daughter, Lyuba, and Lyuba's uncle. That's it over there."

"The child's surname is Koneva, and her patronymic's Ivanovna."

"What's this?" Mrs. Malenkova goes into one of the rooms.

"It's for my little girl, of course! I bought the little bed with my own money, and Mrs. Zhukova and I had a wonderful time selecting the covers and pillows. See this chest of toys? I set up a little ikonostasis for her to pray by, children's books, and a little piggy-bank. Here in this wardrobe are all the clothes I've bought her. I even have little plates, cups, and utensils for her. And see this!" Boris runs into another room and comes back with a long white dress on a pink silk hanger. "Mrs. Zhukova wanted Lyuba to wear her wedding dress, but that poor woman had such a troubled life with her husband. I want my bride to wear something else, so I paid five hundred dollars for this wedding gown. The tailor's making my little girl a pink silk gown. She'll be our flower girl."

"What if Lyuba doesn't want to marry you?" Mr. Malenkov demands.

"And wouldn't it be lying if she wears a white wedding gown when she's not a virgin?" Mrs. Malenkova asks.

"Nobody will care. We'll tell the priest we were separated during the Civil War and had no time to get married."

"We told the people at Ellis Island we were going to our son's house. So we'll be staying here, Boryushka. You would've done better to keep up a bedroom for us instead of a child being raised by another man." Mrs. Malenkova sets her valise down. "Are you going to help your mother unpack, dear one?"

Boris grumbles and opens the valise. In it he finds three changes of clothes, boots, three hundred dollars and fifty-six cents, and a red pencil.

"You were able to get by with just this?"

"You'd be very surprised to find out just how much a person can live without. They paid us dirt wages in the camps, but we saved up. What did you deem important enough to save when you left home?"

"My clothes, shoes, pictures, books, some cuttings from the garden, money, ikons, and a few things to remind me of you." Boris pulls open the top drawer of his mahogany bureau and rifles around through the unfolded, wrinkled undergarments and dirty magazines until he finds a blue prayer rope. "This is yours, *Matushka*. It's been waiting for you to pray with it again all these years. This is your sweater on the bed, *Batya*. Wearing it reminded me of you. Why don't you make yourselves comfortable while I unpack your things, and we'll have supper in three hours? I'm cooking steak and mushroom soup tonight."

"We should work out an arrangement for visiting our granddaughter. Ivan told us he's going to take you to court to force you to give up your claim on the child." Mr. Malenkov picks up *Adventure* magazine, one of many pulp magazines Boris religiously subscribes to, and thumbs through the pages.

"I'm never letting that man adopt my little girl. He tried to kill me so many times! I need to get her back before she's too old to get used to her real father."

"Have another child," Mrs. Malenkova says. "If you've truly repented of your sins, I see no reason why a nice woman wouldn't want to marry you."

"I'm going to wait for Lyuba until she comes back to me."

"Then maybe you should become a monk if you're going to willfully deprive yourself of women," Mr. Malenkov says.

"If you want, your father and I can find you a wife. People may start to wonder if you're homosexual if you stay unmarried."

"I have a daughter. There's the proof I'm not!"

"You'd be surprised what people draw conclusions from. Some people thought we were sinning because we only had you. They didn't know I was left barren from an infection I got from the forceps the doctor used to pull you into the world. You were a very big baby, Borya."

"I was trying to start over with a son."

"Yes, we heard about little Yuriy too."

"Now he's back with his natural mother! She's only fourteen!"

"Why do you want Tatyana so badly?" Mr. Malenkov demands. "Why can't you just marry another woman and have a child with her?"

"Ivan claims it's my fault Lyuba may never have another child, because I beat her during the pregnancy. He says he has medical proof of it, but he's keeping it from her. That's not my idea of love."

"Oh, and beating your pregnant girlfriend is?"

"I did it in the hopes she'd get rid of it or miscarry. But when I first saw Tatyana when she was fourteen months old, I was sorry for every moment I ever beat them."

6

It's just as his parents have said. Lyuba does not show up at

Boris's house. He doesn't see her until the end of June, by chance, when he's strolling through Central Park and enjoying a Gauloise cigarette. Tatyana is in the wading fountain with Nikolay, Ginny is eating a watermelon on a blanket with his mother, and all Boris's former friends are sitting under the trees. He sees red when he recognizes Lena, Antonina, and Sonya.

"My nephew is so cute," Natalya says to Lyuba. "His father is mean for not wanting him and leaving Lena."

Lena takes Yuriy over to the wading fountain too. Boris glares at her.

"Oh, look, it's Boris." Kat looks at him in disgust.

"Are you coming to tell Ivan he can adopt Tatyana without a big fight?" Nikolas asks.

"So what has everyone been up to? My parents came to America and they now live with me, but only until Lyuba marries me."

"I'll never marry you, Boris." Lyuba stands up. "Next week we're all moving to our own apartment, as soon as its diphtheria quarantine ends. We would've moved in much sooner if some of the floors weren't infected by diphtheria. That's the disease I most dread Tanyechka catching. Vanya now has his equivalency diploma, and he's looking for a job. He, Alyoshka, and Kolya plan to work together after they have their equivalency diplomas. Have you noticed Liza's expecting again?"

"That's great news! When's the baby due?"

"My second child's probably due in August, thanks for asking," Eliisabet says. "I've had a wonderful pregnancy for the most part. You know, since Alyoshka doesn't believe in beating the woman carrying his child. Hopefully I won't be scared into premature labor again."

"I'd never beat Kat either," Nikolas says. "Our three families have reserved top-story apartments in the same building, and we can't wait to move in as soon as the quarantine ends. I wish I didn't have to live in a tenement, but the floor plan the landlord showed us is decently-sized, nothing like the cramped tenements from the old days."

"How are you paying for these apartments?" Boris glowers. "I don't think you're as smart as I am. I have a real job, and wouldn't dream of working in a factory. Only during one very brief lapse of reason did I consider it."

"I work at a florist's shop," Kat says. "They don't mind employing a married woman, or a married woman who kept her own name. They said I can still work there after I have children. Liza works at a dress shop, mostly cutting cloth and sewing. You should see the cute little dresses and sweet little baby booties they made for her little girl."

"You can't tell if she's having a girl. She'd better not be too disappointed if it's another boy."

"I know it's a girl," Eliisabet snaps. "I knew Kolyechka was a boy from the very start, and I was right."

Kat puts her hands on the bulge. "Novomira must be a very happy baby. I can feel her kicking."

"What kind of a name is Novomira?" Boris sneers.

"We decided to name her that in Pskov, when I told the other women I was expecting," Eliisabet says. "She'll be born in America, the new world."

"I prayed my baby would be a girl so she wouldn't be a bully like you," Lyuba says. "God heard my prayers."

Boris leaves the park angry and rebuffed.

****

Chapter 26: Scared Back to the Abnormal

Ivan's twenty-third birthday, July 5, Tuesday, Lyuba gets her first sight of the tenement they reserved. They'll be on the fifth and top floor, next to Kat's family and across the hall from Eliisabet's family and Mr. Lebedev and his daughters. Pavel lives on the fourth floor, next to Anya and Leontiy, all of whom have already moved in. Ivan lied to the landlord that they're married, with the caveat it was only a brief civil ceremony in Russia. That way, if he sees their names in the wedding pages after their religious wedding, he won't think they were living in sin and deceiving him.

"Isn't it beautiful?" Ivan asks as he brings the moving wagon to a stop in front of the brick building. "That's our new home. I admit it's not as quiet and secluded as the cabin in Novgorod, but beggars can't be choosers."

Lyuba carries her luggage upstairs, Tatyana toddling behind her, as Ivan, Aleksey, Nikolas, Pavel, and Mr. Lebedev unload the furniture they bought. It's not much, just basic beds, tables, chairs, bookshelves, and davenports, but they'll make do. It was all paid for with the money Lyuba and Ivan made through unspeakable, unscrupulous means. That ill-gotten money was also used to buy basic tableware, kitchen equipment, linens, and other necessities. Their friends are so grateful to have furniture and other household items, they don't care where the money came from.

Lyuba holds her breath when she enters their new home for the first time. The landlord or former residents didn't do a good job of cleaning for the new tenants, as the floor is rather dirty, the kitchen walls are blackened with soot residue, and the windows have dried grime. Lyuba wants to scream when she sees a coal-burning stove instead of the new-fangled gas stove she got used to using at Valeriya's townhouse. This old-fashioned stove is a laughable juxtaposition with the modern electric lights she's grateful for. When she opens the icebox, she finds rotting food which she immediately throws out the nearest window. There's a large main room, which she supposes serves as the living room; the decently-sized kitchen; a small washroom which at least has a flush latrine and running water for the sink and bathtub; a dirty closet full of dust bunnies and caked-on filth; and three bedrooms with not unagreeable proportions. There are a few windows, so they won't be trapped in dank conditions, deprived of fresh air and sunlight. Finally, the fire escape door opens up to a wrought-iron balcony looking down at a concrete jungle. This building doesn't even have a courtyard for hanging laundry or growing a garden. Though the dimensions seem similar to some of the boardinghouses she stayed at, for some reason it feels much more cramped, dirty, and depressing.

"What is that?" she demands when Ivan sets a candlestick phone on a counter by the kitchen.

"Have you suddenly forgotten what a phone looks like? I had to have this for a fancy American status symbol. It's a birthday present to myself. *Pozhaluysta*, don't trouble yourself with cleaning so soon after we arrived. We can clean together later."

Lyuba sighs and heads into the kitchen to get the stove ready for preparing Ivan's birthday supper. She curses her life as she starts a kindling fire and dumps coal into the stove, while Ivan hangs his equivalency diploma on the wall.

"I hope we won't be living here forever," Lyuba frets. "I already hate it."

"You just need some time to get used to it. This is the best I could do without foolishly squandering our precious savings on a fancy uptown penthouse like Katrin's. Aren't you happy our dear friends are our neighbors? Just wait patiently, and before you know it, we'll be in the Midwest, with lots of wide open spaces."

"I miss your aunt's townhouse. Why couldn't you find a house close to hers? She was like a mother to me, and your cousin is so cute. I can't wait till we have our first baby, though I'm not looking forward to raising children here."

Ivan nods guiltily. "Why don't you and Tanyechka go out and buy some groceries? I can't wait to enjoy my birthday supper as my very first meal in our new home." He hands her a list, in his usual smudged, slanted handwriting. "Now that all our things are moved in, I also have to step out for awhile. When I get back, I'll be gainfully employed."

"Your father's very generous offer is still open, Ivanok."

"I want to make an honest living, *golubka*."

"Your father *does* make an honest living, and a respectable one.

Boys from our class never grow up to work in factories."

"He may not cheat people, shirk work, or phony up extra hours he didn't work, but his line of work is illegal. There's nothing wrong with the iron factory where Kolya and Alyosha work. If I work hard enough, I'll get promoted."

"Alyosha told me that boss is a Russian Uncle Tom. He doesn't give a damn about his employees, and treats them worse than dirt. There are only two fire exits, which are practically impossible to get to. There's no heating or ventilation either. What if you got tuberculosis and infected me and Tanya?"

"I'm not going to work there forever, just till we have enough money saved up. I'm smart, unlike most factory workers. This is only temporary, just like this tenement is only temporary."

2

Nadezhda wonders what will happen to her after her temporary stint in Siberia is done. Any possibility whatsoever of future employment will be slim to none, since she'll have a record of a twelve-year prison term for being a work shirker and a prostitute on top of it. She stays in Svetlana's barracks with the other female trusties and fights off the men who try to get her to sleep with them.

"You slept with strange men before," Svetlana says. "Are you suddenly so modest and moral?"

"That was different. I was getting paid plenty, and I wanted to do it. Well, no decent woman ever really wants to be a prostitute, but I was driven to it by circumstance, and voluntarily did it."

"If one of the higher-ups takes a liking to you, you'll get nice quarters, better food, and job security."

"When I sold my body before, I did it with dignity, not to get a better position in a prison camp. I was the one in control."

"Maybe if you make a fake confession to also having been a thief, they'll let you out ahead of time. They love the thieves."

"Great. Another charge, and probably my sentence will be upped to fifteen years."

"How long can they keep arresting people? After they've settled into their precious little atheist government, they'll stop arresting everyone. Things are starting to settle down since the Civil War's finally over."

"I hope they don't stop arresting so many of us until Misha joins our ranks."

"It'll never happen. Misha's protected by his membership in the Party."

"They must want to be left with only people who think and act alike. That doesn't seem like freedom to me."

3

Lyuba comes home at seven in the evening, lugging a bag and basket of groceries. As soon as she's inside, she twists off the wedding ring she wore to cement her charade. When she goes into the kitchen to put away the groceries, she sees the note Ivan left her.

After I got hired, I had to buy a few things myself. After we have dinner, we can send Tatyana across the hall to Liza and Alyoshka. I acted like a coward before, but now I'm ready to be a real man. I hope you won't be offended if I tell you I want nothing more from you for my birthday than to finally become your lover.

"Can you stand to accompany me on one more errand, *knyazhna*? We're going to your real father's house." Lyuba twists off her engagement and pre-engagement rings and leaves them on a small table near the door. "We won't be taking many things with us. I can't wait to get the hell out of this hellhole and back into a real house."

Ivan comes home an hour later to a deserted apartment. As he looks around, he finds the note Lyuba wrote in response, her rings on top.

Dear Vanka—Your note frightened me, and I only knew how to react the way I always react. I took Tatyana, and by the time you read this, we'll be at Boris's house. I'm very sorry I had to leave you yet again, though I still love you always and forever. I can only imagine you're remembering what happened last year on your birthday. I'm deeply sorry for hurting you again. I know I'm not behaving normally or rationally, but I really don't know how to be anything but abnormal. The abnormal has always been my normal. I want so badly to be your lover, but when it's no longer an abstract, idealistic fantasy, I get scared, and want nothing to do with the idea. I'm terrified of being bound to you forever by that act, unable to run anymore after we've done that, since I don't deserve a nice guy who loves and respects me. Pozhaluysta, *believe me, if I could be normal, I would. I hate having these bizarre, irrational, fear-fueled, abnormal thought patterns which have controlled my life since before I could remember. A man who abuses me and treats me as an object for sexual gratification is my normal, even if I know it's wrong. I know what normal families and romantic relationships are supposed to be like, but I never really understood how to make either happen for myself. Maybe I never will, and we're not meant to be together after all. The roast is in the oven.*

"For the love of God! I thought she was never going to leave me again!"

He begins to throw utensils and chairs around, which gets the attention of everyone on the floor. All his neighbors pour into the hall, and Kat opens the door.

"Has Lyuba left you again?" Aleksey guesses.

"Last year on my birthday she left me to be a prostitute, and on my next birthday she leaves me to go running back to Boris, saying I scared her away again! She even took Tatyana this time!"

"How did you scare her away?" Kat asks. "You've seemed rock-solid since you got engaged."

"I had the nerve to suggest we become lovers. It's not like I'd be her first, for the love of Christ! All this Freudian nonsense in this note makes no sense. Maybe I'm too stupid and old-fashioned to understand it."

"Have you ever considered the thought of being with a man she loves must scare her, after a lifetime of abuse?" Eliisabet asks.

"First her father knocks her around and holds her as his concubine for fifteen years; then my drunken father gets in on the act sometimes too; then her wicked, selfish mother scares her away from marrying me; then Basil comes in just as we're leaving to get married; then Boris tricks her into a relationship and she nearly dies because he beat her so much; then Basil rapes her; then Boris comes back; then the Godunov cousins; then she's a prostitute; then she goes and sleeps with Pyotr to make me jealous; and all the while—"

"Calm down! It's your birthday!" Aleksey begs.

"Some birthday! I haven't had a happy birthday in years! Maybe when I was five I last had a truly happy birthday!"

"Are you going back to your aunt's house?" Kat asks.

"I'm staying right here till she comes back to me. She won't be with Boris very much longer. He doesn't treat her with respect like I always have." Ivan begins throwing utensils around again.

"I hope you don't start drinking again," Nikolas says.

4

Lyuba sits at the table eating reheated ham. Boris is delightedly bouncing Tatyana up and down on his knees after feeding her sausages and mushy vegetables.

"Look what my irresponsible son bought you," Mrs. Malenkova sniffs, holding up the wedding gown.

"It's beautiful, Borya. But who says I'm going to marry you? I have no idea how long I'll be here. And it's white."

"Sanya and I said the exact same things. I'm not judging you, but it would be a lie for a nonvirginal bride to wear a white wedding gown."

"The priest doesn't have to know!" Boris wheedles.

"You'd lie to a priest?" Mr. Malenkov asks. "How would you explain away the little girl?"

"If I show him Georgiy Vashington, he'll look the other way."

"Katrin could show him bills of more value," Lyuba says. "Katrin never liked you, Boris, at least not after that day at the restaurant."

"When do you expect Konev will come barging in here to try to take our little girl and you back?"

"How should I know? God, I hope he doesn't start drinking again."

"As long as you're living with Boris, Ivan doesn't stand a snowball's chance in Hell of adopting Tanyechka," Mrs. Malenkova says. "I take it you're no longer going to take Borya to court to get him to surrender his paternal claim to Ivan?"

"Vanya loves Tatyana as much as if she were his biological own. She calls him Papa. She doesn't recognize Boris as her father."

"Will she ever?"

"*Matushka*, stop belittling me. Tanyushenka can't remember yet. In another year or so, it'll be as if she always knew me as her father."

"But Ivan is a grown man and has spent the past thirty months raising and loving her like his own daughter. You're more selfish than I thought if you want to take that child away from him."

"Let him have his own children with another woman."

"Vanya would sooner kill himself than spend his life without me and watching me be married to you," Lyuba says.

"When do we go home?" Tatyana babbles.

"This *is* your home now, *knyazhna*!" Boris says.

"Papa doesn't like you."

"We used to be best friends. I hope someday we can be again."

"By the way, Lyuba," Mrs. Malenkova says. "Since you've given us a grandchild, Sanya and I would like to invite you to use *ty* with us and to call us by our nicknames. Would you honor us by doing that?"

"Yes, I'd be happy to. I'm glad you respect me so much and see me as your friend, not just your son's whore."

"You'll never be a whore in our eyes. These things happen, even if judgmental types always blame and castigate the women while applauding the men who got them pregnant out of wedlock."

Ivan goes to sleep on his twenty-third birthday alone. Lyuba goes to sleep lying next to Boris and thinking about Ivan all alone tonight. She can't remember why she ran away this evening, just that Ivan's note triggered something in her brain and terrified her. The thought of becoming his lover, after so long of fantasizing about it, represented an unknown new reality. The more familiar reality she ran back to already seems like a stupid, foolish, short-sighted mistake.

5

A few days later, Mrs. Malenkova answers the door and finds not Ivan, but Eliisabet.

"Where's Lyuba? I've come to persuade her to return home."

"Let her in, Shura," Lyuba calls from the kitchen. "That's Liza Kutuzova, my best friend. I'm her Kolya's godmother."

"Are Boris and his father home?"

"No," Mrs. Malenkova says. "Sanka has a job loading and unloading crates of fruit, and Borya's somehow a religious school teacher."

"Ivan has been living with us the past few days and taking care of Kolya. He misses Tatyana so badly, he's using your godson as a substitute. When we come home from work, he still won't leave. He goes home to sleep, and returns when I'm making breakfast. He told my Alyoshka he's been sleeping holding your pillow because it still has the scent of your hair on it. And of course, he spends much of the day crying. Why don't you go back to him before he begins drinking again?"

Lyuba looks at her hands in her lap. "I'd love to, but I think this time he may never forgive me."

"When has he ever *not* forgiven you?"

"I've done this to him one too many times. He probably thinks

I'm suit for an insane asylum after that note I wrote, babbling about how I'm not normal and only know how to behave abnormally."

"Ivan starts work next week. When he comes home, he'll be entering an empty apartment. There won't be any supper waiting for him on the table, and there will be no one to greet him with open arms."

"Ivan's a very good cook. He cooks better than I can. He can live by himself. He can also do elementary sewing, so he won't be bringing torn clothes to you or Kat to fix."

"He's been telling us if you and Tatyana come home, he'll forget he ever asked you what he did on his birthday. You should know he'd never force himself on you."

"Vanka's twenty-three now. He's a man, not a monk. Does he expect to remain a virgin till he's thirty?"

"How long has it taken you to get back into Boris's bed?"

"I haven't, not in that way. How can I do that so soon after I left Vanya? And Tatyana misses Ivan so much."

Eliisabet looks into the open wardrobe. "What's this?"

"A wedding dress Boris bought me. I don't intend to wear it, ever."

Tatyana toddles into the room. "*Tyotya* Liza!"

"Yes, I'm here, Tanyechka. Do you want to feel your godsister kicking?"

Mrs. Malenkova puts her hand on Lyuba's shoulder. "You gave me a beautiful granddaughter, but I know as well as anyone Ivan is the man you've loved since childhood, not my pudgy, selfish son. Thanks to his pudginess, I'm unable to have more children. Those rusty forceps would never have been used if he'd been a normal size. Speaking of, I hope so much my son didn't render you unable to have more children after how much he beat you. You and Ivan deserve to have a child of your own."

"We want our first to be a boy. I hope he's just as sweet and kind as his father. Maybe he'll even be a *levsha* too."

"He'll be my honorary grandson. There should be no inequality between Tanyechka and her siblings."

"Maybe we'll call him Ivan Konev the Third."

"How would you tell the three of them apart?"

"Maybe Vladimir, after the saint who's preserved our lives so many times."

"He could have that as his baptismal name and get a different legal name," Eliisabet suggests.

"But there won't be *any* new baby unless you go back to your fiancé," Mrs. Malenkova says.

"I have to go back to work. I hope *you'll* go back to Ivan soon too." Eliisabet sets Tatyana back on the rug. "I don't mean to alarm you, but she's got spots on the back of her neck. Since she's already had measles and rubella, I suspect chickenpox."

"Oh, my Borya prides himself on never having caught it. Even being around children every day, he's never caught it, nor from that abandoned hotel he stayed at last summer. He says the stench of that place was enough to wake the dead twice over."

6

Ivan comes by a few days later. Lyuba looks through the window to see if he looks drunk or angry before she opens the door. Once he's inside, he stands back from her and avoids looking her in the face.

"I start work in a few days. I want to come home each day to you and Tatyana waiting for me. My father came to visit and asked where his granddaughter was."

Lyuba pulls away when he tries to take her hand. "I love you and miss you, but I'm not going anywhere when my child is sick. Tatyana has chickenpox and needs my attention. Boris is also sick. It would be plain heartless to walk out on him now."

"What does he have, the sniffles? And what about the heartless way you left me? You abandoned me on my birthday and broke our engagement, after how long it took to finally get you to accept my proposal. Now I can't take care of my own child when she's sick."

"I explained everything in my note, even if you can't wrap your mind around it. You've barely known a time when your life was normal either, as much as you've always tried to pretend otherwise to the world. And for your information, Tatyana gave him chickenpox."

"Let his mother take care of the big baby. Twenty-one years old and just caught chickenpox, indeed. I'm going to see him to gloat."

"He's very sick, Vanyechka. The doctor said he may be lying

in bed ill for three weeks. I really do want to come home, but I'm needed here, and I'm not ready."

"When will you ever be ready? You've been with Boris, Pyotr, and all those men you serviced, yet it's the scariest thing in the world to take me for a lover. Are you afraid I'll be horrible or hurt you? I'll never be able to become a good lover if I don't get any practice and learn from my mistakes."

"I'm terrified because I never loved any of them, only you. I don't know how to make love to a man, only how to get screwed or raped. You'll never understand what my mind is screaming at me, all these irrational, abnormal thoughts I know aren't normal or sane. You must hate me. I left you one time too many, and now you're mad. You're angry I'm depriving you of my body."

"How could I ever hate my Lyubashechka?"

Boris coughs. "Is that Konev I hear?"

"Oh, Borya knows you're here. Why don't you stop in his room to see him and wish him a speedy recovery."

Ivan storms into Boris's room and yanks the covers off the bed. "What a damn clever excuse to get a month off of work and extra time with Lyuba and my daughter. Are you really sick, you *mudak*?"

"I'm not faking anything! Why would I waste time painting so many spots all over myself or pretend I finally got chickenpox at twenty-one? If I'd had my way, I never would've gotten it."

"Is your colossal pride smashed now that you finally caught chickenpox at age twenty-one? I hope you scratch yourself so much your worthless skin falls off, *dryan*. Lyuba told me the only rational thing stopping her from coming home to me is you being sick. As soon as you get over this, she's leaving you for me. Again! *I'm* the better man. I wonder, did you give chickenpox to my daughter?"

"She gave it to *me*! And if you're the better man, why is Lyuba always leaving you for me?"

"Because you play with her head, you *mudak*!" Ivan seizes Boris by the throat, yanks him out of bed, and begins to slam him against the wall.

"I'll scream for my mother to save me!"

"Oh, lucky you, to be reunited with your mother! How did such a nice woman give birth to a monster like you? Are you sure you're not adopted from the fairies?"

"Oh, good, Ivan's here." Mrs. Malenkova walks into the room. "Are you going to take Lyuba and your daughter?"

"I'll leave the sorry excuse for life to fester in his wounds," Ivan growls, dropping Boris onto the floor. "Where's Tatyana?"

"She's two rooms over. You should see how my son decorated for her, as though she'll be staying here permanently."

Ivan goes into the room and looks down at Tatyana sleeping. Then he sees the little ikonostasis, piggybank, books on the small bookshelf, chest of toys, and wardrobe. Boris has also hung up some paintings.

"You do know when Lyuba and Tatyana come home, these things will come with them, don't you?"

Boris runs into the room, scratching his face and arms. "I decorated this room for my daughter. She's staying here until she's married."

"I'll go to court and prove you abandoned Lyuba and Tanyechka."

"It only counts as abandonment if there's a marriage."

"Who's the man who gave that child his surname and patronymic, you or I? I was the one who helped Lyuba feed her, rock her, bathe her, protect her from the Bolsheviks, and most importantly love her!"

"Well, now I'm in the picture for good. Her name will be changed as soon as Lyuba and I get married."

Tatyana wakes up and sees her two fathers arguing. "Papa, are you taking me and Mama home now?"

"No, Ivan just came over to bait me," Boris says. "*I'm* your true father, not Konev."

Ivan picks Tatyana up and cradles her in his arms. "I'd take you and your beautiful mother home right this very minute if that evil man hadn't given you chickenpox."

"I told you, *she* gave them to *me*!"

"Do you want to tell this awful man what your patronymic is?"

"Ivanovna." Tatyana scratches herself.

"You see how smart my daughter is? Only thirty months old, and she knows her patronymic. Now tell this monster what your surname is."

"Koneva."

"No, your new surname's Malenkova." Boris scratches his chest.

"Tell him what your old surname was."

"Zhukova."

"You see, Malenkov?"

"Now tell Konev who your father is." Boris violently scratches his head and sucks the blood off his fingers.

"You're not my papa."

Ivan smirks at Boris. "Tell Malenkov who you want your mother to marry."

"You. You're my papa."

"I was the one who took care of Lyuba each time you beat her when she was pregnant. I carried her upstairs each time she screamed and doubled over in pain thanks to you. She was losing tissue by the end of her eighth month, you *mudak*! If Lyuba miscarries my first biological child or any other children of mine, it'll be all your fault!"

"Everyone says that to me, and I'm damn tired of it! You, my parents, all our former friends, Katrin, Anastasiya, even my priest! He compared you to God Almighty!"

"I'm flattered your priest thinks so highly of me."

"To him, you're God and Tatyana is Christ!"

"I want my daughter back under my own roof as soon as possible. After Lyuba comes back to me with our child, I'm coming back here to collect my little girl's belongings."

"I bought all these things for her, not you!"

"She won't be living with you anymore soon enough. They'll be put to better use in my apartment."

"I'll do everything a father should. I'll raise her with morals, take her to church, educate her with the right religious values, see to it she's baptized and chrismated, help her to find a good husband, and bestow her in marriage."

Mrs. Malenkova comes into the room. "Did you wake my granddaughter up by your loud shouting? Borya, for the love of God, stop scratching yourself like that. You're going to hurt yourself."

"Konev came to bait me, *Matushka*. He's spewing the usual complaints about how he wants Lyuba and my daughter back under his roof."

"I do too, Borya. Now get back into bed. You're very sick. Why are you making yourself worse by getting up to fight with Ivan?"

"He came storming into my room after Lyuba innocently asked him to see me to wish me well! You walked in on what happened next. I feel a bruise on the back of my head. Put some ice on it."

"I'm afraid you'll have to go home now, Ivan. As soon as Lyuba goes back to you, I'll have Sanya take Tatyana's things to your apartment. If you come to retrieve them, there'll be another fight."

Ivan puts Tatyana back down. "Don't let him hypnotize you, *knyazhna*. Your mother will take you home soon."

Aleksandr Malenkov comes home from work a bit early and sees everyone crowded in Tatyana's room. "Are Lyuba and Tanya going back to Ivan today?"

"Not today." Lyuba tugs at Ivan's sleeve. "Why don't you go home now, my love?"

"Yes, Konev, *pozhaluysta*, go home," Boris says. "You're jealous that as soon as I get better, Lyuba will start sleeping with me again."

Ivan lets go of Lyuba's arm and charges back after Boris, grabs his shoulders, picks him up, and slams him into the nearest wall. "She'll never take you as her lover again!"

"What are you going to do, move into my house and sleep in our bed? Three's a crowd, you know."

"I hope you die of a complication of chickenpox, you dirty *mudak*. At your age, that's highly likely." Ivan holds onto him with his right arm and punches him in the mouth, then begins to punch him over and over in the face. "Now how does it feel to be so powerless against someone who wants to kill you? This was one of the ways you used to beat Lyuba when she was carrying my daughter!"

Mr. Malenkov goes over to Boris and Ivan and manages to separate them. "Boris, stop goading Ivan. Adults are at higher risk for complications of chickenpox. Get back into bed right now."

Boris obeys his massive father.

"I said another fight would break out if Ivan came to visit again," Mrs. Malenkova says. "You're going to take their things to Ivan's apartment after they go back where they belong, with Ivan."

Ivan leaves the house fuming. He doesn't know what to believe anymore, but he has to keep believing Lyuba loves only him and that she's on the level when she insists she wants desperately to be normal but just can't figure out how.

****

Chapter 27: Lovers at Last

Ivan looks over at Lyuba and Tatyana coming into Katrin's penthouse. Tonight there's a party to celebrate the one-month birthday of little Novomira Alekseyevna Kutuzova-Tvardovskaya. At Novomira's age, this party is much more for the adults, and is also a chance for Katrin to show off the beautiful penthouse suite she's just finished settling into. Classical music wafts through the air as Katrin waltzes along with Sandro.

"I hope Katrin didn't invite Boris too," Ivan says when Lyuba approaches him.

"Why the hell would she invite that fat slug after she's hated him almost since they met?"

"I see my daughter's feeling better." Ivan kneels by Tatyana. "Has that awful man who thinks he's your father been behaving himself?"

"No. Mama wants to leave."

"Why don't you go play with your little boyfriend Kolya and meet his new sister? I want to talk to your mother."

As soon as Tatyana has run off to Nikolay, Lyuba wraps her arms around Ivan and kisses him. "Why did I ever stay with Boris for over two months?"

"Thank God, there aren't any bruises on your face. I must be the biggest doormat who ever lived for constantly accepting you back, after how many times you've left me."

"He'd never dare strike me with his own mother in the house. But he has been yelling at me and getting irritated and angry about how Tatyana acts like all two-and-a-half-year-olds. He's even yelled at *her*. If his mother weren't in the house, I know he'd beat me and maybe even her again."

"What has he been yelling at you for? You're not pregnant by him again, I hope to God."

"No, that's why he's angry at me, because I'm refusing to sleep with him. I haven't really been unfaithful to you, *golubchik*. I haven't slept with Boris since last August, and I haven't slept with anyone since I was with Petya last October."

"You never will be with Boris again. Will he be angry if you don't come home tonight?"

"Sanka will bring our belongings to our apartment. And not just you, but every man on our floor, hates Malenkov, so he won't stand a chance if he comes after me."

"I bought a car since I started working at the factory. I'll drive us home in it."

Lyuba hangs her head. "That's an even bigger purchase than a phone! Let me guess, you just had to have an expensive American status symbol."

"It's only a humble Model T, not a fancy Rochet-Schneider or Rolls-Royce Silver Ghost. We've got enough money in the bank to afford it."

"There's nothing I can do about it now, since you already bought it and decided you have to keep it. Since we're already here, why don't we enjoy ourselves before going home?"

Ivan smiles giddily as she drags him into a spare room, pushes him onto the bed, and closes the door.

"I can barely wait till we go home." She wraps her arms around him and greedily kisses him, while her hands wander under his shirt. "You don't know how I felt, going almost a year celibate."

"If you felt that way, why did you run out on my birthday?"

"I was confused."

"That's one of your most common excuses for leaving me."

"You must feel so lonely, coming home to an empty apartment every day. I need you right now." She frantically kisses his neck.

For the rest of the evening, she periodically drags Ivan into the empty room to make out. Even when they're sitting by Eliisabet and Aleksey admiring baby Novomira, Lyuba sits close to Ivan, giving him a back rub and rubbing her foot against his leg. She can barely control herself by the end of the party.

"Tonight you can tuck Tatyana in for the first time since the Fourth of July," Lyuba whispers. "Then you can get your belated birthday present from me."

Lyuba leaves hanging onto Ivan's arm and waits for him to put Tatyana in the backseat of his new car. Then he opens her door and helps her in.

"I'm never going back to Boris." She holds onto his arm as he drives. "Can't you drive any faster? I need you."

"I just know you're going to find an excuse when we get home.

But I'm very grateful you decided to leave Boris and take Tatyana with you before the worst happened."

"If I'd just slept with him once or twice a week, he wouldn't have started arguing with me."

"He never deserved you as his lover. He doesn't deserve that angelic child he fathered either."

"Tomorrow Sanka will take our things to your apartment, where they belong."

"I hope Boris's pride is smashed when his father takes everything out of our daughter's room."

"I'd like to burn that wedding dress he got me."

Lyuba hangs onto Ivan's arm when he stops the car twenty minutes later. Tatyana trails after them.

"We're not going back to that man, are we?"

"No, we'll be safe with your father from now on." Lyuba picks her up after Ivan unlocks the door. "You're going to go right to bed."

"I kept your little bed untouched, *knyazhna*. Look, the doll I bought you when you were a tiny baby is still there waiting for you to play with her and hold her at night again. Tomorrow your *dedushka* will bring all your things here, and we'll redecorate." Ivan pulls back the covers.

"Boris bought me a very big teddybear. I want my bear."

"Your *dedushka* will bring all your things tomorrow." Lyuba sets her down on the mattress. "Boris will probably come here tomorrow, but we won't let him see you. He's not your father."

As soon as Tatyana is asleep, Lyuba goes into the living room. "Put those rings back on my finger."

"*Khotish byt moyey zhenoy?*"

"I'd love to."

Ivan puts the rings back on her finger. "I hope you're serious."

Lyuba drags him over to the davenport and pulls him down beside her. "I've wanted you since I saw you, you know that!"

Very gingerly, Ivan takes her into his arms and slowly begins to kiss her face and neck.

"You can do better than that, Vanyechka." Lyuba starts giving him another back rub.

He slowly runs his hands along her face. "Are you, you know, clean?"

"I've got about two more weeks before that starts again."

Ivan nods hopefully. An ideal time to conceive a child. He begins to unbutton her blouse and kisses her shoulders for a few minutes before the bell rings.

"Just ignore it," he whispers. "I'll lose my nerve if you get that."

"It could be an emergency." Lyuba kisses him on the cheek. "I'll be right back. Don't you move."

Ivan's eyes narrow when he sees the person Lyuba has opened the door for is Boris. "What do you want at this hour, Malenkov?"

"You never came home, Lyuba. My mother thought something may have happened to you."

"I went home with Ivan. I live here. You don't. I learnt my lesson. This time I left you before you began beating me within an inch of my life."

Ivan hides his face, shaking in rage.

"Everything will be different this time. I think Tatyana's starting to consider me her true father, which I always will be."

"She doesn't call *you* Papa. She calls Ivan Papa."

"She just needs a bit more time with me, that's all. I promise you'll feel so loved after you return with our daughter."

"Be quiet. You'll wake my daughter."

Boris drops his voice down to a whisper. "I get paid a comfortable salary. I have a respectable job. I own my own house. I teach religious school at my church. I have solid plans for us to get married. Your mother adores me as the son she'll probably never have. She basically adopted me as her own after she and her sister took me in. Ivan works at a factory for dirt wages. He rents an apartment. He has no solid plans for marrying you. Your only real money comes from savings."

"He's saving up for an expensive wedding. And he just bought a car. You don't have any car."

"Ivan has a very violent temper. How are you to know he won't blow up at you if he has a bad day at work?"

"Ivan only raised his hands against me one time ever, when he was drunk out of his mind. He was instantly sorry the moment he realized what he was doing."

Boris peers around the doorway and inspects the tenement in the dark. "So this is what you want in exchange for material comfort. You're depriving an innocent child of her father!"

"Not anymore. She's back with her father now. He helped me tuck her in."

"Fine, have Konev and starve to death because he barely makes any money and doesn't even have his own house. And his father has an illegal job."

Lyuba kisses him very quickly. "Goodbye forever, Malenkov."

Boris turns around and walks back through the door.

Ivan shakes his head when Lyuba returns to him. "Are you going to leave in the morning?"

"I'm not going anywhere, belovèd."

"I'm not blind. You just kissed Boris."

"I was telling him goodbye forever."

"I know how long your goodbyes are."

"This time I meant it." Lyuba kisses his ear. "That interruption wasn't too bad, was it?"

"Yes it was. I think I lost my stomach and my nerve."

"You don't want me anymore?"

"You can go on to bed. If I change my mind, I'll let you know."

"You're thinking of the scores of men I've been with before."

"I can't possibly be as good as any of them. I'm a twenty-three-year-old virgin who has no idea how to please a woman. I know the basics of what I'm supposed to do, but I don't know anything beyond that. It's a confusing mystery. Go on to bed."

Lyuba sits up in bed reading *The New York Times* and feeling rejected while Ivan lies out on the davenport reading *Life* for the next hour. All the while, he thinks about how tonight might just be the lucky night to conceive his first and possibly only biological child. If Lyuba gets pregnant by him, she won't be able to be confused and run back to Boris with Tatyana ever again. She'd never deprive him of his own child, and Boris would never want Lyuba to come back if she had another man's baby. As the clocks outside strike midnight, he walks over to their room and stands under the lintel.

"I'm finally ready, Lyuba."

Lyuba turns off the lamp and walks towards him. "Are you

sure?"

Ivan pulls her into his arms and kisses her the way he did the night they fled from Mr. Golitsyn's boardinghouse. Pleased, Lyuba unbuttons his shirt to see if she'll elicit another reaction. He throws it onto the floor and lets her caress his chest. Lyuba gets back in bed, waiting for Ivan. He throws the newspaper onto the floor and kisses her forehead, then takes her into his arms again.

"Be my teacher, Lyuba."

"I'm not going to compare you to any of the others. Now enough talk. Be my one and only for the rest of my life."

Ivan hasn't even kissed another woman, not even Anastasiya, but with Lyuba he's as if he's been with her many times. Ivan almost forgets Lyuba has been with hundreds of other men. All that has only been in preparation for being with him. With Ivan, Lyuba is no longer full of the shame that drove her to be with so many other men. Before, she had to get finished with one man as quickly as he demanded it, collect the money, and move on to the next one, or not protest against rape. And she only slept with Pyotr to make Ivan jealous, and that was mechanical every time.

Lyuba quivers as she feels Ivan's hands, mouth, and tongue exploring every inch of her body, and in the dark she can see him smiling like a bashful schoolboy at her involuntary vocalizations. It feels like second nature instead of embarrassing, shameful, humiliating, and degrading as he gently pulls her legs open, climbs on top of her, and slowly enters her. She can feel his whole body trembling as they wrap their arms around one another and join their mouths in a passionate kiss, just savoring this first moment of the most intimate physical connection possible. He moves slowly and uncertainly, trying to read the cues in her eyes and face as to whether he's doing it right. Before he pulls away from her after he finishes, he leans down to kiss her again.

"You've just made me the happiest I've ever been, Lyubonka," Ivan whispers. "I can't believe I finally got to have that experience. I can't describe it, but I feel different now."

"Stay with me, Vanka, me and the child you may have just fathered."

"I won't go anywhere." Ivan puts his arms around her. "You're stuck with me until the day I die. I hope we die on the same day."

"I'm never going to leave you again."

Lyuba contentedly goes to sleep lying beside Ivan, knowing she's made him the happiest he's ever been. She dreams of a cathedral full of candles, and they're walking around the Holy Table with Aleksey and Eliisabet behind them, holding the wedding crowns over their heads. Lyuba is wearing a brilliant blue gown, and Boris isn't invited to the wedding. All their friends are there, and their surviving relatives. In the dream, Mrs. Zhukova is remarried to Mr. Lebedev, who has all ten of his daughters with him. Little Kroshka is on Vera's lap. Kat and Nikolas are in the front row with two little girls, and playing with them are Nikolay, Novomira, Tatyana, and a little boy. Mr. Golitsyn has little Vasya on his lap, and Valeriya is pregnant with her third child. Ivan's mother is in a wheelchair, scars all over her face and hands. Even Pyotr has come in this wonderful dream. Mikhail Kharzin, her uncle, is sitting beside Ginny and Mrs. Kharzina, and even Katrin and Anastasiya are there.

"Vanya, where are you?"

"I'm right here." He ducks back into the room.

"Why did you leave me?"

"I wanted to get a glass of water."

"You didn't leave me?"

"What a question." Ivan lies back beside her. "Our new life is just beginning. I hope you soon come to me to tell me we're going to have our first biological child."

Lyuba snuggles into the crook of his right arm. "I was dreaming of our wedding. Everyone except Boris was there, and even Petya and my uncle had come, and I saw your mother in the dream, and our first child."

"Was it a boy or a girl?"

"It was a little boy, with your brown hair and brown eyes."

"Tomorrow I'll make you breakfast."

"You've done enough cooking by yourself, Vanyechka. Let me."

"I'm going to take care of you the way you deserve."

Lyuba drifts back to sleep and once again dreams of the life she wants so much, with Tatyana finally baptized, marriage to Ivan, her mother remarried to Mr. Lebedev, her uncle safe in America with them, a little boy with Ivan, and no longer being

Miss Lyubov Leontiyevna Zhukova but Mrs. Lyubov Ilyinichna Koneva.

2

In the morning, she wakes alone, and her heart sinks. Surely Ivan wouldn't immediately desert her after a roll in the hay, after how long he's pursued her. And it's still too early for him to be at work. Then she notices the scent of bacon and eggs drifting through the air, and realizes he must've gone to make her breakfast in bed. Lyuba steps out of bed, avoiding looking at her unclothed body, and puts on a smoky purple dress and matching stockings. When she walks into the kitchen, Ivan turns around and smiles his beautiful smile at her.

"I told you not to make breakfast, Vanya."

"I'd do anything you ordered me to, even sit on hot coals for eternity. Making breakfast is much more enjoyable." He gets out a plate. "Do you still respect me?"

"You know I always will. You're more honorable and decent than any man I've ever known, even more noble than Petya, my uncle, or Ilya Nikolayevich. What other man would willingly take on my illegitimate daughter and love her from the moment he sees her, as though she were his own flesh and blood?" Her voice drops a notch. "Do you still respect *me*?"

"I respect you even more now than ever before. I'd never share myself so intimately and vulnerably with a woman I didn't respect. Maybe I'll skip work today and get Alyosha to cover for me, so I can spend extra time with you. If Tanya weren't here, I'd spend the entire day in bed with you, making up for lost time."

Lyuba snuggles against him. "I can't wait to become your wife. Don't worry. Even though you'd never done that before, you were the best lover I've ever had. I never thought that could feel so good." She reaches into his robe and fondles him. "Tonight I'll show you more tricks, and let you have more of a turn at pleasure."

Ivan turns into a giant smile. "Your pleasure matters more than mine, but I'm not going to turn down that generous offer. I'll never miss any of your lessons."

3

That afternoon, Mr. Malenkov makes four trips over. The first two times, he comes with Lyuba and Tatyana's belongings; on the third trip, he lugs over the wardrobe, toy chest, bookshelf, and ikonostasis from Tatyana's room; and on his final trip, he brings the books and framed pictures.

Boris is enraged Lyuba has left him and taken Tatyana with her. He's spent his entire day yelling at his mother and taking it out on her when his father finally comes home early in the evening.

"This son of ours has been terribly-behaved all day, Sanya. Why don't we send him back to live with Lyuba's mother and aunt?"

"Excuse you, woman! I bought this house, not you! I never asked you to move on in here! And I can't move back with Lyuba's mother and aunt now that Ginny's there! That kid hates me for what he thinks I did to his cousin!"

"I wonder why." Mr. Malenkov glares at his son.

"She'll come back to me eventually. She gets restless after too long of suffering under Konev's smothering attention."

"It looked to me like she were enjoying his attention."

"It's a crime for them to keep me away from my daughter."

"What if Lyuba were to have a child by Ivan, would you accept your fate *then?* You wouldn't possibly go so low as to try to win back a woman having another man's baby, would you, son?"

"Lyuba *can't* have another child," Boris scoffs.

"That's not entirely certain. Perhaps she could get very lucky. You seem to forget you're the one who did that to her, damaged her so badly it's nearly impossible for her to conceive again with the man she really loves."

"Besides, Ivan's afraid to sleep with her. It's like a prostitute living with a monk, their relationship!"

"Maybe he wants to be respectable and wait until his wedding night?"

"I hate you, *Batya*!" Boris sulks over to his room.

4

Ivan has never been so happy in his twenty-three years of life before. Every day when he comes home from the factory, Lyuba flings the door open for him and greets him with a bear hug. When Tatyana wakes up from her nap, Ivan plays with her as Lyuba prepares supper. After they've eaten, Lyuba reads to Tatyana while Ivan washes the dishes, and then they sit and listen to the phonograph until they put Tatyana to bed. At eight or nine, Lyuba and

Ivan retire and make love.

About a week into this blissful paradise, Lyuba experiences a strange sensation while they're coupling. This feels like the sensation she often gets while Ivan is caressing her most sensitive areas, but this time the feeling of aching pressure keeps building up instead of quickly dying away. As much as she wants release, she also never wants this divine sensation to end. She breathes hard and fast and clenches her fists, involuntary vocalizations cascading from her throat. Then, just when it feels like she can't handle any more of this tortuous intimate tension, she finds her release and her internal muscles begin contracting. She doesn't care if the entire building hears her loud pleasure noises. Whatever that was, it was well worth its weight in gold. She's ecstatic when Ivan figures out how to produce that sensation in her again and again, every single time after that. Sometimes he takes her to that special place without coupling, with other parts of his body. However and whenever he does it, it always makes Lyuba go to sleep with a big smile on her face.

Lyuba wonders how she ever got along without this. Everyone seems to notice how much happier she is. Eliisabet has told her she's positively glowing.

"I've never been so happy before, Liza. I haven't told Vanya this, but I think I'm already pregnant. Though I don't want to get his hopes up and disappoint him if I'm just imagining things."

Eliisabet knows full well the truth that it's nearly impossible for Lyuba to have a second child. "Why don't you get my midwife to come over tomorrow when Ivan's at work? She came to me highly recommended. Not at all like the ones I was told to stay away from. This woman attended the Bellevue Hospital School for Midwives after coming to this country, so she knows a lot more about modern maternity care and deliveries than the typical midwife. She has the benefits of modern, professional, formal training mixed with an old-fashioned, personal approach you can't get with a fancy obstetrician in a hospital. I hope so much you're really expecting, because that man has been dying to have a biological child with you."

Ivan comes up to them standing by the ikon of Theotokos of Vladimir. "Why don't you come sit down with me, Lyuba? Divine Liturgy starts in about fifteen minutes. I'm secretly glad this used to be a Catholic church. I never liked all that standing, but I was too healthy to merit one of the select chairs."

"*Ya tyebya lyublyu*," Lyuba declares. "I'll never leave you again or make you lonely, no matter what happens."

5

"Has anyone in my family come through here?"

"Your name is Zhukov?" the social worker asks.

"Leontiy Leonidovich Zhukov. I have a wife, a brother-in-law, his wife and son, and my beautiful daughter."

"A few months ago, a striking young woman named Zhukova passed through here. She was with a lot of friends, some children, and an older gentleman."

"Was the name of the man Mikhail Mikhaylovich Kharzin?"

"No one by that name has come through here recently."

"How about Margarita Kharzina and Katya Zhukova?"

"About four years ago, two women with those names were here. We can look them up in the phonebook for you."

"If I find them, I find my daughter. I've missed her so much."

The social worker notices a strange leer in Mr. Zhukov's eyes. "The young Zhukova woman had a man with her, and a small child."

"Couldn't be my daughter then. She knew better than to do something like that."

"You'd be surprised at how many young people these days have embraced free love, Mr. Zhukov."

"That's Lt. Zhukov. I'm a White Army hero from the Civil War."

"The child's surname was Koneva. She also had a boy with her named Kharzin. I believe the boy's her cousin. His name was Mikhail Mikhaylovich."

"Find me my wife and her sister, and I'll find my daughter. I can't believe she went and had a child with that neighbor boy who knew too much. Do you know, Mrs. Ptitsyna, he tried to kill me the last time I saw him!"

"The woman wasn't married, but she was wearing an engagement ring."

"Now I've heard everything. I can't believe she'd do something like that, have a child out of wedlock."

6

Mrs. Kuzmitch, the midwife, buttons her bag back up. "You're definitely pregnant, Miss Zhukova. All the usual signs indicating early pregnancy are present. They're easier to spot after the first pregnancy."

Lyuba breaks into a giant smile, forgetting all about the humiliation she just went through to determine pregnancy. "I sensed it the morning after I was first intimate with my fiancé, and I've felt just like I felt when I was pregnant with my daughter. Now I know."

"Your fiancé won't mind he got you pregnant out of wedlock?"

"He's going to die of joy! I bet he'll soon forget his proud ideas about saving for a fancy wedding. Making me a respectable woman trumps an expensive wedding."

Mrs. Kuzmitch doesn't tell her she's noticed the cervical damage. Instead she brings it up in a different way. "You had many problems with your first pregnancy?"

"Not really, not at first. Only until about my eighth month did I really begin to be afraid I might never have a second child or even carry my baby to term."

"Did you get a viral infection or have an accident?"

"No, the father was beating me around the clock almost during almost my entire pregnancy. He also pushed me down the stairs a few times, sat on my baby, hit me with bricks, beat me over the baby with a crowbar, and battered me in all sorts of other ways. I doubled over in pain my last two months, and began to lose tissue." She blinks away tears at the memory. "But now I'm growing the child of a man who loves me."

"That's terrible. Thank God you got away from such a brute. Why don't you play it safe and try to relax for the rest of the pregnancy? Don't overexert yourself. You don't want to have any problems this time."

"I hope it's a boy. It would make my fiancé so happy to finally have a son and someone to carry on his name."

7

Mrs. Kharzina comes home from work three days later and sees Mr. Zhukov hanging around the property and looking through the windows.

"What are you doing?" Mrs. Kharzina demands. "Who are you?"

"Rita! It's me, Leontiy! I came to America a few days ago. Thank God I got through with that racist new quota. I can't wait to see my wife and daughter. And where's my darling little nephew Ginny?"

"You won't touch my son or my niece. Did you get that scar on your face in the war?"

"Your husband gave it to me. He shot me in the face to prevent me from running after Lyuba and Ivan. Is your husband still alive?"

"I haven't gotten any letters from him in quite awhile."

"I understand I have an illegitimate granddaughter. Did you know Lyuba procreated with the neighbor boy?"

"That's my grandniece Tanyechka, who isn't illegitimate in my eyes, or the eyes of God. Ivan isn't her father."

"Wait a minute. Was the Zhukova woman I was told of my Lyuba?"

"Ivan *is* her father, only not her flesh and blood father."

"Then who the hell did my daughter go out and procreate with? Does she even know who the father is?"

"It's Boris. That man has tried everything possible to weasel his way back into that little girl's life, and Lyuba along with her. I hope you're not going to try to get back into Lyuba's life too."

"Where's my daughter living now?"

"She lives with Ivan and their daughter, and you're never going to touch them or break up their happy home."

"She belongs in this house with me."

"No she doesn't. She belongs with her fiancé and their child."

"Well, I'm going to be living here, like it or not. I've missed my wife and daughter so much. I'm also looking forward to seeing Ginny again. He's out of the house now?"

8

Ginny walks in on a fight between Ivan and Boris when he comes into their apartment early in the evening, carrying his luggage.

"Ginny, what the hell are you doing here?" Boris shouts.

"My mother didn't explain anything. She just handed me my packed luggage and ordered me very sternly to go to your place. She said she didn't want me in the house until she gets rid of an unwanted houseguest who showed up when I was at Hudson River Park."

"What unwanted houseguest?"

"She didn't tell me much. All she said was if a man with a scar on his face approaches me, I'm not to associate with him."

Ivan turns grey. "A man with a scar on his face?"

"My mother will move my bed here tomorrow afternoon. I don't mind sharing with Tatyana for tonight."

"I'm in the middle of having a discussion with Konev, little boy," Boris says. "Come back tomorrow."

"This discussion is over, Malenkov. I want to find out just who Ginny's mother is so afraid of having around her son."

"Well, I want my daughter back!"

"She's *my* daughter, you bully! Lyuba wants to be with *me*!"

"Let her be with you, and give Tatyana back to me!"

"I have to lie down," Lyuba pleads. "All this shouting is giving me a headache."

The door opens just as Lyuba has started towards the master bedroom. Ivan turns white in fury when he sees Mr. Zhukov standing there smiling.

"Who are you?" Boris asks.

"I'm Lyuba's father, you scoundrel! I never dreamt you were capable of procreating outside of wedlock, boy! I want to see my granddaughter right now!"

"No way in Hell," Ivan scowls. "Boris, this is no time to fight over Tatyana. You wouldn't want her coming near this person if you knew what he did."

"What did he do? Tanyechka's playing with the religious building blocks I bought her. I'll let you see my little girl right now."

"Lyuba's father raped her every night for fifteen years. It started a few days after her second birthday and continued until he left for the front when she was seventeen. That's why she thought so little of being a prostitute, and why she's constantly running away from me."

"My daughter was a prostitute?!"

"You did *what* to the mother of my baby?!"

"It's true, Borya," Lyuba says sadly. "He's a very sick man."

"You will never come anywhere near my daughter! At least I can blame what I did on being confused and angry! You knew better! I wouldn't rape *my* daughter!"

Mr. Zhukov strides over into Tatyana's room and picks her up. "I'm your *dedushka*!"

Boris snatches her away and cuddles her tightly close to himself. "You'll live to regret it if you lay a hand on my child, Mr. Zhukov."

"You think you could win in a fight against me? Look how plump you are! Lyuba, come in here. I want to look at you."

"I'm not coming, Leontiy."

"But come without Konev. He tried to kill me the last time I saw him."

"I just told you, I'm not coming."

"I don't approve of what you've done since I went off to war. I want you to accompany me home."

"You're not going to do it," Ivan snarls. "If you try, I'll go to the police and tell them you're a child rapist and a trespasser."

"And I'll tell them in return that my daughter has been a prostitute, had and kept a child out of wedlock, and is cohabiting. The authorities don't approve of living in sin. Better for her to return to her family and be saved."

"I'm not coming," Lyuba repeats. "Are you deaf?"

"I'll give you one last chance to go with me of your own free will."

"And I refuse."

A foul smile appears on his face. "How much do you love your illegitimate daughter?"

"Don't you bring her into this." Lyuba blocks out the image of Misha holding Tatyana over a rock to finally get what he wanted.

"One last chance to leave on your own free will. If you don't, I'll take both you *and* my illegitimate granddaughter back home. And you, Malenkov, and Konev don't want me anywhere near her."

"We'll call the police and tell them what you're threatening," Ginny speaks up for the first time since his arrival.

"Who will they believe, Ginny, an esteemed veteran of two wars or three adults who've taken turns living in sin with one another?"

Lyuba goes over to her father, violently shaking. "I hate you."

"You don't have to go!" Ivan pleads. "We'll all go down to the police right now and tell them everything. You're an adult and can't be forced to do anything anymore."

"I'm sorry, but I don't want this evil man touching my child. I have no choice. I must've been stupid and delusional to believe he was gone forever."

"You said you had something to tell me before Boris came over."

Lyuba looks at the floor. "It wasn't that important." She takes off her rings and pushes them into Ivan's hand, then briefly takes Tatyana from Boris to kiss and cuddle her. "I'm going away for a little while, my love, but I'll be back as soon as I can, and then I'll never leave you again."

Ivan and Boris watch the woman they love walking down the hall with her father in astonishment.

****

Chapter 28: Trapped in a Mad Dream

"What in the world possessed you to come home with this man?" Mrs. Kharzina demands. "What about your little girl, your fiancé, and your friends? How did he get to you this time?"

"He said if I didn't leave on my own free will, he'd take not only me but Tatyana too. I'll murder him if he ever touches my child. She deserves to have a normal childhood and remain a virgin till she's married, or at least in love with someone she's going to marry."

"Oh, that brother-in-law of mine! I wish he'd been shot down in battle!"

"He said the police would believe him over me, Borya, and Vanya, since we've 'taken turns living in sin with one another.'"

"Ivan will probably come here to take you back very soon."

"I don't want him to! My father will kill him if he takes me!"

"But you've loved him since childhood, and fought so hard to be with him! Are you going to live here the rest of your life suffering? If that were to happen, social services might take Tatyana away from Ivan."

"Then Boris would have her, and he'd probably be nice and let Vanka be a part of her life too. He really does love her. He proved it today."

"No, not even Boris would get custody of her if social services stepped in! She was born out of wedlock, and you've never been married to either of them. She'd most likely be taken by an adoption agency and sent away to be raised by strangers."

"Then my friends would take care of her until I came back."

Lyuba suffers through the next week, the same way she lived through her second through seventeenth years. At night, she submits to his degenerate, depraved behavior, praying for it to be over soon, then tries to sleep after he leaves the room. In the morning, after her parents and aunt have gone to work, she goes into the lavatory to vomit from morning sickness. If her father were to find out she's pregnant by Ivan, he'd do something terrible. She talks to the baby in a low voice when she's alone, telling him this will all be over soon and that before long he'll be brought into a loving home with an adoring father, two cousins, a big sister, two great-aunts, and plenty of surrogate aunts and uncles. Her mother wonders why she's been feeling so sick, but she can only shake her head and mumble when asked what's wrong with her.

"Of course she's sick, trapped here with this man, Leontiy Leonidovich, putting up with him raping her every night, and only here because he threatened to take her daughter." Mrs. Kharzina glares at her brother-in-law.

"Maybe it's venereal disease," Mrs. Zhukova says. "She's been with so many men. Or maybe it's from that terrible crowded tenement she's been living in. She'll feel much better now she's in a clean house. Here, have some wine. It does wonders for healing." She passes Lyuba a bottle of red grape wine. "I have my ways of getting around Prohibition."

"No thank you, *Matushka*," Lyuba says in a small voice. "It won't be good for my ill condition."

"Of course, my brother-in-law doesn't care his daughter feels so sick lately," Mrs. Kharzina continues. "He'll just go right on raping her every night like he did when she was a girl, won't he, Leontiy?"

Right now the only sympathetic person Lyuba has access to is her aunt, but she's always at work or out inquiring about her husband. Her mother only sometimes talks to her, and Lyuba is too terrified to confide anything personal. Though they never had a close, loving relationship, Lyuba somewhat pities her, a victim of society's "what's not nice we don't show" motto. Mrs. Zhukova only knows how to look the other way or privately, fruitlessly complain, much like Lyuba only knows how to be sexually exploited instead of remaining with the man who loves her.

"When are you going to let Lyuba leave the house, Leontiy?" Mrs. Kharzina asks. "You're even more delusional than I thought if you think it's normal or acceptable to force a twenty-one-year-old woman to leave her fiancé and child, as though they no longer exist."

"I want her to marry Boris." Mrs. Zhukova becomes animated. "I love that boy like a son. Rita and I took him in when he came to America. He'll be a good provider for our daughter, Leontiy."

"Do you sleep with your Divinely-returned husband before or

after he goes to rape Lyuba?"

Mr. Zhukov sneers. "I haven't wanted Katya for that in years. That's what she gave me Lyuba for. Katya was already too old and washed-up before she was twenty-five. Decent women never expect to sleep with their husbands past the first few years of marriage, unless they're uneducated peasants who can't control themselves."

"You are the sickest man alive, Leontiy."

"And Katya, bride of my youth. Since when can Lyuba get married? She's going to stay here for the rest of her life. I won't let her get married."

"But I want her to marry Boris."

"*I* want her to marry Ivan," Mrs. Kharzina insists.

"She's not wearing his rings anymore, is she?"

Lyuba's heart aches as she remembers the beautiful sapphire and emerald rings which not so long ago adorned her left hand, proudly, lovingly put there by the love of her life. "I left them behind for practical reasons. I'll wear them again as soon as I go home, whenever that may be."

"You'll be here forever," Mr. Zhukov says. "You got really uppity ideas about yourself since I've been away. Thank God I've returned to set you straight about your place."

They have the same fights over supper for the next few weeks, while Lyuba plots her departure to coincide with when she starts to noticeably show. So far, no one except Eliisabet and Mrs. Kuzmitch knows she's pregnant, but already she can feel just the tiniest bulge starting to form.

2

"Open the door. I want to see my son's fiancée."

Mr. Zhukov opens the door for Mr. Konev. "What a wonderful surprise, Ivan Vasiliyevich. But my daughter will be married to no man, ever. Something the other two women in this house just can't seem to grasp. Katya wants her to marry her bastard's natural father, and Rita wants her to marry your son."

"Tatyana misses her mother, to say nothing of how much my son misses his fiancée. What you did was illegal. Now I want to see my son's fiancée."

"Lyuba, Ivan Vasiliyevich wants to see you."

"Alone," he growls.

"My family's about to start eating supper. You can't have a private meeting with my slave." A vile smile appears on Mr. Zhukov's face. "Unless, of course, that's your way of saying you'd like to enjoy her body again."

"I don't drink or rape women anymore. I'm a whole new person."

Lyuba appears in the kitchen doorway. "I can't leave just yet, Ivan Vasiliyevich, but it's nice to see you no longer claim my father as a friend."

Mr. Zhukov spits on the floor. "You'd better leave in twenty minutes. I'll be taking a walk around the garden."

Lyuba steals over to Mr. Konev as soon as her father is out of sight. "Can you keep a secret and not tell Vanya unless you want his heart to break even more?"

"Don't tell me you're really going to stay here forever. You're a free adult, not a slave."

"I haven't been feeling very well. I'm in no shape to go anywhere."

"Ivanok will take care of you until you recover, and not complain. Maybe I can get the prince to come by at night with his fancy Rochet-Schneider, and he'll drive you back where you belong."

"No, it's not that," she whispers. "I'm pregnant."

Mr. Konev turns white. "Your father really crossed the line. You must terminate this pregnancy, and never let my son know about this abomination."

Lyuba protectively puts her arms around her midsection. "No, I want my baby. He's the only thing that helps me endure this. I talk to him during the day when everyone's out. I'm praying it's a boy."

"You want to have your father's child, your own halfbrother? What has he been telling you? Does he know?"

"Calm down. I know for a fact that Vanya's the father. I knew I was pregnant a few days before I came here. A midwife confirmed it. I didn't sleep with Boris since last year."

"You know my Ivanok's the father?"

"I planned to tell him the day I left, but Boris came over and we all started to fight, and then my father came."

Mr. Konev starts trembling. "My first biological grandchild?"

"If my father ever found out, he'd be very angry and try to kill me, Vanya, and our poor little baby."

"I won't tell anyone, but you can't hide this much longer. Sooner or later you'll start to show."

Mrs. Kharzina comes inside. "Oh, good, Ivan Vasiliyevich. Is Lyuba going back home tonight?"

"She refused, and claimed a long, complicated story as the reason. But I want her coming back to my son as soon as possible, whether her father approves or not."

3

Mr. Konev doesn't tell Ivan that Lyuba is pregnant, only that she hasn't been feeling well and her father poses a danger to her health. A few days later, when everyone is at work, Ivan shows up and pounds on the back door.

"Did you forget your lunch, *Batya*?" Lyuba asks as she unlocks the door.

Ivan swings it open. "I'm taking matters into my own hands and acting like a man instead of a mouse for once in my life. You're coming right back home with me this very minute."

Lyuba looks away, frowning. "Oh, it's you." She furtively looks down at her midsection to make sure she isn't noticeably pregnant yet. "What do you want?"

"I can't believe how quickly that *govnyuk* brought you back under his spell. Once I have you safely back home, we'll deadbolt the door and make our friends knock in a code before we'll open the door to anybody." Ivan comes inside and looks at her closely. "You've grown awfully pale. Aren't they feeding you well?"

"No, I just haven't been feeling very well lately. That's why I can't come home yet."

"Why don't you lie down if you don't feel well? I always take care of you when you're sick."

Lyuba nods, goes down the hall to the room her parents have put her up in, and lies on the bed. Ivan shudders when he thinks about what happens in this room every night before sitting next to her.

"So this is where your father comes to rape you every night."

"I don't cry or protest. It's just something that happens to me. This is my normal. I also accept it as the price to pay for Tatyana's safety."

"She constantly asks when you're coming back. At least now I don't have to worry about changing diapers anymore."

"Do you let Boris see her?"

"Every so often he comes to visit her. He knows now not to push for more. Of course, once I marry you, he won't be allowed to visit her anymore. He should enjoy it while he still can."

"I want to come home with you, but I don't feel well, and I can't just leave. My father will know exactly where I went, and he'll react very badly."

"If you're really that sick, I'll take off work and take care of you around the clock. When have I ever not taken care of you when you've been ill? Though I hope to God you're never again as sick as you were when I nursed you during diphtheria. The only good that came from that was your father leaving you the hell alone for a month. How long are you going to torture me and remain with your father?"

"How should I know?" Lyuba's eyes suddenly light up. "Before you only pined for me in your heart, but I bet now you're pining for all of me."

"I always pined for all of you!"

"I let you get spoilt last month." Lyuba kisses him. "You waited so long for me to become your lover, and then you lost me. The others don't get home for hours. We have plenty of time alone till then." She starts to run her hand down his shirt.

Ivan pushes her hand away gently. "I can't do it."

"What, you forgot already?" she teases him playfully. "You got pretty good in the short time we had. No other man ever got me to ecstasy or touched all of my body."

"Why don't you come home, and then we can do this? This is where your father—"

"Well, where else are we supposed to do this, on the floor?"

"I came here on my lunch break, *golubka.* I have about ten minutes left, but Alyosha's covering for me in case I don't get back on time."

"How long do you want to stay here with me?"

"I never want to leave, but if you insist you can't come home with me, I'll stay as long as possible until the evil one returns. I pray you'll someday declare enough is enough and run away again, just as you did when you were seventeen."

They sit there snuggled against one another for the next forty-five minutes, until Mrs. Zhukova comes home early and unlocks the front door.

"Lyuba, I got paid extra today because I did such a thorough job of cleaning for the Halloween party the Rossilinis are having next week. I thought we might go to the marketplace and buy things to decorate our house for the holiday. A woman of your interests would love Halloween."

"Go out the window in the room," Lyuba whispers.

Ivan opens the window and runs away in the chilly late October air. Mrs. Zhukova comes into the room carrying her handbag just as Lyuba has shut the window.

"You still don't feel well?"

"I don't think I'll feel well for a very long time to come."

"What's really wrong with you? You can tell your mother."

"Maybe *Tyotya* Rita, but not you. Don't suddenly start pretending we're close and loving and tell one another secrets."

Mrs. Zhukova closely inspects her. "That's strange. Your face is very pale, but you look like you're gaining a bit of weight."

"Don't bother me about it, *Matushka*."

"You do know about Halloween, don't you?" Mrs. Zhukova quickly changes the subject. "It's an American version of All Saints' Day and All Souls' Day rolled up into one. In America, it isn't religious at all, but more about costumes and carving pumpkins. I want to go to the marketplace to pick up some things for the holiday."

Lyuba breathes in the fresh air once they're outside. She hasn't been allowed out of the house except for church. This feels as exhilarating as when she was in Tartu and finally at liberty to walk about again, no fear of being arrested for merely existing.

"I'll devise a way for you to leave the house," Mrs. Zhukova says as she inspects pumpkins. "You're going to marry Boris. I can't believe your father doesn't see it that way."

4

Mr. Zhukov and Mrs. Kharzina are in a fight when Lyuba and her mother return three hours later, pulling a little cart heaped with pumpkins, gourds, squash, Halloween postcards and decorations, and candy.

"Did you have permission to take my daughter out of the house, Yekaterina Iosifovna? For all we know, she could've run away!"

"I came home early. I got paid a lot of money for making the Rossilinis' mansion sparkle for their Halloween party next week. I took Lyuba out to buy some things to decorate our house for Halloween."

"What in the world is Halloween?" Mr. Zhukov bellows.

"It's an American version of All Saints' Day and All Souls' Day in one," Mrs. Kharzina says. "People wear costumes, carve faces in pumpkins, display autumnal vegetables like dried corn and gourds, bob for apples, tell ghost stories, and give treats to children."

"It sounds like paganism! We're Christians, not heathens!"

"It's all in good fun," Mrs. Zhukova says. "The Rossilinis are Christians too."

Mr. Zhukov grabs the family Bible from the nearby bookshelf. "Let's just see what God has to say about worshipping nature, making graven images in pumpkins, and believing in ghosts and evil spirits."

"Protestants might say our ikons and our grotto for *Matushka* Mariya are graven images," Lyuba says.

"Protestants aren't Christians!"

"They reject Orthodox theology, yes, but they believe in the same core tenants of our faith."

"They don't believe Mariya rose to Heaven both body and soul. They don't believe she was conceived of a virgin and stayed a virgin her entire life. Need I go on? These are not people we want to imitate!"

"The Rossilinis are Orthodox too," Mrs. Zhukova says.

"If you love their mansion so much, Katya, why don't you move there yourself? And if you love that man Lyuba procreated with so much, Boris, why don't *you* marry him instead of delusionally thinking my daughter will marry him someday? I can't believe you want to celebrate a heathen ritual!"

"The Rossilinis are Orthodox. Mr. Rossilini's half-Italian and half-Hungarian, and practices his mother's religion. Mrs. Rossilini's Greek, so she practices it too."

"That's not very surprising. Picking up right where their ancestors left off with stone idols and concocted stories about spirits."

"At least he acknowledges Orthodoxy isn't the only correct way to practice Christianity," Mrs. Kharzina says.

"No I don't. I refuse to ignore the centuries of bad blood between our two churches!"

"My sister and I were in charge of this house long before you showed up, and we always decorated for Halloween." Mrs. Zhukova picks up a large pumpkin. "You'll have to live with our jack-o-lanterns and other decorations."

5

Mr. Zhukov is disgusted by the gourds, dried corn, and jack-o-lanterns his wife puts up around the house. He makes a hex sign every time he sees the decorations and postcards depicting ghosts, witches, demons, black cats, scarecrows, owls, fortunetellers, and pumpkin creatures. To get away from it, he leaves the house on Saturday morning while his sister-in-law is working on a scarecrow with her sister. He wanders downtown aimlessly, until he happens upon Hudson River Park.

"Why is it that you've had to be apart from your parents so much, and my little boy has only been apart from one of us for a few days?" Eliisabet fusses with Tatyana's hair. "Why did you get to be the unlucky one?"

Tatyana recognizes Mr. Zhukov and gets up to follow him when Eliisabet turns to nursing Novomira. Nikolay tries to climb onto her lap and take a turn too.

"You'll be four years old next month. You're a big boy."

***

"If it isn't my daughter's illegitimate child. Why don't we sit over here behind this tree?"

Tatyana obediently follows him.

"My daughter was a little younger than you when I taught her she was forever my slave. Why don't I tell you what you need to do—"

"What are you doing with my child?"

Mr. Zhukov looks up at Boris. "She's my grandchild, and that trumps any claim you have on her. If you cared so much about the fact that you'd procreated, you would've done it properly, within marriage."

"You're a sick, sick man, Leontiy Leonidovich. I was beyond stunned when Ivan told me how depraved you are." Boris picks up Tatyana. "I did abandon Lyuba the night she gave birth, but I never dreamt of doing what you did."

"My wife, daughter, and granddaughter are my property, and I can do what I please with them. Katya got too old and boring, so I had to settle for Lyuba filling her role."

"What you did goes against the Bible. I teach religious school, so I know these things."

"Is it also against the Bible to have relations outside wedlock?"

"You tell me. At least I didn't do it with a relative."

"Do you plan on getting married someday and having legitimate children?"

"I accept my punishment for my sins. I'll probably never get married, and may end up losing my rights to Tatyana. I did ask for it." Boris walks away carrying her.

***

"Where did Tatyana go?" Eliisabet asks after burping Novomira.

"She went with the man with the scar," Nikolay says in Estonian.

Eliisabet gasps and crosses herself. "Holy Mother of God, her *vanaisa* took her. Now Ivan will be worried sick. I'm already imagining what he might be doing to her, and it makes me want to vomit."

6

Boris comes up to the apartment early in the evening, carrying Tatyana, and is greeted by Ivan, Ginny, Eliisabet, and Nikolay.

"Where the hell has she been?" Ivan demands, snatching her.

"She was with me."

"Kolya says she went off with her *dedushka*. He didn't say he saw you come and take her."

"Both of you should be thanking me. I rescued her before he could harm her."

"What a selfish man you are." Ivan swats him over the head with *Life*. "You didn't return her to Liza's care and instead let us worry over her."

"I took my child to an ice-cream parlor, and then we went to the market to buy some things. We stopped by the pond to eat the fruit we bought and then fed breadcrumbs to the ducks. I even took her on a boat ride!"

Ivan's eyes soften. "You're really not a monster deep down. It's almost a shame you'll have to give up your rights after I marry Lyuba."

"You can be nice and let me do what I've been doing."

"Never in Hell. You can leave now and go to your parents. *Spasibo* for protecting my child."

7

Eliisabet comes to see Lyuba the day before Halloween, a Sunday. Mr. Zhukov is at a speakeasy, in spite of his claims of being such a pious Orthodox Christian. Lyuba hopes the police will come by and arrest every patron for violating Prohibition. Her mother and aunt are shopping for groceries in the Lower East Side, where there are more stores open on Sundays.

"You look dreadful," Eliisabet muses.

"Can you tell if it's noticeable yet?"

"Not unless I really look for a long time."

Lyuba sits back down. "I hate to do this to Ivan, but my father threatened Tanyechka. Her safety comes before everything else."

"He did it again yesterday. She went off with him in the park."

Lyuba turns grey and begins shaking. "I hope to God someone, anyone, got her away from him before he could destroy her innocence!"

"Don't worry. Boris came by and saved her before he could do anything to her."

Lyuba's face floods with relief. "It's almost a shame he'll have to sign over his rights to her after I marry Vanya. Sometimes he really does show glimmers of the nice person he used to be."

"But he didn't take her back to me or Ivan. He let us worry all day about what her *dedushka* had done to her."

"That's the old Boris we know at work."

Eliisabet squeezes her hand. "When are you going home?"

"When I start to noticeably show. I can't risk staying after my father discovers the truth. He'll kill me and Vanya." Lyuba strokes her midsection. "I've been praying it's a boy."

"A mother's instinct is always right. I knew Kolya would be a boy and that Mira would be a girl, and you prayed Tatyana would be a girl. Speaking of babies, Kat thinks she's pregnant."

Lyuba smiles sadly. "When Ivan came to see me about a week ago, I couldn't tell him about our baby, since he would've gone even more insane with grief. He would've dragged me forcibly home if I told him, and ruined any chances to get away slowly, when the time is right."

"His father came to see you too, I heard."

"Yes, Mr. Konev knows I'm carrying his first biological grandchild. He promised not to tell Vanya."

"You can't keep it a secret much longer. Kat already looks like she's past the first trimester, though she doesn't suspect she's been pregnant nearly that long. Maybe she just shows more since she's so naturally skinny."

"Maybe she's having a boy too. It's supposed to be a boy if you're carrying all or most of your weight in front."

"No, this is all-around weight, not just in front. Her co-workers are teasing her about how she may be having twins or triplets."

"Some women have even had four at a time."

"Kat would be bursting her sides if that were the case!"

"Even my aunt doesn't know about this yet, and I love her more than my mother. My mother is trying to belatedly be a real mother to me, but if she really loved me, she would've left my father long ago. Even if it's not against the law to rape one's child, and no one decent speaks of such things publicly, she could've run away to a distant locale and pretended to be a young widow. She's never been afraid of working hard, and could've supported us by working full-time."

"She won't have to leave him if Ivan kills your father. She'd be free, without scandal."

"You know who'd be able to save me? My uncle, if he came to America and found out just what's been going on again."

"If he's not dead, he's probably in prison or a camp. Why rely on any man to save you when a modern woman is perfectly capable of saving herself and being the hero of her own story?"

Lyuba leads Eliisabet to a display of gourds and colored, dried corn. "My father's outraged my mother decorated the house for Halloween. He says she's a heathen."

"Then imagine how angry he'll be if he finds out about you carrying Ivan's firstborn child."

"It's best for either not to know just yet. But Vanka has that *groznik* temper of his. What if he overreacts and jumps to the conclusion it's my father's, and that he got me pregnant with both his son and grandson?"

"You knew you were pregnant before your father came back. Mrs. Kuzmitch will back you up if he doubts you."

"And I haven't slept with Boris since last year."

"Oh, just imagine how awful it'd be if you hadn't known for sure! You'd wonder for the rest of your life which one were really the father. I've heard stories about women who only suspected they were pregnant before getting raped, and forever after wondered who was the father."

"It was a very good thing you made me see Mrs. Kuzmitch. I had to know as soon as possible, without waiting for a missed cycle. Knowing so early was worth that humiliation. At least she's another woman, and it was in my own home, not an impersonal doctor's office."

"Kat wants to birth in a hospital, and is using a male doctor. She wants that new-fangled twilight sleep that badly, she doesn't care about compromising her modesty and dignity." Eliisabet looks through the Halloween greeting cards from friends. "Have you decided what to call him yet?"

"I've thought about it, so I can call him something besides Baby when I'm talking to him, but this is Vanka's firstborn child. He should get the honor of naming him."

"Baby Konev will grow up in a happy, loving home environment. Not like this place."

"Vanya probably won't let me leave the house after he finds out!"

"The sooner you come back home, the sooner he can find out." Eliisabet goes back out the door. "Happy Halloween, if you have the presence of mind to be happy about anything anymore these days."

8

By the middle of November, Lyuba is secretly letting out the waists on her clothes to hide the growing small bulge. She tries to always have a handbag over her midsection or to be seen at the table or under the covers, so no one will find out. In her experience, from observing other women, expectant mothers tend to show earlier after the first time. She looks up in alarm when she sees Ivan coming into her room as she's letting out more waists, and immediately shoves the sewing supplies and clothes back into the basket on the other side of the bed.

"The back door was unlocked. Are you still feeling ill?"

"Yes, iller than ever. Why did you come here?"

His face falls. "What, you're not glad to see me? You can't stay here forever. Why don't you get out of bed, and we'll take a walk around this awful house."

"No!" she yelps.

"You're afraid your father will come back, aren't you?"

"You're not supposed to be here, Ivan. Leave me alone."

"I got the day off, and decided to spend it with you. That's not against the law, is it? While I'm here, I'll fix you lunch."

Lyuba lies in bed for the next two hours, picking at the lunch. *He has no idea*, she thinks sadly. *That if he looked at me the right way, he'd notice I'm carrying his child.*

"Tatyana misses you so much, *golubka*. To say nothing of me."

"You're a big boy. You can handle it."

"Once you come back, I'll never let your father take you again. I never should've allowed it to begin with, but I was as much of a pushover as always. I'm a mouse, not a man."

Lyuba ventures a devilish smile. "Oh, believe me, you're all man where it really counts. Before you became my lover, I thought female ecstasy was just a rumor. But getting back to the more important subject, I'll have to enlist my mother and aunt's help if I ever want to get out of here."

"Your mother wants you to stay here forever!"

"No she doesn't. She wants me to leave so I can marry Boris. My aunt wants me to leave so I can marry you."

"Those are two very conflicting interests."

"Don't you know how much I want to leave too? But I have to wait for the time to be right, not just run off whenever I feel like it. Life is about restraint and sound judgment, not doing whatever you want, whenever you want to do it. That's how Boris lives his life, and I don't wish to emulate that."

"What if the time is never right?"

"Trust me, it'll be right sooner than you know it. The time becomes more right every single day."

"Care to let me in on the secret?"

"I can't until I come home."

Ivan grabs her hands. "What, are you dying? Has your father given you a disease? If you're dying, I'll spend all our money to send you to the world's best doctor."

"Leave it to you to get so overly dramatic. You'll find out soon enough, and no, it doesn't involve me dying."

Mrs. Zhukova comes into the house. "Lyuba, care to go shopping again? There's another American holiday coming up at the end of the month, and I want to buy food and decorations to celebrate it."

Lyuba motions for Ivan to go through the bedroom window. "*Batya* wasn't too thrilled with the last American holiday we celebrated."

"This holiday was first celebrated by Christians," Mrs. Zhukova says. "Though since they were Protestants, he won't think they were real Christians. It's a harvest festival called Thanksgiving. People eat a big supper with turkey, cranberries, yams, all sorts of wonderful foods."

Ivan steps through the window and starts walking away. Lyuba gets up to bring her lunch dishes to the kitchen sink.

"You ate in bed? You're still not feeling well?"

"I feel perfectly fine, *Matushka*."

Mrs. Zhukova looks her up and down. "You look like you're still gaining weight. As soon as I get you safely out of the house and back to Boris, you can lose the weight. Weight always comes off the same way it got on, just as a baby always comes out the same way it came in."

Lyuba grows cold with horror as she puts on her borrowed coat and boots and follows her mother outside. She prays that was just an uncharacteristic comment, not her mother's way of trying to say she knows the secret.

9

Mr. Zhukov is enraged with the plans his wife suggests that evening for the American holiday at the end of the month. He stands up at the table and begins a vitriolic rant against Protestants,

American Indian religion, and harvest symbols being eerily similar to pagan holiday rituals.

"I don't even know what kind of animal a turkey is!"

"It's like a much larger chicken," Mrs. Kharzina explains. "This bird has bright, multicolored feathers, and it gobbles."

"The meat is a bit tougher than chicken," Mrs. Zhukova says.

"It gobbles its food?" Mr. Zhukov pours himself more beer.

Mrs. Kharzina salts her meat. "No, it makes a sound like the English word 'gobble.' Katya and I learnt it was almost the official symbol of America in place of the bald eagle. Once you've lived here as long as we have, you'll embrace American holidays too."

"At least you still go to church."

"Of course we do, and we both regularly make confession and don't take Communion without fasting. Unlike some man we could all think of and name right now."

"I confess to God on my own time, Margarita."

"That's awfully convenient, now isn't it? Is it before or after—"

"For the last time, Lyuba is my property, and I can do what I please with her."

"The Rossilinis celebrate Thanksgiving too." Mrs. Zhukova cuts her stuffed cabbage.

"Oh, your halfbreed employer and his heretic wife."

"He's not a halfbreed. He's half-Italian, half-Hungarian. He's not mulatto or anything like that. Very few people in this world are completely racially pure through an entire lineage. Our dear Tsar and his innocent children barely had any Russian blood in their veins, yet they identified as Russians. But that's neither here nor there. We're celebrating Thanksgiving whether you like it or not. I'm obligated to remain married to you, but I'm not obligated to abandon a holiday I've grown to enjoy just because you say so. You can't control every aspect of our lives, and you know it as well as I do. That thought must terrify you."

10

Mr. Zhukov is a real pill about Thanksgiving. He mutters the entire time his wife and sister-in-law's guests are over. None of the guests take any liking to him.

"These are Mrs. Beloborodova and Mr. Myshkin from the bookstore I work at. This is my brother-in-law Leontiy." Mrs.

Kharzina forces a smile as they filter into the dining room.

"How do you reconcile working at a good religious store with celebrating pagan festivals?" Mr. Zhukov glowers.

"There's no conflict," Mrs. Beloborodova says. "Nothing in Thanksgiving is even remotely pagan."

"This is our mailman Mr. Rubin." Mrs. Zhukova smiles icily.

"I can't believe you've become so irreligious since you've been in America."

Mrs. Kharzina laughs. "Wake up, Leontiy. It's called assimilation. You keep your Russian customs and add new ones from America to be like everybody else. Some people even change their names to become more American. Lyuba's friends Aleksey and Nikolas changed the spelling of their surnames, from s-k-i-y to s-k-y, to look less foreign and pedantic."

Mr. Zhukov sits and stews during the entire meal, while Lyuba slips her left hand under the table and rubs the growing bulge. She has absolutely nothing to be thankful for, other than growing the child of the man she loves most of all in this world. If Ivan were to celebrate this foreign holiday, he wouldn't have the money or space to prepare a lavish feast with cranberry sauce, turkey, mashed potatoes, gravy, stuffing, baked squash, pumpkin pie, carrot pudding, and parsnip fritters, but now Lyuba longs for a humble meal in the squalid tenement. She'd be genuinely thankful for such a feast, and it would be in her precious, dear, cherished home, with her belovèd, their child, and all their friends. This meal of plenty makes a mockery of the concept of giving thanks, but hopefully soon she'll be safely back where she belongs and will have a real reason to feel thankful for the simplest things in life.

11

"My poor baby, everything will be normal for you very soon. You'll meet your big sister, your cousins, your other great-aunt, and everyone else as soon as I can possibly go back where I belong. You'll never have to see my father. And you're going to be a beautiful little boy, just like your father—"

Mrs. Kharzina stops cold in her tracks and sees Lyuba cradling her midsection in her arms and talking to it. "Lyuba, you're pregnant!"

"*Tyotya* Rita, I didn't hear you come in."

"Yes, I suspected it, and so did your mother." She marches over and looks. "Your first trimester, correct?"

"Does my father know about it or suspect it? I can't live if he finds out!"

"He never will find out. That terrible man, fathering a child and grandchild by his own daughter! I'll arrange for a doctor to come as soon as humanly possible to get rid of it. It's a bit late, but hope springs eternal. How did you live with yourself, carrying that man's baby?"

"No, you don't understand. This baby is what kept me from losing hope all this time. I love him and want him to be born in a home full of love."

"You can't have this baby. It'll probably have twelve toes, three hands, a brain abnormality, or Mongoloidism. Even I'm not so Christian I believe in forcing a woman to bear a child conceived of incest. That's too diabolical."

"The father is Ivan. I knew it before I came here."

"That's just wishful thinking." Mrs. Kharzina manages to smile. "So you finally took him as your lover, after all that time living together celibately. I thought I saw a twinkle in his eye and a spring in his step."

"It's more than just that. I felt I was pregnant the morning after we were first together, but then a midwife confirmed it. The child is Ivan's. Little baby Konev."

"You've known this child is Ivan's?"

"I felt terrible I couldn't tell him the two times he came here when you were all out."

"Ivan came here? To our house? And you didn't leave with him? Twice?"

"My father would've killed me!"

"I know what *will* kill Ivan. Going a moment longer not knowing he's going to be a father."

"He already is a father."

"As much as he loves Tatyana, nothing will compare to the love he'll feel for his first biological child when you place your baby in his arms for the first time."

"That'll make it all worthwhile."

"I'm getting you out of the house tonight. You didn't bring

luggage, did you? I'll mix something in your father's drink tonight, and when he's out cold and your mother is sleeping, you'll leave the house and take a taxi home. I'll lend you a warm fur coat and boots, so you don't freeze while you're walking a safe distance away and waiting for a taxi. Before you know it, you'll be back where you belong, safe with the man you love. This mad dream will be over."

****

Chapter 29: Home Sweet Home

Lyuba tiptoes out of the house that night, the start of December 3, listening to her sleeping mother breathing and her father lying next to her mother, passed out drunk. Her aunt is asleep down the hall, having been ejected from the bedroom she'd shared with her sister since they bought the house. Lyuba bumps into someone on her way down the hall to the front door, and her heart stops.

"Come to see my father?" She tries to sound normal.

"I got directions to this house, but it took awhile to find. This is where they said my wife, her sister, and my son live."

"*Dyadya* Mishenka, it's you!" Lyuba throws her arms around him. "*Tyotya* Rita will die of joy to find out you're alive! But Ginny isn't here. *Tyotya* Rita sent him to my apartment when my father showed up in early October. That's how long I've been living here, a prisoner of my father. *Tyotya* Rita found out my secret today, so she got my father drunk so I could slip out of the house and go back to Ivan. You must go to *Tyotya* Rita right away, lie down beside her, and let her wake up and find you there. If you wake her up, she'd scream and wake both my parents, and then I'd never be able to escape."

Mikhail Kharzin tries to take all this in. "You're running away?"

"My father threatened my daughter if I didn't come of my own free will! I'm only leaving now because I'm pregnant."

Her uncle turns to stone. "That disgusting excuse for life. I think I'll kill him right now."

"No, Ivan Konev is the father. A midwife confirmed this before my father took me. *Pozhaluysta*, don't hate me for being pregnant out of wedlock a second time, and by a different man."

"Of course I'd never hate or judge my precious niece. These things happen, much as certain people would like to believe only loose, immoral women do that. How far along are you?"

"About three months."

"You shouldn't walk so far in this weather when you're pregnant, no matter how far along you are. Wait right here. I'll put my luggage in your aunt's room, and then I'll drive you home."

"You have a car?"

"I bought it this afternoon on credit. My first payment is due in a month. It was getting dark, and I didn't want to be robbed, so I figured, why not? I'm going to be a real American, and that means having my own automobile."

Five minutes later, Lyuba gets into her uncle's new Model T and begins directing him to her apartment. When they arrive on the Lower East Side fifteen minutes later, she opens her door and climbs out.

"Which is the building?"

"That one. We're on the top floor." She points. "I'll show you in."

Lyuba lies on the floor and goes to sleep almost as soon as they hit the top story. Mr. Kharzin knocks on the last door on the left. He knocks ten times before the door opens.

"What do you want? It's three in the morning." Ivan's accent is heavier than usual after being roused from sleep in the middle of the night.

"You must be Ivan Konev. My poor niece just collapsed on the floor and fell asleep. Don't you recognize her?"

"God has been good to me today," he whispers, picking Lyuba up, carrying her to their bed, and setting her down. "And to you too, of course. You're her uncle, Ginny's father?"

"I came home tonight and heard the whole story from my niece. If I were you, I'd deadbolt the door and not let anyone come in."

Ivan maneuvers Lyuba out of her boots, woolen socks, and fur coat, tucks her in, and drapes a blanket over her. "Not only that, but I'm going to kill your brother-in-law. Do you know he threatened my daughter?"

"Yes, Lyuba mentioned that. Where's my great-niece?"

"She's asleep in that room over there. Ginny sleeps in the room next to hers. Do you want something to eat?"

"I won't bother you. I had supper at a diner in Greenwich Village. When Lyuba wakes up, she'll have something important to tell you."

Ginny shuffles into the living room. "Who's this man who sprung a visit on us so damn late?"

"You don't recognize him?" Ivan asks. "I recognized *my* father the second I saw him again."

Ginny eyes him carefully. "I guess you are my father. It's hard to recognize you when I've only seen you once over the last seven years."

"Tomorrow I'll take you and your mother out for lunch. We have a lot of lost time to make up for, and I won't force you to immediately resume the close father-son relationship we had before I went to war. So many things have happened since then, and we can't carry on as though we haven't been separated for so long."

Ginny walks up to him and hugs him. "You have no idea how much I missed you. I wouldn't have gotten into so much trouble if you'd been there to discipline me. Welcome home."

2

Mrs. Zhukova nearly faints when she sees her sister asleep next to a man the next morning.

"Rita, who's this strange man you dragged home with you? You know Leontiy won't like it very much—"

Mrs. Kharzina sees her husband next to her and screams. "Mishenka, you're home! Thank God!" She wraps him in her arms.

Mr. Zhukov wakes up out of his drunken stupor upon hearing his sister-in-law's screaming and marches down the hall. "What the hell's your problem?"

"Hello, Leontiy." Mr. Kharzin fixes him with a cold, steely stare. "I see you still have that scar I gave you. I've heard you're still as depraved as ever."

"Unlike Katya, I'm happy to see *my* husband is alive. Stop gaping, Leontiy."

Mr. Zhukov spits on the floor. "Joy, a fifth mouth to feed."

"You're getting one in exchange for another," Mrs. Zhukova reminds him. "I'm getting Lyuba out of the house so she can marry Boris."

"We settled that already, Katya. Lyuba goes nowhere." Mr. Zhukov strides down the hallway. "Lyuba, your uncle's here!" He goes into her room and finds it empty. "Katya, you *already* got her out of the house! She's gone!"

"I didn't make arrangements yet. Perhaps she's in another part of the house."

"*I* made arrangements," Mrs. Kharzina says. "She left last night."

"I ran into her on her way out of the house," Mr. Kharzin says. "I drove her back to her apartment."

"You can't do that!" Mr. Zhukov spits again. "I control her!"

Mrs. Zhukova gasps. "I wasn't ready to get her out of the house yet!"

"She was more than ready." Mrs. Kharzina gets out of bed and puts on her slippers. "Just yesterday I found out she's three months pregnant. She had to leave."

"I knew it!" Mrs. Zhukova begins pulling her husband's hair and scratching his eyes. "You crossed the line, Leontiy. You got your own daughter pregnant. And all those years I turned a blind eye to it, thinking it couldn't get much worse. You'd better be willing to pay the money for the doctor to terminate it, and for the possible trip abroad to have it done legally!"

"Calm down. It's not Leontiy's, praise God."

"Then who else could it have been?"

"Ivan Konev, who else? She didn't sleep with Boris even once in the few months she lived with him and his parents, and before your husband took her away, a midwife confirmed she was pregnant. Thank God."

"The baby is Ivan's." Mrs. Zhukova crosses herself. "God has spoken. It surely must be his will for Lyuba to be with Ivan. That's where she is now, isn't she? She can't possibly be going to a doctor as we speak, can she?"

"She's pregnant out of wedlock a second time!" Mr. Zhukov spits on the rug. "She'll have two children by two different fathers! Just how shameful is that? You call that 'God's will'?!"

"But she'll marry Ivan. He'll be my son-in-law, not Boris. Ivan will make her a respectable woman."

"You have to do more than say you accept their relationship and are sorry for not standing up for her ages ago," Mrs. Kharzina says. "That can't undo years of hurt and damage overnight."

"Sometimes people genuinely change suddenly," Mr. Kharzin says. "One of the early *Decameron* stories is about the King of Cyprus being rebuked by a Gascon woman and suddenly waking up as though from a dream. He reformed his character overnight and never went back to his former ways. Time will only tell if Katya is just as genuine in her sudden change of heart."

3

"Why don't you eat the breakfast I made you?" Ivan pleads.

"After that nightmare your uncle rescued you from, you need to eat as much as possible. Praise Christ you're back where you belong. I'll take such good care of you, and spend the rest of my life making up for how I passively let that *mudak* take you away from me, after I worked so hard to finally earn your eternal trust and commitment."

"I don't want to think about last night." Lyuba picks at her oatmeal.

"Why do you look so sad to be home? I thought you got used to this tenement, since it's full of our love in spite of being small and premodern. Are you worried about your father's earlier threat to take Tatyana?"

"Yes, but I also have something important to tell you." Lyuba reaches over and pats Tatyana on the head. "But promise you won't be upset."

"Do you still feel ill?"

"Not as much as I was, no. It's just that—well, it was the reason I had to stay with my father as long as I did—I was afraid for both of us—you see, I knew why I was ill—it's just that—I'm pregnant."

Ivan freezes. Lyuba runs into their room and sits on the bed. Ivan follows her and pulls her into his arms.

"You're furious. I suspected you might be. What, why are you crying if you're angry?"

"Your father is the sickest man in the universe! I'm going to get a doctor here as soon as possible. Fathering his own grandchild and child at the same time indeed. You can finish your oatmeal while we wait for the doctor."

"I don't want to get rid of my baby! I love this dear little boy!"

"I can't ignore that your father did this to you. It's my job to take care of you, and that includes saving you from such a diabolical fate."

Ivan doesn't hear another word out of her mouth and goes to look through the phonebook. He curses when he realizes abortion services aren't exactly publicly advertised, and that midwives no longer advertise themselves as they did twenty years ago. Even then, there's no telling if a midwife or physician offers therapeutic abortions, or if the procedure would involve cotton padding or knitting needles in lieu of a safe surgical procedure. Lyuba sits picking at the oatmeal, and whenever she tries to protest, he urges her to eat.

"I'm not going to break one of the laws of our religion," Lyuba says when he comes back into their room. "Killing your would-be assassin was justifiable, but terminating a wanted pregnancy isn't."

"God will forgive us for this, though he won't forgive your father."

"You can't do this to my baby! You don't understand at all! It's not my father's baby! Don't you think I too would agree to this if it were?"

Ivan's eyes narrow. "Then whose is it? Boris?"

She shakes her head. "I told you the truth when I said I haven't slept with him since last year."

"Are you trying to tell me this isn't your father's or Boris's child, but the child of a total stranger? When did this happen? Tell me his name or where you think he lives, and I'll go there to murder him immediately! I can't let you give birth to a child born of rape. I would've done the same if Basil had gotten you pregnant."

"I'm telling you, I can't do this because I know who the father is!"

"It won't matter who it is soon enough. I'll find an abortion doctor if I have to send you abroad and pay thousands of dollars. You mean that much to me."

"Just let me explain to you why I want this baby!"

"For the last time, give me one reasonable explanation as to why you'd possibly want to carry to term the child of a rape!"

"Because you're the father!"

"Now just because I'm the father—" Ivan drops to his knees. "Did you just say I'm the father?"

Lyuba nods. "Are you angry?"

"You're sure?" he whispers.

"It was what I wanted to tell you the day my father came."

Ivan sits beside her and begins to cry. "Mine?"

"I didn't want to upset you when you visited me, so I didn't tell you."

"Your father would've killed us if he'd known." He kisses her hands. "My first biological child. This is a miracle."

"Don't get too excited, Vanka. You probably feel tempted to quit your job and stay at home till he's born."

"I'll work overtime to afford a second child. When I'm not at work, I'll take such good care of you. I'll snap your father in half if he comes through our door again."

"Baby Konev wants you to say hello." Lyuba places his hands over the bulge. "I'm not able to feel him move or kick yet, but I've been talking to him every day."

"What if it's Baby Koneva?"

"I thought you wanted a firstborn son. I've been praying it's a boy."

"Whatever you give me, I'll love." He rubs the bulge protectively. "If you feel even the slightest pain, lie down right away, and as soon as I get home from work, I'll be your serf."

"Will you do the right thing and make me a respectable woman?"

"I'm dying to be your husband, but we're already married in our hearts. We shouldn't rush our dream wedding just because a baby's on the way. I'll still love you and be your sweetheart. You deserve a wedding fit for a Tsaritsa, not a shameful, rushed affair to avoid wagging tongues." Ivan starts up when the door creaks open. "If it's your father, I'm about to send him to Hell." He kisses her on the forehead and goes to the door. "What do you want?"

"I'm not my uncle, Konev. It's me. I just got back from lunch at a Greek restaurant with my parents."

"Oh, good, Ginny. Why don't you come in and start making food for our guests?"

"What guests?"

"We're going to have a party this evening. Lyuba, tell Ginny and Tanya the good news."

Lyuba smiles down at her daughter. "Tanyechka, guess what! You're going to have a little brother!"

"A real brother?" Tatyana asks excitedly.

"You'll probably meet him around June, and you'll be such a big helper. I know you'll be the best big sister ever, and love your little brother so much."

"Who are you having a baby with?" Ginny demands. "My uncle?"

"He's mine." Ivan goes across the hall and pounds on Eliisabet's door.

Eliisabet greets him. "What's the matter?"

"Lyuba came home last night with her uncle and told me the most beautiful news ever. Where's your husband?"

"Lyuba's home? And do you know she's having your baby?"

"Do I know? I'm going to die of joy! And I'm inviting everyone we know for a party."

"Can all of us fit in there?"

"Who cares! I'll make us fit!"

"Alyoshka, come here," Eliisabet calls. "Ivan's inviting all of us over. Lyuba came home last night, and she just told Ivan they're having a baby. I've known for awhile, but I've been keeping it a secret from you."

Aleksey scratches his head. "Are you sure it's his?"

"She wasn't sleeping with Boris, *golubchik*, and she knew before her father came. Konev isn't as bashful as he used to be!"

Aleksey smiles at him. "So you finally became a real man and never let on. I knew I saw a spring in your step and mysterious smiles in September. I should've known what caused that."

Lyuba sits on the davenport and greets their friends as they come in one by one. After Eliisabet and Aleksey have come in with Nikolay and Novomira, Kittey comes in with Nikolas, and then Kat waddles in, looking six months pregnant.

"Lyuba, how exciting! Mine will be born just a month before yours!"

Lyuba has a good long look at Kat. "Aren't you concerned how you look more pregnant than you really are?"

"My abdomen itches a lot, but everyone says that's normal. Yet I can't help thinking I'm having twins or triplets. I hope to God the woman who makes up my schedules is dead wrong and that I'm not one of the few women who've had four babies at once."

After that, Pavel, Mr. Lebedev, his daughters, and Kroshka, Leontiy and Anya, and Alya and Anya Furtseva come over.

"Do you think we should invite Katrin, *golubchik*?" Lyuba asks, snuggling against Ivan.

"That shallow woman who cared more about material possessions than saving her own life?"

"No, Vanya, I'm serious. She wanted me to be with you. Boris fell out of her favor a long time ago. And we didn't have such a long wait on Ellis Island because she curried favor with Sandro."

4

Katrin loves her penthouse suite on the Upper West Side. In the morning, she wakes up as late as possible, usually a good hour before her spoilt best friend, and goes to the table to partake of breakfast. Her cook, Mrs. Oswald, always has a lavish spread waiting—eggs, bacon, ham, cottage cheese, sheep cheese, goat cheese, pancakes, waffles, fruit salad, hash browns. After breakfast, Katrin focuses on typing her latest articles for the Estonian-language paper. Sometimes Sandro stops by for lunch, after which she reads the Estonian, Russian, Lithuanian, Latvian, French, and German newspapers until it's time to eat supper. Every so often, she interrupts her reading to chat with her maid, Mrs. Samson. Right now she's working on a scathing editorial denouncing the so-called Emergency Quota Act, while Anastasiya sits gazing over the latest issue of *Vogue*.

"Who's on the phone, Katya?"

"Lyuba Zhukova."

"What does she want?"

"She wants to use our suite to host a party in about six months, since her apartment's so small. And they're inviting me to a little party they're having at their house today."

"You mean Ivan let her back in after she left him again? What a pathetic doormat that man is."

"You know as well as I do she had no choice but to go with her father. He threatened her daughter, Nastya!"

"Don't tell me they're getting married in six months."

"Ivan still insists she deserves a wedding suit for a Tsaritsa, and won't hear of rushing things. Their landlord believes they're civilly married and are saving money for a second, religious ceremony."

"But I'm the better woman!"

"Oh, get over yourself already. He was only using you to try to make Lyuba jealous. And it sure worked. Besides, Ivan wouldn't dream of leaving her when she's carrying his first biological child."

Anastasiya turns grey. "That's not fair! And I thought Lyuba couldn't have more children."

"It's not impossible, just a miracle."

"But I wanted to be the lucky one!"

"Oh, read the personal ads in one of the Estonian papers."

"Those things are for people who are too desperate to do anything else! Only luckless, unattractive people place personal ads."

"Maybe you could get together with Boris."

"Never! He's already been with a woman, has a child by her, and he's too chubby."

"What about that fellow who came over on the ship with us, Maksim? You seem to enjoy playing the role of a helpless, fragile damsel, and he's as old-fashioned as they come."

"He's Russian, and I want an Estonian. I may be very Russified, but I haven't forgotten who I really am."

"Then whyever are you so obsessed with Konev?"

"Because he's good-looking. What woman wouldn't want such a handsome man?"

"But he never wanted nor loved you."

"I'll make him want me again."

"You'd be so low as to try to win over the heart of a man with a fiancée who's pregnant with their first child together? Give me a break."

"So you told her she can use our suite for a party."

"I was just about to before you began your little sulking fit. Why don't you run off and see that movie you've seen every day since it came out, the one with that handsome Italian fellow? That way you'll be having fun, and none of us will have to deal with your sulking at this party."

"Rudy Valentino's just a fantasy man, like Grand Duke Dmitriy! Ivan is real! I have a chance with him!"

"No you don't. Now why don't you run along to the theatre, and with any luck, you might find a sheik of your own who doesn't have a pregnant fiancée and an unofficial stepdaughter."

5

Lyuba impatiently waits for Ivan to come to bed that night. He's been at the door for twenty minutes, fooling with the new locks.

"Isn't the door locked enough yet?"

"Not locked enough to keep your unworthy father out, my love."

"Whatever happened to your plan to murder him instead of arresting him? I'll sleep a lot more soundly if he's dead."

"If he comes around here again, I'll give him one warning. If he disobeys me, it's time to send him to Hell."

Ivan comes to bed five minutes later. Lyuba sits up and runs her hands under his pajama shirt, but he gently pushes her away.

"Don't you want me anymore now that I'm pregnant?"

"What a question. I wanted you every single day of your other pregnancy."

"You won't crush the baby, if that's what you're afraid of. My father never crushed him."

"If he *had* crushed our baby, I would've marched over to his house and snapped him in half."

"Is it because Ginny's here? Even if he's old enough to understand we must be doing that, he's probably trained himself to not think about it if he happens to overhear something. And not that I want to be overheard, but if it happens, it sends children a positive, healthy message about sexual relations, instead of thinking it's so shameful, dirty, and secretive."

"It's too soon after your father. I don't feel right. You yourself stopped me from finishing what we'd started the first time, since you thought it was too soon after what our fathers did. You've already made me the happiest I've ever been. Tomorrow, we'll visit my aunt and tell her the good news."

"Who else is left to tell after that?"

Ivan smirks in the dark. "I can think of the perfect person."

6

The next evening, Lyuba puts on Lyolya Lebedeva's coat and waits for Ivan to finish washing his hands of the soot from the factory. He's in the bathroom for over ten minutes with the water running.

"Are you okay in there?" Lyuba opens the door and peers in. "Why are you letting the water run if you're not using it?"

"I didn't want to upset you."

Lyuba sits beside him on the narrow bench. "Why are you crying? Are you upset because you wanted me to have an abortion?"

"I was just thinking about what your father did to you."

"But that's not a problem anymore, Vanya. He can't do it ever again."

"I knew something was off about him from the moment I met your family, but I was too young and stupid to figure it out until I was thirteen. And I had my father's drinking to deal with too. I was unable to protect you from that terrible man when he came back, because I'm a coward. I let you endure those awful things for too long, and just passively accepted it. If I'd just done something, anything, to try to stop it sooner, you might not think the abnormal is normal."

"I don't think even a priest could've stopped my father."

"How long did it take before you came to accept that? All those unspeakable things he made you do and that he did to you, how scared and confused—" He wraps his arms around her and sobs into her hair.

"At least I saved Tatyana."

"I can't forgive him. You know what, I'm going to take a knife with me in case we bump into him. I'd purchase a gun, but I'd probably be scared to fire it. You know me, I'm a coward."

"You weren't a coward when you killed Basil or all those times you beat up Boris or anyone else who threatened me."

"I too was frightened by your father's threats to go to the police and have Tatyana taken away."

"Our baby won't think you're a coward. He'll worship you and think you're the most wonderful example of a real man in this world."

"I must've done something right. You picked me to love over everyone else who wanted you."

7

Mr. Konev leaps up to open the door as Valeriya dusts off the framed pictures of her husband's family. Ginny heads for a rocking chair and begins looking at a Russian magazine.

"What do I owe the pleasure of this visit to?" Valeriya asks, picking up her eight-month-old son. "Anything besides your fiancée coming home?"

"Most first-cousins once-removed are a generation apart." Ivan carefully holds little Vasya. "But this little one will only be fourteen months older than his. Maybe they'll be best friends growing up."

Valeriya looks at Lyuba. "Vasya's first-cousin once-removed—Lyuba, are you pregnant?"

"I knew it for a long time," Mr. Konev says. "I was the third person to know she's carrying my first grandchild."

"She knows it's mine," Ivan says. "I love Tatyana like my own, but this child will be flesh of my flesh and blood of my blood!"

Everyone except Lyuba and Tatyana knows it's a wonder and a miracle she conceived again, let alone has carried it this far. Ivan intends to keep the secret that way. Afterwards, when they're old and grey and have hopefully had a few more children, he'll tell her, and not fear her adverse reaction at finding out.

8

"What do you want, Konev?" Boris demands, opening the door.

"I'm home, Borya," Lyuba says.

"That's great news!" He turns to Ivan. "So you're going to return Lyuba and my daughter, I hope. Why didn't you tell me sooner, or did she just escape?"

"She came back to me at three in the morning yesterday," Ivan says. "I don't think she'll ever return to you."

Mrs. Malenkova comes into the room and gets an eyeful of Lyuba. "You're pregnant!" She clutches the back of a chair to prevent fainting.

"It's Vanya's. Don't worry, Shura."

Boris turns red. "That's not fair! I wanted to marry you and give you a second child! Not him, that Konev! Now you'll never marry me! Unless of course you agree to let Ivan raise the mistake and come back to live with me, or marry me and let me pretend it's my child too."

Ivan gives him a push. "My unborn son is not a mistake, Malenkov. I'm going to start working overtime to afford a second child. Unlike Tatyana, *my* baby was created out of consent and love. Two things which never happened any of the times you were with Lyuba. You're not coming anywhere near my son when he's born, nor will you lay a hand on my pregnant fiancée."

"Can I at least have some time with my daughter? Come here, Tanyechka. I've been looking forward to visiting you again."

"Those visits stop as of today. She'll get confused if you keep coming to see her when she's being raised by Lyuba and me, with a little brother on the way."

"But I was finally building a relationship with my child! No fair!"

"Vanya finally forgave his father," Lyuba says. "Maybe when Tatyana's a grown woman, you can come around as a father again too. You can see her every year."

"That child will be three years old next month! Like hell I'm waiting twenty years to finally have a fatherly relationship with her again!"

"Don't be such a baby," Ivan sneers. "You can always find a woman who'll have you at church."

"I only want Lyuba and Tatyana! Can't you see?"

"But of course, Shura, you and Sanya will be this baby's grandparents too," Lyuba says. "Since Tatyana's your granddaughter, her little brother shouldn't be treated any differently."

"Oh. And meanwhile, the father of this baby's older sister gets to have no contact with said older sister!"

"Exactly. We'll manage to work something out by the time he's born."

"I'll tell Father Spiridon what you're doing and find a lawyer! I refuse to give up my only child!"

"If you're so against ever finding another woman, why don't you adopt?" Mr. Malenkov sighs.

"Oh, I tried to, you know I did try! I told you about how I came back from Russia with a baby boy, Yuriy. Lyuba's mother and aunt promptly took him away from me the first time I was out of the house."

"They didn't take him away from you because he was never yours to begin with."

"The boy's aunt had a note pinned to him, saying whomever found him could take him and raise him. She gave me permission when she saw I'd found him. I'd grown to love him so much by the time I came back to America. I was held over in Europe because of the baby."

"You told us you were forced off the ship when it passed Denmark because they discovered you were an illegal immigrant."

"I walked and took crowded trains from Denmark all the way to Belgium, and then we were held in quarantine for two weeks so they could make sure Yuriy didn't have any diseases before we boarded the ship."

"And you left that child alone in the house, after how much you claimed to love him."

"I did not! I washed, fed, and diapered him before I went to work!"

"But you knew Lyuba's mother and aunt also worked."

"It was Mrs. Zhukova. I'll get her yet. She was the one who left him on the floor, didn't change his diaper, and ignored his cries."

"Would never have happened if you'd found a nanny."

"Mrs. Kharzina came home because she forgot her handbag, and saw the work of her evil older sister. After changing his diaper and soothing him, she took him to an orphanage, where he languished for months, and then had the nerve, *Batya*, the *nerve*, to read my private mail!"

"Why didn't you mail it right away if it was so private?"

"Shut up! It was a letter to you, Lyuba, telling you about what happened to me and Yuriy on our way back to New York."

"Like I would've cared if I'd read that letter."

"I would've torn it up and thrown it into flames," Ivan agrees.

"At least now Yuriy's back with his mother," Mrs. Malenkova says. "And one of his aunts, and his mother's two friends."

"I hate you, *Matushka*! Yuriy was my child! That girl is only fourteen! At least in the orphanage, he could've been adopted back by me or a couple."

"A few centuries ago, most Russian girls *were* that age when they got married and started having babies."

"Oh, this is not fair! I'll tell Father Spiridon about you, and you'll be sorry."

"Maybe while you're there, you can make a pit stop to confess and tell him about how you recommended Ivan let you raise his firstborn child, told your father to shut up, and told your mother you hated her. Don't forget to add you engaged in hateful speech against everyone in this house except Ginny, and spoke ill of the mother of Yuriy Yeltsin."

"This is not fair! I want to marry Lyuba and start over!"

"You do know you're expected to confess regularly, don't you, son?" Mr. Malenkov asks. "What will those impressionable students of yours think of you if they see their teacher hasn't confessed?"

"Why don't you go to Hell, *Batya*."

"He's always this disrespectful to his parents, Vanka," Lyuba whispers.

"I don't think we should have to put up with this behavior,

Sanya. It would be a good thing for everyone involved if Boris moved out and found his own place as soon as possible. He's always bragging about how much money he makes and how comfortably he can afford to live."

"Crazy woman. This *is* my own place! I bought it! You were the ones who moved in on me without an invitation! Find your own house and leave me here in the house I bought with my own money! Like hell I'll leave my house!"

Before Boris can move, Aleksandr Malenkov strikes him and sends him flying onto his back, then begins whacking him with a fire poker. "I am not going to put up with a son who disrespects his parents and his former friends so much. You're going to pack your things and be out of here by tonight, boy."

"My house. I can prove it in court."

"Then go back to where you came from until you can learn to respect other people besides yourself."

9

Everything has come out for the better, Ivan can't help thinking as he puts away the dishes the next evening. Mr. Kharzin is alive and in America, Mr. Konev has turned his whole life around, Valeriya has remarried and had a baby, Mr. Zhukov hasn't come around again, Boris has been thrown out by his parents and come crawling back to Mrs. Kharzina and Mrs. Zhukova, and now a baby on the way.

"You need me to help you with anything, *golubka*?"

"You do enough work at the factory. Don't bother me."

Ivan puts away the last of the dishes and comes into the washroom. The bathtub is full of fresh, hot water, and Lyuba is in the process of removing her clothes. Her off-white blouse and brown wool socks are on the floor, and she's slowly unbuttoning her ankle-length calfskin skirt. Ivan's heart rends when he sees a number of scratches on her upper body.

"Your father did that to you, didn't he?"

She nods, looking away.

"Praise Christ you're back where you belong, so I can take care of you again. I'll do everything in my power to make sure you're never hurt again."

He helps her out of the rest of her clothes, then helps her into the bathtub. Lyuba softly smiles at him as he tenderly bathes her.

Afterwards, while the tub is draining, he dries her off with a fresh white towel and disinfects her cuts and scratches with iodine and ointment. He looks at her curiously when he finds a pale blue silk nightgown on top of the hamper, in place of the purple pajamas or regular white cotton nightgown she usually wears.

"Where did you get this?" he asks after he slips it onto her body.

"I bought it at Macy's when you were at work the other day."

"You left the house?"

"I was perfectly safe. My father works during the day, and if he'd approached me, I would've shouted for a police officer or run into the nearest building."

"I hope you don't mind if we're not able to get married before the birth. I really want to make you a respectable woman in everyone's eyes, but we shouldn't rush our ideal wedding just because of this."

"*Pozhaluysta,* don't keep me waiting very much longer. I can only bear so much of being an unrespectable woman."

"I respect you, and so do all our friends and most of our relatives. It's not the concern of strangers to judge situations and people about which and whom they know nothing, *golubka.*"

That night Lyuba falls asleep safely beside Ivan after they've made love, and she dreams about bringing home little Baby Konev from the hospital, and all of them standing in a circle, except Boris, as Father Yakim baptizes him. She'll never worry again about having to leave Ivan, because with a baby on the way, their love has finally been solidified, with no worries whatsoever about getting scared.

****

Chapter 30: Consequences for Mr. Zhukov

"They don't want me doing any bending or lifting now that I'm heavily pregnant." Kat pats her midsection. "You want to feel her kicking?"

It's now February 1922, and Lyuba and Kat are in a store on the Upper East Side, buying baby things. Kat looks about ready to give birth, despite being three months away from her guess month, and Lyuba is now five months pregnant.

"You can feel mine kicking too. He's been waking me up in the middle of the night. The first few times we felt him moving, it was amazing, but now all he does is kick, kick, kick. I think he'll grow up to be as strong as Vanka."

"Mine doesn't kick quite so much, but she moves around an awful lot, like she's fighting against something."

The proprietor takes a good look at Kat. "How far along did you say you are, Mrs. Vrangel?"

"Six months, I think."

"Either you really miscalculated when you got pregnant, or you're having twins or triplets!"

"I don't want to think about having more than one. This is my first as it is."

"It'll all be over before you know it. Thank God, there's a new drug that lets women go to sleep and forget the pain. You'll love twilight sleep and the hospital."

"Yes, thank God for modern medical miracles."

2

Svetlana hasn't yet served five full years, but she's being let out a bit early for good behavior. She picks up a small satchel of things and squeezes Nadezhda's hands at the gate of their camp in Uelen, Russia's easternmost settlement, very close to the Bering Strait.

"You're a very good escape artist," Svetlana pleads. "Why don't you come with me and make it look as though you weren't escaping with me? I don't want five more years pasted onto me. I'll wait for you in Alaska Territory. There are many Russians there."

"You can't go to Alaska Territory. Your family's in New York. Imagine how your father's eyes will light up when he discovers a sixth daughter is still alive. Little Kroshka's there too. You can get a job in a hospital, helping the im-

migrant women and their babies. I don't want to get my whole brigade in trouble by escaping or attempting to escape. You go now and go to your father and your five sisters. You know how loyal dogs are. Kroshka will doubtless leap at your legs and lick your face."

"I'll tell Pasha you're still alive."

"Tell him I'm waiting for him too, that I haven't been with any other men since I left prostitution."

"If he still loved you while you were a prostitute, I don't think he'd mind very much if you were to be with men again here."

"You know that's out of the question. Anyway, after you go to America, there will only be four more of your sisters left to find."

"Dina and Fima are probably still alive, but I don't know what happened to Lyolya. To say nothing of Motya."

"He'll still get the majority of his daughters back. I'll look out for the babies here. You were a very good nurse to them, actually giving a damn about each little baby, unlike most of the mothers and the other nurses."

"If you see Dina or Fima, tell them I'm alive and went to America."

"Of course. I'll also tell them their father, Galya, Alla, Vera, Natalya, and Dora are there. Knowing they're not sole survivors would do their spirits such beautiful good."

3

Lyuba is on the davenport, reading Lermontov's *A Hero of Our Time*, when she sees her father standing there. Blood rushes and pounds through her ears just as when Basil came back. "What do you want?"

"I wanted to visit my daughter, so I picked your locks. Wow. What an awful lot of locks you have on that door."

"You're not allowed to come here, *Batya*. Tanyechka, run across the hall to your godparents."

Tatyana scampers over to Eliisabet and Aleksey's apartment.

"I can't believe you got pregnant out of wedlock a second time, by another man. What a disgusting slut I raised. Are you going to go live in sin again with the father of your first child after this second one is born, or find another man to have a third illegitimate child with? I can't stand that man living in my house. He eats all our food, sleeps late, whines and moans about how his parents threw him out of his house, wastes his money on trinkets for you and presents for your illegitimate daughter, and cries out his prayers. That such a person is a teacher at a church school."

"Did you come to beg forgiveness for the unforgivable?"

Mr. Zhukov smiles his vile smile. "You know, there are drugs to induce labor. Once you're no longer pregnant, you can come back to live with us. What I wouldn't give to enjoy your luscious body again right this very minute."

Lyuba wraps her arms around her midsection. "I'm only five months along. He'd never survive. And you can't force me to take drugs against my consent."

"You don't need another illegitimate child to add to your rap sheet."

"It's not your business I chose to keep both of my children. Unlike you, I adore my children."

"After I get a lawyer involved, you'll have no choice but to give it up."

Ivan comes into the apartment and glares at Mr. Zhukov. "What business do you have coming here? Who let you in?"

"I picked your locks. Everyone was out. Don't worry, I haven't touched my daughter. Like I'd want to, even in my dreams, when she's pregnant with her second illegitimate child!"

"Where's my daughter?"

"Lyuba sent her across the hall."

Lyuba is shaking. "Vanya, do you know what he was ordering me to do?"

"I can guess. He wants you to come back to your mother's house and be his slave again."

"He said he'd get a lawyer involved and make me give up our baby."

"Yes, I mentioned she can come back to live with us once she's no longer pregnant. You haven't married her yet. It'll be pretty hard to convince the authorities for me to stay away from her when she's not your wife."

"Unluckily for you, it's far too late for an abortion. When my son comes in four months, you won't be allowed anywhere near him."

Lyuba tightly pulls her arms around herself. "He suggested drugs to induce labor, but our baby would die if he were born so early. I want to meet our baby so much, and to give you your own blood child."

"Get out of our apartment. If you come here again, I'll kill you."

Mr. Zhukov sneers. "How are you going to kill me, Konev? The evidence will point right to you! I can go to the police and say you threatened my life."

"You speak English worse than I do. No cop will listen to you." Ivan picks Mr. Zhukov up and throws him down the stairs. "That was only a foretaste of what's to come if you threaten Lyuba and my child again. Do you understand me?"

"You should've thrown him upside-down and killed him," Lyuba says.

"No one can suspect me if I have to kill him. I can't bear for someone to witness it and turn me in to prison again."

"If you do end up getting arrested, I'll go with you like I did before."

"The three of you need me. I'm not going to go to prison for killing him."

"Maybe you won't have to kill him. You might've scared him away this time."

"Why don't you put on the bracelet and necklace I got you for Christmas, and we'll go out for supper to put our minds on much nicer things. Ginny comes home soon."

"Didn't you tell Glazov you're working overtime to afford baby supplies instead of buying expensive jewelry for your fiancée?"

"I can do both. I didn't spend much on our Christmas tree."

"That wasn't a tree. That was a twig that held five ornaments."

"I put away a hundred million of those rubles in a savings account. Mr. Golitsyn helped me with it. As soon as possible, we'll be married."

"The sooner the better. I want to show off our baby in style, but I'd feel better about going out in public with him if he were legitimate. Maybe we can dress him in a tiny silk suit for his welcoming party. Voroshilova will turn green in envy."

"Maybe she's changed and no longer wants to chase after me. Don't sink down to her level."

"Katrin has told me Anastasiya still harbors delusions about getting back together with you. I don't think she'll give it a rest even after we're married."

4

Katrin tosses aside the Estonian weekly for the lowest of the low immigrants. Her nationalist group will be there in an hour, and after that the weekly secret meeting of immigrants who'll join the Socialist Party as soon as they become citizens.

"Is that comic relief, Katya, the poor trash newspaper?"

"Nope. Just wondering if my parents ever came here and were looking for me. Probably were executed or sent to camps, though."

"At least there's a possibility yours might still be alive. I witnessed mine being murdered in the middle of the night, along with my big brother."

"Every week I look in this paper for any mention at all of my parents. Though I still know in my very heart of hearts I did the right thing by turning them over. Goddamn imperialists."

"Don't you feel at all badly about how all your little brothers and sisters were killed when you turned in the names of your parents?"

"No, not a bit. There were so many of them, they were always in my way. Look, as hard as this may be for many people to believe, not everyone loves their families. It doesn't mean I actively hated my siblings and wanted them dead, the same way I always hated my traitor parents, but I only shared a loving, special bond with Vika. In addition, it was a great way to control the population. Nine less people to fill the Earth with more people who in turn will breed too, on until infinity. But if you really want to know, I'm sorry innocent children had to die in order for population control to be achieved. I'll have kids when I'm older than just twenty-two, and not ten like my parents did."

"With Sandro, I assume. After nearly a year, I hope you plan to marry him, or you're leading him on and behaving like a common slut."

"For your information, Sandro and I are in love, but not sleeping together. When has he ever come here when I've been alone, and when have I ever gone to his place alone? He didn't even kiss me for the first time until we'd been courting for five months. I made him earn it. We haven't done much more than French kiss and neck. We don't even pet, since we know what might happen if we get too carried away. Anyway, I'm far too busy to worry about planning a wedding or having a bunch of mewling, vomiting babies tugging at my legs." Katrin adjusts her pants. "Lots of American women wear pants nowadays, Nastya. I think you should too. I can take you to Macy's to help you to select the right pants. We came to America at just the right time, with so many wonderful modern developments, and just before that beastly quota discriminating against Eastern and Southern Europeans. Women get to vote, wear men's clothes, and have short hair. The worst thing about this country is that alcohol is illegal."

"You never drink much, only at parties. And you rarely wore pants before."

"But I always had short hair, and I was a feminist before there was a word for it."

"I think you're wearing pants now just to shock people."

"No, I feel free, wearing pants. I can't very well maneuver around the newspaper office wearing feather boas and tango shoes, now can I? I have different priorities, just as a woman acquires new obligations when she goes from being a co-ed to a working woman, or from a gay bachelorette to a wife and mother."

"You've stopped wearing makeup too."

"Just not as much as I did before. I want to be taken seriously, like an equal to men. I was as good as shooting myself in the back by dressing like a spoilt *knyazhna* and wearing so much makeup. Like everyone always told me, it was bizarre to profess to be such an ardent Communist while living like an out of touch *knyazhna*."

"You never hung up your pictures of all the handsome men we loved to swoon over."

"Take them. They're yours. I'm far too old to get giddy over famous men I'll never know. Besides, half of the nobles are probably dead or in prison for being in Comrade Lenin's way."

"My favorite picture is the one of Grand Duke Dmitriy in his full uniform, all those beautiful medals and tassels. He's still alive."

"Yeah, he's handsome, but a Romanov. A Socialist doesn't display pictures of her oppressors."

"You don't live like a Socialist."

"Just because I'm rich doesn't mean I can't be a Socialist too. You never complain about living like this, do you? *I* should be complaining about how you've been leeching off me for the past three years."

"I'm your best friend, not a leech!"

"The night Lyuba gave birth, you turned up at my back door, saying Ginny kicked you out. Tatyana just turned three last month. So it's been over three years you've been leeching off me. You're a leech, Nastya."

"You let me eat all those nice pastries, cookies, and cakes, drink those expensive teas you stock, and borrow some of your best clothes. A leech wouldn't have permission to do any of that."

"You don't participate in my activities, though. I hope you don't whine when I host the party for Lyuba's baby."

"I should've had a baby with Konev by now."

"He prefers Lyuba. Haven't you figured anything out by now about them? They've been in love since childhood. You, you were only a distraction for him."

5

Svetlana has taken a train through Alaska Territory and now gets on one travelling through Canada.

"Where's your final destination?" the Russian translator asks.

"New York City. My father and five of my sisters are there."

"How old are you, Miss Lebedeva?"

"Twenty-two. I was a nurse in Siberia, helping with the newborn babies in particular. I'm going to work at a hospital when I get to New York."

"How much money do you have to declare?"

"Five hundred rubles and thirty kopeks, Sir. I can also work on the train with the babies. The only thing I can't do is deliver one."

"You can go to Car Number Eleven for the medical personnel. Expect to cross down into Maine in about two months."

Svetlana goes to her designated car and begins to unpack her few things. Besides her clothes, money, and passport, she also has a first aid kit, some food, a couple of blankets and sheets, a hand-drawn ikon she made in a camp at Magnitogorsk, and a notebook about all the babies she worked with.

"Will you be interested in the religious services on the train?"

"I don't think so. I forget how to behave at Divine Liturgy."

"They're run by Old Believers, if you're interested in just observing until it all comes back to you."

"I'm not an Old Believer, Sir. I don't like them. They cross themselves

incorrectly, misspell the name of Jesus, and do all sorts of abominable things in their services."

"Many of the Russians you'll find in Canada are Old Believers, just like the ones in Alaska Territory. They settled here when they were chased out."

"Are you an Old Believer?"

"No, I only came here in 1915. It's not as if they're as heretical as the Protestants or Catholics."

"No, but they still hold onto rituals and things which have long since been proven incorrect."

"The Catholics and Protestants think we're nuts because we boil our ikons if the saints bring bad luck to us. Crazy is in the eye of the beholder."

"Protestants don't even have ikons, and the Catholic ikons are poor imitations of our true ikons."

"So you remember all this *business, yet you don't feel like you could remember what goes on at Divine Liturgy."*

"I remember religious teachings, but if you'd been away from church for going on five years, you'd feel a bit shaky too about all of a sudden going back. I haven't even confessed anything since 1917."

"You'll get the hang of it again before you know it, Svetlana Ilyinichna."

6

To celebrate Ginny's fifteenth birthday on the fifth of March, Mrs. Kharzina has baked and frosted a chocolate cake. Since it's not safe for Ginny to return home, she and Mr. Kharzin have come over to Lyuba's apartment.

"Didn't *Tyotya* Katya want to come too?" Ginny asks.

"She can't come unless your uncle follows her, and nobody wants that. Besides, Leontiy thinks celebrating secular birthdays is the work of the Devil. You should've seen the fits he pitched when we celebrated Halloween and Thanksgiving."

"Ginny got this in the mail," Lyuba announces. "Though I don't know if he'll want to read this letter now."

"Why, who sent it?"

"Georgiya."

"Is that the girl who almost got you and your friends killed?"

"In spite of how she indirectly caused the invasion of the valley, she saved our lives when the Reds were at our door. She was so helpful on numerous other occasions. She comes from such a good family, even if they've chosen to be Bolshevik."

"How could she send this? Now people will accuse her family of having contact with foreigners, and they'll be kicked out of the Party!" Ginny says.

"I wasn't under the impression travelling abroad or sending mail to people in other countries was illegal."

"No, it's not. But somewhere down the line, you never know. Comrade Lenin can't be around forever."

"Comrade Lenin?" Mrs. Kharzina demands. "Is that how you talk now that you're in America?"

"Oh, just give me my damn letter."

"I'd like to get a letter from Petya, but it's far too dangerous," Lyuba says. "I pray he got back home safely and his father didn't find out what he was really up to all those years."

Ginny tears open his letter.

10 February 1922

Dear Grigoriy:

I didn't know where to send this, so I used the address you said your mother lived at and wrote 'Forward' on the envelope in case you live somewhere else. You'll probably get this on or around your birthday. Aleksandr Shepilov told me in the strictest confidence what he did for you, your cousin, and her friends. He saved your lives, or at least saved you from prison and orphanages.

I'm the top pupil in tenth class, and Leonid hopes to have a future in politics. He plans on running for local office in the next election. Our family is honored by Comrade Lenin because of all five of us. Yes, five. In December, my parents gave me a little sister, Nelya. Comrade Lenin likes almost nothing better than a family with many children and membership in the Party. More enlightened minds to spread the word about Communism.

Don't worry about a censor reading this and getting Aleksandr in trouble, though I know you hated him most of the time you knew him. Pyotr Litvinov got it sent through secret channels that didn't require a censor. Although Comrade Lenin is enlightened enough to know visiting friends and family in other countries and writing them letters isn't wrong or illegal. I don't know about some of the crooks surrounding him, though. He's been feeling not himself lately, with his strokes. If I were still a Christian, I'd pray every night for him, but I instead ask our great Communist saints to save him. Saints like Marx and Engels. I'd die of grief if Comrade Lenin were to die before his time. Of course, all of Russia will be heartbroken on the day he does die, but if he goes before his time and doesn't recover soon, it'll be ever sadder. I cannot stand the Party

Secretary he's taken. Some filthy Caucasian with terrible manners.

I enclosed a picture of my family—me, Leonid, our parents, and Baby Nelya. Papa is really after Leonid to take a wife. He's almost twenty-eight. All the important people in Comrade Lenin's inner circle are married. Lyonya's disobeying the savior of our great and mighty nation of Russia, and twisting his words around to try to justify remaining a celibate, childless bachelor.

If I'm able to, I'll come and visit you in America, or we might meet in another country without people who want to track down your cousin's boyfriend. Even if we never meet again, I'll always keep you in my heart, Grigoriy. I love you and will never forget you.

All my love and Communist greetings,

Georgiya Yuriyevna Savvina.

"I'm going to write right back to her this very instant," Ginny announces.

"You can never be together unless Russia restores the monarchy or Georgiya defects," Lyuba warns. "Each letter will only make both of you sadder. If the higher-ups find out from any of the people who were after Vanya, they'll bring her in and interrogate her. She's almost old enough for prison."

"Mrs. Zyuganova sent girls to prison at thirteen," Natalya Lebedeva shudders. "Sick woman."

Ginny is already writing a letter to Georgiya.

"There are nice girls in your class, aren't there?" Mrs. Kharzina goes on. "How about Kittey or Natalya?"

"I'm too old for those girls."

"I feel the same way," Kittey says from across the room. "I have nothing in common with the other eighth graders."

"My Natasha's smart. She's one grade level above her age," Mr. Lebedev boasts.

"Zhora's a year ahead too, the top pupil in tenth class," Ginny says.

"Is that a picture of her family?" Lyuba inquires.

"Yeah. Isn't she even more beautiful than the last time we saw her in Novgorod?"

"Who's the baby? Leonid's?"

"No, it's her little baby sister Nelya. She was born in December."

"Most women don't have babies that late in life unless it's a second marriage like mine," Valeriya says. "Nelya was probably an accident."

"I don't think Zhora would be very pleased if you told her that, Mrs. Golitsyna! The extra child has added even more honor and reward to her family. Leonid's going to run for local office when the next election rolls around, though their father doesn't think he stands much of a chance unless he takes a wife."

"You know who else just had a birthday?" Ivan asks.

"Yes, Boris turned twenty-two four days ago," Lyuba says. "You couldn't want to send him a belated birthday gift, do you?"

"I sent him something even better."

7

Boris has spent the last few days in a foul mood. He's snapped at the children in religious school, snarled at his parents when they've come to visit, and lashed out at Mrs. Zhukova, the only person left who still loves him.

"Even *I've* accepted that Lyuba will never marry you, and you know how long I wanted that to happen. What is that thing you keep reading?"

"A sick, twisted birthday letter from Ivan, telling me in no uncertain terms what'll happen to my daughter after he marries Lyuba."

Mrs. Zhukova grabs it from his hands and reads it.

To one of the most disgusting creatures to ever walk the planet:

Happy birthday, you svoloch. *Many unhappy returns to you, you* dryan. *Have you seen Lyuba lately? She's entering her sixth month of pregnancy. My child will be born in June, and you won't go anywhere near him (or her). I'll tell Father Yakim to lock you out if you show up at the baptism and the wedding. I believe you love my daughter, but it's too little, too late. As soon as I can, I'll marry Lyuba and make my children legitimate. Right after the wedding, I'll be writing the final draft of a letter to be sent to a judge who'll give me full rights over the child you never wanted. I'll legally adopt her long after I adopted her in my heart. The second the judge rules in my favor, you'll have lost your rights to her. Don't put up a fight over signing the legal documents when the day comes, or I'll break you right in half, you* morda. *Maybe you have suggestions on how to improve the letter to the judge? For the sake of my daughter, I pray our day in court won't be very much delayed. I've heard about how cases get stuck in the American legal system for years before the people get their day in court. But don't count on it, bully.*

Dear Judge:

This letter is to request a hearing be held in court to grant me legal guardianship of my stepdaughter, whom I've been raising as my own since the night she was born. Her biological father left her mother moments before she went into labor with my child. He told me to take care of her mother and to tell the baby I was her father. He didn't care what happened. He sent no letters. He beat the love of my life when she was pregnant with his natural child, and she almost miscarried at least five times. Because of him, it's a miracle she was able to conceive my first biological child. (And you'd better pray he's born alive, Malenkov, or I'll die of grief!)

When my daughter was fourteen months old, he rushed back into our lives. He left America illegally and came into Russia illegally too. After a week of playing mind games with my daughter's mother, he left again. Illegally. When she was eighteen months old, he came back again, but this time thankfully never got to enter my daughter's life. He did, however, play more mind games with my child's mother and beat her very severely on his last day in Russia. He kept threatening, during this second illegal visit, to take my daughter back to America. This man's name is Boris Aleksandrovich Malenkov, a chubby fellow, rather short for a man, black hair, black eyes, date of birth the first of March 1900. He teaches religious school, unbelievably. It's supposedly part of his penance for his life of sins. Do you know, Your Honor, he caused a young girl to take her own life many years ago?

Sincerely Yours,

Ivan Ivanovich Konev

In the final draft of this letter, Malenkov, we'll add an additional page or two of signatures of people who'll be our witnesses in court. Good luck finding witnesses of your own, scum. We know we can count on my aunt, her new husband, your parents, Mr. Lebedev, his daughters, Alya, Anya, Kat, Nikolas, Kittey, Liza, Alyoshka, Lyuba's aunt and uncle, Ginny, my father, possibly some of the people with whom my father works, our priest, Pasha Teglyov, Anya Godimova, her brother Leontiy, Lyuba's mother, Katrin, Lena and Natalya Yeltsina, and a few others we'll dig up. We also may convince Anastasiya to sign as a witness against you. Look out, Malenkov. Your mind games are coming to an end.

May you burn in Hell,

Ivan

"He can't get you to sign such a petition, Mrs. Zhukova! You love me!"

"I want my daughter to be happy. I'll have to sign the petition. You've been a horrible father to Tatyana."

"That's not fair! My own parents won't sign such a thing either!"

"They threw you out of their house. They're furious at how you behaved while they were away."

"I'm just as furious at getting tossed out of my house! I bought that thing with my very own money! I could kill them!"

"You'll have more daughters with a woman who loves you someday."

"I want Lyuba to love me! She's mine!"

"Come now. Are you really going to try to win back a woman who's going on six months pregnant with another man's first child?"

"Will wonders never cease. I find it very hard to believe that child is Ivan's. Lyuba never wanted to sleep with him before, and now suddenly he got her into bed?"

"Isn't that because of the mind games he speaks of in this letter?"

"I should take that letter to the judge and tell him that man is threatening to take away my daughter!"

"Does Father Spiridon have any daughters or nieces near your own age, Borya?"

"I'll have no part of other women. I've only been with Lyuba my entire life."

"Do you know what Lyuba's going to call one of her future daughters, if she's able to have more children after this one?"

"Don't tell me. After Ivan's mother. That woman raised him to be a coward and a passive man!"

"No. After me and my *babushka*. Little baby Katya Koneva."

"Aren't you special. I didn't know Lyuba thought of you so highly."

"We can't pretend we have a perfect relationship, but she's always respected what I've gone through. Someday, we'll hopefully be much closer and recover from the past."

8

Lyuba wakes up in the middle of the night, sensing someone lurking outside the door. All the guests are gone, and one of their friends wouldn't lurk if there were an emergency.

"Vanya, wake up. I think someone's outside our door."

"You're probably just dreaming."

Tatyana comes running into their bedroom and climbs into the bed. "Mama, I heard someone at the door."

"Could it be Boris? Or maybe Ginny snuck out and is now trying to sneak back in?"

"I have a sinking feeling it's not." Ivan leaps out of bed and goes to open the door. "Hello, you disgusting *svoloch*."

"I wanted to see my daughter."

"You're not going to see her ever again."

"Oh, come now, *golubchik*," Lyuba calls. "Boris does love her deep down."

"This isn't Boris. It's your father, may he drop dead and burn in Hell for all eternity along with the regicidists who murdered the Tsar."

"I want to see my daughter right away. I've been kept away from her long enough."

Ivan seizes Mr. Zhukov by his neck and begins to bang him against the wall. "Last time you dropped by, you suggested Lyuba take drugs to induce labor. You may not give a damn about your grandchildren, but I do. You'll never live to see my son. Don't worry about your wife. Lyuba and I know a widower who'll be a wonderful second husband for her. In fact, he lives right across the hall. Just be warned. You may want to go to a priest for your Last Rites, because you won't outlive this week. Got that, dirty pile of *govno*?"

Mr. Zhukov slithers out in total fear of Ivan.

"That was my father?" Lyuba demands.

"I told him what's what. He won't outlive the week."

"Tanyechka, you can run along back to bed now. Your unworthy *dedushka* will never bother us again."

Mr. Zhukov runs down the stairs, through the door, and down the street into the nearest church he can find. It's three in the morning, so none of the priests are up and about. This doesn't stop Mr. Zhukov. He grabs a directory from the lobby bulletin board, then goes up to the third floor and begins banging on the first door.

"What do you want? It's three in the morning."

"I need a priest for Last Rites. Anyone will do. You'll do."

"Are you a member, or is your church closed for the night?"

"No time to explain. I'm going to die very soon, *Batyushka*, and my not-yet son-in-law ordered me to go to a priest for my Last Rites, since I won't outlive this very week!"

"You don't look like a dying man to me."

"He's going to kill me, that's why."

"Wouldn't you be better-off going to see a police officer than a priest?"

"I'm afraid of this man. But I'm very religious, so I had no other choice." Mr. Zhukov crosses himself thrice. "I probably will go to Hell, but at least I'm making the extra effort to try to get myself situated in one of the better circles of Hell, not the very last one."

"Why do you feel you'll go to Hell?"

"Just hear my confession, *Batyushka*. And put up a curtain. I don't want to see your face when you find out just how evil I am."

***

Lyuba rolls over and smiles at Ivan after Tatyana has gone back to bed.

"You can smile after your father was here?"

"I want you. We haven't been together for too long."

"That's because it's far too dangerous. You told me about how Boris sat on Tatyana when you were carrying her, and I don't want to take any chances."

"Even you surely know there are many different positions beyond missionary. It'll give you strength for what we're going to do tomorrow night, kill my father."

***

The priest gets up and pours himself a glass of vodka. Irritated, Mr. Zhukov storms over and glares at him.

"Father Morodenko, by this time tomorrow I could be dead! We don't have time to drink vodka!"

"Unless you have a strange way of showing it, I don't think you're one bit remorseful about what you did to your daughter and threatened to do to your granddaughter!"

"So? It's my right. It's right there in the Bible. Pavel said that just as Christ is the head of the Church, so too is a man the head of his household and all must obey him and bow down to his authority. His wife, daughter, and granddaughter are his property."

"Find me anything in the Bible to support your actions. Isn't there a rather long section about whom you can and can't marry?"

"Marriage is different than sexual relations."

"In those days, sexual relations indeed made two people married."

"Regardless, I can do what I want with my daughter."

"Including telling her to take drugs to induce labor?"

"She doesn't need a second illegitimate child, much less one with a different father."

"You know you have to feel sincere contrition for a confession to be valid. I can't absolve you of anything if you're not truly sorry."

"At least tell me I can get a place in a nicer circle of Hell than the last!"

"I don't think I can do that."

"Then at least give me my last Communion!"

"I can't do that unless you feel true contrition. I don't think I can help you anymore."

"Tell me to say the entire prayerbook forty or fifty times and I'll do it starting now! I'll do it on my way home!"

"Penance means nothing without true contrition. But you knew that, didn't you?"

***

Lyuba wraps her arms around Ivan. "I bet you enjoyed that far too much to feel emasculated. It takes a real man to accept a non-dominant position. You can't complain about how it left your hands free to do whatever you wanted to me."

"You're truly incredible. I missed so much all those years."

"Wasn't it worth the wait?"

"Still, I don't think we should try that again until after our baby's born. I don't want to induce early labor if we do that too close to your guess date. Not to brag, but the way I always get you going, I'm afraid those, you know, personal contractions might lead to the other type of contractions."

"That sounds like an old wives' tale. Anyway, I can't wait to start spoiling our baby rotten after he comes home from hospital."

"Who said anything about going to a hospital? What if they take him away because he's born out of wedlock, and we never see him again?"

"We've pulled off the charade very well so far, as much as I hate having to lie. Don't you want me to be safe in a modern hospital, particularly in case something goes wrong?"

"I want you to be here when you have him. Or her. When I come home from work in the afternoon, I'll see the baby for the first time. Just like it should be, the way it's been done for all of human history."

"You don't want to be here for the birth?"

"Nothing would make me happier. I hope he's a good boy and doesn't decide to make his entrance when I'm at work. That's a special moment I'll never get back."

9

The next afternoon, Lyuba drops Tatyana off at her paternal grandparents' house and then sits at home waiting for Ivan, Aleksey, and Nikolas. They arrive at six in the evening. Aleksey is holding a small briefcase, Nikolas has hauled in a heavy iron weight attached to an even heavier chain, and Ivan has a small paper bag.

"A pen, paper, and pre-blessed Communion bread and wine," Ivan explains. "It'll be pitch black rather soon. Then we'll go down to the car and do it."

"What's in that briefcase, Alyoshka?" Lyuba asks.

"A gun and ammo. I won't shoot the *mudak*. That would be too simple and would give away clues about who did this. It's just to scare him."

"How did you manage to get a gun?"

"I got it from one of the fellows who works in the liquor store with Mr. Konev. I'll give it back to him shortly."

Mr. Lebedev comes in holding a large brown burlap sack and rope. "Are we going to bury him at sea tonight?"

"Yes, Ilya Nikolayevich. Everyone we know has the same story straight, and Tanyechka's with Boris's parents. We'll go right after we eat supper. I made *pelmeni* stuffed with potatoes and cheese."

"Then we'll let you really meet Lyuba's mother," Ivan says. "I can't wait for you to become the father Lyuba deserved all along."

Lyuba crosses herself before they sit down to eat. "In the name of the Father, the Son, and the Holy Ghost, forgive us for what we are about to do, and let my father burn in the last circle of Hell. Amen."

"We'll order him to drive to the East River at gunpoint," Aleksey says, sitting down. "Ivan will order him to write a suicide note and take his last Communion."

"Maybe we should take pictures so we can show your mother and aunt he's really gone," Ivan suggests.

"No, Vanyechka, that'd be very dangerous," Lyuba says. "And none of us has a camera."

"After we get done with that, I'll fasten the chain on the anchor around his neck, and Mr. Lebedev will stuff him inside that burlap sack and tie it shut with the rope," Nikolas goes on. "Who wants the honors of sending him to his doom?"

"I'll do it," Ivan says. "Lyuba can help, but only if she feels up to it. I don't want her to push or throw him too hard and lose our baby."

Lyuba pours herself a glass of water. "You've thought of everything. I can't wait."

10

Mr. Zhukov is shaken awake at 11:00 by his brother-in-law. He opens his eyes and sees Lyuba, Ivan, Aleksey, Nikolas, and Mr. Lebedev standing there.

"Hush, you dirty *mudak*. If you scream, I'll shoot you on the spot." Aleksey points the handgun at him. "Do everything we say, and there won't be any unnecessary trouble."

"But I was turned away in the middle of my Last Rites earlier this morning!"

"I said hush." Aleksey stuffs a sock in Mr. Zhukov's mouth. "Ivan figured no priest would want to administer Last Rites to someone so despicable after he found out what you'd done, so he got pre-blessed bread and wine. Let's go. Ivan's car is waiting, you dirty little *svoloch*."

"I haven't dressed or had a last meal yet!" he mutters through the sock, petrified.

"We figured you might want to get dressed. Go." Aleksey continues pointing the gun at him.

"What if my wife wakes up!" Mr. Zhukov pulls out the sock. "That worthless Malenkov lives here too!"

"I put Katya out like a light at supper. Mixed a little heavy proof liquor into her wine. As for Boris, that man could sleep through the outbreak of another war." Mr. Kharzin pulls open the wardrobe. "What would you like to wear to your death, Leontiy?"

"This really isn't a joke, is it, Mikhail?"

"I wonder what gave you that impression," Ivan snarls. "Now start getting dressed, or Aleksey will shoot you. Hurry up, you dirty old man."

"I'm only forty-three! I haven't lived yet!"

"Neanderthal man lived about as long as you. Even now, people die young all the time. You'll make it look like a suicide. Now go." Ivan yanks a random suit off a hanger.

Mr. Zhukov strips off his pajamas at the speed of light and begins getting dressed.

"Perhaps you'd like to be castrated too and write in the suicide note I've memorized that you did it out of shame for what you did to your daughter?"

"Don't push me, Konev. *You* should feel a lot of shame for getting my only child pregnant out of wedlock with her second child by a different father!"

"Don't push *us*? I'm the one holding the gun on you." Aleksey smirks.

Mr. Zhukov is hustled out of the house fifteen minutes later with Aleksey holding the gun to the back of his head. He opens the driver's side door of Ivan's Ford and tries to start driving.

"You'll drive to the East River," Ivan commands, pointing to the starter button on the floor. "You'll need to push this, *dryan*."

"I don't think I know the way there."

"Nice try. I do. I'll give directions the entire way there." Aleksey slides in next to him and continues holding the gun to his head. "Begin."

Mr. Zhukov is shaking in terror by the time Aleksey announces they've reached the East River. Nikolas lights a lantern and holds it in front of Mr. Zhukov as Aleksey still holds the gun to his head.

"Remember this gun is loaded, *mudak*. Ivan's going to give you more orders, and if you don't obey them, I'll shot you on the spot."

Ivan hands him the pen and the paper. "Write every single word I say to you, *svoloch*. 'To my wife Katya—'"

"I want to write 'Dear Katyushenka' instead."

"You do and I'll murder you," Aleksey growls. "You never

loved your wife."

"'To my wife Katya.' Don't forget to write today's date, the sixth of March, the year of our Lord one thousand nine hundred twenty-two. Now. 'Recently, I have grown very ashamed of my life of unforgivable sins against God, you, our daughter whom I do not deserve to look in the face, my granddaughter who luckily won't remember what I almost did to her, my unborn grandson whom I told Lyuba to induce labor on so I could use her for more sinning, your sister Margarita, her husband, Lyuba's fiancé, my nephew, and the whole world. I can no longer live with myself. I went to a priest for my Last Rites earlier this morning, but he sent me away before we were finished because he knew I'm not sorry for all I've done. Don't worry, Katya, I'll have taken pre-blessed bread and wine. First Communion is a joyous occasion, and Last Communion is a sad one. I'm not a true Christian. I don't deserve to take Communion one last time, but duty calls me. I'm fully aware of the fact that I'll end up in the last circle in Hell. You can collect the insurance and my money in the bank after the police recover my body. Then you can remarry. I recommend Ilya Nikolayevich Lebedev. I don't deserve to live. I don't deserve a Christian burial. Goodbye. Leontiy Leonidovich Zhukov.'" Ivan grabs the papers and begins reading them. "Excellent job, piece of scum. You follow orders well."

"Now cross yourself and begin praying," Nikolas orders, taking out the pre-blessed wine and bread. "You're about to get an abbreviated version of Last Rites, scum."

Mr. Zhukov crosses himself thrice and begins to make up his own prayer. "Dear God, *pozhaluysta*, spare my life from these five men who want only to harm me, and I will never see my daughter again—"

"Don't make up your own prayer, or I'll pull this trigger," Aleksey snarls in his right ear. "You're going to say the Our Father, a Hail Mary, and the Nicene Creed the fastest you ever said them."

Mr. Zhukov trips over the words in his race to say the three prayers, slurring words together, putting the wrong case endings on many a word in his absolute terror, and forgetting some of the words altogether, which Ivan has to supply for him. It's almost midnight by the time he's taken the wine and bread, crying in pure terror.

"Very good," Nikolas says. "Ten minutes before midnight. You won't outlive the sixth of March, *mudak.*"

"I haven't even left a will!"

Nikolas slips the chain around his neck and tightens it a bit. "Now pick up the weight and hold it while Mr. Lebedev puts you into that sack."

"I want to leave a will!"

Ivan pokes him in the eyes. "It'll all go to your widow, Lyuba, Tatyana, and my unborn son. Not like you have very much to leave, besides insurance money that automatically comes to the widow of the deceased party. Lyuba and her mother will work out who gets your possessions, though I hope they decide to burn most of them. Now pick up that weight and stop sniveling. A grown man like yourself, crying. At least I cry when I'm sad, not because I'm a coward!"

Mr. Zhukov picks up the weight mutely as Mr. Lebedev unfurls the sack.

"Cross yourself," Aleksey reminds him, still holding the gun to the back of his head. "Every Christian must cross oneself right before he meets his doom. Even you, about to enter the lowest circle of Hell."

Mr. Zhukov automatically crosses himself thrice more and begins to gasp in terror as Mr. Lebedev stuffs the sack over his head and knocks him off his feet to tie it shut.

"I'm having a deathbed repentance!"

"Nice try." Ivan picks the sack up and throws it into the East River. "So long, excuse for life."

Mr. Zhukov screams as the sack plunges into the water and begins to sink rapidly.

11

Mrs. Zhukova wakes up in the morning with a terrible headache and finds her husband gone. The note he wrote under coercion last night is on his pillow. When they came back to drop Mr. Kharzin off, they tidied up the mess and put all the clothes back in the wardrobe on hangers.

"Rita, Mishenka, Borya, I just found a suicide note from Leontiy!"

"Whatever does it say?" Mrs. Kharzina gasps.

Mrs. Zhukova reads the note, her voice shaking. The further she reads, the fainter she feels.

"In his handwriting?"

"Yes, this is his writing!"

"I'll look for him in the house." Mr. Kharzin pretends to be helpful and goes off to "search."

They look for two hours and find absolutely nothing. No body hanging from a pipe or rafter, no limp, lifeless body with a gunshot or slit wrists, no empty bottles of pills or poison, no knives with blood on them, no body hanging outside from one of the trees, no nothing. Boris bores of searching after only fifteen minutes and goes to make himself his usual extra-large breakfast of scrambled eggs, ham, herbed goat cheese on sourdough bread, and spicy sausages. The other three are still searching over and over when he pulls on his new tweed suit and leaves for work.

"Do you think he went somewhere else to do it?" Mrs. Zhukova asks.

"Maybe he drowned himself," Mr. Kharzin suggests. "But first we must go to the police and tell them what we suspect."

They go to the police station twenty minutes later. Mrs. Zhukova hands the note to the first police officer she sees.

"This is a suicide note from my husband. I found it this morning when I awoke. My sister, my brother-in-law, and I searched our house and yard for two hours and turned up absolutely nothing. The only possibility left, we believe, is that he drowned himself."

The Russian police officer reads the note over and over again. "No mention of how he planned to kill himself or where he might've gone to do it."

"Try the Hudson River first," Mrs. Kharzina suggests.

"Is it possible he took my car?" Mr. Kharzin asks.

"Who would've driven it back?" Mrs. Zhukova asks. "Unless he had an accomplice."

"Do you know what priest he would've seen for Last Rites, the one who turned him away?" the cop asks. "Find that priest, and you may find out what he was planning to do."

"He just says he went to see a priest. He doesn't say he went to see our priest. And he took pre-blessed Communion before he died. How could Leontiy do this without leaving a will?"

"He's a new immigrant. What did he have of worth to be left to anyone?" Mrs. Kharzina asks.

"It sounds like he was planning this right down to the last detail. He even suggests I remarry that widower Lyuba and her friends are so fond of."

"You'll get insurance money." The cop feeds a piece of paper into his typewriter. "Would you like to stay here until we get some answers?"

"Yes, *pozhaluysta.* This isn't something I *ever* suspected from Leontiy, not even once! He took pride in what he describes as his 'life of unforgivable sins'!"

There are cops out in boats searching the Hudson River and the East River all day long, pulling up a number of bodies, but none of them belonging to Mr. Zhukov. Finally, at five in the afternoon, the burlap sack stuffed with the body of Mr. Zhukov is pulled up in one of their recovery nets in the East River. A cop cuts it open and calls to Mrs. Zhukova.

"Is this one your husband?"

"That *is* Leontiy!" Mrs. Zhukova faints.

"So he pulled this sack over his head and tied the rope around his feet," Mrs. Kharzina says. "And he sank with that weight."

"Suicides don't get Christian burial," Mr. Kharzin says. "Leontiy himself wrote that he didn't deserve one."

"You want to bury him at sea again?" the cop asks.

"They have a section in our church cemetery for the unbaptized, suicides, and various other cases. Put him there," Mrs. Kharzina says.

No priest wants to preside over the burial of a presumed suicide, even one who took a semblance of Last Rites before dying. The shame and dishonor Mr. Zhukov brought to Lyuba for so long in life is now finally revisited upon him in Death.

****

Chapter 31: A Terrifying Ordeal

"Come right in, they're both beautiful."

"Well, of course you say that. It's your duty as Kat's husband to think she's still beautiful after she's given birth," Lyuba says.

"Well, in that case, all three of them are beautiful."

"Three of them?" Eliisabet asks.

"Kat had twin girls!"

"That's wonderful!" Lyuba says.

Nikolas leads the way into Kat's room. She's lying on the bed with two identical baby girls on her left side. One baby is in pale green, and the other is in pale blue.

"Which one came first?" Lyuba asks, immediately sinking into the nearest chair.

"This little one in blue. Lyudmila, after Kolya's mother. Look how plump she is. She must've been taking most of the room and food away from her little sister!"

"The second one came fifteen minutes later," Kittey says. "Kolya named Lyuda after our mother before she was born, because Kat thought it was a girl, and Kat named the other one Raisa."

"Lyuba, don't you want to come closer to look?" Eliisabet asks. "They look like they take after their mother."

"No, I'm having a bit of pain right now. It'll pass."

"Do you want me to take you home?" Ivan asks. "Just to be safe?"

"I'm sitting down. I'm safe now. If something were to happen, I'm far enough along to produce a healthy baby. We're in a hospital, the perfect place to be if anything goes wrong."

"I'm giving the baptismal gown my sisters and I wore to Eliisabet for beautifying," Kat says. "It's thirty-six years old, but I know you can make it look beautiful again, as beautiful as the day my mother finished making it for Grafya. You have everything you'll need for mending it in the fabric shop."

"What will the other one wear?" Lyuba asks.

"Would you or Liza mind making one for Raisa? Kittey and Kolya were taken in the middle of the night, and didn't have time to grab anything. What a tragedy, how dear little Kittey's baptismal gown is forever lost and unable to be passed down."

"I'd be honored to make Raya's baptismal gown," Eliisabet says.

"Have you wondered lately what became of your family?" Kittey asks. "I imagine you're thinking about them a lot, since you just became a mother."

"I miss them, but it's never occurred to me to wonder about their fates. In my mind's eye, I'll always see them standing there waving as I climbed into the wagon heading to the valley. They're frozen like that for all time. In reality, they've probably been absorbed into the Communist machine. It really doesn't matter to me, just like Lyuba wasn't bothered by how her father killed himself."

Everyone in the room smiles except Lyudmila and Raisa.

"My mother picked up five hundred dollars in insurance money after the body was recovered," Lyuba says. "Now all we have to do is wait for her prescribed mourning period to cease, and we can introduce her to Ilya Nikolayevich. I hope she uses the money to pay for their wedding."

"His funeral was priceless." Ginny starts to chuckle. "The one priest they could find to bury him in the non-Christian section just watched the hired help digging the grave, filling it with extra lime, and dumping him in without a coffin. After they filled it up and packed it over, he didn't sprinkle holy water over it. I doubt he'll do it either when the headstone comes. People forbidden Christian burial don't get nice headstones, just very thin, short, ordinary pieces of rock with their names and dates chiseled on. I wonder if they'll even chisel a cross onto the pathetic little headstone he'll get."

"Then he spoke at length about the sin of suicide," Ivan says. "He rehashed the pedophile's whole litany of sins and why such a person doesn't deserve a Christian burial. I could barely keep from smiling when the priest talked about how there would've been no Christian burial either if he'd been killed, because his killer would've been doing society and his family a great social and moral service. It says right in the Bible to kill those who are found guilty of the worst kinds of sins. Guess I was in the right when I killed Basil too."

"Maybe Eliisabet can make my mother's wedding dress too," Lyuba says. "The rest of the insurance money can go to the wedding banquet, entertainment, and flowers."

"These two will never have to ask for anything like I did, being the last of fifteen daughters," Kat says. "Within the next ten years,

Kolya, Kittey, and I hope to move away from New York and go somewhere less crowded, after we have enough money. I don't want to live on the top floor of a tenement my whole adult life. What'll happen when I have my next child? There will be five of us when I'm discharged, and where would we stick a sixth person in that small apartment of ours? And in addition, we have a dog."

"Many families have six or seven people to a room or apartment," Eliisabet says. "With enough hard work, all of us can save up enough money to travel to a better place and raise our families there."

"Yes, I also want a better life for my two babies," Lyuba says.

2

Lyuba feels slight cramps again the next morning, but thinks nothing of it. They gradually begin to grow worse during breakfast, and as Ivan is opening the door to leave for work shortly thereafter, she walks quickly to their room as the pain grows even worse. She can't help screaming in agony and lying on the floor.

"What's wrong?" he demands.

"This is exactly how I felt at the end of my pregnancy with Tatyana!"

Ivan picks her up and sets her on the bed. "I'm going to be late for work today."

"You don't need to do that just for me."

"I'll call the midwife and order her to come as soon as possible."

"I'm far enough along to deliver safely if that's what we need to do."

"You almost started to miscarry Tatyana at least five times!"

When Mrs. Kuzmitch comes in twenty minutes later, Ivan directs her into the room.

"I swear to you I haven't done anything to her. I'd never beat a pregnant woman the way the father of her daughter did. I do most of the housework so she won't have to exert herself."

Mrs. Kuzmitch goes into the room. "Do you feel any better, Miss Zhukova?"

"As long as he stays safe until June is all that matters."

She again finds the cervical damage but says nothing about it. Ivan stands outside the door, quaking in terror. He crosses himself when Mrs. Kuzmitch announces the fetoscope has picked up a normal heartbeat.

"I want you to stay in bed until June and only leave if you must. You've lost tissue, and the uterine lining may be starting to tear."

"I am going to murder Malenkov!" Ivan shouts.

"I lost tissue before too, when I was carrying Tanya." Lyuba rubs her bulge. "All I ask is that my dear little boy stay safely baking inside me until June."

"It may be very risky from here on out. Maybe you shouldn't try to have a third child, since this may happen again. If you want, I can refer you to a good doctor who can sterilize you after you give birth."

"You can't sterilize my fiancée," Ivan says. "I want nine children, and we've got seven more to go."

"You can always adopt."

"But I don't want to adopt. At least Tanyechka is Lyuba's blood child, not a complete stranger. It's also against Orthodoxy to use birth control or get sterilized."

"We'll see what happens," Lyuba says. "All things are predetermined by God."

3

Ivan doesn't allow Lyuba to walk anywhere from here on out. He does all the housework and cooking, and carries her to the table for meals. Sometimes Mrs. Malenkova comes over during the day to take care of things and look after Tatyana.

"You're carrying all the weight in front," she smiles. "It's a boy."

"Isn't that an old wives' tale?"

"I carried all my weight in front."

"That's probably because Borya's so chubby!"

"Ivan's dear late mother carried him in the front too, and so did Mrs. Vishinskaya when she had her boy and Mrs. Tvardovskaya when she had Aleksey. Mrs. Litvinova and Mrs. Beriya carried all their sons out in the front too."

"Some people say it's bad luck to announce the name before the baby's born, but we know what his Christian name will be. Vladimir, after the saint who saved our lives so many times. But that won't be his given name. Vanya will pick a first name."

"What if it's a girl? Vladimira?"

"I feel it's a boy, but there's always that chance I'm wrong."

"Boris told me your mother's getting sick of him and that he's overstayed his welcome. I told her she can hand him back to me only if he proves beyond a shadow of a doubt he can respect his parents."

"As long as he doesn't put up another fight about how he doesn't have the right to have Tatyana."

"Father Spiridon told me his third-born daughter is only two years younger than Borya and that we might get them to meet each other. Granyechka, her name is. She has a voice like an angel in the church choir. We may force the meeting a little by having her start to 'assist' Borisko with the children in religious school. Granyechka's a student at New York School of Applied Design for Women. Her artistic passion is weaving. We went to Father Spiridon's house to talk more about this matter, and he showed us all the beautiful wall hangings, tapestries, and blankets his lovely daughter made. She also makes quilts. She'll do that from home after she's married, and spend the rest of her time raising as many children as God allows her to have. Borya better not insult Father Spiridon by turning down his wonderful daughter after so much trouble."

"Will this woman mind Boris has a child and isn't a virgin? Won't she want someone more pure in character? And what if he beats her when she's pregnant like he did with me?"

"She knows about his past sins and how much penance he's done to try to absolve himself of everything in the eyes of God."

"At least if he marries this woman, she'll give him more than enough children to take his mind off Tatyana for good."

"She has black hair and brown eyes. About five foot three. She's sort of slim. Her other talents are singing, dancing, and reciting Scripture. Her proud father bragged to us that his Granyechka practically knows the whole Gospel by heart."

"If he marries her, will she mind you have a relationship with me and Tatyana?"

"This is a woman who truly knows the meaning of forgiveness. Every night, she prays for the souls of the Bolsheviks to be saved so they won't go to Hell. She's the third of seven. There are Yevdokiya, twenty-five; Yelena, twenty-three; Granyechka, twenty; Pyotr, nineteen; Roza, seventeen; Marta, fifteen; and Filipp, ten."

"What's wrong with Yelena that he didn't offer her first?"

"She's already married."

"Something I wish *I* were, Shurka. Ivan's taking his good old time making me a respectable woman. Once the baby's born, we'll be too busy taking care of him to be much concerned about anything else. I love him so much, I don't give a damn if we have an expensive wedding. All I want is Vanya, and the security of being a respectable woman."

4

In the middle of May, about an hour after Ivan has left for work, Lyuba goes into active labor, after having felt sporadic contractions since last night. She throws orders to the wind and goes to Kat's apartment. Eliisabet is at work, but Kat's allowed to stay home until July, with a generous paid leave allotted to her by the florist's shop.

"Ivan says you're not supposed to be walking around."

"He'd keep me locked up in a glass box if he could! Kat, you must know something about delivering babies, because mine's about to be born, almost a month too early! You surely were there when your older sisters gave birth."

"Yes, but not in that way! Why don't you go back to your apartment and phone your midwife?"

Lyuba waddles back next door and places the call, for once grateful Ivan splurged on that telephone instead of making do with public phones like normal people. Mrs. Kuzmitch's phone rings five times before Mr. Kuzmitch answers it.

"This is Lyuba Zhukova. Is Mrs. Kuzmitch in? I went into labor early, and I really, really need her."

"I'm sorry to say, but she's out of town for a week. If you want, I can give you some numbers for other midwives."

"That's a nice offer, but not necessary. My friends and I can handle this by ourselves."

"How deep into labor are you?" Kat asks after she hangs up.

"I think I'm in active labor. I've felt contractions since last night, but they didn't start getting really bad till just now."

"I can call for the hospital to take you to their maternity ward.

It's much cleaner to give birth in a hospital. I got a drug that put me to sleep. I woke up with my babies, no memory of any of that pain. It was kind of weird how the nurse insisted on wrapping gauze around my head, putting earplugs in my ears, and putting a kind of straitjacket on me, but I guess it's done for your own good so you won't hurt yourself while you're thrashing about during the worst of the pain. Kolya hasn't seen me naked since before the birth, so he has no idea I was shaved to make things cleaner for the doctor. The worst part was having, you know, a suppository, to make things as clean and comfortable for the doctor as possible."

"Vanya doesn't want me to have our son there. He says they'll take him away from us as soon as he's born. If he knew what you just told me, he'd be even more against letting me go there."

"You're not an unwed mother in the true sense of the word. That only happens to girls who give birth after being abandoned. You've got a loving fiancé, and aren't a dirty, wanton slut. In spite of having to wear a straitjacket and have gauze over my head, I got to stay there for two weeks. I felt like a *knyazhna*, and when Kolya and I put up enough of a fight, the staff let us have our girls in the room most of the time instead of keeping them in the nursery. The nurses thought I was a bit strange for breastfeeding instead of taking their lessons on preparing bottles and accepting free samples of artificial milk, but they accepted that too after enough of a fight. They're not used to immigrant women who are so assertive and educated."

"Tatyana came rather fast after hard labor started. Maybe five or six hours total."

"Eliisabet comes home in a few hours for lunch. She can help us then. From what I know about labor, I don't think your baby will make his entrance before then."

***

Eliisabet comes up to the top floor a little before noon and is promptly greeted by Kat, carrying towels and sheets.

"Lyuba's been in active labor for about four hours, since eight in the morning, and the midwife's out of town for a week. She refuses to let me call an ambulance to bring her to the hospital."

"Did you call Ivan?"

"The boss said he doesn't take calls for workers in the middle of their busy day."

Lyuba comes to the door as white as a sheet.

"I told you to lie down and relax."

"My water just broke."

"Why don't we call Mrs. Malenkova or Ivan's aunt to help you?" Kat begs.

"They'll get here too late. My contractions are closer together now. We've had almost six children between the three of us, and don't need so much outside help."

Lyuba lies back down and begins to feel more and more feverish by the minute. Though she got on all fours when she had the urge to push with Tatyana, this time she's too weak to move, and has no choice but to push flat on her back. She's barely aware of Kat holding a cold cloth over her head or of Eliisabet telling her to push more gently so she won't tear. She's delirious by the time Eliisabet hands her the baby.

"Didn't you hear me? I just told you it's a boy."

"A...boy?" Lyuba briefly comes back to her senses. "And I just gave birth to him?"

"Don't you feel well?" Kat asks. "You have a dazed look in your eyes."

"Vanya will be so happy when he comes home!"

"You're burning up. I'm calling a doctor right away."

"He's so beautiful. I knew he'd look just like Vanya." Lyuba takes one of his tiny hands in hers. "*Ya tyebya lyublyu*, my precious baby boy."

The baby suddenly stops his squalling and goes limp against her chest.

"Why is he no longer crying?" Lyuba demands. "He's breathing shallowly."

Eliisabet puts her ear over his face. "That's why we're calling a doctor. Kat, rub his chest to keep him breathing."

Eliisabet calls the hospital as Lyuba delivers the placenta, explaining there's no time to waste by sending an ambulance. The baby might die en route. A doctor needs to come immediately, and if it's serious, they can go to hospital. The receptionist gags when Eliisabet supplies the address, and mutters something about sending a nursing student who just came from Russia, someone who won't mind going into *that* neighborhood and treating immigrants from home. Eliisabet then starts calling every doctor in the phonebook, only to be met with similar disgusted reactions when she speaks with a foreign accent and provides the address. By the time she finally reaches a doctor in the S section who says he'll be right over, she no longer cares he has a German name. A doctor is a doctor, and it's possible his family immigrated long before the war.

After a miniature eternity, a green-eyed, russet-haired nurse comes in, followed very closely by a kindly-looking doctor with off-blonde hair and bluish-green eyes. Both have large bags full of medical supplies. Lyuba tries to get up to greet them and crashes to the floor. Through her hazy senses, she hears little Kroshka hysterically barking across the hall.

"What's wrong with this little guy?" the nurse croons. "Sometimes they just need a little jump-start to help along the breathing. At least you kept his cord attached. That helps with resuscitation. It's obscene how American doctors immediately sever it and yank out the placenta."

"He was crying just fine when he came out!" Lyuba says. "Don't let my baby die so soon after I fell in love with him."

"What's wrong with my new brother?" Tatyana demands.

"Whatever it is, I'll get him fine in no time. I'm not a registered nurse yet, but I worked a lot with babies for the past five years in Siberia. I never lost an infant." The nurse pulls out a stethoscope and listens to the baby's shallow breathing. "He'll be fine with a little extra oxygen. Don't you worry, I'll have him hale and hearty in no time. You just lie down and relax. Pregnancy and childbirth aren't diseases, but they're not a walk in the park for all women. Some women just need a little extra time to feel themselves again, and that involves not moving unnecessarily."

Lyuba looks away as the nurse puts a small oxygen mask over the slightly undersized baby's face. "What's your name, and where in Russia are you from? I'm from Petrograd, but I lived in Moskva most of my life."

"I'm Svetlana Ilyinichna Lebedeva. I was born in Pskov, though like you, lived most of my life in Moskva. Some babies are just a bit weak when they come into this world. It has nothing to do with where they're born. Many of the hospital babies I've worked with aren't as healthy as the ones I worked with in Siberia. A lot of hospital babies come out groggy or not breathing due to the drug cocktail they give all the laboring mothers nowadays, since it depresses the baby's central nervous system. You didn't hear me say that, though. I value my job, particularly since I'm a new immigrant."

The doctor extends his hand. "I'm Dr. Scholl. How good is your English?"

"I must've been about thirteen when I began learning it at gymnasium," Lyuba says in her completely unaccented English. "I learnt very quickly and well, though we learnt British English, not American English."

"If you're cognizant enough to have a normal conversation, you can't be that ill, though sometimes these things can be deceptive. I can rule out puerperal fever right away, since you in all likelihood wouldn't immediately be showing signs so soon after birth. There's always an incubation period. When did you start feeling feverish?"

"After my water broke. I also had cramps, bleeding, and lost tissue last month. My fiancé wouldn't let me do any housework or even walk."

"Your fiancé?"

"Poor thing's so feverish, she meant to say husband," Kat jumps in.

"I'm not here to judge you if you are unmarried. I'm so radical, I offer sterilizations and birth control, and am moving away from hospital deliveries because I strongly disagree with the non-evidence-based nonsense most of my colleagues have unthinkingly embraced, like automatically giving all women episiotomies and not allowing laboring mothers any food or water." Dr. Scholl wraps a blood pressure cuff around her arm. "That's not good." He slips a thermometer under her tongue, and turns pale when he removes it several minutes later. "That's even worse."

Lyuba slumps over on her side and starts lapsing in and out of consciousness again. She doesn't register the baby crying furiously in the background after Svetlana announces he's out of the woods, and is only vaguely aware of being lifted into a chair, pushed into the living room, and maneuvered onto the davenport, where her head and legs are propped up with pillows. Dr. Scholl sets a bottle of some kind of medication on the coffeetable.

"Open all the windows," Dr. Scholl orders. "She needs as much fresh air and sunlight as possible. I'd order her onto the roof if I weren't afraid she might walk or roll off in her state. The bed linens and her clothes need to be washed immediately, and she needs cold compresses around the clock."

"What kind of dog is that making so much noise across the hall?" Svetlana asks. "A giant wolfhound or Mastiff?"

"It's a little Pomeranian," Kat says. "Normally she doesn't make nearly this much noise. She's always so good and calm, and only makes a lot of noise when she's very excited."

"I had a Pomeranian too. They're my favorite breed, since they're so little, cute, and fluffy."

"When do you think our friend recovers?" Eliisabet asks.

"There's no telling," Dr. Scholl says. "She has a fever of one hundred six degrees, which isn't promising at all. Even if you move her to a hospital, there wouldn't be much that could be done beyond monitoring, cold compresses, and injected medication. I assume you can't afford a lengthy hospital stay. If she's going to die, at least she'll die in the safety of her own home. She'd be alone among strangers in a hospital, which isn't as antiseptic as many doctors like to promote it as. There are all sorts of diseases and infections floating around in there, whereas even a home like this can be cleaned well enough to keep away the worst microscopic offenders."

"Will you and Svetlana stay until her fiancé comes home? Knowing him, he'll go crazy if he comes home to find her like this, without anyone to explain anything."

"Of course. I'm a full-service doctor, not someone who just shows up, gives a diagnosis, writes a bill, and leaves."

***

Ivan comes home to laundry strung through the apartment, the smell of chicken dumpling soup, baby cries, two strangers in his living room, and his fiancée lying unresponsive on the davenport, a cold compress on her forehead.

"Papa, I'm very hungry," Tatyana announces. "Did you buy me candy after you left work? I didn't eat any lunch."

In a daze, Ivan opens his metal lunchpail and hands her two Goldenberg's Peanut Chews, with the wrappers open for her convenience. "Can someone care to explain to me what in the world happened today?"

Eliisabet pulls him aside and begins whispering. He falls into a chair as Dr. Scholl and Svetlana provide more medical details. Before Ivan came home, they all agreed to let him find out for himself it's a boy, so they only refer to "the baby" and "it."

"So my fiancée and baby are dying?"

"Baby is fine," Svetlana says gently. "Baby just had a very uncertain beginning. Your friend Kat is nursing Baby in another room, but you can meet Baby when she comes out. As for your fiancée, it's anyone's guess."

He gets out of the chair and stalks over to the davenport, making the sign of the cross over Lyuba. "Malenkov did this to her. I'm going to break all the bones in his body, starting with the pinky finger on his writing hand. Twentieth century women in America aren't supposed to die in childbirth."

"Vanya, did you just come in?" Lyuba flutters her eyes open, sits up, and puts her hands up to his face. "I can barely see anything, even you, *golubchik*."

"Lie down and relax, *golubka*. You'll be fine now that I'm here to take care of you. I'll take off work and get someone to cover for me so I can take care of you and our baby around the clock."

"I'm dying, aren't I? I'm going to join our beautiful baby in the grave. *Pozhaluysta*, don't ever forget me." Lyuba kisses Ivan on the cheek, lies back down, and closes her eyes.

"You're just delirious. I'll save you from the grave just as I did when I nursed you with diphtheria. As soon as you recover and I have enough money, I'll marry you, we'll baptize our children, and we'll all live happily ever after in the Midwest."

Lyuba doesn't answer him. Ivan hears her breathing shallowly, but when he checks her wrists for a pulse, there's none. He feels for a pulse over her heart, but there's none there either. His screams bring everyone in the apartment and on the hall running. Dr. Scholl pushes through the crowd and presses an adult-sized oxygen mask over her face, while Ivan huddles in a corner, praying every prayer he can think of.

"There's no telling how long she'll remain like this," Dr. Scholl says after Lyuba's heart starts again. "If she continues to be this unstable, I'll have to recommend moving her to a hospital. She'll need continuous monitoring."

"I want her at home," Ivan says. "Our special saint Vladimir will intercede for her and restore her to full health." He takes Lyuba's hand, grateful for the weak pulse.

"Vanya, what's happening?" Lyuba raises her head.

"You're very sick, but you're going to get better. You always get better. You have to get better."

Lyuba falls back on the davenport and doesn't move or speak again. Ivan feels a very faint pulse coming from her wrist, but observes no other signs of life. He stands back in terror as Dr. Scholl checks Lyuba's vital signs again, pries her eyelids open, and shines a small flashlight onto her eyes.

"Sometimes a high fever can cause a coma. She could come in and out of her senses, or remain like this for awhile. As long as she's otherwise stable, I'd still recommend keeping her comfortable here and closely monitoring her. Even the best modern medicine can't work miracles. With all the wondrous advances my profession has made over the last hundred years, we still can't effectively treat and cure many infections."

"Why do these nightmarish things only happen to *me*?" Ivan kicks the wall. "And where the hell is my baby? Am I to lose both the woman I love and my one and only blood child in the same day?"

Svetlana gently lays her hand on his arm. "Your baby is fine. I got Baby to breathe again, and all the vital signs are excellent. Baby is in your daughter's room, being nursed by your friend with deep blue eyes. I'll go to check if nursing is over, and I'll come back with Baby."

"Can you all leave?" Ivan pleads. "I want to meet my baby privately, without so much company." He switches to English. "Doctor, please wait in hall."

After everyone has left, Ivan sits in the chair near the davenport, his head in his hands. This was supposed to be one of the happiest days of his life, not a complete nightmare. At the rate things are going, the baby might die in his arms as soon as he's seen it.

"Don't you want to see your baby?"

Ivan looks up, and his heart melts at the sight of the small newborn nestled in Svetlana's arms. "Mine?" A lump forms in his throat, and he bursts into tears when Svetlana gently puts the baby in his arms.

"Don't let go of Baby's head. Newborns are very fragile, and this one's only six pounds."

Ivan's hands shake as he unpins the diaper. His eyes widen in disbelief when he realizes he's gotten the firstborn son he wanted so badly, and he can barely see straight as he repins the diaper.

"I got a boy? A little Konev to pass on my family name?"

"You sure did."

"He's perfect and beautiful just the way he is. A living reminder of how much I'll always love my Lyubochka." He looks guiltily at Lyuba, still unresponsive but steadily breathing. "You have no idea how long I've waited to hold a blood child of mine in my arms. For so long, I thought this day might never come. I can't believe he's mine." He rubs his hand over his eyes, but his tears keep flowing. "The most wonderful gift Lyuba could ever have given me. I'd die for you, little guy. I'm going to give you all the love, affection, attention, and protection my father denied me. I'll be the exact opposite of my father. If you genuinely act up, I'll reason with you or only discipline with love. I swore to myself long ago I'd never raise my hands or voice against any child of mine. Besides, you're too cute to hurt with spankings, beatings, beltings, or switchings. You depend on me to love and protect you, not abuse you."

"I hate to interrupt you, but would you like a lesson on preparing bottles before I go home tonight? He'll need to eat during the night, and I imagine you won't want to interrupt his wetnurses in the middle of the night."

He nods. "I love cooking. Learning how to prepare bottles can't be that much harder than learning how to prepare meals. Might I be so bold as to ask you to come back to check on my baby while I'm at work? It was a pretty stupid, short-sighted idea to take off work. My fiancée and I have enough friends to monitor her throughout the day, and lots of other relatives who can come over. My aunt has a thirteen-month-old baby, and I'm sure she'd be happy to volunteer wetnursing services too." He gazes into the baby's face adoringly. "Don't worry, I already know how to change diapers. Anything this little guy wants, I'll do."

Ivan refuses to let go of the baby as Eliisabet and Kat come back in to take the soup off the stove and pull the potatoes out of the oven. He keeps sitting by Lyuba, gazing down at the baby, as Tatyana, Kat, and Eliisabet eat dinner. Only very reluctantly does he hand the baby back to Eliisabet for wetnursing. After she shuts the door to Tatyana's room so Ivan won't die of mortification, Dr. Scholl goes over the instructions for monitoring Lyuba, making it absolutely clear Ivan is to immediately call a hospital if her condition worsens. Right now, the most important thing is to make sure her fever doesn't climb any higher, if it won't go down. Then Svetlana gives a lesson on how to prepare and sterilize bottles, and both of them leave. Kroshka finally stops barking as their footsteps recede down the rickety stairs.

"What's his name, Vladimir?" Eliisabet asks as Ivan picks at the dinner she set at his place.

"That'll be his baptismal name. I don't know yet what his legal name will be."

"When do you think you'll know?" Kat asks. "Shall we call him Volodya in the meantime?"

"I'll think of something soon."

"Lyuba was thinking of naming him after you," Eliisabet says. "Or you could name him after your uncle."

"I have more important things to think about, like the fact that my fiancée is dying instead of enjoying our beautiful little boy's precious first moments. I wish it were possible to take off work until Lyuba gets better. I brought her back from death's door when she had diphtheria as a girl, and I can nurse her back to health with fever too."

"What if you get fired! You can't afford to support two children and a sick woman if you lose your job. And don't talk about all that money in savings. That's meant to be your nest egg, not for everyday expenses."

Ivan sighs. "I'll have to make do with a bunch of babysitters in the meantime. Lyubochka has to come back to me. I hope this isn't Divine punishment for refusing to marry her before she gave birth."

"Of course it isn't," Kat says. "These things happen, just like many children sadly die of measles, whooping cough, diphtheria, polio, and chickenpox. All it means is medicine has many limitations, not that they're being punished for supposed sins."

Eliisabet goes to the phone and relays the news to Lyuba's mother and Valeriya as Ivan finishes his dinner at a snail's pace. Ivan hears Mrs. Zhukova and his aunt screaming at the other end of the line. Feeling like the unluckiest guy in the world, he deposits his tableware in the sink, runs some water over it, and retreats back to his chair by the davenport. Eliisabet puts Tatyana to bed, while Kat prepares enough artificial milk formula to fill all the bottles Svetlana gave them, according to the recipe provided, and deposits them in the icebox. He's relieved when they go home to their own children. As soon as he's finally alone with his family, he rests his hand on Lyuba's shoulder and starts telling her about the farm they're going to have someday. She's still alarmingly feverish, but her breathing has become steady, and her heart hasn't stopped again.

"Ivanok, can you let us in?"

He jumps in his seat when he recognizes his aunt's voice. "The door's open."

Valeriya, Vasya, Mr. Konev, and Mr. Golitsyn stream into the apartment. Just earlier today, Ivan would've been mortified to let visitors see dirty dishes in the sink and laundry hanging all through the apartment, but that's a minor detail now.

Mr. Konev crosses himself. "I can't believe what happened. Lyuba wasn't due until next month. Thank God my grandson's alive. I can't imagine how terrified Lyuba must've been. We just had to come over to see the baby and Lyuba when we heard the news."

"If she dies, Malenkov is ever going to pay. He took her away from me so many times, but if I lose her this time, it'll be permanent. He isn't worth the air he breathes."

"Think positively," Valeriya implores him. "This is no time to fantasize about settling a score with that short, fat bully."

"What's his name?" Mr. Konev asks. "I was afraid our family name would die."

"I haven't decided yet, but his baptismal name will be Vladimir." Ivan gently rocks the baby in his arms as the baby starts fussing. "I think he takes after our side. He looks just like me. So much for the old wives' tale about how all babies are born with blue eyes."

"If Lyuba recovers, I hope you won't try to have more children," Mr. Golitsyn says. "Not after what happened today."

"I don't really care at this point. If Lyuba wakes up, we'll concentrate on the two we've got and adopt more. I'll let her think she isn't able to have more children because of what happened today, not because of what Malenkov did to her."

"Watch where you're going, you stupid, clumsy oaf!" Mr. Lebedev shouts in the hallway. "What the hell are you doing here, and at this hour?"

"He never needs reasons for anything, Papa," Vera says in disgust. "He gets an urge, and just runs with it."

Boris opens the door and comes in. "Lyuba's mother just got a call from Liza. What a horrible, horrible tragedy. I'll do anything I can to help Tatyana until Lyuba gets better. If it were up to me, I would've had her delivering in a modern, antiseptic hospital, not that filthy hovel you call home."

Ivan advances towards him. "What a generous offer. Too little too late. Don't you remember *you're* the one who caused her to nearly die, and *my son* along with her?! Get the hell out of my house this instant! I have more than enough assistance! You dare try to offer help when you were the one who beat her so much she was nearly unable to have more children! I'd be breaking every bone in your body right now if my innocent son had died thanks to you!"

The baby begins screaming along with Vasya. Ivan kisses the baby on the head and begins walking back and forth with him.

"You see what you did to your cousin and your new baby?"

"That man is your big sister's biological father," Ivan whispers to his son. "You'll never see him again after I marry your mother and have you and your sister baptized. He won't dare break up your family."

"If Lyuba dies, Tatyana goes right to me. I'm going on supervised dates with my priest's daughter Granyechka. She wants lots of kids, as many as God lets her have, and I've already got one, so it works out well for both of us."

"Any judge in his right mind will give me permission to adopt Tatyana! I'm raising her, and she trusts me! Just like my son already trusts me when he's only a few hours old, you *mudak*!"

"What kind of father are you if you're screaming at the top of your lungs so close to that baby? Look how much he's screaming!"

"I think he might want to eat again." Ivan hands the baby to his aunt. "Would you mind being a wetnurse?"

"Of course not." Valeriya smiles down at the baby. "This little guy does take after our side, Ivanok. He has your hair and eyes."

"And you take after my Anyechka," Mr. Konev says proudly.

"If you want, Ivanok, I can stay here overnight to help you with feeding the baby and redding up. Then maybe tomorrow everything will be better."

"Everything will be better for me only after Lyuba gets better and Boris learns to stay the hell out of my life!"

"You know you're not seeing the last of me," Boris growls before he goes back out through the door.

****

Chapter 32: Truth and Consequences

Eliisabet and Svetlana come running at the sound of a gunshot from the bedroom. It's late in the afternoon on the third day of Baby Konev's little life, and Lyuba still hasn't woken up yet. In one of his rare generous acts, Mr. Glazov, the Russian Uncle Tom who runs the iron factory, has permitted Ivan to take off work, albeit without pay, to take care of his children while his fiancée is indisposed. Anastasiya has dropped by, barely able to conceal her delight at Lyuba being out of the picture for at least a little while.

"What are you doing?" Eliisabet demands. "Give me that gun!"

"I'm such a failure, I can't even shoot myself. I flinched, and it went into the wall. The worst it did was graze my shoulder." Ivan throws the gun on the ground and kicks it under the bed. "She'll never wake up or get better. She'll get even worse and die, and I can't live without Lyuba."

"You almost shot yourself!" Svetlana admonishes. "Where did you get that gun?"

"My father's workplace. They always keep a couple of guns around in case the police come by to try to arrest them for violating Prohibition."

"Thank God you misfired. Think about that darling little girl and that helpless little baby boy who already loves you and trusts you with his brand-new life. You can't leave them fully-orphaned." Svetlana shakes her head at the fresh bullet hole in the wall. "If you'd aimed properly, you might be already dead."

The baby begins screaming at the top of his lungs. Ivan tries to get up, but Eliisabet holds him back. "Sveta will take care of you, and I'll see to him. Why haven't you given him a name yet?"

"I told you, I care more about taking care of Lyuba than minor things like naming a baby."

Svetlana begins to take things out of her bag. "Take your injured arm out of the sleeve, and I'll see how seriously you hurt yourself."

Ivan looks away as he unbuttons his shirt, his left arm smarting in pain, and lets her look at and touch his bare shoulder. "I know you're a nurse, but I don't want you getting too personal with me."

"Take it easy. I'm a professional, not a pervertess."

Eliisabet snatches Baby Konev out of Anastasiya's eager arms and speaks to her in Estonian. "What the hell are you doing with Ivan's baby? You don't even like children!"

"But I love Ivan, and as soon as he marries me, I'll be the baby's stepmother."

"You're still living in your little fantasy world, Stasya, because Ivan will never marry you. If Lyuba recovers, he'll marry her as soon as he has enough money. Look at her, lying there unconscious!"

"As soon as she keels over, I have another chance with Ivan."

"Even if she does, Ivan will never marry. She's the one great love of his life, and he'd never be unfaithful to her even after death."

"He still wants me, no matter what he otherwise professes."

Eliisabet trots back into the bedroom after Svetlana calls her in. Tatyana is now sitting on the edge of the bed, looking at a religious picture book Boris got her in January for her birthday.

"You don't want to read that," Ivan says. "It's from Boris."

"Maybe you can find a name for my little brother in here."

"Why don't you name him Dmitriy?" Anastasiya asks. "After handsome Grand Duke Dmitriy. This little guy is rather good-looking himself."

"I caught that woman holding your son, Ivan," Eliisabet says. "She claims you're going to marry her after Lyuba dies."

"I want that woman out of my apartment," Ivan orders. "She isn't allowed to be near my children."

"In the meantime, you need to get back to the question of names. How about Arkadiy?"

"No, I never liked that name. It has a sharp, nasty ring to it."

"Innokentiy?"

"I don't much like that one either."

"What about Pyotr, after our savior whom we owe our safety in America to? Or Mikhail, after Lyuba's uncle?"

"I'll think of something."

"She considered naming him after you. How do you feel about a little namesake?"

"It'd be too confusing to tell him, me, and my father apart, and why would I deliberately give a kid the most common male name in history? Every time I introduce myself, I might as well say, 'Hi, my name is Generic.'"

"He's three days old, and you still haven't named him. Why not just use his baptismal name as his regular name too?"

"Viktor, after my father." Anastasiya grins like a fool.

"I'd sooner name him after Boris!" Ivan recoils.

"If I had a son, I think I'd name him Dmitriy Rudolf or Rudolf Dmitriy, after the two most handsome men in the world. I think so many impure thoughts when I look at my pictures of Grand Duke Dmitriy and see Rudy at the movies."

Eliisabet hangs her head in embarrassment for her former close friend.

"This birth certificate form won't go away by itself," Svetlana says. "We need to put a name on it soon to register his birth."

2

Late that night, Ivan sits with the baby in the rocking chair. There's a bandage on top of his shoulder, but he doesn't feel very much sustained pain. Svetlana said he got lucky, and the bullet grazing isn't very serious or likely to form a permanent scar.

"Do you know some people say I behave like my namesake's grandson, Ivan Grozniy, with my *grozniy* temper and fits of rage?" he whispers. "But he didn't start out as a bad Tsar. He was very enlightened. He only became *grozniy* in the last twenty years of his reign, after he lost the love of his life, his first wife Anastasiya Romanovna. The last Tsar in the Ryurikovich Dynasty after him was his only surviving legitimate son, Fyodor. Fyodor was taken advantage of by his evil brother-in-law, and his only child died young, but he was a living reminder to his father of his love for his first wife. Why don't I name you Fyodor too? Even if I lose your beautiful mother, there'll always be you in the world to remind me of her, just like Fyodor the Blessèd was a reminder to Ivan Grozniy of his belovèd Anastasiya for the rest of his days."

The baby falls asleep with the fingers of his left hand curled around Ivan's left thumb, but as soon as Ivan gets up to put him in the bed, he wakes up again screaming.

"Maybe you're a *levsha* too, my little Fedya. You always curl your left-hand fingers around my left thumb. Your mother wanted to give me a fellow *levsha* for a son, and God must've heard her prayers."

Ivan feels like a walking dead man, up at all hours of the night preparing bottles until Eliisabet, Kat, or Valeriya can come during the day with real milk, then putting the baby to sleep, only to be woken several hours later by his cries for more milk, and then having to do it all over again. Even Kat and Nikolas aren't as deprived of sleep with their month-old twins. He can barely function during the day after barely sleeping a wink, but he pushes himself to keep going so he can take care of his children and keep the household smoothly running. Lyuba wouldn't be very happy to wake up this very moment and see everything has gone to shambles.

3

Mrs. Zhukova and Mr. Konev come over the next morning at nine. Tatyana is playing with a teddybear as Ivan cleans up the breakfast dishes.

"What about Iosif, after my dear father who died in the flu pandemic in 1889?" Mrs. Zhukova asks. "I told the Rossilinis I wouldn't be coming until this afternoon because I wanted to see my new grandson. Your father told the same thing to his employees at the liquor store this morning."

"He's asleep in our bed. You can take over until Kat comes by in an hour. Then Svetlana comes over in two hours to help some more. You should hear how much Kroshka barks across the hall when Sveta's here. It's like she thinks there's an intruder in our home."

"How are you today, Lyuba?" Mrs. Zhukova kneels beside her daughter on the davenport. "You need to wake up and recover so your poor fiancé doesn't have to take care of two very young children all by himself."

"I don't think she'll ever wake up. We might as well bury her and get it done with. Most people don't recover from such a high fever, let alone come out of comas. All we can do for her at this point is inject her with that medicine Dr. Scholl left, and put cold compresses on her around the clock. There are only so many miracles one person can have in this lifetime, and Lyuba ran out of her supply. She's special to me, but not any more special than all those other people who've died of fever over the centuries. I just wish I understood how those personal problems had anything to do with the fever, or if this is just a coincidence and wasn't caused by her personal damage."

"She's still burning up. If she were dead, she'd be cold and clammy. Maybe this is just a silly old wives' tale, but I've heard a fever is the body's way of fighting off an infection. I'm frightened at how high this fever is, but maybe it's just taking awhile for it to run its full course and get out of my daughter's body. When she wakes up, she'll want to see her beautiful little boy."

"How about Afanasiy, after your mother and aunt's father?" Mr. Konev suggests. "This little man probably can't wait till he's safely back in his mother's arms."

"His name is Fedya, after the last Ryurikovich Tsar."

"Couldn't you have picked a more noteworthy Tsar, like Aleksandr the Third or Pyotr the Great?" Mr. Konev picks up the baby. "Fyodor was a moron who rang church bells. Boris Godunov did all the ruling for him, and we all know how well that turned out."

"He was a living reminder to Ivan Grozniy of his love for his first wife, the love of his life, just like this little man is a living reminder of how much I love Lyuba. And you know how people always tell me I should've been named for Ivan Grozniy."

"I can't wait to show him off at my job, Ivanok."

"I'd like to show him off to the Rossilinis," Mrs. Zhukova says.

"He's not a Fabergé egg," Ivan says. "He's a tiny baby who had a very scary start. I don't want him leaving the house until he's a little bit bigger and stronger, except for brief walks in his perambulator so he can get fresh air and sunlight. He's never been away from me, and I don't want him separated from his loving, adoring father any sooner than he's ready."

***

Svetlana comes in an hour after Kat. Ivan is washing clothes in a wooden tub as Tatyana watches Kat feeding Raisa and Lyudmila. Mrs. Zhukova is talking to her unconscious daughter as Mr. Konev thumbs through a cooking magazine written in English for housewives. Almost on command, Kroshka starts barking hysterically again.

Ivan drops a handful of soap crystals into the water. "Fedya's in bed, waiting for you to check his vitals. Still no change in Lyuba."

"You named him Fyodor? You hesitated so long, I was starting to think you'd pick a common name to get it over with, like Aleksandr or Stepan."

"He's named after the last Ryurikovich Tsar."

Svetlana forces a smile. "Well, that's certainly an interesting namesake."

"He's a symbol of my eternal love for Lyuba, just as his namesake was a living reminder of his own father's love for his mother."

"I have an idea," Mrs. Zhukova says. "Her fever may go down if we cut off her hair. The Grand Duchesses and Tsesarevich had their heads shaved after they got the measles, shortly after their dear father was tricked into abdication."

"I cut her hair rather short some years back. I guess I could do it again, though scissors are torture for a *levsha*."

"How are you, Fedyushka?" Svetlana picks him up. "I bet you can't wait to see your mother again."

"He'll probably grow up without her. He's lost his mother the same way I lost mine. Only I have eighteen years of memories. He has none. He'll never even have a stepmother."

"She comes back to you every time," Mrs. Zhukova says. "She'll come back to you again, and then you'll marry her and raise my two beautiful little grandbabies. Maybe God will smile on you and give you a couple more too. After all, you said it was nearly impossible for her to have a second. Who's to say there can't be another miracle or two?"

"There's no life for me without my Lyuba. I can't live the whole rest of my life without her."

"She'll recover and come back to you. She wants to see that beautiful little boy you created. Not all people die of fever. She's got such a strong life force, and must be holding on because she's got such a wonderful family to come back to."

4

Ivan is rocking Fedya at 5:30 when Kroshka comes running into the apartment, right to Svetlana, stirring a pot of beef stew at the coal-burning stove. This can only mean Mr. Lebedev forget to lock the door when he and his daughters left this morning, and forgot to close the door all the way. Such carelessness isn't typical. In Russia, he only locked his door at night, and felt safe leaving it unlocked during the day because of that phony smallpox quarantine sign. Now he keeps it locked all the time, though most people trust their neighbors too much to bother with locks.

"I'm really sorry for her behavior," Ivan says as he gets up. "She's normally so sweet and gentle. Maybe it's true lapdogs have fantasies of being as mighty and powerful as big guard dogs, and this is her way of trying to do just that. She must be sensing a stranger's presence, and wants to protect her friends."

Kroshka is now jumping at Svetlana's feet, and won't stop till Svetlana picks her up. Once she's in Svetlana's arms, she frantically starts licking her face.

"She looks just like the little Pomeranian I used to have," Svetlana says wistfully. "My cousin told me my sweet little Kroshka went to America with my father and five of my sisters. Praise God, I'll be reunited with my dear little dog soon, if she's still in this world at her age."

"What did you just say your dog's name was?"

"Kroshka, since she was as tiny as a crumb when she was a puppy. I thought it was such a cute, sweet, appropriate name."

"Well, isn't that something. This dog's name is also Kroshka."

Svetlana smiles. "Perhaps I wasn't as original as I thought. May I feed her some meat?"

"Of course, go ahead." Ivan sets Fedya on a pillow and changes Lyuba's cold compress. "I don't think Mr. Lebedev or his daughters will mind if you quickly go into their apartment to get Kroshka's brush and dishes. She prefers to eat from her dishes instead of being fed by hand, and she loves being brushed."

"Your neighbor's name is Lebedev? I'm a Lebedeva!"

"Come to think of it, one of his missing daughters is also a Svetlana. He had ten daughters, but only five are safe in America, the oldest and the four youngest. God knows what happened to the others."

Galya comes up the stairs holding onto Alla's arm. They work at an orphanage, Alla with the children and Galya in the kitchen. Galya has learnt to find her way around the kitchen pretty well, though she can't use the stove. She's promised to make the children a sumptuous meal if she ever gets taken off the waiting list for an eyesight restoration operation. Vera works there after her continuing education classes, reading stories to the children. When Fyodora and Natalya get out of school, they walk down to their father's rug factory. Natalya is allowed to weave smaller rugs, and little Fyodora sits on a bench beside Natalya and reads her schoolbooks. The family is generally home before six, though sometimes Mr. Lebedev can't help stopping to buy his youngest daughters candy, chocolate, popcorn, or pastries, or to take them to the moving pictures. Today they're coming from the moving pictures, since Natalya and Vera begged to see *Beyond the Rocks*, starring Rudolph Valentino and Gloria Swanson, for the umpteenth time since it opened not quite two weeks ago.

"Ivan Ivanovich, did no one notice I left my door open this morning?" Mr. Lebedev asks, appearing at the doorway. "There are enough people around to have corrected that embarrassing bit of carelessness."

"It was unlocked, not open," Ivan says. "Kroshka pushed the door open and ran to my place just now. The door wasn't wide open; the doorknob must've just not been closed properly."

"Can you please make sure it doesn't happen again?" Mr. Lebedev asks. "I understand you have more pressing priorities right now, but I wouldn't appreciate coming home to find myself robbed blind, after Nadya was so clever as to save everything in my house."

"Sure thing. Say, do you mind stepping inside for a moment? You haven't met Fedya's wonderfully talented nurse yet. It turns out you have the same surname, and her dog had the same name as yours."

"What?"

Svetlana turns around and gasps at the sight of the older man with one blue eye, one brown eye, and brown hair with copper highlights. "Papa?"

"Sveta?" His voice trembles, and his eyes cloud over.

Svetlana leaps into her father's arms, while her sisters cross themselves. "Thank God you're alive. Nadya told me you six had gone to America, and I couldn't rest easily until I found you."

"You've seen Nadya? Where is she?"

"Still in Siberia, sadly. She was too scared to try to come with me when I went from Uelen to Alaska Territory. I wish I could tell you more about my other sisters. All I know is Fima and Dina were sent to another camp, and Lyolya got pushed off a bridge. I'd like to believe she was spotted and rescued in time. She landed on a rock, not in the water, thank God."

Mr. Lebedev releases her and holds her at arm's length. "You look so grown-up. I haven't seen you since you were seventeen, and now you're already twenty-two. God has been so good to me to return another daughter to my hearth. How long have you been in New York?"

"I just got here earlier this month. I've been taking classes to become a real nurse and working at a hospital, though for the last few days, I've primarily been working as little Fedya's nurse. I live in the dorms they provide to the nursing students."

"*Pozhaluysta*, you must leave that dorm and come live with me and your sisters. A dorm is no place for a nice Russian girl. I'm sure they don't object to nursing students living off-campus if they're with family. I'll write you a note or go there in person to make sure you get out of those dorms. Kroshka looks ecstatic to see you again. I kept all her dishes, her leash, and her brush. I'm sure she'd love you to give her a bath tonight, and to be taken for a walk on Sunday."

"That's a very nice offer, but there are already six people and a dog in your apartment. I don't want you to be even more crowded."

"It's certainly not the nicest place I've ever lived, but it's nice to be among so many friends. Although eventually I hope to move into a real house." His eyes grow soft. "Your dear mother…"

"Nadya told me about *Matushka*. I know what happened to her."

"I don't remember you," Fyodora says.

"I'm your big sister Svetlana. You were only three when we last saw each other. But now there are six of us, and one day, God willing, there will be ten of us again."

5

"One day there will be four of us," Ivan whispers to Fedya on the sixth night of his life. "Your mother's going to get better, and she'll be so happy to see how well you're doing. You can't live your whole life being taken care of by friends and relatives. At least I lost my mother when I was a great big boy, eighteen years old."

Fedya has become so attached to his father by the time Ivan stops pacing the room and sets him down on the bed, he begins screaming again. Ivan begins pacing back and forth again, telling him a story about his patron saint, Vladimir. Each time he tries to set him back down, Fedya begins crying again. Ivan ends up falling asleep in the rocking chair with Fedya on his lap, and is woken up at five in the morning by more screams. He dutifully gets up and goes into the kitchen to get some milk.

"I can't believe I wanted to get rid of you. I should've known you were mine without question. The only thing wrong with you is that you don't let me get a good night's sleep. Your sister was such a good sleeper."

6

An hour before Kat is due to come over, the door opens and Boris comes in. He begins to open a very large box.

"What the hell are you doing here?" Ivan demands. "Can't you see Lyuba is very, very sick?"

"My courtship with Granyechka is going better than I hoped, so I decided to splurge on presents for my daughter. I thought I might be allowed to take my little girl out this afternoon to meet her future stepmother. Father Spiridon has been paying me extra every week because I'm his future son-in-law."

Tatyana hides behind Ivan. "You're not my papa."

"I was planning to go out this afternoon with my children. There will be a number of people in today to look after Lyuba, so don't worry about her. Not like you ever did, though. You certainly didn't worry about leaving her alone except for Ginny to bring my daughter into the world, now did you, *mudak*?"

"Look. A music box, a paintbox, a little crystal snowglobe, a book of stories about the Ryurikovich Tsars, three new dolls—"

"You can keep them all, Malenkov, and give them to your own children."

"This *is* my own child!"

"My right foot it is." Ivan sets Fedya in the perambulator. "My children and I are going out now."

"Then I can help."

"My right foot you can help. We're going to my aunt's house first, then out for our walk. You can get lost in the meantime."

"We'll work something out by the time Lyuba gets better."

Ivan pushes Boris out the door and waits for Kat to come over. When she does, Ivan gives her orders not to let Boris inside.

7

"She's not getting better, *Tyotya* Lera. Why do I even bother to go on living when Lyuba will never recover? That damned fever probably attacked her brain, and any day now it'll give her meningitis or something even worse. I'm delusional to keep thinking she'll be the exception, not the rule."

"That vulture of a man will swoop in and snatch Tatyana, that's why! And whatever will happen to that darling baby boy once both his parents are gone? Social services will take him away, and we'll never see him again!"

"He's got plenty of other relatives to take care of him."

Tatyana hands Ivan her hairbrush and the orange ribbon Boris got her. "Braid my hair, Papa, like Mama does it."

Ivan absentmindedly begins brushing her hair. "You'll help your *babushka* and grandaunts take care of Fedka, won't you, *knyazhna*?"

"Mama will get better. Then you can go back to the factory."

"She'll never get better. One person can only have so many miracles in this lifetime, and hers have run up. I might as well ask Dr. Scholl to come by and give her an injection to end her suffering."

8

When Ivan comes home at eight in the evening, Lyuba is gone. At first, Ivan wonders if one of his helpers moved Lyuba onto the excuse of a balcony for fresh air and sunlight, but she's not there. He checks the other rooms, and she's not there either. Quickly, he puts Tatyana to bed and makes Fedya a bottle, then goes to see all their friends on the fifth and fourth floors. No one has any idea Lyuba has disappeared, or who might've taken her. When he phones all their friends and relatives who don't live in the building, he gets a similarly resounding negative response. He begins to wonder if someone from the health board dropped by and took her, perhaps because she finally succumbed and was taken to a hospital for an autopsy, or, worse yet, already buried. If Lyuba is dead, he doesn't want to live anymore either. After putting Fedya to bed, he takes his borrowed gun out of his hiding place, checks to make sure it's still loaded, and heads off to their church's cemetery. He hopes he and Lyuba can be buried together when they find him in the morning, dead as a doornail.

The cemetery is gated and locked for the night, so he enters over a low stone wall around back. The wall isn't so low to people of normal height, but to someone over six feet tall, it's not a challenge to scale. His eyes have by now adjusted to the dark, and he quickly finds his way to the part of the cemetery reserved for those ineligible for a proper Orthodox burial. He kneels, crosses himself, asks for forgiveness for what he's about to do, and pulls the gun out of his pocket.

"What are you doing with that gun, Vanya?"

Ivan drops the gun and looks up. "I must be dreaming or hallucinating, imagining myself already dead."

"Tell me what you were doing pointing a gun at yourself!"

"Will I come back to the reality of having to kill myself if I try to touch this mirage?"

"I am no mirage! Tell me what you were doing about to kill yourself!"

Ivan reaches out and touches her cheek. "You feel so real."

"That's because I *am* real! What in the world were you doing, Ivan Ivanovich Konev? We have a little girl at home! I leave you alone for one moment because I'm a little feverish, and this is what happens the next minute I regain consciousness? You really do need a woman to look after you every moment of your life, or you do something crazy like this!"

Ivan gets to his feet. "I'm not dreaming?"

"Don't you know what would've happened if you'd killed yourself?"

He begins to cry. "You're real, my love. I'm not dreaming. This must be a miracle, though I don't know what I could have ever done to deserve this." He puts his arms around her and won't let her go. "Don't you know how terrible the past week has been for me?"

"I've been out of it for a whole week?"

"Our friends and relatives have been taking care of you for the past week, trying to do everything to break your fever."

"But I wasn't dead, Vanya. I'd never die before you and leave you so lonely."

"I tried to kill myself earlier this week, but it only grazed my shoulder. I am so sorry I wasn't at home when you went into labor."

"I'm still a bit feverish, and weak in the knees."

Ivan carries her to the gazebo in the graveyard and sits her down. "Take as long as you like to recover fully, *golubka.* I'll never let anything like this happen to you again. I'll never sleep with you again if it means you'll almost die every time you get pregnant."

"Did you lock the door when you went out?"

"Of course."

"Is anyone at home looking after our daughter?"

"No, she's there by herself."

"You left a three-year-old girl at home all by herself?" Lyuba begins hyperventilating. "The only thing I could think of when I woke up was where they'd taken our precious baby, so I walked down to our cemetery. I thought I might find him in the section for unbaptized babies. What happened to our little boy? Where did they bury him? I'm not going home till you show me where my baby was buried!"

"Calm down. It's bad for your heart, and might make you fall back into a coma."

"I don't care about that! I only care about seeing where our baby was buried!"

"He's fine." Ivan smoothes her hair back. "Svetlana Lebedeva saved his life. He's a fine, healthy little guy, and is he ever feisty. When he's not sound asleep, he's screaming his lungs out. I bet he can't wait to be back in his mother's arms and to finally get to be nursed by you."

"He survived?"

"And he's beautiful. I think he takes after me and my mother. Everyone loves him."

"I want to see him right now! I can't believe you were moments away from orphaning him and Tatyana both!"

"I'll take you home right now." Ivan picks her up. "This is a miracle."

Ivan helps Lyuba over the wall and carries her home, his legs shaking the entire way. He only very reluctantly sets her down after he unlocks their door, though he keeps holding onto her.

"What a zoo it's been in here the past week. Everyone has been coming over to help with you and the baby."

"I'm still a bit feverish. I don't want to infect the children."

"You're no longer burning up. In the morning, we'll get the

midwife to make sure nothing went wrong." Ivan opens the door to Tatyana's room and shakes her awake. "Look who's up again, *knyazhna*."

Lyuba sits beside her. "You must've missed me so much."

Tatyana jumps into her mother's arms. "We missed you, Mama. Very much. Papa said he wanted to die."

"He'll never do anything crazy like that ever again, *knyazhna*."

"Papa had to do a lot of chores while you were sleeping."

"I did everything I could, Lyuba. I gave the baby bottles when none of the other nursing women were here, and became a walking dead man when he kept me up at all hours of the night."

Lyuba ruffles Tatyana's hair. "I want to meet your baby brother now and make sure he's healthy and alive."

"I love my brother." Tatyana climbs off her mother's lap and pulls her old doll back into her arms.

Ivan leads the way to their room. "There he is." He picks Fedya up and sets him in Lyuba's arms. "The most perfect, precious gift you've ever given me."

Lyuba sits on the bed and cuddles him, making sure he's got ten fingers and toes. "He has no health problems?"

"He's making up for lost time. If he starts crying during the night, I'll take care of him. You need to sleep, so long as you don't fall asleep for another week."

"He's the most beautiful gift you've given me too, Vanya."

"My father's crazy about him. He wants to take him to work to show his first grandson off, and your mother wants to show him off to the Rossilinis."

"Your father will do no such thing! If he wants to do that so badly, he can invite his coworkers here to see him! The police might come in and arrest them for violating Prohibition!"

"He loves me so much. It's really overpowering to think of how new this little guy still is, only a week old."

"I don't want to have a third child until you marry me."

"Of course." Ivan nods guiltily. "If you want a third child, I hope it's another girl. That way, I'll have a biological daughter too."

Lyuba sets Fedya back on the bed. "I want to go to sleep now."

"Don't worry about a thing. You'll always be taken care of. If the baby wakes up during the night, I'll take care of him."

"He does take after you, *golubchik*. You and your mother. What did I ever do to deserve someone so kind and full of unselfish love, my precious Vanka? Even after everything I've done to you and been through."

"I don't know. Maybe we deserve each other because of everything we've been through, both together and apart." Ivan squeezes Fedya's left hand.

9

In the morning, Ivan changes Fedya's diaper and dresses him, then gently puts him on top of Lyuba's chest.

"Someone wants to say hello to you."

Lyuba stirs awake and reaches down for her baby. "Good morning, little man. I still can't believe you're my baby." She gently positions him at her breast. "Drink as much milk as you want, my love. From now on, God willing, you'll only have to drink your *mamashka*'s milk."

"His name's Fyodor Ivanovich Konev. If you're not happy with the name, you can change it. I only named him on the third night of his life."

"No, it's fine. I wanted you to name him. It's not like you gave him a horrid name like Arkadiy, Genrikh, or Zakhar. I could never stand those names."

"I named him after Tsar Fyodor the Blessèd."

Lyuba grimaces. "What for? He was Boris Godunov's puppet, and because his only child died young, the Ryurikovich Dynasty ended and the *Smutnoye Vremya* began!"

"Yes, that's indeed true, but he was also the last living Ryurikovich, and the last living reminder to Ivan Grozniy of his belovèd first wife, just like I feared Fedka would be my last living reminder of my love for you."

"That's incredibly sweet. I bet he's the first little boy to take his name after Tsar Fyodor the Blessèd in recent memory."

"He probably is."

"You probably don't remember me, do you, Fedya?" Lyuba whispers. "I'm your mother. I almost made the ultimate sacrifice so you could live, just like your papa's mother did for him."

"I want to kill those dirty Bolsheviks who killed my mother like an inhuman piece of trash!" Ivan snarls. "Nobody should ever die so barbarically, like they're vermin or scum who don't deserve to live and grow old and see their grandchildren!"

"Calm down, Vanya. You'll upset the baby."

"I'm guilty of that already. I've made him scream or cry because of how loudly I yelled at Boris. That *mudak* dared come over here uninvited several times."

"I hope you don't grow up to be a hotheaded bully like your papa."

"I hope he does grow up to be just as strong as I am, though. The people at Ellis Island said I'm as strong as ten men!"

"I also hope he becomes just as sweet and sensitive as you. Though not as passive as you can be far too often."

"He takes after my mother like I do. I wish so much she'd lived to see this day. Well, my father was supposedly dead too, and now he's as alive as ever."

"Boris, Ginny, and I saw her being murdered. If you hadn't run away, you would've joined her, and Fedya would never have been born. She died to protect her darling only child."

"Thank God we're all safe in America now. Nobody will orphan our baby the way I lost my mother."

10

"I'm very sorry to have to tell you this, Miss Zhukova."

Ivan stares at Mrs. Kuzmitch in horror.

"What, is something wrong with Fedya? Svetlana hasn't reported anything wrong since he was able to breathe again."

"No, little Fyodor is indeed a feisty baby. But even if I hadn't been out of town, things still would've turned out the way they did. You probably won't be able to have a third child."

"We'll see what happens. I don't want a third until after I'm married. I don't want to have three children out of wedlock."

"I don't think you'll be able to have a third child. It's a miracle you were able to conceive Fedya and have him born alive."

"Is it something that can get better by the time I'm married?"

"I don't think it'll ever get better. You have serious cervical damage that makes it nearly impossible to have more children. Maybe one or two more if you're really lucky and don't let the medical facts bother you. That's probably why you were able to have a second child, because you didn't know about this and weren't bothered by it. If you do manage to conceive a third child, it'll probably miscarry. If it somehow makes it all the way to term, you may not be as lucky as you were this time. You may die, and the child may be stillborn or die soon after birth. But there are lots of children waiting for good homes in orphanages. Several of my clients who also were unable to have more children completed their families by going to orphanages. You can request a full-blooded Russian child, and a baby even younger than Fedya."

"I'm unable to have more children?" Lyuba's voice grows more panicked.

"How could you tell her that?" Ivan demands.

"I didn't tell her until now. If I'd told her when I first found out, she might've thought about it constantly and miscarried."

"I won't get to be a respectable woman and have children as a married woman? I have to have a third child!"

"It may take awhile for that to happen successfully. But even if you never do, you've still got two beautiful children. Many women would love to have just a girl and a boy, if it were easier and legal to have access to birth control methods."

"I never wanted any children until I was an adult. This must be a punishment for that selfish, sinful wish. But I loved my daughter from the moment I found out I was going to have a baby, even with a man I didn't love. And now I've failed the man I really love by giving him only one natural child." Lyuba's voice trembles.

"Your daughter's father beat you a lot when you were pregnant with her, you've said. It must come from him, though I have a hard time picturing how that could lead to cervical damage. It must've been an indirect injury. But you've got two beautiful children, a girl and a boy, and you might be able to have another one or two down the road. Sometimes women who are unable to have children go about their daily lives, adopt a few, and then just when they least expect it, they find themselves pregnant because they weren't obsessing about it every single day. You and your fiancé are both only children, and so is your daughter's natural father."

"Mrs. Malenkova can't have more children because of an infection she got from rusty forceps used to yank out that chubby boy of hers, and my mother and Ivan's late mother didn't get that way from being beaten constantly when they were pregnant!"

"I think I'll take a walk this afternoon," Ivan says after Mrs. Kuzmitch has left. "I can't believe she told you that."

"You have my full permission to walk as far away from here as possible, Vanya. You won't want to come back home to me after you know I've failed you."

"You haven't failed me. All you need to do is not think about it, and then when we've been married for fifteen or twenty years, another child or two might show up."

"I never wanted any children, but these two aren't enough for you. You wanted seven more babies."

"I'm officially changing my mind now. Any more we may end up having will be counted as happy, lucky surprises. Better to have just one of each than die giving birth."

11

Ivan shows up at Mrs. Zhukova's and Mrs. Kharzina's house at three in the afternoon, storms in with a wild look in his eyes, drags Boris out of his room, and begins to slam him against the wall.

"You deserve an eye for an eye, Malenkov. Lyuba now knows she's almost totally unable to have a third child. As you might expect, she's devastated. She knows you're the reason why. How do you feel about that woman from your church you've been seeing? Do you want to have a lot of children with her?"

"Granyechka wants as many as God allows us."

"I wanted nine children. I never thought I *could* have a biological child by Lyuba after I found out what you did to her. One adopted daughter and one biological son are very nice, but it wasn't the family I always wanted. You not only deprived Lyuba of the chance to have a lot more than just two children, you also deprived *me* of the chance to have more children."

"There's nothing wrong with you that I know of. You can always have an affair with another woman, like Anastasiya, persuade her to move in with you, secretly have the children, and you and Lyuba can raise them together."

"Nice try. But you know I could never commit adultery."

"Time changes everything."

"If Lyuba and I are unable to have a third child within the next ten years, I'm coming back after you to break all your fingers and toes. If there haven't been more children by May 1932, you'll live to regret you decided to beat a pregnant woman. But in the meantime, you deserve to have the same amount of pain." Ivan drags Boris by his shirt into the hallway and opens a cabinet. "Take a seat right there, Malenkov."

"What are you doing?" Boris begins hyperventilating.

"Oh, just something I should've done the moment you snuck back into Russia illegally when Tanyechka was fourteen months old." Ivan opens a bottle and holds it away from his face. "Just remember this pain will be like nothing compared to the pain Lyuba and I will feel if we don't have a third child." He casually pours the carbolic acid onto Boris's lap, ignoring the resulting squeals. "This serves you right for what you did. May you never have another biological child with that priest's daughter."

"Mrs. Zhukova, Ivan is torturing me in a cruel and unusual way! I might need an emergency circumcision thanks to him!"

Mrs. Zhukova marches into the hallway. "What's going on here?"

"Lyuba found out she probably won't be able to have more children and that it's a miracle she had Fedya. Malenkov deserves to be punished with the pain of knowing *he* won't be able to have more children either."

"You'll have a third child, Ivan. God was already good to you by giving you my grandson. Since Boris is able to live as comfortably as he always says he is, he can afford to spend some of the money on someone other than himself. After you're married, I hope he starts saving to afford a doctor who might be able to cure my only child. I would've liked more children, but that deceased husband of mine made it impossible. He barely touched me after Lyuba was born, and I didn't want to get pregnant again after I found out what he was doing to her. Thank God he's dead now."

"You're still young enough to have another child or two." Ivan puts the bottle back in the cabinet. "We've all had a nice widower in mind for you. We'd like you to meet him."

"Would he be interested in a suicide's widow?"

"I have a little secret, Mrs. Zhukova. We like each other now, and it's obvious you never loved your husband, so I feel safe telling you this. I killed him. Mr. Lebedev, myself, Lyuba, your brother-in-law, Aleksey, and Nikolas were all there. I was the one who threw him into the river. The priest himself said at the funeral that it's only right to kill such sinners."

"You did that for Lyuba?"

"Not just Lyuba. For you, Tatyana, and Fedya."

"I should've known it wasn't really a suicide. You're going to make my only child a respectable woman. You're all but married already. When you finally put a ring on her finger and have your children baptized, everyone else will consider you married as well."

"Ivan only has *one* child!" Boris begins whining again. "Lyuba gave me the girl and she gave him the boy!"

"What, you think you own Tanyechka and I own little Fedka?" Ivan snarls. "If anything, *you* gave her Tanyechka and Lyuba in turn let me share her. God willing, we'll also have at least one more child together, hopefully a biological daughter. You're damn lucky Lyuba was able to carry Fedka so far and have him born alive! Don't you know he nearly died shortly after he was born because of you?!" Ivan starts for Boris's throat again. "I couldn't be there because I was working to make money to support Lyuba and my children, but I sure *was* there when she first began to double over in pain thanks to the damage you gave her when she was carrying my daughter! Thanks in no small part to you, the Konev family name could've died out!"

"There, you see? You finally have that firstborn son you wanted for so long. Why aren't you home taking care of that baby instead of doing this to me?"

"That baby boy may very well be my only natural child ever. Consider yourself warned if he dies before he can have his own firstborn son." Ivan stalks off in a huff.

12

Lyuba is sitting in a rocking chair and nursing Fedya when Ivan comes home. Tatyana is looking at a picture book.

"Oh, you came back."

"How could I desert such a beautiful woman after she nearly died, and in addition this beautiful little girl and perfect baby boy?"

"I may never give you another natural child, Ivan. I'm worthless."

"You'll never know that for certain till we try again."

"Mrs. Kuzmitch said at least five months."

"Until you're completely healed?"

"Yes."

"Five months without being able..."

"Yes, at least five months before you can sleep with me again."

"How could I go that long?"

"You went the first twenty-three years and two months of your life without sleeping with any women just fine."

"I know we can have another child someday. But for now, these two are just fine."

"You can marry me after the five months are up and make me a respectable woman. I won't sleep with you again until we're married."

"It's not as if we're casually living together and not thinking it's any big deal to have children out of wedlock. We're doing it respectably, not dishonorably, no matter what society thinks. We're getting married eventually, not involved in that crazy free love movement."

Lyuba gazes down at Fedya. "I'll guard him with my life, Vanka. Your only natural child is not going to die of any childhood diseases, bad food, or anything!"

"I'd just as readily die for him too." Ivan takes one of Fedya's little hands in his own. "I think he likes you."

"He'd better like me. I'm his mother!"

"He screamed when Voroshilova picked him up."

"That vain woman was trying to still get her claws into you while I was unconscious, and even trying to get her claws into my son?"

"She suggested I name the baby after her father. But don't worry, she'll never come here ever again. You're the only woman I've ever wanted, no matter what I led her to believe."

13

That night, Lyuba is unable to fall asleep due to Ivan crying loudly beside her. This in turn wakes up Fedya.

"I kept a terrible secret from you for three and a half years, my love."

"Does this secret have anything to do with Voroshilova?"

"God no. I never even kissed her!"

"Is this a crime you committed?"

"I've known all along, *lyubimaya*. The other midwife told me you were practically guaranteed sterile. I told the others in a fit of rage that night Boris came back, right after you went to work for the Godunovs. My aunt, Mr. Golitsyn, my father, your mother and aunt, Boris's parents, and Father Yakim know too. I knew it was a miracle you had Fedya. I never told you for fear you'd leave me and declare yourself useless to me because of what that *mudak* Malenkov did to you."

"Wait a minute. So you've known all along I didn't have very good odds of getting pregnant, and you stayed with me and told me it was all in my head I might never be able to have any children by you when you knew full well it was all a lie?"

"I felt terrible keeping it from you!"

"That must've been killing you inside, my Vanyechka. That's the most beautiful thing you've ever done for me. You finally became my lover knowing you might never get me pregnant. Even now you want to stay with me. Now I really have no doubts about how much you love me."

Ivan picks Fedya up. "I should've known God would be good to us and grant us little Fyodor. Just as long as you can keep yourself from running back to Boris every six months or so from now on, the four of us are a family in every way that counts."

"A family living in sin!"

"Your father lived in true sin with you and your mother, and the fact that they were married didn't take away from the sin. Two people living together who've loved each other since childhood and have extenuating circumstances aren't living in sin."

"It was a sin how Tatyana was conceived."

"Only on the part of her unworthy natural father. I committed no sin, and neither did you, when we conceived Fedya. How can love be a sin when Christ himself said there's nothing higher than love? Soon enough, we'll be a legal family, and Malenkov will sign over his undeserved paternal rights to Tanyechka. Maybe we'll have a third child too. Malenkov knows what'll happen if there's no third child within ten years."

"What do you mean by that?"

"Nothing you need to know."

14

When Fedya is three weeks old, right after Ivan has returned to being exploited by Mr. Glazov at the iron factory, Ivan comes home to the kind of beautiful family scene he's long dreamt of. Lyuba is sitting on a pillow on the floor by Fedya, playing with his hands, as Tatyana happily scribbles in one of the stupid storybooks Boris got her at a dime a dozen last year. Ivan smirks with pride upon seeing this, but regrets his arch-rival can't see it in person too.

"Do you know why I love you?" Lyuba whispers to Fedya. "Because you're little and sweet and so brand-new. And you look just like your good-looking papa, the same way your big sister looks like her average-looking mother, only a whole lot prettier than I'll ever be."

"What a thing to say." Ivan closes the door and sits beside her. "You're just as beautiful as Tatyana."

"Boris thinks I look like he does," Tatyana says.

"He's delusional. Malenkov is short for a man, chubby, with large eyes and sickly-colored pastel skin most of the time, except for when he blushes, he's a coward, a bully, a joke—"

"Malenkov has no bearing on our lives," Lyuba says. "Even my mother and aunt are getting tired of him leeching off them. He must be jealous of you because you have the love of the woman he wants, and get to have your family name passed on through the firstborn son you always wanted."

****

Chapter 33: Resentment Brews

Lyuba sits rocking Fedya, who's now three months old, as Ivan comes home from the factory. She ignores his return and holds Fedya tighter.

"Did you have a bad day?"

"Kolya was five months old when Alyosha made Liza a respectable woman. He didn't waste much time. They didn't care it was a very simple, small ceremony. Money wasn't an object for them. Here we are, engaged on and off for nearly a year and a half, I now have two children out of wedlock, we had a chance to be married on Ellis Island, but you oh-so-stubbornly chose to wait until you had enough money saved up to afford a fancy, expensive wedding. Don't you know how strange this situation is? I thank God every single day we've got such modern, sympathetic, understanding friends and relatives, and that outsiders haven't questioned my phony wedding ring when I go out. Many other fallen women aren't nearly that lucky, and are taunted with accusations of sluttery and whoredom."

"That was a different situation. Religious ceremonies were illegal or suspect, and we were all on the run from the Bolsheviks and didn't have much money."

"When are you going to make me a respectable woman?"

"I can't give you an affirmative answer."

"Praise Christ it's too soon to resume sleeping together. Then I'd really feel like I wasn't a respectable woman, living in sin with the father of my second child."

Ivan takes a step toward her. "Can I hold the baby?"

Lyuba clutches Fedya tightly. "What if your son is upwards of three years old, like my Tanyechka, when you finally decide to get around to marrying me? How do you think he'll react upon finding out his father wasn't man enough to marry his mother before he was born?"

"You're already my wife in every way but the most important way."

"A true wife would wear her husband's wedding ring and live a respectable life with him. Anybody could do the job of cleaning, taking care of two small children, and cooking."

"I would've married you by now if you hadn't kept running back and forth. We would've been married five years ago if you hadn't listened to your mother."

"Then there'd be no Tanyechka, and we'd have more than two children, since I wouldn't have been rendered so barren."

"Just to make you feel better, on the day you found out you might not be able to have another child, I went to your mother and aunt's house to visit Malenkov."

"Why does that not shock me? Did you beat him up or just threaten him?"

"Both. And I poured acid into his lap. I hope I made him sterile."

Lyuba stands up. "You can take the baby. I might as well start supper."

"I'll do that for you. I know how much you hate that coal-burning stove."

"You work enough at that awful factory being exploited by that awful man." Lyuba hands him Fedya and saunters off to the kitchen.

"How's my little guy this afternoon?" Ivan lifts Fedya into the air. "Pretty soon you'll be big enough to play with your cousin Vasya!"

Lyuba does her best job of ignoring Ivan over the next few months. She ignores his little gestures and rarely ever sleeps in his arms.

2

Matryona Lebedeva purposely fell behind on a forced march to another ore-mining camp in Eastern Siberia in September. As soon as the last zechka *vanished, she smuggled herself onto a truck leaving for Uelen. She managed to pass for one of the passengers boarding a ship headed for Alaska Territory by walking very close to an older man with three children. Now she lives in a tenement on Chicago's Devon Avenue, surrounded by people who've also been alone in the world since the Revolution. To make a living, she cleans floors at Angel Guardian Orphanage. It was founded by German Catholics, both historical enemies of the Russians, but money is money. She prides herself on being a modern, university-educated woman, but that diploma is worthless when she's not a citizen and speaks very poor English. Cleaning floors will have to suffice in the meantime, until she proves herself worthy of a position befitting her education and experience.*

Matryona grows misty-eyed when one of her friends passes around old family pictures one evening, as a cool breeze blows through the windows. Before long, everyone is sharing stories about dear ones left behind, either dead or with God knows what fate.

"I was the second of ten sisters," Matryona says. "Only my older sister Galya was left when I was taken. It'll drive me crazy if I think about what may have happened to my relatives. As far as I know, I'm alone in this world, and it's impossible to ascertain what happened to anyone after I last saw them."

"If your four littlest sisters went to an orphanage, they may have been adopted and are living nice lives with new families, alive and well."

Matryona shakes her head sadly. "Only my two youngest sisters would still be young enough for an orphanage. The older two must be in jail or camps by now. My baby sister might not remember any of us. She was barely three when they took her away."

"You don't think any of them might've escaped or been freed like you? Why so pessimistic?"

"Like I said, it's best to not think about such things. I don't want to imagine the dead, raped, burnt bodies of my sisters, parents, or cousin."

3

"Why don't you remarry Mrs. Zhukova, Papa?" Galya asks after they've gotten back from the hospital, where they were informed it'll be at least another three months before her eyesight can be restored. "It's been long enough since the dirty Reds murdered *Matushka*."

"I have four daughters still out there somewhere, and Nadya. I cannot remarry until I know Nadya and my last four living reminders of Yevgeniya are safe and alive. How could I disrespect my first family like that? And I'd never love another woman nearly as much as I loved my dear Zhenyushka."

"If Lyolya were found by good people in time, she may very well be able to rehabilitate herself and come to America. God knows what happened to Dina, Fima, and Motya. There's a hole in my heart for my other four sisters too, but six out of ten isn't a bad survival statistic. I want you to be happy and start over."

"You're a good-looking man for fifty, and such a good family man," Svetlana says. "Lyuba's mother would be very lucky to have you for her new husband, and finally know what it's like to have a husband who loves and honors her like she deserves."

"Don't you believe life was intended for the living?" Vera agrees.

4

Boris goes smiling into the urology clinic with Granyechka and Father Spiridon. Mrs. Zhukova walks behind them with Mrs. Malenkova.

"Once I marry Granyechka, you and *Batya* will move out of my house," Boris snarls at his mother. "I bought that house with my own money, and it was mine, all mine, until you decided to be horrible parents and kick me out. I'm humiliated living with Mrs. Zhukova and Mrs. Kharzina again. I only did that before I became a real man by making a living to support myself, when I had no choice. And I know full well you get to have a relationship with Tanyechka while I'm forbidden to even talk to my own daughter!"

"That child is our granddaughter, Borya. We didn't abandon her when we found out about her like you did. And of course your father and I will continue to live where we're living now, unless you want to take responsibility and buy us a house."

"What the hell would I do that for, woman? I don't owe you anything!"

"That's right, I only gave birth to you and spoilt you because you're the only child I'll ever be able to have, which is partly your own fault—"

"Lyuba's problems might be my fault, but I haven't got anything to do with *your* sterility problems, woman!"

"If you weren't so chubby, the doctor wouldn't have needed to yank you out using those rusty forceps."

"I'll pray to God you'll try to begin to talk more respectfully to your mother." Granyechka picks up an issue of *The Journal of Urology* and promptly turns as red as a beet when she begins reading.

The doctor who comes up twenty minutes smirks when he gets an eyeful of Boris. "Aren't you an ugly man."

"Just for that, I don't think I'll pay you, bastard. I can lose the weight, but you can't lose your mean attitude."

"So you're here for medical advice on how to lose weight? Did you ever pick the wrong type of doctor. You're also rather short for a man. What are you, five-one?"

"Five feet one inch tall? That's as short as some women. I'm five feet eight inches tall."

"In boots, with wooden inserts," Mrs. Zhukova smirks. "Doctor, this man is five feet three inches tall in his bare feet, though he's always wearing those stupid inserts and high-soled shoes to try to appear much taller."

Mrs. Malenkova begins speaking in her pronounced accent. "I'm this man's mother, and that's his fiancée. Other man is her father, and his priest. My baby wants to make sure he'll be able to have children after the wedding."

Boris follows the doctor into a room down the hall.

"Name, age, reason why you think you can't have children?"

"Boris Aleksandrovich Malenkov, twenty-two years old, date of birth the first of March 1900. My former best friend poured acid onto my lap recently. This man has also brutally assaulted me in ways such as throwing me down an entire flight of stairs and smashing my head against a rock, all because I want a relationship with my little girl, she's three and a half years old."

"How did this daughter come about?"

"Don't tell me you don't know how babies are created."

"You were married?"

"What does it matter? My daughter's here now, isn't she?"

"Is her mother still living?"

"Yes, though my former best friend won't let me forget some bad things I did to her when I didn't think properly."

"Are you with this woman now?"

"Didn't you pay attention when my mother said the woman in the waiting room is my fiancée? She's not the same woman. My daughter's mother is engaged to my former best friend. They have a baby boy now, he's five months old. Because of me, she probably won't have more kids."

"You know this how?"

"Everyone in our circle of friends knows this. Even the mother of my child finally knows this. Apparently I did her some personal damage when I beat her during her first pregnancy."

The faces of Granyechka and Father Spiridon fall when the doctor comes back out two hours later and talks to them. Boris limps out on his injured leg and sits beside his mother and Mrs. Zhukova.

"I'm being punished, *Matushka*, for what I did to Lyuba when she was pregnant with Tanyechka. Why should she be able to have another child with Ivan if I can't have more children myself?"

"Now you know how Lyuba and I feel."

"It wasn't just the acid. It was all my sustained injuries from the things Ivan's done to me, and the anti-Slavic punks who beat me up. I'll die alone."

"You teach all those children, Borya, and there are always new ones coming in. That's a great way to make up for not being able to have more children."

"It's better work than the hotel, where everyone hated me and laughed at me. Now my children at the religious school love me."

"Praise God you work with our own people now, Borya," Mrs. Zhukova says. "I can't imagine how you'd be living if you were still a bellboy."

"You're not going to tell Konev about this ever. He'll laugh in my face."

"I'm sorry, but I don't think I want to marry you anymore, Boris," Granyechka says.

"I understand completely," Father Spiridon says.

"No!" Boris shouts. "Konev thought I'd left Lyuba unable to have more kids, and now they've got that five-month-old son."

"Why should I waste my time hoping eventually we'll have even one child when I could be with a man I know can easily give me many children?" Granyechka asks. "God loves the infertile just as much as the fertile, but I shouldn't have to voluntarily marry someone unable to reproduce when I want children. Even I'm not as otherworldly pious and devout as the infertile women of the Bible."

"Your father is a damn priest! That's a great reason to believe a miracle will happen!"

Father Spiridon shakes his head. "I'll still let you teach religious school, Borya, and pay you well, but you cannot marry Granyechka. I can't let one of my children marry someone who isn't very likely to be able to give her children."

Boris starts crying.

5

One of Matryona's fellow tenants approaches her one evening shortly after she comes home from work. "I hope you don't take any offense, but I was very moved by the stories you've told about your family. Unlike a lot of these other people, you can't say with any certainty your dear ones are dead. I traced the name Lebedev and found a man with your father's name, Ilya, living in Manhattan."

"Ilya's a fairly common name, and so is Lebedev," Matryona says. "Perhaps not as common as the English name John Smith, but not the most unusual name combination either."

"His household includes six daughters, Galina, Alla, Vera, Fyodora, Natalya, and Svetlana. My contact also informed me he came to this country in May 1921 with five of those daughters and a little dog named Kroshka. He has four more daughters who could be alive or dead."

Matryona crosses herself. "That has to be my father!"

"Why don't you take the next train to New York to see if he's one and the same as your father? If not, at least you'll know, and you can come back here if you don't want to remain in New York. But if he really is your father, he'll soon be reunited with his seventh daughter and only have three more to search for. Even if you could be the last to be found, seven out of ten isn't bad. I'm sure he can't wait to welcome you back to his hearth."

"I'm thirty, Sir. That's too old to live with my father, even if I'm an old maid. I've gotten used to living by myself, and I'm a modern, university-educated woman. Twentieth century spinsters have earned the right to live independently."

"You can think about all these things in more detail later. The sooner you start packing and get on that train, the sooner you can find out if this is indeed your father, and the sooner he'll know seven of his children are still alive."

6

It's December 1922, and Fedya is seven months old. They've been in America for a bit over a year and a half. It all seems like a strange, sometimes brutal, sometimes lovely dream, with the horrors of the Revolution and Civil War so far behind them, at least in waking life. There are still the nightmares about the burning buildings, the Cheka, the riot in Pskov, the narrow escape into Estonia, and the escape to America, but it was all worth it in the long run.

"Look how big he's getting," Tatyana says.

"Most normal men marry the mothers of their children long before they're seven months old." Lyuba glares at Ivan.

"I'm coming home with back pain, iron residue all over me, poor wages, and a cough for you. Show me some respect for these thankless sacrifices."

"Look at these beautiful children. Tanyechka's always asking why her belovèd father hasn't married her mother yet, after everything we've been through together. I knew this would happen when she was old enough to understand."

"We'll be married as soon as I have enough money saved up, *golubka*. You deserve the most beautiful wedding ever, and I'm not going to waste our savings on something we don't need as badly as food and coal. It's bad enough that *mudak* doesn't pay enough for me to afford rent without constantly dipping into our savings. Then boarding Branimir at that stable is another twenty dollars a month we can't afford without savings. If this damned tenement had a courtyard like some of the other ones I've seen, I'd get our four-legged buddy out of that damned stable and move him here to save that monthly expense."

"If I didn't have a son by you, Vanya, I swear to God and Christ I'd walk out of this door with my daughter and go back to Boris right this very moment. At least *he* had plans for us to get married."

"You could never do that because you love me too much. You'd never destroy our beautiful family."

"Boris bought me a wedding dress. He has his own house instead of a squalid, filthy tenement. He has lots of money to afford a fancy wedding. We've been engaged for almost two years, and there's still no wedding in sight."

"At least you've gone ages without running away from me and getting scared about how much I love you, *golubka*. That baby boy you're rocking is proof you finally decided once and for all to never run away from me again."

"If you're so in love with him, you can have a turn rocking him while I make supper." Lyuba hands Fedya to Ivan and goes into the kitchen. "Thank God we haven't slept together since I was seven months pregnant, or I'd feel like a totally shameful woman."

"Why haven't you married Mama yet?" Tatyana insists as her mother fries fish. "*Tyotya* Kat and *Dyadya* Kolya got married by a priest when we came to this country, and they didn't care it wasn't huge and expensive."

"Sometimes grownups have complicated things going on in their lives they need to set right before they do something serious like getting married. Real life isn't a Krylov fable."

"Don't you love her enough to marry her? Mama tells me she feels like a shameful woman, because respectable women are married instead of living in sin, she called it. She's afraid people will find out she's not really married. They'll be mean to her and ask why she couldn't get married."

"If only she'd been in this much of a hurry and this impatient years ago, we would've been married for almost six years." Ivan smiles as Fedya wraps his left hand around his father's right thumb. "I think our baby's a *levsha* too, Lyuba."

"Mama wants Fedyushka and I to be baptized like Kolyechka, Mira, Lyuda, and Raya. She says we can't be baptized till you get married."

"I'm married to your mother in every way that counts, *knyazhna*."

"She says something called a social service agency can track us down and take us to an orphanage. We all love Fedyushka so much, and I don't want my baby brother to be taken away and given to total strangers."

"They can have the son I wanted for so long, this baby who was conceived by nothing short of a medical miracle, when they pry him from my cold dead hands."

"Mama says they don't care if you love us. They don't want children to be raised by unmarried parents."

"Fine!" Ivan stands up, startling Fedya, and walks swiftly into the kitchen. "I *will* make you a respectable woman by the end of next year!"

"I can't bear going very much longer without being your legal wife, Vanya."

"We'll get married in September, the anniversary of the night we became lovers, the night we created this beautiful little boy who grew inside of you and miraculously didn't miscarry or die at birth. Of course, I'd never share such a personal reason with anyone else. I'll let them think we liked that date more than any others. Once we're finally married, you won't have any more excuses to run out on me and blame our problems on someone else."

Lyuba nods. "I'll leave you forever if September comes and goes and I'm still not your real wife. I may very well take both of my children with me and go back to Boris."

"You know you'd never do that because you'd shatter my heart."

***

That night, Ivan tries to pull Lyuba closer to him, but she pulls away. She ignores him caressing her hands tenderly and stroking her long sable hair.

"I know we were told five months, but since you had so much trouble, and were so weak after you had Tanyechka, I wanted to wait a whole seven months."

"You're going to have to wait even longer. I'm afraid I won't give you my body again until we're husband and wife."

Ivan lies there in shock. "You would never be so cruel to me!"

"You're being crueler to me, depriving me of being a respectable woman who wears a wedding band. And I'm dying to shed my awful surname, the name of the so-called man who fathered me and did so many awful things to me. If we ever get so lucky as to have another child, I want it to be born to married parents. Don't you know how awkward I feel when Tanyechka asks questions about why we aren't married yet? She already knows we live in sin." Lyuba leans over and kisses him briefly. "There, that ought to keep you until you decide to be a real man, put a wedding band on my finger, and make me a Koneva."

Ivan lies there in disbelief, longing for her body. He knows she knows full well he's too chivalrous to force himself on her. And so he lies there, in utter agony, over the fine mess he's sprung.

7

"You have another bad day?" Aleksey inquires the next day at the iron factory.

"Lyuba won't make love to me again until I marry her! Now even Tanyechka's harassing me about why I won't marry her mother. I'm so tired of explaining I can't marry Lyuba till I have enough money saved up for a fancy wedding."

"Don't you think you've once and for all finally proved your love for each other after everything that's happened?" Nikolas inquires. "I hate this job. I wish I could get moved to the book-keeping department or another managerial task instead of standing all day over scalding hot liquid iron. I'm an intellectual, not someone meant for manual labor. I had a hard enough time in the labor camp."

"I told Lyuba I'd marry her next September, only nine months from now, and she still doesn't fully believe me."

"You're too noble to force yourself on her," Aleksey says. "Not that I've ever had that problem with Liza. Even if I had, I wouldn't be able to live with myself if I did that to her."

"I can't stand a chance in court against Boris if I tell the judge glibly I'm not married to Tanyechka's mother, I just live in sin with her."

"Don't you remember how happy you were when you found out Lyuba was having your child? Don't you think she'd feel that same exact happiness if you put a wedding ring on her finger? You already know she'll never leave you again."

"She said she'd leave me and take the kids if September ends and she's still living in sin with me."

"I can't help but wonder if you're suddenly holding yourself back from marriage as a mental reaction against how many times Lyuba left you before. Maybe deep down, you're terrified she'll go through that same cycle of leaving you and coming back, and putting off marriage for such a shallow reason is your subconscious way of avoiding what you believe to be many more impending betrayals. Perhaps deep down, you're still not sure if she really wants to stay with you forever."

Ivan shrugs.

"Tell Father Yakim you're getting married next September and that you'd like Tatyana and Fedya to be baptized after the ceremony. Then you'll contact a judge. When your big day in court comes, that beautiful little girl who's your daughter in every way that counts will be legally yours. You'll have it in writing, and that slug Malenkov will be forced to relinquish his paternal rights over her, not that he deserves any. Then we'll wait a few more years to save up our money for the most important thing of all, splitting the hell out of here and moving to the Midwest, where we won't have to be exploited all day in this godawful iron factory."

8

Lyuba has continued to deny Ivan her body at night. She knows full well he feels completely tortured on her twenty-third birthday; when they ring in 1923 at a party given by Katrin, who's now engaged to Sandro; on Orthodox Christmas; on Tatyana's fourth birthday on the twenty-third of January; and every day in between. Fedya is now nine months old, and she only feels a little sorry for Ivan. He did bring this on himself, and now that the tables are turned, he kind of deserves it.

"Are you in such a hurry to start another day of exploitation that you're going to forget your lunch?" Lyuba pesters, running down the stairs after him and through the entrance door. As soon as she sets foot outside the tenement, she slips on a large patch of ice, landing on her side. "Now you see what you made me do?"

Ivan picks her up and opens the entranceway. "Even if you're not being so nice to me, I still love you."

"I can walk, Konev. All you need to do is get your lunch, and then you can be off for another day of exploitation by that traitor."

Ivan ignores her protests and sets her on their bed, putting ice on her leg. "There's probably already a bruise forming. You're not going anywhere today."

"Yes I am! I have all these chores to do in our little game of playing house!"

Ivan sets Fedya beside his mother. "So you won't have to walk back and forth all day whenever he needs you."

"Tanyechka's four years old, and he's nine months old. You've had ample time to marry me since Fedya came into this world."

Ivan goes back down the stairs to the iron factory.

"I don't want those people you told me about to take me and my brother," Tatyana says. "Why won't Papa marry you after you've had two children?"

"I won't let anyone take either of you from us. I'll make sure that man puts a real wedding ring on my finger by the end of this year."

"At least *Tyotya* Kat and *Dyadya* Kolya didn't have their babies before *they* were married."

"Some people know the meaning of respectability," Lyuba says darkly. "Whatever was I thinking, allowing myself to have a second child out of wedlock when your father and I were nowhere near solid plans for an exact wedding date?"

9

Ivan comes into the factory growling and takes his place near Aleksey and Nikolas in the most dangerous area.

"I can't *believe* she'd be so mean to me after everything we've gone through together!"

"Why couldn't you just do what Kat and I did?" Nikolas asks. "Finally being married mattered far more to us than the where and how."

"I want a fancy, expensive wedding to make her happy."

"Seems to me Lyuba would be much happier just to have a wedding ring on her finger, regardless of what kind of ceremony it is, as long as it's a proper religious ceremony." Nikolas steps aside from the scalding liquid iron being poured down from overhead. "Why couldn't I get a job at the library like that stiff Gromyko?"

"Who would you rather work with, someone we always hated for being all brain and no fun, or the two of us, lifelong friends you've gone through thick and thin with?" Aleksey challenges.

"I'm going to be the first of the three of us to quit this terrible job in this horrible factory. I don't think I can go another year and a half of being exploited like this."

"Come on, that's too soon to quit this job to run away to the Midwest. We'll leave together, the same way we came to America together."

"Kolya did the right thing," Ivan says darkly. "Not having any kids by Kat till after they got married."

"I had to wait two months to consummate our marriage," Nikolas says. "There was never any way we could've been alone together until we had our own place, even if it is a dirty little tenement. Why couldn't I find a penthouse like Katrin?"

"Because you're not that rich!"

"I never thought I'd be jealous of a woman, but I am now. She gets to sleep late; she wears nice clothes and doesn't live in a filthy, crowded tenement; she writes for newspapers instead of working in a damn iron mill; she gets to buy gourmet food; she's always throwing parties; she can afford to go to a salon every week; she has a maid, cook, and butler; she eats ice-cream and fancy pastries every day; and she never once has to put her life in daily jeopardy. She doesn't have any kids to worry about, since she's only engaged, and as far as I know, she isn't sleeping with her fiancé. Even she isn't so radical she believes in free love. If she did, I'm sure we would've heard all about it by now."

10

Katrin is going through several library books from the Baltic section of the main library branch, reading up on Estonian wedding customs, baby names, and cuisine. Some of the books are written in Latvian and Lithuanian, but so long as they have sections on Estonian culture, she doesn't discount them.

"You're going to design my wedding dress, Nastya. Think of it as your first real fashion design assignment. Everyone in Manhattan will want to wear the same dress I wore on my glorious wedding day." Katrin admires her dark blue opal engagement ring for the umpteenth time since Sandro proposed while they were ice-skating at the 59th Street Pond in Central Park on her birthday in December.

"Your wish is my command. I'm forever beholden to you for how you probably saved my life. You never once abandoned me. Will it be white or red?"

"I like green best. You're going to buy a whole large roll of medium green silk. I should also like roses to be made out of the silk and sewn onto it. Just to be prepared, you'll also start sketching some possible designs of highly fashionable maternity clothes."

Anastasiya almost chokes. "You think you're pregnant? I never once suspected you were such a slut you'd fornicate outside of wedlock, as cute as Sandro is."

"I'm only twenty-three, and still a virgin. Of course not. And I've heard talk of clinics in this wonderful country that provide things to prevent having as many kids as my parents did. I want you to have designs ready when that day finally comes. You have such a talent for design, yet you've never put it to any outside use. This is your chance."

"How can you get married when you don't go to church? A traditional Estonian marriage ceremony has a strong religious element."

"I don't need to go to church. Whatever kind of impression would that leave upon the people who come here for our secret Socialist meetings? Though sometimes I go to a Unitarian church, mostly composed of immigrants. I was always shot down by our childhood priest for daring to question such ridiculous beliefs as a virgin having a baby, how a crucified person could talk, devil spirits possessing people, a geocentric universe, bringing the dead back to life, and most of all how God, who's supposedly beyond all human descriptions, could have a flesh and blood child. It's highly lazy to decide you can sin all you want because some dead guy took responsibility for your own actions. If you'd like, I can lend you some of the books I received from a friend of Sandro, on how Christianity is nothing more than a highly-evolved, socially-accepted, great huge myth, with tons of similarities to ancient polytheistic cultures. You'd be surprised."

"How can you just abandon Orthodoxy like that?"

"Most of our fellow Estonians who became Russian Orthodox did so because they thought they'd get treated better by the thugs in charge. I'm positive the majority were not motivated by sincere religious conviction, just like most Jews who converted to Christianity throughout history were motivated by the promise of social advancement."

11

Nikolas always looks at the scant amount of postings on the factory bulletin board during lunch break to see if there are any openings in less hazardous positions, such as the book-keeping department. There are still none for workers who've been there less than five years.

"Maybe I could work with Liza and not have to do this every day. I could work a sewing machine instead of standing around boiling hot liquid iron."

"The thug who runs this place doesn't look kindly on workers who leave before five years. We don't even have a union," Aleksey says.

"At least you have wives," Ivan sulks. "I couldn't be happy getting married earlier than I wanted to in some cheap affair."

"Do you think I liked having to learn a strange new language for Liza, from a completely different language family than Slavic or even Indo-European? For the love of God, I had to learn fourteen cases, nominative, genitive, partitive, illative, inessive, elative, allative, adessive, ablative, translative, terminative, essive, abessive, and comitative. My five-year-old son speaks the language better than I do, and I've been learning it longer than he's been alive."

"Kolya was rejected by Kat at first, but he wasn't as unlucky as

I was. I wonder, if I never come home from this factory again, will she still love me."

"She's threatening to leave you by September if you haven't married her. You're going to get cracking right away. People really will start to think horrible things about you if they discover you've been lying about being married. You're damn lucky Glazov turns a blind eye to it and hasn't reported you. Liza told me Katrin wants to take all of us down to the coast this summer for a vacation. How do you think people will react if they discover this couple with two children lives in sin?"

"Their judgmental reaction will say far more about them than me."

12

Ivan goes home expecting the usual tongue-lashing. Tatyana and Fedya are listening to the phonograph as Lyuba sets the table.

"Sit down, or the food will get cold, Konev."

"What are you doing up?"

"I'm not your wife. You can't tell me what to do. We're only playing this game of keeping house with two kids and no marriage. At least back in Novgorod, it didn't feel like we were just playing house, since we weren't sleeping together."

"Where did this champagne come from?"

"Your father. He brought it over last week, remember, in the black leather briefcase so people wouldn't see he was transporting an illegal substance?"

***

That night, Lyuba beckons to her fiancé instead of coldly turning over in bed when she sees him coming in like she usually does.

"Someday they'll make you a saint, my belovèd, for your level of otherworldly patience, goodness, everything you've ever done for me, and how you always forgive me and take me back no matter what's happened. I want to believe I'll be your true wife in nine months, not just someone you live in sin with. No matter what society thinks, I don't believe Fedya came about as the result of a sin. That was a beautiful, loving act, and it's not fair to either of us to have to be celibate for nine more months. Come here and remind me of all the reasons you're the best lover I've ever had."

Ivan eagerly takes her in his arms and kisses and caresses her greedily, coupling with her four times before he tires himself out. Lyuba's heart melts when she sees the sweet smile he gives her afterwards.

Lyuba goes to sleep that night beside him, still not happy over the cohabiting, but at least now assured that in nine months she'll be a married woman instead of someone who's living and sleeping with a man to whom she's not married. And how could she have willingly deprived herself of such a sweet, gentle lover who's only ever been with her, yet makes her feel like she's only the latest of thousands of women he's slept with?

****

Chapter 34: Changes for Katrin

Lyuba looks down at the wedding invitation before going out to Katrin's bridal shower. She can hardly believe she's going to both a shower and a wedding for this woman whose values seem so diametrically opposed to hers.

You are most cordially invited to the wedding of Katariina Nikonova, daughter of Kaarel and Martina, and Aleksander Kalvik, son of Priidu and Asta, on 14 March 1923, at Miss Nikonova's penthouse suite. The wedding was planned for a hotel, but it was cancelled after the manager found out all the guests and people in the wedding party are immigrants. The most serious occasion of matrimony shall be presided over by Reverend Ernst Zimmer, a Unitarian clergyman, with minimal religious references. It is not required, but highly smiled upon by bride and groom, that all guests donate a small fee of ten dollars to be used towards their honeymoon. Both bride and groom will wear outfits designed by Miss Anastasiya V. Voroshilova.

The food to be served will be, for an appetizer, potato salad with beets, stuffed mushrooms, and roasted vegetables. The main course will be mutton in peppermint garlic sauce, roe deer in herb-wine sauce, salted herring, black bread, black pudding, goose, and smoked salmon on ice. All female guests are invited to Miss Nikonova's bridal shower a week before the wedding. Mrs. Samson, Miss Nikonova's maid, will gladly provide babysitting at the wedding. Pozhaluysta, *RSVP.*

The wedding invitation is written first in Russian, then Estonian, and finally English. Katrin didn't want to spend too much money, so she left out Latvian and Lithuanian.

"How can she claim her parents when she happily turned them in and got them arrested, and was responsible for the murder of her nine younger siblings!" Ivan shouts.

"She certainly didn't do that deliberately. How was she to know what was going to happen? As we both know, sharing blood doesn't always mean you love someone. We weren't in Tartu the first seventeen years of her life, and have no way of knowing why exactly she hated her parents so much, and felt so little for eight of her siblings."

"I'm certainly not giving that selfish, vain woman ten dollars for her to go on her honeymoon when we all know damn well she can easily afford it!"

"One rarely earns a millionaire's salary by writing for newspapers, no matter how many of them she writes for. She might be worried her money may soon be all used up if she doesn't watch it." Lyuba picks up her wrapped package. "Tanyechka, Fedya, be good for your papa while I'm gone."

2

Katrin's penthouse suite is enormous, with proportions befitting a one-story mansion instead of merely a large apartment with more rooms than usual. The home décor includes a Steinway grand piano with framed pictures of Katrin, Anastasiya, and Sandro; a large, airy drawing room with two easels holding Anastasiya's sketchbooks; a large cherrywood box of A.W. Faber-Castell Polychromos colored pencils, arranged into darks, lights, earths, and pales; three huge cartons of *Vogue* and *L'Officiel*; pictures of celebrities; pictures of Russian royalty; and a big jar of candy or mints in every room, each jar bearing a different type of candy. The floor is littered with newspapers from the Baltic and Russian émigré press, leftist publications, Katrin's rough drafts of her articles, and Anastasiya's rejection letters from various fashion schools. So far, no fashion school has accepted her because she's an immigrant.

"That's an ankle watch," Eliisabet says as Katrin unwraps the small parcel. "Some moviestars wear them, and you must want to emulate them."

"Why would Katya show her bare ankles in public?" Anastasiya asks in horror. "It's bad enough she sometimes wears pants and skirts with a bit of her lower legs showing, even covered by heavy stockings."

"I'll be showing my ankles on Long Island and Coney Island after I get back from my honeymoon. Isn't this a wonderful bathing suit Maarja got me?" Katrin giddily holds up a peacock green satin swimsuit without the sleeves and long skirts they're accustomed to, let alone the wool fabric most swimsuits are made from.

"Oh my goodness, it goes clear up to nearly your waist!"

"It only stops a quarter of the way down my upper leg, dolt. It's not like it's nearly as revealing as Annette Kellerman's swimsuit outlining her legs and crotch. This is modern without being too scandalous. Besides, I want to swim instead of sitting on the shore looking beautiful." She reaches for Kat's present and unwraps several Macy's boxes. When she lifts the tissue paper, she discovers silk stockings in a variety of colors; garter belts; several straight, loose dresses with hip-level waistlines, lightweight fabric, and very short sleeves or mere straps; several skirts ending just above the knees; and glovelettes.

"Do you like them?" Kat asks. "I don't know why you of all people haven't picked up the latest fashions yet."

Katrin squeals in delight, but Anastasiya groans again.

"These clothes show your knees and elbows! It's bad enough you sometimes wore strap dresses to balls, but that was a special occasion, not really public."

"You've seen my elbows and knees thousands of times since we were little girls."

"Strange men haven't!"

"Wow, now I won't need to pack twenty trunks of clothing. I can take maybe three small suitcases on my honeymoon. These outfits must weigh no more than two pounds apiece."

"We already paint our faces. You can't go around looking like these American women showing their elbows and knees to the world! Even the most scandalous of these modern American women aren't so brazen they showcase their knees. That's a piece of harlotry reserved for only the most impudent strumpets."

"They're called flappers, and hemlines and sleeve lengths don't make one a whore. I really like this look. How could I have gone so long wearing heavy, dragging dresses, a proud twentieth century woman like myself? So many of my clothes are so out of touch with current reality, even after I've started wearing pants and shorter skirts."

"You can sure say that again. Even I think some of your wardrobe is ridiculous. How about that hat with packs of playing cards glued on, your feather boas, or your wigs?"

"Once I get back from my honeymoon, I'll start in earnest on acquiring more modern clothes. I already paint my face and wear short hair; why not go one step further and start dressing the part too? Some of my outfits are truly ridiculous. I'll never forget how Petya humiliated me in Tartu by throwing all my clothes and hats around, and even you, Nastya, laughed at them! Petya was right when he said I didn't need nonsense like those stupid clothes, pictures of celebrities, and nonsense like the hat with stuffed birds. I had a deep-seated emotional attachment to them, and couldn't give them up no matter how many times I was called on my hypocrisy."

Anastasiya shrieks again when Katrin comes out of her room modeling one of the outfits, a smoky-grey chiffon gown with little red hearts along the neckline. Her arms are exposed well above her elbows, her legs are showing to a bit above the knees, and the clothing is loose instead of tight-fitting. Lyuba meanwhile is shocked to see Katrin's bare legs for the first time.

"You shave your legs like these modern flappers?"

"I always liked to be hairless even before it became the fashion and safety razors were invented. People in places like Egypt and India have been doing it for thousands of years as a matter of cleanliness. Back in Estonia and Russia, I used sugaring to remove body hair. If you want a lesson in either sugaring or shaving, I'd be happy to teach you all my secrets."

"Aren't you going to at least put a corset on?" Anastasiya asks.

"I've never worn one. How many ladies here have ever worn a corset? We came of age just as they fell from favor, and modern, progressive women stopped wearing them a long time ago, even when they were considered *de rigueur*. If I must wear a supportive undergarment, I'll wear a brassiere. I don't want shortness of breath, crushed ribs, displaced organs, and flattened breasts." Katrin smiles devilishly. "Sandro can't wait to finally touch my voluptuous breasts on our wedding night. I'm not going to deny him that pleasure by deforming myself to conform to a mindless fashion."

"I don't even know you anymore since we came here! You flat-out refuse to hang up your pictures of celebrities and cute royalty; you claim you no longer support Communism yet have secret weekly Socialist meetings with other immigrants; you stopped reading *Vogue* and *L'Officiel*; you wear pants; you don't wear most of your old clothes anymore, just stuffed them away in a dark corner to gather dust; you read lowly rag publications not for comic relief but to see if your parents, whom you willingly turned in, are here and looking for you; and now you want to wear immodest clothing showing excess flesh!"

"I had every right to turn in those traitors. I hope they finally learnt their lesson in prison. I also got rid of nine excess people while I was at it, as unfortunate as it was children had to die. I don't even remember their names, except the oldest two, Karl and Nikita, and little Viktoriya. My parents didn't give any of us Estonian names except me, the big traitors. You yourself don't have an Estonian name."

"I also don't like how you're asking all the wedding guests to give you ten dollars for your honeymoon. You can most easily afford it all by yourself!"

"My only money comes from the articles I write for the radical publications. Now who's next?"

"I bought you twenty cartons of cigarettes," Anastasiya says in a very small voice.

"What for? You know I don't smoke."

"But see, each carton has a different picture of a celebrity. All the handsome screen sheiks, and the stylish ladies. You can sell the cigarettes and keep the pictures."

"And you wonder why we thought you were the most expendable member of our band," Lyuba says. "Even Katrin wasn't running from the Bolsheviks in Jeanne Paquin gowns, tango shoes, and full makeup."

"I wonder sometimes why I saved your life," Katrin says. "You denounced me at the victory ball and pushed me away when I was trying to hug you and ask what happened to you in the labor camp. You said you hated me and wanted nothing more to do with me, but guess who came crawling back fourteen months later! I nearly got killed because I stayed loyal to you, against my own better judgment. You were definitely the most disposable member of our band. Everyone else said I was intelligent and had a brain underneath my deceptive exterior."

"I don't know, maybe the fact that I got back from the worst seven months of my life only to find my lifelong best friend became a Bolshevik, turned in her parents, got them arrested, and was responsible for the murder of nine helpless little children, while my parents and older brother were killed and I was in a labor camp for seven months, had a little something to do with it!"

"The oldest ones probably would've reproduced by now. I never rejoiced over their murders, but it had the macabre blessing of controlling the population a little bit."

"What if one day your oldest child turns against you, gets you arrested, and has all the rest of your children murdered!"

"As soon as I get back from my honeymoon, I'll schedule an appointment at one of those secret population control hospitals."

"For all you know, you could get pregnant on your honeymoon!"

"Now is too soon for you to be able to comply with my instructions. But I'm warning you right now. As soon as I get back from my honeymoon, you're out of our penthouse suite. There are lots of nice places you can live on the Upper West Side. If I were you, I'd start looking at real estate and the female help wanted ads. With your interests and talents, I'm sure any bridal salon would be more than happy to employ you as a seamstress."

Anastasiya sits crying for the rest of Katrin's bridal shower.

3

Lyuba gets back from the shower to find Mr. Lebedev in her apartment, animatedly talking with Ivan while Tatyana plays with her dolls and Fedya crawls around making his cute baby noises.

"To what do I owe the pleasure of this visit, Ilya Nikolayevich?"

"I want to get to know your mother as soon as possible. Maybe you're right and we'd be a perfect match. Earlier today, my daughter Matryona showed up at my door, praise Christ. My Zhenyushka left me seven out of ten of our beautiful children, and they'll always be a tangible symbol of the love I had for my dear wife. Now that I've been reunited with the majority of my children, why shouldn't I try to find love again and be happy? Zhenyushka would want me to be happy, not sit about forever mourning her. And that disgusting waste of life who fathered you shouldn't be your mother's only memory of a husband. I'd love to be your stepfather."

Lyuba crosses herself. "Praise God. If my mother wants to marry you, would you move her into this tenement? She and my aunt got out of their tenement as soon as they had enough money to get a house, so I don't think she'd be happy to return to tenement living."

"I'll buy my own house, of course. Your aunt's family and that man who fathered your daughter would keep their house, and your mother and I would find our own house nearby."

"I'll ask Katrin to seat you next to my mother at her wedding next week. I don't want your meeting to look too obvious, though my mother knows I want her to meet you."

"Katrin's the one with hair cut as short as a man's, who wore all those ridiculous clothes, hats, and accessories on the boat?"

"She's the one. Once I started getting to know her better, I began to realize she's not as bad as I assumed. She's extremely intelligent and progressive, even if you might not guess it from some of her silly outfits and rather naïve, knee-jerk opinions. And yes, she caused the arrest of her parents and the deaths of her younger siblings, but as she says, that wasn't done deliberately. She really had no idea that was going to happen from such a simple act as telling the principal her parents' names. I'd like to think she thought they'd just be taken to an orphanage."

"She talked proudly and openly about how much she admires those traitors to the Tsar, said Lenin's wife is her hero, wants to join the Socialist Party as soon as she becomes a citizen, and never apologized for turning in her own family. Apologetics aren't the same as genuine apologies."

4

Katrin turns over one of the few family pictures she still has, taken as afterthoughts when she was packing the night before she left home. Herself, Karl, Nikita, Sergey, Viktoriya, Lev, Yegor, Larisa, Olga, and three-month-old Manyeshenka. When she came home from gymnasium that fateful day, she went about her business of studying her Russian grammar, trigonometry, and political history, and did homework for French, English, and economics. In the evening, she went to her little sister Viktoriya's room, asking her if she wanted to join the Red cause and fight for Estonian nationalism and the overthrow of the provisional government, since Viktoriya had been displaying signs of rebellion against the family lately. Katrin told her very sternly she needed to answer right away, but Viktoriya said she was too young to be of any use to the movement. Instead of saying goodnight, Katrin told her little sister goodbye. In the morning, when everyone but Katrin was herded downstairs, there was no chance to try one more time to intervene and get her to defect also.

Mr. Rhodes, the sandy-haired, dark hazel-eyed butler, answers the door to a wavy-haired young brunette holding a suitcase. "May

I help you? Are you here for Miss Nikonova or Miss Voroshilova?"

"I come to see Katariina Nikonova." The young woman strides into the penthouse and addresses Katrin in Estonian. "I got your address from the major Estonian émigré paper that publishes your articles."

Katrin looks up from her fried squid. "Now isn't a good time. Try me again after my wedding, exactly a week from now. I have weekly meetings here to discuss Socialism, but tonight isn't the regular night."

"You have more right to want to kick this complete stranger out of our house than you do me," Anastasiya sulks.

"Is that Anastasiya Voroshilova?"

"You see her picture in the society pages of one of the Baltic publications?" Katrin asks.

"I knew her for the first nine years of my life!"

Katrin turns white when she gets a closer look at the young visitor.

"Do you know this person, Katya? You look like you're seeing a ghost."

"I am! I watched her death with my own two eyes!"

The visitor puts her hand on Katrin's. "I'm no ghost. The one assigned to murder me was a lousy shot and misfired. I knew I had to play dead until the coast was clear. A neighbor came by as soon as you'd left and found only me still alive. After I recovered from smoke inhalation and nerves, I lived on a farm near Tashkent, far away from the political and military turmoil, until things seemed normal again. Now here I am."

Katrin breaks into a huge smile. "I knew it! A friend of mine told me she swore she saw slight movement from you and a bullet hole in the wall behind you, but there was no way of knowing if you were able to get away before the whole house went up in flames. I was left homeless two years later. I temporarily lost my Party membership because of this prim little fashion plate, and a year, later our boardinghouse was pillaged and burnt. Nastya and I had to escape through a back window, and then it was running from one place to the next, every time right before the police came. We had an especially close call in Tver." She enfolds her little sister in her arms. "You're safe now, and we'll never be apart again. I hope you don't hate me for almost getting you killed. You have no idea how much I've missed you all these years, forced to keep my real emotions bottled up inside so I wouldn't appear weak."

"I never held anything against you, Katrin. You were right to turn them in. I was only nine, and didn't realize what you were saying to me that night."

"This harebrain is out of my penthouse before I come home from my honeymoon. I can fix you up with an annex to the main suite. Though at least Nastya's worth something. She's making my bridal gown and will be my maid of honor. The things I've gone through because of my lifelong loyalty to her."

5

Mrs. Samson and Mr. Rhodes have fancied up the suite even more than usual by next week, March 14. Katrin rented fifty mahogany chairs for the guests, bedecked with white silk roses and with a small present underneath. In the kitchen, Mrs. Oswald slaves away making the appetizers, the Estonian main course, and the desserts that haven't been previously bought at the bride's favorite bakery—chocolate Jell-O, the wedding cake, and an ordinary cake spiked with dessert liqueur from Mr. Konev's store. Anastasiya is heard wailing as Katrin cuts off a good portion of the sleeves on the green silk wedding dress, leaving them barely covering her shoulders.

"I found my own place like you ordered," she sulks as Katrin sniffs the bridal bouquet of brilliant blue cornflowers and baby's breath. "The best I could find was a crummy old apartment in the Upper East Side, with none of the perks nor spaciousness of our lovely penthouse suite."

Ginny hops over and deposits ten dollars in the basket one of the Estonian radicals is holding.

"I barely make ten dollars a month!" Ivan shouts. "There's no way in the world I'll let that spoilt, pampered traitor get her hands on any of my money so she can finance her honeymoon!"

"I gave her ten dollars," Eliisabet says. "I get paid twenty dollars a month."

"Well, you had to! You, Katrin, and that little brainless excuse of a woman Anastasiya were best friends growing up!"

"You may never believe me, but she's a good person, albeit a bit hypocritical, especially when she spouts off Socialist viewpoints while living like a royal and swimming in millions of dollars. I think you're threatened by a strong woman."

"Besides, she doesn't like me because she thinks I want Lyuba to be a substitute for my mother; she made a very ignorant pronouncement about my mother on Tanyechka's first full day of life; and she thinks I'm weak-willed and not very masculine because I can cook."

"She's very generously offered to take us all on vacation with her and Sandro this June."

"Who's this man berating my sister?"

"Who the hell are you?" Ivan demands.

"I'm Viktoriya Nikonova, Katrin's sister. I'm fifteen. The Bolshevik who was assigned to kill me misfired, and I was saved by a neighbor after they left the burning house. I live here now, in a little annex to the main suite. Why won't you give my sister ten dollars so she can go on her honeymoon?"

"I barely make ten dollars a month! And it's horribly bad manners to ask your wedding guests to give you ten dollars each so you can go on a stupid honeymoon!"

"Does your wife work?"

"I'm not married. My fiancée's job is to stay at home, look after our kids, and do housework."

"You're not married, yet you live with a woman and have more than one child by her?"

"Her four-year-old daughter isn't my blood daughter, but our ten-month-old son is. We're getting married this September."

"How shameful!"

"It didn't happen this way on purpose. You're not in my tenement! You don't know why this happened!"

Nikolas too is refusing to give Katrin ten dollars for her honeymoon.

"I gave her ten dollars," Kat says. "Don't be stingy."

"You can! You make twenty-five dollars a week! I make only twelve dollars a month, up from eight when I started working at that factory. We have five mouths to feed, and the dog. If I can't get work in a safer, higher-paying job at that godawful factory, like bookkeeping or accounting, I'll look for work in a garment factory like Pasha Teglyov."

"You'll get a raise sooner or later, Kolya. Maybe one day you'll be able to live as comfortably as Boris."

Boris also has been invited to the wedding. He's sitting with Mrs. Zhukova, far away from all the others.

"I'm glad this wedding was moved from the hotel because they hate immigrants. That was the hotel I worked in when I got here," he whines like a little baby. "I have a gimpy leg thanks to the creeps who went to that stupid hotel. Now I'm impotent too!"

"Oh, yes, being a bellboy was such a step down for you," she says sarcastically. "You told me you were a drug trafficker and village tough, and beat up people who trespassed into your valley."

"We also made and sold cigarettes, forged things, and manufactured official documents."

"Why does that woman have her hair cut so short? That's even shorter than Mrs. Rossilini recently cut her hair!"

Katrin walks down the long red carpet as the remaining guests take their seats. There are no religious articles present. Even the Unitarian clergyman is devoid of a cross.

"Is she a Lutheran, a heretic?" Mrs. Zhukova asks in a horrified whisper. "I know most Estonians are Lutherans."

"She's Russian Orthodox by baptism, but she's at best an agnostic now. Even a Lutheran heretic is more religious than a Unitarian."

"Marriage isn't recognized unless done in a religious ceremony pleasing to God."

"It's a legal marriage. They're not going to live together for seven or eight years to become common-law married like some people we know."

"Speak for yourself. You also aren't married, yet you have a four-year-old daughter."

Boris glares across the room at Ivan during the ceremony, which is conducted in English. "He's stealing my daughter!"

"Pipe down and listen. This woman invited you to watch her wedding, not to stir up old grudges against your former best friend."

Mrs. Zhukova is horrified the vows are so generic and completely devoid of any religious significance, and instead of a fancy ceremony involving candles, crowns, a walk around a Holy Table with a cross and a Gospel, and drinking from a common chalice, all bride and groom have to do is say "Yes" to the questions posed by the Unitarian clergyman. The rings come very late in the ceremony, instead of before the actual marriage ritual begins. He even pronounces them husband and wife instead of man and wife.

"Presenting you with Mr. Aleksander Priiduvich Kalvik and Mrs. Katariina Kaarelovna Kalvik-Nikonova!"

Ivan is still holding onto the money in his pocket as the guests are led into the dining hall.

"*Matushka*, you must sit next to Ilya Nikolayevich," Lyuba insists. "We really think you'll get along great."

"I'd like to make a toast." Flagrantly flouting the laws of the nation, Katrin fills her glass with an openly-displayed bottle of wine. "To the future of Socialism and all the workers of the world, most especially my guests, who are just the people Socialism means to help."

"Why did that woman leave Russia if she's this pro-Socialist?" Mrs. Zhukova demands of Boris, sitting on her left.

"I told you, she refused to leave her best friend. Anastasiya wanted to leave, and she wouldn't leave without Katrin, so there was no choice."

"Now if only you'd refused to leave without *your* best friends."

"I did what I did. The past is over and done with. There's still time. I can easily persuade Lyuba to come back to me before Ivan gets his claws any further into my daughter."

"This child is mine!" Ivan shouts from across the table. "I'm glad you were dumped by your priest's daughter! You don't deserve more children!"

"That's my only child, Konev, my only child ever! I'm impotent now, and possibly sterile!"

"It serves you right. It was the acid I poured onto your lap, wasn't it?"

"Yes, and the doctor also said it might've been partially caused by how late in life I had chickenpox."

"Why are you here? Katrin likes you even less than she likes me!"

Katrin shrugs as the doorbell rings. "I invited Malenkov to be polite. I still don't like him. Why doesn't Malenkov put himself to some use now and answer the door. Can't imagine who would be so unspeakably rude as to come that late to my wedding."

Boris hobbles over to get the door. Ivan rolls his eyes at how his former best friend exaggerates his limp.

"An older couple to see you, Katrin!"

"Do either of you have an invitation to my private wedding?" Katrin demands in Russian. "I know I have lots of admirers from the things I write in the radical publications, but I can't very well cater to every fawning admirer who has the utter nerve and gall to drop by at my suite for an autograph or just to see me."

"All guests are expected to give bride and groom a gift of ten dollars in cash for their honeymoon," Anastasiya says. "Produce the money or leave, scum."

The man steps forward, his face ashen. "Do you know how humiliating it was to go through the last six years of our lives, Yekaterina, known only by numbers and forced to do horrible things like empty barrels of human waste and cart out dead bodies to be burnt or buried after the snow had gone, all thanks to our selfish, radical firstborn child who turned out to be the entire cause of our misery?"

Anastasiya gasps. "You're Katrin's parents!"

"That's that shallow best friend of yours, Katyenka, the one who was dragged away to a labor camp of her own days before we were arrested? How is it a shallow, brainless excuse for life like that could survive and happily come to America while we were slaves the past six years?"

"My name is not Yekaterina or Katyenka. My proper Estonian name is Katariina, and everyone calls me by the nickname Katrin. I've decided to stop letting people call me Katya, though Nastya hasn't quite gotten used to this change yet. I never should've let anyone call me that Russianized nickname to begin with, but at least I finally put a stop to it. Don't expect a tearful hug hello, traitors. Mrs. Samson!" Katrin claps for her maid to appear and switches to English. "I want you to show these two to the door right away."

"Is that Viktoriya?" the woman asks.

"Fuck off, traitors," the fifteen-year-old sister says in Estonian. "Katrin and I are much better-off without people who kowtowed to oppressive rulers."

"What Katrin says goes," Anastasiya says.

"A Negress for a servant?" Mrs. Nikonova gasps in downright horror. "What for, Katyushka?"

"She's teaching me the latest jazz dances," Katrin responds calmly. "And she's great around the house. You should see what a miracle-worker she is about cleaning even the most horrific stains on clothes and carpets."

Everyone resumes eating except Ivan, who's absolutely horror-struck at what just happened. He now hates Katrin more than he did before, and when it comes time to leave, he still refuses to part with any money for her honeymoon fund.

6

Mr. Lebedev escorts Mrs. Zhukova home after the wedding. As they walk arm-in-arm, his heart flutters. It's nothing short of a miracle for such a sensation to be awakened in a man of his age. For almost six years, he's been forced into unnatural, early celibacy, finding little choice but to repress his longing for female companionship and physical connection. Seven daughters and a dog can never take the place of a wife. As much as polite society would deny it, or castigate him for such thoughts, sexual and romantic desires don't automatically stop at a certain age. And right now, he feels such long-repressed feelings miraculously awakening, as Mrs. Zhukova chatters on a mile a minute.

"I cannot believe that woman who got married! Throwing her own parents out after she sees them again for the first time in six years, outright asking guests to give her ten dollars each for her honeymoon, getting married by a godless Unitarian preacher, having a completely secular ceremony but for some vague references to God, and that gown! Her arms were exposed clear up to her shoulders! My Lyuba tells me that woman, the ungrateful, vulgar bride, didn't get her hair cut that short because it's how all the girls wear it now. She's had it cut short as a man's for years. At least girls with bobbed hair style it femininely instead of cutting it like a man wears his hair. I'm shocked her new husband was even remotely attracted to her with hair shorter than his."

"My oldest daughter Galya had hair barely longer than that when we were reunited. I never judged her unfavorably. I was too happy she was still alive and had been Divinely returned to me."

"How old is your oldest daughter?"

"She'll be thirty-three in two months. I'm fifty-one, if you're curious or want to figure out how old I was when I became a father."

"I'll be forty-one. We've both kept our age well, considering what we've lived through."

Mr. Lebedev gets a faraway look in his heterochromatic eyes. "I haven't been with anyone since my wife Zhenyushka was brutally raped and murdered in front of me six years ago."

"I can top that. I haven't been with a man since I was twenty-three. My late husband last slept with me late into Lyuba's fifth year. I thought it was a phase, but when I looked into our daughter's bedroom about three months after her sixth birthday and saw what he was doing to her, I was disgusted. He claimed I got too old and boring, at only twenty-three, and that's why I 'gave' him Lyuba, to sleep with. My own daughter, my only child, at best resented me and at worst hated me for never intervening or taking her, leaving him, and going far away so he never could find us. Who would've believed Leontiy was capable of such lewd, diabolic things? He never even confessed it to a priest till that night before you and the others murdered him, and even then only to try to save himself from one of the lower circles in Hell. I set a horrible example for Lyuba. I'm the reason she let Boris beat her when she was pregnant. Ivan is the best thing that's ever happened to her, and while neither I, Lyuba, nor my granddaughter are happy about how Ivan won't be a man and marry her immediately, at least he's not beating her, and he's treating her like an actual human being for a change. I wish I'd found a man to treat me like a human being. At my age, it's hard to hope."

Mr. Lebedev looks around nervously for a few very long moments, then takes his chances and kisses Mrs. Zhukova. That long-forgotten sensation makes his heart flutter even faster. "Why don't you marry me, Yekaterina Iosifovna? You deserve a husband to honor and love you better late than never, and I'm longing for female company to take away my loneliness. Having seven daughters, I'm surrounded by women, but that doesn't mean anything without the kind of love and companionship a man can only have from a wife."

Mrs. Zhukova struggles to find her tongue. "I wasn't expecting you to do that at all, but I'm glad you did. It's been so many years, I truly forgot what that felt like. But my husband has only been dead for a year. It's common courtesy to wait at least two years for a woman to remarry, especially if she's a widow."

"Based on speaking to you just now, and going on what I've heard about you for so long, you really do seem like an ideal match for me. And Lyuba and Ivan will never leave me alone if I don't marry you. They've had this idea for years, particularly Lyuba. She really wants me to be her stepfather. But don't think I'm only interested in marrying you because other people have suggested it. We'd still seem like an ideal match independent of that. We can always grow to love each other like a husband and wife over time, even if we're not in love now. The most important thing is I'll take care of you, honor you, and protect you as you deserve, and we'll take away one another's loneliness. You'll never be the bride of my youth, but I want someone to grow old with, perhaps someone I'll eventually grow to love in a more mature, deeper way than I ever loved my Zhenyushka."

"I want more than anything to know what it's like to have an honorable husband and to be loved by a man. At forty-one, it's a miracle any man would want to marry me. And at my age, a ten-year age difference isn't a big deal. A man who's had ten daughters has to know how to treat women better than my first husband. Lyuba and Ivan will get their wish. I'll drop the name Zhukova, in September Lyuba will follow suit, and then that evil man will finally be out of our lives for good, forever. Sometimes when one door closes, a much better, unexpected one opens."

7

Katrin returns from her honeymoon to Cape May at the end of March, wearing her new lightweight clothes baring her elbows and knees, a cloche hat, and rolled-down black silk stockings, looking noticeably pale and spent.

"What's eating you?" Anastasiya asks. "I'll be out of our suite in no time, now that you're back. The lady who runs the floral section of the bridal shop I work at noticed my design of your wedding dress in a local paper, and loved it to death. I protested and said that wasn't how I originally designed it, that you chopped off the sleeves all the way up to the shoulders at the last moment, but she said all the fashionable women these days don't mind showing a bit of excess flesh. She ordered me to start working full-time in the main part of the bridal shop, doing nothing but designing that very same dress in different variations all day. As time passes, I'll start designing different types of wedding dresses. Once I make enough money, which I hope is very soon, I'm going to start my own salon so I'll have all the fame for myself. When I get famous enough, I might get to go to Paris and see my designs displayed in a fashion show. I've come a long way from the labor camp. If only those godless Bolshevik bastards could see me now."

"I'm pregnant," Katrin announces soberly.

"Excuse me?"

"I went to the secret population control place when Sandro and I got back, and the nurse informed me it was probably a little too late for a diaphragm, since I'm two weeks late. I expected my menses a few days after the wedding, and they never arrived. It's far too early to detect pregnancy, but it seems obvious. I'm already fatigued and am having headaches."

"You didn't want to start breeding till you're thirty. Are you going to go back to get it removed?"

"You can start designing baby clothes when you have some free time. I myself was a firstborn child, and I'd never discard another firstborn. Little Marek or Oliivia will probably come in mid-December. Well, have a nice day." Katrin walks into the kitchen and pulls out a box of Babayevskiy chocolates. "Some maternity clothes would be a very nice gesture too."

Anastasiya goes through the door carrying her luggage in utter shock.

****

Chapter 35: Tension Mounts

Natalya, Vera, Fyodora, Svetlana, Galya, Matryona, and Alla are all wearing dusky pink bridesmaid gowns designed by Anastasiya. Anastasiya's designing career has taken off like a rocket, and she's already earned enough money to afford rent on a building she's in the process of converting into a bridal salon, christened Voroshilova's Weddingland Creations. Scores of prospective brides have come to her dying to wear what Katrin wore. Some want a different color, usually red or white; some want a different design over the gown, like a layer of lace studded with artificial diamonds or a series of thin, delicate silk ribbons; some want a higher hemline, much to Anastasiya's utter horror; and some want the sleeves a bit longer. Along with the prospective brides have come their bridal parties, also wanting dresses. Anastasiya grins and bears it when her customers tell her they want shorter skirts and sleeves, for it's paying her bills at her new upscale apartment on the Upper East Side and getting her established as a player in the fashion world. In the next few years, she hopes to have her first showing in Paris.

"Your soon-to-be-stepdaughters are wearing dresses made by that brainless woman, *Matushka*?" Lyuba demands in horror.

"A brainless woman couldn't make such beautiful gowns. She may only care about fashion, moviestars, and other trivial pursuits, but she's an excellent seamstress and fashion designer. Some fashion designers have other people make their clothes for them, but this woman does it all by herself." Mrs. Zhukova admires her vintage engagement ring for the umpteenth time, a round garnet on a copper band.

"At least your wedding gown wasn't made by her."

"It's your aunt's. Since she's had such a happy marriage, it might rub off onto me for my second marriage. I can only find one thing slightly wrong with your Ilya Nikolayevich. It's taken me awhile to get used to looking him in the eyes, because his right eye is brown and his left eye is blue. I thought I was seeing things at first."

"It's unusual, but very charming. You can't forget a person like that, no matter how long it's been since you've seen him."

***

Vera and Natalya are poring over a letter they've just received, postmarked Minsk. The address simply says "*Pozhaluysta*, forward to Alla, Vera, Natalya, and Fyodora Ilyinichna Lebedeva, New York, New York, USA."

3 February 1923

Dear Alla, Vera, Natalya, and Fyodora:

It's such a happy life now for me and my new sisters. I languished in the dirty orphanage in Yaroslavl for seven or eight months, till February 1921, with little Karla Gorbachëva and Valentina Kuchma, and then Dyadya *Dima came to my rescue with the most happy news that mean* suka Tyotya *Dasha was thrown in prison with her oldest daughters, Lyudmila, Ivana, Kseniya, and Rufina, for running that horrible orphanage and pretending to the authorities and my uncle it was a hospital. The authorities were especially furious at how she sent girls to prison as soon as they became teenagers, and that no one was older than a rare fifteen or sixteen because of this most barbaric practice of hers. She should've sent them out in society to start working, kept them as paid helpers or teachers, or released them into the custody of relatives or friends of relatives. They were only in orphanages because their parents were supposed enemies of the people, but they themselves did nothing wrong other than being born into the wrong families at the wrong time.*

Dyadya *Dima managed to take custody of those of us who'd been mistakenly shipped like cattle to the hellhole in Yaroslavl, and now little Karla is back in Kiyev in Mrs. Brezhneva's orphanage with her cousin Naina and their friend Katya. He also adopted our friends Olga Kerenskaya, little Valentina Kuchma, Klara Nadleshina and her brother Fyodor, and Zofia Kwaśniewska. I very much wanted Inna to also come with us, but she refused and said she liked Mrs. Brezhneva and wanted to continue helping her with the children, especially all those foreign children from places we'd never heard of, like Ingushetia, Chechnya, and Dagestan.* Dyadya *Dima no longer works in that awful coal mine, and now has a job at the Belarusian State Library, in the section on Marxism and the struggles of the proletariat. Every night before I go to bed, I kiss the photo of Comrade Lenin hanging above my bed, to thank him for all the good things he's done for me.*

Sadly, five of my cousins died in the Civil War, Alyaksandr, Ilko, Yakiv, Danylko, and Kindrat. Lukhym and Nykyfor came home, though, and are now busy raising their own families. That makes eleven of my cousins you know about, and there are sixteen more. The other older girls, Nyura, Odarka, Malanka, and Alena, all have their own families too by now. Katarina and Matviyko are away at university in Poland, and Dyadya *Dima also must support ten more. Kista's sixteen, Petrusho's fifteen, Prokip's fourteen, Roman's thirteen, and all of them are away at a fancy Communist private school. It's sort of like olden-days religious school, only instead of being taught by nuns and priests and learning about religion, it's taught by high-ranking Party members with teaching degrees, and they learn about Marxism and Comrade Lenin all day. Rustam's twelve, Yuliya's eleven, Ulyana's ten, Kilina's nine, Oksana's eight, and then finally little Vladlena is only seven years old. In addition to all those,* Tyotya *Dasha also had seventeen miscarriages and three abortions. I'll never enslave myself to a man like that, not even one as nice as* Dyadya *Dima, having children, getting pregnant, losing pregnancies, and arranging to get rid of pregnancies artificially every time I turn around.*

Comrade Lenin hasn't been in great health lately, and I fear we might not get as enlightened of a ruler after he passes away. Pozhaluysta, *write back soon in case writing letters to foreign places is no longer officially allowed.*

With much love and Communist greetings,

Inessa A. Zyuganova.

***

"Are we all ready to go to the vestibule?" Mr. Lebedev asks. "I can't believe I'm as nervous as I was when I was a young man of seventeen on my first wedding day."

"I wanted to see you on your wedding day, and to see how my soon-to-be-stepmother looks in her wedding gown," Galya says. "That stupid doctor can go to Hell for constantly moving my operation date."

"Are we going to move in with Mrs. Zhukova?" Fyodora asks. "I don't want to be moved again. The tenement isn't very nice, but it's been our home for almost two years."

"We're all going to move into a much bigger house as soon as we've got enough money," he promises. "Me, your stepmother, Natashka, and maybe Verushka too. You and Natashka are my only daughters left who aren't old enough to live on your own."

"I can't leave Natasha and Dora," Vera insists. "I was all they had for four years, Papa, for four years! I was always with them when we were shuttled from one orphanage to the other, and most of all Alla and I were together with them when we escaped from Kiyev with Anya and little Lyonya and slowly made our way to freedom."

"You don't want to live with your father for the rest of your life, do you, Verushka?"

"All three of us were apart from you for four whole years. We don't have our mother anymore. We're lucky you and *Matushka* had so many daughters. If you'd only had three or four, you might've lost all of us, or only been reunited with one. Being together in little groups is why we survived. I feel bad for Galya and Motya, surviving alone."

"You're about to get a wonderful new stepmother," Mr. Lebedev beams. "And she's about to get seven new daughters as part of the deal."

Mrs. Zhukova stands counting the Lebedeva sisters. "What have you and Ivan talked me into, Lyuba? Becoming a stepmother to seven girls, most of whom should be married by now?"

"Galya's the oldest, almost thirty-three, the one with scars on her face, arms, and hands," Lyuba starts explaining. "That's Matryona, two years younger than Galya, the one with light brown hair that curls at the ends. Svetlana's the one who saved Fedya's life. She's the one cradling the dog in her arms, little Kroshka. She's only two months my senior. Alla's nine months my junior, and then come Vera, eighteen, Natalya, fourteen, and Fyodora, nine."

"Come on," Mrs. Kharzina tells her sister. "It's time to become Katya Lebedeva, finally drop that disgusting name carried by that sick-minded excuse of a man you were married to, and get on with your life. For the first time in nearly twenty years, you're about to have a husband who loves and wants you, and you'll also be giving your daughter, your only child, a wonderful stepfather who's long regarded her as a surrogate daughter."

2

Boris doesn't take well to the three new additions to "his" household. When he comes home from teaching religious school the next day, he finds Vera, Natalya, and Fyodora there as well. They've made themselves at home in the room he formerly slept and lived in.

"What happened to the sheets on my bed, little girls?"

"We're not little girls, you short fat man, you. I'm eighteen, Natashka's fourteen, and Dora's nine."

"I'm a bit on the portly side! So what! And like hell I had control over only growing up to be five foot three inches tall! I'd love to be as tall as that bully Ivan!"

"We're washing the sheets we brought from our tenement," Natalya announces. "You can find your sheets in the hallway. We can't sleep in sheets a grown man slept on."

"This looks like a girly room now! What the hell happened to all my masculine articles, like my posters of the shebas of the silver screen, my sporting equipment, and my men-only literature, if you get my drift?"

"Your posters of the American actresses I pulled off the wall, rolled up, and stuck into three large cardboard tubes so they won't get ripped or wrinkled on the way to your new house, or your old one, if your parents still claim you as their son," Vera tells him. "The sporting goods are lying on the floor all around the cardboard tubes. And the trashy smut with obscene jokes, stories, and God forbid illustrations we tossed in with your sporting clothing. Have a nice time moving."

"Mrs. Zhukova and Mrs. Kharzina adore me as though I'm their son! And Mrs. Zhukova's known me since I was barely eight years old, little girls! She barely knows you!"

"This is our room now. We're going to be living here until our father buys us a new house."

"My parents kicked me out over a year ago! I can't go back to them after they took over my house and evicted its rightful owner, namely me!"

"We packed the rest of your things for you," Natalya says. "Your clothes, religious articles, non-smutty books, magazines, newspapers, personal photographs, photo albums, soap, other cleaning articles, and last but not least your towels. It isn't too far to your old house, is it?"

Boris grumbles and snatches his things. He has to hop a streetcar to get back to his house and then be helped off with all his things by several other people.

"Who said you get to come back here?" Mr. Malenkov asks his son.

"Mrs. Zhukova's three youngest stepdaughters invaded my room when I was at work, and made it over into a completely unrecognizable girly room! They stripped the room bare of all my things! So now instead of my favorite actresses hanging all over the walls, my sporting equipment, and my adult books just for men, I come back home to find the walls smothered in posters of actors like Valentino, girly junk like pink pillows and white lace curtains, and stupid little advice manuals on how to get a suitor!"

"You've finally come home, Borya. Sit down, and I'll make you some warm soup." Mrs. Malenkova gets up and opens the cupboard.

3

Boris doesn't get to go back into the house until Mrs. Zhukova and Mr. Lebedev return from their honeymoon to Staten Island a week and a half later. He stands by hugging the wall as everyone else welcomes Mrs. Zhukova home, even Mr. and Mrs. Rossilini. The newlyweds are hand-in-hand, constantly smiling and gazing at one another, looking the happiest and liveliest anyone has seen them in years.

"Are you going to keep him?" Lyuba asks her mother, smiling.

"More importantly, are you going to keep *them*?" Boris demands. "These three little imbeciles invaded my room the day after you got remarried!"

"Can you be my mother?" Fyodora begs. "I was only three when I last saw mine, and I've come to realize she's dead. That's what my papa meant when he said she went to a happier place with golden water and harps and things. And he couldn't remarry unless Mama were dead. I don't remember my mother, not very much."

"Excuse me, little girl, but Mrs. Zhukova and I share blood! She's the *babushka* of my precious daughter, that beautiful little girl that bully Konev's holding like she's his damn own! *You* are only one of her seven new stepdaughters!"

"What's this man doing in our house?" Mr. Lebedev asks. "You said he'd go back to his parents after our wedding, Katyushenka!"

"More importantly, who gave him the authority to raise his voice against such a sweet little girl?" Mrs. Zhukova asks.

"Come on, Mrs. Zhukova! You've known me since I was eight years old! That's fifteen years, woman! You've only known these little twerps for a bit under two years, and you don't know them that well, not like you know me! I'm your honorary son-in-law! You and your sister have treated me like a son for the past four years!"

"I cannot believe Katya and I let you freeload off us that long," Mrs. Kharzina says. "My sister does still love you as though you were her own, because you fathered my darling grandniece and her granddaughter, but that's where the obligation ends. Ivan Konev has been that little girl's father since before she was born."

Boris stalks out of the room in disgust, throwing a wrapped package at Mrs. Zhukova on his way out. He spends the entire rest of the welcoming-back party sitting and sulking in the yard in front of the grotto. He begins to pray, his voice barely audible over the sounds from inside.

"I'm never getting married, Holy Mother of God. The mother of my daughter apparently will never come back to me, though I'm still willing to wait and see if she ever gets around to marrying Ivan before I completely abandon hope. I could become a priest, since I'm religious and already have been teaching religious school for two years. But priests can marry in our correct version of Christianity. Granyechka no longer wants to marry me since my diagnoses with infertility and impotence, though perhaps the latter obstacle could eventually be overcome through psychotherapy. I'm far from the ideal candidate for the priesthood. If Lyuba goes through with it and marries Ivan, I'm all but assured of losing my only child unless I hire the best lawyer in New York. I could always become a monk after the inevitable, losing my child to that bully Ivan, a man I can't believe used to be my best friend until a couple of years ago when he suddenly started to hate me uncontrollably and wanted to kill me, Mother of God! So since I cannot have children or even sexual relations anymore, I'd better become a monk so people won't think wrongly I'm God forbid homosexual. Better to eventually shift myself over into a totally asexual lifestyle than go around lusting for women, namely the mother of my only child, yet not being able to marry since I only love her and want my daughter back and have people wrongly jump to the completely false conclusion I prefer men. I'll talk with my priest about this matter before the day is through, *Matushka*."

***

Everyone leaves through the front door of the house three hours later. Mrs. Zhukova beckons to Boris.

"You want to spit on me some more when I'm down?"

"The set of porcelain dinnerware depicting the life of Christ was very lovely, Borya. Ilya and I will especially like it during the holidays. But you must go back to live with your parents. You'll always be the father of my lovely granddaughter, but you'll never be my son-in-law unless Lyuba decides to leave the best thing that ever happened to her and go back to you, against her better judgment. I'll be testifying against you when Lyuba and Ivan finally are married and get their day in court against you. I'll say I believe my granddaughter will be much better-off with Ivan as her adoptive father instead of letting the court grant you even small paternal rights over her."

4

Boris walks into church an hour later and waits for Father Spiridon to come by. He reads the latest church bulletin with pure anger. Granyechka has just become engaged to another young man of her father's choosing, Georgiy Valeriyevich Likachëv, and the wedding is in three weeks. The children in the religious school, it goes on to mention, will be making decorations, both religious and secular, to hang all around the church on her wedding day. Boris resolves to forever hate Granyechka and her father, his own boss.

"How could you, *Batyushka*! I trusted and really liked you! You believed in me and gave me a second chance at a good life! Even your surname means 'forgiveness'!"

"Oh, you saw our just-published bulletin. You must surely understand why Granyechka couldn't marry you, not after she found out about your medical problems."

"Everyone these days is so damn in love with Freud, I could've easily cured the impotence with a psychotherapist! And Granyechka's naturally more spiritual, since her father's a goddamn priest, so we could've had lots of children by mere virtue of the fact that I would've been married to a priest's daughter who could've become my living miracle! Now on to why I really came here, before I found out you stabbed me in the back. I'm interested in becoming a monk."

"With your outburst just now, complete with a few curse words sprinkled in there? Who would accept *you* into a monastery?"

"I can't very well be a priest like you, since our priests are allowed to get married, unlike those mildly heretical Roman priests.

Everyone in my congregation would look at me funny, wondering why the hell young Father Boris isn't married or doesn't have legitimate children."

"In time, you'll grow to realize the error of your ways and decide to try getting married."

"Who wants a man who can't get her pregnant or even have relations?!"

"I'm going to testify on your behalf when that case you're always ranting about finally gets its day in court, after your former best friend marries the mother of your daughter and they're able to bring what they want to the attention of a sympathetic judge. Of course I want your child to remain with her mother and future stepfather, but I'll tell the court you deserve partial rights over her. I'll tell them that despite your warts, such as mild cursing every now and again, rudeness towards your parents, and your shameful past in Russia, such as how you were involved in drug trafficking and beating the woman who was pregnant with your child, you've shown yourself to truly love your child, and become a mature adult in the short time I've known you."

"You won't talk to the nearest monastery and let me become a monk, *Batyushka*?!"

"Isn't it enough I'll take your side when your desperate plea for rights to your only child, that cute little girl in the pictures you're always showing me, finally goes to court? Everybody else you know, including your parents and the *babushka* of your daughter, will tell the prospective judge you're a bad father and negligent human being in general." Father Spiridon walks upstairs.

Boris makes the *dulya* sign at virtually the only person left on his side after his back is turned, then runs away muttering curses.

5

Mrs. Zhukova, now officially Mrs. Lebedeva, comes to Lyuba's tenement at the end of April. Ivan has just come home from another day of exploitation at the iron factory and is sitting grumbling on the davenport, next to the phonograph.

"You'd think he hadn't just gotten a raise," Lyuba says. "Everyone who works lower-level jobs at that stupid factory will now bring in fifteen dollars a month! We'll soon be able to afford much nicer things, if we save and spend all our money wisely. I'd like a washing machine and gas stove, and it'd also be very nice to get some vanity things, like replacing that outdated phonograph. Soon enough we'll be laughed at for using such an outdated machine. We'd like a gramophone that plays records instead of cylinders."

Ivan glares across the hall. "My own best friend has betrayed the way we were raised! I can't believe he would stoop so low as to join ranks with the ilk of people who overthrew God's anointed as though he were the lowest scum on Earth for daring to be a kind and loving Tsar! Did you know, Mrs. Zhukova? Alyoshka was, behind the backs of both me and Kolya, agitating for months to form a union, and today the boss finally granted it! And guess what! Today Mr. Glazov held a vote to decide who ought to be the president of our brand-new union. I didn't dare to participate, though Kolya was persuaded by Alyoshenka to vote. The winner was our Alyoshka! Only three of us voted against him—I abstained from voting, one man voted for himself, and the third wanted Mr. Glazov to lead the damn union. That man replaced that *mudak* Malenkov as my best friend, and he turns around and does this to me! He's even been talking about how he'll register to vote when we're granted citizenship. He wants to be a Democrat, and even Kolya wants to be one! The American political party most in line with our beliefs is the Republican Party!"

"You're not going to register Republican, Vanya," Lyuba says authoritatively. "We've had to change the way we think about politics here in America. We're no longer upper-middle-class. We live in a squalid little tenement, though it's a sight better than they were forty years ago. We make a pittance compared to most other people in this great country. Lyosha wants to stand up for our rights, and you can't get it through your thick head this is how it must be now. Republicans want to keep the rest of our people out of America. We got here just in the nick of time, before the government began passing more and more restrictions against who can and can't enter. They especially want to keep out our fellow Russians and Slavs, anyone from Southern Europe, and everyone from Asia. Katrin's completely right. If I weren't restrained from the mere thought of it by how I was raised, to love the Tsar as Christ on Earth, I'd also consider joining the Socialist Party once we're citizens."

"Speaking of citizens." Mrs. Zhukova changes the subject. "This little guy's getting big. It's so special how he was born an American citizen. I'm so glad Ivan is Fedya's father."

"He'll be a year old next month," Ivan says proudly. "Can't you tell Fedyushenka's my boy?"

"I'm going to have one of my own," Mrs. Zhukova announces in a trembling voice.

"You and Ilya Nikolayevich want to adopt?" Lyuba asks. "Did you want a child of your own that badly?"

"I'm forty-one, so this was a big surprise. I've only been married three weeks, but missing my menses for almost that entire time can only mean one thing. And I'm far too young to be having change of life already. I'm no spring chicken, but I'm not ready to hobble away in the night just yet."

Lyuba gets up and leaves the room with Fedya in her arms.

"You're the second woman to tell her about a pregnancy," Ivan says gloomily. "My aunt was just by the other day to inform us Vasya will be getting a little brother or sister."

"Katrin's pregnant too," Lyuba says. "I have to give you another child, Vanya, preferably a blood daughter the next time. Wouldn't you like to have both a blood son and daughter in addition to our little Tanyechka to love?"

"Aren't you happy with the two you've already got?" her mother begs. "So many women would love to have just two. Don't you remember Mrs. Vrangel always looking as if she were just a lowly, hovel-dwelling peasant instead of a high-society woman, because she had fifteen daughters to take care of? And Mrs. Minina with five children, Mrs. Furtseva with six, Mrs. Litvinova with a dozen, and Mrs. Beriya with thirteen? You already have a boy and a girl; you don't need more."

"Vanya's dream was for us to live in the Midwest on a big farm and have nine children. Now we only have two, and the first isn't even his by blood."

"You're getting married in September. Maybe God will smile on you and permit you to have more children. And what woman needs nine children? Are you afraid you'll lose these two to diphtheria or whooping cough when the time inevitably comes?"

"Orthodoxy forbids birth control, unless a priest permits it in extreme circumstances. All the children would've done chores on the farm we'll probably never have, since Vanya oh-so-stubbornly refuses to quit his job and go for a higher-paying one, like the one our friend Pashenka Teglyov has. Pashenka goes to school during the day, and almost as soon as school gets out, he reports straight to a garment factory. He started out just working a sewing machine, and by the next year, he was up to office labor, like stock inventory and keeping track of the weekly profits. Instead, my Vanya's content to let Glazov walk all over him, refusing to listen to reason."

"Alyoshka stabbed us in the back by forming a godless union and getting himself elected as its president!"

"You're not that naïve, Vanyechka. We're living a different reality now. We're suddenly the class of people who overthrew the Tsar, and need things like unions and higher wages. We don't live in fancy big houses anymore, eat gourmet food, and never have to worry about money like back in the old days."

"I refused to join the union. Alyoshka's having a little celebration across the hall, but I told him flat-out after work today I wouldn't be caught dead joining in his irreverent spitting in the face of all we used to hold most dear to our hearts."

"That sounds like it might be enjoyable." Lyuba stands up and goes into the living room. "Come across the hall with us, Tanyechka. Your *Dyadya* Alyoshka's having a little party to celebrate being elected president of the new union at the horrible factory he, your father, and your *Dyadya* Kolya work at."

Tatyana obediently scampers across the hall with her mother and baby brother.

"Look what I got, Ivan!" Aleksey taunts across the hall. "Your father sold me eight bottles of high-quality champagne!"

"I almost wish that father of mine would get found out by the police and be arrested for breaking Prohibition!"

"I can't believe how much money we'll make now. It's his loss if he refuses to join our new union." Aleksey pats twenty-month-old Novomira on the head. She has wavy brown hair like her proud father and lively green eyes like her father's mother. "I was thinking, between Liza and myself, we'll earn enough money to afford a third child."

"You're pregnant?" Lyuba demands of Eliisabet.

"This is the first I've heard of him wanting another child."

"How did you smuggle so much champagne here?" Kat asks.

"I was taking my little *knyazhna* for her afternoon stroll after I got home from the factory, where I'd just been triumphantly elected president of the new union. Ivan's father told me to take out the baby and put the champagne bottles underneath her."

"How can you even think about having a third child?" Lyuba demands of Eliisabet, not caring Aleksey just admitted to using his baby daughter to smuggle champagne. "I'd look at you and want to hate you because you can have as many more children as you want! I'm stuck with only two!"

"Soon we'll have enough money for Ivan to take you to the best doctor money can buy," Aleksey promises. "I was thinking, our first two kids have names beginning with N, so why not go for three and give the third one an N name too?"

"We're going on holiday starting in early June," Eliisabet says. "I don't want to be away from you for several months if I'm pregnant."

"Well, Kolya was an accident, and Mira was quite a surprise as well. It would be nice for once to actually plan a child."

"What do you mean I was an accident?" five-year-old Nikolay demands of his father in Russian.

"You'll understand when you're a bit older."

"It happened like this, Kolya." Eliisabet glares at her husband. "Your *isa* ran into a burning house to save me. He had to carry me and my suitcase, and strapped my rosebush to his back. When we got to his house, his parents were gone and everything was a mess, so he packed up his things, and we ran and ran and ran until we saw a wagon driven by Anya and Leontiy's parents. They saved our lives, and Lyuba, Ivan, Ginny, and Boris. We were taken to an old abandoned house near Ryazan. Your *isa* and I were so happy to be alive, we confessed our love for one another and inadvertently created you."

"Sometimes I wish Boris had been caught so Vanya and I could've hidden together," Lyuba says. "Then I'd still be able to have him those nine children he wants. We have seven more to go, but it'll be a miracle if I give him even one more."

"What are you doing thinking about having another child?"

Kat demands. "Fedya's only eleven months old. My Lyuda and Raya are only a year old, and I don't intend to have another child until they're quite a bit older."

"He claims he loves me, not my ability to have children, but I know he'll leave me if I don't have another child."

"He kept that secret from you for such a long time, and because you didn't know it, you were able to have this darling baby boy!"

"I don't know if Vanya could love an adopted child as much as he loves my Tanyechka. The woman he loves is her mother. An adopted child wouldn't be my own blood child. I'd feel just awful asking Vanya to go through the motions with another woman just so he could have more children of his own."

Alya and Anya exchange funny looks.

"I didn't feel I could look Vanya in the face after I found out I was having Boris's baby. He'd look at that child and hate her, and imagine his belovèd in the arms of another man, though I was drunk out of my mind when it happened. I didn't know what happened, I only guessed. My guess was right."

"Has Ivan ever given you even *half* a reason to make you believe he's *ever* hated or resented this little pumpkin?" Eliisabet asks.

"However much he might refuse to admit it, he loves Fedya more because Fedya's his blood son."

6

Lyuba goes back across the hall with the children that evening, feeling miserable, and picks at the roast chicken Ivan made. She ignores his shouts to look at Fedya trying to feed himself with his little left hand.

"What have I been telling you, Lyubonka? My boy's a *levsha* just like I am!"

"Sure you're happy with him now, but what about ten years from now when these two are still all we've got? You're as old-fashioned as they come, Vanyechka. You want me to stay at home cooking, cleaning, and shopping, and you would've been crushed if our first blood child together were another girl. You'll become angry I haven't given you seven more sons."

"I don't care what the rest end up being, if we do manage to have any others. I could truly care less if the rest are all girls and all

I've got is Fedyushka."

"All men want replacements for the firstborn son. You know it as well as I do."

"How could I want a replacement for this cute little guy?"

"You know, if there's another major war, and he goes off to fight and is killed, or, worse yet, if he's struck down by a disease or a fever."

"What an imagination. The very fact he was conceived is of itself a miracle. Why would God punish us by taking away this adorable little baby?"

***

That night, Lyuba demands his attentions five times. Ivan can barely keep up with her, and wonders if she might be drunk.

"You've never wanted me more than four times in a row before. Not that I'm complaining about making up for years of lost time, but that really tires a guy out in ways you can't imagine."

"If that didn't conceive another baby, nothing will," she says before turning over to sleep.

7

Vera and Natalya are up late in bed, Fyodora sound asleep beside them, writing a letter to Inessa with light from five very large candles.

30 April 1923

Dear Inessa:

We're most happy to report we reached America safely, and with our father, whom we met up with in Estonia after we successfully crossed the border of the Motherland. Our oldest sister Galya was with him, and our sister Sveta's little Pomeranian Kroshka. Kroshka's now fifteen and slowing down a bit, but she's still an adorable little bundle of love and fur. Since our triumphant arrival in America in May 1921, which will be exactly two years ago by the time you receive this letter, we've also been reunited with two more of our sisters, Svetlana and Matryona. The only ones we're still missing are Dinara, Lyolya, and Serafima. Earlier this month, our father remarried a widow named Yekaterina Iosifovna Zhukova. In January, she'll give us a baby brother or sister, though we all hope it's a brother, since there are ten of us sisters and no brother.

We do have our troubles, though. Galya has been blind since 1917. The Red mudaki *threw her into a box and set it on fire, and she lost her eyesight. We're getting sick and tired of the American doctor constantly moving her opera-*

tion date to restore her eyesight. Every couple of months, he tells us a new date for her operation! Our other big sister Sveta says she's so tired of this nonsense, if he dares to reschedule Galya's big operation yet again, she'll do it herself, and she probably can *do it herself, since she's a nurse!*

We came to America with the daughter of the woman to whom our father just remarried. Her name's Lyubov Leontiyevna Zhukova. Her father was a very sick man and was murdered thirteen months ago by her fiancé, a murder that was assisted by our father, Lyuba herself, her uncle, and a few of her male friends. They came to his house by night last March, and her uncle put our now-stepmother out like a light by drugging her drink, so she'd sleep through them ordering the disgusting mudak *to change out of his pajamas and into decent clothes. They forced him, at gunpoint, to drive down to the East River, where they made him write a suicide note they'd prepared and do an abbreviated version of Last Rites with wine and bread. They had to smuggle the wine, since alcohol is now illegal in America, except for medical purposes or unless it's something called "near-beer," which nobody wants to drink. They don't even permit people to use wine for church purposes. It's insane. And then Lyuba's fiancé threw her father into the river after our father stuffed him into a sack. The* mudak *also had a weight on a chain that went around his neck. The next morning, the police found him in the river after Mrs. Zhukova, her sister, and her brother-in-law reported it after she found his "suicide note" on his pillow.*

We also came over with a whole lot of interesting characters. Besides us, our father, Anya, Leontiy, and a sweet little girl we picked up on our flight into Estonia, Natalya Yeltsina, we also travelled with our now-stepsister and her friends. One of her friends, an Estonian, is a raving Socialist. She claims she was betrayed by the Party, and tore up her Party ID and threw it into the water, but she plans to become a member of America's Socialist Party once she's a citizen. She lives in a penthouse suite and just married another Estonian, and writes for radical Baltic, Estonian, and Russian émigré presses. I can't read a word of her Estonian articles, since it's not close to Russian except for a surprisingly large number of cognates. This woman has started dressing like a lot of modern American women, they're called flappers. And her best friend is a whole other story!

On the ship, we got weird feelings about two women with whom Lyuba has been friends since the age of eight. Anya Furtseva and Aleksandra Minina were presumed dead, or in prison or a labor camp, since they weren't heard from for two years. They lived together until they split off into separate houses—Lyuba, her cousin, the flapper's best friend, and Lyuba's two male friends, one of whom is now her fiancé, were in the original house; a young couple with a baby son (they now have a daughter as well) in a second; another young couple who were then engaged (they got married at Ellis Island at something called the Kissing Post and have year-old twin daughters now) and the young man's little sister in a third; and these two other women in the fourth. They still live together. We don't know them that well, but we pick up a lot of strange feelings when we see them together. If they don't find husbands soon, or start seeking young men who'll court them, we'll really truly start to believe they prefer each other! The redhead, Alya, was at one time engaged to a young man who also came over with us, who works in a library now. She ran away to be with her friends, because she hated this man and couldn't bear the thought of being married to him. He's disgustingly old-fashioned.

Our stepsister Lyuba was the one who set up our father with her widowed mother. She has a beautiful little girl, four years old, and an eleven-month-old little boy, both by different fathers, but she's not a whore who had two children out of wedlock by two different men because of a lack of moral character. At her age, and with the extenuating circumstances she and her fiancé have been under for such a long time, she has every right to have her little boy. The girl was conceived when she was gotten purposely drunk.

We're all having a lovely time in America. Maybe you, Olga, Klara and her brother, Zofia, and little Valentina can leave Belarus sometime to visit us in America!

Love,

Vera and Natalya

****

Chapter 36: Ins and Outs of Prohibition

Mr. Konev comes into the tenement in time to see his future daughter-in-law knocking over the large wooden washbasin full of soapy water and clothes.

"Is this a bad time, Lyubov Leontiyevna?"

"Your son *could've* been making enough money for me to afford a real washing machine like so many other American women! Instead he only brings in fifteen dollars a month, and has the nerve to whine about how one of our best friends got their evil boss to raise their salaries by a few dollars a month and formed a union to stand up for workers' rights! Vanya won't let me work, since he's so old-fashioned, albeit a sweet, lovable old-fashioned guy who wants his woman to stay at home cooking, cleaning, shopping, and taking care of the kids."

"I can easily arrange for you to start making thirty to fifty dollars an hour." Mr. Konev pulls up a chair at the table, takes down a glass, uncaps his cane, and pours a glass of beer.

Lyuba instinctively backs away from him. "You're supposed to be a teetotaler! We all know what happened before when you were an alcoholic!"

"I drink from time to time. I'm not out of control about it now. I'm deeply ashamed of what I did to you and my son when I drank." He takes off his belovèd bowler, pulls out a false bottom, shakes out a plain white paper bag, and unties the top. "Care for some champagne truffles?"

"You certainly have a lot of clever ways to get around the law," she manages to say.

"All that money you want to buy nice things like a real washing machine, and the money my son wants to afford an expensive wedding, I can easily see to it that you come into. One of my leading smugglers was busted by the police for violating Prohibition yesterday. Maybe you can take over his job?"

"Vanya would never allow it. It would put us all in jeopardy."

"My son will probably never find out, he's so pure and innocent about the real world. If you agree, I'll have a co-worker come by tomorrow with a still and an instruction manual. He'll also provide empty bottles. You simply follow the directions in making the beer and gin, put it into the bottles, transport them into two buckets of ice, strap the buckets to your legs, cover them with a big floppy overcoat, come to my store, pass through the false front, untie the buckets, and put them on the shelf. Once in awhile, a local gang leader comes by to threaten us and tell us who we can and can't get our alcohol from, but there's never been any repercussions from the local mobsters."

"Why do you need to work in a liquor store when you know full well it's illegal, and in addition you're a former alcoholic? You already tempted Fate once by bootlegging instead of finding a respectable job."

"I worked in a liquor store before. I stayed with what I knew. Besides, I'm very experienced in bootlegging, having done it for three years. I'm not a greenhorn who just wandered in off the streets, hoping to make a quick buck under the law of supply and demand."

"How about enough money to afford a decent doctor who'll fix me? I'm crushed because I'm not pregnant. I thought five times in a row would ensure I'd become pregnant, even with my damage from Boris, but I chose the wrong time in my cycle." Ordinarily she'd never speak about her sex life so openly with a man, but given what happened between her and Mr. Konev, that horse is already past the gate.

"You can have relations with my son a hundred times in a row and it'll still be highly unlikely you'll get pregnant. This little fellow here was surprising enough." Mr. Konev picks Fedya up off the floor and sets him in his lap. "Your friend Aleksey just bought eight bottles of champagne from me. He smuggled them by taking his little daughter out of her pram, putting the bottles under her blankets, and putting the baby back in."

"I'm not having Fedya come anywhere near your liquor store. Maybe Alyoshka doesn't care if he puts his little girl, my goddaughter, into danger from mobsters and federal agents enforcing the law, but I *do* care Fedya might be killed by a stray bullet or taken from me if the police come by and discover he was born out of wedlock and I haven't married the father."

"Do you or don't you want the extra money?"

"Vanya certainly isn't doing anything about improving his job, and this might be the only time ever I'd be allowed to earn money without him finding out. I know he's old-fashioned, but compared to a lot of men, he's an egalitarian angel. He likes to cook; he's not afraid to show tenderness towards Fedya and Tanyechka; he's never once snapped at me because the tenement wasn't completely clean, I didn't pick up something he wanted, or I didn't have supper finished in time; he never demands my body or forces himself on me; and he doesn't mind I have political convictions that differ from his. I'll have to start breaking the law to get money. You can bring the still and instruction booklet here as soon as possible."

2

The next morning while Ivan is at work, Mr. Konev's associate comes up to the tenement, bearing a large wooden crate. Lyuba lets him in.

"You'll get thirty dollars if you successfully deliver all the beer and gin you'll make with this today. You are to report to your father-in-law's store tomorrow morning after your husband leaves for work. I'm your father-in-law's closest associate, after the other one was arrested. My name's Zakhar Lavrentiyevich Lazhenitsyn."

"What do I need to make beer and gin?"

Mr. Lazhenitsyn opens the crate and takes out the still, an instruction manual, and several large glass jars. "These three are near-beer that need to be mixed with these ones of wort, yeast, Vine-Glo, and malt tonic from the local drugstore. You can use various household products to make more liquor, like apples, dry oatmeal, and barley. You get thirty dollars tomorrow morning." His eye catches on Fedya sitting on the floor. "You can use this little guy to do more smuggling, if all the bottles don't fit into the buckets to be strapped under the coat."

"Why does such a little boy need to be dragged into breaking the law too? He's not even a year old yet."

"From what I hear from your father-in-law, your husband's very weak-willed, passive, and happy with less than what he deserves. Do you honestly think he'll be able to bring in half the money you'll get by the end of this month smuggling alcohol?"

"Fine, you can use Fedya to smuggle alcohol back and forth."

3

When Ivan comes home from work, he finds three iceboxes in

the kitchen and goes to investigate. Lyuba slaps his hands when he tries to open the two new additions. Tatyana has been ordered to keep quiet about how her mother was making moonshine and mixing things together to get various types of alcoholic spirits in the morning and early afternoon.

"What are you hiding from me?"

"You don't need to know."

His eyes catch on the still stuffed into the bathtub. "Just what is that thing?"

"You don't need to know about that either."

"Does this have anything to do with my father? Last week he propositioned me to smuggle alcohol back and forth. He took me to the docks and showed me all these boats anchored about three to five miles offshore, and showed me all these people rowing back and forth in rowboats, canoes, skiffs, and motorized boats to get the alcohol back to shore. He said I should go in a rowboat with him to see if I'd be interested, then I watched, stunned, as he got into a speedboat and returned twenty minutes later with what must've been a good fifty bottles of various types of alcohol."

"Oh, what an imagination. I'll tell you what this is all about later, when I'm at liberty to divulge what I'm doing."

4

The next morning after Ivan has left for work, Lyuba begins placing the bottles into the two buckets full of ice. Some of the alcohol is pure moonshine; some is moonshine made from grain, water, and essence of juniper; some has been made from wort and yeast; some is Vine-Glo mixed with near-beer; and the rest is malt tonic mixed with near-beer.

"Why are you tying those buckets to your legs, Mama?" Tatyana asks.

"Your *dedushka* will give us a lot of money if we can do this for him, take certain things back and forth between his workplace and our tenement."

"The weather's too nice to wear that long coat."

"Other people mustn't find out what I'm doing for your *dedushka*. This coat will easily hide these buckets." Lyuba places the last three bottles into Fedya's pram and then puts the baby in. "Remember, your father must never know anything until and if I decide it's safe to tell him. He'd never allow us to do this otherwise, and then we'd be in the same place we were a few days ago, without a lot of money guaranteed."

***

They arrive at Mr. Konev's secret liquor store thirty minutes later. The only customers in the store now are a couple of police officers having a drink with Mr. Konev and Mr. Lazhenitsyn.

"Not to worry, Lyubov Leontiyevna, these nice three men are on our side. You'd be amazed at how many so-called officers of the law, both federal agents and policemen like these fellows, openly enable us to continue breaking the Volstead Act."

"That's a cute little baby," one of the police officers says in English.

"He'll be a year old in another week." Lyuba throws off the coat and unties the two ice-filled buckets. "Another three are under the baby."

Mr. Konev delightedly lifts his grandson into the air. "This is the grandson I've been telling you officers about week after week! Fyodor Ivanovich Konev, named after last Ryurikovich Tsar, not for any of his political accomplishments, since he was simple-minded fool controlled by Boris Godunov, but because he was only reminder left to his father of his mother. My unofficial daughter-in-law was in coma after she had Fedya, and my son thought she was going to die. He looks just like my son."

"When is your son going to come around here, Mr. Konev?" a second police officer inquires. "You're awfully proud of him too."

"My son is weak-minded person too good and moral for his own good. He's teetotaler and only drank during one very bad time in life."

Lyuba touches the spot on her face where the scar used to be.

"And this is my granddaughter Tatyana, named after one of the late Grand Duchesses. She has four years. She takes after her mother."

"Your son seems like he has the perfect family, a beautiful fiancée, a lovely daughter, and a baby son. Why won't he do the right thing and marry this woman?"

Lyuba sighs. "He wants an expensive wedding, Officers. He says we're getting married this September, but he hasn't informed our priest about this."

"Every day longer he waits to marry her, girl's natural father gets more and more hope to be man who does marry her," Mr. Konev says.

"September's only four months away. Forgive me if this idea is too crass for mixed company, but maybe they can celebrate finally getting married by having another child," the third officer suggests.

"I'm nearly unable to have more children, Sir," Lyuba says. "Fedya's a medical miracle."

"If you want and pray for it badly enough, Lyubov Leontiyevna, you and my son will have another child someday. In the meantime, here's the thirty dollars you get for smuggling this alcohol here today."

"I want you to show me the boats Vanya told me about."

"You're already that warmed-up to breaking the law? Let's go see them right now." Mr. Konev lapses back into Russian.

"I want to go out on a boat to smuggle alcohol ashore. More money."

Lyuba walks down to the harbor with her future father-in-law, who pushes Fedya's pram as Tatyana skips behind them. There's a long line of ships anchored three and half miles away from the shore, constantly being boarded and unboarded by alcohol connoisseurs in various types of boats. Some of the local policemen and mobsters are casually standing by, enabling this to happen in broad daylight.

"You'd feel up to coming back here as many times as I'd need you to get alcohol to supply my store with? You could keep making moonshine and mixing things together to get alcohol, and smuggling them to the store."

"How much money for going onto one of those boats to get liquor?"

"You'll of course have to pay for it. But I'm in the invariable habit of paying back that same amount of money to my employees who risk their legal freedom to go out and do this for me."

"Has your store ever been raided by the police?"

"Never, only a handful of far and few between run-ins with local mobsters. Sometimes they post their fellow thugs on the roads to steal alcohol from the people who went to Canada to get it for us. They always claim there'll be a price to pay if we don't buy all our liquor from them, but nothing has happened in the way of violence or financial repercussions."

"Maybe I could work at your store when Vanya's at work?"

"My son would be furious."

"Vanya doesn't suspect what I started doing behind his back."

"No. For now, you just need to manufacture liquor at home, bring it to me, and go out to the boats from time to time if need be. You could also start going to drugstores to get legal malt liquor. I'll forge a doctor's note saying you need it for medicinal purposes." Mr. Konev steps into a rowboat at the water's edge. "Coming, Lyubov Leontiyevna?"

"Fedya's pram can't fit into that little thing."

Mr. Konev takes the baby out and lashes the pram down to the other end of the boat.

5

Ivan has zero idea over the next week of where all this extra money is suddenly coming from. So far, a modern washing machine and gas stove, new kitchen and cooking appliances, and six pairs of silk stockings have materialized without an explanation.

"Your father's giving it to me," Lyuba replies elusively.

"And we all know where he gets his money from!"

"You know Father Yakim oh-so-illegally gets our Communion wine from mixing water with huge bricks of grape concentrate."

"That's for religious purposes, not making a living out of breaking the law. I'm disgusted my father has the gall to break the law like that when he could just as easily work in a factory like I do. As if he didn't learn his lesson from the first time he bootlegged."

"The illegal dispensation and production of alcohol pays so much better than your little factory job ever will."

"My father never would give anyone money for free. You have to be doing something in return for all this money suddenly floating in to us out of thin air."

"Maybe he actually loves his son and wants you to be able to live comfortably and have enough money to afford that expensive wedding you want in September."

"Why can't I go near those two new iceboxes?" Ivan marches into the kitchen and finds them gone, replaced by a brand-new appliance. "When did that get here?"

"That's a General Electric refrigerator, my love, and it came this afternoon. It only needs to be plugged in. No hassle with belts, drains, fans, or anything. Look how much bigger it is than the old, tiny icebox! Now I won't need to go shopping so often! The man who installed it told me the top will never get dusty. You can't look inside just yet. Not till I feel safely at liberty to tell you just why."

"My father is like a caricature of a modern American man, only he's an immigrant who just thinks he's as close to a typical American man as a Russian immigrant can ever hope to get. He never wore white gloves in the Motherland like he does now! And he carries a cane, as though he's crippled, wears fancy suits, breaks Prohibition, and that ridiculous bowler hat seems to be glued to his head, the way he never takes it off."

"Your aunt bought it for him because he was so taken with how all the actors in the vaudeville movies wear them, remember?"

"I'd like to knock it off his head!"

"Your father keeps alcohol in his cane. It's a hollow cane. He visited one day, and uncapped it and poured a glass of beer. Then he took his hat off, removed a false bottom, and took out a bag of champagne truffles."

"At least alcoholic candies are more harmless than resuming heavy drinking."

"He's not a heavy drinker anymore. I know, because I'm around him so much lately, since he's been giving me all this money out of his love for you, his only child."

Ivan's eyes narrow. "Are you ever around him alone for extended periods with the door closed?"

"I'm never alone with him. There are always Tatyana and Fedya, and of course his work colleagues. He's deeply ashamed of what he did to me before."

"If I were him, I couldn't even bring myself to look you in the eye, after he raped you!"

"Only when he was very drunk, and it couldn't have been more than ten times tops. He never did it while sober, just like he never beat you when he was sober either."

"Well, our dear friend Aleksey has convinced Mr. Glazov, that *svoloch*, to give us money for nothing! His little union he's president of successfully petitioned that *dryan* to give us two weeks of paid vacation this June!"

"You know how much he pays you. Your father has given me well over a hundred dollars in the past two weeks alone for simply being engaged to you."

"There will be lots more money yet, *golubka*, when we move to the fertile Midwest and get a farm. Then I won't have to work in that dangerous sweatbox anymore."

"Keep telling yourself that. Now I see why my mother always wanted me to marry Boris instead of you."

6

Boris has been in a foul mood for the past three weeks. He's not only snapped at the children in religious school, but screamed at them and reduced most of them to tears for minor infractions like getting a minor point of theology wrong, forgetting one word of a prayer, daring to express sympathies for people in other denominations, crossing themselves in the wrong direction or with two fingers instead of three, and not being able to name all the saints with May name-days. He's also threatened to beat the children who say they'll tell their parents or Father Spiridon how he's been mumbling bad things under his breath about Father Spiridon, sometimes when he's right there in the classroom with them. Boris has also lately been demanding the children stop hanging the ikons and religious paintings crooked. He's been seen kicking the box of decorations his students made for the big wedding this afternoon.

"Get down off that wobbly ladder, Sashura, or you'll break your goddamn neck!" Boris thunders at a little girl in first grade. "Here, let the older children hang up these ugly decorations for that slut Granyechka."

"We worked so hard on our decorations, Borya!" Her little friend Nyushenka begins to cry. "Father Spiridon and Granyechka told us they're beautiful!"

"That whore jilted me for that ugly mug her father dragged in from the gutter for her to marry," Boris snarls at the children. "You are to call me Mr. Malenkov or Boris Aleksandrovich! It's very rude and horrible manners for a child to call an adult, much less a teacher, by a diminutive!"

"You always let us call you Borya and Boryushka before," eight-year-old Danya whines.

"Shut your mouth, little boy! That was before that *suka* Granyechka jilted me!"

"May I, *pozhaluysta*, be excused to go to the toilet?" four-year-old Dusyechka begs. "My little sister Asyechka already wet her skirt."

Boris grabs the oldest girl, eighteen-year-old Kseniya, by the wrists. "Go direct these little rodents to the nearest water closet."

"Can you lift me up to hang these ones up?" nine-year-old Yegor asks.

"What do I look like, a goddamn serf?"

"What the hell is going on in here?" Father Spiridon comes storming into the nave by surprise. "Granyechka's marrying Gosha in three hours, and the church isn't even a quarter decorated yet!"

"Mr. Malenkov's yelling at us, *Batyushka*," four-year-old Yulyechka pipes up.

"The hell I'm not going to cooperate in decorating this goddamn church for that vile traitor's wedding, *Batyushka*!" Boris snarls.

"You're lucky I'm not angry at you because I know this is only your hurt feelings and not the real Boris talking." Father Spiridon grabs a bag of the secular decorations and starts climbing up the ladder to hang them up.

Boris nearly dies laughing when Father Spiridon falls off the ladder twenty minutes later, after stringing up three bags of butterflies, birds, and hearts made from colored tissue paper. He laughs even harder when the oldest students run to try to help Father Spiridon up and he can't move.

"What kind of man are you, Malenkov, to laugh at a priest when he might be dead?" Kseniya sobs.

"I'm alive." Father Spiridon sits up. "But I think I broke my legs."

"Hooray! Now Granyechka won't be getting married today after all!"

"I am not going to stand up everybody who's coming here today to see my daughter and her fiancé getting married just because of a few broken bones! The oldest students will continue decorating the church in their honor, while Boris calls for a doctor as quickly as possible so I can still perform the ceremony."

"Do I have to?" Boris whines.

"You sure as hell will, Malenkov, if you value your job, your high salary, and most of all my support when your case for partial custody of your illegitimate daughter finally gets to court!" Father Spiridon threatens in a low growl.

Boris runs off to use the phone, emphasizing his limp on the way. He's relegated to the backmost row when Granyechka walks into the vestibule, her father in a wheelchair.

"Whatever happened to your legs, Papa?" Granyechka asks in a whisper when she takes her place besides Gosha.

"I broke them while hanging decorations."

Boris begins praying something terrible will happen, like a ring that's too big or small, a fallen candle that burns Granyechka's dress and skin, Father Spiridon accidentally dropping one or both of the crowns onto their heads, someone tripping and falling during the walk around the Holy Table, the wine going down the wrong pipe, anything. He curses Father Spiridon's entire family when the wedding is triumphant and the two are successfully married.

"Punk *mudak*, I'm the one who should've married her and had kids with her, not you!" Boris saunters over, still emphasizing his limp, to punch Gosha's lights out when the couple are about to cut the cake.

"You're jealous of our happiness. But God will forgive you. God always forgives everyone for everything." Granyechka continues cutting the cake.

Boris sits mumbling obscenities for the entire rest of the day. He kicks his students underneath the table, throws food at them, and spills his wine into their laps.

"Who let this man teach our children?" one of the mothers demands.

"Father Spiridon."

"This man is a truly horrible influence! He curses, uses vulgar language, does mean things to little children, growls at everybody, and had the nerve to punch a groom on his wedding day!"

"You should've seen me in action in Russia," Boris smirks. "What awful things didn't I do then."

7

Mr. Konev delightedly plays with Fedya as Mr. Lazhenitsyn carefully cracks open the eggs Lyuba just brought over. There are a total of four dozen eggs per each of the four boxes, each egg carefully drained of its contents and refilled with various types of alcohol.

"Vanya wonders why we've eaten almost nothing but eggs recently, but he's not complaining about how we've gotten over five hundred dollars by now!"

Mr. Lazhenitsyn gets to the last of the eggs. "Now these ten boxes contain coconuts. You are to bring them back in the next two days, following the same procedure you did this time." He puts one under the blankets in the pram. "The rest we'll bring to your tenement by tomorrow afternoon, before your fiancé gets home from work."

Mr. Konev looks through the peephole of the front door. "Not these people again."

"Federal agents?" Mr. Lazhenitsyn guesses.

"I want you to take my grandson and go into the wine cellar in case these characters sneak their way inside. My son would kill me if he found out his son could've been threatened by these people—"

"Hello, Ivan Vasiliyevich."

"Who are these people?" Lyuba demands. "And how do they know your name?"

"These five men are the leaders of a local Russian gang." Mr. Konev gulps. "They've been by to threaten me and Zakhar before, but nothing terrible ever came of it. It's all empty words."

"It's later than we thought," Mr. Lazhenitsyn says. "Shouldn't Lyuba be getting home? Your son usually gets home from the factory around five-fifteen."

"Is it liquor you want this time?" Mr. Konev cajoles. "I'll give you every last ounce of alcohol in this place if it's what you want!"

"You don't understand this store is supposed to be under our tutelage, Ivan Vasiliyevich. You aren't buying your alcohol from us and only us. Having our men hijack your employees who brought booze over the border from Canada hasn't been enough. You get your liquor from Canada, make it yourself, have employees make it and bring it back to you, and use the ships anchored off the coastline, bootleggers in the area, the drugstore, all sorts of neat little ways of getting around the suspicions of the feds, everywhere but from us!"

"I really think Lyubov and her children ought to go home,"

Mr. Lazhenitsyn says, his voice shaking. "This is no place for them, and whatever will Ivan Vasiliyevich's son think if he finds out about this?"

"I won't let Vanya know," Lyuba says. "I'll tell him I was shopping and ended up being later than I thought."

"It's already seven at night," Mr. Konev says. "Knowing my son, he'll think you left him and took the kids."

8

Ivan has come home to an empty tenement. There's no note and no food on the table. He goes to the Vishinskies, Aleksey and Eliisabet, the older Lebedevas, Pavel, and Anya and Leontiy, and none of them knows anything. He phones Lyuba's mother and aunt, who also don't have a clue. When he calls their church, Father Yakim says she hasn't been seen there either. He begins to panic and phones Boris.

"Admit Lyuba returned to you and you're setting up house as we speak, and that she brought my daughter *and* my son this time!"

"Don't tell me she's run out on you yet again."

"I came home and nobody was here! And you are in for a *major* surprise if you think you'll be raising my son as your own! That's my only blood child, you *mudak*, and you're the reason I won't get more!"

"I only wish Lyuba *had* come back to me." Boris hangs up.

Ivan calls Katrin's penthouse, and once again is told she hasn't been there. Valeriya hasn't seen her either. The last number he tries is Alya and Anya's.

"What is it? We just had supper and are settling down for the evening."

Ivan swears he hears Anya breathing rather heavily. "Has Lyuba come to visit you?"

"Not that I'm aware of."

"Anya, who's that on the phone?" Alya appears by her side, wearing a black lace nightgown. "I want you to come back to bed."

"What the hell did Alya just say?"

"Nothing important. She isn't here, Ivan." Anya hangs up.

Ivan sits there frozen. The two years they were apart from the others have always been explained away innocently, that they found their way to a major White stronghold where they were safe until they came to Estonia in early 1921. But several times on the ship, he saw them holding hands under the table at meals, and once he even spied them taking a walk in the moonlight with their arms around one another, and now they're still living together, with no suitors in sight...

9

Mr. Konev is cajoling and pleading the mobsters for his life as Mr. Lazhenitsyn categorizes all the money from the register into their values. For the first time in his life, Mr. Konev is crying genuine tears.

"How about weapons, Ivan Vasiliyevich?"

"I need them to protect my store from the likes of you!"

Mr. Lazhenitsyn hands over all the money. "Now can Ivan Vasiliyevich's grandchildren and their mother go home? It's nearly nine o'clock!"

"I'm hungry," Tatyana announces.

"You'll get to eat as soon as your *dedushka* does exactly as these men say," Lyuba says.

"I'm not handing over my weapons to the likes of you," Mr. Konev repeats.

"Wouldn't you feel bad if you were to be killed tonight and then disappeared, no body ever recovered, and your son became completely orphaned?"

"My son's nearly twenty-five. He survived for years without parents. And since when do you know about my wife being murdered?"

"We know everything about everybody."

"Give them the weapons!" Lyuba commands.

"I'm very hungry," Tatyana repeats.

"Fine. Your son's fiancée and her daughter get to leave," the lead mobster finally declares. "Have a nice evening, Miss Zhukova."

Lyuba turns to take Fedya from Mr. Lazhenitsyn.

"I didn't say anything about the baby returning home with you."

"Let my grandson go home, or my son will have all your heads on a platter! He's barely one year old!"

"I can't return home without my baby. My fiancé will automatically assume the worst, and he probably already has."

"They're being chivalrous," Mr. Lazhenitsyn pleads. "Ladies first."

"It's supposed to be women and *children* first, and Fedya's barely a year old!"

"What if he gets hungry or needs his diaper changed?" Mr. Konev pleads. "I bet you anything my son will come charging over here as soon as he finds out where my grandson's being kept!"

"Are you going to give us your weapons and promise to start buying all your alcohol from us and only us?"

"Of course not!"

"Then the baby stays behind." The head mobster opens the front door.

"I won't let anything happen to him," Mr. Lazhenitsyn says as Mr. Konev is pushed into a chair and tied up.

"Get in the pram, Tanyechka," Lyuba says.

"I'm too old for that."

Lyuba picks her up and carries her on her left arm, pushing the pram with the other hand, empty now except for the blankets and the crate of coconuts.

10

Ivan is on the telephone to Boris again, screaming at him and threatening him. In the background, he clearly hears Boris snapping at his parents when they ask him to talk more civilly.

"I bet you anything my daughter is sitting on your lap as we speak, and that Lyuba is moving her things into your bedroom, and you must already be making plans to train my son into thinking you're his father!"

"Don't you think I'd be honest with you if that were the case? We used to be best friends! And we let a woman come between us!"

"Borya, I made your favorite cake for dessert," Mrs. Malenkova says in the background.

"Is it triple chocolate frosting with candied cherries on top?"

"Yes it is, my baby boy."

"I'll talk to you later, Konev. I have a very pressing matter to attend to right now."

"No wonder you're so chubby." Ivan slams the phone in disgust.

11

Lyuba returns home at 11:00, dragging the pram up the steps. When she unlocks the door, Ivan is standing there in his work clothes.

He hasn't even washed off the iron residue from the factory.

"What in the world are you doing still up, and dressed like this? Have you even eaten supper?"

"Did you just come back from Malenkov's house?"

"I haven't even seen Boris today. Aren't you paranoid. The one time I come home a little bit late from my daily errands, you jump to the wild conclusion I left you for him. Just let me get to bed. I already stopped at a late-night restaurant, where Tanyechka and I ate our fill."

Ivan takes Tatyana from her arm. "Why didn't you call home?"

"I just told you, you always jump to the wrong conclusions. *Knyazhna*, you can get into your pajamas, go to bed, and sleep as late as you'd like, since we've been out so late. In the morning, I'll make you a great big breakfast of whatever you'd like."

Tatyana jumps to the floor and runs to her little room.

Ivan reaches into the pram and finds only blankets. He lifts them up and finds the crate of coconuts.

"Where's Fedya? Did somebody steal him?"

"Don't be crazy. He hasn't been kidnapped."

"Somebody must've snatched him as you were coming home, and you didn't even realize it, that bandit was so snappy! Where's my son?"

"You're scaring me, Vanya."

"What happened to my son? Does Malenkov have him, or was he snatched?"

"Stop yelling at me."

"And what's in this box?"

"Coconuts."

"I won't even ask why. But I have to demand an explanation for why you haven't come back home with my son in his pram!"

"Don't be selfish. He's my son too. I'm the one who almost died giving birth to him. You didn't even know I was pregnant with him till the end of my first trimester."

"Where's my son?"

"He's with your father, *golubchik*. You know how much your father adores Fedya. He'd never let anything happen to him."

"You were with my father again!"

"Yes, just look at all this good money I got today." Lyuba removes one hundred forty dollars from her pockets.

"Were you at my aunt's house?"

"All you need to know is I was with your father the entire day."

"At his little illegal liquor store!"

"Yes, at his store. I tried to leave with Fedya too, but your father wouldn't allow them to permit it, since all three of us could've left together if he'd just turned over his weapons to the mobsters who came in to threaten him—"

"My son is not only in an illegal liquor store that could get raided by the police at any time, but in the same store with mobsters?!"

"He was being held by Mr. Lazhenitsyn as they tied your father up."

"Who's Mr. Lazhenitsyn?"

"The second-in-command at the store, right after your father."

"So all this time this money has been coming from bootlegging, smuggling, moonshining, and breaking Prohibition right and left!"

"Yes."

"I'm going over there right now to get my son back home!"

"You'd dare make the mobsters even angrier!"

"My father will never see Fedya ever again! He's been putting you, Fedya, and Tanyechka in danger for weeks, and I never even knew it!"

"You're going to go to bed now, and in the morning we'll discuss this matter again."

Ivan lies in bed shaking with rage and barely sleeps at all. Lyuba and Tatyana are still sleeping in the morning when he leaves the house and runs toward his father's liquor store instead of Mr. Glazov's factory. Aleksey and Nikolas are completely ignored when they try to steer him in the other direction.

The mobsters are still holding Mr. Konev and Mr. Lazhenitsyn at gunpoint when Ivan gets into the store. Mr. Konev is tied up in a chair, and next to him Mr. Lazhenitsyn is holding Fedya in his lap, his legs tied to the chair.

"Now who's this?"

"Don't drag my son into this, he's a teetotaler except for drinking Communion wine, he's morally repulsed by how I'm violating Prohibition, he never knew I was paying his fiancée for smuggling alcohol here and making the stuff in their house!"

“You sure dragged *my* son into this, though!”

“You can clearly see the baby isn’t hurt a tad! He’s been in Zakhar’s lap all night, though he’s had to shush him periodically when he got hungry. Sure they tried to scare me into giving up my weapons and making vows to buy only their alcohol, taking target shots at him but only shooting right over his head or next to his arms—”

“Just let me take the baby, and I’ll make sure you never see your grandson again!”

“They won’t allow that, Ivanok! What you need to do now, before they tie you up too, is to step into the cellar and wait there for all this to be over. Sooner or later, a customer will come, and then the mobsters simply must release us!”

“I’m not going anywhere without Fedya!”

“I’m ordering you to go into the cellar right now!”

Ivan goes downstairs and finds three phone numbers scrawled on a piece of paper by the telephone, with “Alcohol-friendly cops” written overhead.

“Is this Officer Harry Baron?”

“Who is this?”

“You know my father, Mr. Konev. He runs an illegal liquor store with some guy named Zakhar. They’ve been held at gunpoint since last night by Russian mobsters, and now my son, who barely has one year, is at gunpoint too, since my father chose not to surrender his weapons and to swear to the mobsters he’d begin buying liquor only from them. The baby could’ve been home by now if my father weren’t so stubborn!”

“You’re the one who gets only fifteen dollars a month at an iron factory, the guy who refuses to make his fiancée a respectable woman instead of indefinitely living in sin with her even after you’ve had a son together and you’re raising her four-year-old daughter like your own? The same guy who won’t let his fiancée get a job of her own because he’s so paranoid about men at work making advances on her, and as a result forcing her into danger like this, where she had to resort to breaking the law to pump extra money into your household?”

“My father’s tied up in a chair, and his business partner is half-tied up!”

"You must be in the wine cellar?"

"Don't tell me this has happened to my father before."

"No more than ten times. It's never been this awful, only empty threats from mobsters previously. We'll be right over."

The police van drives up fifteen minutes later. Mr. Konev begins shouting curses at the mobsters as the police come through the front door and force them to the floor. Mr. Lazhenitsyn unties his legs and stands up, hands Fedya to one of the officers, and unties Mr. Konev next.

"The hell this won't ever happen again!" Ivan shouts, coming back upstairs as the head officer leads the mobsters into the waiting van outside. "You're never going to see your grandson again!"

"Thanks to me, my grandson was getting good food and nice things in his excuse of a house for the first time ever! You make fifteen dollars a month, Ivanok, and most men in this great country make that much a week! You have a refrigerator, your fiancée has nice things to wear, you're eating very nice food, there's extra money in the bank for that wedding you want, modern appliances for the kitchen, no more outdated coal stove, and Lyubov Leontiyevna told me she was finally able to afford wallpaper for your squalid tenement! I may not live in my own place, but I live in a house! You live in a dirty little tenement!"

"Compared to some tenements, I have a great place to live! We have three bedrooms, a kitchen, a washroom, a closet, and a big living room! You, you only live in a back room in my aunt's house, stashing away illegal alcohol every chance you get!"

"What are you arguing about?" Officer Baron inquires.

"My son is furious at me for giving a damn about his family! Here I was giving them money, very good money, which enabled them to buy nice things like modern refrigerator, good wallpaper, and silk stockings for the lady, and he's angry because it violated that stupid Volstead Act!"

"You're never going to see your grandson again!" Ivan snatches Fedya back from Mr. Lazhenitsyn and pulls the baby close to himself. "I'm taking you out for ice-cream for being such a brave little boy."

"What about that belovèd job of yours?" Mr. Konev snaps. "Now you'll get less than that saintly fifteen dollars a month, since you're a few hours late to work!"

"I'd rather have my family starve in dignity and by living honestly than live like a rich man by breaking the law, even with the full approval of crooked cops like these!"

"Here, have some more money, Ivanok, for helping out today. I don't know if I would've lived much longer if you hadn't come charging in here like a madman!"

"This is a hundred dollars! And you're giving it away like it's nothing!"

"Maybe you can buy something nice, like one of those newfangled radios, new car parts, or a nice new suit or hat—"

"Like that idiotic bowler that seems to be glued to your head? I wish you'd been murdered and *Matushka* had really been alive all along! She wouldn't be living like this!"

"You know as well as I do, Ivanok, your mother would've fully supported what I'm doing now, earning money for my family."

"*Tyotya* Lera has a job, and so does her new husband! They don't need any help!"

"I earn hundreds of dollars every week instead of getting paid only three dollars and seventy-five cents a week! How do you look at yourself in the mirror, earning such horrible money?"

"I have a lot of money in the bank, and so does Lyuba! I'm down at the bank every week taking our money out so we can have significant money to supplement my poor weekly paycheck!"

"Do you want one of these kind officers to drive you down to that sweatbox you labor away in? It's a wonder that *mudak* gives his workers a ten-hour day instead of a sixteen-hour day."

"First I'm going to deposit Fedya at home, and then go to work."

Mr. Konev sighs in disgust as Ivan leaves the store clutching Fedya. "Harry, this is address of iron factory my son works by. You're going to go there right now, before my son gets there, and say you'll arrest boss unless he starts paying my son fifteen dollars a week instead of fifteen dollars a month."

12

Officer Baron pays a visit to Mr. Glazov as he's eating Cadbury chocolate, reading *True Story* magazine, and every so often taking little peeks at the exploited workers through ten different glass peepholes. Mr. Glazov's personal office is more like a suite, and even has air conditioning, something he denies his laborers.

"Is this the Mr. Glazov I've heard so many terrible things about?"

"One of the workers sent you to inspect the factory?" Mr. Glazov speaks perfect English. "I never should've let them start that stupid union. They're lucky I'm not making them work sixteen hours a day instead of only ten, and that I'll start giving them paid vacations this year."

"I'm a frequent visitor to a store owned by the father of one of your workers. He says you only pay his son fifteen dollars a month, which averages out to three dollars and seventy-five cents a week, sixty-two cents a day. You're going to start paying all your workers fifteen dollars a week from now on."

"I already let them have a union and now paid vacations. They'd walk all over me asking for more special favors if I began to pay them more than they deserve."

"My friend's son is friends with another man who works here. Not the agitator who just started the union, the other man he comes in with every morning, the pale, scrawny, bookish guy who's always reading the bulletin board to see if there are openings in positions that don't involve so much danger. He's also threatened to walk if he won't get a higher salary."

"He can walk. It's no great concern of mine. I can continue to pay my workers only fifteen dollars a month as long as none of them complain en masse."

"You'll pay them fifteen dollars a week from now on, or else I'll run you in," Officer Baron threatens.

Aleksey comes marching into the office, brandishing a petition. "Mr. Glazov, I spent the past few days gathering signatures of fellow workers who want—"

"Speak English. We may both be Russian, but we're in America now."

"You know as well as I do you understood what I just said perfectly. Only five people refused to sign this petition to go on strike until you begin to pay us fifteen dollars a week for risking our lives in your stupid factory."

"I've already told your boss I'll arrest him if he doesn't start adhering to basic rules by paying all his workers money they can actually live on, instead of money that would only satisfy a child laborer."

13

Ivan comes back into the tenement and takes Fedya into the washroom. Lyuba has just woken up and started to make Tatyana breakfast. Ivan sees red when Lyuba goes to get the door and one of his father's co-workers is standing there with ten crates.

"You know what to do with these, Miss Zhukova," he whispers before disappearing.

"What the hell is in these crates?"

"Coconuts."

"I bet you're going to hollow them out, refill them with alcohol, and smuggle them to my corrupt father and those crooked cops protecting him from getting busted by the feds!"

"What did happen with your father?"

"His hide was saved because he ordered me into the cellar, where I saw a phone number for three 'alcohol-friendly cops'! I can't believe there are officers of the law protecting people who dare violate Prohibition!" Ivan goes back to Fedya and changes his diaper.

"The mobsters are gone?"

"They were arrested."

"So I can deliver the next shipment of goods without worrying there'll be another incident."

"I'll deliver those coconuts in my car, and that's the last you'll ever break the law to get money!"

"Several days ago, I begged Alyoshka to start a petition at the factory. He told me he'd do anything for me, since he's practically my brother. With any luck, he'll generate enough signatures for a strike for higher pay."

"I'll refuse to join in! I can't believe how much you've been going behind my back!"

"You have to join in that strike, Vanya, or I'll leave you for good this time and take the kids with me. I'll find another man who knows how to be a good provider for his family."

Ivan goes off to the iron factory shaken and furious, and arrives just in time to see Mr. Glazov addressing his workers, flanked by Aleksey and the vice-president of the union, twenty-five-year-old Daniil Gavriilovich Karmov.

"I've been threatened with arrest if I don't begin to pay you fifteen dollars a week. That's the last pay raise I'll ever grant anyone. Along with this latest concession to the scum I employ in my nice factory, there must be an equal and opposite reaction in the form of more hours a day."

Ivan is shaking with rage by the time Mr. Glazov gets done speaking. He runs after Aleksey as the crowd begins to disperse.

"You and my fiancée conspired behind my back to start a strike for higher pay!"

"That money in the bank won't last forever, Ivan. Sooner or later, you'll have to become like Liza and I, with only the money we earn to get us by. Lyuba's like a sister to me."

Ivan's eyes narrow. "Do you have designs on her?"

"I've been very happily married for five years! I was never in a million years one of the guys who had his eyes on her! Lyuba's always been just a dear friend, a friend I'd do anything for."

14

Ivan comes home to more moonshining. Tatyana is putting the alcohol-filled coconuts back into the crates. He sits on the davenport waiting for them to finish, and as soon as they are, he swoops over to grab the boxes and runs down to the street with them two at a time.

"That's good alcohol, and a lot of money!" Lyuba shouts in protest.

"I'm driving this illegal junk to my father's store, and that's the last we'll participate in breaking the law again!"

Mr. Konev looks up in surprise as he and Mr. Lazhenitsyn are closing the store for the evening, as Ivan begins honking the car's horn over and over again.

"Now what do you want, Ivanok? Didn't Officer Baron force your evil boss into upping your pay rate to fifteen dollars a week?"

"Yes, and I found out he might've done it anyway, since Lyuba and my other best friend were conspiring behind my back the entire time about planning a strike to get a higher salary! The alcohol in the coconut shells is in the car. Take it out yourself. I refuse to touch it more than I have to."

"You brought it yourself! You're only steps away from full-out joining me! I'll pay you a thousand dollars a month if you come to work for me!"

Mr. Lazhenitsyn carries the ten crates into the store.

"I don't want any of your money, *Batya.* Just give me what you would've given Lyuba."

Mr. Konev hands him one hundred thirty dollars and watches him driving away, unable to believe anyone, even a greenhorn, could be that naïve about the truth of the ins and outs of Prohibition.

****

Chapter 37: Coney Island

Katrin, Viktoriya, and Sandro take the lift up to the thirty-fifth floor of the fancy apartment where Anastasiya now lives in the Upper East Side. Today they're taking the subway down to Coney Island, and Anastasiya hasn't even started packing yet.

"Nice bird. Are you leaving it in the care of a neighbor while you're away?" Viktoriya goes over to Anastasiya's new yellow canary, housed in a fancy, large bamboo cage. "Wow, you'd think someone my age lived here instead of a twenty-four-year-old woman. Your walls are covered in pictures of celebrities instead of wallpaper."

"Dmitriy and Rudy *are* my wallpaper." Anastasiya starts slowly packing her clothes into three trunks.

"You obsess over the most current celebrities, like that Valentino guy and your precious Grand Duke Dmitriy, whom I see you still very much have a crush on, yet you think and dress like someone from your *ema*'s generation. My big sister only had to take half the amount of suitcases for her clothes on her honeymoon, because she wears regular clothes now instead of huge flowing skirts, heavy blouses, and those stupid-looking hats. You work now, so you ought to be very worried about your long sleeves getting caught in the sewing machine or tripping on your skirts."

Anastasiya takes an hour to sort through all her clothes, then stuffs her magazines, three bags of celebrity pictures without adhesives already stuck to the backs, a Mahjong set, and plenty of perfume, makeup, and hair accessories into another valise. She carelessly throws a pink silk covering over the birdcage and then departs the apartment.

"Why don't you find a hobby for a modern, intelligent woman?" Katrin suggests. "My Sandro is very interested in radios. We have a Crosley Ace, and he subscribes to all the publications about radios under the sun. He's also greatly interested in flying machines, and is always bothering me to go with him to a place where they charge civilians to take a ride on a real flying machine. His father was also interested in new-fangled technological contraptions. You should see the stash of ancient automobile magazines and catalogues my father-in-law has lying around his house."

Viktoriya goes through Anastasiya's picturefold in her wallet on the subway. There are three pictures of Anastasiya's late parents and brother, while all the rest are pictures of Anastasiya, popular actors and sports stars, and an inordinate amount of pictures of Grand Duke Dmitriy and Rudolph Valentino.

"Why aren't there any pictures of my sister if she's your best friend and the only family you've got left in this world? You would've been out on the streets, dead, or back in prison if it weren't for her."

"I have plenty of pictures of Katya in my apartment."

"She's also told you to stop calling her Katya. She's done answering to that Russianized nickname."

"It's hard to break a lifelong habit. I'm not trying to disrespect her."

"So." Katrin quickly changes the subject and switches out of Estonian. "I decided last Sunday I'm going to baptize Oliivia or Marek. It was a very inspiring sermon by Reverend Zimmer that swayed my opinion of Christianity, though I'll baptize the kid Unitarian instead of Orthodox."

"Even a heartless heretic can find God for the sake of her unborn child," Ivan says. "Though I hope you knew your baby would've gone to Hell if you hadn't baptized it."

"Vanya!" Lyuba chides.

"His sermon was about how Jesus was the original Socialist. I have such a high opinion of that dead guy now."

Ivan's jaw drops.

"Even if he's just a myth and combination of gods like Tammuz and Mithras, the person we're taught about was indeed the first Socialist. If he did exist, I don't think he was the son of God, though that doesn't take away from how he was a Socialist before it had a name."

"How much longer to Coney Island?" Ivan asks.

"Want to bet Katya will get arrested for indecent exposure the second we set foot on the beach?" Anastasiya asks. She covers her ears when her canary begins chirping. "Be quiet, bird! We'll be there before we know it, and you can sing all you want when you're alone in our hotel room."

"Thank God you only got a bird instead of a husband and baby," Katrin says. "I'd hate to see how you'd behave if you ever have an actual child."

"I bet she'd name her kid, if it's a boy, Dmitriy or Rudolph," Viktoriya smirks.

"Just because I'm in love with a handsome prince and a handsome moviestar isn't a reason to make fun of me!"

"Put that wedding ring on, Vanya," Lyuba snaps. "I don't want the people at the hotel to know we live in sin."

"This is the man who refused to give my sister and brother-in-law ten dollars for their honeymoon fund?" Viktoriya asks.

"Oh, coming from someone whose older sister thinks Christ was a Socialist, and the first Socialist at that!"

"We'll sign in as Mr. Konev and Mrs. Koneva," Lyuba goes on. "People would wonder why Miss Zhukova's signing into the same room as Mr. Konev, and why in the world they have two children if they're not married."

"Do you think your mother would be pleased to learn her only child grew up to live in sin?" Katrin joins in. "It's almost a good thing she's dead. If I'd lived in sin with Sandro, I could've never faced my mother if she'd been in my life at the time."

"Speaking of that vile traitor, do you know what's happened to her and our father?" Viktoriya asks.

"About a week or two ago, I saw them at the publishing house for the main paper I write for. They were there to place an ad asking anyone who knows anything about their other eight children to contact them. I had to tell them the ugly truth, and that you only got away because your assigned assassin was a lousy shot and misfired. They broke down crying and ran out of there as quickly as they knew how."

"Lyuba, Ginny, and that *mudak* Malenkov saw everything," Ivan says. "You watched, dry-eyed, as the *mudak* Bolsheviks broke the neck of the three-year-old and threw her against the wall, then walked all over her on their way to do the same to the other two little girls. If Viktoriya hadn't magically shown up in March, you wouldn't have cared."

"Why is it that whenever a woman asserts herself and does something that violates Western society's taboos, like get divorced, refuse to get married or have children, or do what I did, they attack her so viciously, like she's the Devil incarnate?" Katrin asks. "Well, I have some news for you, Konev. Maybe this won't happen too often by the time your son's a man, but rest assured, by the time your grandkids are your age, things will be a whole lot different, and you old-guard men won't be in control any longer. Your granddaughters won't be content to play the role you want your poor fiancée in, a full-time housekeeper who isn't allowed to earn her own money."

"I have no objections to Kat or Liza working, or even to you writing for those crazy newspapers."

"Vanya doesn't want me to work not because he's opposed to a woman with a family working, but because he's so afraid my male co-workers would make unwanted advances on me," Lyuba explains.

"Are you even going to let her vote when we become citizens?"

"I'll have to do some serious talking to Vanya before I let *him* vote! He's delusional, Katrin. He wants to register Republican when we get our citizenship papers, and thinks they best represent our interests."

"Republicans don't care for poor immigrant factory workers in tenements. You'll be better served by joining the Socialists or Democrats. I convinced Stasya to register as a Democrat when we get citizenship." Katrin looks over at Anastasiya, very close to swooning over her billfold of pictures of the sheiks of the American silver screen. "Stop that, Stasya. You'll have more than enough time to fall into a faint over Grand Duke Dmitriy and all those American actors when we're in the hotel."

"Maybe I'll meet a man on Coney Island, a Russian or Estonian, who looks just like Grand Duke Dmitriy."

"A man would notice you sexually or romantically when almost your entire body's covered by a bathing suit that went out of style years ago?" Viktoriya giggles. "I'm surprised you don't wear bathing socks and shoes."

Katrin puts her arm around Viktoriya. "I'm glad her assassin misfired. Vika's a great help with my articles, essays, reviews, and exposés. She even does a little to contribute to the income, though my greatest boost in income has come not from her dishwashing job at a Catholic girls' school in Greenwich Village, my article-writing for the immigrant publications, or Sandro's job at Ellis Island, but from what I've begun doing on a piece of advice from my mother-in-law. What a sage woman. I wish she were my blood mother. She's so egalitarian and liberated. She gives me all sorts of advice on investing in the Stock Market. Now my riches will never cease."

"Don't you think you're a huge hypocrite, writing for crazy left-wing rags and having Socialist secret meetings, yet living like a *knyazhna* in a fancy penthouse suite and not doing a lick of work besides using a typewriter to spew insane Socialist propaganda?"

"Hush up, Vanya," Lyuba says. "You won't have to see Katrin very much as soon as we're in our hotel room."

2

At the hotel, Lyuba signs herself in as Mrs. Lyubov Koneva and waits for Ivan to sign. On the subway, she slipped the wedding ring onto her finger, the one she used when they previously pretended to be married, and wears in public to avoid judgment. Even if the custom is to only use the title Mrs. with a woman's actual name if she's a divorcée, Lyuba is supremely uncomfortable passively identifying herself in relation to Ivan. If anyone dares question her, she'll say it's the Russian custom, and women's surnames take different endings anyway. Calling herself "Mrs. Konev" wouldn't be grammatically correct, and would invite strange looks.

"Is your husband illiterate?"

"Sign the ledger, and let us get on with our happy vacation!" Anastasiya shrills.

He picks up the pen and reluctantly signs, smudging his signature a bit in the process, then realizes he's signed his name in Cyrillic, and the style of Cyrillic that's been outdated since the Revolution, with letters that don't exist anymore. He crosses it out and manages to print his name in Roman letters this time. Perhaps someday he'll master Roman cursive and be able to sign his name like a normal grownup.

"I've never seen anyone write with that hand before. I thought all the teachers beat it out of their students before they got older."

"This is how God made me," Ivan says defiantly, turning away from the sign-in desk.

Eliisabet is furious that, even after presenting the marriage certificate attesting to the fact that she's been married for five years, she still must write “wife of Aleksey Tvardovsky” after her name. Kat is forced to write “wife of Nikolas Vishinsky.”

“You should’ve done what your other radical friend did and given your children your husband’s surname, instead of sticking them with hyphenated names,” the desk worker says to Eliisabet, a snide look on her face. “It’s not normal for a woman to keep her maiden name after marriage. Do you think you’re superior to your poor husband?”

“The Spanish and Portuguese have somehow managed just fine with multiple surnames for centuries, and many countries have the custom of women keeping their birth names,” Katrin says. “You remember me, Katariina Nikonova. I stayed here last July. I’m married now, and Mrs. Kalvik-Nikonova. This is my nice husband Sandro Kalvik and my little sister Viktoriya Nikonova. I’m birthing my first child at the end of this year. This is my best friend Anastasiya Voroshilova. She’s bringing a pet canary. We’re checking into the room I stayed by last year.”

“I remember you and the blonde woman with curly hair. She still dresses like it’s 1900!”

“The woman married to Mr. Tvardovsky is my second-best friend. Don’t give her any trouble, or I’ll sue this establishment.”

Ivan cannot truly believe the thoughts and words that spew from Katrin’s mouth. Every so often, while he and Lyuba are supposed to be unpacking their things, he darts down the hallway to Katrin’s huge suite to see what’s going on in there. She has everything a modern society person ought to have, plenty of expensive clothing, and hoards of left-wing literature and memorabilia.

“You spying on me, Konev? Going to report me for ‘heretical’ political beliefs? I’m an enlightened rich society woman who gives a damn about the world and politics because of how I grew up, not a rich woman who just became a Socialist because she thought it’d be sophisticated or an ideal way to rebel against her parents just for the sake of rebelling. I was like this since I was a girl, only I didn’t know it had a name till I was about twelve.”

Anastasiya goes into mini-swoons every time she glues up another picture on her bedroom walls. Viktoriya comes by to look and sees two very large pictures hanging right above the head of the bed.

"Wow, are you actually kissing Grand Duke Dmitriy in that picture and in the arms of Valentino in that other one?"

"Don't I wish, child. No, they're cosmographs. All the tabloids use them. I have a lot of tabloids I brought along for reading material, if you're interested in seeing some more examples."

"Is that *True Story Magazine* on your bed?"

"I read these magazines as practice for my English, and also because their line of reporting is right up my alley. I myself have a juicy story I might sell to this magazine, about how I was jilted and used by Konev."

"You were involved with that cheapskate who lives in sin?"

"We never slept together, but he deceived me for a good long while about how I was his girlfriend and about us having a future together. All along, he was only using me to make that other woman jealous, the one who lied and signed herself in as Mrs. Koneva when she's really Miss Zhukova."

"You really haven't moved on yet? Hasn't he been with her for the past three years at least?"

"She's always running away and leaving him. I'm the better woman."

3

Out on the beach, Anastasiya draws stares and loud gales of laughter due to her outdated bathing dress, a heavy black wool outfit with a hemline falling to her ankles and sleeves extending past her elbows. It's painfully severe and old-fashioned even by the standards of the typical bathing dress. No matter what, Anastasiya refuses to show her ankles and elbows in public. Her few concessions to practicality are her lack of bathing stockings, lace-up bathing slippers, and a cap. Katrin meanwhile enjoys the flirting glances of other men, though she's wearing a wedding ring and is just starting to become visibly pregnant. Kittey, Viktoriya, Alya, and Anya also have modern, lightweight bathing suits which allow them to move freely and actually swim, while Kat, Eliisabet, and Lyuba have more demure bathing dresses, made of satin, with shoulder-length sleeves and hemlines just covering their knees.

The four men have the normal black tank tops falling to their mid-thighs, over snug-fitting shorts, made of ribbed cotton. Ivan typically has the most conservative bathing suit, paranoid he'll be arrested for indecency if the wind or water clings to him too tightly or blows anything out of place. He's also made sure his top isn't loose and that the sleeves are as relatively long as possible, so no one will see any of the thirty whiplash scars still emblazoned all over his back. The children meanwhile run and toddle about in homemade bathing suits, unburdened by worries of looking either fashionable or immodest.

Ivan's eyes lower when he sees Alya and Anya walking ahead of all the others, frequently whispering and even holding hands. Of course, no one would ever think anything of two close friends doing such things, because they're best friends and women instead of men...

"Have you ever thought the two of them aren't quite right in the head?"

"Why not? Because they haven't married yet?"

Ivan hangs his head, expecting another tongue-lashing from Katrin.

"It may come as a shock to many men, but there are actually some women who have no use for marriage and feel it's an anti-woman, oppressive institution. Don't you remember how Liza and Kat had to add 'wife of' after their names in the hotel ledger because they kept their own surnames? Married women lose their jobs, legal rights, identity, and all their rosy hopes and dreams. Thank God my husband doesn't want me in the kitchen round the clock or picking up the penthouse for him."

"You have servants to do that, you big hypocrite."

"If we didn't, he wouldn't make me become his slave. If this baby's an Oliivia instead of Marek, I sure as hell won't raise her to be a submissive doormat whose only identity is her husband's."

"You're frightened of an assertive woman like my big sister." Viktoriya skips down to the shoreline, wearing a bathing suit showing just as much flesh as Katrin's.

"I know you'll be arrested for indecent exposure before the end of the day!"

Alya and Anya sit down on two beach chairs. Ivan watches them out of the corner of his eye as he and the others come down to join them.

"What don't you like about them?" Nikolas asks. "If it weren't for Anya, my little sister might not have survived the labor camp."

"Doesn't it strike you as a bit odd neither of them has married yet? They've had all the time in the world to find husbands since we came to America. Soon they'll be too old to be desired by men, and they'll have to enter a nunnery or be old maid schoolteachers."

"As if there's something wrong with that," Katrin says.

"If this baby's an Oliivia, won't you want her to marry before age twenty-five?"

"Anastasiya still isn't married, and she's twenty-four. Do you suspect *her* of being wrong in the head?"

"I always suspected she *was* goofy in the head!"

"Well, yes, she certainly is delusional, like about how she's the better woman for you, and she has her share of little quirks, and she's very shallow, but she's very much sane otherwise. Do you think a crazy woman would be allowed to have her own fashion design company? That was her dream since childhood, to be a famous fashion designer, and since she designed my wedding gown, it's all come true faster than she could blink. Maybe you can forgive her a little for having unrealistic designs on you and let her design Lyuba's wedding gown, if you ever get around to making her a respectable woman."

Kat moves to sit closer to Alya and Anya. "Maybe you could meet your matches at a dance at the amusement park!"

"I was engaged once before, and we all remember what a disaster that was," Alya says. "I'd be married to that lifeless bore Maksim if I hadn't run away to escape that awful fate."

"American men are different from most Russian men," Lyuba says. "They may be old-fashioned like my Vanya, but nowhere near the way that boring stiff Maksim is."

"Every time I'm at the library, I see Maksim looking in my direction the entire time I'm there. After so much time has passed, he still thinks he has a chance with me."

"If you don't get married soon, people will start to think you prefer each other!" Kat says.

Anya laughs nervously.

"That would be crazy, to assume two women who are best friends, sharing an apartment, and unmarried prefer each other!" Alya laughs, equally nervously. "Maybe we just don't like the idea of marriage. There are plenty of successful women who've never married, despite how society casts them."

Ivan still has his suspicions as their party goes to have hotdogs at Feltman's. Alya and Anya pull their chairs very close to one another and look as though their feet are intertwined underneath the table.

"I've started to wonder about what really happened to them during the two years we were apart. If it turns out they're deviants, we must stop associating with them at once. Don't even start to contradict me, Katrin."

"Don't you have a fiancée and two children to be paying more attention to?" Katrin asks.

"I would've never lived in sin with you, Ivan."

Ivan glares at Anastasiya across the table. "You're another one who needs to get married, though any man insane enough to want to marry you would be in for a lifetime of torture."

"You're damn lucky I'm able to think of you on two different levels," Katrin says. "The one level I view you on is the reason I'll be testifying on your behalf when you go to court against Malenkov for full paternal rights over Tatyana. On that level, I view you as a good, decent person, but on the other level, you're so unenlightened."

"Does your daughter know what's going on?" Viktoriya asks. "About how you and her mother live in sin?"

"I'm marrying Lyuba three months from now!" Ivan shouts in his defense. "I wish your assigned assassin had fired correctly. Then I'd be spared your big mouth and having to be in the company of a younger version of Katrin."

"What a horrible thing to say! And for your information, Konev, I tried to save Vika the night before. I asked if she wanted to join me in becoming a Bolshevik, and said she had to answer right away. I was going to try again in the morning, but it was too late. The Bolsheviks were already looting the house. Now I have someone to help out with my work for the émigré publications and the secret weekly meetings. Viktoriya will also be a nanny for Oliivia or Marek."

4

That night, Ivan refuses to come to bed, and stands on the upper-level patio watching the blinking lights of Coney Island in the dark. Down the hall, Katrin is playing a jazz record loudly on her brand-new gramophone and making Anastasiya wind it up. He's imagining what Alya and Anya might be doing in their own hotel room. At least when Alya was engaged to Maksim, however much of a farce it was, there were no doubts about her true nature, and Anya used to openly have her eye on boys in gymnasium...

"You know Katrin will be a part of our lives as long as we live in New York, just like she was in our lives during the Civil War."

"She, that stupid, brainless best friend of hers, and that big-mouthed little sister who reappeared three months ago all should've died long ago. When Katrin got kicked out of her mansion, she and that idiot Anastasiya had to go and oh-so-suspiciously decide to hide out in the same place as our band. All because that shallow blonde still has a delusional crush on me. That woman had more than enough money to get a ship to America, with fare left over for her idiot friend, right then and there. Instead they chose to tag along with us."

"I sure don't see you getting a job with a much higher salary that can afford train fare to the Midwest, a big farm, machinery, and animals, if you hate living in such close vicinity to Katrin and Anastasiya. Why don't you come to bed?"

"Everyone hates me. Katrin can't stop berating me for being a bit old-fashioned; my father thinks I'm stupid for staying with my job and never protesting about my salary or the working conditions; Alyosha won't get off my back about how I won't join his stupid union; Alya and Anya practically bit my head off when I asked them about how I think they might be wrong in the head; and you seem to be berating me a lot too lately."

"I'm on vacation with *you*, not Boris. And you're returning to Manhattan in two weeks, so you'll have lots of time to plan our wedding. When I'm on Long Island with the children and Katrin, I expect you to make frequent calls to tell me every new development. I already know Alyoshka will be your best man—"

"The way he went behind my back to form that damned union and almost put me out of a job, had the guys stupid enough to go along with the union started striking for higher pay?"

"Liza will be matron of honor, of course. Kat, Kittey, Alya, Anya, and my younger stepsisters will be the bridesmaids. And then this wedding ring on my hand will be there because you put it there in a real ceremony, instead of me putting it on my own hand because I don't want people to know I live in sin."

"I'll get you a much nicer one. Maybe we'll be blessed and be granted another child after the wedding. If we have another child by some miracle, I hope it'll be a girl. Not everyone is meant to have as many kids as your stepfather."

5

Galya flutters her eyes open in the doctor's office. Svetlana and Matryona are sitting on the doctor's right side, and the four youngest are on his left.

"I can finally see again!"

"Do you recognize us?" Alla asks hopefully.

"I recognize Allochka, Sveta, and Motya, but not the younger ones."

"This finally happened because I threatened to report this doctor to the state health department for continually moving your surgery date up." Svetlana looks meaningfully at the doctor.

"You must be Vera and Natalya. I haven't seen you since you were twelve and eight!"

"You've heard us since we were sixteen and twelve, though. Now you can see the lovely children at the orphanage too," Vera says.

"This must be Fyodora. She's grown so much."

"Now you can see our new little brother or sister at the end of this year!" Natalya says. "If it's a girl, Papa will name her after Mama, and if it's a boy, he'll be Osip, after *Dyadya* Osyenka. I don't know what Mrs. Zhukova would think, to always hear the name Yevgeniya or Zhenyushka and think of her husband's former wife."

Fyodora puts her head in Alla's lap. "I want there to be ten of us again, though most of you are old enough to be my mother instead of my older sisters."

"*Matushka* isn't coming back. As more and more time goes by, there's less and less of a reasonable chance Dina, Fima, and Lyolya are still alive somewhere."

"Why don't we name the baby after one of them if it's a girl?" Natalya asks. "It'll be more palatable to *Machekha* Katya if it were named for one of her stepdaughters she'll never meet, rather than the woman to whom her new husband was married for twenty-eight years."

"Or maybe it's a little Osyenka," Alla says. "Nothing in this life is guaranteed. Sometimes I think God has a very dark sense of humor and enjoys springing surprises on us when we least expect them."

6

The next evening, Kat darts into Alya and Anya's room to borrow a dress to wear to the dance she and Nikolas are going to at one of the dancehalls. Kittey will be putting on a puppet show to entertain Lyudmila and Raisa while their parents are out dancing.

Kat has just found the dress she wants when Alya and Anya walk into the room and draw the drapes. Kat draws farther back into the closet in case they assume she was spying on them.

Anya sits on the bed. "This is the biggest quandary I've ever been in. We're in love with each other and don't prefer men anymore, yet we can't very well have children unless we find a man who'll sleep with us for the sole purpose of giving us children."

Alya sits beside her. "We can have cover marriages. It's been done before. That overly intellectual stiff Maksim is out of the question, since he'd assume the wrong thing and think I finally changed my mind. How about Boris? He still isn't married."

"I won't hear of it, Alyechka! We'd be cheating on each other, even with the very best of intentions! I couldn't bear to think of you in a man's arms after these past four years of loving only one another! Besides, we now know what Boris did to Lyuba when she was pregnant with Tatyana. Thanks to his brutality against an innocent, defenseless pregnant woman, Lyuba probably will never have another child. She's lucky she got a second child after what that awful brute did to her. What if he did the same thing to one or both of us?"

"Then how about eventually declaring we realized we weren't meant to marry, and enter a convent?"

"I might get jealous of the other nuns and think they had designs on my girlfriend!"

"Some nunneries are rumored to be hotbeds of lesbianism. We could find one that is and join them."

"Most of our friends have begun to get suspicious. Very soon, we must join a convent that's a hotbed of lesbianism, find men who'll have us for cover marriages, or seek out an area of this country that won't stone us to death if we were to live openly like we are."

"This afternoon on the Ferris wheel, I so wanted to kiss you the way some of the young men on the other cars were doing with their wives and girlfriends. It's not fair we can't show our love openly like other people."

Kat sits down in horror in the closet as Anya and Alya begin unbuttoning one another's blouses and kissing one another. She slowly crawls into a corner, shuts her eyes, and plugs her ears to prevent the sights and sounds she fears being an unwilling witness to. She sits there that way for the next hour, until she hears the door slamming and footsteps padding down the hallway and away from the room.

"We're late," Nikolas tells her when she runs back into their room. "You didn't even get the dress you wanted to borrow."

"I can't very well wear a dress when I now know who was wearing it! I was in the closet, about to leave, when they came in and began an awful conversation, about how they needed to have cover marriages or enter a nunnery because they prefer each other and not men! Right before I crawled back into a corner, shut my eyes, and plugged my ears, they were kissing and undoing each other's buttons! I never once suspected either of them of deviancy, but there they were, unashamedly professing to love each other instead of men! They're homosexuals!"

"That can't be possible! Anya was like a mother hen to me in the labor camp!" Kittey shouts. "Someone with something so wrong in her head wouldn't have been so mothering, kind, and protective. And she had crushes on a few boys in gymnasium. Alya also had crushes on boys, and was engaged, even to someone as irritable as Maksim."

"You're sure you saw them doing that and carrying on such a deviant conversation?" Nikolas asks, his face white.

"I don't want Lyuda and Raya to be around those two pervertesses!" Kat wails. "They might corrupt their sweet little minds away from normalcy and convert them into homosexuals too!"

"If that's the truth, then for the love of Christ, I won't let them be around my little sister anymore either."

"How about the other children? Kolya, Mira, Tanyechka, and Fedya are equally impressionable. We must never see them ever again." Kat runs down the hallway into Lyuba and Ivan's room.

"What's wrong?" Ivan asks.

"Anya and Alya are homosexuals!" Kat sobs. "I saw and heard the proof just now! None of our children can be allowed near them ever again!"

"I knew it!"

"Knew what, *golubchik*?" Lyuba comes up behind him and slips her arms around his waist.

"Furtseva and Minina prefer each other! I've had suspicions for such a long time!"

"We can't let any of our children be around them ever again," Kat pleads. "We have to tell Liza about this too, and even Katrin might show some moral decency and agree her baby won't be allowed near those sexual deviants ever either."

***

When Alya and Anya get back from the restaurant across the way, everyone is standing in their hotel room. Kittey is watching the six children in her brother and sister-in-law's room, unable to believe the truth about Anya.

"My wife was in your hotel room of sin and corruption to innocently borrow a dress to wear to a dance tonight, a dance which we never departed for, because she was made late when you came in unexpectedly and she had to hide in the closet." Nikolas can hardly believe he's asserting himself when so often he's more passive than even Ivan usually is. "Kat overheard and oversaw some things that upset her very much. Are you going to give us an explanation for your deviancy, repent and go back to preferring men, or claim my wife is a liar?"

"What are you talking about?" Alya turns as red as her hair.

"You're sexual deviants!" Kat shouts.

"I can explain what you saw and heard," Anya starts.

"I shut my eyes, plugged my ears, and crawled back into a corner of the closet right after I saw you kiss each other. I wasn't spying on you in your greatest moment of deviancy."

"Yes, we prefer each other, and it's been that way for the past four years," Alya says. "It began after Boris left for America and we fled the valley. We found our way to a safe haven with lots of other displaced Whites. We soon were living in another house together, with no other houseguests, and then one thing led to another."

"One day Maksim came looking for Alyechka, along with her parents," Anya goes on. "Neither of us had any idea how they found out where Alya was. Luckily, the three men who were guarding our area from the Bolsheviks managed to scare them away and said they had no idea where she was. Alya was of course noticeably shaken over this, since she ran away to avoid marrying that man who wanted her for display purposes and bearing him only sons. Suddenly, during the conversation we had that evening, it just happened. Alya and I fell into one another's arms, and that was the first night we realized we were in love with each other. Exactly a week later, we first made love."

"The lesbian Sappho produced a lot of great poetry," Katrin says.

"You're defending them?" Anastasiya shrieks. "You just were saying Oliivia or Marek won't be allowed near either of these sexual deviants!"

"Only because I don't know either of them very well, and I'm all booked up on progressive causes to espouse and promote. Socialism, ending Prohibition, doing more for women's rights, even now that American women can vote, the plight of the proletariat in America, and a whole cornucopia of issues pertaining to Russian and Estonian immigrants."

Anastasiya's jaw drops.

"I'm the one paying for their vacation, and it'd be too cruel and senseless to send them back to Manhattan after only two days on Coney Island. Their co-workers might also get suspicious about why they returned so soon. They get to stay here in the same room. If I see them, I see them, and as for their friends who know them a lot better than I ever will, it's their personal business whether or not they choose to associate with them any longer. I wired ahead for a five-story beach cottage on Long Island, so I'll have to continue paying for their vacation."

"Now I *really* know you're insane!" Ivan yells. "First it was only nutty radical causes like Bolshevism; now you're defending deviants!"

"Like I said, it's your private business if you no longer want to associate with them."

"Had I known you were a deviant then, I never would've allowed my little sister within a hundred *vyorsty* of you!" Nikolas thunders. "I would've found someone else in the women's section of the labor camp to watch out for her!"

"You're going to Hell," Ivan says. "But we'll leave it up to you to explain to people why you're unmarried and childless. We decided not to tell anyone in Manhattan about your sexual deviancy."

"We want children," Alya says. "We'll figure out a way to do it somehow."

"That is disgusting," Nikolas says. "That'd be twice as worse as a pedophile like Lyuba's late father having children! The state would take those children away from you!"

"God will forgive you," Kat says. "If you did what you did out of sheer desperation, because no men took romantic notice of you, and you feared you'd never amount to anything more than spinsters, you could either join a nunnery, if you still think that way, or a club where you'd be bound to find some nice Russian bachelors."

"We go to church every Sunday and feast day," Anya says. "The God we worship doesn't hate or despise us for simply loving one another."

"What's the use of going to church if you don't want to repent of such disgusting sinning?" Ivan asks. "You're both going to Hell."

"Coming from someone who lives in sin and has a thirteen-month-old bastard son! Cohabitation and out of wedlock children are also considered sins in Orthodoxy!" Alya protests.

"I'll turn you in to the police if I catch you near my children," Ivan warns.

"You'll never be allowed near my little sister again either," Nikolas says icily.

"I never suspected either of you of being deviants. I guess you can't go anywhere near my two kids either," Aleksey joins in.

"Even crazy Katrin isn't jumping to your defense," Ivan says victoriously. "Thank God she's already too booked up with daffy Leftist causes to want to bother with advocating for homosexuals. You should've both been murdered by the Bolsheviks."

Alya and Anya watch the others storming out of their hotel room and back to their own rooms in shock. The only one who approaches them in the morning is Katrin.

"All of us are going to Luna Park today, so you can't tag along unless you want another scene like last night. You'll be going to Steeplechase Park instead. For the record, I don't think you're deviants, though I do feel a bit strange around you now, though I barely know you, knowing you prefer women instead of men like everyone else."

Anya and Alya are alone when they march down to the hotel's restaurant. The others in their party sit far away from them.

"Weren't you with all those other people?" the waiter inquires.

"We were, but we had a very serious disagreement last night," Anya says vaguely. "They ended our friendship, and only that blonde woman with short hair and flapper clothes will talk to us now."

Kat is holding onto Lyudmila and Raisa at their table, looking warily over at the scorned lovers. Ivan glares at them when they briefly look over at the others.

"They're not pedophiles like Lyuba's late father or woman-beaters like that scumbag Malenkov," Katrin says.

"What they're doing is even worse! What Lyuba's unworthy father did to her went against everything good, right, and proper in the world, but these two are going against everything good, right, and proper tenfold!"

"Does everyone want to go on the Wonder Wheel again today?" Eliisabet asks, changing the subject. "I liked it, but I don't understand why eight of the cars are stationary while the other sixteen move. I'm used to Ferris wheels where all the cars move."

"I want to go on the Ben Hur Race," Katrin says.

"Are you crazy!" Anastasiya shrills. "You're pregnant!"

"I went on the Rocky Road to Dublin yesterday with Sandro and Vika, and I'm still pregnant now."

Anastasiya casts a glance back at the scorned lovers. "Perhaps they reacted out of confusion and desperation. It was wartime, not too many men around, always having to run, no room to develop a romantic relationship with a man. Anyway, I want to go to Henderson's Dancehall this evening. There are a lot of our fellow immigrants coming here since the subway made the fare only a nickel. I hope I can yet find a nice man like Katrin did, either Russian or Estonian, it doesn't matter. Though the only one I want still has time to change his mind and come back to me."

"Get it through your head, blondie," Lyuba says sharply. "Vanya only used you to make me jealous, the same way I used Malenkov to make Ivan jealous. This September I'll be a respectable woman, and your wild delusions will have no basis in reality."

"Was part of the plan to make Konev jealous getting pregnant out of wedlock with that?"

"I didn't dream what I was getting into would become so over my head. I hadn't planned to sleep with Boris or get pregnant, much less have him beating me when I was pregnant."

Ivan pushes Anastasiya's cup of hot tea into her lap. "You dare refer to my beautiful daughter as 'that,' you vain little witch? You must be jealous you don't have any children, and you're sure not getting any younger. Lyuba gave birth to Tanyechka a month after her nineteenth birthday, and had my little boy when she was twenty-two. You're twenty-four years old, still no husband or children in sight."

"Unlike your fiancée, I don't believe in having children out of wedlock and by two different fathers."

"Your bleeding-hearted best friend had her husband lined up since she was twenty-one. Couldn't you have done the same?"

"I think she's still delusionally dreaming her Grand Duke Dmitriy or Sheik Rudolph will come to her and propose marriage," Viktoriya says.

"It's normal to have crushes on unattainable men, little girl!" Anastasiya snaps.

"And most normal women have moved on to dreaming about attainable men by the time they're your age. If they're still unmarried and having crushes on unattainable men, they know nothing will ever come of them, unlike little girls who wildly believe they'll someday walk down the aisle with one of them."

"I think those cosmographs are encouraging you to not start to focus on men whom you actually know," Katrin concurs.

"Well, at least we'll never have any doubts about Anastasiya preferring only men."

"I know it's odd to be unmarried at twenty-four, but just give me time, and I'll have my own family."

After breakfast, while riding on the Wonder Wheel, Anastasiya begins to think about her waning prospects for marriage. She now has her own bridal salon that's brought in a whole lot of money in the not quite three months it's been in business, and it has her name in its title. Having a husband might mean giving up her career for the sake of supporting a family, even with servants. Children would be an even greater distraction taking away from designing time. Anastasiya silently vows to become a stylish spinster with loads of money and a famous bridal salon, so no one will feel pity for her in that great, esteemed position. She's never been too keen on the idea of having children either.

7

"Sometimes I wonder how you can look me in the eye after I've had another man's child," Lyuba says as they walk to lunch. "I'm still surprised you never resented Tatyana because she's not your own."

"I would've been less able and quick to forgive you if you'd been unfaithful when we were romantically involved, but we weren't together when it happened. And she's an innocent child. It's not her fault how she was conceived. She never asked to be born."

"I never wanted children. Now that I finally want more children than the two I've already got, I'm being punished for my earlier selfish wish. Just another one or two and I won't feel like I failed you. If we have another child and it's a boy, we'll name him Igor, after your uncle. I was surprised you didn't name Fedya after him."

"Two is enough for now, and we're not married yet. I remember going to Kat's house for her birthday parties, name-day celebrations, and visiting, and her mother, when she made an appearance, always looked half-crazy and like she had no life left in her."

"Petya's mother was never driven half-insane because she had a dozen children."

"When I'm back in Manhattan, I'll only spend as much money as I need to, and by September, we'll have a lot of money for our wedding. The sooner we get rid of all that shameful money in the bank, the better."

"You're ashamed of the gruesome thing you did to Basil's corpse for money?"

"I'll never feel ashamed of that. I just don't want your money in the bank to remind me of when you were a prostitute."

"We can also invest in stocks. Katrin is more than happy to

give us pointers on which ones to invest in and how much."

"That woman is hardly a paragon of virtues."

"Not our kind of virtues, no, but someday she feels the things she believes in will be common across the land, among more than a small but determined minority."

8

Katrin hasn't given up her day job just because she's on holiday. In the evening, while she and the others are poolside at their hotel's indoor pool, she's brought her typewriter and a stack of paper to write more articles. The one she has with her now is her Estonian typewriter. The Russian typewriter is back in the hotel room, a brand-new typewriter she bought shortly after her arrival in America two years ago. Katrin glued shreds of paper inscribed with the older pre-Revolution equivalents to the keys with the new, unfamiliar letters. When she goes to type the letter she grew up with, she can quickly access the right key without having to look it up in a book on the new lettering system. She especially misses Yat, Ѣ ѣ, which was replaced by a much less pretty letter, Е е.

Anastasiya plops down beside her. "I've been thinking all today my fate has been staring me in the face for ages. I'm coming to see what you've been preaching all these years, Katya, about how one need not marry to feel whole. I have a business now, with my name in the title—"

"Can you please stop calling me Katya? That's the equivalent of an American Negro's slave name." Katrin continues tapping away at the typewriter.

Viktoriya starts splashing several of the children in the indoor pool and shouting curses at them in Estonian.

"You see, children are obnoxious, whether it's being an inconsiderate brat, like these children refusing to share the pool, or an all-and-out crass, loudmouthed teenager like your long-lost sister."

"Yes, children sure are obnoxious, but not if you raise them correctly. I'll make sure Oliivia or Marek is raised to know what an indoor voice is, and most of all to recognize what behavior is obnoxious and uncivilized in public."

"Katrin, these little brats almost killed me!" Viktoriya shouts as she comes out of the water. "These merry pranksters were doing stunts underwater, inconsiderate of how I was trying to swim! And like hell I want to swim around those girls every time I do a lap!"

"Excuse me." Katrin stands up and walks towards the parents of the brats in the pool, holding herself as regally as she can. "Are you not aware the behavior of your children is rude and inconsiderate to people who want to use the pool for swimming? My little sister expects to be able to swim back and forth peacefully, instead of unexpectedly bumping into people doing pranks underwater! I'll personally pay for a pool your little savages can fool about in."

"They kicked me when they were underwater," Viktoriya goes on in Estonian. "You don't want them to make you miscarry if they do the same to you when you're trying to swim too."

"Look at that crazy woman, causing another public scene!" Ivan shouts. "And this must be more of her insane left-wing propaganda she's so keen on! She can't even leave it behind when she's on holiday!"

Aleksey's eyes nearly fall out of his head when he sees Katrin's latest efforts. "From what I can understand of this, she's oh-so-openly advocating a sterilization operation for women after they think they've had enough children! She even supplies the names and addresses of doctors who'd stoop so low as to do this thing, and other doctors who gladly terminate pregnancies!"

"I can't believe how selfish she is! My cousin Vasya wouldn't be here if my aunt had gotten sterilized!"

"Sterilization doesn't sound half-bad," Kat says. "My mother was always having nervous breakdowns because she had fifteen children. Her mental health would've been fine if she'd gotten sterilized after, say, Likonya, her sixth child."

"If she *had* gotten sterilized after Likonya, you wouldn't have been born," Nikolas says in a timid voice.

"We're not having more children until our twins are at least five years old," Kat says. "Likonya said things only got worse after her. Each time a new daughter arrived like clockwork each year, until I finally came along and she was able to get sterilized with the permission of our priest, she just screamed crazily for the midwife to take it away. She tried suicide several times, because she didn't want to deal with having fifteen children."

"That was extremely selfish. Petya's mother never fell apart because she had a dozen children! My own mother would've loved to be in your mother's position," Ivan says.

"Mrs. Litvinova had help in taking care of all those children, because their family was well-off. Even with us being upper-middle-class, we never had even a housekeeper or nanny. It was just my mother and her increasingly large menagerie of girls."

Anastasiya sighs in disgust when the three lifeguards come over and escort the troublesome children and their parents out of the pool area. Katrin and Viktoriya are smirking triumphantly.

Coney Island has become a weird nightmare for Ivan. After two whole weeks of Katrin's public and private scenes, strange food, long lines at the rides, an accident with a train which leaves six people injured, frightening people in the circus freak show, and studiously avoiding Alya and Anya, he's more than glad to finally go back to the dirty tenement with Aleksey and Nikolas.

****

Chapter 38: Long Island

"I can't believe I didn't make Lyuba come home with me after that nightmare. I'm never going back to that island Hell again. Praise Christ they're in a private cottage in Sea Cliff, instead of a place swarming with insane people, social degenerates, and nightmarish attractions. I can't believe Katrin didn't care Fedya was crying hysterically when we went into Hellgate, or that your twins were likewise frightened by that grotesque freak show with bearded women, dwarves, toothless Negroes, giants, and children with faces like dogs and elephants!"

"I don't want to go back next year either," Nikolas says. "I also wanted Kat, Kittey, and the twins to come back with me. I don't want to leave any of them in the same company as those twisted deviants we thought we knew."

"They should've kept it secret so we wouldn't feel strange around them," Aleksey agrees. "At least they're not homosexual men."

"I hope Lyuba doesn't change her mind and decide to be unfaithful to me while she's away," Ivan says. "She swore to me she'd never commit adultery. Today after work, I'm going to church to arrange a September wedding."

"Look at that *svoloch*, watching us through his glass peepholes." Aleksey glares up at the corner of the ceiling. "Like he thinks we'll steal molten iron ore, tongs, or trays on wheels. We should've been working in a garment factory instead of here."

"That's women's work."

"You're the one who doesn't bat an eyelash about cooking and taking care of small children!"

"My small children are now apart from me, where I can't protect them from the evil influences of Katrin, her big-mouthed little sister, or those twisted deviants who need medical help so they'll start preferring men again! Fedya won't see me for two whole months!"

"I've always been with Kolyechka except that time in Pskov, and I'm not having hysteric fits about whether or not he's being taken care of well. Liza even willingly sent him over the border into Estonia with Kolya and Kat while she waited for me to return."

"He wasn't in the company of those deviants or that insane woman. I can't believe she thought it was exciting when she was on that miniature railroad and that trestle ten feet up collapsed! She's pregnant, and could've been one of those six people who got injured!"

"Look, it *is* Katrin's money, and it *is* her business if she's chosen to continue paying for Alya and Anya's vacation, despite knowing they're touched in the head and prefer women, most notably each other."

"At this rate, I'd prefer Lyuba take her holiday with Malenkov!"

2

Boris stands alert at afternoon Divine Liturgy with his students, making faces at Granyechka and Gosha as they stand beside Father Spiridon. He's convinced himself he wouldn't have wanted her anyway, since she's too otherworldly and moral for the likes of himself, always saying God will forgive everyone for everything, even praying for the souls of the Bolsheviks he had to go into hiding from.

"My daughter would like our congregation to, if the spirit so moves them, make prayers as often as they see fit for her health, and the health of her unborn baby, in the coming months. She's about two months along, and feels it's overly superstitious to put off announcing such news until the end of the third month."

Boris drops his candle in rage and pushes his way out through the standing crowd, kicking his smaller students to the ground.

"The carpet is on fire, Borya!" Sashura screams.

"Put it out yourself, you *suka*."

"This man is a teacher at your religious school?" an angry woman demands of Father Spiridon.

"He used to be engaged to me, and is angry I wasn't able to marry him after his diagnoses of impotence and infertility," Granyechka says. "This isn't the real Boris talking. But God will forgive him. God always forgives everyone for everything."

Boris turns red in shame upon having this personal news revealed. And of course, the next special extracurricular assignment for his students is to make congratulatory cards for Granyechka and Gosha, and to pool their money to buy a group present for the baby and each of the parents. Boris thinks darkly that Granyechka's next move to spite him will be to take a job teaching at the religious school, or worse yet, decide to become his student teacher.

"We want to know how Granyechka came to be having a baby,"

Dusyechka says. "Nothing in the Gospel explains about it."

Boris drags the four-year-old to the corner of the room where the smaller children have their art time and plunks a block of soap into her mouth. "That will teach you to never ask such a vulgar question again."

"Granyechka isn't vulgar!" Nyushenka protests. "She's sweet, kind, and always says wonderful things when she visits our classroom!"

"I can understand how you'd call *yourself* vulgar for having a child out of wedlock, but not Granyechka!" fifteen-year-old Zhenya shouts.

"Nice, polite schools don't dare teach their young impressionable students horrible things like reproduction! Anyone else who wants to open his mouth to talk about that slut Granyechka or her unborn baby that should rightfully have been *mine* is getting a thrashing with that stick!"

3

Katrin's servants have joined the others at the five-story cottage in Sea Cliff, Long Island. Kat is positively horrified Mrs. Samson, the maid, is Negro. Lately, Kat has been seen going into little outbursts, usually directed against Alya and Anya or Anastasiya, and prefers to sit alone on the beach or go out in the water with only Kittey. She also refuses to talk on the phone to Nikolas after Kittey makes the call with Katrin's money, since Nikolas can't afford long-distance calls.

"Did you have a fight before he went home?" Kittey pesters out on the rocks one morning. "Or are you driven crazy being away from my brother for this long?"

"I don't know if I can face him when we go home!" Kat cries. "I'd never divorce Kolya, since he's a good person and I love him dearly, but he has this crazy idea having another baby is a great idea! Lyuda and Raya are only fifteen months old, and I'm still nursing them!"

"Are you sure he meant right away?" Kittey asks. "I told him I'd like you to put about four years between your kids. What if you have twins again! You'd have your hands full, and couldn't work anymore. You're lucky you get to bring Lyuda and Raya to work. Where could you stick a third baby, with Lyuba? She's got her own hands full."

"Kolya told me, in no uncertain terms, the moment I get back, he wants to start trying for another baby."

"You already bring Lyuda and Raya to work every day. They'd fire you for sure if you added another baby."

"My mother couldn't handle more kids, yet my father persuaded her they needed to keep trying for a boy. He told her to her face that Grafya, Agnessa, Adaliya, Alina, Yuliya, and Likonya were 'just for practice' when she was pregnant with what they hoped was finally a boy after six daughters, but turned out being Dina. Maybe women like Mrs. Litvinova pulled it off without completely losing their sanity, but we all know she was special if she could give birth to such a saint as Petya. I know she loved all fifteen of us, but she didn't want to partition her attentions fifteen separate ways all the time."

"You could fool Kolya and use an artificial method like a diaphragm."

"It isn't allowed by the Church. You know that. But there *are* means of preventing unwanted pregnancies by natural methods."

"My parents must've done that if they only had Kolya and me, and put seven years between us."

Kat shudders as she sees Anya walking on the rocks another beach down, hand in hand with Alya, laughing gaily about something, as though they haven't been excommunicated from their former friends. "I cannot believe that degenerate took care of you in the labor camp. Thank God Kolya never felt he owed her a relationship because of that. Look at what might've happened if they'd married and he'd found out he'd been played for a fool, used in a cover marriage like they talked about when I unwillingly spied on them, while his wife pursued unnatural sexual dalliances behind his trusting back."

"I know. When we all lived together in the valley, I was closer to Anya than you. I still can't believe she could be so loving and nurturing to me and turn around and do this behind our backs for oh-so-many years."

"You were lucky they disappeared, so you could become my little sister and I could steer you in the right direction. I can't bear to think about her being there instead of me as you've become a young woman."

"They're still in our cottage, though!"

"Yes, and to think they're staying on the floor right above ours! If Katrin were any sort of decent woman, she'd have sent them packing instead of continuing to finance their summer holiday!"

"She did say she feels strange around them now, since learning their dirty little secret, though she doesn't consider them deviants."

"Katrin is still swept up with the spirit of youthful rebellion, instead of putting it away after becoming a married woman with a baby on the way. When one becomes an adult, one must put away all vain illusions of youth, like overthrowing governments, espousing radical political ideologies, and flagrantly flouting the Establishment. Dressing like a flapper is one thing, since those clothes are easier to get around in, but not the radical left-wing rhetoric!"

"Now that I'm older, I understand but don't agree with her anger at our murdered Divine-righted. The rulers they dispatched to her country were indeed foreigners in a land they had no true linkage to. But now she's in America, and needs to put away such crazy ideas."

4

Katrin has put away none of her ideas. Right now she's evaluating several local radical organizations that jive with her beliefs, deciding which one she'll become a temporary member of while on Long Island.

"Your husband lets you do this crazy stuff, Katya?" Anastasiya is whining.

"Unlike many men, Sandro has no qualms whatsoever about a working wife. This isn't our parents' generation. Nowadays, in most places, an unaccompanied woman is no longer arrested or chased away for daring to want to eat at a restaurant or stay in a hotel room alone. And I've told you over and over again to quit calling me Katya already."

"Sometimes I wonder why you're still my best friend."

"Because I saved your hide on at least three distinct occasions. Let's not forget how no one but me wanted you in the band. And then you continued to leech off me in America. Until I got home from my honeymoon, you were living it up in my penthouse and not doing a lick of work, not even light housework. You also owe all your possessions to me. I snuck into your house, hysterical, and saved your most important possessions—family photographs, your numerous sketchpads, your favorite clothes, and everything else you brought to America. You would've been left with only the clothes on your back if you hadn't had me."

"I don't even know you anymore."

"You always knew the real me. I'm just a little older, wiser, and less hypocritical now. As it says in the Bible, 'When I was a child, I spoke as a child, I understood as a child, I thought as a child, but when I became an adult, I put away childish things.'"

5

Kat and Kittey have now abandoned the rocks and are walking the beach with their friends, keeping close watch over Alya and Anya three beaches down.

"This is a whole sight better than that Coney Island beach," Eliisabet comments. "With that ugly tan sand they pumped in to make room for a stupid Boardwalk."

"Tanyechka and I are making boxes with seashells glued on," Lyuba says. "One for my mother, one for my aunt, one for Vanya's aunt, one for Sveta, one for Allochka, and the last for little Natasha Yeltsina."

"And one for *Babushka* Shura!" Tatyana adds.

"It shocks me when you call Boris's parents by their diminutives," Kittey tells Lyuba. "It seems like it'd take years of friendship for someone to start calling her elders by such affectionate appellations instead of the usual first name and patronymic."

"They invited me to use *ty* and to call them by their nicknames two years ago. Shura said it would be an honor, and I was more than happy to adapt to it."

"Are they invited to your wedding?" Eliisabet asks.

"If I ever have a wedding. Yesterday on the phone, Vanya said he still hasn't talked to Father Yakim, saying maybe we should do it at a different church, because Father Yakim knows we live in sin and I have two children by two different fathers."

"You should've said yes when he first proposed six years ago," Kittey says. "Then you would've been safe in America all this time and able to have as many children as you wanted."

"I really will leave him if he still has no date set for our long-overdue wedding by the time we get back to Manhattan."

"But you went through so much heartache and grief since

you've known one another!" Kat protests. "You could honestly just take your kids and leave, and never feel the slightest bit tempted to come back?"

"Vanya would probably kill himself if I left him for good and it became clear I'd never come back, ever again, but I could start making a life for myself and my kids. I could work instead of sitting around at home all day long doing chores while my partner in living in sin gets exploited with a smile, bringing home only a pittance a week."

"You'd willingly have the suicide of the love of your life on your conscience for the rest of your life?" Eliisabet asks.

"I'd always have happy memories of him. We've been through so much together, but that man takes me for granted, thinking I'll always come back to him after I've left him or that it'll all work out for better in the end. Out of the three of us, Liza, you're the only one who has a happy marriage that never once had any rough spots. Alyoshka didn't fool around about making you a respectable woman, nor has he ever been on your back like Kolya is with Kat now, hassling her about having more children long before she's ready for it."

"And how would you go about raising Tanyechka all by yourself? She'd miss Ivan, and Fedya's far too young to remember his father."

"I'd write Vanya letters every so often, of course. But if he finally does the right thing and marries me in two months, I won't have to worry about how I'll manage if we have to walk out on him."

6

Everyone is woken on August 3 by the screams of Katrin's cook Mrs. Oswald. Her screaming soon sets off Anastasiya's bird, and then Anastasiya begins hollering as well.

"A national tragedy has struck, Mrs. Kalvik-Nikonova! The President of the United States has died!"

Katrin grabs *The New York Times* from her. "Well, he's dead. He was bad for my fellow immigrants. I wish we didn't have to get another Republican in his place."

Anastasiya starts screaming too. "Now everything will fall into utter ruin, just like when the Russian Empire changed governments and the Tsar was murdered in cold blood by those awful, godless Bolsheviks!"

"We have a vice president, Nastya. Everything's set up perfectly to avoid chaos in situations like this. Why are you crying? A shallow fashion plate who cares more about clothes, celebrities, fads, and fashions than important matters like politics can't care too deeply about someone you never voted into office, or voted against, for that matter."

"What's going on here?" Viktoriya asks.

"President Harding died. Now we have President Coolidge."

"What wonderful news. I hated that man from the very moment I began reading about him in the newspapers!" Viktoriya skips off to the breakfast table set by a huge window overlooking the ocean.

"And I've pretty much hated your little sister from the very moment she reappeared," Anastasiya says.

"Would you have preferred I kick her out and make her live out on the streets like a homeless person?"

"Hello? You did that to your parents when they appeared at your penthouse during your wedding banquet!"

"They're grown adults, and very much capable of finding work and a place to live. Vika's only sixteen, and needs adult care and supervision. Besides, I love her and am thrilled to have a second chance to be sisters."

Lyuba comes down the stairs to use Katrin's phone, still clad in her rumpled white pajamas.

"I think I'm going to have a celebration tonight for the passing of the torch to Vice President Coolidge," Katrin says. "Did you know that clown Harding died, Lyuba?"

"The President is dead?"

"And he's never coming back." Viktoriya grins.

"This could be the start of something awful! After those godless regicidists murdered the Tsar, things only got worse and worse!"

"There's no violent revolution brewing in America," Katrin says. "Why haven't you put on your day clothes yet?"

"I'll do that later, after I'm off the phone and Vanya gets on the next ferry with my stepsister Sveta."

"Are you going to demand he marry you right here and now? If Sandro had done that to *me*, playing around with my feelings like that for as long as Ivan's been pulling your strings and refusing to marry you, I would've walked out on him."

Lyuba picks up the receiver and gives the operator the address and apartment number, then listens to the phone ringing and ringing with no reply.

"He's probably already run off to that stupid job of his," Katrin says.

"Hello?"

"Why didn't you pick up as soon as it began ringing? And why are you home at this hour? Doesn't your job start at seven in the morning, and here you are at eight in the morning still at home!"

"Mr. Glazov declared a day off after he found out President Harding died."

"You're going to have as many days off as it takes, because right now you're going to grab my stepsister Sveta and hop on the next ferry. I need you here right now!"

"If you miss me that much, why don't you come home?"

"If I tell you why you must come at once with Sveta, I doubt you'll be able to make it off the ferry without having a heart attack of panic. Do as I say, and you can panic to your heart's content once you're where you're needed, with Sveta at your side."

"What does your stepsister have to do with any of this, love?"

"This is an emergency, and you know what her nursing specialty is."

"Infants!"

"I can hear you starting to panic. Hold that thought until you're here and can see with your own two eyes just what I need you to be here for."

"What was that all about?" Katrin asks after Lyuba has hung up.

"When I woke up after your cook started screaming, I picked my baby up, and he was hotter than the Devil! When I took off his nightshirt and wrapped him in a wet hand towel, I heard his skin sizzling, and I think he's got a fever! And he's as limp as a rag!"

"For that you call Konev all the way out from Manhattan?" Anastasiya asks. "Fevers come and go."

"You don't have any kids, so you can say that." Katrin glares at her.

"You don't have children yet either!"

"Just what the hell do you think this bulge I'm carrying around with me is, decoration?"

"I don't even know you anymore since we came to America!" Anastasiya stalks away to her room and comforts herself with her pictures of Rudy and Dmitriy as she starts picking out black clothes to wear.

"Did you leave your daughter in the same room as the baby?"

"I sent Tanyechka downstairs to Liza and her children."

"My siblings and I were always catching things from each other. I know how cruel this sounds, but childhood mortality is Nature's way of controlling the population and ensuring survival of the fittest. When you only have a few kids instead of a huge pile of brats, there should be a modern way. Modern people can control the size and spacing of their families, and there should likewise be modern inoculations against these things. We're long past the days when it was normal to lose eighteen out of twenty kids to measles, scarlet fever, or diphtheria, but I long for a day when there's no childhood mortality and all diseases have been completely eliminated. There won't be any need for natural population controls then, since decent, educated people will have stopped having a whole slew of brats and will only have four or five."

7

Anastasiya is sitting on the front veranda, sipping a lemonade and absolutely sweltering in the early August heat, draped head to toe in black, when Ivan arrives with Svetlana.

"Who died, the grand duke or the actor?" he asks.

"Don't you joke around about my Rudy or Mitya dying! President Harding is the one I'm in mourning for!"

"You never even elected the man!"

"Vanya, get in here and stop talking to that woman," Lyuba commands. "I figured out God is punishing me for the great sin I had to go and commit twice."

"Your bastard son has a very high fever," Viktoriya says. "I can completely sympathize with having a child out of wedlock in the prior circumstances, but why'd you have to make her have a second child out of wedlock too? I'd feel dirty if I had two children by two different fathers."

"Why don't you shut your mouth, you little agitator, and stop dwelling on things you know nothing about!" Ivan snaps. "You're not in this relationship!"

"My sister would've left Sandro if he'd done what you're doing to this poor, innocent woman, skinflint."

"Your sister was the really skinflintish one, little girl, ordering all her wedding guests to offer up ten dollars each so she could go on her honeymoon! That woman is wealthy enough to easily afford twenty honeymoons! I wonder if she'll make her baby shower guests pay her ten dollars each too, so she can afford her hospital bills for giving birth!"

"That sounds like a good idea!" Katrin says.

"If I were your delivering doctor, I'd give your baby up for adoption so it wouldn't have you for a mother."

"Vanya!" Lyuba chides. "I ordered you to come here so you could be with your only blood child in case he dies, not to start fighting with Katrin again!"

Viktoriya sits reading Anastasiya's latest issue of *True Story* and all her precious English-language tabloids, with their cosmographs and wildly exaggerated news of the latest comings and goings of the sheiks and shebas of the silver screen, as the two new house-guests go upstairs with Lyuba.

"I wish the two of them would get struck down by lightning!"

"Everyone knows someone like Katrin and her little sister, the people who rub them the wrong way because of their vastly differing viewpoints on the world." Lyuba scoops up Fedya. "I drew all the shades in case it was heat exhaustion, but his skin still sizzles whenever I change the wet towels I've been wrapping him in."

"He's probably too little for most medicines," Svetlana fusses over her stepnephew. "In Siberia, I had to wait it out whenever a baby fell ill. There were always the days when a baby in the camp hospital would die, and the camp directors had to pitch the tiny bodies into one of the mass graves."

"He's too tiny to die," Ivan pronounces. "God made him so cute so the Angel of Death wouldn't take him before his time."

"This is a punishment for what we did that awful night. I should've learnt my lesson and not willingly done that. I should've insisted you use a prophylactic."

"You sure didn't think it was awful at the time! And you know now it's a miracle you had this little guy!"

"That very same miracle could've happened after I was a married woman. Speaking of, have you talked to Father Yakim yet about our wedding next month?"

Ivan hangs his head in shame.

"What are you waiting for? I'll walk out on you with my children if you don't have a date set by the time I return to Manhattan!"

"I'll talk to him as soon as I get back," he mumbles sheepishly.

"Everybody's aghast at how you're keeping me an unrespectable, fallen woman—myself, my mother, my aunt, your aunt, my stepfather, Ginny, Liza, Kat, Alyoshka, Kolya, Kittey, your aunt's new husband, my daughter, my uncle, Katrin, her little sister, my stepsisters, Pasha, those two deviants Alya and Anya, even that vain blonde woman on the front veranda!"

"Weren't you horrified at how you got my stepsister pregnant out of wedlock?" Svetlana asks. "Most men would drop to their knees and say they'd marry that woman as soon as humanly possible, not wait until that baby was fourteen months old!"

"Sveta, you saved his life before, and countless other babies, so you must know how to save him once again." Lyuba glares at Ivan.

"If the fever gets any worse, I'll have no choice but to find a priest to do Last Rites or Extreme Unction."

"He can't do Last Rites when he's unbaptized! My Tanyechka couldn't do Last Rites either!"

"Then if the worse comes to worst, the priest will baptize this little guy so he won't have to be denied Christian burial." Svetlana checks Fedya's vitals and shakes her head. "My guess is viral meningitis."

Over the ensuing week, Lyuba and Svetlana continuously push Ivan aside whenever he tries to take charge of the situation or offer a differing opinion. He ruminates darkly that it would've been better if Lyuba had just made Svetlana come. Now every hour he spends on Long Island in Katrin's fancy beachfront cottage equals out to less and less money earned from the exploitative Mr. Glazov for the entire month of August. The only person there who pays him any attention at all is Tatyana, who's delighted to see her father has joined them and makes him read her stories every night.

"Is it okay with you now if I return to the city?" he begs Lyuba toward the close of the second week of the meningitis. "You don't want me here. You said so yourself. You told me you only ordered me to come here in case Fedya died."

"You'd go back to the city and leave this feverish little boy who's barely fifteen months old to die alone but for his mother and his nurse?!" Lyuba screams. "Thank God we were never married, so we don't have to go through the trouble of getting a divorce or annulment. It's grounds for divorce if the wife can't bear the husband any children."

"The purpose of Orthodox marriage is the union of two people. Whether or not they have children has nothing to do with it. Why would God take this little guy away from us after he was kind enough to give him to us in the first place, *golubka*?"

"To punish us for having this bastard son out of wedlock. Katrin's little sister is right. I *do* feel dirty for having children by two different fathers."

Fedya starts screaming from the heat.

"You'll be out of your misery soon, baby," Lyuba whispers over him.

"What was that supposed to mean?"

"Nobody has fevers or meningitis in Paradise, *golubchik*."

"I told you, God made him so cute so the Angel of Death wouldn't dare snatch him before his time!"

"He's getting hotter and hotter and limper and limper every day. Sveta and I have been doing nothing but keeping all the shades and drapes drawn around the clock, wrapping his little, fragile, feverish body up in cold, wet hand towels, even sticking him into buckets full of ice water with freezing blocks of ice, and he's still burning up like the Devil! I've been forced to stop nursing him and start giving him bottles of bland store milk because he's so hot!" Lyuba sets him back on the bed. "Now you'll leave me because I gave you a dead baby."

"Before our Divine-righted were brutally slaughtered by the atheist Bolsheviks, that damned German woman had a hysterical pregnancy, and the Tsar never left *her*."

"They already had four daughters, none of whom had died."

Lyuba's face falls and starts shaking uncontrollably.

"Why don't you and Sveta go someplace nice this evening and leave me to sit with the baby. You're starting to have hysterics like Kat, though at least your hysterics are understandable. I can't believe Kat is so selfish, the thought of her loving husband wanting to start trying for more children is sending her into hysterical fits."

"Our baby is going to Hell!"

"No he's not. He's not going to die either."

"He's unbaptized, and unbaptized babies go directly to Hell!"

"Then why not have him baptized by the nearest priest if you're so concerned?"

"Because respectable priests refuse to baptize a baby who was born out of wedlock so long as the parents remain unmarried!"

"Pyotr the Great and Yekaterina the First's daughter Anna was also born out of wedlock, but made legitimate after her parents married."

"Something I sure as hell haven't seen you making any motions toward! Next month, you'll slip a wedding band onto my finger and make me Mrs. Koneva, enable my children to finally be baptized, and put an abrupt stop to us living in sin, or I'll walk out on you and take the kids with me, and you'll never see us again!"

"I told you, I'll talk to Father Yakim as soon as I return to the city!"

"Nothing's stopping you from doing it right now! You can march downstairs at any time and use the phone!"

"I don't like having to look at Katrin and that evil little sister of hers, or that vain blonde thing she brought with her. The only one in their party I can bear to talk to is Sandro, and even *he* doesn't like how I haven't married you yet."

8

That evening, Ivan comes back upstairs from using Katrin's phone and finds Lyuba and Svetlana screaming and weeping on their knees. The contents of Svetlana's medical bag are strewn all over the floor.

"He's dead," Lyuba informs him.

"Are you sure? Maybe he's in a coma like you were."

"He's dead, Ivan. As dead as my mother and the Tsar are dead," Svetlana says. "Now this poor little boy has gone to Hell, because you were selfish and refused to do the right thing by marrying Lyuba and enabling the baby to be baptized. That poor little innocent baby, all alone in Hell without his mother to hold him as he's being tortured by the Devil, and maybe running into that sick psychopath who was Lyuba's natural father!"

"I want to die too," Lyuba sobs. "I'm destined for Hell as well, since I killed that man who would've killed you. You're going to Hell also, for killing Basil and my father. If we kill ourselves, Fedya will soon have both his parents there to continue loving him. Well, there's no reason now for me to stay around. I'm going downstairs, and then we'll figure something out about how often we write or visit one another. Thank God I still have one child left, though her natural father is a man I never loved." Lyuba flies out of the room with Svetlana at her side.

"But I just called Father Yakim and have a date set for our wedding!"

"It's far too late," Svetlana says. "You can call him back right now and cancel."

Lyuba runs downstairs into Eliisabet's story of the cottage and scoops up Tatyana, who's playing pretend with Nikolay and Novomira.

"I'm leaving Vanya. There's no reason for me to marry him next month. My baby is dead. Thank God I still have Tanyechka."

"Who came to that conclusion?" Eliisabet demands. "What if it's just a coma like the one you had?"

"His fever is gone. He's as cold and clammy as a dead person. I'll spend the night here, and leave with my daughter in the morning. I can't bear to look at his tiny little body all night long. Sveta and I will take the pull-out bed in the davenport."

"Oh, no. You and your stepsister may have my bed, and I'll take the pull-out."

"I can't evict you from your rightful bed. I'll only be here tonight, anyway. After we take breakfast, I'll go back upstairs to get my things, and then I'm leaving. Perhaps I can stay with my mother and stepfather until I figure something out."

"You can stay with me across the hall," Svetlana offers. "Galya, Motya, and Allochka won't mind a new roommate."

"If you're going to refuse to take my bed and don't want me to sleep on the pull-out, my bed can take the three of us," Eliisabet says.

"I promise I'll write to you often, and if I end up living near enough to you, I'll call frequently also. You're my best friend, your kids are my godchildren, and my children would've been your godchildren if I'd gotten married and made them legitimate."

"Why are we leaving?" Tatyana asks.

"Something very awful happened to your baby brother. We're staying here tonight, and in the morning we're going home until I can figure out what to do with our living situation."

"I can't leave Kolya."

"We're not going to break off contact with Liza, Alyoshka, and their children. We'll visit and write often, and call if we live close enough. I don't want you to be a disgraceful fallen woman like your mother's always been. When you're old enough, you'll marry a man who knows how to be a good, honorable person, like Kolya."

9

Ivan is holding the small, limp body when he feels a very faint, infrequent pulse on the left wrist, but no breath. Svetlana has taken her nursing bag, and he has no idea how to jump-start an infant's breathing.

"Maybe you really were only meant to live for fifteen months," he says as he taps Fedya on the back lightly several times. "Your mother may think I'm a heretic for believing this, but I don't believe unbaptized babies go to Hell. That evil woman Katrin had a little sister who was only fifteen months old too, and she died a more horrific and terrified death than you."

Ivan glares at one of Katrin's recent Russian-language articles for one of the émigré presses, about how infant mortality isn't a tragedy, but a great way to control the population. He can't believe Lyuba has begun to read the things Katrin spouts off for the left-wing immigrant presses.

I am about to share with you, dear Readers, something which I have never shared with you before. You may already know I, Katariina Kaarelovna Kalvik-Nikonova, formerly just Nikonova, was the firstborn child of fairly wealthy Estonian parents who kowtowed to the Tsar, and that very recently, shortly before my wedding, I was most surprisingly reunited with my favorite sibling, fifteen-year-old Viktoriya. But I've never spoken at length with you all, most loyal dear Readers, about how my other siblings met their end. They were murdered by the Bolsheviks as I watched, and I didn't shed a tear, though, most thankfully, the assassin assigned to darling Vika misfired, and she survived without my knowledge for many years. There were five boys and three other girls, Karl, Nikita, Sergey, Lev, Yegor, Olga, Larisa, and Mariya. The boys were shot or stabbed, and the three girls had their necks broken and were flung most violently and brutally against a wall. The man in charge of murdering them walked all over little Olga on his way to do the same to Lara and Manyeshenka.

Am I a heartless person for watching this most grotesque and horrifying spectacle without shedding a tear or making a martyr of myself by trying to save even my favorite one, little Vika, who was but nine years old at the time? And would I not have wanted someone to do the same for me, or try to do the very same, if I'd been among their sorry little ranks? Well, I'm a firstborn child, and therefore more valuable, which was why I got away with my new friends the great Bolsheviks. Firstborn children are always the most valuable, which is why, though I'm currently pregnant without planning it, I decided not to have an operation to get rid of the unplanned child-to-be. This will also be a firstborn child, just like its mother.

Some cultures, like the Eskimos, kill all their daughters, even if they're firstborn children, because they want to have two boys in a row before they get the "luxury" of having girl children. But really, while barbaric, infant mortality, stillborns, abortions, and miscarriages are simply a fact of life and have been since the days of prehistoric human beings. This even happens in the animal kingdom, and was common practice in certain foreign nations. For example, fratricide was the law of the land in the Ottoman Empire, since there could only be one Sultan, and he didn't want all his hundreds of brothers from all different mothers constantly challenging or threatening to kill him to seize power for themselves at every turn.

My little Oliivia or Marek will be the firstborn of no more than five children at maximum, possibly six, if I have another accident years after I may think my family's complete. Just think of how many children some agrarian and extremely religious families have. If a newly-married Amish couple, for instance, eventually have a total of thirty children, after marrying at only fifteen or sixteen, and each of those children has thirty children also, and on and on ad infinitum until the world ends after the Sun has burnt out all its massive energy many billions of years down the road from now, just think of how many people the planet will be bending under the weight of. There are simply not enough resources to feed, clothe, and in general take care of so many trillions and up-

wards of people.

Now, if you've deliberately chosen to have more than five or six children, that's your own personal business, but just remember, not everyone wants to make the same choice you have, because they care about world overpopulation. By now, my three oldest little brothers, Karl, Nikita, and Sergey, would've been old enough to be married and have children of their own. I shudder to think of how many more people there might be in the world today, even that very small amount, if eight of my nine younger siblings were still alive.

Ivan throws the article onto the floor in disgust and starts whacking Fedya on the back violently. "Just to spite that disgusting woman so in love with secular humanism and upsetting the natural social order, I hope you recover and go on to have more than her precious five or six children!"

Fedya begins coughing, then crying.

"You're probably too young to know you gave your mother and her stepsister quite a scare. I can't believe your *Tyotya* Sveta just gave up on you after she saved your life when you were a newborn." Ivan pulls back the covers on the bed. "In the morning, we'll go down to your mother and sister and tell them the good news." He pulls his shoes off and lies beside Fedya, pulling him into the crook of his right elbow. "Your mother won't need to be scared anymore about you going to Hell. Early next month, on the second anniversary of your conception, you'll finally be made legitimate, better late than never, and baptized with your big sister."

10

In the morning, Ivan wakes up alone in the bed. He sits up to see if Fedya hasn't rolled under the bed, and he isn't there, nor by the little bed Tatyana used before her frantic mother sent her downstairs to Eliisabet and her children. The window was shut and locked for the evening, and Fedya is too short and undextrous to reach up, unlock, and open it all by himself...

"Where have you disappeared to, Fedyushka? I don't recall your mother coming back in here during the night, or anyone else for that matter."

Fedya toddles up and pulls on his father's left pant leg. "*Vot ya, Papa.*"

Ivan pulls the baby onto his lap. "You don't seem to have a fever now, and you're not cold and clammy anymore either."

"*Ya khochu Mamu i Tanyu.*"

Ivan goes downstairs to Eliisabet's floor, and nobody is there. Katrin's floor is empty as well, except for the canary. He picks up a huge rough draft of a "morality story" she's working on for a leftist Russian-language children's magazine, featuring a tale about a little Socialist girl who's rewarded for teaching her classmates at church about how evil the Tsar was and about the myths that make up Christianity, and tosses it onto the floor, hoping it takes her hours to put the plus-fifteen pages back into their proper order.

The others are down at the beach. Lyudmila and Raisa are at the water's edge with Kittey, collecting shells, while Kat is sitting under a large shade umbrella downing some sort of pills. Tatyana, Nikolay, and Novomira are building sandcastles. Viktoriya is out in the ocean, the water up to her mouth. Ivan hopes she slips on a patch of seaweed and drowns. Sandro and Katrin are reading the local radical English-language newspaper. Anastasiya is swooning over her belovèd pictures of Rudy and Dmitriy. Lyuba, Svetlana, and Eliisabet are having a heated conversation, which he suspects is about himself and his reticence to stop living in sin.

"What kind of an infant nurse are you to just give up on a little boy when he's not dead?" Ivan demands. "Did you not feel a very faint, infrequent pulse? I'm not a doctor, but I just hit him on the back to start him breathing again!"

Svetlana stands up. "Fedya's alive?"

Ivan pushes him at her. "Your stepnephew doesn't have a fever anymore. I saw a lunatic article that crazy Bolshevik flapper woman wrote, about how infant mortality isn't a tragedy but a great way to control the population, and I decided I'd try to save his life just to spite her."

"Did you like my work?" Katrin asks.

"I hope that child you're pregnant with dies of infant mortality or is stillborn, so you'll learn it *is* a tragedy when any child dies or looks like it's going to die!"

"I don't want Oliivia or Marek to die, since my baby will be a firstborn child. And I was speaking of people who have far more children than is proper, not modern, normal people who wisely have only four or five kids."

Lyuba grabs Fedya from her stepsister and hugs him tightly to herself. “I’ve had enough of this vacation, Vanya. I want to come home with you.”

Lyuba desperately begins to hate the tenement again the moment she sets foot back in it that night, and the poor money Ivan drags in, and how they can’t live as extravagantly as Katrin and Anastasiya, but she’s come home to be with the only man she’s ever wanted, loved, and needed, the father of her son and the soon-to-be-stepfather of her daughter. With that in mind, she begins to think about their coming wedding, when she’ll no longer be a fallen, unrespectable woman, but instead Lyubov Koneva, a woman with baptized, legitimate children and a wedding ring on her finger.

****

Chapter 39: Cold Feet

"Are you sure you don't want Anastasiya to design your wedding gown?" Eliisabet insists in the changing room of the Upper East Side bridal shop. "As a way of showing her past involvement with Ivan, however transitory and meaningless it was—they never even kissed!—is just water under the bridge now and all is forgiven? You saw how fabulous Katrin's wedding gown was, and all the hundreds of women she's made gowns for can't be wrong."

"Knowing that awful, superficial woman, she'd probably rig it so the buttons start popping off during the ceremony!"

"You'll have to give her a break sometime. After all, you forgave Katrin."

"Katrin was never after Vanya, and underneath all her radical politics and near-godlessness, she's a highly intelligent, educated woman. And her walls aren't covered in pictures of actors and handsome royals."

Lyuba sits alone in the changing room after Eliisabet goes to pay for her matron of honor gown, thinking about how she's but one week away from being made a respectable woman. The stability and finality of it all have never come to creep into her thoughts until just now. Once she's married, she'll never be able to commit adultery or run away from Ivan because she feels scared of his love for her. Anastasiya would've never sat around for so long, content to remain unmarried and living in sin before Ivan married her almost as an afterthought after so long of premarital cohabiting. Boris was ready, able, and willing to marry her long ago. He really does seem to have changed his ways, and her rejection of him is the only reason he's being so mean, bitter, and vindictive towards his students...

"Please wrap this up and send it back to my place," Lyuba instructs the shop owner. "I already paid for it. I have to go somewhere for awhile before I return home, and I don't know for certain how long I'll be gone."

"Your wish is my command, Miss Zhukova."

Ivan has already returned home from the bridal shop and is now anxiously waiting on Lyuba. Eliisabet has just dropped off Tatyana and Fedya, and he cannot see Lyuba leaving him and the children as well...

2

Boris looks up in delighted surprise when he sees Lyuba entering his house that evening, without Tatyana. His parents are trying their hand at an English-language crossword puzzle in the newspaper two rooms over.

"I don't know if I can marry Ivan next week, Borya."

"Where's our daughter?"

"Liza sent her and Fedya back to Vanya. I'm staying here until I figure out whether I can stomach being married to Ivan for the rest of my life. I never once thought about just how final this would be!"

"Of course I still want you to marry me so we can raise our daughter together, but if you marry Ivan, you'll stand a bit of a better chance of someday having more children than if you marry me. Together, we're nearly unable to have further children, and there's nothing wrong with Konev that I know of."

"But with you, I wouldn't have my hopes built up for more children."

"What about your existing children?"

"Ivan can have both of them forever. Besides, you always were the boy all our friends thought I preferred over Vanya, Petya, and that vile Basil. If I decide I want to marry you, there will simply be some murmuring when Father Yakim sees a different groom than the one he expected."

Mrs. Malenkova comes into the front room. "What's Lyuba doing here?"

"It's a last-minute miracle!" Boris shrills like an overeager schoolboy. "Lyuba says she may yet decide to marry me instead of Ivan before it's too late and she'll have to go through an annulment! I always knew she'd pick me instead of him! When you choose the one you love, you're always happier in the end. Only she didn't bring our daughter, and I don't want Ivan raising her, since she's mine, and Lyuba will be marrying me instead now."

"That's craziness!" Mrs. Malenkova declares. "Sanya, come hear what our irresponsible, juvenile son is saying!"

"Lyuba says she may possibly decide to marry me instead of that bully Konev!" Boris is beaming a mile a minute. "Praise the

Lord!"

"This poor woman is just having cold feet! Shame on you for encouraging her instead of ordering her to march right back to her fiancé and children! I had cold feet before I married your father, but thankfully was spotted running away from the church that morning and had some real sense talked into me by my three older sisters!"

"Boris *is* the sensible choice, Shura," Lyuba says softly. "He's financially secure, lives well, makes a lot of money, a lot more than I'll ever see if I marry Ivan, was ready and willing to marry me quite a long time ago, he's like a son to my mother, and I truly believe he's repented of all his horrible sins."

"You haven't been with Boris for two years! The last time you were together, I feared he'd begin abusing you again because of the way he was yelling at you and your little daughter!"

"He was yelling at me because I didn't want to sleep with him, not because he was angry at the political situation or using drugs."

"And you *could* sleep with him now? This man is impotent and unable to have another child! With Ivan, you at least stand a little chance of having a third child. There's no medical problem standing in the way of *him* having more children!"

"I know what I'm getting with Borya. He knows he won't be able to have more children, while Ivan's always wanted nine children and tells me we have seven more to go, despite the fact that I'll be lucky if I ever have a third."

"Don't you want a third child and even a fourth?"

"Of course, but I know that's impossible. If I dwell on it too much and too often, I'll launch myself into melancholia."

"But Boris isn't only infertile, he's impotent too! That would be an entirely celibate marriage!"

"We already have a child, *Matushka*," Boris says. "What, are you blind?"

"You talk as though that innocent little child was born out of love! She wasn't! You could've easily killed her many times before she was born because of how you beat Lyuba! And you got Lyuba drunk when it became clear she didn't want to sleep with you!"

Lyuba nods. "That's true, and I don't remember what happened that night. I only remember the next morning, waking up in the bed in the cabin beside your son and feeling horrible once I realized what happened after I lapsed out, since I'd slept with the best friend of the man I loved."

"And now you're going to be marrying his best friend too," Mr. Malenkov says in disgust.

"That man isn't my best friend anymore, but once I marry Lyuba and he once again realizes she was always mine and never truly his, I do so hope we can begin healing and rebuilding our friendship. I'll pay for all three of us to attend psychotherapy together."

Lyuba goes into Boris's bedroom. "Are you really ready for marriage when there are posters of other women plastered all over your walls?"

"Of course I still have all my pictures of you and Tanyechka on my night table," Boris gushes like a little boy. "You shouldn't have any rational reasons to be jealous of my posters of the shebas of the silver screen."

"I don't have any pictures of the sheiks of the silver screen!"

"You do know men are the weaker sex, Lyubashechka."

Lyuba bristles. "Only my mother and Vanya have ever called me Lyubashechka."

"Though we probably can't have more children, I can go to a psychotherapist to cure my impotence, and we can have a normal marriage. Everybody these days is in love with Freud, so I've been looking over some of his stuff, in both German and English, at nights when I come home from work. Some of it does seem a bit out there, but all the rest is right on the mark."

"Is that the man who thinks all children are sexually attracted to the parent of the opposite sex and feel threatened by the parent of the same sex?" Mrs. Malenkova asks. "By that standard, you're sexually attracted to *me*, your own mother, and afraid your father will castrate you."

"I said not all of it makes a great deal of sense."

Lyuba's eyes grow sad. "I'd still feel a little bit guilty, though, about how if I decide to go through with it and marry you instead of Ivan, Fedya would have to take your surname and be raised by someone who's not his father."

"That would serve Konev right. He'll soon see what it feels like when another man he thought was his best friend begins raising his own flesh and blood child like it's his damn own and turning the child against him. He did it for four and a half years with our precious little Tanyechka, and now I have the perfect opportunity for revenge."

Mr. Malenkov gives his son the evil eye. "Konev never abandoned his child moments before the mother went into labor."

"You keep quiet and keep out of this, *Batya*!"

3

Ivan is furious Lyuba has run away to Boris again, after such a long time without any relapses. He's gotten the infuriating news from none other than Boris himself, late at night, leaving almost no time to figure out where to stick Fedya and Tatyana until Lyuba comes back to her senses. Everyone he knows works, even the women. Kat, who hasn't returned from Long Island yet, and Eliisabet, who bring their children to work with them, are allowed that privilege because they only have two children apiece, not four. He finally gets eighteen-year-old Vera to make the trip back to their seedy part of the Lower East Side to watch the children for the next ten hours.

Boris meanwhile has made a total metamorphosis at the religious school. He's been nothing but sweet, kind, polite, and humoring to even the youngest children. He reads the religious storybooks in a honey-sweet voice; personally escorts the younger ones to the lavatory with an older companion; gets out a broom and sweeps away the crumbs left from lunch in the classroom; doesn't bat an eyelash at three ikons which are hanging slightly crooked; takes on a baby-talking voice of delight and pretended emotion when the younger ones talk about asinine matters like their new clothes; goes over the menu the oldest students have drawn up for their graduation supper without grumbling at a one of them; and talks well of Granyechka when several of the intermediate-aged students show him the satin pillow with ribbons and lace which they're making for her baby-to-be.

"Did you have a religious experience?" Danya asks towards the end of the day. "You're being so nice to us instead of mean like before."

"The mother of my child has moved back in with me!"

The older students all gasp in unison and begin crossing themselves.

"Isn't your illegitimate child's mother supposed to be only one week away from marrying another man?" Zhenya asks.

"The man she'll be marrying in a week's time is myself, not Konev. Is that the final question on this line of subject matter?"

Father Spiridon comes into the classroom. "Well, Boris, today when you had the students in the chapel for prayer, you were better-behaved than you've been in at least six months!"

"I am extremely well-behaved and happy today, *Batyushka*, because at long last the mother of my child has moved back in with me and my parents, and we're getting married next week! It was a last-minute miracle!"

"Did you manipulate her into this shocking last-minute change of heart?"

"She came over all by herself last night. I didn't know she was on her way over until she walked in the door. She left our daughter and her son with Konev, so we'll have to work out the transfer of the children very soon."

"What is this, you tried to ruin Granyechka's marriage, and now you're going to bring scandal to a marriage that was supposed to be only a mere week away?"

"Now we won't have to go through court begging Konev to relinquish that iron fist he's got over my rightful flesh and blood daughter."

"You think he can just give up on raising that cute little girl as his daughter after she's been with him for the past four years and seven months?"

"Since I'm marrying her mother very shortly, no judge in his right mind would want to break up a family and hand over a newly-married couple's sweet little daughter to be raised by a man who's no relation to any of them."

"I hope you realize she's very possibly only exhibiting a case of cold feet and deciding to have one last hurrah with you. Don't let your hopes get dashed after unrealistic building-up if she does indeed decide to leave you and go back to her fiancé before any more scandal is thrown into her hard life."

4

Mrs. Lebedeva is stunned and furious as well at what her

daughter has done. That evening, she goes through the wedding presents everyone in her household bought for the impending bride and groom, and thinks in disgust just how much money it cost to foot the bills, and that the nametags will all have to be changed. And what use does Boris have for all these divine wedding presents when he makes enough money to live comfortably and lives in a house instead of a squalid tenement? He has sports equipment; posters of all the shebas of the silver screen; many books, a bunch of which are quite scandalous and titillating in nature; fancy, expensive, gilded photo albums; a new-fangled gramophone that plays 78s; nice bath articles, like colored, scented soaps shaped like various seashells and sea creatures; a fancy, exquisite, illuminated Bible with the cover entirely in gold leaf, with a very expensive crucifix glued on; expensive ikons; and now a $500 orange leather Ottoman recliner, because Freud has one just like it for his patients. To say nothing of the things Boris has bought for his parents.

"You could paint over Ivan's name and replace it with Boris's," Ginny suggests.

"Would you want *your* gift tags on *your* future wedding presents to have another man's name painted out with yours written over on top?" his mother asks from the other side of the room.

"What wedding, *Matushka*? I'm only sixteen!"

"You don't notice any girls at church yet who suit your fancy?"

"I know you don't approve of my doing this, but I still write letters back and forth with Zhora, and I told her about Lyuba's wedding. In her last letter, which I received the other day, she sent a little card of congratulations and said Lyuba and Ivan will get a surprise present from Pyotr. I guess Petya's package should arrive any day now."

"Oh, even that Bolshevik Litvinov would've been a better man for her than Boris!" Mrs. Kharzina laments. "Between the three of them, Ivan was always the best thing that ever happened to your cousin, but Pyotr came a close second place."

"Lyuba said she would've married him instead of Ivan if she had to stay behind in Russia. They even had a brief relationship while we were in Tver."

"What do you mean by 'brief relationship'?" Mrs. Lebedeva asks suspiciously.

"For about three weeks, they were lovers."

Mrs. Lebedeva's jaw drops.

"She was a grown woman, *Tyotya* Katya. She came to him and seduced him. He was nearly twenty-one, and saved himself for her. Lyuba was Pyotr's first lover."

"Thank God Boris gave her that internal damage! Any other woman would've had a lot more children than just two with that much rampant fornicating going on!"

Vera comes through the door. "Ivan paid me a quarter for watching his kids today!" She holds up a shiny new Liberty Standing quarter. "I'm putting this into my piggybank with the other money I'm saving to afford a Hunter education."

"And you. Aren't you ashamed for your stepsister? Now we'll have to get completely new gift tags for all her wedding presents, since it'll look cheap and tacky to paint over Ivan's name and substitute Boris's. I told her over and over again, after I finally came to my senses, Ivan is the best thing who's ever happened to her, and here she is, a mere week away from her long-anticipated wedding, running back to Boris!"

"She's just having cold feet," Mrs. Kharzina says. "Trust me, she'll be back with Ivan within the next few days, when it all hits her."

"What I want to know is why she'd even consider marrying a man who's not only infertile, but impotent too! I was there in the waiting room with his mother, his priest, and that sweet girl he used to be engaged to until that moment, when the doctor came out and told us the bad news."

"If you try really hard, and you really want to have relations, it can happen," Vera says. "Not that I would know from personal experience, of course."

"Where have you learnt such bawdy things?" her father asks, his eyes wide.

"In the orphanage, we older girls snuck in books of a certain nature, sometimes Russian, but usually translations of British books from the Victorian era, or sometimes French erotica."

Mr. Lebedev's jaw drops also.

"I'm eighteen, Papa, old enough to be married." Vera slips the quarter back into her dusky purple beaded pocketbook, slung over her left shoulder. "To get back to the subject, I agree Lyuba's probably just having cold feet, but we can't force her to do anything. She has to decide to come back to Ivan because her heart tells her. If I had a fellow, I'd start to miss him powerfully if we were apart for too long."

5

Kat is less than enthusiastic when she, Kittey, and the twins go to meet Nikolas when they unboard the train that took them from the ferry the day after Labor Day. Katrin gives Nikolas a very dirty look before sauntering off on Sandro's arm. Viktoriya also makes a nasty face at him before skipping off with her sister and brother-in-law. Anastasiya gets into the streetcar with her bird and the other three people and gets off at her high-rise apartment. Katrin's three servants go the rest of the way back in a cab.

Kat shivers violently as Alya and Anya step off the train last of all and hail a cab. She prays that's the last time she's subjected to the sight of her two former friends.

"Why were that twisted Bolshevik woman and that crazy little sister of hers making such juvenile faces at me?" Nikolas asks.

"Word gets around fast, Kolya," Kat says.

"If anything, they should've made faces at those twisted sexual deviants, not me!"

"Public is no place to have an argument about how much in disagreement I am with your plans. I pray so much you've changed your mind since the last time we spoke."

"About having a third child? Lyuda and Raya are almost seventeen months old, and if you get pregnant right away, the new baby will only be two years apart from them."

"Oh, Kolya, you know how my dear mother practically went crazy on account of having fifteen children in a row!"

"I'm not suggesting we have fifteen."

"I'm not ready for another child."

"That's crazy talk! You've been hanging around Katrin far too long, I can tell. But I'll retrain you. You're not supposed to be prepared for more children, even if you want them. Children ideally are supposed to just happen as little miracles from God. We've got two already; what's one more or even a second set of twins if God so wills it? We'll *love* having more children! Think of it as a little playmate for Lyuda and Raya." Nikolas takes her luggage and carries it back to their tenement.

Kat lies in dread that night as Nikolas walks around their living quarters, checking on the windows and the lock on the door, and putting away the newspapers and books he spent the evening reading. If only he'd go back to reading his precious philosophy treatises, or rereading one of the classic Russian novels for the umpteenth time...

"I know everyone thinks of me as this purely philosophical guy who likes to spend all his free time reading, debating, and thinking, but I just couldn't resist myself when your parents found out I was back in Moskva and decided I had to start courting you. And obviously you saw something in me, otherwise you wouldn't have stayed with me for so long. I know you wouldn't have if you only felt sorry for me like you initially did."

"Don't think I'll consent to having another child long before I'm ready to start considering such an insane suggestion, just because I initially might feel sorry for you again."

"Oh, what nonsense. You'll *love* having another child!"

Kat just lies there and lets Nikolas do whatever he wants with her, knowing he's so submissive and weak-willed he won't mind her complete lack of reciprocation. In the morning, before heading to work, she goes to the library to check out a book on predicting the safe and unsafe times to have relations. She doesn't mind Maksim's horrified look when he sees the title of the English-language book she's checking out. Katrin's views on controlling the population may be a little bit extreme, but they're more in touch with most wives' personal reality than Nikolas's cavalier attitude of how babies "just happen" and that Kat will automatically love having another child long before she's ready.

"What if I tell your husband you're reading such an awful, immoral book behind his back, Mrs. Vishinskaya? I'm stunned the library carries such an evil book in broad daylight, without hiding it in brown paper wrappers."

"Mrs. Vrangel, you pig. My identity didn't disappear simply because I married. No one ever assumes a man should suddenly give up his lifelong name because he's married. Kolya's so enamored of philosophy, he'll probably think I'm expanding my knowledge of how my body works. If you tell him the real reason why I got this book out, I shall stab you to death with scores of thorns from my roses."

6

Lyuba wakes up in Boris's bed the morning of what would've been her long-awaited marriage to Ivan. Boris is out of the house, going for an early morning walk. The suit he bought for the wedding is hanging on the back of their bedroom door. Mr. Malenkov has already left for work.

"Shura, do you mind if I return to Vanya's house? I just realized I was a fool to move back in with Boris against my own better judgment. I hope Ivan can forgive me one last time and not throw me back out. I did abandon my children this time too."

"I think he'll find it much harder to forgive you if you marry my son this evening."

"I have your blessing?"

"You're already my unofficial daughter-in-law, and always will be, because of Tatyana. I'll be there at your wedding tonight, and so will Sanya. We'll also testify on your behalf when your case goes to court, to disallow Boris to have even partial paternal rights over Tatyana."

"But what if Vanya finds it in his heart to still forgive me one last time, and Boris finds out and gets angry because I led him on mercilessly this past week, and decides to spoil our wedding?"

"I'll speak to Father Yakim and order him to not let my short, pudgy son anywhere near the premises. If he does, Father Yakim shall call for police and have him arrested for trespassing. Knowing Ivan, he probably hopes you're having a last-minute change of heart and waiting for you to return to him. I expect to see you marrying him tonight, not my son. I have no qualms about the Malenkov family name dying out with Boris. It's my husband's family name, not mine. I was a Dobrolyubova in girlhood, not a Malenkova."

7

Ivan comes to the door with Fedya on his right arm and Tatyana by his right leg. Lyuba steps forward to try to hug her children, but Ivan takes them into Tatyana's room and shuts the door.

"You come to pick up your things?"

"I came to apologize and see if you'll forgive me one last time for running away from you."

"You were so impatient for us to get married, and then one week before I would've finally made you a respectable woman, you ran away again. Today was supposed to be our wedding day."

"It still can be. You said you didn't schedule the ceremony until tonight, so there's plenty of time to get down to the church."

"How can I tell if you won't commit adultery because you feel restless or afraid of how much I love you?"

"I can't commit adultery with Boris. He's impotent."

"This was my dream since I was nine years old, when I saw the beautiful new neighbor girl. But maybe it's finally time for me to admit you're more dream than reality. You got restless again because you'd been with me for two years straight without a single interruption, except for those terrible few months with your late father. I'm so monogamous, pure, and moral it's truly sickening. How many men besides monks go twenty-three years without sleeping with a woman? I promise you too much. It's time for me to give up my longtime dream and let you go to Boris."

"No, Vanya, we have too much history, and everything we went through together during the Civil War!"

"You'll still get married today, though with a different groom. But, *pozhaluysta*, don't let that *mudak* Malenkov raise Fedya as if he's his own. I understand you have to take Tatyana, because she needs to be with her mother, and Boris is her natural father, as much as I hate to admit it. But you know very well I'll never even consider sleeping with another woman for as long as I live, and Fedya's the only natural child I can ever have. I don't want the Konev name to die out because of that little man's selfishness in wanting to snatch away a little boy from the only father he's ever known."

"You're also the only father Tatyana's ever known!"

"But she knows Boris cares for her."

"Yes, he loves her, particularly since she's the only child he's ever going to get."

"I don't think there's really any easy way to do this, *golubka*."

"Stop crying, Vanya. If you really no longer love me and want me to get out of your life, you wouldn't be crying!"

"I will always love you, Lyuba. I will think of you at night, you will be in my dreams, I will think of you when I'm being exploited in the factory, I will think of you when I look at Fedya and when I catch glimpses of Tanyechka from afar, I will think of you when I see old pictures and your handwriting, and I will be thinking of you when the wind will be crying your name. And when Fedya becomes a man and gives me grandchildren, I will still be thinking of you and how this little boy will always be a forever memory to me of how much I love you and of how much I believe you tried to love me. I still believe in my heart that I'm the only man you've ever slept with out of love. And I will always be tortured by how close I came to finally realizing my dream completely, with you as my wife and the farm I always promised you in the Midwest, but had to turn you away because I love you so much I finally had no choice but to release you and send you back to the man you should've been with all along. We've tried so many times to make things work, but you always kept running away from me, and that's no way to have a marriage, with such an awful track record." Ivan wipes his eyes with his sleeve. "I know you'll have a celibate marriage with Boris, and I certainly will become celibate again, so at least I won't have one more torture added to my already very long list of tortures. I won't have to drive myself crazy picturing you in another man's arms, since your husband will be impotent and on top of that infertile." Ivan leads her to the door.

"You're not thinking rationally! We'll get married tonight, and I'll never run off and leave you lonely again!"

"I'm sorry, *golubka*. This was my dream, but this is the only way we can end things peacefully now, before we have even more history together."

Lyuba is still protesting when Ivan swings the door open and there stands Boris.

"Working out arrangements with the jilted fiancé over when he can visit Fedya, or breaking the news he can't ever see his son again?"

Ivan suddenly changes his mind once he sees his former best friend, now his enemy, standing there in the flesh. "I was just discussing with Lyuba how we're going to get married tonight no matter how much you try to ruin the occasion."

"That's not what you were saying a moment ago! You said you

had to give me up because you love me too much to marry me when you think I'll leave you again periodically!"

"I wasn't thinking straight. I'll let this scumbag marry you when Hell freezes over."

"Lyuba *has* to marry me, Konev!" Boris begins whining like a little child. "I slept with her first, three and a half years before you got around to it, and I used to believe I was her first man just like she was my first woman!"

"Well, surprise, surprise, I'm the only man she's ever slept with out of love, unlike you getting her so drunk she couldn't remember what you did to her that first night together!"

"Speaking of that very night! Our daughter came out of that night! Lyuba *must* marry me because we have our firstborn child together!"

"I've been raising that daughter as my very own since the night she was born, you *mudak*, and Lyuba has a son with me!"

"Well, where do you think our daughter came from? It didn't just materialize out of thin air!"

"'It'? You dare refer to that beautiful little girl you somehow sired as 'it'?"

"Since I'm going to have a celibate marriage, I won't fill Lyuba's head with unrealistic expectations about how many more children we can have, since we're both infertile, and I'm even impotent thanks to you."

"At least with *me* she'd stand a slightly better chance of having another child someday, since *I'm* not impotent or infertile. Oh, and by the way, she says I'm the best lover she's ever had. Unlike you, I know how to produce certain reactions in her."

"I make more money than you. I'm in great standing with my priest. I can let my daughter, your son, and most of all Lyuba live very comfortably for all the rest of their lives."

"At least I'm poor with dignity and happiness."

"Back in our gymnasium days, all our friends always believed that out of all the guys with their eye on Lyuba, I was the one she preferred above everybody else."

"Well, little did they all know she'd always secretly been in love with *me*! You were just the other neighbor boy, the short, ugly, fat one!"

Boris starts crying. "I don't sit around all day gaining weight! I play sports with the boys I teach in my religious school and go for walks! I'm naturally just a bit pudgy! And short guys like myself don't appreciate tall guys like you constantly ragging on our height! I'm five feet three inches tall, five-seven with my shoe inserts and thick-soled shoes, not some little midget man who's only five feet! In the winter, I pass for five-eight with my even-higher boots plus my inserts."

"You made a young girl kill herself."

"I never knew Lyusha was planning to hang herself, you big dolt! Even if I'd known about it, I never handed her that piece of rope!"

"You were always the last to flee when we were in hiding, and you beat a pregnant woman, the mother of your natural daughter!"

"I have truly repented! Even my own goddamn priest says so!"

"For the love of God, stop arguing over me and who deserves me more as though you're still two boys in gymnasium!" Lyuba thunders.

"You see how upset you're getting her?" Ivan glares at Boris.

"I had a girl, and you had a girl! I'll marry Lyuba tonight, and we all know Anastasiya still wants you. We'll have a double wedding if you want."

"If you're going to turn a serious matter like matrimony into a juvenile, boyish contest over who deserves me more, I don't think I'll marry either of you," Lyuba declares.

"What, you'd punish me by not marrying me and not let Konev marry you either?"

"I'll ask both of you to answer the same question I'm about to pose, and whoever answers it the most to my liking will be my husband by the time the day is over. Boris will answer first. Why do you love me?"

"Haven't I given you enough reasons over the past six years and even before?" Boris starts his whining routine again. "We have a daughter together, you're the first and only woman I've ever slept with, you're beautiful, our daughter's beautiful, you'll make a most wonderful wife, my parents adore you as the daughter they'll never have, your mother loves me like a son, and I know deep down you love me more than you ever loved that pipe dream Konev."

"What do you say, Vanya?"

Ivan looks at the floor, shaking. "I can't explain."

Boris begins giggling.

"I don't believe love should be explained in concrete terms. It's more like the feelings I've gotten from all the things we went through together, and how I'm the only man you've ever slept with out of love and nothing else, the fact that I'm nothing without you! I just can't explain all the reasons why I love you without having to think long and hard on how to accurately describe them. Well, I guess I'll never see you again, since Boris is clearly the ultimate winner in our longtime battle for your heart."

"That's right, Konev!" Boris gloats. "I won and you lost!"

Lyuba turns around and takes Ivan by the hand. "Why, Vanya, that's just what I've been waiting for a man to tell me my entire life!"

"What?"

"If you'd told me something like that long ago, I might never have gone through all that confusion and periodic running!"

Ivan looks Boris right in the eyes. "I won, Malenkov, and you lost!"

"Lyuba, are you serious? That pathetic answer is what you always wanted to hear from a man?" Boris asks.

"Yes it was, Malenkov. Now kindly get out of our tenement. By the end of the day, it will no longer be seemly for you to fantasize all the time about a married woman."

Boris leaves the building rebuffed and angry.

"I can't believe this!" Ivan says. "I'm finally going to make you my wife after fifteen and a half years of longing for you!"

"Enough stalling for time. We should start getting ready for our wedding right now. I'll carry the boxes with our clothes out to the car, and you'll take the children down. All the other things for the ceremony and reception are already at the church. And then the last fifteen and a half years will have all been worth it, *golubchik*."

Ivan dashes into Tatyana's room. "Guess what! Your mother and I are still getting married this evening!"

8

Lyuba almost runs into someone when she opens the door on her way to take the boxed clothes down to the car. A woman of somewhat above average height, five foot five, with scars all over her face and hands, is sitting there in a wheelchair.

"Is this where Ivan Konev lives? I read in the paper today he was getting married, and I had to see if it were true," she says in Muscovite Russian.

Ivan freezes when he sees her.

"Aren't you Ivan Konev?"

He drops onto his knees and crawls over to the woman. "This surely isn't possible! It's been nearly six and a half years, and there were at least three witnesses who saw what happened—"

"Vanya, who is this woman?"

Ivan has dropped his head onto the woman's lap and is sobbing from deep in his soul. "My mother is alive, Lyubonka!"

Lyuba comes over to the wheelchair-bound invalid. "Mrs. Koneva? But everyone saw how you met your end—"

"I thought I was dead too, but I just slipped into shock. Some neighbors rifled through the pit of bodies that night to see if there were by chance any survivors. I regained my consciousness the next morning, though I was covered in burns and lost the use of my legs. Sometime later I was sent to America, and I've lived in a hospital for invalids ever since."

"*Matushka*, you've come just when I needed you most!" Ivan is sobbing. "Today is my wedding day, and at the age of twenty-five, I'm finally going to marry the beautiful neighbor girl!"

"Your husband is still alive too," Lyuba says.

"That old goat eluded the authorities? However did he do that?"

"He switched places with a corpse. He put on the dead man's clothes and switched their nametags. He lives in your sister Valeriya's house, illegally working in a liquor store. I helped him this May."

"Who are these children?"

"This is your grandson, *Matushka*," Ivan sobs, putting Fedya into her lap. "*Pozhaluysta*, forgive me for having a child out of wedlock."

"Looks like you've had more than just one child out of wedlock!"

"The girl is not my blood," he whispers. "Her natural father is Boris Malenkov, but he abandoned her moments before Lyuba went into labor with her, and I've been raising her as my own ever since."

"This is my daughter Tatyana," Lyuba says. "We usually call her Tanyechka instead of Tanya."

"Are you sure we have to get married today, Lyuba?" Ivan asks. "I want to stay here and tell my mother about everything that's happened since we were separated."

Lyuba gives him a warning look. "Do you not recall that big scene taking place just minutes ago between you and Boris?"

"Yes, Lyuba. I'll finally make you a respectable woman today."

9

When they get to the church, Boris is nowhere to be found. Mrs. Malenkova assures them she's talked to Father Yakim about how Boris isn't allowed anywhere near the premises or he shall be arrested.

Tatyana looks down the hall as her parents and brother are heading off towards the changing rooms, and begins screaming in delight. "*Dyadya* Petya!"

Lyuba looks up and sees Tatyana running right towards Pyotr, who scoops her up and throws her up in the air. She can barely believe her eyes.

"Holy Mother of God, Petya, I never thought I'd see you again!"

"I'm here, aren't I?"

"Oh my God, Petya, I'm so glad to see you!" Lyuba throws her arms around him. "However did you find out about my wedding and manage to come here?"

"From her." He motions towards Georgiya standing near the stairs.

Ginny squeals in delight and runs towards Georgiya, falling into her arms and hugging and kissing her for the first time.

"This is the surprise Ginny told me about? I thought you'd just send us a present!"

"I had to use my baby sister as an excuse to take a trip to America. My father bought the monumental lie that Yaroslava wants to write an independent paper for extra credit for her political theory class, about how the American Socialist Party works. He does have ten other children to keep him busy while we're away." Pyotr motions towards thirteen-year-old Yaroslava.

Lyuba retires to the dressing room with Tatyana, Eliisabet, Kat, and Kittey, crying her eyes out over how horribly the day began and how Ivan has agreed to forgive her one last time and finally do the right thing by marrying her, and on top of all that, Ivan's mother is alive, and now Ginny has been temporarily reunited with his girlfriend, and to top it all off, their savior Pyotr has come to America just to see her wedding!
****

Chapter 40: Finally Husband and Wife

"My Alyoshka bought you very nice weddings rings," Eliisabet whispers as she leads Lyuba up to the vestibule. "He had enough money for them, since he gets extra salary for being the president of the union."

"You have to be jealous of me, Liza. You and Alyoshka had to wear ordinary clothes for your wedding, and there was barely any religious symbolism." Lyuba inhales her bouquet, blue, white, and red roses.

"It is what it is. The most important thing to me was to marry the man I love."

Ivan and Aleksey have already got to the vestibule. The best man and groom are no longer arguing or fearing for their friendship. Right before the ceremony began, Ivan told Aleksey he'll join the union, because he's realized the benefits outweigh the fear of looking like a traitor to the causes he was brought up to believe in.

Besides Boris, the only people absent are Alya, Anya, and Anastasiya. Lena, Natalya, Antonina, Sonya, and Yuriy have come down from Canada for the occasion. Yuriy is now four years old, and Lyuba slightly winces when she walks past the pew holding their family, knowing that cute little boy's father is Misha.

"I'm jealous," Pyotr whispers to Mrs. Lebedeva. "If things had been any different, she might've been my wife. She belongs with Ivan, but I can't just turn off my feelings for her overnight." He glances at her obviously pregnant midsection. "By the way, my utmost congratulations on your new marriage and the baby on the way."

Mrs. Malenkova is smirking with delight at how Lyuba isn't wearing the white gown Boris bought her. She's wearing a full-length indigo blue gown, made of sturdy cotton, without any fancy embellishments or long train. After all, why blatantly lie to a priest and a whole house of worship about her nonexistent purity? The four-and-a-half-year-old flower girl and the sixteen-month-old honorary grandson on her lap are certainly not adopted children!

Father Yakim takes the wedding rings Aleksey bought. They're made of three circles, to represent the Trinity, and are white, blue, and red, to represent the colors of the now-extinct glorious Russian tricolor flag originally used by Pyotr the Great. Making the sign of the cross over their heads, he begins, "The servant of God, Ivan Ivanovich Konev, is betrothed to the maid of God, Lyubov Leontiyevna Zhukova, in the name of the Father, the Son, and the Holy Ghost." The purpose of the rings is to show each person in the marital union is incomplete without the other; now the weaknesses of one will constantly be made up for by the perfections of the other.

Lyuba discreetly steps on Ivan's foot when she feels his hand shaking as he slips the ring onto her finger. "You are not going to embarrass yourself at the age of twenty-five by crying in front of everyone!" she whispers.

"To think that was almost my son up there with her," Mrs. Malenkova whispers. "I wonder if they even make wedding rings big enough to fit over his chubby fingers."

Following the exchange of rings, they're led into the nave, and Father Yakim chants Psalm 128. Quaking with nerves, Lyuba starts her declaration of intent, knowing Ivan would probably be too nervous and emotional to go first.

"I, Lyubov Leontiyevna Zhukova, have come of my own free will, without any constraints or prior commitments, to be joined by God to Ivan Ivanovich Konev as husband and wife. He has been my best friend for fifteen and a half years, the one constant I had to protect me, comfort me, and take care of me during our Motherland's modern-day *Smutnoye Vremya.* I couldn't imagine taking any other man as my lawfully-wedded husband and my partner in life from now until eternity."

"I, Ivan Ivanovich Konev, have come of my own free will, without any constraints or prior commitments, to be joined by God to Lyubov Leontiyevna Zhukova as husband and wife. When I met my Lyuba fifteen and a half years ago, in March 1908, I was nine and she was eight. Ever since a month after we met, we've been inseparable best friends, and never cared how unconventional it is to have a best friend of the opposite sex. Starting when I was eighteen and she was seventeen, we had an on-and-off romantic relationship as well, which was interrupted a total of eleven times, but even when we weren't romantically linked, we still held each other as best friends. I can't believe what an *udachnik* I am to finally have the honor of making my best friend since childhood, the only girl I've ever loved, my lawfully-wedded wife from now until eternity."

Kat bought the candles which they're now handed by Eliisabet and Aleksey. These candles represent the five women in one of the parables, whose lamps had enough oil to see Jesus when he visited them at night. These candles are one of a kind and sold very specially at Kat's floral shop. They're made of gold leaf, and as they slowly burn down, the tops constantly crinkle over.

To symbolize the oneness of the couple, Father Yakim joins their right hands before he begins the prayer that begs God "join these thy servants, unite them in one mind and one flesh."

"The servants of God, Ivan Ivanovich Konev and Lyubov Leontiyevna Zhukova, are crowned in the name of the Father, the Son, and the Holy Ghost. Amen." He repeats the individual blessing thrice for each one, then proclaims, "O Lord, our God, crown them with glory and honor" as he lifts up both crowns and switches them back and forth thrice.

"My parents have been made a Tsar and Tsaritsa of their own little kingdom!" Tatyana whispers in delight to her paternal grandmother.

"If anyone needs those crowns' symbolism, it's your parents," Mrs. Malenkova says. "They've endured so much self-sacrifice and near-martyrdom."

***

During the reading of the Epistle and Gospel, describing the first miracle of Jesus, turning water into wine at the wedding at Cana, the smaller children grow fidgety, and Lena and Antonina take Yuriy into the hall with Tatyana, Nikolay, Novomira, Fedya, and the twins.

"I'm glad Mrs. Malenkova ordered the priest to not let her irresponsible son come anywhere near this house of God during this wedding," Lena says. "Who knows, he might try to steal my son again."

"He never kidnapped Yura. Your older sister gave him full permission. She probably would've let any stranger take him to a better life."

"I can't find a priest to baptize my Yura, since he was born out of wedlock. But how I am to go about finding a man who'd want to marry an unwed mother?"

"Sonya doesn't need any man. She hasn't rushed to remarry since losing her husband. She also doesn't feel the need to have more children to make up for losing Mikhaila and Karla. Although I'd like to believe she'll see Karla again in this lifetime. As for you, some priest somewhere is bound to understand that situation eventually."

"Yura has started to ask questions about where his father is. I vaguely tell him he's back in Russia. When I deem him old enough to understand adult matters, I'll take him to see Pasha, since he was sort of friends with Misha, lived with him and Kostya, and has pictures of him. I don't want Yura to get an idea of his father as a hero or good man, and then feel betrayed when he finds out the truth."

"In an ideal society, we won't need men anymore. All they're good for is fathering children. Good men are hard to find, the kinds who don't think it's their God-given right to drink excessively, stay out at saloons till midnight, beat their wives, have affairs, and try to bar us from entering the world of work."

"But how will you have children without a husband? It's bad enough I'm an unwed mother and that my darling little Yura is the product of a rape."

"With the right male for a friend, and the right kind of kitchen instrument, you can have a baby more or less on your own and still be as pure as *Matushka* Mariya. I'd like to do that. I like boys, but most of them change after marriage and start denying their wives basic rights, cheating on them, drinking, and beating them. And in the Anglophone world, married women don't even get the common respect and courtesy to be referred to by their own names. Everyone has to know they're Mrs. Husband's Name, a man's property."

"Sonya and my mother changed their surnames. It was just what women did in those days. If I ever found a husband to take a fallen woman, I'd probably add his name to mine with a hyphen, like a modern woman."

"In Russia, it would be ludicrous to refer to a married woman like that, since we have feminine endings on our surnames, and it's inaccurate to refer to a woman without the feminine ending unless she has a name of foreign origin, like Latsis or Shaffer."

"The bride is changing *her* name."

"Only to get rid of her father's name, because he was such an evil deviant."

"Don't you remember how we had to get Sonya to pretend to be Yura's mother so we could get him signed out of that orphanage and put back into my care, because no sane person under the sun would've let a thirteen-year-old girl reclaim a baby she had out of wedlock!"

"I think you know by a certain age whether or not God has predestined you to get married. I don't feel I was predestined."

"That evil man who stole my son sure was fighting *his* predestination, that's for sure! Thank God he soon abandoned his hopes of raising Yura as his own and turned his full attentions to his own out of wedlock child."

"Sometimes I think Orthodoxy is too strict and unfair to people who don't do exactly as they're told. At least the Catholics have loosened their theology up a bit, like no longer believing unbaptized babies go to Hell. I hope by the time our grandchildren are our age, they'll live in a world that doesn't blanketly condemn women for doing things like having children out of wedlock or cohabiting before marriage."

"At least you don't have a mother around to tell you to stop thinking in such an unfeminine way."

"Sonya supports me. She's only thirty-three, which is old enough to be our mother, but a young mother, not an old one like yours."

Antonina has recently begun to dress like a flapper, with knee-high skirts, powdered knees, cloche hats, and shirtwaists that only go as far as the elbow. She's also taken to wearing her galoshes unbuttoned, in addition to makeup, fake jewelry, and rolled-down silk stockings.

"What will people say when you carry out your unorthodox plans?"

"Canada's always been less restrictive than America." Antonina picks up the Vishinskaya twins and walks back into the nave.

***

Mr. Konev sits smirking as his son drinks wine from the common cup after the readings conclude. This ardent teetotaler except for religious purposes must know the church has been smuggling in all its wine and making the rest from mixing water with bricks of grape concentrate ever since Prohibition's been in effect!

"What are you smirking about now, you old goat?" Mrs. Koneva hisses.

Mr. Konev's smirk fades, and his state of utter shock at seeing his wife alive again comes sweeping back into his body. "At what a hypocrite my boy is."

"Because he's drinking an illegal substance? You're a bigger hypocrite! My sister told me you claim to rarely drink at all anymore, yet you work in a liquor store!"

"It's sure well-protected from the feds raiding it." Mr. Konev motions to his three police officer friends, whom he invited to the wedding.

"I can tell we'll have a lot of things to talk about after this ceremony is over, Ivan. Like about whether we should stay married. We were apart for six and a half years and both thought the other was dead. After the first five years of our marriage, it was all downhill faster and faster each new year. Twenty years of marriage we had before the Revolution. Since I'm an invalid now, I'll have to stay with my sister and her new husband."

"I've repented. Even our son knows that! You're going to stay married to me, Anyechka."

"Not once I go to a lawyer and tell him about the past six and a half years."

"But I was never dead, so I'll refuse to give my consent."

Father Yakim leads Lyuba and Ivan thrice around the Holy Table containing a Gospel and a cross, Eliisabet and Aleksey following behind as they hold the crowns over their heads, while a hymn to the Holy Martyrs is sung. Their bridesmaids, Kat, Kittey, Alla, Vera, Natalya, and Fyodora, follow, holding lit candles. During the processional, the guests throw flower petals and rice at them. After they proceed to the ikonostasis, it is finished.

"Be thou magnified, Ivan, as Abram, and blessed as Isak, and increased as Yakov, walking in peace and working in righteousness the commandments of God. And thou, Lyubov, be thou magnified as Sara, and glad as Rebeka, and do thou increase like unto Rakhil, rejoicing in thine own husband, fulfilling the conditions of the law;

for so it is well pleasing unto God."

"Gorko!" Tatyana urges her parents from Mrs. Malenkova's lap, and they oblige her until the best man pulls on the groom's sleeve to remind him to get his hands off the bride for the time being.

"Do not embarrass yourself or me by crying in front of all these people at our reception," Lyuba whispers.

"Did you catch me crying when I married Liza?" Aleksey asks as they walk toward the reception hall.

"You'd only waited a year! I had to wait for this day for fifteen and a half years! If Lyuba's mother hadn't interfered six and a half years ago, we would've been married at only seventeen and eighteen, not twenty-three and twenty-five!"

"What did my new son-in-law just say about me?" Mrs. Lebedeva demands, coming up with Mr. Lebedev and his seven daughters.

"He's blaming you for not marrying me six and a half years ago, *Matushka*. When he *could've* married me at Ellis Island the same way Kat and Kolya were, or any time since then."

Georgiya comes up on Ginny's arm. "I want to apologize for how I indirectly caused the raid on your valley."

Lyuba smiles at her. "I know you're sorry, and it never would've happened in the first place if there hadn't been the Civil War. I always admired how intelligent and progressive you were, even as a girl. It was only natural you followed your family's political beliefs and didn't realize you made a bad decision that one time, to say the least."

"She would've stayed in that asylum if the dirty Reds hadn't come back to the area and 'liberated' their fellow dirty Bolsheviks." Ivan holds his bride's arm a little tighter. "We all know she was the one who squealled on us."

"I was an eleven-year-old child, Konev. Now I'm nearly seventeen."

"Speaking of children, where are ours?" Ivan asks. "And where did Alyosha and Liza go?"

"Katya, Rita, Lera, and I arranged something," Mrs. Malenkova says elusively.

Lyuba turns around in shock as she hears Father Yakim in the middle of a prayer she hasn't heard since Kat and Nikolas took their twins to be baptized. Her children have just been baptized themselves.

"Shura, the least you could've done was to tell us you were doing this!"

"It's what you wanted, wasn't it? To have your children made legitimate?"

Tatyana comes running to her parents with her little brother by the hand. "Now we've all stopped living in sin, since you and Papa are married, and Fedya and I are baptized."

"Did your daughter really want to be baptized, or did you force it on her?" Georgiya asks.

"All children need baptism," Ivan says. "Even that crazy woman Katrin decided to baptize her baby!"

"Oh my, Comrade Nikonova! I always admired you so much, and now you've turned around and done this?"

"Not to worry, little Georgiya. The child will be baptized Unitarian. I was inspired after my reverend gave a very stirring sermon on how Jesus was the first Socialist. Even if I don't believe he was the son of God and have doubts about his existence, I can still be inspired by how he, whether myth or actual real man, was the first Socialist to ever live. By the way, it's Mrs. Kalvik-Nikonova now."

Lyuba's eyes light up at the sight of all the food arrayed around the banquet tables—salmon, lox, *selyodka*, all sorts of *zakuski*, several kinds of soups, both hot and cold, *bombonieras, shashlyk, pelmeni, pirogi, pirozhki, draniki*, stuffed mutton seasoned with mint, roasted duck, lots of contraband champagne, with enough mocktails for the guests who refuse to violate Prohibition, plenty of roasted vegetables of all types, fruit salad, tomato and carrot salad, noodle pudding with raisins, sourdough bread, a wide array of jams and jellies, caviar, and soft, herbed goat cheese. The dessert table looks even more divine, with *chak-chak, pastily, vatrushki*, chocolate and cherry Jell-O, several shining silver platters piled high with a wide assortment of truffles, chocolates, and candied fruit slices, a bowl of roasted peanuts coated with chocolate, *limonnik*, cherry pie, and chocolate meringues. In the center of the dessert table sits a mammoth five-layer wedding cake with strawberry icing. A fancy silver knife with an embellished ivory handle sits off to the side. On every table, there are centerpieces of Gerbera daisies, daffodils, irises, freesias, snapdragons, zinnias, and sunflowers, with a few creative centerpieces made from seashells, decorative buttons, paper flowers and butterflies, and small Christmas bulbs. So this is the expensive wedding Ivan kept insisting was worth waiting and saving up for.

"Does it meet your approval, Mrs. Koneva?" Ivan whispers as he helps Lyuba into her seat at the head of the main table.

Lyuba's heart skips a beat. "It sure does. This is the best reception I could've dreamt of. I can't believe you're finally my real husband. It's such an honor to be a real Koneva after so long of pretending."

"I'm glad the name agrees with you." Ivan smiles, caressing her hand. "You're going to be answering to it for the rest of your life." He cups her face in his hands and kisses her as several people start shouting *Gorko* again.

2

Halfway through the banquet, Georgiya vanishes from the table with Ginny.

"Did Ginny just leave the table without excusing himself?" Mrs. Kharzina asks. "At his only full cousin's wedding?"

"I won't be his only full cousin for long," Lyuba says. "That honorary title will only belong to me for another four months." She looks jealously at her mother, wishing she could become pregnant just as easily.

"Maybe he's tired and decided to go home early," Mrs. Lebedeva says.

***

Ginny and Georgiya have rushed into the abandoned priests' quarters upstairs. The church's priests haven't lived there for ten years, but they left their furniture and mattresses.

"There's no chance of me defecting unless Comrade Lenin dies or is overthrown and horrible people come to power," Georgiya whispers. "I very much doubt you'd risk coming back overseas to visit me after all the trouble you and your cousin went through to leave the country. This could very well be the only time we see each other again, Grigoriy."

"My parents were missionaries," Ginny tries to protest as Georgiya leans in closer and puts her hand on his thigh.

"I thought you'd renounced Christianity for Communism."

"I'm back in church now, though I still harbor some of my old views. That said, I don't believe in what you're implying we do!"

"I can never defect. My family's destiny is tied up with the new Russia. The current political realities are things my parents worked for and wanted desperately since they were teenagers. Leonid and I, and now baby Nelya, have been raised to believe in the same things they do. When I met Comrade Lenin in the flesh, it only served to crystallize my political views. I'll graduate from gymnasium, attend a nice university, and teach school. Maybe I'll someday get over you and be able to marry someone whose fate is also in the new Russia, not the old one you, your cousin, and her friends are trying to recreate in America. But for now, I want to know what the big grownup mystery is all about, and not have to wait who knows how long before I have another chance to know a man."

3

Ginny and Georgiya are still noticeably absent as Lyuba and Ivan begin unwrapping their wedding presents.

"My sister was oh-so-nice to get you a wedding present, Konev, after how unspeakably rude and impolite you were at *her* wedding," Viktoriya says.

"Correction, big mouth. I've had some very intelligent conversations and debates with your heartless older sister."

"This is a gramophone," Katrin says. "You crank the arm like a phonograph, only it doesn't play cylinders. This one takes big, flat, round black discs, called records, which rotate seventy-eight times per minute. You have to flip them over sometimes to hear the rest of the song or another song. If you're interested in starting a record collection, I can refer you to some great music shops in Harlem where I buy all my jazz records. No one else sells most of the ones I have, since they're labeled as 'race records.' And there are always records with classical music instead of modern jazz."

"And I'd want to listen to music made by colored people for what reason?"

"Vanya!" Lyuba chides. "You're already so terribly old-fashioned, even in a good, sweet way instead of a bad way; need you give Katrin yet another reason to dislike you?"

"And my sister was so good to get you something for your household, full well knowing you lived in sin for years," Viktoriya says.

Natalya Yeltsina steps forward with Lena. "My big sister and I found this at a religious shop in Toronto."

Ivan pushes Katrin's gramophone off to the side of the presents table to make way for the miniature grotto Lena and Natalya bought. Viktoriya makes yet another sour face at him.

"The little accessories that came with it were like things in a dollhouse," Natalya says. "The woman who sold it to us assured us these tiny little candles can actually light, and I thought this doll-sized prayer rope was very cute, just like these mite-sized little silk flowers."

Viktoriya stands and surveys the oncoming presents, most of them religious or mundane in nature. The only modern present so far, besides the modern kitchen appliances, has been Katrin's.

"Here. This present has Ginny's name on it," Mrs. Kharzina says.

Lyuba uncovers a photo album with a note on top, "Once again, I'm deeply sorry for how I behaved in the old days. I made a bad situation even worse by my bad behavior. The only thing that matters now is we're back on good terms and not dwelling on the ugly past or holding anything against one another."

Pyotr presents them with a large framed oil painting depicting St. Vladimir's conversion, alongside a little colored booklet about the lives of all the rulers of Russia, both Ryurikovich and Romanov.

"You said your favorite saint had become Vladimir, so I found this painting at one of the few religious art stores still left in Moskva, though in my heart I believe God is dead. And even though the monarchy's dead, I always wanted a constitutional monarchy. There were some very interesting characters on the throne, which I'm sure you'll want your children to learn all about as they get older."

"You're really not going to defect," Lyuba muses.

"Not unless there's a complete turnaround and I find myself in the position you were in, suddenly out of favor politically and in danger for my life. Besides, however would I be able to get this cute little pumpkin back home if I defected?"

"You're embarrassing me, Petya," young Yaroslava says.

"Having a sister a good eleven years my junior might be the closest I'll ever come to having paternal feelings," he confides. "I don't know if I'll be able to find someone to marry. I've known for a long time I didn't have a chance of marrying you, but I'll have the memory of Tver to keep me company in my old age."

Lyuba squeezes his hand. "You've always been so selfless to put your friendship above romantic feelings, even when it meant persuading me to leave you and go back to Vanya. That showed you would've been a wonderful husband."

"It's a shame Malenkov wasn't more noble about losing the girl he wanted since boyhood too," Ivan says.

"I want to go to sleep," Tatyana says.

"Maybe it's time for us to get them home." Lyuba smiles at the sight of Tatyana's new baptismal cross. "It's getting very late."

"Let Alyoshka and I have them tonight," Eliisabet says. "Tatyana and Fedya are now our official godchildren, and we won't mind having them over for their parents' honeymoon night."

4

Pyotr catches up to Kat in the church hallway as she's about to leave with Nikolas, Kittey, and the twins.

"I didn't give you this news earlier because I didn't want you to become upset in the middle of the party. Another reason I risked my father's and brothers' suspicions to come overseas was because this news would never reach you any other way, and I didn't want to risk writing a letter."

"What is it?" Kat asks.

"It's your mother. She recently came down with some sort of cancer, and the doctor said she'll be most likely dead within three years."

Kat crosses herself. "Does she want me to come back to Russia so I can be with her?"

"Once today's pictures are developed, I'll give her some of them so she can see you and her twin granddaughters."

"But you do know my parents and sisters are all safe and still alive?"

"I think they've become used to the new Russian landscape. Now that the Civil War is over, most of them have come to like Comrade Lenin. He's no longer doing things even I was ashamed of him for, like seizing land from the peasants, that he was forced into doing because of so-called emergency wartime measures."

"Besides sending pictures, Petya, *pozhaluysta*, tell everyone in my family I'm doing quite well here, I'm a married woman of two years, and I've got twin girls, one of them named after Kolya's late mother."

"Also make sure to tell them that by this time next year, hopefully, we'll have another baby," Nikolas says.

"I hope we don't," Kat growls.

"If it's a boy, I want to name him Andrey, after my father," Nikolas continues, ignoring his wife's pleas to put a hold on further childbearing yet again. "If it's a girl, why don't we call her Anzhelika, after Kat's mother?"

"I'll be here in Manhattan for a few more days with my baby sister." Pyotr slips them a small piece of paper. "If you have any further questions you'd like to ask me while I'm still here, about the whereabouts of your family, or any other people who didn't immigrate, like Alya's parents, this is the hotel where I'm staying. Speaking of Alya, why didn't I see either her or Anya at the wedding?"

"They're sexual deviants," Nikolas says. "We don't want our children or ourselves around such horrible, disgusting, twisted people. Did you know, Petya, during the two years they were apart from us, they entered into an unnatural sexual relationship with each other? Women homosexuals. I never dreamt of such a sordid thing."

"Oh my. I don't have any religious basis for calling them deviants, since I no longer believe in God, but I feel strange knowing they prefer each other instead of men!" Pyotr strides out the door with little Yaroslava by the hand. "Tell Lyuba and Ivan I hope they're married for a hundred years, to make up for all the things they went through before they were married, and let them know once again I think their little boy is the cutest little boy I've ever seen."

5

"I'll be in Manhattan for a few more days, with Petya and his sister." Georgiya hands Ginny their hotel number written on the back of one of her father's business cards. "If you want to visit in addition to calling me, you should come by again when Petya and Slava are off exploring the city and researching the types of Socialism prevalent here, in the late afternoons most likely. But we're leaving by the end of the week, so make sure you stop by often and soon if I mean that much to you. That kind of hurt and felt awkward, but I'm glad I had that experience. I assume it only gets better and doesn't hurt so much when you try it more often."

Lyuba catches sight of Georgiya walking downstairs, then skipping to catch up with Pyotr and his sister. Ginny appears five minutes later, tucking in his shirt and furtively looking around.

"What gave you a reason to disappear like that?" Mrs. Kharzina demands.

"I wanted to be alone with Zhora."

"You do know you'll very soon have to start getting interested in other girls. I want grandchildren. You'll be seen as the family disgrace if you continue pining away for a heretical Bolshevik girl thousands of *vyorsty* away and never marry and have children."

"Zhora's here now, *Matushka*."

"Not for very long she won't be. Better get used to the prospect of how you'll inevitably have to start finding other, more appropriate, local girls to chase after when you become a man."

"I already am a man," Ginny asserts.

"Just because you're sixteen does not equate adulthood, young man. You're still in school."

Ginny catches up to his cousin on her way outside, under the guise of wanting to help to transport all the wedding gifts into the backseat of the car.

"Where in the world have you been?" Lyuba demands.

"If you must know, Zhora and I were upstairs in the old priests' quarters. But promise not to tell anyone."

"Doing what? Something more important than celebrating our wedding day?" Ivan asks. "Couldn't you take her to explore the church another day? She's not leaving immediately."

Ginny looks at the ground. "I can't trust him, though he himself committed the same so-called sin I just did, and has proof of how guilty he is. Can we, *pozhaluysta*, speak alone, cousin to cousin?"

"What proof of what sin? Now that you've started to tell us the story, why stop there and insist only Lyubonka can hear the complete version?"

"Unless I am very much mistaken, Fedya's your flesh and blood son, and I very much doubt that was an immaculate conception."

Lyuba turns white. "You slept with Georgiya!"

"Had to happen sometime. Besides, she'll soon be returning to Russia. It would've been very unfair to both of us to just be a memory of a romance that occurred in the first blushes of adolescence and nothing more ever."

"What if Georgiya returns to Russia pregnant?!"

"I sincerely doubt that. If she were, she'd do what a nice girl does and give it up for adoption. No offense, Lyuba. You were an adult when you became an unwed mother, and under much different circumstances."

"Give me some money, or I'll tell your mother about your shameful behavior tonight," Ivan says.

"That's not fair! You yourself aren't a wedding night virgin!"

"I was twenty-three the first time I slept with your cousin, not sixteen!"

"Come on, we did what was natural! Not everyone has such incredible willpower to deny themselves sexual knowledge that long!"

"If you won't give me money, you have to give me your absolute word of honor you'll absolutely slaughter Malenkov's character when we put you on the witness stand when we go to court to force him to give up his paternal rights on Tatyana. You liked him at one point. Do you still like him?"

"Not after he walked out on us the night Lyuba gave birth."

"Good boy. You're going to say he totally destroyed your trust for him and that it was twice as painful as how he abandoned his child before she was born. Or else I'm going straight to your mother with the news her sixteen-year-old son is now sexually knowing." Ivan opens the car door.

"He and Georgiya slept together on a bed that used to belong to a priest!" Lyuba opens the driver's side door. "Don't wait for me over there, Vanya. I'm driving home tonight."

"You're a woman. You can't drive."

"All evening long I kept having to step on your toes to prevent you from crying in front of everyone. Now that I no longer need to do that, you'll probably be too blinded by tears to see the way back home."

"Since when have you ever driven?"

"My uncle taught me in May."

"But it's my role as the man to drive a car."

"If someone isn't stuck in the Victorian era." Lyuba climbs into the driver's seat.

"You probably won't let me carry you across the threshold either," he sulks, closing his door.

"It'd defeat the whole purpose of the tradition, since we've already lived in that tenement for over two years. That horribly dated tradition also harks back to the time when the groom had to carry the bride into their new house, since he had to kidnap her to marry her."

"I almost *did* resort to kidnapping many times because I wanted to marry you so badly!"

"You finally got me in the end, didn't you?"

"I never thought I'd be that lucky, after so many rejections, all the other men you've been with, and how many times you ran away from me."

"I couldn't run forever. The only thing I can find to harp at you about now is that horrible low-paying job of yours and the tenement we live in. My days of bothering at you to finally make me a respectable woman are now over."

6

It's the same tenement they enter into that night. There's no new house waiting for them. It'll always be this tenement to which they'll be chained so long as Ivan refuses to look for better, higher-paying work, but it's a far better first married home than the one Kat and Nikolas had in the boardinghouse or the one Eliisabet and Aleksey had in the crowded house in the valley.

"Tomorrow while you're at work, I'll go through all the paperwork." Lyuba sinks onto the davenport and takes off her shoes and silk stockings with the tops rolled down. "With my last official signature on the last piece of paperwork, my disgusting father's name will finally be as cold and dead as he is. I'm also changing my patronymic to Ilyinichna, after my wonderful stepfather. I wanted to do it as soon as he became my stepfather, but I thought it made more sense to take care of both name changes at once. We've already long changed Tatyana's surname from Zhukova to Koneva, my mother's now a Lebedeva, and I'll be the last Zhukova to shed that horrible name."

"So this whole day wasn't a dream," Ivan whispers, sitting beside her.

"Well, the morning did seem like a nightmare."

"I can't believe I actually wanted to give you up so Boris could have you! As though I'll ever fully forgive him for his past sins."

"You were willing to give me up, though, just like Petya. Boris was never willing to give me up so you could have me."

"Now we only have to write to a judge and ask we be granted our day in court against that scumbag Malenkov. Once I'm Tanyechka's legal adoptive father, our lives will be perfect but for my low-paying job."

"Today you became her stepfather, Vanyechka."

"I almost expected something to go wrong at any minute. There have been so many times in the past where we almost were together, but something stupid split us up again. According to my reckoning, it's been eleven times total."

"May there never be a twelfth time."

"I still have to go to work tomorrow at seven sharp, and won't be home till ten hours later. This isn't the perfect wedding night and morning after I always dreamt of, Lyubonka."

"One day there will be that farm in the Midwest you always wanted for us, maybe even another child or two. We'll get Branimir back from the stable on Long Island, and maybe we can convince Liza and Alyoshka and Kolya and Kat to move with us. Luckily for you, I don't think radical Katrin or her big-mouthed little sister would adapt well to life in a farming town. But most of all, no Anastasiya. I would've preferred Boris to be a wedding guest. Thank God she had no interest in attending our wedding, not even to try to spoil it."

"Neither she or Boris can ever again attempt to get back together with either of us. You're my legitimate wife now, no longer the woman I live in sin with, the mother of my children!"

"One day they'll make you a saint for everything you had to go through for my sake. But for now, it's the moment that should've occurred six and a half years ago. Why don't we make believe, just for tonight, it's our first time all over again and we're unspoilt wedding-night virgins?"

"Nothing would make me happier."

****

Chapter 41: The Pain of a Barren Womb

The past few months have been absolutely idyllic. Lyuba now wears a real wedding ring in place of a fake one; she's become Mrs. Koneva and now proudly bears a patronymic from her stepfather; her children are finally legitimate in the eyes of the Church; Tatyana and Fedya have begun taking Communion; she's effectively gained two mothers-in-law; and, most of all, Lyuba now has the security of being a respectable woman instead of a fallen woman. She also now has a week-old baby halfbrother, Osip Ilyich Lebedev, named after Nadezhda's murdered father and Mr. Lebedev's brother, with one blue eye and one brown eye like his father, and Ivan has a new baby cousin as well, Vasya's also-week-old sister Vasilisa Grigoriyevna Golitsyna.

It's January 1924, and Lyuba is at Katrin's penthouse with the other women. One-month-old Oliivia Asta Kalvik is being bounced up and down on her *Tädi* Viktoriya's knee while the proud mother looks on.

"And to think I once never wanted children until I was thirty. She's a firstborn just like her mother, and most importantly a girl! I know it's a horrible stereotype and assumption, but I've found it's true that most normal women enjoy having a firstborn girl more than a boy simply because it's a member of their own sex. Oliivia will look so cute in her little frilly dresses and hairbows, with that beautiful golden curly hair. I'm getting Stasya to start a whole line of flapper baby clothes."

"I wouldn't have time to do all this designing at your beck and call if I had a kid to run around after all the time like you do now." Anastasiya reaches for a honey cookie.

"Vika and the servants will chase around after Oliivia after she starts crawling. Of course, she's always welcome on my lap when I'm writing my articles. Who knows, I might want a second one a lot sooner than I thought. Liza's on her third child, and she'll only be married for seven years this April."

Lyuba jealously looks over at Eliisabet, now four months pregnant. Kat is also four months pregnant, and hating every minute of it, even more so because she deeply suspects she's having twins again.

"I got my hands on that book on safe and unsafe days too late, apparently." The life has started to drain from Kat's deep blue eyes, and her skin is even paler than usual.

"You've already got two kids." Katrin takes Oliivia back from her sister. "I don't know why you didn't take my advice and find a doctor to do the deed the moment you first suspected you were pregnant again."

"I didn't want another pregnancy so soon after my girls were born, but I didn't want to commit a sin by killing these two I've got inside me. It's not their fault their father was overly aggressive about having another baby so soon or that their mother wasn't ready for another baby yet."

"Pretty soon they'll be viable. Kolya was born twelve weeks early, and nothing's wrong with him as far as we know, but they wouldn't have been viable by any stretch of the imagination when you found out."

"They're Kolya's children too. He wanted them so badly."

"I think mine is a second girl," Eliisabet says. "If my maternal instinct's right a third time in a row, we're calling her Nina, after my Alyoshka's mother."

"I hope my maternal instinct's wrong. I don't want twins again! Kolya wants to call a boy Andrey, after his late father, and if it's a third girl, she'll be Anzhelika, after my poor mother."

"At least you're all lucky enough to be able to have more children without a miracle," Lyuba says darkly.

"When is your trial to have that *mudak* Boris sign away those paternal rights over your daughter that he wants so badly?" Katrin asks.

"March."

"He was the one who did this to you, rendering you almost unable to have more children. I know I'm not alone when I say I'm absolutely going to slaughter his character once they put me up on that witness stand. I never liked that short, chubby man."

"Why should I even be there?" Anastasiya asks. "It's a good idea the child know who her real father is. The second time he was in Russia illegally, he was ready and prepared to take her back to America with him, a notion I fully supported all along."

"Coming from somebody so selfish she won't even have children on her own!"

"A daughter would steal the spotlight from me. I don't want to run the risk of having a daughter who's more beautiful than I am. No matter if it's a boy or a girl, I'd have to devote a lot of time and energy to running around after the unwanted thing, even if I hired a nanny to do it all, right down to telling the child she was the real mother."

"A selfish person would logically want at least one child, to carry on her bloodline," Eliisabet says. "You're even more selfish than I always thought if you think that way."

"Having Oliivia dispelled my last vestiges of selfishness," Katrin says. "Now, though I have a nanny to take care of her, she's my number one priority, even greater than my newspaper career."

"Well, *my* number one priority is myself," Anastasiya says.

"Sooner than I hope, my Oliivia will start asking all sorts of questions, and one of them is bound to be why her *Tädi* Anastasiya doesn't have any little children for her to play with."

Eliisabet begins reading Katrin's latest article in progress for one of the Estonian-language newspapers, on the proposed new immigration quotas. "Soon your Sandro might be out of a job, from the looks of this!"

"He still processes a lot of people every day, but it's getting lesser and lesser, compared to the huge hordes he used to lead through. Before long, only immigrants from the socially-approved places, like England, Ireland, and France, will get to come through. We got here just in time. The racist men in government don't like people from Eastern and Southern Europe, and they want only a small fraction of us to immigrate, about two percent of the number who were here prior to 1890, when barely any of us *were* here. Of course, that really favors Western Europe over Asia and Eastern Europe. It's bad enough that nauseating, so-called Emergency Immigration Quota that passed just after we arrived already restricts our kind to three percent. I like how those racists think it's such an emergency for their precious purebred country to be flooded by people from other lands, while it's not an emergency for many of these immigrants to remain in their homelands under hostile conditions. God forbid they have to learn to live with people beyond their own kind."

"Immigrants achieve great things, like political office, or me becoming a locally famous fashion designer," Anastasiya says. "My reputation is growing throughout the whole city. They'll see America is made great by its immigrants, and change their minds about denying entry to our brethren."

"It's far too late to turn back the tide of sickening nativism and xenophobia being whipped up by the racist men in government and local politics nationwide. My wedding had to be held here because the hotel cancelled after finding out everyone attending is an immigrant."

Anastasiya turns her attention back to her crossword puzzles and her little wallet-sized pictures of Rudy and Dmitriy.

"That actor you like so much is an immigrant," Katrin goes on. "Had he been born at a different time, your precious Valentino would be languishing in Italy instead of a famous moviestar sheik in America."

"You're always agitating for loopy left-wing causes, and very strong on letting more people immigrate from the less socially-approved-of places. Why don't you do something about it beyond ranting to us or writing about it in the left-wing press?"

"Even *I* know some things have been skewered by the government to such a great degree, nobody but independent thinkers would agree with things like Socialism or letting in more immigrants from Asia or Eastern Europe. I have to pick my battles."

2

Sandro comes in from work at six in the evening and goes right for Oliivia, bouncing her up and down on his knee.

"You wouldn't remember every immigrant you process, would you, Sandro?"

"Only the memorable ones, and I forget them soon. The only one I never will forget is you." He rubs her arm.

"So you don't remember processing Malenkov the three times he came to America? You worked on Ellis Island at that time."

"If I did process him, he didn't make a memorable impression. There are many men with black hair and eyes I've processed, and he wasn't the only one a bit on the short side or slightly chubby."

"Do you by any chance remember processing Konev, or if you observed how he was treating his daughter?"

"I remember he had the little girl on his lap the entire time you were in the waiting pen, and that the older gentleman was reading a book of poetry. I didn't see him again after your group left the holding pen and went upstairs to see the doctors and interviewers."

"So your testimony wouldn't do Lyuba's case much help."

"But I do distinctly remember three of the women I processed today, because their surname is the same as the little redhaired girl who travelled with you, Yeltsina. A woman in her late fifties, with two daughters in their thirties. The younger daughter was a bit on the chubby side."

"Mrs. Yeltsina and her daughter Zina ran the boardinghouse we stayed at in Tver in autumn 1920. She had four daughters, but Zina was the only one left."

"Apparently she found another daughter."

"Zina was certainly what I'd call a bit hefty. Not obese by any stretch of the imagination, but hefty."

"I told them I might know the whereabouts of the two younger girls and the little boy they were questioning everyone about, so I made arrangements for them to stay the night on the island."

"The little Yeltsina girl and her older sister live in Toronto."

"It's a pity. Both of the older sisters are soon to be ending their most fertile years, and old maids."

"Zina was engaged during the Great War. She studied abroad in Sweden, returned to Moskva to teach chemistry, and was a student teacher for a couple of years. Then came her fiancé, whom she was with for only two years. He was murdered by my fellow Bolsheviks, sadly. Barbarous things, they made her watch it. Now she's a luckless spinster for life."

"That's more than can be said for the oldest sister, Valya."

"At least they won't end up selfish old maids, like Stasya wants to be now. She still loves men, but told me today she wouldn't want a daughter to steal the spotlight from her beauty; either a son or a daughter would make irritating demands on her precious time; and a husband might get jealous of Grand Duke Dmitriy and Rudolph Valentino, whom she spends so much time swooning over at her age, it's so damn ridiculous."

3

Lena, Yuriy, Natalya, Sonya, and Antonina have come down from Toronto and been ferried over to Ellis Island to see the older Yeltsinas. Sandro is standing with them as Mrs. Yeltsina, Zina, and

Valya walk over to the Kissing Post with their luggage.

"Those *are* my mother and two big sisters!" Lena runs away from the others and towards Zina.

"*Tyotya* Tonya, who are those women?" Yuriy asks.

"The oldest one is your *babushka*, Yura! And that's your *Tyotya* Zina, and I don't think you ever saw your *Tyotya* Valya."

"I don't recognize them either," Natalya says.

"Hello, Mrs. Yeltsina. I'm Aleksander Kalvik, one of the people who processed you yesterday. I wouldn't have thought twice about you, but my wife was an immigrant I processed through these gates, so I remember her friends. I've gotten to know most of them very well since that fateful day. One of them was this little girl, Natalya Yeltsina. She was travelling with the group, though she had no relatives. She was in the care of a woman named Lyuba, whom she'd grown very fond of during the ocean voyage, and lived with her until Lena came down from Canada for her. You may remember some of these people if I gave their names, since they stayed at your boardinghouse in Tver for three weeks."

"I want to stay with Lena, Tonya, Sonya, and Yura." Natalya hides behind her big sister.

"Look how big my grandson's gotten!" Mrs. Yeltsina scoops up Yuriy. "Thank God he got to America safely and wasn't permanently separated from you."

Lena chooses her words carefully. "I'm obviously very glad to see you again, *Matushka*, but I've lived in Toronto for the past three and a half years. Toronto is where I've made my new life. I was just about the only person Natasha remembered from our old life, and she's grown very attached to Tonya, Sonya, and Yura. She only knew her surname and patronymic from the ID the orphanage hung around her neck. Natasha knows Toronto as her home. Even if you settle in Toronto instead of New York, my baby sister can't just magically readjust to living with a mother and two sisters she no longer remembers. She's happy and secure in the family we've built for ourselves, and couldn't handle being uprooted again after all she's gone through. This is tantamount to taking an adoptive child away from the only family she's ever known. My God, she hasn't seen any of you in nearly seven whole years!"

"Are you going to settle in Toronto so you can all be together?"

Sandro inquires.

"We're damn lucky we were allowed to come here," Zina says. "After that ridiculous new nativist immigration quota, it's almost impossible for Eastern Europeans to enter this country. We wanted to come to America, not Canada. I'm sure Canada's a lovely country, but America's the land of promise we dreamt of. We're so lucky to have come here with the quota, and don't want to spit in the face of our good luck by immediately abandoning our new country."

"Why are you in Canada?" Mrs. Yeltsina asks.

"It was the only deal Klarisa could get for us," Antonina says. "She also knew Canada's more open to receiving immigrants."

"Who's Klarisa? And who are you?"

"I'm Antonina Borisovna Petrova, and that's Sofya Mitrofanovna Gorbachëva. Lena and I left our orphanage through the wiles of the deranged orphanage warden's pet. Klarisa used being that sick old woman's pet to her great advantage, like sneaking girls out of the country on a regular basis. She snuck Natasha out too. Sonya met us on the ship leaving for Canada, and agreed to pretend to be our mother. She also posed as Yuriy's mother to get him back from an orphanage here in New York after a terrible man kidnapped him."

"The man with the limp to whom I gave my full permission to take Yuriy?" Zina asks. "Thanks to that man, Yura got a chance at a happy life."

"You don't know that man like I know him," Lena says. "Come March, I'll be back in Manhattan to testify against him in court, as a character witness. He wants to have paternal rights over his daughter whom he had out of wedlock, but the mother and her new husband won't let him. I'll most gladly, cheerfully assassinate that awful man's character."

"Why don't you start looking for work and a place to stay in Manhattan?" Sandro suggests. "From time to time, you can take turns visiting each other. You don't need a passport to travel from Canada to America, or the other way around."

"Don't worry, *Matushka*, I'll write regularly," Lena promises.

"I want to stay with Sonya," Natalya says. "She's like my mother now."

Mrs. Yeltsina turns white.

"I had two little daughters of my own, Mikhaila and Karla.

Tonya was there the night my Misha died. She was beaten by a sadistic orphanage warden named Mrs. Voznesenskaya, and stopped breathing three days later. Then that sick woman turned around and began to pretend Misha were her daughter, keeping her poor little dead body in the same bed other girls slept in." Sonya crosses herself. "My beautiful Misha is an incorruptible, chosen by God to serve as a witness to the inhumanity of Bolshevism."

"'I'm barren, so I like to pretend she's my daughter,'" Antonina mimics.

"I don't know what's become of Karla, but I pray we might meet again in this lifetime. I'm old enough to be little Natasha's mother, though she's never called me Mama, and Lena and Tonya also look up to me."

"How old are you?" Mrs. Yeltsina asks.

"Thirty-three."

"You're still plenty young enough to have more children with a new husband. I myself had Natasha when I was in my late forties. As grateful as I am you've been a surrogate mother to my younger daughters, I can't fathom the thought of having them taken away from me all over again."

Lena shakes her head and takes her mother's hands. "I love you, Zina, and Valya, but my home is in Toronto now, with Sonya and Tonya. Natasha will always be well taken care of, since she's with her big sister, the only person she recognized from her old life. And Yura worships her." Lena writes something on a small piece of torn-out notebook paper. "Here's our address. You can start writing us at any time, and I'll start filling you in on what's happened to us since we've been away. Do remember all of us will be here again come March, to help Lyubov Koneva and her new husband secure full rights over Lyuba's young daughter. I hate that man who wants to take her daughter away from her, and who almost succeeded in me never seeing Yura ever again, with every fiber of my being. I hope he rots in the last circle of Hell."

Natalya doesn't look at her mother and two oldest sisters as her group begins moving away.

"It could be worse," Sandro says. "My wife turned in her parents' names after they moved to Russia, and shed no tears as they were arrested the next morning and eight of her nine younger siblings killed. She thought they'd all been killed, until her favorite sister turned up by total surprise ten months ago, shortly before our marriage."

"What an awful woman!"

"Yeah, my wife seems cold, heartless, and even a bit crazy at first to outsiders, but she ends up growing on you after you learn to understand what makes her tick and how she didn't do things like that out of pure meanness. She's never rejoiced over her siblings' deaths, even if she believes they had the macabre blessing of controlling the population."

Stunned, Mrs. Yeltsina strides away with her two oldest daughters.

4

That night, Lyuba is racked with a nightmarish dream about the night Tatyana was born, only with a more sinister, horrific ending. Pyotr has gotten to her in time, *sans* doctor, pushing that vain witch Anastasiya out of his car, and he and Ivan help Lyuba into the backseat, with Ginny right beside her. She's walked into the hospital by Ivan and Pyotr, and then the nightmare really begins.

"Hospital regulations say no one can be in the delivery room except for the mother and medical personnel. Step aside, all three of you."

"What kind of hospital makes a poor young woman alone in the world give birth all alone but for a strange doctor?" Pyotr barks. "That woman is barely nineteen years old, and the father of her child abandoned her moments before she went into labor!"

"An illegitimate child?"

"It's not her fault she's pregnant out of wedlock," Ivan jumps to her defense. "She wasn't lying there all by herself when she got pregnant!"

"What about this boy? Does he have no parents either?"

"His mother's in America, and his father's God knows where."

"So he's in the care of you three?"

"I don't live with them," Pyotr tries desperately to explain. "I'm just a very good friend."

"If this young man doesn't live with you, how many men does *that young woman live in sin with?"*

"We know the paternity of this child," Ivan says. "I've never slept with Lyuba. The only one she slept with was that scumbag who abandoned her tonight to go sailing off to America!"

***

Inside the delivery room, the nurse holds the baby up. "It's a girl."

Lyuba sits up slowly and reaches her arms out, her heart melting at the sight of the newborn. "Can I hold her?"

"No, you'd grow attached. Hospital policy is to put up all illegitimate children for adoption as soon as possible. You're very young. You might find a man who'll marry a fallen woman and have a lot more children with him. Perhaps one of those two young men you came in with would be so willing."

***

Pyotr and Ivan come into the delivery room ten minutes later with Ginny. Lyuba is lying there alone in the bed, sobbing hysterically.

"They took my baby because she was born out of wedlock!"

"She can't have left the hospital yet." Pyotr pats her on the head. "Maybe Ivan can pretend to be married to Anastasiya, and they can adopt her back."

"It will be a cold day in Hell when I even pretend *to be married to that selfish, vain blonde woman!"*

"They can't take my baby, Petya! You've saved us so many times, you must do it again and put my baby back into her mother's arms before she's given away to total strangers and possibly beaten or abused by them!"

"No respectable woman keeps an out of wedlock child," Ginny says smugly. "Of course Pyotr will have no part of letting you get away with defying society's rules for the natural order of things by keeping a baby born out of wedlock."

Lyuba sits up with a jolt and feels for the wedding band on her finger, then reaches over to feel Ivan's wedding ring. A married, respectable woman no longer in danger of having her children snatched from her because they were born out of wedlock, and by different fathers no less. Then she rushes into Tatyana's room and kneels by the bed to see her sound asleep, holding her doll.

"You've already been through so much in your not quite five years on Earth, Tanyechka, and your nine months before you were born too, but you've been loved and relatively safe your entire time on Earth, except those few times we were separated. You've never done anything wrong. You never prayed to God you should be born out of wedlock or to a woman who was barely nineteen. And you've always had a great father who loves you, though you're not his flesh and blood. Not very many men in the world would gladly do that, love a child who was fathered by his best friend and the woman they'd always both been in love with. Your father was never absent from your life, since the man who's raised you from the night you were born is your father. His love for you has always transcended biology."

She quickly moves back to her room and gazes down at twenty-month-old Fedya sound asleep. The beautiful little boy that logically should never have been conceived thanks to Boris, with his father's dark brown hair and eyes, and looking every day more and more like he's a *levsha* like his handsome father.

"I heard you screaming in your sleep, *golubka.* Though I don't know which of the children you were begging the people in your dream not to take, him or her."

"I dreamt it was the night I gave birth to Tanyechka, only in my nightmare, you and Petya were able to get to me in time and take me to the hospital. You were all barred from the delivery room, and I was pinned down to a cold, sterile hospital bed as a strange male doctor delivered her. When the nurse told me it was a girl, I wasn't allowed to hold her, since she could only be given up for adoption since she was born out of wedlock!"

"You're just worried about our court case against Malenkov in two months. But we've had such a wonderful four and a half months since finally becoming husband and wife; why ruin it with nightmares?"

"We have more than enough witnesses to totally destroy his character, I hope."

"I think the testimony both you and I will happily provide will be more than enough to throw the judge's decision, and they'll also hear from crazy Katrin, who never liked Malenkov; Lena Yeltsina, who's hated him since she met him; and Liza, Alyoshka, Kat, Kolya, and Kittey. Ginny must slaughter that man's excuse for character, or else I'm going right to his mother with the news her only child lost his virginity at the age of sixteen on our wedding day. Boris's parents aren't too keen on his behavior, and neither are your mother and aunt. We might be able to pull in a number of others also."

"My three youngest stepsisters also don't like how he treats them when he visits."

"I promise you, if we're blessed with a third child, that child will be both conceived and born in wedlock, and none of us will ever have to worry about that possible child being snatched from us by a mere incident of birth."

5

Mr. Lebedev has worked his way out of the lower level of the rug-making factory, and for the past five months has worked as a salesman on the middle level, where the rugs are sold. When things in the store slow down considerably, he sneaks in an umpteenth reading of one of his precious books of prose or poetry, some inscribed with the names of his three daughters who are still unaccounted-for. Well, at least now he has Osyenka. Finally, at age fifty-one, and after ten daughters, he's been blessed with his very own son. Fyodora especially is most delighted with her brand-new baby halfbrother, so much so she persuaded her father and stepmother to let her be the godmother, with Ginny serving as the godfather.

Ginny is preoccupied lately with reading and rereading all his many letters from Georgiya over and over again until he can recite them backwards and forwards in his sleep. In her last letter, which he received a week ago, she was very vague and almost off-putting. She didn't enclose her usual pictures of the family—her wizened parents who've lived nearly half a century; Leonid, the almost-thirty-year-old bachelor heavily involved in politics but not women; Georgiya herself, a beautifully-matured sixteen-year-old young lady; and last of all, two-year-old Nelya, now starting to resemble more and more a toddler instead of a tiny baby. Her only mention of anything more than vague news about the family or herself was that she hasn't been feeling well and that perhaps it was a mistake for them to sleep together.

A rather striking woman with a baby in a pram and a husband by her side enters the factory and brushes the thick snow off her silver fox coat. "My husband and I are interested in buying the nicest Persian rug possible as a present for ourselves. It's our first anniversary." She speaks perfect Russian, in a Pskov accent. "This is the Russian area of the neighborhood, isn't it, Sir? Don't you understand me?"

"How much money can you spare?"

"My husband's a rather well-off businessman, though we've only been in America for a year. He can probably afford most of your selection of Persian rugs."

"Are you wearing a glass eye?" the husband asks. "I don't mean to embarrass or upset you, but I couldn't help noticing your eyes are different colors."

"I naturally have one blue eye and one brown eye. My newborn son does too."

"Our daughter has one blue eye and one brown eye also. She gets it from my wife's father, who also had such an ocular condition. After seven years, my wife forgets what most of the people in her family look like, but she'd never forget her father had two different-colored eyes. You only see something like that once in a blue moon!"

Mr. Lebedev sits up at attention, his heart racing. "Did she ever find out what happened to the rest of her family?"

The woman crosses herself, a faraway look in her eyes. "I was in Siberia with three of my sisters, Sir, but one of them got pushed off a bridge and was left there as the rest of us were forced to move on. Later, one of my other sisters was put on a work transport and separated from us. I was freed last year around this time, and had no choice but to leave my remaining sister. My husband and I met in the harbor where the ship picked us up to go to California. Thank God we were admitted despite that racist new quota. We've been in New York since the birth of our daughter."

"How old is she?"

"Three months. Her name's Yevgeniya. We call her Zhenyushka."

Mr. Lebedev smiles. "You wanted a boy and would've named him Yevgeniy? Not that I'm one to talk, since I have a Fyodora, but some feminine forms of names sound more forced than others. I'm sorry, you probably don't like people saying negative things about your child's name."

"No insult taken. It's normal to wonder after names we rarely see in the feminine form. I also had a sister named Fyodora, so you weren't the only one to like the name. My baby's named after my mother."

Mr. Lebedev's eyes nearly fall out of his head. "Holy Mother of God, your story is hitting closer and closer to home."

"You recognize something in my story? Sir, if you know what happened to my family, *pozhaluysta*, tell me. I just came here to buy a rug, but getting information about my missing dear ones is even better."

Mr. Lebedev's hands are trembling. "Was your father Ilya Nikolayevich Lebedev, originally from Pskov, and you were the third of ten girls?"

"How did you know that? Are you trying to tell me you know some of my dear ones and that they're safe in America? I'm not the only one?"

"My wife's name was Yevgeniya. We lived in Pskov and had ten daughters, Galina, Matryona, Dinara, Serafima, Yelena, Svetlana, Alla, Vera, Natalya, and Fyodora. Seven of them are safe with me. Even little Kroshka's still alive and well. Now I have a little boy named after my murdered little brother, and a stepdaughter who's about the same age as Svetlana. You have to be my dear Dinara. My dear Sveta said Lyolya was pushed off a bridge, and Sveta was put on a work transport. You must be my Dina, since Serafima's hair was strawberry-blonde, and yours is coppery-brown like mine."

Dinara falls onto her knees and hugs her father's knees, putting her head on his lap. "I never dreamt you were still alive!"

"Praise Christ. Praise Christ. God has been so good to a nobody like me to bless me with the safe return of eight of my daughters. Having eight out of ten daughters returned to my hearth is an even greater miracle than finally fathering a son. You're safe here, and no one will ever hurt you again. I hope this husband of yours is an honorable fellow who protects, loves, respects, and provides for you as you deserve."

"Yarik's wonderful, Papa, the best husband I could've wanted. He's even modern enough to accept how I became a Lebedeva-Sheltsova instead of giving up my single name entirely."

Her husband extends his hand. "I'm Yaroslav Markovich Sheltsov."

Dinara dabs her eyes. "*Matushka* must be dead if you've remarried."

"You don't want to know the details. But she's in a better place now, and now I've got a brand-new baby and a stepdaughter who's long regarded me as a father figure. Even better, eight of my daughters are alive."

"Who are the other seven?"

"Galya, Motya, Sveta, Allochka, Verushka, Natasha, and Dora. I can't believe you're the only one who's married and a mother. My other adult daughters are all old maids."

"I'm sorry Fima had to stay behind, but I couldn't dare fight the executive decision enabling my release unless I wanted to spend another six years in hard labor camps. My freedom was more important than staying with my only sister left. If I'd stayed, we might've both died together, but now at least one of us is still alive."

"She'll come eventually, just like I hold out hope for Lyolya to come back. It must've been hard to leave her, but I didn't raise my girls to be martyrs." Mr. Lebedev takes his three-month-old granddaughter onto his lap. "Thank God I finally have a real grandchild."

Mrs. Lebedeva comes into the store pushing Osyenka's pram. "Who are these people, Ilya? You normally never get so friendly with customers."

"Allow me to introduce my daughter Dinara, her husband Yarik, and my three-month-old granddaughter Zhenyushka."

"This is your new wife, Papa?"

"Yes, and that's your baby halfbrother in the pram. The woman is your stepmother, Yekaterina Iosifovna."

Mrs. Lebedeva shakes her head affectionately. "I still can't believe how many daughters you have. Every time I turn around, another one reappears!"

"God wanted me to have ten children in my first marriage, and was kind enough to restore eight of them to my hearth. Since today is Dina and Yarik's first anniversary, why don't we organize a small affair for them?"

"I can't wait!" Dinara proclaims, clasping her hands together. "I thought I'd never see any of my sisters again, and now seven of them are here waiting!"

6

Lyuba feels mildly sick when she sees her three-month-old stepniece at the dinner table that evening, a reminder of something she may never know or experience again. She constantly averts her eyes to avoid looking at Eliisabet and Kat's pregnant bodies. The past four and a half months of married life have been wonderful, but now again Lyuba is starting to have doubts about herself and Ivan. Eliisabet, who's never had any trouble with conceiving, is four months along with her third child. Kat, who's complaining so miserably about how it's far too soon to handle another pregnancy, at least has the ability to have more children and is also four months along with what she feels is another twin pregnancy, no less. Even Katrin, who once was so adamant about not having any children until age thirty, is now so in love with month-old Oliivia and can't stop chattering about how she can't wait to have another one, maybe getting pregnant again before the year is up. And Lyuba, the one who once never wanted even one child, now has two children, and now that she wants many more children, she's being tortured and taunted by the awful, horrific knowledge she may never have a third child, let alone get pregnant again.

Her woes are only monumentally added to when Mrs. Koneva pays a visit the next evening after Ivan is home from work, telling them how, though she never thought it possible, she and Mr. Konev have finally reconciled the pain of the past twenty-plus years. They're reunited and getting along as well as they did in the early years of their marriage, when Ivan was a little boy, before his father took to drinking to get away from the pain of having a *levsha* for a son and a wife who wouldn't get pregnant again. She caps off the latest news by revealing that in September, Ivan will finally become a big brother. Lyuba breaks down screaming after her mother-in-law wheels herself out of their tenement and carefully navigates her way down the stairwell.

"What are you so upset about, Lyubonka? Sure I'll be twenty-six by the time it's born, but I'm still going to become a brother after all these years as a lonely only child! And you're going to get a sibling-in-law, though we'll be old enough to be the parents!"

"My mother, your aunt, your mother, have all beaten the mounting odds of getting pregnant in their forties—in fact, your aunt beat the odds twice!—; our dear friends Eliisabet and Kat are four months pregnant; and I wouldn't be surprised if my sixteen-year-old cousin also got Georgiya pregnant! Even Katrin's done a complete turnaround and declared she can't wait to get pregnant again, not even wanting to wait six months after the birth of little Oliivia! At least my aunt and Boris's mother haven't yet rubbed it in my face by getting pregnant at their ages too!"

"We'll get through this together, just like we went through everything else together since we were children." Ivan pulls her up off the floor and takes her into his arms. "You'll gradually come to accept this is how you are now, and after you've crossed that bridge, when you least expect it, we'll have a third child."

"This is the worst thing that ever happened to me, even worse than what my father did to me!"

"Now I know you're not thinking rationally, if you really believe infertility is worse than rape and incest. We've still got two kids, a girl and a boy, to love. I love our family just the way it is right now, and you should too."

7

Sandro bursts in on Katrin's regular afternoon soirée, holding *The New York Times*. "I wanted you to hear this disturbing news from me, Kati." He's taken to calling his wife Kati, an Estonian nickname, lately, and Katrin has eagerly adopted that as her new secondary nickname. "Somebody whom you've long cared about very much died."

"Who are you talking about?" Anastasiya asks. "The only people Katya truly cares about are me, you, Oliivia, and that big-mouthed little sister of hers!"

"Are you going to tell me who?" Katrin gives Anastasiya a sharp little kick. "How the hell many times do I have to tell you to quit calling me Katya already? That was my slave name."

Sandro braces himself for her reaction. "Vladimir Ilyich Lenin."

Katrin screams and crosses herself, barely realizing what she's doing after years away from Orthodoxy. She then slumps over.

"He's dead?" Eliisabet asks.

"He just died of another stroke."

"Now, now. Let's not start panicking and jumping to wild conclusions," Viktoriya says. "Who was second-in-line to Comrade Lenin all those many years? Comrade Trotskiy. He'll assume power after the funeral."

"He was only fifty-three!" Katrin blubbers. "I bet someone sneaky, with evil, sinister, ulterior motives, did this to him. He had an awful fear of poison. Comrade Lenin had taste-testers for his food just to make sure. People very close to the one in power can become insanely jealous and want that power for themselves. Empress Livia poisoned Augustus Caesar to get her son on the throne. What's the name of that crude-mannered outsider whom Comrade Lenin hated and wanted to get rid of? He's Caucasian, and can't speak proper Russian."

"I think I remember who that was," Eliisabet says. "The one with big illusions about his power and importance. I think he's Georgian."

"Oh, that nobody. Iosif Vissarionovich Dzugashvili, called Stalin."

"You think Comrade Lenin met his sudden, untimely end by being poisoned by a Georgian nobody?" Viktoriya asks.

"We'll see what turns up in the papers covering these tragic events. I hope Comrade Trotskiy assumes power and gets rid of this pretender in his midst."

"He must've never expected to die so young, especially if he really were poisoned. Wouldn't it be horrible if the masses decided the past seven years were only an experiment and they wanted a Tsar again?"

Katrin grimaces. "That sleazy schemer Kirill is unfortunately first-in-line, and most people never liked him or his family. I wouldn't want to be ruled by such a creature. Forget how he saved his own hide by supporting the provisional government. His repulsiveness goes far beyond that. If the people insanely wanted the monarchy restored, I hope they'd finally revise the House Laws to circumvent the next-in-line and put a decent person on the throne. The Tsesarevich would've been nineteen now, a full grown man. Now we'll always wonder if he would've been a kind, enlightened ruler or an iron-fisted, bloody-handed tyrant like his awful father."

A number of the Leftist enclaves which Katrin is so keen on have put on black clothes by the end of the day and are holding vigils and memorial services. Katrin alone seems worried about the stranger in their hero's midst, the Georgian who possibly poisoned Comrade Lenin. She starts praying for his widow, Comrade Krupskaya, to stand up for her late husband's memory and make sure Comrade Trotskiy assumes power and kicks the schemer out of the Kreml, never to be heard from again.

8

Lyuba has had enough of looking at the pregnant bodies of Eliisabet and Kat, listening to Katrin's enthusiastic raves about how wonderful motherhood is and how she hopes to get pregnant again very soon, seeing Osyenka and Vasilisa, and putting up with Ivan going on and on about how he can't wait to finally become a big brother and how wonderful it is that his Divinely-returned mother is pregnant again at her age. Friday morning, she leaves the tenement before Ivan is awake and begins walking towards Lifegiving Font, the church they found their way to their first real day in New York, where they were able to confess for the first time in a very long time, even Ginny, and light candles for their departed dear ones. Long before Lyuba found out about her near-barren womb.

"Are you waiting for Divine Liturgy to start?" a nun asks.

"I came to mourn for something I once never wanted but now want more than ever. No offense, but you're not the ideal person to give counselling on this matter. You have the same situation I do, only you chose yours, and I didn't."

"Which situation, not being married or not having children?" The nun motions towards the hallway. "Father Yakim is busy with other duties, so we can speak privately in the chapel. It seems this is a personal matter you might not feel so comfortable discussing with a priest. Everything we say is in as much confidence and secrecy as if it were a sacramental confession. My name is Sister Serena."

Lyuba follows Sister Serena and closes the door. Once inside, she sinks onto a red cushioned divan and starts pouring her heart out.

"I've been married the past four and a half months, and I have two children. They were both born out of wedlock and by different fathers, but they're baptized now and have been made legitimate since my marriage. I'm unable to have more children. My daughter, who just turned five, was in constant danger for her unborn life when I was pregnant with her, because her natural father wouldn't stop beating me. I nearly miscarried five times, and by my eighth month, I started losing tissue and having terrible cramps. It was a miracle she came out alive. Several days later, my now-husband and a midwife learnt I was very unlikely to have more children. That man who fathered my daughter and abandoned us moments before I went into labor gave me serious internal damage because he beat me so much. I didn't know until several years later, about a week after I had my son, who's twenty months old now. It was a miracle I had him."

"Do you think your husband will leave you if you don't have another child?"

"This man adores me so much it's unreal, ever since he was nine and I was eight. He stayed with me after he found out about my damage, and keeps insisting he loves me and not my ability or lack thereof to produce more healthy children, but he always wanted nine children, and I know he's very disappointed and upset I won't be able to give him more children unless another miracle takes place. He threatened the father of my daughter after I found out what he did to me. As a foretaste of what he said was to come if I haven't had a third child within ten years of the birth of our son, he poured a bottle of acid onto his lap. Since then, this other man has found out he was made infertile and impotent by that, though another contributing factor, he insists, was a complication of chickenpox."

"If your son's only twenty months old, there's a good long time before those imagined ten years are up."

"My mother beat the odds and now has an infant son by my stepfather, and my husband's aunt also has an infant daughter that same age, as well as a thirty-three-month-old boy. And my mother-in-law just announced she's pregnant again, though my husband will be old enough to be that baby's father. My two best friends are each four months pregnant, one of them with what she feels is a second set of twins. Another friend has a one-month-old daughter, and can't stop talking about how she can't wait to have another one."

"Many women would love to only have two children, a boy and girl like you've got. The grass isn't always greener, as envious as you are of these other women."

"I always wanted none, until I had my daughter. While I wasn't very happy about being pregnant out of wedlock at only eighteen, I grew to love her. She never did anything wrong, never asked God to be born out of wedlock one month after her mother's nineteenth birthday or to a woman who never wanted any children."

"You look plenty young to have another child before it's too late."

"I'm a month past my twenty-fourth birthday, though after the things I've lived through, I must look closer to thirty. I know there are tales of infertility being healed in the Bible, but I'm not a paragon of virtues like Sara or Khanna. I was a fallen woman for most of my life. I can't remember when I was a virgin. My husband was the last man in a line of several hundred to sleep with me. That's a very long story, but suffice it to say, my husband is the only man I've ever loved."

"He knows all that, and he still wants to stay married to you?"

"He's too good for this world. He's a saint, wanting to stay married to a woman who's failed him in the most important way, someone useless to him, and most of all a fallen woman."

"The purpose of marriage in Orthodoxy isn't to produce children, though that is a nice side benefit. It's about the union of two people completing one another, making one another perfect, halving one another's sorrows, and doubling one another's joys. We'd never turn away a prospective couple because of infertility or being past childbearing age."

"But you chose deliberately never to marry or have children."

"There were many struggles before I achieved a sense of peace about my calling. Your husband seems to be above and beyond a saint by how accepting he is of your past and your current medical status."

"He'd never leave me, though I often left him before we were married, because I didn't want to believe he loved me that much. After a lifetime of abuse by men, I was too used to being hurt and used. The abnormal was my normal."

9

Ivan sent Tatyana and Fedya to his aunt for the day and now has invited Eliisabet over, after calling Boris and getting a negative on his accusations that Lyuba has left him for Boris again. Finding his bride is more important than picking up his daily pittance from Mr. Glazov. He can always find another job, but he can't find another wife.

"You're closer to her than almost I am, Liza. Don't you know where she might've gone if she hasn't left me for Boris again?"

"You're all but keeping her in a glass box here, Ivan, though I know you don't see it that way. The only things she does are housekeeping, childcare, shopping, and visiting friends and relatives."

"You don't think she could've taken her own life, do you?"

"She's only tried that once before. I have no idea how anyone could survive taking thirty barbiturates and wake up with just a stomachache and vomiting. God must really want her to stay alive.

For whatever reason, her time isn't up yet."

"This life isn't the rosy paradise I promised her over and over again, but it's far better than if we'd stayed in Russia, politically out of favor and now swarming with chaos after that raving lunatic Lenin died. Working ten hours a day in an iron factory for that *svoloch* Mr. Glazov and living in this tenement aren't the stuff dreams are made of, but there's always tomorrow."

"Alyoshka's been talking of quitting the factory too, maybe in a few years. When he feels the right time has come, he'll hand over the leadership of his union to Daniil Karmov and walk. There will be five of us come June, and we can't support a family that size with peanuts from an iron mill. We'd eventually like a fourth child, but the Lower East Side's no place to bring up children. My Kolya and Mira deserve a better life and happier childhood. This isn't the American paradise we imagined."

"You'd really come with us when we leave New York?"

"How could we not, after the past seven years together? As it says in the Book of Ruth, 'Where you go, I will go.'"

"You have such a perfect marriage. No fights, infidelity, threats to leave, disagreements over how many children to have, insecurities over things that don't matter in the long run, nothing. You were magically thrown together, and a year to the day after you met, you were married."

"We have problems you're not privy to, like money concerns. A happily-married couple with a placid home life isn't immune to disagreements and struggles."

"Lyuba probably doesn't want to look at you, because she gets jealous whenever she sees your pregnancy, but I'm begging you to search for her, bring her back to me, and convince her it doesn't matter she can't have more children. We've fought too hard to finally become husband and wife to lose our beautiful pair bond now. You can't kill a swan's pair bond, and my beautiful swan belongs with me, no matter what Fate decrees."

10

Eliisabet finds Lyuba at Lifegiving Font at five in the afternoon, after looking for her in the libraries, various stores, Katrin's penthouse, the parks, and her mother and aunt's house. Lyuba is immobilized on a kneeler, before seven candles she's lit. Only a few other people are in the church, in various other corners, staying away from this hysterical woman who's been praying and sobbing all day.

"Your husband has been very worried about you."

Lyuba stands up and squeezes Eliisabet to herself. "Today has been the darkest night of my soul, Liza, but I've finally realized no amount of praying, screaming, crying, having hysterics, or having relations with Ivan one hundred times in a row will ever change the fact I'm barren."

"You're really ready to accept your fate? Actions have to speak louder than words, and we need to see a constant pattern of changed behavior."

"I won't like it, and it'll always hurt powerfully, but as long as I don't dwell on it for too long, I won't have such emotional breakdowns. I've already got a girl and boy. So many women would love to have only two children, one of each. I should feel grateful I won't end up like Kat's mother. It was a miracle Tanyechka was born alive, and another miracle Fedya was even conceived. I can't expect a third miracle so Ivan can have a blood daughter, or for Fedya to have a brother."

"Starting right now you feel this way?"

"The worst of today isn't over, but once the morning comes, I'll start accepting it little by little. Someday I'll have no more sorrows."

"Oh, I know how long Ivan has been waiting to hear you say that!"

Lyuba sighs. "He didn't think I left him for Boris again, did he?"

"Of course, it was his first instinct to call Malenkov to accuse him of having you in his house!"

"Now if only Vanya would get over *his* problem too, always thinking I've left him for Boris whenever I disappear too long!"

"You do have of a track record of doing just that. He's not going to forget that easily or overnight."

"I already have what I still sometimes think I don't deserve, a loving husband and two precious children. Most of all, I've got a great big family. We might not all be rich, and some of us aren't blood, but we've become family after all the shared experiences of the past seven years, and through deep-seated love. Maybe I'll also stop being so jealous of the older women in our family for having babies."

"Right now we need to get you home. Do you know Alyoshka and I decided to join you and Ivan when you move to the Midwest?"

"That's always been Vanya's dream of life in America, taking me to the fertile Midwest and living on a farm. But Alyoshka's the union president..."

"Wherever you, Ivan, and your children go, Alyoshka, I, and our children will go. Eventually we want a fourth child, and New York is no place to have so many children, especially not in a tenement."

Eliisabet leads Lyuba back into her tenement thirty minutes later. It's almost beautiful because of the presence of Ivan and the children. She senses their dream of relocating to the Midwest is still a long time coming, because Ivan is so stubborn about not quitting his job and being content to be exploited by Mr. Glazov day in, day out, but since Aleksey persuaded Ivan to join the union, and wants to eventually move to the Midwest and take up farming, perhaps they won't be stuck here much longer...

"She was in church the whole time."

Ivan rushes forward and pulls her into his arms. "Praise Christ you've come back to me. You always come back to me. I should stop doubting you'll come back to me every single time."

"I've fully accepted my fate as a barren woman. It won't be easy, but after I get my worst grief out of my system, it'll only begin to get better and better. Someday I'll only feel occasional twinges of guilt and grief. It'll always be very painful to think about, but so long as I don't dwell on it, I'll one day be able to accept it, come to terms with it, and be at peace with how God only wanted me to have two children, one of each."

"You can't imagine how long I've been waiting to hear you say that, *golubka*. I told you I love you, not your ability to reproduce."

"I know you're not lying, because I know you better than that. We've known one another for almost sixteen years. I won't need a fancy American psychotherapist to cure me, because you're too patient for your own good, and I'll always have two children. God willing, they'll survive all those horrid childhood diseases."

"What's a psychotherapist?"

"It's a therapist who uses Freud's teachings to help mind problems. Boris is seeing one to try to resolve his grief and anger over losing Tatyana, and to possibly cure his impotence and infertility."

"Isn't Freud the man who believes all men are sexually attracted to their mothers and want to kill their fathers to marry them, that girls are sexually attracted to their fathers and want to kill their mothers to do the same, and that all little boys are afraid of being castrated by their fathers?"

"Shura tells me her son loves him."

"We all know how crazy Boris is. Wouldn't put it past him to take an avid interest in the rantings of a sex-crazed pseudoscientist."

Lyuba forlornly plays with her food when they sit down to eat fifteen minutes later, ignoring how Fedya keeps trying to climb into her lap. One last time, she grows envious over how Eliisabet, Kat, and her mother-in-law are all pregnant. As a final means to try to draw herself out of it, she begins praying for Anastasiya to someday feel the same pain over how she won't be able to have children, never feel a tiny future life growing inside her, feel the quickening, or see the end result in that tiny little baby. If Anastasiya did get pregnant, she'd probably live up to her word and drop it off in an orphanage.

Lyuba retires to bed early, right after Tatyana and Fedya. Ivan is looking through the jazz records Lyuba has out from the library, and looking in distaste upon the new-fangled gramophone Katrin got them, when Lyuba begins screaming, like nothing he's heard before, as though it's coming from her soul instead of the back of her throat. Slightly frightened, he stays right where he is.

"You've never ignored me before when I needed you, Vanya!"

He goes into their bedroom and stands by the door as she continues screaming uncontrollably out of her soul.

"Vanya, my husband, come to me, and reassure me you really don't care I'm barren! In the morning, I really will finally start to come to terms with it, and before long, I'll never bring it up again!"

Lyuba's soul sings in joy when she feels his wonderful arms around her, the same safety she's felt since the first time she was in them at eight years old. He was spying on her doing yardwork from over the fence between their houses, when she sank down on an empty crate and started crying. Then and there, he promised her for the first time he'd never abandon her and would protect her from her father, though he had no idea why she was so afraid and hateful towards her father.

"You really were right," she manages to say in a normal voice. "How your arms were meant for holding me."

"Of course I was right. You need to have a little more faith in me."

"You should have more faith in me too, like not always calling Boris whenever I've been gone too long, to accuse him of having me in his house and thinking I've left you for him. I know what my track record is, but I'll never commit adultery."

"Anything's possible after your announcement today."

"After you've helped me through tonight, I promise I'll slowly begin to achieve peace with my fate as a barren wife." Lyuba pulls his head towards her and kisses him.

"You're kind of hysterical tonight. Are you sure you want to?"

"I don't want to, I *need* to. This is more about comfort than love."

***

Lyuba wakes two hours after Ivan has gone to Mr. Glazov's factory, feeling a strange spark. She goes about her usual routine of picking up the house, making breakfast and lunch, taking care of the children, and the few odd errands in town, all with the spark still burning away inside of her. For once, she doesn't berate Ivan about how little money he makes or how much she hates living in a tenement. Her whole attitude is immensely turned around for the rest of the month and well into February. She doesn't fall apart when Katrin announces she's pregnant with her second child, nor does she any longer feel insanely jealous of Eliisabet and Kat, the latter of whom is now hugely pregnant for only twenty-five estimated weeks and positive she's having twins again. Even Ivan's exuberance over how he'll be a big brother in September no longer fazes her.

11

"You weren't just imagining things or having hallucinations, Mrs. Koneva. I have no idea how this is possible, but you're definitely pregnant. If you don't miscarry, and if your suspicion of the exact conception date is correct, it'll be born in October."

Lyuba sits bold upright. "But I've come to terms with how I'm barren, and you and that other midwife both discovered the same internal damage! I can't believe I beat the odds so soon after having my son!"

"If I were you, I wouldn't get too attached to it. It's highly likely you'll miscarry. I wouldn't tell your husband this strange, miraculous news until you reach at least your fourth month, so he doesn't get his hopes up any greater than yours."

Lyuba gently strokes her midsection. "I expect I won't be blessed with a third child. I won't tell Vanya about this unless I make it past the first trimester. Any day now, I'll miscarry, and he'll never know. I won't get too attached to it. I've come to accept being barren, and now that I've accepted my fate, I won't be so upset."

Lyuba remains in shock over the news. She doesn't want to believe it, let alone tell Ivan anything about it. The only other people besides herself and Mrs. Kuzmitch who know by the beginning of March are Kat and Eliisabet. She doesn't want to grow attached to the future baby growing inside her, yet she can't help it as each day goes by and there hasn't been a miscarriage yet. If Ivan knew, he'd probably want it to be a girl, so he could have his first and possibly only biological daughter, but he already has a full daughter as far as they're concerned, whom they'll all be in court on behalf of in two weeks, to decide whether she stays with her mother and the only father she's ever known, or if Boris gets partial paternal rights over her, despite how the only people left in his corner and willing to testify on his behalf are Granyechka and Father Spiridon.

****

Chapter 42: Who Will Stand, Who Will Fall?

Boris enters the courthouse on March 14, flanked by Father Spiridon; Granyechka, carrying her month-old-daughter Manya; and his mother, the lattermost of whom quickly deserts him once they're at their designated bench. Boris looks back in terror and sees the eyes of everyone whom he's offended or made an unending enemy of over the past seven years—Katrin, Lyuba, Ivan, Ginny, Lena, his parents, Mrs. Lebedeva, Mrs. Kharzina, Eliisabet, Aleksey, Kat, Nikolas, Kittey, Mr. Lebedev, Mr. Kharzin, the Lebedeva sisters, Pavel, Viktoriya, Sandro, some of his students, the priest who'd been ready to employ him until Mrs. Lebedeva told him all about Boris's life of sinning, in the misguided view she was doing a good thing by being honest about how Boris had made a real effort to turn his life around. His only allies left in the world are Granyechka, Father Spiridon, and his lawyer.

Ivan and Lyuba have a lawyer paid for by Katrin. Boris has read the letter they wrote to the judge, demanding a court trial, and the number of people who've signed off approving Tatyana not be allowed a relationship with her biological father nauseates him. Even his own parents have agreed to slander his character if they're called upon by the lawyer, and Mrs. Lebedeva and Mrs. Kharzina, who've treated him like a son for years.

Boris's lawyer is being paid for out of his own pockets. Though he makes enough to live comfortably, he's furious Father Spiridon flat-out refused to pay for the lawyer. He's sick with rage at the entire situation, even more so when he realizes Tatyana isn't in the courtroom. She and the other children are downstairs, to protect their innocent ears from these very age-inappropriate testimonies. Only Dinara's five-month-old Zhenyushka, Katrin's three-month-old Oliivia, Valeriya's two-month-old Vasilisa, and Lyuba's two-month-old halfbrother Osyenka are allowed in. Boris looks away in mortification when he sees Katrin breastfeeding, as though she isn't surrounded by scores of other people, including complete strangers.

There is absolutely nobody whom Boris can cling to for support, not even Granyechka or Father Spiridon, when the judge enters the room and the bailiff announces the case, Konev and Koneva vs. Malenkov. *All because I ran away from responsibility five years ago*, he thinks darkly, *and because nobody wants to forgive me*. Even the few who've somewhat forgiven him, like Mrs. Lebedeva, have refused to stand by him in his darkest hour. He tries to reassure himself with the knowledge that, knowing Ivan's volatile temper, his former best friend might be held in contempt of court for any number of outbursts due to how Boris's lawyer might bait the other side's witnesses.

"Why did Konev have to be the plaintiff?" Boris begins whining to his lawyer and Father Spiridon. "Now I look like the bad guy to the judge because I'm the defendant, when I'm the one who had the better case, wanting to take *him* to court to force him to give me back my daughter! Konev beat me to it, like a spoilt child!"

Boris's lawyer stands up and faces the judge. "During the course of today, my client, Boris Aleksandrovich Malenkov, will prove to you, through the testimony of his witnesses and the cross-examination of the witnesses brought by his former best friend, that he's a changed man who loves his daughter Tatyana very much. It's a given that people often do irrational things during wartime and civil upheaval, and afterwards feel extremely guilty about what they did during a crisis, such as rape, pillage, and stealing. My client was barely seventeen when he was thrown out of Aleksandrovskiy Gymnasium, where he was completing his penultimate year, all because he and his parents, who were arrested shortly before his expulsion from school, supported the Tsar, who had recently abdicated. He held up valiant hope against hope during the ensuing months, while he, the mother of his child, his former best friend, and his daughter's cousin were in hiding outside Moscow—"

"My home city is called Moskva!" Boris interrupts.

"Not in America. As I was saying, after the October Revolution of 1917, my client and his friends felt safe to return to Moscow, under the protection of a Bolshevik friend. They all lived together in a big house in a valley for several months, until they broke off into smaller groups and got their own smaller houses in the valley. My client was left in the original house with the original group he'd been in hiding with, in addition to an Estonian woman who survived a labor camp. My client was by that point involved in a romance he'd long been dreaming of with the mother of his child. His former best friend, Ivan Konev, was in a romance with the Estonian woman.

"During this period of time, my client began to feel very angry about how, while the Whites seemed to be winning the Civil War during much of 1918, he and his friends had to live in an isolated valley instead of in the center of their home city, all because of the godless Bolsheviks. To relieve his newfound rage, he got work as a village tough, protecting his new home from would-be Red intruders, beating them up if they tried to get in, stealing, and getting involved in run-of-the-mill drug trafficking. During April 1918, my client's daughter was conceived. My client wasn't thinking straight, with everything going on around him, and did some things he very much regrets. He took out his rage on a defenseless unborn child, did leave the mother of his child moments before she went into labor, but not on purpose, and went to make a new life for himself in America in anticipation of eventually bringing over his girlfriend and their daughter so they could have a wonderful new life together someday.

"My client will talk about his two trips back into Russia, when he grew to love his daughter and resent that his former best friend had all but officially taken his place as that baby's father and male guardian. My client did some very bad things, but they're excusable since they happened during a war and civil upheaval, when almost no one is thinking straight."

The lawyer paid for by Katrin stands up next, giving Boris's lawyer a dirty look. "My clients, Ivan Ivanovich Konev and Lyubov Ilyinichna Koneva, will prove to you that that man is not only a bully and a coward, but does not deserve to be a father. You'll find out how Mrs. Koneva was never in a romance with him and how Mr. Konev was never in a romance with the Estonian woman. They got involved with those people to make the other jealous, not out of love for Mr. Malenkov or Miss Voroshilova. While it's true that, ever since both men met Mrs. Koneva sixteen years ago, when she was Miss Zhukova, they were both smitten with her, there were plenty of clues she always preferred Mr. Konev and only felt a strong friendship towards Mr. Malenkov. They were all best friends until Mrs. Koneva got pregnant with her daughter and Mr. Malenkov began to beat her.

"That child whom Mr. Malenkov claims to love so much might

never have been here, as he told Mrs. Koneva over and over again while she was pregnant that he didn't want a baby, didn't want to do the respectable thing and marry her, and beat her and pushed her down stairwells to try to make her miscarry. She almost did, at least five times. He also told Mr. Konev, when he caught up to him at a nearby railroad station, to take care of Mrs. Koneva and tell the baby he was the father.

"You'll hear all about his two intrusions into their happy lives during his subsequent illegal returns to Russia, how he left Mrs. Koneva with almost no chance of having another baby, and how he won't leave my clients alone about the daughter whom they've been raising together since the night she was born. Mrs. Koneva doesn't remember the first time she slept with Mr. Malenkov, the night her daughter was conceived, since he got her too drunk to remember after it became clear she wanted no part of sleeping with him. She guessed what happened when she woke up in the morning. Apologies and repentance came too late for Mr. Malenkov."

"Even if you lose your case, God will forgive you," Granyechka whispers.

"To demonstrate how Mr. Malenkov can't be trusted to responsibly take care of his own daughter, let alone a child that isn't his, we'd like to call our first character witness, Miss Yelena Vadimovna Yeltsina."

Lena, who's now seventeen, gives Boris a look of pure hate as she walks up to the witness stand and is sworn in.

"Miss Yeltsina, do you remember the first time you met Mr. Malenkov?"

"The first time I *met* him and the first time I *saw* him were two different times, though they happened only months apart. I first saw him in late March 1920, and I first met him in June of that same year."

"What was your first impression of him when you actually got to know who he was?"

"I remembered him right away when I saw him, because of his limp, his kind of chubby face, and how he was a bit short for a man. Those thick-soled shoes didn't fool me for a minute. I was on a boat getting ready to leave Russia for a new life in Canada, and my best friend and I saw this man charging off a steamship, pushing away everyone in his path, and running onto our boat. Many people on the boat he unboarded had a chalk X marked on their clothing."

"Aren't people who have an X marked on their clothing the rejects from Ellis Island who have to be sent back unless they get a second opinion from a higher board of doctors? What was he doing on that ship if he didn't have any X on his clothes or hadn't chosen to be deported with a rejected loved one?"

"He was snuck onto the boat illegally, to get back into Russia. I later found it was his second time sneaking back illegally. Once he was on our ship leaving for Canada, he demanded to know if anyone had seen his daughter and her mother. I remembered him because he had a limp in his right leg. I immediately got suspicious when he told me the name of my son. He proceeded to tell me, without any remorse whatsoever, that he'd taken my son to America and abandoned him to illegally return to Russia. I soon found out his daughter's great-aunt took him to an orphanage because his daughter's grandmother, the other woman's older sister, left him alone in their house while she went to work and hadn't changed his diaper. Thankfully, that very same great-aunt was able to help me get my baby back once I was in North America. I will never forgive or forget that evil little man for how he kidnapped my son and almost was the reason I might never have seen him again!"

"Do you think Mr. Malenkov can be trusted to raise his own daughter after the cruel way he kidnapped your son and didn't take good care of him, and was the reason he was temporarily languishing in an orphanage without his mother to take care of him?"

"One hundred percent. In my eyes, that man is pure evil and has no business having children, not even adopted ones. I hope he burns in Hell for kidnapping my son."

Boris's lawyer steps up next. "Wasn't your son born out of wedlock?"

"Yes, but so was Mr. Malenkov's daughter."

"How old were you when you got pregnant?"

"Eleven. I was twelve when I had my son."

"Isn't it a bit hypocritical to berate him for his behavior when you've done the same thing?"

"You yourself said it. People do things in wartime they'd never consider in peacetime. I did what I did to get food for my mother and sisters."

"Do you recognize this man?" Boris's lawyer holds up a picture of Misha.

"That man is Mikhail Yakovlevich Godunov, my son's father, though I use the words 'man' and 'father' only in a literal sense."

"He looks like a grown man, and this was taken possibly four or five years ago! You don't look too old yourself. How old are you?"

"Seventeen."

"And how old is this man?"

"He'll be twenty-seven in June."

"So you were eleven years old and whoring yourself with a man ten years your senior!"

"I met Misha a week before the February Revolution. He saw I was hungry and gave me some water. Later, he promised me a lot of food. He didn't really mean it, though he didn't always lie to me. He often gave me enough food to help my mother and sisters survive. My son was conceived of rape, but I came back later, giving my body to that older man in exchange for food and water. I did it because it was wartime, like you yourself argued your sick client beat a pregnant woman because of wartime. When you're starving, food is food. You don't care what it is or how it gets in your stomach. I was so hungry I would've eaten roasted rats or crawled through tetanus-infested rust and broken glass. You've always lived in a country of plenty, and have no idea what food shortages and hyperinflation are like."

"Did Mr. Malenkov ever endeavor to explain the purely altruistic reasons for taking your son to a better life in America?"

"He claims my sister Zina gave him full permission. I'd been sent to an orphanage, as I was too young for prison, because I made mutual funny faces as a young circus clown dressed like Lenin. My mother and Zina couldn't care for my son anymore, and Zina left him on the ground with a note pinned to him. The first person to stop by and pick him up was Boris. Zina approved of this action after learning he was going to America and had just left his daughter again. She had no idea about his immoral character."

"How about a little girl who sleeps with a grown man, gets

pregnant, keeps the baby, and defends those immoral actions, while slandering a man who came to think of Yuriy as his own son by the time they landed in America and wanted to adopt the boy as his own?"

"No girl voluntarily sleeps with an adult man. You're morally repulsive if you truly believe I had consensual sexual relations at that age and that I was a whore. Something tells me you'd never accuse a man of such immorality if he'd done the same thing. I did what I had to do to get food for my family."

"Just like my client did what he had to do to feel better about his personal situation during the Civil War. I rest my case."

"That's damn right! And that boy would be calling me Papa if she hadn't persuaded Mrs. Kharzina to get him back from the orphanage for her!" Boris shouts to Father Spiridon.

"We'd next like to call Mrs. Katariina Kalvik-Nikonova to the stand."

Ivan looks away in horror when he sees Katrin breastfeeding Oliivia for the whole world to see. She sits down in the witness stand, oblivious to the gasps.

"Please put your hand on the Bible—"

"That is a blatant violation of separation of church and state. I worship Unitarian and don't believe in most of the Bible. I'll raise my left hand and affirm."

"Why do we have to put that crazy woman up there?" Ivan pesters. "I know full well Boris must've told his lawyer the perfect thing to destroy her credibility!"

"She's paying the bills for our lawyer, Vanya, and you're beholden to her for how she let you stay in her house," Lyuba says.

"What a pretty little baby. What's her name?"

"Oliivia Asta Kalvik. She has three months, and already I have two months pregnancy with my second child. It's hard to believe when Mrs. Koneva was pregnant with her daughter, I didn't want any children till I had thirty years!"

"Were you in close contact with Mrs. Koneva during her first pregnancy?"

"Not at all. I wasn't even in contact with my own best friend, who lived by her house at the time."

"When did you first meet Tatyana Koneva?"

"The morning after she was born. My best friend came crawling back to me the night before, but in the morning we took the train back to their house. She left after it quickly became very clear Mr. Konev wanted nothing to do with her, but I stayed and soon realized how much he loved that tiny newborn baby who wasn't his natural child. He and Lyuba took turns holding the baby until she began breastfeeding, like I'm doing now. He looked away in embarrassment and went into the kitchen to make lunch."

"After that, did you have many chances to get acquainted with the baby?"

"I didn't see her again until March of that year, 1919, when my friend and I were thrown out of my house, along with Mrs. Koneva's cousin Ginny, who'd been living in my garage on and off for quite some time, and my maid, who died the next morning."

"And of course, Mr. Malenkov had already long since abandoned both his girlfriend and the new baby by that time."

"Yes, it was just Lyuba, Ivan, the baby, my other best friend Eliisabet, her husband Aleksey, and their baby Nikolay. We had to sleep in Khimki Forest and walk all day for several days, until three friends found us. Then Aleksey and Ivan stole a car and dumped Ginny far away from us, and we moved to a boardinghouse. It was unbelievable how loving and attentive Konev was to this baby who wasn't his. Most guys would leave if the woman he loved had a baby with his best friend."

"There was no resentment on the part of Mr. Konev about any of this?"

"The girl has always regarded him as her father. He might not have initially instantly regarded her in his heart as his full child, but he did instantly love her. My friend and I stayed behind when the others left that August. When we rejoined them next June, it became even more abundantly clear how much Ivan adores that girl. By that time, he'd long come to regard her as his daughter in every way that mattered. When Lyuba was away working that summer, he learnt how to diaper the baby, sat with her nights when she had violent croup attacks, measles, and rubella, fed her, rocked her to sleep, and protected her from Boris when he returned illegally a second time. He was like a demon that night, so full of rage it was frightening, jumping down thirty steps in one jump, pulling out a knife, ready to die for that baby."

"And now that Mr. Konev is the girl's stepfather and has a biological son of his own, has there been any inconsistency in his feelings of love for the girl?"

"Absolutely not. That girl is the light of his life, along with his son and wife."

"But now on to Mr. Malenkov. When did you start to dislike him?"

"Almost from the very moment we met, like the Yeltsina girl. We were eating lunch by a restaurant, and my friend and I said we were cold. Boris put his coat around me, and Ivan put his coat around Anastasiya. Then Lyuba's cousin said Boris and Ivan liked her, though they weren't her beaux, and that her mother wanted her to marry Malenkov. I was so disgusted and enraged a boy with his eyes elsewhere would give romantic attention to another girl. I told him what I thought of his disgusting behavior when he ran after me and tried to grab my sleeve."

"And your hate only grew from that point forward?"

"I didn't have much of anything to do with him for a long time after that, though I saw him from time to time until he got expelled from gymnasium and then again at two victory balls on consecutive nights, which I hosted after the October Revolution. This guy was scum. I sensed evil emanating from his entire being, and had doubts about how much Lyuba enjoyed dancing with him. She looked like she wanted to be with Ivan instead, who'd been trapped the previous evening by Anastasiya. Nastya delusionally, instantly assumed they were now courting."

"What was your reaction to finding out what the child had been named when you saw her the morning after she was born?"

"I was very pleased Lyuba gave the baby her surname. When she had about eighteen months, her surname became Koneva. I was also pleased to discover her patronymic, which has never been altered, was Ivanovna instead of Borisovna. That child didn't need that evil man's surname or patronymic."

"And in your eyes Boris has never been a father to this child."

"His way of being a good father is buying lots of expensive presents, like books, dresses, hair ribbons, dolls, toys, teddybears, paintboxes, coloring books, and religious items. He never changed her diaper, cradled her in his arms after she got injury, or took care of her when she was fighting to breathe during croup attacks. He is the lowest scum on this Earth. He even made a big scene at my wedding, one year ago today! He was having a screaming argument with Konev about the girl, again. I only invited him to be polite."

Boris's lawyer steps forward. "Your child is three months old?"

"Yes." Katrin transfers Oliivia to her shoulder and burps her, then places Oliivia in her lap and buttons her blouse back up.

"Isn't that the same age your youngest sister was in April 1917?"

"Yes, but that baby is long dead, and mine is alive. I've never thought about my baby sister since she died. I barely knew her."

"Didn't you all but sign your family's death warrants?"

"My parents are alive. They made a surprise appearance at my wedding last year. They were only in prison."

"How many siblings did you have?"

"I had nine, one of whom is still living. Viktoriya has sixteen years, and sits between my husband and Anastasiya, with long, wavy, light brown hair."

"Did you ever mourn your other eight siblings?"

"Not a bit. I never told anyone to kill them, though I felt something bad might happen. I told Vika, who had nine years, to answer me right away and tell me if she wanted to join me in becoming a Bolshevik and breaking away from our kowtowing family, but she refused. I was on my way to try to beg her to join me again the next morning when the Bolsheviks broke in, and I never looked back, though I'm glad Vika survived."

"You were a Bolshevik?"

"It's no secret. Everyone in this courtroom knows it. But I'm not the one on trial! That short, chubby man Malenkov is!"

"Mr. Malenkov, Mrs. Koneva, and her cousin all saw the scene in your house that morning, Mrs. Kalvik-Nikonova. Mr. Malenkov states you were standing by very calm and collected as your parents were herded out of the house and pushed into a police van. He also saw how your younger siblings were murdered one by one. The oldest boy was shot in the head and died right away. The others were shot or stabbed, and then the three little girls had their necks broken one by one and were thrown against the wall and walked all over, the sound of their breaking bones audible, as you stood by without a tear in your eye."

"Malenkov seems to remember it well for someone who wasn't in that house, but only watching it from the street. I'm the one who has to live with those images and memories for the rest of my life. And he was never in my family to understand why I hated my parents and never felt love for my siblings but Vika. It's no sin to not love everyone in your family, as unpopular a sentiment as that might be in the West."

"Aren't you a rather wealthy woman?"

"Yes, I was born into a rich family, and took much money to America. I make good decisions with investing and saving to remain rich."

"But wouldn't a good Socialist such as yourself give away all your money to live like one of the people whom you claim to be?"

"I do good things with my money. It's not impossible to be a good Socialist and wealthy. I really believe these things, and didn't take up radical politics to rebel against my parents or because I had boredom."

Boris begins to grow more and more afraid of losing Tatyana as the afternoon wears on. Next up are his parents, his mother testifying first, and both royally tearing into his behavior towards them for the past few years. They express horror at how he left a pregnant woman moments before she went into labor with his child. His fate only worsens when Mrs. Lebedeva and Mrs. Kharzina rip into his bad behavior, adding good credit to Lena's earlier testimony about how wrong he was to take Yuriy when he didn't have a job, much less a place to stick him while everyone was at work. His shock only worsens when Mr. Konev takes the stand and he finds out the judge might've been selected by Katrin too.

"How long have you known the defendant, Mr. Konev?" Boris's lawyer demands after Mr. Konev has effectively painted Ivan as a saint.

"His whole life. He was born year and eight months after my son, and they were best friends growing up. I never liked how his parents let him get away with bad behavior. Do you know it's his fault his mother never had more children? His fat head was so large, doctor had to use forceps to yank him out, and forceps were rusty and gave Aleksandriya infection which made infertility."

"That's not my fault, that's the doctor's fault for using rusty equipment!" Boris shouts.

"That boy was lazy, thankless mama's boy. My son was mama's boy too, but he was good, not spoilt. Boris always got his way, even if he wanted three portions of dessert. He wasn't punished for failing marks from gymnasium, learnt curse words at tender age of eight, caused big scenes for inappropriate behavior with girls at school, made fights he knew he couldn't win, and always tried to blame other people, even his best friend, my son, for what he did wrong. And he's sore loser. He fought inevitable marriage of my son and Miss Zhukova right up till morning of wedding."

"Where do you work, Mr. Konev?"

"In a store. You didn't ask anybody else where they work."

"Isn't your store illegal?"

"You can come and see it yourself. It's not illegal."

"Don't you work in a liquor store?"

"You can answer affirmatively," the judge announces. "I'm a very alcohol-friendly judge and despise Prohibition."

Boris begins crying in rage.

"I do work at liquor store."

"Didn't you almost get your grandson killed there last May?"

"There was incident with mobsters. They let my daughter-in-law and granddaughter go home, but they made me stay with my partner and grandson. Situation ended happily next morning, when three alcohol-friendly cops who frequent my store saved us after my son called them from basement."

Boris's ill fortune continues to increase. Eliisabet, Aleksey, Kittey, Kat, Nikolas, Mr. Lebedev, and Valeriya all take turns ripping into him next. He spends the entire recess fuming and cursing at his lawyer, then sweats bullets while Ginny takes to the stand. Ginny is also sweating bullets, fearful Ivan might not be convinced enough of the sincerity of his character assassination and proceed to go straight to his mother at the next break to tell her what happened six months ago.

"How long have you known Mr. Malenkov, Ginny?"

"One month shy of seven years." Ginny's voice shakes. "I met him before I could remember, but my parents didn't move back to

Russia from East Prussia till the war broke out, when I was seven. My mother and I only moved into my aunt's house in April 1917, after my uncle enlisted. My mother refused to live under the same roof as my degenerate uncle, so we lived in a neighborhood on the other side of the city. When we started living together, I got to know Boris very quickly, because he visited my cousin every day after school."

"Were you initially friendly with him, despite the seven-year age difference?"

"Boris was like my big brother. He always defended me, excusing my bad behavior by saying I was only ten and children shouldn't be expected to be good all the time. He even laughed at a poem I wrote for Ivan on his nineteenth birthday, a rather vulgar little poem concerning Lyuba, Ivan, and Boris, only I didn't name them in the verses, with equally pornographic illustrations. I really looked up to him and thought he was a great guy. I approved of him and Lyuba becoming a couple in late 1917."

"When exactly did your opinion of Mr. Malenkov change?"

"When Boris walked out on us like a coward. Our plan was to immigrate together! I defended him for a short while after he abandoned us, but then I grew to hate him blindly. He was the reason I became so out of control, wild, naughty, and evil. I knew he was involved in drug trafficking, roughing up the Reds who dared try to trespass into our village, forging documents, making cigarettes, stealing, distributing weapons, even using some of the drugs, but I still defended him and confided in him like a big brother. He told me about his plans to sleep with Lyuba, how they were going to a cabin, but if Lyuba started to protest, he'd get her intoxicated with mixed liquors and drugs. Russia had Prohibition too, so he got this liquor from the black market. I hate what he did to my cousin, how Tatyana was born out of wedlock and got a natural father who's such a bully and coward, and how it most of all made me act for so long, like an uncivilized savage with no regard for the rules of proper society, even during wartime! Everything was like a twisted, weird nightmare for so long, and it was all thanks to him!"

"Do you have any feelings left for Boris now?"

"Only pure unadulterated hate for how he threw our lives into a crazy, nightmarish whirlwind. I look back on those long-ago days with pure disgust. I don't even recognize the person I was when I did those things I did only because I was so mad, furious, and hurt over how Boris betrayed us, but especially Lyuba and his child, in the worst way possible. My father was away, I wasn't too keen on the other guys we lived with, and I didn't much like being surrounded by so many women either. After Boris left, I had absolutely no one left I could confide in or be with. I was like a young, unleashed demon."

"What a batch of lies!" Boris mutters.

His credibility and skills as a father slip even further when Svetlana, Alla, Vera, Natalya, and Fyodora take turns on the witness stand after that. He hangs his head in rage when the priest who fired him before he could start working at his religious school takes to the stand and rehashes the big litany of sins Mrs. Lebedeva laid before him.

"We're going to call a surprise witness," Boris hisses during the next recess. "Anastasiya."

"Does she know you want to call her?" Granyechka asks.

"No, she doesn't. But her delusions are still strong about her past relationship with Konev, and she truly believed Lyuba and I were happy together. She'll easily admit to being jealous of Lyuba, that she still has feelings for Konev, and that she's always believed Tatyana belongs with me, being raised by me and only me."

"Aren't you scared Ivan will destroy you?" Father Spiridon asks.

"You, Granyechka, and Anastasiya combined may yet swing it for me, in addition to all the bad things that were revealed about some of their character witnesses, like Katrin and that girl who had a baby when she was only twelve years old."

***

Boris sits smirking as court reconvenes ten minutes later.

"The defense would like to call Miss Anastasiya Viktorovna Voroshilova to the witness stand."

"What!" Katrin shrills. "She wasn't set as a witness for either side!"

"If your best friend doesn't testify, we will hold her in contempt of court."

Anastasiya reverts back to biting her nails after she's sworn in. She lowers her gaze from that of Boris's lawyer, feeling he's looking at the lower-than-usual neckline Katrin has finally persuaded her to start donning in place of her last-generation outfits revealing usually not a micrometer of flesh except her face and hands.

"How long have you known Mr. Konev, Miss Voroshilova?"

"One month shy of seven years," she says in perfect English.

"Didn't you have a romantic relationship with him for quite some time, during the same time Mr. Malenkov had his relationship with the woman who's now Mrs. Koneva?"

"Yes, he was my boyfriend. At one point, we were engaged."

"When did it start?"

"I had a crush on him the moment I saw him, though I was also as enraged as Katya was when we found out both of them had a crush on Lyuba, and we stormed off that bench and went to find another place to eat our lunch. But then I was taken to a labor camp and somehow survived, and I saw him at a ball Katya gave. I ran right over to him and convinced him to dance, and we spent the evening talking about everything under the sun. I convinced him I'm not superficial just because I'm a delicate blonde. Our romance continued to blossom at the next night's ball, one thing led to another, and before long I was living with him!"

"Living in sin?"

"My God no! There were many other people in the house, and even by the time it dwindled to just a few in the original house after the others got smaller houses, there were still other people there!"

"Do you believe Mr. Malenkov and Miss Zhukova had a good relationship during this time period?"

"They got along great. Always together, getting closer and closer, and of course they were certainly very much in love if they slept together out of wedlock and conceived a baby. All while Ivan kept buying me fancy, expensive presents, driving the sleigh for my ride as Snegurochka on Christmas, getting me a diamond ring, and continuing to have deep, meaningful talks with me. He would've proposed to me if Ginny hadn't thrown me out of the house after Lyuba gave birth!"

"Why did that little boy have the authority to evict you from the house?"

"He said so himself. He was a bad little boy back then, and everyone was scared of him, myself included. Ginny couldn't wait to get rid of me, and that seemed the perfect excuse. I took the train back in the morning after spending the night at Katrin's house, but Ivan, obviously confused and delirious, insulted me and told me he wanted me gone. We made up a few days later when he came running to Katya's mansion with Ginny, staying there for about two days. He left because of a misunderstanding involving *besprizorniki* Ginny invited in.

"I didn't get another chance to win back his love until July 1920, a year and a half later, when Lyuba was off being a prostitute and had left him with the kid. He told me we were engaged shortly thereafter, and we had a great relationship until I had to leave with Katya after our Bolshevik helper-friend told us we were in danger and needed to go to Tver. We shared some wonderful times in Tver, but unfortunately he picked Lyuba and her out of wedlock child over me. It's creepy how loving and tender he is towards that girl, as though he's her mother instead of her stepfather. One time, when we were all sitting outside except Lyuba and our Bolshevik friend, his affection towards the girl frightened me so much I had to leave. It's a woman's job to nurture small children, not a man's!"

"So then you assert Lyubov and Boris were indeed madly in love at the same time as your and Mr. Konev's relationship?"

"One hundred percent. May I go back to my seat now?"

"Not till you're cross-examined," the other lawyer informs her.

Anastasiya sighs.

"How far did things go with Mr. Konev? Was your relationship just puppy love, or was it a full-fledged affair?"

"We never slept together during the entire time we were together. I'm twenty-four years old and a virgin. Unlike *some* people, *I* am completely against premarital relations."

Ivan gives her a dirty look worth a thousand dirty looks.

"Did it ever make you suspicious, in the past few years you've had time to think about it, that you and Mr. Konev were only supposedly a romantic couple while he and Miss Zhukova were on the outs?"

"Why should I be suspicious?"

"The very moment you came home the night Mrs. Koneva gave birth to her daughter, her cousin pushed you out."

"Because he hated me and wanted any excuse to get rid of me. Several days later, Konev came to Katrin's house, and we were back together again until he left our boardinghouse in August 1919. The others stayed at the next boardinghouse for almost a year, but he left very early on with Lyuba, her bastard daughter, and her demonic cousin, who was using cocaine at the time."

"Would you kindly describe the circumstances of his leaving that residence?"

"Nobody knew they were leaving except my other best friend Liza and her husband. Originally, I later found out, only Lyuba, her cousin, and the baby were to have gone. Konev came along with them at the last minute."

"Did that make you suspicious?"

"Even the most disgraceful fallen woman who knows what's what would never travel with only a baby and twelve-year-old boy. She needed male protection."

"How about the time you claim you were engaged?"

"Lyuba was off being a prostitute, and in her absence, Konev proposed to me and we began our relationship again."

"How far did this relationship go during any given point of its so-called existence?"

"I already told you, we never slept together. We held hands, went places together, had meaningful conversations, and loved to dance."

"No petting parties for you?"

Anastasiya turns bright purple. "What do you take me for, an immodest flapper who exposes her knees and elbows and drives cars? I have *never* engaged in *any* immoral behavior such as that!"

"Did you ever kiss?"

"No."

"Then how can you claim he was your boyfriend and fiancé?"

"The love I feel for him is real."

"Wasn't this an unrequited romance born out of desperation?"

"Much later, I found out, to my horror and misery, that Konev used me, at least the first time around, to make Lyuba jealous so she'd break things off with Boris and come running back to him. The second time we got involved, like I said, she was off being a prostitute, and he wanted to move on with me. I don't understand why he kept coming back to her after I proved over and over again I've *always* been the better woman."

"Could it be said you're jealous of Mrs. Koneva?"

"Yes!"

"And so, angry over finding out you'd been used to make the love of his life jealous while she was involved with another man to make the love of *her* life jealous, you developed delusions about the true nature of your relationship."

"I know what I experienced, Sir. This was as real as it gets."

"Are you still pining for a married man with two children?"

"He has *one* child. That other child belongs to Boris, and I've always been completely supportive of her being raised by her true father."

"Isn't it a regular habit of yours to pine for unattainable men?"

"There's nothing unhealthy about having a crush on someone."

"What about these?" The lawyer holds up Anastasiya's two cosmographs.

Anastasiya gasps. "Where did you get those!"

"They're not the originals. I have my ways."

"What normal bachelorette has never had unrequited passion for a high-profile man?"

"It's one thing to put up posters and photographs of your dream men on your walls, and another to make cosmographs like this!"

"I'm not on trial here! And last time I checked, millions of women are also madly in love with Rudy Valentino, and my crush on Grand Duke Dmitriy dates back to when I was a young girl!"

"Those other women don't make cosmographs of themselves being kissed and embraced by the two men in question. I think we all know now you suffer from delusions, though your delusions are harmless and not enough to have you put away. You may step down."

Boris is furious Anastasiya has just been discredited and humiliated so thoroughly. He's still shaking in rage as Granyechka and Father Spiridon take turns giving their glowing testimony and painting him as a man who indeed made some terrible mistakes but feels awful about it and has fully repented.

All that is shot straight to Hell, however, as soon as Ivan takes the stand at the behest of the lawyer Katrin is paying for. Boris feels his former best friend's eyes boring holes into his own eyes, and the hate in them is undeniable.

"How long were you best friends with Mr. Malenkov, Mr. Konev?"

Ivan speaks slowly, his accent as heavy as ever, to avoid making mistakes. "I am a year and eight months older than he is. He always viewed me as a big brother. We grew up together, and our friendship lasted till I discovered he was beating the love of my life, who was pregnant with Malenkov's undeserved natural child. I harbored residual feelings of friendship for five or six months after my baby was born."

"How did you discover he was beating a defenseless pregnant woman and, along with her, her even more defenseless baby?"

"In August 1918, I took Miss Voroshilova to a market, and came home to loud fight upstairs. Boris said he didn't want to take responsibility, how dare she get pregnant out of wedlock, and it was entirely her fault she was pregnant, since she didn't tell him when to stop. That was impossible, since he made her so drunk she didn't know what he was doing to her and didn't remember it the next morning. He pushed her down the stairs and said he hoped the baby would be dead by the time he came home, and he went off in a car to his double life involving drug trafficking, hooliganism, stealing, and forgery. I put my hands over the baby and felt she was still moving."

"Didn't you have suspicions about this terrible behavior of a father towards his unborn child for months before you saw it in action?"

"When Lyuba had three months pregnancy, we went to a ballet, and after the show, she came to me furtively and whispered she was scared for her life, and her baby's life. I also had been secretly noticing her putting greasepaint on her face, as if to cover bruises, and sitting alone crying. There were times Boris turned back into the pretty nice guy I formerly knew, but then he began to beat her again, with disastrous results. After he left for work, she often doubled over in pain and screamed in agony. She told me she lost tissue."

Boris is forced to sit and listen to his whole lifelong litany of sins yet another time, as if his pummeling at the hands of the other priest, Ginny, Lena, his parents, his former friends, Mrs. Lebedeva, and Mrs. Kharzina weren't already enough. He listens to the story of Lyusha Zubova and her suicide; his two illegal visits back to Russia; how he beat Lyuba and raped her on his last day in Moskva during the second illegal visit; how he told on Ivan to Officer Bulyakov after he was beaten up in revenge for what he just did to Lyuba; how he broke and entered into the final Muscovite boardinghouse, and the loud, violent confrontation which ensued, during which the manager took Ivan's side even after the pulling out of the knife; his continued attempted interference in Tatyana's life; how he was a sore loser when Lyuba chose to marry Ivan instead of him; how Ivan suspects he gave Tatyana chickenpox instead of the other way around; his delusions that went as far as making up a room for Tatyana full of toys, religious articles, books, dolls, a little bed, and clothes; his blanket refusal to face the truth about how Ivan has been Tatyana's father since she was born; his cowardice; his alleged drug habit during 1918; his manipulation; and his disrespect of everyone, even the children in his religious school. Ivan dispenses a token gesture of affection by saying he truly believes Boris loves Tatyana, but it's far too late, since the damage has already been done.

He weathers a further character assassination when Lyuba takes the stand next and completely corroborates her husband's telling of the past seven years, right down to his pathetic attempts to win Tatyana over with presents; how she was conceived while her mother was dead drunk; how Boris wouldn't stop raising his voice to his daughter when she behaved like a normal little girl; and how Lyuba believed if Mrs. Malenkova hadn't been there, Boris probably would've started to beat her again. She's unfazed by Boris's lawyer's attempted goading of her by bringing up her shameful past, saying she was a prostitute for only a few months, to make money, and that if she were a man, everyone would praise her for having several hundred partners. Boris is now crying in rage and disappointment. Only near the end of Lyuba's testimony does his heart soften a little, as she relates how her childhood traumas led her into very dangerous, unhealthy relationship choices.

"My blood father was a pervert who used me for his degenerate, immoral desires and sins against the natural order of the world from the time I was very young. I never knew anything but a man who abused me and treated me as an object for sexual gratification. I knew what normal families and romantic relationships were supposed to be like, since he didn't keep me locked up, but I never understood how to make either happen for myself. Moreover, I didn't think I deserved a good man who'd treat me like his Tsaritsa, protect me from harm, and put my desires above his. As a result, for many years, I made very unhealthy choices about relationships and sexual behavior. My whole life, abnormal was normal. I didn't know any other model. My mother was too much in shock and disgust, and just looked the other way from the time she discovered what her husband was doing to me. She always told me to choose a man who could financially provide for me, even if he were abusive, immoral, and lacking in social graces, since she gave up her youthful love and his idealistic promises for my blood father. Women of her generation had even less rights and choices than we do today. She didn't know any better. My aunt was radical for marrying for love, going to art college, postponing motherhood, and only having one child. My mother, not my aunt, was considered the normal woman for their era. Only now, with the wisdom of her accumulated years and a healthy new marriage, does my mother understand what her choices did to me where no one can see it. We both deserved better than an abusive, immoral man who made us believe it was acceptable and normal to have such a dysfunctional relationship with each other. Now we both understand we deserve to be married to kind, loving, nice, protective men. I finally have an honorable husband who treats me like gold, and a stepfather whom I wish had been my natural father."

"I want to testify," Boris growls to his lawyer after Lyuba steps down.

"Are you sure that's wise, Mr. Malenkov? Mrs. Koneva, her husband, mother, stepfather, aunt, uncle, and cousin, all your former friends, Mr. Konev's aunt and father, Mrs. Kalvik-Nikonova, that other priest their side pulled in from somewhere, the girl who had a baby when she was twelve years old, and even one of *your* witnesses managed to all but clinch the verdict in your disfavor."

"That vain blonde woman should've done what was best for me and her by taking the Fifth instead of making it seem like she's delusional about her past relationship with Konev and her strange obsession with Grand Duke Dmitriy and that actor guy!"

"I hope you take the Fifth too when they start asking you the hard questions." His lawyer rises. "The defense is going to call Boris Aleksandrovich Malenkov to the stand."

Boris sits grinning like a schoolboy after he's sworn in. "Don't ask me questions, since I plan to tell it like it is in the hopes of getting my daughter permanently put back in her father's arms and raised knowing I'm her real father instead of that bully who has on innumerable occasions nearly killed me in his blind fits of rage. I don't trust someone with that boiling hot temper to raise a child. I love my daughter, and I'll never deny I had my priorities jumbled when I was put in the unwanted position of being a father to a child conceived out of wedlock, but now that we're in America and it's peacetime, I have truly changed.

"I was trying to prove just how much I'd changed by adopting Yuriy Yeltsin until my daughter's great-aunt shuttled him off to an orphanage. That seventeen-year-old girl doesn't have the right to be the mother of a five-year old-boy! At least Lyuba was nineteen when she gave birth! I bought an orange hairbow and a book of fairytales by Krylov and Pushkin for my daughter when I went to see her for the first time. I didn't care I didn't know her name, how old she was, or if it was a boy or girl.

"I've always wanted what's best for my only child. I make enough to live quite comfortably. I teach religious school instead of slaving away in a godforsaken iron factory. I'm sickened everyone rushed to judgment because I did a bunch of unsavory things during a time of extreme crisis. That seventeen-year-old whore who had a baby at only twelve years old claims she slept with a man ten years her senior because it was wartime, and nobody's judging her! Konev's father breaks Prohibition for his career and used to be a major alcoholic who beat his son and verbally berated his wife, and Ginny was a little vagabond and wild child all by himself. He's lying through his teeth by trying to pin all his bad behavior on me and my disappearance. He was acting like an uncivilized, wild little animal long before I left. Lyuba may have chosen a life with a man who works for fifteen dollars a week being exploited in a factory and living in a filthy tenement, but I want my daughter to come back to live with me so I can give her the life she deserves."

"Jerk." Katrin makes the *dulya* sign.

"I'm finished," Boris announces as he walks back to his seat.

"I don't have any more witnesses to call," his lawyer says.

"Neither do I," the other lawyer says.

"There's a final person involved in this complicated situation who needs to be heard from," the judge announces.

"We've already called everyone!" Boris protests in a loud, angry whine.

"Miss Tatyana Ivanovna Koneva."

"You can't do that, put my five-year-old daughter on the witness stand!" Ivan shouts. "She doesn't need to know such a huge battle is being fought over her!"

"Go and get your stepdaughter or you will be held in contempt of court."

Ivan goes down to the basement to find Tatyana playing with Nikolay and Yuriy. She's never been told Boris is her real father, only that he wants to be her father. She knows Boris is determined to be her father, but she has no idea why he believes he's her father when she knows her father is the man who's been with her since the night she was born, whom she's hardly ever been away from in her entire five years of life.

"The judge wants to hear from you too, my little *knyazhna*."

"I'm tired. I want to go home."

"The judge will hold me in contempt of court if I don't appear with you very soon. I don't know if you know English well enough to answer all their intense questions."

"Mama's teaching me English, though I don't get much opportunity to practice it."

"You've been through so much, all because you were born in the wrong time and place, in the midst of the wrong kind of people. I promise you, this is the last trial you'll have to endure in your precious young life."

Ivan appears carrying Tatyana five minutes later and puts her on the witness stand in a standing position. Boris begins tearing up at seeing his daughter.

"Will you tell us all who your father is, Miss Koneva?"

"Ivan Ivanovich Konev is my father. I love my papa. He's the best papa in the world. He protected me from lots of bad guys when we lived in Russia. My papa was very brave and jumped off a roof covered in ice and ran across the border into Estonia in ice and snow, carrying me and my mama, to save us from bad guys who wanted to hurt us. He carried us all the way to safety. He reads me stories, plays with me and my baby brother, takes me for walks, buys me ice-cream and candy, takes care of me when I'm sick, and changed my diapers when I was a baby and my mama was away working. My papa was brave enough to go to a toy store to buy me my first doll when there was something my parents call a flu pandemic, when I was a tiny baby. My papa isn't a rich man, but he always buys me the best toys because he loves me so much."

Boris groans loudly.

"Has he always been your father?"

"When my mother and I lived with Boris and my grandparents, Boris pretended to be my father."

"If Boris isn't your father, how can his parents be your grandparents?"

"My parents will tell me when I can understand."

"Why do you think Boris wants to be your father?"

Tatyana's somewhat limited English leaves her. "*On revnuyet k moyemu papu. Yemu zavidno smotret na nevo so mnoy, potomu chto Boris vlyubil b moyu mamu, no ona vybirala moyevo papa, i nye Boris.*"

Boris's ears burn in shame. "That's only half the truth, Your Honor!"

"Why don't you translate this 'half-truth,' Mr. Malenkov?"

Boris's face begins turning red in shame too. "She says I'm jealous of Ivan and envious when I see him with her, because I was in love with her mother, but she chose Ivan instead of me."

"Do you think Mr. Malenkov loves you, Miss Koneva, even if he isn't your father?"

"He gives me many presents, but my godfather Alyoshka does too, and *he's* never pretended to be my real father."

"How would you feel about living with Mr. Malenkov for part of the year, or visiting him on the weekends or once a year with supervision?"

"Boris is an evil, bad man. My parents, my grandparents, all my other relatives, and my parents' friends don't want him in my life."

"Do you think Mr. Malenkov would kidnap you if you were allowed to spend some time with him every now and again?"

"Yes, like he did to Lena Yeltsina's son Yuriy."

Boris storms out into the hall following the judge's announcement he'll take another brief recess and come back with his decision. He glares over at the people on the other side coming back from upstairs with their young children. He's even more infuriated when he hears Yuriy Yeltsin start crying to his mother.

"All these other boys and girls have fathers, Mama!"

"You have a father too, Yura. He's in Russia. When you're old enough, you can talk with Pasha about your father. Pasha was rather good friends with him and can tell you more about him than I can. He could even get you to see your father's good side. I never saw much of any good side, but he can't be completely evil."

"Why isn't he here with us? Why didn't he love me and want me?"

"Pasha will explain when you're capable of understanding."

"That boy *would've* had a father if Mrs. Kharzina hadn't schemed with you to adopt him out of the orphanage and refused to give him back to me!"

"I despise you. I would've trusted Misha more to raise his son alone than I'd ever trust you to raise any child." Lena turns away.

***

Boris sits shaking all over when the judge returns to the courtroom. It's by far the worst day of his entire twenty-four-year life. Everyone has turned on him so viciously. The fact that he could only find three witnesses for his side, one of whom was thoroughly discredited as delusional and humiliated for the heights to which her crushes on Valentino and Grand Duke Dmitriy soar, surely must not reflect well. He starts thinking that if he'd brought another character witness for his side, his new psychotherapist Dr. Seelenfreund, maybe things might've been just a little bit brighter...

"I have decided in favor of the two plaintiffs, Ivan Konev and Lyubov Koneva. The defendant, Boris Malenkov, is hereby ordered to never again have any contact with the child in question, Tatyana Koneva, except in the form of sending her those gifts he's so fond of. When she's of majority age, she may of her own free will decide whether or not she wants Mr. Malenkov in her life, but till that day, Mr. Malenkov must break off all contact with the child. His parents, however, are free to continue an active relationship with their granddaughter."

Boris gasps.

"Please come up here and sign these papers."

Boris, fearing being arrested if he doesn't comply, signs away all his paternal rights over Tatyana and stands off to the side as Ivan and Lyuba sign the document. When they're back at their seats, Boris falls onto his knees and down into the kowtowing position, sobbing hysterically, like an infant. Granyechka, Father Spiridon, and the lawyer all move away.

"Your bill for me will be in the mail," the lawyer informs him before leaving the courthouse.

Boris continues to howl until his mother pushes through the crowd on the other side of the courtroom and kneels by him, pulling him up into her arms.

"My only child, *Matushka*, since I'm impotent and infertile now, and I just lost her! I've loved that little girl since I saw her, and because I made some really horrible mistakes, she was taken away from me!"

"This must be a horrible shock for you, Boryushenka. I know what it's like to only have one child your whole life. Maybe you can ask Father Spiridon for a sabbatical and spend some quality time at home with me and your father. We'll get through this together."

Boris continues to weep uncontrollably as his mother holds him at the opposite end of the courtroom.

"Finally that man is out of our lives forever!" Ivan says. "Now he'll never come to our tenement again or stalk us on the street unless he wants to be arrested! It's really late, but we should have a celebration in honor of the judge finally recognizing Tanyechka has always been my daughter! I can't think of anything that would make me happier!"

"Look at that fat, short man crying like it's the end of the world," Katrin says. "I don't hold any grudge against his mother for comforting him, but he has to show some restraint when he knew damn well this was coming!"

"You're about to be made even happier, Vanya," Lyuba says.

"What could possibly make me happier than the verdict that was just delivered, ordering Boris to stay the hell out of our lives forever?"

"In seven months, we'll have a third child!"

Ivan cannot believe his ears. "What?"

"I'm pregnant with our third child!"

"Are you positive?" His eyes begin filling with tears.

"I've known since last month, but only told Liza and Kat in case you might get too attached to it. I'm still worried, but now that I'm this far along, I'm less and less scared something bad will happen."

"So soon after Fedya was born?"

"I thought I was going crazy, imagining things, and having delusions, but Mrs. Kuzmitch confirmed it."

"So we're going to have another child in October?"

Anastasiya, turning green in jealousy, runs out of the courtroom and hails a carriage going her way, longing for the moment when she can drown the day's sorrows and humiliations by gazing at her pictures of Rudy and Dmitriy, men who may be unattainable but who won't use her to make another woman jealous.

"This is even better news that what the judge decided!" Ivan kisses Lyuba on the eyelids. "I hope it's a girl."

"I knew you'd want it to be a girl. But if it's another boy, we'll name him Igor, after your late uncle."

"Now weren't the past sixteen years really worth it in the long run, *golubka*? Instead of having an ordinary romance and marriage like so many other people, we had to wait so long before we became husband and wife, let alone lovers, and by that time our love had been tested in so many ways. Whenever we may have problems in the future, we'll only need to remind each other of what we went through the last sixteen years and how any couple who makes it through a Revolution, Civil War, meddlers like Boris and Anastasiya, your evil late father, and everything else including today can go through anything. Just like I told you that long-ago day we skipped gymnasium and spent the day at Patriarch's Pond, the swan mates for life."

Epilogue: You Cannot Kill a Swan

It is now gathering dusk in Siberia. Serafima Lebedeva, utterly alone in the world for the past fourteen months since Dinara departed for America with Yarik, cannot remember the faces of her nine sisters, her parents, her aunt and uncle, or her cousin Nadya. She forgets their voices, how they walked, their house, the little dog Kroshka. Now that everyone is gone, there's no reason to live, but the Orthodox Church forbids suicide. It's been nearly seven years since her family was together. She doesn't have any idea her mother, aunt, and uncle have long been dead, nor what happened to Matryona and Galya. She doesn't know how many of them are still left alive.

But if she can find a way to break out of camp in the dark, when the sadistic wardens aren't watching her, she may yet survive. In camp, there's no reason to survive now that everyone is gone. No one is left to survive for or give hope to for surviving. Even if she found her way back into civilization after nearly seven years away from it, she'd be too shell-shocked to function properly. She'd most likely become a ward of the state. If she'd gotten away earlier, snuck away with Dinara, run away, or dragged farther and farther behind on a forced march, maybe there could've been even one little glimmer of hope...

2

In the small three-room log house in Bulun, for the past several years, Lyolya has been thriving and coming back to a small part of the civilized world after her three years apart from it. The four Smirnov children who dragged her in from that icy river are still at home. Bella is now nineteen and teaches at a nearby one-room schoolhouse, while seventeen-year-old Vsevolod, sixteen-year-old Manyechka, and fourteen-year-old Rostislav are students at Bulun's excuse of a gymnasium, which isn't called a gymnasium anymore after the Revolution. Slowly but surely, Lyolya has begun to use her legs again, though the Smirnovs never allow her to leave the house, not for fear of being recognized and arrested, but because she hasn't completely regained the use of her legs and can't walk very far on her own.

But one day, she keeps saying, she wants to move to America, California, and become a dancer, like she always dreamt of as a girl. Mrs. Smirnova brings her books, magazines, and articles about all the great Russian dancers, both past and present, and lets her design costumes for the girls in a local ballet troupe put together by the three nearest schools. Lyolya swears every night in her prayers that when she's finally granted the full use of her legs back, she'll return to dancing with a vengeance, to show those godless Bolshevik bastards how miser-

ably they failed when they beat her over the kneecaps with their filthy iron crowbars and then pushed her off a bridge into icy water, leaving her there to die. She's full of anger over this situation, but there's more hope lately than anger. She only has to think of her surname, Lebedeva, and how it means "swan," a symbol of so many good things, like eternal love and hope.

3

Two hours after the sun has set, Serafima begins her trek away from the camp she's currently imprisoned in. She's starting to go crazy after nearly seven years in captivity, with not even one sister left to give her one good incentive for surviving.

There it is, right after the large rocks the camp wardens have put up as a roadblock to escaping. The signs of a nearby hick town, any town, even one that doesn't qualify on any major map. With people who live in real houses, eat real food, and have real, lasting relationships with other people, with no ulterior motives. A place with real hospitals, where dying people aren't tortured, buried alive, sent to the cooler for five days as punishment, or forced to dig through rubbish bins to find a little something to eat.

But unlike how Alla was able to escape from prison, Serafima's departure hasn't gone undetected until it's too late to do anything about it. The head warden scrambles up on top of the largest rock and takes aim at her, the unluckiest of ten otherwise very lucky sisters.

Serafima plummets down to the sharp rocks below, her senses fuzzy, her back screaming from the bullet, with only enough energy after her seven-year ordeal of Hell to scream:

"You may be able to kill me, but you cannot kill a swan!"

The End

31 January 1993–26 August 2001
Conceived, planned, and begun in a very juvenile form circa 1990–1992
Polished, edited, rewritten, and revised 23 April 2011–18 October 2014
Second edition edits December 2014
Third edition edits July–August 2015
Fourth edition edits August 2018
Fifth edition edits January–February 2019
Final polishing May–June 2019

Glossary

Vulgarities and insults:

Blyakha-mukha: An exclamatory expletive of surprise
Chyort: Devil
Dryan: Good-for-nothing
Durak: Fool
Govno: Shit (only used literally)
Govnyuk: Shithead
Khuy: Vulgar word for penis
Morda: Dog-face
Mudak: Bastard; dickhead
Suka: Bitch
Sukin syn: Son of a bitch
Svoloch: Swine
Yebarishka: Despicable person (literally, "small-time fucker")
Zhopa: Ass (not anatomical)

Other words:

Analogion: A lectern or slanted stand with ikons or the Gospel, often near the ikonostasis.
Babushka: Grandmother
Batya: Father (formal form), only used in direct address.
Batyushka: Literally, "dear little father." Used to address a priest and to refer to the Tsar.
Besprizorniki: Literally, "neglected; uncared for; homeless; stray." Colloquially, it refers to the bands of wild children which sprang up in the wake of the Civil War.
Bolshoye spasibo: Thank you very much
Dedushka: Grandfather
Dobroye utro: Good morning
Dom gorit: The house is on fire (literally, "burns").
Dulya: An obscene gesture in Slavic and Turkic cultures, also varyingly known as *kukish*, *figa*, and *shish*, formed with the thumb between the index and middle fingers.
Dyadya: Uncle
Ema (Estonian): Mother
Golubka, golubchik: Darling; sweetheart (when used in direct address;

literally, pigeon)
Gorko: Literally, "bitter." This word is shouted at weddings to get the newlyweds to kiss.
Gromyko: Chatterbox
Groznik: Roughly, "thunderstorm man" or "dreadsome one," derived from *groza*, thunderstorm. It was once the nickname for July.
(Ya) Khochu: I want
Knyazhna: Princess (usually translated into English as "Duchess")
Levsha: A left-handed person
Lyubimaya: Darling; belovèd
Ma armastan sind (Estonian): I love you
Machekha: Stepmother
Mamashka: Mommy
Matushka: Mother; literally, "dear little mother." This term of endearment is only used for a priest's wife in modern times.
Nevesta: Fiancée
Papashka: Daddy
Pozhaluysta: Please
Prababushka: Great-grandmother
Prapradedushka: Great-great-grandfather
Spasibo: Thank you
Spasite: Save me
Tädi (Estonian): Aunt
Tata (Ukrainian): Father
Ty: Familiar form of "you"
Tyotya: Aunt
Udachnik: Lucky man
Ukhodite: Get lost; get out of here
Vanaisa (Estonian): Grandfather
Versta (plural *vyorsty*): A unit of measurement used until 1924, slightly more than a kilometer.
Vot ya: Here I am
Vy: Formal form of "you"
Ya tyebya lyublyu. Khotish byt moyey zhenoy?: I love you. Do you want to be my wife?
Zechka (plural *zechki*): GULAG slang for female prisoner.
Zek (plural *zeki*): GULAG slang for male prisoner.

Food:

Beignets (French): Deep-fried fritters with powdered sugar
Blinchiki: Small, thin, dessert pancakes
Bombonieras: Little bags of confectionary treats, particularly Jordan almonds, traditionally distributed after a baptism or wedding
Canelés (French): A small pastry with a soft custard center and thick, dark caramel coating
Chak-chak: A pastry of Tatar origin, made of deep-fried unleavened dough rolled into balls, put into a special mold, and covered with hot honey. Dried fruits and/or hazelnuts may be added to the dough.
Draniki: Potato pancakes
Limonnik: Lemon pie
Olivier salad: A smorgasbord salad. Prior to the Revolution, it was typically made with crayfish, cold meat like tongue or ham, cucumbers, grouse, capers, potatoes, lettuce, caviar, duck, aspic (gelled meat stock), and olives, and dressed with gourmet mayonnaise.
Pastily (singular *pastila*): A sweet made from apples, honey or sugar, berries, nuts, and egg whites
Pelmeni: Ravioli-like pasta generally stuffed with potatoes, cheese, onions, and sometimes vegetables, with very thin dough
Pirogi: Pies filled with fruits, berries, cheese, nuts, honey, fish, mushrooms, meat, rice, cabbage, poppyseeds, potatoes, or groats. Not to be confused with Polish *pierogi.*
Pirozhki: Small, individual pies or buns filled with fruit, jam, cheese, fish, meat, cabbage, onions, potatoes, or mushrooms
Rassolnik: Soup with pickled cucumbers, pearl barley, and pork or beef kidneys
Selyodka: Herring
Shashlyk: Lamb shishkebab
Solyanka: A thick fish or meat soup
Vatrushka: A soft, round bun made with sweet dough and filled with soft cheese, cottage cheese, raisins, and fruit
Zakuski: Appetizers; *hors d'oeuvres*

Historical references:

Acmeism: A school of poetry which began in 1910, characterized by clarity of expression and compact form. Their name came from the

Greek *acme*, "the best age of man." The major Acmeists frequently met at the Stray Dog Café in St. Petersburg.

Basmachi (literally, "Raiders"): Participants in a Muslim, largely Turkic, uprising against Imperial Russian and Soviet rule in Central Asia between 1916–1931.

Aleksandr Aleksandrovich Blok (1880–1921): A major poet of the Russian Symbolism school.

Ivan Alekseyevich Bunin (1870–1953): Russia's first Nobel Prize winner in Literature.

Cheka: The earliest incarnation of what eventually became the KGB. It was in existence from 1917–1922 and was replaced by the GPU.

Dagestan: A region in the Caucasus north of Georgia and Azerbaijan, between Chechnya and the Caspian Sea. Most of its people are Muslim and speak Turkic, Caucasian, or Iranian languages.

False Dmitriy: A succession of pretenders to the throne during the Time of Troubles, all claiming to be Tsar Ivan IV's dead son Dmitriy, who would've been the rightful heir after Tsar Fyodor's death.

Grand Duke Dmitriy Pavlovich (1891–1942): Tsar Nicholas II's first-cousin; grandson of Tsar Aleksandr II. He was saved the fate of many other Romanovs when he was sent to the Persian front as punishment for being involved in the murder of Grigoriy Rasputin. He was known as a great womanizer throughout his life.

Grand Duke Nikolay Konstantinovich (1850–1918): A grandson of Tsar Nicholas I, declared insane and exiled to Tashkent after stealing jewels from his mother. He and his descendants were the only Romanovs allowed to remain in the USSR.

Tsar Fyodor the Bell-Ringer, usually called Fyodor the Blessèd in Russian (1557–1598): The only surviving legitimate son of Ivan Grozniy, a simple-minded ruler whose failure to produce an heir caused the end of the Ryurikovich Dynasty and the start of the Time of Troubles.

Ingushetia: A region between North Ossetia and Chechnya in the Caucasus. The Ingush people refer to themselves as Ghalghai and are predominantly Sunni Muslims.

Ivan II, called Ivan the Meek (1326–1359): Grand Prince of

Moskva and Vladimir. He wasn't considered a very strong or proactive ruler by his contemporaries.

Tsar Ivan III, called Ivan the Great (1440–1505): The first Russian ruler to call himself Tsar, one of Russia's longest-reigning rulers, and a very successful leader. Under his rule, the Golden Horde was finally expelled from Russia, the size of the empire tripled, the Kreml was renovated, and the foundations of the Russian state were laid.

Tsar Ivan IV, called Ivan Grozniy (1530–1584): The last consequential Ryurikovich Tsar. Though his appellation in English is "Terrible," Grozniy truly means "awe-inspiring; fearful; dreadsome," a far more accurate depiction of his personality and reign than the misleading "Terrible."

Kadets: Members of the Constitutional Democratic Party, mostly intellectuals and professionals. The party was formed in 1905.

Ivan Andreyevich Krylov (1769–1844): Russia's foremost fabulist.

***Izvestiya*:** A daily newspaper which began in 1917. Its name literally means "delivered messages," but is usually translated as "News" in the context of newspapers.

Jaani Kirik: St. John's Church, a very old Brick Gothic Lutheran church in Tartu. Parts of it date from the 14th century, when it was a Catholic church.

Aleksandr Fyodorovich Kerenskiy (1881–1970): Minister of Justice, Minister of War, and second Prime Minister in the provisional government; a member of the Socialist Revolutionary Party. He very narrowly escaped the Bolsheviks after the October Revolution and fled to France, where he lived until 1940. After the Nazi occupation, he escaped to America and settled in New York City.

Grand Duke Kirill Vladimirovich (1876–1938): Declared himself Emperor-in-Exile. Though some supported his claim, most opposed him for his support of the provisional government and certain Soviet policies, his overall personality, his scandalous marriage to his divorced first-cousin, a general disdain for his branch of the family, and his mother's refusal to convert to Orthodoxy until her children were adults. His granddaughter is the current pretender to the throne.

Kunstkamera: Russia's first museum, founded by Pyotr the Great and finished in 1727. It contains many medical curiosities, and anthropological, ethnographic, and mineralogical exhibits. The macabre exhibits could best be compared to those of Philadelphia's Mütter Museum.

Mikhail Yuriyevich Lermontov (1814–1841): Russia's most important national poet after the death of Aleksandr Sergeyevich Pushkin.

Okhrana: The Tsarist version of the KGB.

Old Believers: A group who rejected Patriarch Nikon's reforms of 1652–1666. They continue to follow practices such as using different wording in some prayers, spelling the name of Jesus differently, and crossing themselves in a different way. Many fled to Siberia and Alaska to escape persecution.

Tsar Pavel (1754–1801): Yekaterina the Great's firstborn child and successor, who reigned from 1796–1801; best-remembered for the draconian House Laws he established to get back at his mother for deposing his supposed father, Pyotr III. He was assassinated by a band of dismissed officers.

Peetri Kirik: St. Peter's Church, a brick Gothic Revival church in Tartu, built in the 1880s.

***Pravda*:** A thrice-weekly newspaper which officially began in 1912, with origins in 1903. Its name means "Truth."

Provisional Government: A coalition government formed immediately after the February Revolution, recognized by the U.S., Italy, Great Britain, and France. It was overthrown by the October Revolution.

Ryurikovich Dynasty: The ruling family prior to the Romanovs, who ruled from 862–1598. The dynasty took its name from their original ruler Ryurik, a Varangian prince.

Smutnoye Vremya: The Time of Troubles (1598–1613), between the end of the Ryurikovich Dynasty and the start of the Romanov Dynasty, when many pretenders to the throne and other unsavory would-be rulers appeared. This era also included a famine, occupation by the Polish–Lithuanian Commonwealth, and civil uprisings.

The Church of Saint Simeon and Hanna the Prophet: A

wooden Russian Orthodox church on Tallinn's Ahtri Street, near the harbor, built in the 1750s by Russian sailors.

Snegurochka: The Snow Maiden, a young girl who helps Dyed Moroz (Grandfather Frost) distribute Christmas presents to children.

Telleri Kapel: Teller Chapel, one of Tartu's houses of worship, built in 1794.

What Is to Be Done?: A political pamphlet written by Vladimir Ilyich Lenin in 1901 and published in 1902. It argues that the proletariat should become Marxists with help from a political party formed to educate them, and partly caused the split between Bolsheviks and Mensheviks.

The Story Behind the Story

The genesis of this story arose sometime in the early Nineties, as a picture book about a beautiful 17-year-old ballerina and balalaika-player named Amy, and her 10-year-old cousin Ginny. They lived in Russia in 1917, and Ginny was so upset about being poor, he rushed out the door when someone mentioned their poverty. Either later or around that same time, I had to do a report on Russia for my sixth grade social-studies class, and my Russophilia slowly began developing. Then, in late 1992, I discovered the late Ida Vos's *Hide and Seek*. This was the first time I'd read a book in present tense, years before every other writer jumped on it. It was a revelation to discover books could be written in the present tense. The action seemed so much more dramatic, tense, gripping, compelling, right in the moment the entire time, never knowing what was going to happen next, unsure if there'd be a happy ending or not, since everything was constantly unfolding instead of already finished and related after the fact.

From that book, I also got the idea to write a similar story, only my characters would be Russians hiding from the Bolsheviks starting in 1917. As I developed this story in my head, I remembered the hotel my family stayed by on Cape Cod in the aftermath of Hurricane Bob. I thought about my characters having a place like that, without electricity, ice, or running water, cut off from much of civilization, signs of devastation all around. The old dacha near Ryazan was very loosely based on that two-story hotel room I stayed by in August 1991.

The false names Boris gives to the visitors in autumn 1917 also had their origins in *Hide and Seek*, when the characters in hiding have obviously Jewish names temporarily replaced by regular Dutch names. Originally, Katerina Godimova (then called Kathleen) gave them "American names" to use if Bolsheviks ever came around, along with a ridiculous story about how their great-aunt Aleksandra Stalina wanted them to return to Russia to spread the word about Communism and create a people's government. At that age, I didn't know what Communism was, only that it was supposed to be bad.

I knew jack about Russian anything when I started the book at the end of January 1993, with painful evidence such as a plethora of

Western names, ridiculous discrimination against Tsarist students that read like the increasing persecution and stigmatization of Jews during the Shoah, and a complete disconnect from the historical and cultural setting. (I didn't know women's surnames have feminine endings, nor about patronymics or nicknames!) It read like a silly, fluffy soap opera about early 1990s American teens who just happened to live in Russia in the late 1910s. I didn't even deliberately make Katrin, Eliisabet, and Anastasiya Estonians. It was just a random country from the former USSR. But thanks to that Divinely-ordained choice, I ended up becoming a passionate Estophile in 2001, so it wasn't really an accident.

Lyuba was called Amy all the way into 2011, when I finally figured out how to convert and reformat all those old files which had been trapped on disks, in obsolete file formats, for years. I engaged in some powerful cognitive dissonance to justify keeping Western names for certain characters long after I knew better. At least I eventually wrote it into the story that her legal name was Lyubov, and Ivan sometimes called her Lyuba, Lyubonka, Lyubochka, and a few other diminutives. It was another beautiful, Divinely-ordained miracle that I named her Amy, since its Russian form is Lyubov (Love). I love the wordplay it creates in Russian when Ivan calls her "my love." Not only is she his love, she's also his Lyubov. It's also a very fitting name for a woman who's in desperate search of love and its healing power.

Other Western names originally used were Alexis (changed to Aleksey in 1996), Elizabeth/Lizzy (changed to Eliisabet/Liza in 2011), Catherine/Cathie (changed to Katariina/Katrin in 2011), Al (changed to Alya in 1996), Kathie (Lyuba's mother; changed to Katya in 1996), Margaret (Lyuba's aunt; changed to Margarita in 2011), Peter (changed to Pyotr in 2011), Paul (who became Pavel as soon as I put him on the page in 1996, after envisioning him since 1993), Anne (Ivan's mother; changed to Anna in 1996), Vallerie (changed to Valeriya in 2011), and Leon (changed to Leontiy in 2011). In the original 1993 material, I also used the Westernized spellings Tatiana, Nikolai, Georgia, Alexander, and Anastasia (who was sometimes called Stacy). Nikolas started out as Nicholas, then became Nickolas in the prequel stories I wrote in 1993–94, and finally emerged as Nikolas, with the caveat that his real name is Nikolay. He was frequently called Nicky, until I changed his nickname to Kolya in 2011.

It just seemed right to keep the old, non-Russian names for Ginny, Kat, Nikolas, and Kittey. Ginny is Ginny, and I can't think of him by any other name, so I created the story about that being his childish mispronunciation of his baby nickname Genie. Since he lived in East Prussia for so long, it makes sense his family would've become less Russianized, as evidenced by how he also has an actual middle name, not just a patronymic. It totally fits Nikolas to go by the Greek form of his real name, and Kat rightly needed some way to stand out from the crowd of fifteen sisters instead of being just another Katya. As for Kittey, there's the precedent of Kitty in *Anna Karenina*, where the nickname is written phonetically in Russian and not used as a "translation" of Katya. English, like French, was a fashionable language among upper-class Russians at the time, so it wouldn't have been that unusual for some people to adopt such nicknames.

In my defense, I'd read a lot of books which "translated" Russian names, had read a number of historicals set in Russia which used non-Russian names, and knew the Romanovs and other nobles frequently used their Western names. I copied what I saw, not realizing that wasn't accurate. Even a very Westernized, upper-class Russian wouldn't have gone by a name like Peter, Elizabeth, Catherine, Amy, Margaret, or Leon. At least there are plausible reasons for Kat, Nikolas, Kittey, and Ginny to go by non-Russian names.

The insipid original title was *Amy and the Boys*, a title I ditched sometime during autumn 1996, during my second major period of working on it. It was such a relief when the new and improved title came to me, along with the symbolism of the swan. The first major period was January–October 1993 (including some mostly prequel stories I handwrote), the second was September 1996–circa June 1997, and the third must've begun sometime in late 1998 and went through to August 2001. I couldn't have written Chapter 15 any earlier than September 1998, since I learnt the croup relief trick from my Spanish professor. In between the first two periods, I continued writing supplemental stories and edited a printout of the first seven chapters, the entire story up till that point. Over the last twenty-one years, this book has been written, edited, rewritten, revised, and polished on six different computers, all starting with my dear 1984

128K Mac. So many years later, I still miss that sweet, simple machine.

Going through the first draft (which I went back through and tinkered with multiple times as I got older, starting in 1995), it's obvious there are several distinct writing styles, representing myself as a writer at several different ages. Probably 99% of the original 1993 material was junked or radically rewritten, but a little bit is still there. That was by far the worst, most epically cringe-worthy material, with so many stupid, pointless scenes and so much unrealistic dialogue. There were also some scenes which came from that notebook of supplemental stories, written in 1994, and material I wrote onto the print-out in 1995 when I did my first real edits and revisions. In the material written during 1996–97, the dialogue became overly, unnaturally formal and stilted, rather mismatched with these characters. This was also after I found out just why the Revolution happened, and why so many ordinary Russians hated the Tsar so much. So in went a lot of awkward, infodumpy, preachy historical and political lectures, mostly delivered via dialogue. During this time, I also began outlining what would happen in each chapter from there on out, based on the storyline I came up with in 1993. Then, slowly, during the third and final major period, there's an increasing maturity and complexity, with characters coming more and more into their final forms. It's obvious I wrote the final ten or so chapters plus the Epilogue when I was twenty-one, since the writing style is like night and day next to everything which came before. I had so much fun researching and writing the Part II chapters which strongly feature aspects of the Roaring Twenties, and transforming Katrin from a shallow Communist of convenience to a strong, principled woman who lives her convictions and gives up childish things.

The handwritten prequel stories began with a fairly long story called "How Amy Met the Boys," set in March–April 1908. It began with 9-year-old Ivan in Khimki Forest at night, desperately praying for someone to love him and be his friend, and to take away the pain of being brutally abused by his drunken father. There was lots of purple prose in this story, along with ridiculous scenes like Ivan frequently skipping school, befriending stray animals, and sneaking them into the classroom, including a horse he tries to hide in the cloakroom. It also featured a number of scenes of Ivan being physically abused by his father, in several different ways, Mr. Konev's flaring temper against both his son and his brother Igor, the attempts of many of the boys at school (including Misha and Kostya) to turn Lyuba's head, and Lyuba's coldness towards Ivan, whom she starts off thinking is a stupid, hotheaded, self-centered chatterbox. The story ends when they finally become friends and each realize the other is a fellow wounded soul, with secrets not yet ready to be shared.

Other prequel stories included Lyuba and her friends starting English lessons around 1912–13, during which Ivan struggles mightily and acquires his thick, heavy accent; a gymnasium ball (originally a school dance) probably around 1914; the murder of Ivan's cousin Liza in 1913, during a siege Mr. Litvinov and his older sons orchestrate during Sunday services at St. Basil's; and the night Mr. Konev murders his brother Igor in a fit of drunken rage, in September 1914, as Ivan watches from a tree outside. The original 1993 material of the actual book also included a long, pointless flashback to a school picnic in 1908, where Boris badly misbehaves and gets in lots of trouble, Anastasiya is visiting for some reason and causes a scene of her own, and Lyuba starts reaming Ivan out for fighting Boris and then finds out Ivan is being horrifically abused by his alcoholic father. She runs off to tell a teacher, and Mr. Konev is arrested that night for child abuse. This bit of backstory was later changed to several years later, and Mr. Konev was hit up for public drunkenness. I didn't realize child abuse wasn't a crime in 1908.

The 1993 versions of these characters were so one-dimensional. Lyuba was entirely too passive; Ivan had an even-worse temper, had been an obnoxious chatterbox and very popular at gymnasium, was always telling Ginny dirty stories, actually liked Anastasiya, and was pretty damn obnoxious; Boris wasn't so crass or pudgy, and was the guy Lyuba really did like most; Anastasiya was even more harebrained; Katrin was as shallow as they come; and Ginny was way too over the top and psychotic. None of these people exhibited any real motivations for such behavior. They were just names on a page. I'm going to take the Fifth on whom I based Ivan's original incarnation on!

Sometime during 1993, I came upon the idea of Lyuba gradually falling in love with Ivan, and eventually marrying him in America, after they had a son together. Their latest romantic reunion the night they leave Mr. Golitsyn's boardinghouse was originally the first time they kissed or Lyuba declared her feelings. One time before, when Boris was out checking on the news of the October Revolution, Ivan tried to get her alone and begged her to kiss him, but she called him crazy and went into the other room with Ginny. It didn't take very long to stumble into the idea of Ivan being madly in love with Lyuba all along, not just having a crush on her, and of Lyuba secretly being in love with him all along too, not just falling for him all of a sudden. The plot got even better when I hit upon the idea of them being together before, unbeknownst to almost everyone, only for Lyuba to dump him under pressure from her mother. Along with these new plot developments came the backstories about Ivan being physically abused by an alcoholic father and Lyuba being sexually abused by her own father. (I actually think that was inspired by an after school special I saw in 1993!) They became two wounded souls who understood one another like no one else, and it also did worlds for explaining some of their seemingly confusing behavior. These scarred survivors of childhood abuse put on façades to the world, and don't know how to be normal. In the process, I also had to make Boris more and more of an antagonist, far from the nice guy he started out as. Sorry, Borya!

I got the idea for the orphanage girls from the film *The Inner Circle*, which I discovered in July 1996 and immediately fell in love with. I've watched that film so many times. I wasn't exactly a typical teenager, since I passionately followed Russian news, read Russian literature, and wrote research papers on Russian historical topics instead of being interested in anything current or from my own country. It was a foregone conclusion I'd study history and Russian and East European Studies at university. My senior year of university, I did a research paper on Estonian nationalism and the Estonian people's struggle for independence, inspired by my love for Katrin. Who knows what might've happened if I'd decided to make Katrin and her two friends Ukrainians, Kazakhs, Uzbeks, Tajiks, or Azeris instead. I might've fallen madly in love with the culture and history of those places, and never felt pulled towards Estophilia.

Lyuba's embarrassing scene on the tram, in the first section of the first chapter, was based on something which happened to me shortly before I began writing the book. I too was standing on the city bus home, and when a friend (whom I based Alya on, in terms of physical appearance) motioned to me to sit with her when the seat became free, I ended up on a boy's lap. It happened again when I tried to get up. Unlike Lyuba, I didn't ring the bell to get off long before my stop.

Lyuba's birthday, December 11, was given in honor of my favorite writer, Aleksandr Isayevich Solzhenitsyn, of blessèd memory.

Aleksey's surname was originally Trotskiy, then changed to Tvardovskiy in honor of Aleksandr Trifonovich Tvardovskiy, the longtime editor of *Noviy Mir* and a well-known poet and writer. While Trotskiy is a real surname (albeit not very common), there's really only one association people have with that name, and I only chose it because it was one of the Russian surnames I found in the old 1965 encyclopedia I got from my father. Georgiya's family were originally the Stalins, with many comments about how they shared their name with the Georgian nobody who had delusions of grandeur. I changed it to Savvin after realizing no other family had that name. Ginny's surname was originally Herzen, but changed to Kharzin to sound more Russian. (That's what happens when you're a 13-year-old know-nothing who randomly picks names from an outdated encyclopedia!)

Had I begun this story as an adult, or later in my teens, I probably would've started the story closer to the October Revolution, even in 1918, and set it in Petrograd instead of Moskva, but it is what it is. To avoid major unraveling and reconstruction of the core outline of the first two chapters, I invented the plot elements of a left-wing gymnasium, vigilantes roving the neighborhood, and other reasons for Lyuba and her friends frequently moving from place to place while they're in hiding, along with turning the unexpected houseguests and intruders into deserting Bolshevik soldiers and punitive forces dispatched by Kerenskiy to put down the numerous peasant rebellions against their landowners. It makes more historical sense, and didn't require a complete rewrite of the first two chapters. At thirteen, I naïvely believed the February Revolution meant an immediate Bolshevik takeover and Red Terror sweeping the land. I had no idea the February Revolution established a provisional government, and that it was the October Revolution which established Bolshevik rule. I also didn't realize what an out of touch minority monarchists were, and that almost no one still supported the Tsar by 1917. Making the characters upper-middle-class was the most realistic way to explain why they'd support the Tsar in spite of everything.

If I hadn't Divinely stumbled into that storyline of Lyuba and Ivan being madly in love since childhood, and Boris being such a scoundrel, I honestly don't know if I would've been able to salvage a halfway-decent story from the immature mess this book was in 1993. The mass of garbage I cut will never see the light of day. You don't want to know how psychotic and over the top Ginny was; how dickish Ivan came across as; the silliness of Ivan, Boris, Pyotr, and Basil constantly fighting over Lyuba; how divorced it was from Russian culture and the historical era; how shallow and apolitical Katrin was; how obnoxious Georgiya was; or how Kittey really became crippled. I didn't even realize Nikolay was born twelve weeks early, having no idea pregnancy is measured in weeks, not a span of months. At least Eliisabet's pregnancy came out to twenty-eight weeks, which wasn't an automatic death sentence in 1917, provided the baby were relatively healthy and very well taken care of. I made him two and a half pounds, so he'd have a fighting chance, and had a progressive doctor from the women's medical school examine him off the pages.

Much of the stuff from the 1996–97 period was crap too, though not as bad as the 1993 material. The few concurrent stories from the handwritten notebook which found their way into the text were rather cringeworthy in their original forms, but decent enough to be salvaged with some reworking. These scenes include Ivan's heartbroken, romantic pleas to Lyuba right after Tatyana is born, and the scene of Lyuba, Ivan, and baby Tatyana at Sokolniki Park in spring 1919. Ivan became such an annoying, simpering pansy in those handwritten stories, always speaking and thinking in such over the top, flowery, poetic, sappy language, and becoming such a passive doormat. Just because he often acts like more of a mouse than a man doesn't mean he should be completely passive and spineless!

Nothing in this life is really an accident. I didn't just stumble into this immature idea of a story at such a young age, any more than I stumbled into Lyuba really preferring Ivan, making three Estonian characters, creating Mr. Lebedev and his ten daughters and niece, or creating my orphanage girls.

About the Author

Ursula Hartlein, who also writes as Carrie-Anne Brownian, was born on the fifth night of Chanukah in 1979. Though a proud native Pittsburgher, she's lived most of her life in Upstate New York and has also lived in Pittsfield and Amherst, MA.

She earned a bachelor's degree from UMass–Amherst in History and Russian and East European Studies. Her areas of historical expertise are Russian history, the World War II/Shoah era, and 20th century American history. Her ultimate goal is a Ph.D. in Russian history, with a focus on GULAG and the Great Terror.

She is the author of *And Jakob Flew the Fiend Away*, a Bildungsroman set from 1940–46; its sequel, *And the Lark Arose from Sullen Earth*, set from 1946–47; *And Aleksey Lived*, an alternative historical saga about the greatest Tsar who never ruled; *The Twelfth Time: Lyuba and Ivan on the Rocks*, the sequel to this book, set from 1924–30; and *Journey Through a Dark Forest: Lyuba and Ivan in the Age of Anxiety*, a four-volume saga spanning 1933–48. Under her other pen name, she is the author of *Little Ragdoll: A Bildungsroman*, a contemporary historical family saga set from 1959–74, and has had work published in the anthologies *Campaigner Challenges 2011*, *Overcoming Adversity: An Anthology for Andrew*, *How I Found the Write Path*, *The Insecure Writer's Support Group Guide to Publishing and Beyond*, *The Cat Who Chose Us and Other Cat Stories*, and *Masquerade: Oddly Suited.*

www.ingramcontent.com/pod-product-compliance
Lightning Source LLC
Chambersburg PA
CBHW020303030826
48979CB00027B/2018/J
* 9 7 8 1 9 2 7 9 6 7 3 2 4 *